Apollo Rises

"Evolution of a Patriot"

Rigney Page Missions:

For
Muz and Ace

Author's Introduction

When Apollo first went undercover during the Cold War, his mission was classified and the U.S. Navy cryptographic systems that were his mission to protect were classified. Those classified cryptographic systems were valuable targets for foreign espionage operatives. Now, decades later, Apollo's mission files and those cryptographic systems have been declassified, allowing me to tell Apollo's story to the detail that I always wanted to tell it.

Apollo Rises chronicles the travel and events of a young navy man who experiences a unique adventure. His story is more than the telling of venturesome episodes. His story is also a journey of discovery through the U.S. Navy of the Cold War Era—a journey where reality battles perception.

While writing *Apollo Rises*, I enjoyed reliving my early years in the United States Navy. I vividly remember my friends and my foes. While writing Apollo's adventure, I was compelled to include characterizations of those I knew. Some are unsung heroes, and I honor them in this story. Some were friends who helped me understand my environment, and I creatively and appreciatively include them in Apollo's journey. The women I knew significantly affected my life, and I honor them with creative portrayals of meaningful and intimate relationships in Apollo's experience. Some of the people I knew were evil demons, and I spare few details while exposing their indecent, brutal, and uncivilized behavior.

Please enjoy this adventurous, sometimes sensual, and sometimes amusing trek through the U.S. Navy of the Cold War Era.

For my non-navy readers, I have included a Glossary of Navy Terms and the Navy Rank Structure at the end of this story.

. . . Michael R. Ellis

Prologue

March 1961

March 1961

Jonathan Lacrosse's house stands on the eastern slope of a hill on the island of Barbados. A wide wooden deck wraps around the backside of the house. The deck provides an unobstructed view of the Caribbean Sea. Today, few clouds hang in the sky and a six-mile per hour wind blows inland from the dark blue and white-capped sea. Private yachts and commercial vessels are visible on the sea.

Jonathan suns himself on a fully reclined deck chair. He covered his body in sun block. He only wears cotton shorts. His body beads sweat. Occasionally, he sips from the large glass of ice water that sits on a small table next to him. A smile of satisfaction crosses his face as he thinks about how he fooled them all. How he fooled the U.S. Air Force, the U.S. Government, and mostly how he fooled Javier. He prides himself on his ability to move about the Caribbean under fake identities and unnoticed by his enemies and U.S. authorities.

Jonathan thinks back to the time he served in Germany. He thinks of that German woman who claimed she loved him—the one who tricked him into giving her FOR OFFICIAL USE ONLY documents. The documents were not classified, but they were documents that should not find their way into the possession of a German civilian. Then, Javier appeared one day with pictures of Jonathan and the woman together and proof that the woman was an East German intelligence agent.

In exchange for a few CONFIDENTIAL classified documents, Javier promised not to tell the Air Force about Jonathan's espionage activities. As an added incentive, Javier promised to pay well for each document.

CONFIDENTIAL is the lowest level of classified material and sneaking copies of CONFIDENTIAL documents off the base involved low risk. Later, Javier asked for more and more documents. During the next two years, Jonathan supplied SECRET and TOP SECRET documents to Javier on a regular basis. Most of the documents were Air Operations Plans and procedures for high-altitude intelligence flights. The TOP SECRET documents were more difficult to photograph and sneak off the base.

On several occasions, he came close to being caught. Although he lived dangerously, he appeared adept to it and was sometimes stimulated by it.

Nevertheless, after three years the stress and pressure to meet Javier's demands became too much for Jonathan. He had accumulated over $78,000.00, which he figured was enough money to buy him a new life and a new identity. He designed a plan to escape Javier, escape the U.S. government, and escape a life of fear. He looked into the future and foresaw a life of anonymity living in far off lands. Over a six-month period, he planned every detail of his escape.

Obtaining a fake passport with a new identity became the most dangerous and most costly effort in his escape plan—dangerous because of the number of criminals he had to involve—costly because Americans seeking such passports paid the highest price. The fake passport was essential. He had to take the risk and pay the price.

During an evening while eating in a Munich restaurant, Jonathan went to the men's room and changed into a disguise. He exited the restaurant; then, he took a cab to the train station. He traveled under his new name. *How easy it was to escape Javier's grasp*, he thought.

His escape occurred three years ago. Then, for five months, he wandered South America and Central America and lived in cheap backstreet hotels. While in Argentina, Jonathan purchased another identity and false passport. He traveled to Panama where he purchased another identity with a matching passport. Protected by two, fully credible, false identities and a proficiency in conversational Spanish, he traveled with no concern that an American military deserter named Jonathan Lacrosse could be tracked through Central and South America.

He settled in Costa Rica. He portrayed himself as an adventurer of meager means and worked several general laborer jobs. His knowledge of the Spanish language landed him a job on the concierge desk at a beach resort hotel. He lived on the money he earned, which allowed him to keep his emergency stash of sixty-two thousand dollars and his other passports in a safe deposit box. Life was safe and life was comfortable.

Then, six months ago, he sensed that someone followed him. He became afraid of being discovered when several of his coworkers informed him that some hotel guests were asking detailed questions about him. He retrieved the contents of this safe deposit box, executed his escape plan, and disappeared from Costa Rica.

He changed his identity for a third time just before traveling to Barbados. Jonathan now feels comfortable and safe. He feels that this time he covered his trail well, and no one can find him.

The sound of shuffling feet on the deck transports Jonathan's mind to the present. Alarmed, he jumps to his feet and faces the direction of the sound. Terrified at what he sees, he begins to tremble. His heart races and his body sweats.

Three men stand on the deck facing him. Javier stands in the middle. Two large and sinister looking men stand on each side of Javier, and each points an automatic pistol at Jonathan.

Javier stares coldly and menacingly into Jonathan's fright-filled eyes. "Jonathan, you cannot escape me. You and your kind can never escape me."

Jonathan's legs wobble. He falls to his knees. He begins to cry.

One of the sinister looking men walks over to Jonathan and points a gun at Jonathan's head.

Javier walks over to Jonathan. He stoops down and violently grabs Jonathan's chin. He glares angrily into Jonathan's eyes and warns in a menacing tone, "Where is the money? You should tell me now because if you do not tell me now, you will be begging to tell me later."

PART I

EVOLUTION
OF A
PATRIOT

Chapter 1

May 1967

The U.S. Navy warship cruises through a calm sea on a westerly course 45 miles to the south of Puerto Rico. The warship's captain and *Officer of the Deck* stand on the port bridge wing and look to the south through binoculars. Both officers focus on a point three thousand yards away.

"Do you see the periscope?" the captain asks the OOD.

"No, Captain."

The captain queries, "Did you confirm the bearing and course?"

"Yes, Captain. Sierra One bears one-nine-two on a course of two-seven-zero."

"What about the radar?" the captain asks. "Has the EMO fixed it yet?"

"No sir. The ET who specializes on the radar went on emergency leave the day we departed Norfolk. The other ETs are having difficulty finding the problem."

The *Junior Officer of the Deck, JOOD*, steps onto the bridge wing and reports, "OOD, CIC reports another submerged contact—designate Sierra Two—bearing one-seven-two—at five thousand yards—course two-seven-zero—classified as a Soviet Whiskey Class Submarine."

"Any idea as to her depth?" the OOD asks the JOOD.

"CIC says Sierra Two is at one-five-zero feet, and her actions indicate she's preparing to come to periscope depth."

"Now, we are all going in the same direction," the OOD states the obvious in a flat tone.

The captain and OOD return to the enclosed bridge.

The OOD hears a voice behind him. "Sir, I have an immediate precedence message for you."

The OOD turns in the direction of the voice and sees the *Communications Messenger of the Watch*.

The OOD takes the message board and reads the immediate precedence message. Then, he looks up to locate the captain's position on the bridge. The captain leans over the dark de-energized radar repeater screen. He shakes his head and expresses dissatisfaction.

"Captain, a contact message from COMNAVFORCARIB," the OOD advises as he hands the message board to the captain.

The captain scans the message. Then, he directs, "OOD, this message is forty-five minutes old. Which means the information on the Soviet destroyer is probably ninety minutes old. The Soviet destroyer is headed our way. Have CIC plot the destroyer's position specified in this message. Assume the same course and speed and calculate when that destroyer will be in visual range."

"Aye, aye, Captain."

"And tell the EMO to report to me."

"Aye, aye, Captain."

The OOD turns to walk away; he turns back around and faces the captain and comments, "Interesting. At the same time that we are scheduled to rendezvous with one of our own submarines to conduct ASW exercises, two Soviet submarines and a Soviet destroyer arrive at our rendezvous position at the rendezvous time. Just like the last MED cruise, Soviet warships were often at our rendezvous points—waiting for us—as if the Soviets read our operation orders."

The captain casts a stern stare at the OOD and warns, "Keep those conclusions to yourself. I don't want the wardroom speculating about what they don't know and coming to incorrect conclusions."

"Aye, aye, Captain." The OOD walks off.

Thirty minutes later, the captain sits in his bridge chair. He watches the Soviet destroyer, which now cruises twelve-thousand yards off the forward starboard quarter.

"You sent for me, Captain?"

The captain turns his head toward the voice and sees the Electronics Material Officer.

The EMO, who wears threadbare and grease stained wash-khakis, waits for a rebuke from the captain regarding the nonoperational radar.

The captain looks the EMO in the eye and asks, "Dan, are you aware of our tactical situation?"

"Cap'n, the OPS Boss tole' me that we got a Russian destroyer tailin' us."

"And two Soviet submarines also" the captain adds.

The EMO nods acceptance of the additional information.

"Dan, I am at a tactical disadvantage. I need that radar to pinpoint periscopes. At night, that Soviet destroyer over there can move about without me knowing where she is. Without the radar, our ship must restrict its speed and movements. Do you understand that?"

"Yes, Cap'n. Myself and three ETs have been workin' 'round the clock to get the radar fixed, and I assure you that we are doin' our best to troubleshoot the radar and fix it."

"Dan, I've known you for fifteen years. I recommended you for the LDO program. I do not doubt your effort. I need an estimated time of repair. I may need to CASREP the radar, cancel this exercise, and go back to Puerto Rico for repairs. That will look bad for the ship."

"Cap'n, I just don't know. We're chasin' a ghost in that equipment.

3

It's an intermittent power problem. We've swapped power supplies, transformers, and power cables. Just when think we have the problem traced down to a subassembly, the unit powers back on. Thirty minutes later, it powers down again. In 25 years, I've seen nothing like it."

"You have made no progress during the last twenty-four hours. If you don't have it fixed twelve hours from now, I must send a CASREP and seek assistance from a repair facility."

"I understand, Cap'n."

"Okay, Dan. Go back to your duties."

"Aye, aye, Cap'n."

The captain sits in his bridge chair and watches the Soviet destroyer. The OOD updates the captain every fifteen minutes on the position of the Soviet submarines.

The Soviets knew where to find us, again, the captain concludes. *That is the real danger here . . . and has been the danger since last MED cruise. The radar problems exacerbate the real problem. Our operation schedule is known by the Soviets.*

The OOD walks to the captain's chair. "Captain, the EMO reports that one of his ETs just took a high voltage shock while working on the radar. The ET is unconscious and is being taken to sickbay."

"Give me a report on the ET's medical status every 30 minutes."

"Aye, aye, Captain."

"I am going to my sea cabin. Tell the operations officer to report to me there."

"Aye, aye, Captain."

The captain paces the deck of his sea cabin. A knock on his door causes him to stop pacing.

"Enter!" the captain orders loudly.

The door opens and the operations officer enters.

"Frank, this ASW exercise is eight hours late in starting. Our submarine will not come close for fear of being detected by the Soviet destroyer or those Soviet submarines. Do you agree with my assessment?"

"Yes, Captain. I do."

"Why are we in this situation with the radar?"

"If I could pick one major reason, I would say lack of schooled and experienced technicians. We only have 50 percent of allotted ETs, been like this ever since before I came aboard a year ago. I call BUPERS several times a month to see if I can convince them to send more ETs. Their response is always the same. Higher priority billets elsewhere."

The captain considers the operation officer's words; he responds, "Every department on this ship is undermanned. Our superiors expect us to complete every mission, regardless of manning problem."

"I understand that, Captain, but we keep getting assigned missions that require a 100 percent manned crew. My whole department stands port and starboard watch rotations of eight hours on and eight hours off. The engineering department and weapons department are also port and starboard. My men are exhausted, and they are making mistakes because of it."

"Frank, I cannot go to Admiral Melton and tell him we cannot meet our missions because of under-manning. We must succeed with what we have."

"I agree, Captain. I'm not making excuses. You asked me the cause of the radar problem. I'm just telling you the cause."

The captain's phone rings.

"Captain."

"Captain, OOD here. That ET that got hurt is unconscious and has second-degree burns. The doctor says he needs to be sent to the nearest hospital, ASAP."

"Okay. Tell the doctor to request med-evac via helicopter."

"Aye, aye, Captain. Will do. Also, MAIN COMM just handed me another immediate precedence contact report. A Russian Trawler is headed our way and should be here in three hours."

"Very well. Give me position updates on all Soviet vessels every 30 minute."

"Aye, aye, Captain."

The captain cradles the phone handset and turns back to the Operations Officer.

"Frank, who is your offline encryption officer?"

"That would be Ensign Rowing. You gonna send another message to the Office of Naval Intelligence?"

"Yes. I want Rowing to make the Adonis offline encryption ready to go. I will do the actual encryption."

"Aye, aye, Captain. I will get Ensign Rowing started."

After the Operations Officer departs, the captain considers his options. He previously reported his suspicions that his ship's operation schedule is always known by the Soviets.

The captain is not the only officer aboard his ship that suspects espionage. *At first, it was just the XO and operations officer. Now, junior officers like the OOD this afternoon are speculating. I must know what The Office of Naval Intelligence is doing about this!*

Chapter 2

November 1967

Radioman Third Class Rigney Page stares out the third-floor classroom window. The dreary November weather reflects his depressed mood. The gray overcast sky dims the sunlight. A cold, brisk wind blows in from Long Island Sound and up the Thames River Basin. The wind whips between multistory brick buildings of the New London Submarine Base, producing swirls of the few leaves missed by base cleaning crews.

To the west on the Thames River, Rigney observes several nuclear-powered submarines moored to piers on the Lower Base. Each submarine's *Top-Side Watch* wears a thickly padded jumpsuit with hood over his head. Over their jumpsuits, they wear kapok life jackets. Rigney can make out the black leather holsters of their .45 automatics.

Beyond the Thames River, Rigney views the suburbs of New London.

He shifts his attention to the street below. Only a few sailors walk about, and they are bundled in peacoats and wearing insulated black gloves to protect themselves from the blustering cold. Occasionally, a strong gust of wind blows a sailor's Dixie Cup style white hat from his head, and the sailor runs hunched-over chasing his white hat rolling on the ground.

The sound of chatter and multiple footsteps cause Rigney to turn around to face the interior of the classroom. Some of his classmates are returning from break. They attempt to include him in some joke telling. He declines. His depressed mood distracts him.

He had carefully planned the next phase of his life. When he was a young teenager, he studied radio electronics from books that he found in the local libraries of Orange County, California. At the age of fourteen, he easily repaired radios, tape recorders, and phonographs. He built Heath Kits at the rate of one every two months. He learned early in life that most skills could be acquired by reading books and then experimenting hands-on.

At the age of fifteen, he decided to join the navy after high school and take advantage of the advanced electronics courses offered by the navy's Submarine Radioman Program.

Now that he nears the end of his technical training, he worries that something has gone wrong. His classmates have their orders to submarines, but he does not.

He made several trips to the Personnel Office to inquire about his orders. The personnelman phoned the Submarine Assignment Branch at the Bureau of Naval Personnel. The Bureau responded that Rigney's file had been routed to the Special Assignments Branch. The Submarine Assignments Branch advised that Rigney's file had been flagged – *No assignment until approval of top secret clearance.*

"You're being considered for a special assignment," the personnelman told Rigney.

Rigney also wonders about the top secret clearance. Last month, the Personnel Office ordered him to complete the Top Secret Clearance Application. He became curious because all his classmates who already received orders completed the Secret Clearance Application Form—the classification level below top secret. He became increasingly concerned after the personnelman told him that it took six months for a Top Secret Clearance Application to be processed. That means more delays in achieving his goal of serving in a submarine.

Rigney *tested out* of the eight week Basic Electronics course in four weeks. His next scheduled course was the six-month-long Radio Repair Course, which he *tested out* after only three months. Impressed by Rigney's achievements, the Director of Submarine Radioman Schools offered Rigney an additional course. Normally, a submarine radioman attended only one repair course; then, the radioman was sent to a submarine. So, the offer of another repair course was unusual.

Rigney had asked the Director if he completed the next repair course in half the time could he then attend all remaining submarine-radioman repair courses. The Director agreed. Rigney chose Antenna Repair as his next course, which he knew he could finish in half the time, and he did. He completed the Teletype Repair Course in half the time. Now, he attends the Cryptographic Equipment Repair Course. Rigney will complete all his training at the end of the month, and he anxiously awaits orders to a submarine.

The instructor returns to the classroom, which signifies students must return to their workbenches and continue their lab exercises.

"RM3 Page," a voice announces.

Rigney sits at his workbench and turns his head toward the sound of his name. He sees the second class petty officer who is the school's administrative yeoman.

"Here," Rigney replies as he raises his hand.

"You're wanted in conference room," the yeoman advises.

Rigney weaves his way through the maze of desks and lab stations. He notices the eyes of his classmates watching him. His six-foot and one-inch tall, broad shouldered, one-hundred-eighty-five pound build casts an intimidating image. His wide, muscled chest and thick biceps cause his uniform jumper to stretch tightly across his upper torso. Light green eyes and reddish brown hair accentuate his rugged good looks.

The yeoman escorts Page to the conference room. When Page enters the conference room, the yeoman does not follow.

The square shaped conference room measures fifteen feet by fifteen feet. The window blinds are shut. The overhead lights illuminate the room. An American flag stands in one corner, and a U.S. Navy flag stands in the other corner. Paintings and prints of historic naval battles decorate the walls. Navy blue colored carpet covers the floor. An eight-foot-long conference table, surrounded with wooden armchairs, stretches through the center of the room.

Two men sit casually at the far end of the conference table. One man wears Service Dress Blues with lieutenant commander stripes on the sleeves. Rigney notices that the officer does not wear the gold dolphins of an officer qualified in submarines. The other man wears a dark blue business suit. A tape recorder and microphone sit on the conference table in front of the two men.

The officer appears to be about 30 years of age. The crew-cut blond haired officer's most noticeable feature is his thickly muscled neck.

The civilian appears much older—fifty or more—with peppered gray hair and a closely cut, all gray beard. Flab hangs from his chin, and his fat belly strains the buttons of his white shirt.

"I was told to report here," Rigney states with purpose and in a strong but mild tone. Rigney always attempts to sound confident and assured.

Both men cast appraising stares at Rigney, as if he is a job candidate.

Rigney stands straight and returns each man's stare. The officer and the civilian each have an open folder on the tabletop in front of them, which they study between glances at Rigney.

Rigney looks down and across the table at the folders. He sees his name *Page, Rigney Michael* in bold black letters on each folder. Rigney also sees that both folders are opened to a page with a five-by-seven-inch photograph of him. Rigney recognizes the photo as the one taken for his Navy Identification Card when he was advanced to radioman third class.

"I am Commander Watson, and this is Mister Barton," the man in the officer's uniform informs. "Sit there," the officer directs as he points to a chair that will seat Rigney directly across the table from the two men.

As is Rigney's manner, he does not allow gravity to slam his butt into the chair. He places both hands firmly on each arm of the chair and employ his arm muscles to slowly lower himself into the chair. Rigney read somewhere that this action conveys self-control to those who are watching. Rigney watches the two men as he seats himself. The two men do not appear to notice.

The navy officer says, "Page, I need to verify your identity against your I.D. card."

Rigney takes out his wallet and hands his I.D. card to the officer.

The officer compares the I.D. card to Rigney's face. Then, he compares the I.D. to the photograph in the file folder. Then, he explains the purpose of the meeting. "Page, last month you submitted an application for a top secret clearance. Our meeting with you today is a part of the process for completing that application. Our questions and your answers will be recorded. Are you willing to have your answers recorded?"

"Yes, sir," Rigney answers confidently.

The civilian, Mister Barton, reaches over the table and presses the record button on the tape recorder. The two tape reels begin their circular motion.

Mister Barton speaks into the microphone. "This is Charles Barton. Today is Wednesday, November 8, 1967. The current time is 9:37 a.m. With me is Commander Brad Watson, whose identity I have verified. I also have with me Radioman Third Class Rigney Michael Page, whose identity I have verified." Barton pauses and looks toward Rigney and directs, "Page, state your full name and your service number."

Rigney responds calmly, "My name is Rigney Michael Page, and my service number is 1198107."

Charles Barton states for the record. "The purpose of this interview is to finalize the process for granting Rigney Michael Page a top secret security clearance."

Rigney is curious about Mister Barton's words. He remembers the personnelman saying that the top secret security clearance process takes six months.

Mr. Barton queries, "Page, your personal profile-sheet lists *None* for *Religious Preference*. Why is that?"

Rigney flinches and blinks his eyes, conveying surprise at being asked such a question. "My recruiter told me that I should never be asked that question. He said the navy would not care about my religious preference."

"*None* for *Religious Preference* is unusual. I just want to clarify. Is it true that you have no preference?"

Rigney does not like the direction of this interview. He becomes agitated and considers it unfair that he must answer such a question. Rigney looks at Commander Watson for some guidance. Rigney thinks that another navy man will understand, but the commander does not respond.

Rigney asks, "Does my religious preference have anything to do with the special assignment?"

The civilian shoots a glance at the commander.

In a challenging tone, Commander Watson inquires, "What do you mean by special assignment?"

"The personnelman called BUPERS to find out why I do not have orders. Everyone else in my class got their orders weeks ago. The personnelman had to call around. Finally, someone he knew told him that my file had been sent to the Special Assignments Branch, and that my tickler file had been marked *no assignment until approval of top secret clearance*, or some words like that."

"What is the name of the personnelman?" the commander demands.

Rigney realizes that the personnelman must have done something wrong. Rigney also knows that he must cooperate. He knows that having a top secret clearance is not something to be taken lightly. "I do not remember his name. He is a second class, fat, with black hair and glasses."

The commander spends a few moments writing in his notebook. Then, he asks, "Have you told anyone about this special assignment?"

"No. I thought that because a top secret clearance is involved, I should not talk to anyone about it."

The commander quickly writes in his notebook. Then, he looks over at the civilian and smiles. The civilian smiles back and nods.

Mr. Barton explains, "Rigney, now that you know you are being considered for a special assignment, you need to understand the purpose of my questions. The content of your answer to religious preference is not important. What is important is that you explain. If you are selected for this assignment, the commander and I will have periodic contact with you over the course of your assignment. The commander and I need to know you well. We need to understand your background."

Rigney becomes more curious. "So, this meeting is more than just part of the top secret clearance process? You are interviewing me for the special assignment, right? What is the special assignment?"

Barton responds, "Yes. This interview is part of the screening process for special assignment. I cannot inform you of the special assignment at this time. I must caution you not to mention the content of this meeting to anyone. Are you now ready to answer my questions?"

Rigney feels more comfortable.

"Yes sir. I will answer your questions."

Barton resumes. "Rigney, it is unusual for a person with your background to list *None* for *Religious Preference*. You went to Catholic grade schools. Please explain."

"I do not practice any religion and have not since the sixth grade."

Barton asks, "Next year you will reach the age of twenty-one. Do you plan on registering to vote?"

"Yes."

"What political party will you register?"

Rigney hesitates.

Mr. Barton directs with an insistent tone, "Please answer. As I said before, it is not important what you say, only that you explain fully."

"If it's not important, why do you need to know?"

"Let me clarify," Barton offers. "On your navy application and on your Top Secret Clearance Application, you swore that you did not belong to any organization whose purpose it is to overthrow the legally formed government of the United States. If you plan on joining the Communist Party next year, we need to know about it."

Rigney nods understanding. "I will register Republican."

Barton asks, "Who is the President and Vice President of the United States?"

"Lyndon Johnson is President. Hubert Humphrey is Vice President."

"Name the Secretary of the Navy and the Chief of Naval Operations."

"The CNO is Admiral Moorer. I do not remember the name of the Secretary of the Navy. I do remember that someone new took over last summer."

Commander Watson leans forward in his chair with a questioning look on his face and motions that he wants to ask a question.

Barton nods to Watson.

Commander Watson looks directly into Rigney's eyes and speaks in a questioning tone. "Page, I know many young sailors on their first hitch, and I do not believe that any of them know or care to know the names of these government and military officials. So, it makes me wonder why you know."

"I read *Navy Times*, *All Hands*, and *Proceedings*."

"When did you start reading Proceedings?" The commander appears to be impressed.

"Ever since my sophomore year in high school I wanted to join the navy and receive advanced electronic training. Since my first look at a submarine, I wanted to be a submariner.

"My home is next to the Naval Weapons Station in Seal Beach,

California. My parents have many navy friends. From our recreation-room window on the third floor, I watched the ships and submarines come and go. Those sailors looked impressive in their dress uniforms. My parents' navy friends would talk about the foreign countries they visited. They talked about their lives at sea. I found it fascinating.

"My mother asked one of her navy friends what publications I should read to keep me informed on the navy. A chief petty officer recommended *Proceedings*. I have had a subscription since I was fifteen."

Commander Watson asks, "Do you understand what you read in *Proceedings*?"

"I understand the articles that explain weapons systems and other electronic systems. Many of the articles about political and military strategy concepts that confuse me. I figure that with time I will come to understand them."

Commander Watson sits back in his chair and nods approval toward Charles Barton.

Mr. Barton states, "I am finished with my questions. The commander has more questions for you." Charles Barton sighs and moves farther back in his chair.

Commander Watson leans forward and folds his arms on the tabletop. He comments, "Page, I have been studying your Quarterly Performance Evaluations. You get four-O in all categories, except Leadership, which you get three-eighths and three-sixes. You are academically at the top of all your classes. Your instructors report that you are intelligent and are a fast learner. Informally, however, your instructors believe you are cocky and have a know-it-all attitude. Why is that?"

Rigney casts a bewildering expression and responds, "I did not know that they think that, and I do not know why they think that. I hardly talk to anyone in school. When I do, it's about class stuff. Except for a few class parties at the enlisted club, I do not associate with my classmates outside of school. I spend most of my off time in the base library and the base gym."

"Are you bothered by what your instructors think of you?"

"I am not bothered by it." Rigney's voice is calm and sincere.

"You are not concerned about what your instructors think of you?"

"Sir, you said *informally* they say that. I average 3.8 performance marks, which is near top notch. What difference does it make what they think informally? I am not obliged to perform to some unspecified standard that exists in the minds of others. Are not my Quarterly Performance Evaluations the formal and official report of my performance?"

Watson ignores Rigney's question and informs, "Your instructors say that some of your classmates think the same thing. Does that concern you?"

"No, I am not concerned."

"You do not care what others think of you. Is that correct?"

Rigney feels that the officer is trying to trap him into saying something that disqualifies him from the special assignment. *Whatever that might be.* "Sir, I do not understand what you're getting at."

"I am trying to understand how you respond to what others think of you and say of you. Especially, if what they say may be insulting or a lie or both."

Rigney spends a few moments formulating his response. "Sir, I am not responsible, nor am I accountable, for what others do and say. What people do and say belongs to them, not to me. I am not responsible for the actions of others, and I am not responsible for how others react to me. I am only responsible and accountable for how I act, and for what I say."

Watson nods understanding; then asks, "When someone tells a lie about you, how do you react?"

"I do not react. I do not feel obliged to react to lies and misperception. What possible reaction can there be that makes sense? Those who peddle lies and misperception are not interested in the truth. Why should I spend energy to convince them of the truth? Those who would judge me based on what others say are not worthy my time. I do not consider it healthy to torment myself over what others may think of me.

"My Evaluations report that I am conforming to the standards prescribed officially by the navy. I agreed to those standards when I took my oath. My expectations of myself are aligned with what the navy expects of me. The navy expects me to be a good sailor and a good radioman, and that is what I want to be. I cannot waste my time worrying about those who do not care about reality and would rather wallow in deceit. I wasted too many years of my childhood worrying about what others thought of me."

The commander asks, "What caused you to change from a person who cared what others think of you to a person who does not care?"

"Sir, it's a long story. In short, I found it objectionable for others to design my path and set my goals. Too many people close to me tried to manipulate me. I went my own way and suffered the criticism of others because of it. I insulated myself against the words of others and did what I wanted."

"Be specific," urges Watson in a demanding tone.

Rigney sighs deeply and expresses annoyance at being ordered to describe events from his past. He spends a few moments recollecting. Then, he explains. "During the summer before my sophomore year of high school, I let family and friends talk me into playing football. I didn't want to because I don't care about football and because August is when the Southern California surfing competitions take place. Also, August is some of the best times for snorkeling and scuba diving off Southern California beaches. Spear fishing competitions take place the last two weeks of August.

"Anyway, I skipped some football practices so that I could compete in surfing and spear fishing tournaments, which caused the football coach to jump on me. He yelled and criticized me in front of the team. Then, school started, and football games were played on Friday nights. During the week, I would skip some football practices and physical endurance sessions, so that I could attend surfing competitions.

As punishment, the coach assigned me to third-string center-linebacker. During the first three home games, I only played a few minutes in one game. The coach did not allow me to travel to away games.

"Then, one Wednesday afternoon in early October, I showed up late for physical endurance training. I was late because I was competing in the semifinals of a surfing competition. The coach pulled me aside and started yelling at me for being a loner instead of a team player. He said I was third string because of my tardiness and my absences from practice and training. He said that unless I was in top physical shape and stopped missing practice, I would never get a better position on the team. I explained to him that no one on the team was in better shape than me. He said he was the best judge of that. I told him that I did not believe a fat and flabby thirty-year old was a better judge of physical fitness than me. He tried to embarrass me by nearly shouting that I was never late or absent for a Friday night game. I responded that those activities more important to me than football were never scheduled for Friday nights. He responded that I needed to get my priorities in order and do what he told me. He claimed I would never be successful in life by being a loner and a nonconformist. He told me I was on probation, and should I be late or absent for one more practice, I would be dropped from the team.

"After a day of thought, I decided that I should not put a lot of value in the opinion and expectations of a high school football coach. The next day in school, I searched out the coach. I found him in the hallway outside his classroom. I asked to talk with him in private. He said that I had not earned a private conversation with him.

14

"With a bunch of other teachers and students watching, I gave him the keys to my uniform locker and told him I was not playing football anymore. I told him that I was not willing to meet his expectations or anyone else's expectations. I told him that from now on, I would dedicate my time to meeting my own expectations.

"The coach did not say anything. He turned his back on me and walked away. He was also my history teacher. Later, in history class, he spent at least ten minutes trying to humiliate me in front of the class. He called me a quitter . . . said I did not have what it takes to be a winner, but I was not humiliated. I was not embarrassed. He was trying to manipulate me through guilt and embarrassment. I just smiled at him throughout the entire tirade.

"For several weeks after that, I endured the sarcasm and harassment of friends, my girlfriend, and family. They called me a quitter and a coward. I broke up with my girlfriend and disassociated myself from my so-called friends. I became a real loner. I think what frustrated them the most was that I did not try to justify my actions. I believe they were offended that what I thought important was not the same as what they thought important. They could not tolerate someone not wanting to be the same as them. I felt that I had no obligation to justify my actions to others. I knew they would not understand.

"Anyway, I went back to activities I enjoyed. I was happier. Ever since that football incident, I have lived my life to my own expectations. I ignore the name-callers and the liars. They are ignorant and lack self-respect. I just don't see any value in being concerned by it all."

Watson asks, "You said that you endured the sarcasm and harassment of family. How did your parents react to your open rebellion?"

"By family, I didn't mean my parents. I meant my uncles and cousins. My parents were supportive of what I did. I was a straight-A student and never got into any trouble. I succeeded in winning at the activities I enjoyed."

The commander questions, "Appears to me that you avoid team sports. Why is that?"

"Not true sir. I play a lot of basketball."

"In high school, did you play on the school basketball team?"

"Not the high school team. I played in the city sponsored leagues, like Elks and Masons. I also played in the church leagues."

"Were you not good enough for the school team?"

"I never tried out for the school team. After that incident with the football coach, I didn't want any part of serving the masters of high school sports. The city leagues allowed me to set my own schedule and provided me more freedom to play and practice when I wanted."

Commander Watson states, "The navy requires you to conform and be a team player. I hope you understand that."

Rigney chuckles and comments, "Sir, I chose the navy and I chose submarines. I am more than willing to do what is necessary to be successful in the navy."

"But will you do what is best for the navy and what is best for your country?"

Rigney expresses bewilderment.

Commander Watson states, "I have no more questions."

Mr. Barton states, "Interview concluded at 10:24 a.m., November 8th, 1967." He reaches over the table and turns off the tape recorder.

Watson stands and advises in an official tone, "That's all for now, Page. One of us will get back with you within a few days."

Rigney rises from his chair and stands at attention for a moment as he says, "Aye, aye, sir." Rigney performs an about-face and departs the room.

As Rigney walks back to class, thoughts race through his mind. *What was that all about? Who are those two? Why are my religious beliefs and political beliefs relevant? Good thing about the top secret clearance investigation almost done. The officer was not a submariner. So why was he there? Who was the civilian? And what was that business about how I react to insults?*

Rigney enters the classroom. His instructor advises that Rigney is 30 minutes late for the lab test. The instructor also tells Rigney that the electronic problem has been placed into the Jason cryptographic equipment and that he has only 30 minutes to find the problem and write it down along with the corrective action.

This Cryptographic Equipment Repair course is the last course that Rigney needs to complete prior to assignment to a submarine. When he completes this course, he will have completed two-years of electronics schools. He will be trained to repair all equipment in a submarine radio room, including transmitters, receivers, teletypes, crypto, and antennas.

Rigney powers up his oscilloscope. As he progresses with troubleshooting, he occasionally looks at his instructor. His instructor is a first class radioman with eight years in the navy and a total four years in submarines. Rigney wonders if this instructor reported him as having a cocky and a know-it-all attitude. He wonders which of his past instructors reported the same thing.

He finds the problem in the Jason equipment in seven minutes and spends only one minute writing down the problem and the fix.

Rigney sits at the test bench and wonders about the events of this morning. He knows that his philosophies are not typical. He believes that he will probably not qualify for the special assignment because he is too much a loner and free thinker. *That's fine with me,* he reasons, *I am ready to serve on a submarine.* Rigney senses impatience within himself to start his submarine adventure. Five years have passed since he first decided this is what he wants. *Finally, the day is near!*

Chapter 3

After school each day, Rigney walks to the base library. He spends 30 minutes studying the day's lessons and notes he wrote. Then, he reads newspapers and news magazines for another hour.

As usual, the librarian, Sally Macfurson, smiles at Rigney as he walks through the double doors. She is a slim and petite woman of twenty-six. Her thick, auburn hair is her most striking feature. She wears her hair straight and long. Her hair hangs over her ears and flows to a taper at the back of her neck where it is held in place with a wide and circular black clasp. From the black clasp, her hair flows in a thick ponytail to the middle of her back. Sally stands five feet and two inches. Her face is round with a small upturned nose over a small and full-lipped mouth. Her dark green eyes are widely set. Most of the time, Sally wears loose fitting sweaters and skirts. While working, she wears reading glasses perched on the end of her nose. Normally, her bearing and behavior is best described as collegiate. She recently received her master's degree in European History.

Tonight, however, Sally wears a tight, lightweight black turtleneck sweater that accentuates her bust and narrow waist. Instead of a skirt, she wears tight, light-gray colored ski pants that show off her small and rounded hips and buttocks. Tonight, her manner is sexy. Her dark green eyes, looking over the top of her reading glasses, follow Rigney as he walks toward her desk.

As Rigney approaches, he recognizes her lightly scented perfume. Tonight, she looks sexier and more attractive than ever before. He stares into her eyes and whispers, "Hi, Sally. How are you this evening?"

Sally leans over the desk and calmly whispers back, "You come in here every night and ask the same thing. Then, nothing else from you for the next hour-and-a-half. Do you really care how I am? When you leave each afternoon, it's with a wave to me from across the room." Sally pauses and expresses regret. In a yearning tone, she says, "I want to talk with you after the library closes."

"I don't think that's a good idea," Rigney responds in a tone of confident sincerity.

Sally looks around the library. No one is paying attention to them. She motions Rigney toward the door. Rigney reluctantly follows her through the glass paned doors and into the building's main corridor. He walks behind her and cannot help noticing her swaying hips.

"Rigney, why are you avoiding me? Since our last date three weeks ago, you have been distant. Have I done something wrong? Is there something that I have said?"

Rigney stares into her eyes for a few moments. *She sounds like she really cares, but does she?*

Rigney decides to be honest with her. "Sally, I do not understand your interest in me. You're six years older than me. You're pretty, you're intelligent, and you're educated. I think that there must be men around here that are more your type. I'm 20 and do not have a college degree. I will probably depart New London in a couple weeks. You seem interested, and you appear attracted. But that night we were last together, you made excuses about not having sex. None of it makes sense to me. I think it better if we just let it go."

Sally begins to respond, but she looks through the glass panels of the library door and sees a line growing to check out books. "I must go back to the desk. Please meet me later."

Rigney does not intend to meet her later. He follows her back into the library. Again, he cannot help but notice the sway of her hips and the fragrance of her lightly scented perfume. Her tempting presence excites him.

Sally began working at the library several months ago. From their first meeting, Rigney and Sally were attracted to each other. Their first conversions were flirtatious to the point of sensual. They went to the Navy Exchange snack bar a few times for coffee during her thirty-minute break. They often stepped outside the library door to have short conversations.

After four weeks of just having coffee and having short conversations, Rigney asked her for an off-base date. She agreed. They decided to see a movie in New London. Rigney does not have a car, but Sally does. Sally picked up Rigney at his barracks. She drove a large 1967 Mercedes sedan. The car belongs to her. Rigney discovered that Sally is rich. Her parents descend from old New England money and affluence.

He asked her why she had kept it a secret. He thought that she lived with her parents. Rigney thought she was hiding her wealth because he had told her that he comes from a financially challenged background. He had told her that his parents survive from payday to payday, and that he had to work part time during the summers to pay for his surfboard supplies, take girls on dates, and maintain his 1951 Ford pickup truck. Rigney had told Sally about his Southern California upbringing. His family lives a beach lifestyle. He spent most of the summers surfing the shores from Seal Beach to Newport Beach.

Sally insisted that she did not keep her wealth secret and never thought about keeping it secret. It just never came up in conversation. Sally honestly thought that Rigney already knew. She asked Rigney if he had not noticed her expensive rings and other jewelry that she wore. She asked him about noticing her expensive clothes. Rigney replied that he did not know enough about jewelry or clothes to determine expensive from inexpensive.

He emphasized that his family lives a beach lifestyle. That means they mostly wear casual clothes. In the summertime, it is always shorts and sandals. Only his father wears a suit and that was only in the wintertime. Rigney told Sally that jewelry and clothes do not matter to him.

Sally rationally responded that it never mattered to her either. She explained that what she wears and what she drives is just part of her family lifestyle. She never thought much about it, either. Yes, she lives with her parents. She explained that she lives in a four-room apartment in the east wing of her family home. The apartment has private access. Except for weekends, she seldom sees her parents.

They dropped the issue and did not bring it up again. They enjoyed their first date. After the movie, Sally took Rigney to a nightclub on the beach. Rigney looks older than his actual age, and no one questioned him about his age. They both drank soft drinks. They sat out on the beachside patio until closing time. They sat next to each other and held hands and snuggled. They kissed a few times. They expressed their goals in life. Rigney violated his own rules by telling Sally why he thought the way he did about many things. He told her about the high school football incident. Sally shared her deepest thoughts. They discussed politics, religion, and Vietnam.

Several nights later while parked in the barracks parking lot, they started kissing. Their kissing became deep and passionate. Sally offered to take them to a motel.

Rigney's last sexual activity had been the previous summer. His passion overcame his every thought. He tremendously ached for release. Rigney had suggested that they climb into the backseat, instead of waiting the long drive to a motel. It was 10:30 p.m. on a weeknight. He was tired, and he had lab tests first thing in the morning. Sally was tempted, but she told Rigney that she would rather do it in the comfort of a bed.

Rigney apologized. He gently told her that he had to get a good night's sleep. She pulled away from him and agreed to a motel on another night, maybe the next weekend. To Rigney, it sounded like a put off. She appeared to be disappointed that Rigney turned down the offer of going to a motel. Or was she faking. Rigney did not understand. Since entering the navy, Rigney did not have sex as often as he did when in high school. He had never been put off. He said goodnight to her and exited the car.

Since that night, Rigney avoided conversation with Sally. He also would make excuses not to go on dates. He was confused by her interest. *Why is she interested in me? She is six years older than I am. She has a master's degree. She is educated and smart. Why is she not interested in the bachelor officers? Rigney thought the officers would be more her type—college graduates and her own age.*

He also did not appreciate her actions to get him totally aroused, then not finish it. That never happened with the girls he knows back home in Seal Beach. He wonders if she is a tease. He knows the type.

Sally came to the barracks several times looking for him. He was never there, but he got the messages.

Rigney sits at his study table in the rear of the library. He tries to study, but he cannot. His mind wanders. He looks to the front of the library and follows Sally's movements. *Does this woman want me?* The question makes him uneasy. He needs to maintain control. *I stay in control by avoiding her. Avoiding her is difficult because she works at the library four nights a week. She is totally desirable!*

Rigney knows that he cannot be in control if he gives himself to another. He knows that he must remain distant to be in control. He knows that relationships with others make him vulnerable.

As is his normal routine, Rigney departs the library at 1730. He walks to the base dining facility for dinner. After dinner, he walks to the barracks. He deposits his books in his locker and changes into jeans and a hooded sweatshirt. He grabs his gym gear and goes to the base gym.

Normally, Rigney spends one hour playing vigorous basketball and another hour lifting weights. Tonight's activities are different than his normal routine. He mostly just watches the basketball pickup games. He plays for fifteen minutes, but he cannot concentrate. His mind is preoccupied with this morning's interview. He spends some time lifting weights, but he does not follow his usual routine. At 8:00 p.m., he decides to shower and get dressed.

He exits the gym at 2030—too early to go back to the barracks. Rigney does not like going back to the barracks until after 2200, which is *lights-out* time, and the barracks goes dark. He avoids sitting around the barracks during the early evening. Too many of his classmates want to engage Rigney in conversation about things in which he has no interest. Rigney could not care less about which cars are the fastest,

21

which professional football team has the best chance to win next weekend, or the sexual conquests of his classmates.

Rigney decides to go back to the base library, which does not close until 2200.

At 2045, the library is mostly empty. Only two sailors are sitting at tables and reading.

Sally's face illuminates with joy when seeing Rigney enter the library.

Oh, no. She thinks I came back to meet with her. Rigney had forgotten about her request to meet after the library closes. He decides to stay and talk with her later. He does not want to offend her, nor does he want to appear rude.

He checks the magazine rack and selects a recent issue of a news magazine. He wanders back to his table in the rear. Within a few moments, he is absorbed in an article regarding the Israeli attack on the USS *Liberty* that took place last June. The article reports the *Liberty* did not receive the message to cruise more than 100 miles away from the Israeli coast until after the *Liberty* was attacked. Navy investigators are blaming processing errors within the navy communications system.

The library's overhead lights go dark. Lights from the street and the lights from the outside corridor cast a dim illumination into the library. Rigney looks at his watch. The radium glow tells him it is 2145, which is fifteen minutes early for the library to close.

Rigney hears Sally's light footsteps coming closer.

She comes around the closest bookshelf. The outside light is behind her. Her petite silhouette casts a shadow as she walks toward him.

Sally has removed the barrette that normally holds her long red hair pulled back, and she is not wearing her reading glasses. She walks over to where Rigney sits; she lowers her head and kisses his neck. Then, she moves her lips to his and kisses him firmly. She holds her lips to his.

He becomes aroused. He stands and wraps his arms around her waist. Sally's hands hold his biceps. Rigney is too tall for her to put her hands around his neck.

Sally looks up into Rigney's green eyes and smiles at him. His eyes are wide, and his face is flushed. He bends down to kiss her again. She holds up a hand to stop him.

She takes his right hand and leads him through the library and into the library office. An overhead light brightly illuminates the room. A large, worn and beaten, overstuffed brown-colored leather couch stands against one wall. A small door on the opposite wall leads to a bathroom.

Sally leads him to the leather couch.

He stands with his back toward the couch; he faces Sally. She pulls up the bottom of his sweatshirt as a signal for him to remove it. As Rigney pulls the sweatshirt over his head and tosses onto a chair a few feet away, Sally loosens his belt buckle.

Sally takes a step back. She kicks off her shoes. Then, she pulls her sweater over her head and tosses it onto the same chair. She stands topless, except for white bra that surrounds her breasts. Then, she removes her own belt and pulls down on the side zipper; her ski pants fall to the floor. Sally is not wearing hose or stockings.

Naked, except for her white bra and white panties, she steps toward him and turns her back to him. She lifts her flowing red hair to her shoulders. Rigney fumbles with the bra clasp but gets it done. Sally slips the bra off her shoulders; then, she pushes her panties to the floor. She tosses both items onto the chair.

With her back still toward him, she takes several steps.

The rear view of her shapely, petite body increases his excitement.

Her red hair hangs halfway down her back and sways side to side as she walks. Her thin waist accentuates her small and firmly rounded buttocks.

After three steps, Sally turns and faces Rigney. She wants Rigney to see her fully naked body from head to toe. Her hands are on her hips and her shoulders are back. She stands with her legs slightly apart.

Rigney stares at her. He sees that her face is flushed. Her hair falls back behind her shoulders. Her breasts are firm and perfectly sized for her body; her nipples are pink, hard, and round. He moves his eyes slowly down her body. He takes in every shape and curve. His penis expands to its limit.

He takes a step toward her. She moves forward and pushes him lightly back toward the couch. He stares at her. *What a beauty!* He leans forward to kiss her, but she holds up a hand.

"First things first," Sally rasps lightly. Her voice sounds husky and sexy.

She kneels in front of him and removes his shoes and socks. He lifts each foot a few inches to allow the removal. She places her hands on both sides of his waist and pulls down on his pants along with his underwear.

Rigney looks down at her as she pulls down his pants and underwear. Her face is just inches away from his exposed, erect, and throbbing penis. His heart starts pounding harder and his knees become weak as he fantasizes her sucking his penis into her mouth.

Sally looks up as she notices him breathing faster. She asks softly,

"How about stepping out of your pants, sailor?"

Rigney lifts each foot as Sally removes the pants from around his feet.

She tosses Rigney's pants and underwear onto the pile. Then, she stands up and steps back about four feet.

Rigney feels disappointment. *She did not blow me.* He believes he did something wrong to destroy the moment.

Sally stands four feet from Rigney and evaluates his physical attributes from head to toe. *What a rugged and handsome man. His shoulders are wide, and his biceps are large. A thick covering of reddish brown hair spreads over his body from his neck to his ankles. His torso is hard, and his stomach his taut. His hips are narrow, and his buttocks are flat.* She spends a few extra moments staring at his erect penis. She moves her eyes to meet his. She has fantasized about this moment. She likes what she sees. Her face forms a sexy smirk.

"What, Sally?" Rigney rasps between rapid breaths. The sight of this woman's naked body drives him crazy.

Sally walks toward him and places her hands on his chest and gently pushes him down to a sitting position on the leather couch. She grabs two of the couch's throw pillows and stands over him. She instructs, "Put these pillows under the small of your back for support."

Rigney complies.

Sally gets on her knees, spreads his legs apart, and moves between his thighs. She lowers her head and sucks his penis into her mouth.

This moment is the most erotic moment in his life.

They remain in the library most of the night. Rigney surprises himself with the number of times he accommodates their lovemaking. Sally introduces Rigney to sexual activities that he has never experienced. She teaches Rigney how to properly place his head between her thighs and where and how to use his lips and tongue to bring a woman to groaning, shuddering, and pleasurable orgasm. In Sally's case, loud and guttural and moaning orgasm. She also teaches him the best way for conventional sex with her straddling him while he lies on his back.

During their fifth and final sexual act of the evening, Sally again takes Rigney's penis into her mouth. The act is the most sexually satisfying that he has ever experienced.

Rigney does not realize that this night he is not in control of himself. He completely turns himself over to this woman.

During this night, Sally knows that she could ask Rigney for anything, and he would give it.

Chapter 4

The Submarine Base Officer's Club bar is quiet at 10:30 p.m. on this weekday evening. Paintings of WWI and WWII submarines at sea and in battle hang on the oak paneled walls. The thick, deep-blue colored carpet adds a touch of elegance. Subdued lighting provides an atmosphere of privacy. A few junior officers in their Working Blue uniform sit at the bar and speak softly about the events of the day. The bartender, a young man wearing a white shirt and black vest and a red bowtie busily wipes down the bar top with a white cloth. In a back corner booth, hardly visible to those sitting at the bar, Lieutenant Commander Bradley Watson and Mister Charles Barton sit quietly.

Conforming to the Brad's suggestion to be as anonymous as possible, both men are dressed in casual civilian clothes. The only discernable sound is the clinking of ice when they sip their drinks. Occasionally, one of them swirls the glass to better mix the ice and the alcohol.

Charles Barton leans toward the Commander Watson and speaks softly with a concerned voice, "Brad, are you sure this is the best place to discuss this Rigney Page business? What if someone hears us? What if the place is bugged?"

"Do not worry, Charlie. You're on my turf now. No one will hear us, and this place is swept for bugs daily."

"What if it is bugged by our own people?"

"Take it easy. I am with the Office of Naval Intelligence. I know about these things. The place is not bugged."

Charles sits back and looks somewhat relieved, but some doubt lingers. As an experienced field agent and, now, a Field Supervisor in the DIA—Defense Intelligence Agency—Charles knows that he must always doubt. Nevertheless, he knows that Brad would not say that he is with naval intelligence if he were not confident of privacy.

Brad asks Charlie, "What do you think of Petty Officer Page?"

The DIA Field Supervisor ponders the question for a few moments; then, replies, "He's an independent thinker and too unconventional. He's a loner. You said it yourself. He does not think like other young sailors think. He is too young to think deeply, and he questions too much. It's the nature of young people today. They are not educated in the ways of the world and are too quick to question authority. I worry that Page will question orders at a time when quick, unyielding obedience is necessary. Besides, he has no training in this line of work. Counterintelligence work requires years of training and experience."

Brad Watson considers Charlie's words; then, he responds, "Buddy got hurt because he was undertrained. He was not. . ."

"What do you mean undertrained?!" Charlie raises his voice. "Buddy Pearson has eleven years' experience. He is one of my best field agents."

Brad understands Charlie's protest. Charlie is protective of his agents. Buddy Pearson is a DIA field agent, not an ONI counterintelligence agent. Buddy served as an officer in the Army and knew little about the navy. Brad perceives Charlie to be a member of that ageing breed of intelligence professionals who believe experience in intelligence gathering is more relevant than experience in the environment where you gather intelligence.

"Let me finish, Charlie. What I mean by undertrained is that his specialty is intelligence gathering, not electronics. Buddy is 33. Because of his age, he was placed undercover as a first class petty officer. Most ETs are chiefs by the age of 33. But if he were placed undercover as a chief ET, his lack of electronic knowledge would have been even more noticeable. He only has a working knowledge of electronics. You know, the little theory and practical application we get working with electronic intelligence gathering devices. It had to be obvious to those Buddy worked with that he did not have the electronics knowledge typical of an ET1. His lack of electronics knowledge probably made him standout. Today's navy is much more technical than it was ten years ago. Someone must have noticed.

"Charlie, you and I have been collaborating for years. You know that the older agents can no longer pass for junior enlisted men. Most of our agents have four years or college and several years as an officer before we recruit them. Men in their late twenties and early thirties can no longer go undercover as junior enlisted. During the thirties and forties, they could pass. In those days, there were many older men in the lower pay grades. It just does not work anymore. We cannot have them go undercover as officers because they will not be close enough to the technical environment. I understand that the DIA was the first agency in on this thing, but now it's time to turn it over to the navy."

Charlie contemplates Brad's words. He shakes his head with disagreement. "So, you think Rigney Page is the answer? You said yourself that he is unusual. You don't think he will be conspicuous?"

"Actually, I am counting on him being conspicuous," Brad advises. No one will expect an egotistical, conspicuous sailor who brings attention to himself to be a counterintelligence agent. We assign him simple discovery and collection tasks, nothing to put anyone in danger. We need someone of Page's intellect, youth, and electronics knowledge. We are running out of time. We must have someone in place by the end of December. We have researched other candidates. Page is the most qualified. With Page, we need not put him in the ET Shop. He will be assigned to the ship's radioman division."

Again, the DIA man reflects doubt, but he relents. "Okay. The direction from the Joint Chiefs is to come up with something unique this time because too many of our counterintelligence agents are being detected. If I agree to your plan, then the navy directs this one. My position will be one of DIA coordinator. I still question Page's value. He has no navy experience other than two years in navy schools. He has a lot to learn about his technical job and about the navy. How will he recognize an unusual technical situation when he encounters one?"

Brad Watson answers confidently, "I know using Page has some risk, but he is the best qualified. I will train him on recognizing unusual technical situations."

The DIA man counters, "Page wants to serve in submarines. He might not agree to this."

"I know," Brad Watson acknowledges. "I will convince him tomorrow."

Chapter 5

During a troubleshooting lecture, the school yeoman pulls Rigney out of class and tells him to report to the Director's Conference Room. Rigney's classmates become even more curious than the day before.

Rigney enters the conference room. This time, however, only Lieutenant Commander Watson is present. The officer stares out the window. The commander is in shirtsleeves. His coat drapes neatly over the back of a chair.

Rigney comes to attention and recites in his best military voice, "Radioman Third Class Page reporting as ordered, sir."

As the officer turns from the window, he points to a chair.

Rigney lowers himself into the chair, using his arms to control the movement as he did the day before. Again, the officer does not appear to notice.

Brad Watson

Rigney senses a less formal manner from the officer. The officer does not stand erect. His shoulders are drooped.

Watson states, "You look like you had a bad night."

"Actually, sir, I must say it was the most pleasant evening that I have had in a long time."

"Glad to hear it. Did you think about what we talked about yesterday?"

Rigney replies mildly—without emotion. "Yes, sir. I figure that my personality disqualifies me. That's okay, though; submarines are what I want."

"Page, the navy has a special assignment for you. If you decide to take it, you will be assigned to a surface ship for a period-of-time. We know that you want to go to a submarine. However, the navy needs your qualifications. I believe that you are our best chance for a successful mission. Your top secret clearance is approved. What I am about to tell you is classified top secret. Do you know how to protect the classified information that you carry in your head?"

Rigney sits stunned. His mind focuses on the words *surface ship*. He worries that his five year quest will be for naught.

"Rigney!" Brad Watson snaps. "Are you paying attention to what I am saying?"

Rigney returns his attention to Mister Watson. He realizes that the officer addressed him by his first name. The informality causes Rigney to refocus on the officer's words. "Sir, please repeat your question?"

"Do you know how to protect top secret information that you have in your head?"

"Yes, sir. I may only discuss with those who have a top secret clearance and who also have a *need to know*."

"Correct."

Watson advises, "I work for the Office of Naval Intelligence— ONI—Counterintelligence Branch. We believe that someone on a navy surface ship is passing classified information to the Soviets. We do not know whom or how he is doing it. Nevertheless, the evidence is solid that the information is coming from that ship. We need someone to go aboard that ship, gather intelligence on how the material is being compromised, and identify who is doing it."

Rigney interrupts by asking, "Gather intelligence? You mean like James Bond? You mean like a spy?"

"No!" Brad Watson snorts in an irritated tone. His face reddens slightly. "Real intelligence agents work anonymously. They are not flamboyant, and they do not have sex with every pretty woman they encounter. And, they do not blowup large enemy complexes at the end of every mission."

Rigney attempts to grasp Mister Watson's meaning. He does not understand how he fits into all of this. He responds, "Yes, I know that James Bond is fantasy." Rigney pauses, expressing that he is formulating a question.

Brad knows that another question is coming, and he permits Rigney ask it.

Rigney's face contorts into an exaggerated quizzical expression with one eyebrow raised. He queries, "You want me to become an intelligence agent?"

"Counterintelligence operative to be more accurate."

Unsure of the difference, Rigney decides to research it later. He asks, "But, what about submarine duty? What about all these schools? What about my six-year obligation? I was guaranteed the Submarine Radioman Program." Rigney becomes agitated and the volume of his voice increases.

"Calm down, Rigney," Brad Watson orders in a low tone. "You are not obligated to do this. If you do not want to do this, then there is no problem. You go to your submarine and forget me and forget yesterday and today. There will be nothing in your record. Declining this mission will not be held against you.

"If you do accept this mission, you will be assigned to the surface ship for about six months at the max. Then, you can go to your submarine."

Rigney expresses concern. "Mission? That sounds dangerous."

"Sorry," Watson responds, "Mission is the word we use to describe these kinds of actions. There will be some risk. Someone on the ship is passing classified information to the Russians and will not want his identity known. He might become violently protective of his identity. Your mission would not be to apprehend that person. Your mission involves only determining how it is being done and reporting who could be doing it. ONI analysts will make the final determination as to whom. Your contribution to this mission provides valuable technical knowledge beyond that normally expected of such a young sailor. Your youth will protect you. You can back out of this at any time, including after you go to the ship."

Puzzled, Rigney asks, "How do I go about this? What do I do? What ship?"

"All of that will be explained later. If you accept, I will arrange orders for you to come to the ONI Maryland facility for two weeks of indoctrination and training. In Maryland, I will provide the details. I must also tell you that even if you accept now, you could be found unsuitable while in Maryland when you go through some mental and psychological screenings."

"Sir, I complete crypto repair school at the end of this month, I was hoping to go home to Seal Beach for the Christmas Holidays."

"I can have you home by December 20th. You would not report to the ship until December 28th."

"Sir, won't it be suspicious that I spent two years in Submarine Radioman School and then be sent to a surface ship?"

"You must trust me. ONI knows its business. Near the end of your crypto school, you must go through a final physical exam that verifies you are still medically qualified for submarines. If you accept this mission, you will flunk that physical."

"But what about after those six months, sir? You said I could go to a submarine after that?"

"I said trust me. A later physical will find you were incorrectly diagnosed." Brad Watson sits down next to Rigney, looks directly into Rigney's eyes, and asks, "Well, Rigney, can we count on you for help in this matter?"

Rigney understands that he is under no obligation. However, he also knows that he obligated to serve his country and follow the orders of the officers above him. This officer did not give him an order, but this officer said that Rigney is needed elsewhere.

"Sir, how much time do I have to decide?"

"You have about 60 seconds."

Rigney wonders if being a counterintelligence agent can be as exciting and adventurous as serving in submarines. *It's only six months.*

He considers that this situation provides an opportunity for him to experience that which he would not otherwise experience. He desires to experience as much of life as possible while he is young. "Okay, sir. I'll do it. What's next?"

"You are scheduled to finish your school on December first. Correct?"

"Yes, sir. That's correct."

"And you planned on flying to Los Angeles and take 30 days leave."

"Yes, sir. I already have the airline's tickets."

"Where are the tickets?"

"In my locker, sir—in the barracks."

"Go get them and bring them here."

"Yes, sir."

Rigney stands and departs the room.

Brad contemplates the wisdom of his strategy to use young sailors as counterintelligence agents. They lack maturity and experience, but it is that lack of maturity and that lack of experience and their youth that will make them unsuspected. This strategy is unique and new and is Watson's creation. His credibility and career are on the line. His peers criticize him for the idea. This new strategy was a hard sell to his superiors. However, his superiors allowed Watson to pursue this approach because no one else had any ideas on how to make field agents less likely to be discovered. Who better to act and think like a young sailor than a young sailor? But Page is not the typical, young sailor. Page's unconventional philosophies and behavior might make him too conspicuous. On the other hand, enemy agents would not consider a conspicuous person to be a counterintelligence agent.

Ten minutes later, Rigney returns with tickets in hand and gives them to Brad Watson. Brad sticks the ticket packet in his shirt pocket.

Brad advises, "One week before you graduate, your doctor will report that your physical reveals a problem, and he will recommend that you be sent to Bethesda Naval Hospital in Washington DC for evaluation. You will be allowed to graduate, and you will be given orders to report to Bethesda Naval Hospital in Washington DC. You will travel by train. You will be met at the DC train station and taken to an ONI facility."

"What will be my medical problem?"

"I don't know yet. ONI must contact the CO of the SUBASE hospital and arrange for a properly documented medical problem. I promise you. The problem will not be terminal."

They both chuckle at that comment and smile at each other.

"Seriously, Rigney, whatever the problem, it will disqualify you from submarines, but not surface ships.

"You will return to New London on December seventeenth. I will take care of changing your plane tickets to depart on December 20 for Los Angeles. At that time, you will also be given plane tickets to depart Los Angeles on December 28 with a destination of Norfolk Virginia.

"If someone you know asks where you are going after graduation, say that you do not know. Say that you have not received orders, yet. If they ask about your medical disqualification from submarines, just say that you do not want to talk about it."

"Sir, the only person that would care is a civilian friend of mine."

"What's his name?"

"It's a she, sir. Her name is Sally Macfurson."

"The librarian?"

"You know her?" Rigney shows surprise.

"No, but I know who she is from the nametag she wears. I have been to the base library a few times. I mean, who would not notice her? Is she more than a friend?"

"Yes, sir. We go out occasionally."

"She is much older than you, right?"

Rigney becomes defensive. "Only six years older, sir."

"Well, if she asks about your orders, just stick to the story. She must not know the truth."

"Yes, sir." Rigney does not convey sincerity.

"Look, Rigney. You must not tell her the truth about all this. Do you understand?"

"Yes, sir. Excuse me if I do not sound sincere. I just don't understand your concern. I understand the nature of classified information, and that I should not discuss it."

"Okay, Rigney. Apology accepted. I'm convinced that you are sincere."

Rigney objects strongly. "Sir, I did not apologize. I never apologize for my actions. I will ask people to excuse my actions, but I'm never apologetic."

Brad stares into Rigney's face for a few moments. He tries to understand Rigney's outburst. He makes a mental note to have this part of Rigney's behavior analyzed during indoctrination in Washington.

Brad informs, "Soviet agents are thick as flies in this neighborhood. Enemy agents are tasked to find out where transferring sailors are going. They engage young sailors in conversation. What you say to your girlfriend may seem meaningless to you. However, enemy agents who specialize in putting together many pieces of so-called meaningless information uncover many secrets. Many self-important people, officer and enlisted alike, mistakenly believe that others find them interesting. So, they talk too much. Too many sailors just talk too much, and they do not think about the significance of what they are saying.

"Anyway, if someone you don't know starts asking questions, just tell them that you are not allowed to discuss personnel movements. And please understand that these foreign agents can be the prettiest and sweetest girls you have ever met, or they can be nice old women who appear to be engaging you in casual conversation. Do you understand?"

"Yes, sir. I understand."

Lieutenant Commander Watson stands and says, "Okay, Page. I will see you in Maryland."

Rigney stands and walks toward the door.

"Wait, Page," Brad Watson orders in an official tone. "Here is the first lesson. Whenever we are together and both in uniform, all rules of formal navy protocol apply. During those occasions, you must address me as *sir* or *Mister Watson*, and I will address you as *Page* or *Petty Officer Page*. Do you understand?"

Rigney turns around and faces the officer and replies. "Yes, sir. I understand, but why did you call me by my first name today?"

"To gain your trust," Watson replies. "I thought if I was less formal, you would be more likely to agree to my proposal. You and I will be working closely. There will be occasions when we will not be in uniform, and we must be informal."

Rigney considers Brad Watson's words. *He is being honest about trying to manipulate me. I will trust this officer—for now.* "Okay, sir. I understand."

Rigney snaps to attention and recites, "Request permission to leave sir?"

"Permission granted," Brad replies officiously.

Rigney performs a smart about face and departs the room.

Lieutenant Commander Brad Watson stares at the closed door and thinks seriously about RM3 Rigney Page. *I hope I am doing the right thing. Sometimes Page appears perfect for this assignment and sometimes he appears lacking. What was that thing about never apologizing? What's the worst that can happen? My approach can be used as reason for my superiors to write a bad fitness report. My peers will tell me 'I told you so.'*

Chapter 6

During the following weeks, Rigney spends most of his liberty time with Sally. On weekends, Sally takes Rigney to historic sites around the New London area. On Saturday nights, they attend small production stage plays.

Sally and Rigney have sex nearly every night, engaging in at least three sex acts each time. Sometimes they have sex in the library office and sometimes in Sally's apartment at her family home.

They both agree that the oral sex is the most pleasurable act. When sexual ecstasy is what they want, they perform oral sex on each other but simultaneously. Rigney performs oral sex on Sally, first. Then, Sally performs oral sex on Rigney. It is more pleasurable that way. The one performing can concentrate on properly giving, and the one receiving can just lie back and enjoy it.

On those occasions when they want to be more intimate and share each other, they have sexual intercourse in the traditional positions.

Sally educates Rigney on how to be a better sexual partner. Rigney is a willing student. He considers the lab work the best part. He often wonders where Sally learned it all.

As each day passes, they share more and more of themselves. Rigney opens himself fully to Sally. He tells her everything about himself, his family, and his philosophies. Sally does the same.

They never mention Rigney's pending transfer. Rigney follows Commander Watson's orders and never even hints to Sally that he knows he will transfer from New London.

Sally hopes that Rigney gets orders to a submarine home-ported in New London. Rigney tells her that he hopes so too.

The amount of time he spends with Sally cause his grades deteriorate. Most mornings, he drags his tired and drained body to class. He is not concerned. He could fail the remaining tests and still get a "C" in the course. He would rather be with Sally than study.

Rigney and Sally lie naked in each other's arms. A low wattage nightstand lamp provides the only illumination in her bedroom. They just completed their third sexual act of the night. They shared themselves intimately and completely during a traditional, face-to-face act of lovemaking.

"Rigney?"

"I'm right here," he answers softly.

"What is your opinion of draft dodgers? Do you hate them a lot?"

"I don't hate anyone," Rigney explains. "I disrespect draft dodgers. I see them as people unwilling to contribute to the preservation of the freedom they enjoy. They want a free ride. Draft dodgers dishonor those millions of American men and women who have willingly served when their country called. Draft dodgers define the military draft as involuntary servitude as justification for not fighting in what they have labeled as an illegal and immoral war."

"You don't think that they truly believe what they say?"

"I think a few do, but I think the majority use those words as an excuse to justify their unwillingness to serve. They break the law by not reporting when drafted. They will eventually be prosecuted."

"But thousands have fled," argues Sally. "How could the government prosecute that many?"

"It's the government's obligation to prosecute them. Otherwise, the government dishonors and disrespects those who did serve and those who died. Veteran's groups and Congress would never allow the government not to prosecute."

"What about those boys who have fled to Canada?"

"They will be prosecuted someday," Rigney declares confidently.

"But Rigney, you wanted to serve in the military. You wanted to be in the navy. Why should those boys who do not want to be in the military be forced to do so?"

"Because it's their duty."

"Who says it's their duty?"

"The law of the land."

"What if you were ordered to Vietnam?"

"I would go because it is my duty."

Sally challenges, "But not your first choice?"

Rigney un-wraps his arms from around Sally and slides his body away from her to get a better look at her face. "No, not my first choice. What are you getting at? What point are you trying to make?"

"The boys who are conscripted have only one choice . . . Vietnam."

"No, not if they plan it properly," Rigney retorts.

"So, you're saying that only the stupid ones go to Vietnam."

"Sally, that's not what I mean."

"So, you avoid Vietnam with proper planning, and draft dodgers avoid it by running away . . . sounds like a fine line to me."

Sally's voice is trembling. She becomes emotional and starts weeping.

Rigney responds tenderly and in a sincere, consoling tone. "Sally, what's the matter. Please tell me."

Sally pulls several tissues from the box on the nightstand. She dabs her eyes. She looks at Rigney with wet eyes and a concerned and sorrowful expression; she says, "I've told you about my brother, Willie."

"Yeah. He's away at college."

"He flunked out last semester. He hid it from my parents. They kept sending him money to live on, and he kept writing letters about how well school was going. Without school, he lost his college deferment from The Draft. A few days ago, his draft notice arrived here at the house. My father called Willie, and Willie told my father the truth. Willie came home yesterday."

"When does he report?" Rigney asks.

"January."

Rigney studies her face. She cannot look him in the eyes. Rigney understands. "He's planning to evade The Draft, right?"

She nods and reveals, "After Christmas, my Dad is driving Willie to Canada and will set him up in an apartment there."

"There are legal ways to avoid The Draft. Since the Draft's inception, the rich and affluent have legally avoided The Draft through deferments. That's why it's called a selective service draft. Your father has powerful friends. He could easily get Willie a deferment."

"Willie refused my Dad's offer of a deferment. Willie says that he wants to protest selective service by fleeing from it."

Rigney does not understand Willie's logic. "What's offensive about serving a few years in the military?"

"Willie believes the selective service law permits slavery. He wants to do his part to protest it."

Expressing disgust, Rigney opines, "Protesting by living in a comfortable luxury apartment in Canada and all his needs subsidized. I have more respect for protesters willing to experience discomfort to support their cause."

"But the government has no right to force Willie to serve in the military."

Rigney shakes his head, conveying his disagreement; he declares, "Every American has a duty and an obligation to serve and protect. A few years of service are not too much to ask to preserve our republic."

Sally looks deeply into Rigney's eyes and responds, "You don't think that selective service is unfair?"

"Yes, I believe it's unfair."

"Then, why do you support it?"

"Because it's federal law and because I think The Draft is necessary. American citizens cannot pick and choose which laws they want to obey. Otherwise, there would be anarchy. I hope that someday our leaders in Washington will pass laws to make selective service fair. Until then, the law must be obeyed."

Sally retorts, "Hope! Laws don't get change on hope! Then, more softly, she says, "Our political leaders in Washington designed the selective service law to protect their own children from The Draft. Don't you see that?"

"I know some who take advantage of deferments. I also know some who could take advantage of deferments but volunteer to serve anyway."

"You never considered a deferment."

"No. I am now doing what I have wanted to do since I was fifteen. Besides, my social and economic background makes me the exact candidate that the selective service law was designed to draft."

"And you still haven't decided what you want to do after the navy?"

"No, that's almost four years away. I will think about all that later."

Sally instructs, "You need to take more charge of your future. You should start planning now."

"Should I?" Rigney quips sarcastically. "How old were you when you decided what you wanted to do with the rest of your life?"

"Your age . . . during my second year in college, I decided that I wanted to teach history at a prestigious university."

"Then why aren't you?" Rigney challenges.

"I need to earn my doctorate, first."

"Oh."

They lie in silence for a few minutes.

Sally breaks the silence. "In a few days the whole family goes to our house in Cape Cod. We spend Thanksgiving through Christmas there. It's a family tradition. We do it every year."

"You're staying here, right?" Rigney asks because he worries that Sally will leave soon.

"No, Rigney. I must go to Cape Cod. We don't know when we will see Willie again. I must be with my family."

Rigney asks, "When were you going to tell me?"

"Rig, I did not want separation levying sadness our thoughts. We don't know if your submarine will be home-ported in New London. We have avoided that subject."

Ironic, Rigney muses. *We both knew we would be separating soon, but we did not want the other to be saddened by it.* He accepts Sally's words with a nod.

Sally suggests, "You are taking leave after school. You can come and visit me in Cape Cod. By then, you'll know about your submarine assignment. You can stay with me in Cape Cod before going out to California for Christmas."

Rigney knows that he cannot go to Cape Cod, but he cannot tell Sally that. He must play along. "Yes, I will do that."

Sally stares sorrowfully into Rigney's eyes and says, "Tonight is our last night until you come to Cape Cod. Please spend the whole night."

"I will stay. You must get up early and drive me to the base."

"No problem," Sally responds happily.

They wrap their arms around each other and kiss tenderly.

Chapter 7

During the last week of school, the base hospital performs Rigney's pre-transfer physical. Two days later, he is informed that he has been medically disqualified from submarines. He has a scarred eardrum. The problem is not severe enough to prevent duty in the surface navy but severe enough to disqualify him from the submarine navy. The hospital schedules him for an evaluation at the Bethesda Naval Hospital in Maryland, near DC, for a more thorough evaluation. The timetable requires Rigney to depart New London several days after he graduates from school.

Rigney goes to the base Western Union Office. He sends a telegram to Sally's address in Cape Cod. In the telegram, he tells her that he cannot come to Cape Cod, and that he has been ordered to the Bethesda, Maryland Navy Hospital. He says he will put more detail in a letter.

Two days later, Sally arrives at the base library. She drove down from Cape Cod when she got the telegram. She finds Rigney reading a magazine at his usual table.

She is three feet from Rigney when he looks up and sees her. He jumps to his feet and hugs her. They kiss hungrily as lovers do after an absence.

"Will you come to my house where we can talk in private?"

"Yes, of course!" Rigney already pictures them both naked in her bed.

Sally pictures the same thing.

Several hours later, they lie spent in Sally's bed.

"We must talk about some things," Sally says seriously. "I will make some coffee." Sally climbs out of bed, puts on her robe, and walks to the kitchen.

Rigney puts on the robe that Sally keeps for him, and he walks to the kitchen.

"Tell me what happened with the physical."

Rigney explains the eardrum problem.

"When do you come back to New London?" she asks.

"I'm being transferred from New London. I don't know when I will be back."

Sally puts down her coffee and says sadly, "This is it, then."

"Yes, Sally, for a while anyway."

Sally responds with sadness in her voice, "Now I understand why some of my friends avoid relationships with navy men. How do navy wives suffer through the heartbreak of long separations?"

"I never thought about that," Rigney admits.

Sally stares into space while she thinks about how to say what she needs to say. Then, she says it. "I've been thinking about starting my doctorate studies. I have been offered fieldwork in Europe, which starts after the first of the year. I have put it off too long. I am going to accept it."

Rigney nods his head in agreement and acceptance. "I think that's a great idea. How long will you be gone?"

"One year. So, it looks like it will be a long time before we see each other again."

Rigney thinks about what that means, and he responds, "Sally, we need to be free to experience what life offers us. No commitments. Do you agree?"

"Yes, Rigney. I do. I'm glad you feel that way."

Sally reaches over and takes Rigney's hand. She smiles and says, "When our paths cross again, we will see if we still feel the same way about each other."

"I hope we do," Rigney responds sincerely.

"And, Rig, I appreciate that you never said anything negative about my family regarding Willie."

Rigney does not know how to answer. Saying something negative never occurred to him. He had thought about Willie's fleeing to Canada and realizes that he now feels differently about draft dodgers. The subject is not as black and white to him as it was before. Not that it is okay, but now the draft dodger is the brother of someone he cares about.

"I must drive back to Cape Cod tomorrow. Will you stay the rest of the night?"

"Of course!"

They stand and walk arm in arm back to the bedroom.

Chapter 8

On December 1st at 0930, a short graduation ceremony begins in the Submarine School auditorium. In attendance are Rigney, his 22 classmates, the Director of Radioman Schools, and several instructors. Also present are wives of the four married students. All military members wear Service Dress Blue uniform.

Lieutenant Commander Driscoll, Director of Radioman Schools and a mustang with 26 years naval service, walks to the podium. Driscoll wears seven rows of decorations above his left breast pocket—the Navy Cross at first precedence. The scuttlebutt flows that Driscoll earned the award while serving on a submarine in WWII. The story goes that he repeatedly dove back into the water to bring aboard wounded and dead shipmates during a surface battle with a Japanese gunboat in the Marianas. After a depth-charge attack that damaged all propulsion systems, the submarine surfaced and was dead in the water. The submarine fought the gunboat with all its diminishing strength. The story continues that the Japanese gunboat obsessively strafed both the submarine and the water around it. Finally, the submarine deck-gun crew blasted away the bridge of the Japanese gunboat. Driscoll had saved the lives of five shipmates and returned two dead shipmates to the deck of the submarine.

Rigney admires Driscoll. The Director's positive attitude and military correctness inspires all of whom he comes in contact. He is slim in stature and is of medium height. The Director always remembers Rigney's name. Whenever they pass each other in the halls, their verbal exchange never alters. Page would say, "Good morning, Mister Driscoll." The officer always responded cheerfully with, "Good morning, Page. How are you?" Rigney would always respond with, "Just fine, sir. Thank you for asking."

The Director reads some notes on the podium. Then, he looks around at the crowd and says, "Good morning. For those of you who do not know me, I am Lieutenant Commander Driscoll. I am the Director of the Submarine Radioman Schools. I welcome our graduates, their instructors, and guests.

"Every several weeks, I am honored to conduct the graduation ceremony for those who have successfully completed difficult and demanding courses. These courses are specifically designed to challenge and test the ability of our submarine-bound students. When a student completes his course of instruction at this school, I am confident that student is ready to solve any problem within his area of technical expertise that he may encounter aboard a submarine.

"This class successfully completed the most difficult of repair courses . . . the Crypto Equipment Repair Course. Especially significant for this graduating class is that all those who started the course finished the course in the scheduled time. Such accomplishments are rare. Usually, one third of our students are either set back or dropped for academic reasons. This graduating class set several records. First, the class average is the highest average ever recorded for the Crypto Equipment Repair Course. Second, the class honor man achieved the highest average ever recorded for the course. Third, a member of this graduating class is the first ever to complete all Submarine Radioman Courses in continuous attendance and in the shortest period-of-time.

"We are proud of these sailors who achieve these records. Submariners are challenged every day to substantiate their elite image. Today, we send new submariners to the fleet. We have trained them well. They have learned well. I am proud to say that I have served with them."

The Director's words inspire Rigney. He vows to perform at his best, regardless of where he serves. The Director provided Rigney with the opportunity to achieve even higher than Rigney had originally hoped. He promises himself that he will not disappoint Mister Driscoll, Mister Watson, or the navy.

Rigney wonders if Mister Driscoll is the epitome of navy leadership. Rigney hopes so. He hopes that all officers are like Mister Driscoll. Although Rigney does not plan to stay in the navy past his obligated six years, he hopes that should he ever lead sailors, he will be able to inspire them as Mister Driscoll does.

The Director continues. "I call attention to the class honor man, RM3 William Wilson. Petty Officer Wilson has completed the Crypto Equipment Repair Courses with the highest average ever recorded. Before the ceremony, I had an opportunity to converse with Petty Officer Wilson's wife. Mrs. Wilson told me that her husband studied four hours every night and eight hours on both Saturday and Sunday. Well, the effort paid off. RM3 Wilson has set the standard by which all future students must attempt to surpass."

Billy Wilson's face is beet red with embarrassment. He has never been in the limelight before. He is 24 years old and comes from a Pennsylvania farmland background. He joined the navy to break the generations old tradition of toiling on the family farm.

Rigney looks toward the guest section where Celeste Wilson sits. She holds the Wilson's two-year-old daughter. Celeste stares toward her husband and beams with pride.

Lieutenant Commander Driscoll directs, "Petty Officer Wilson, please come to the podium."

42

Billy Wilson, his face still red from embarrassment, walks up to the podium.

The Director looks at the audience for Celeste Wilson. The Director asks, "Mrs. Wilson, please join your husband at the podium."

Celeste shyly shakes her head no.

"It's okay, Mrs. Wilson. I will not embarrass you. Please, join your husband at the podium."

Celeste Wilson walks to the podium and stands by her husband. She still holds her child in her arms.

The Director, with a knowing smile on his face, continues his comments. "We are often told and reminded about the sacrifice made by men in uniform. The sacrifices made by navy wives, family, and, yes, girlfriends seldom get attention. Submariners could not meet the demands or overcome the challenges of their service without the support of those who love them. Loved ones must endure the long separations, the long hours, and raising children mostly on their own.

"Petty Officer Wilson studied for hours into the night and long hours on the weekend to achieve these grades. We must also recognize the contribution of his family. On behalf of the navy and the submarine service, I thank you, Mrs. Wilson, for your contribution toward making your husband a better submariner."

The Director lightly claps his hands. Attendees join in light applause. Celeste Wilson blushes and her eyes become moist. As the Director hands Bill Wilson his certificate and shakes his hand, a navy photographer snaps a photograph that includes the Wilsons's and the Director.

The Director indicates to the Wilson's that they should step down from the podium and return to their seats. Instead of returning to his seat with his classmates, Billy takes a seat next his wife in the guest area. Billy Wilson looks down at his Certificate. He reads *Class Standing: 1 of 23*. He shows the Certificate to Celeste. Celeste puts her hand on his arm and smiles with admiration into his face. This accomplishment substantiates their decision to leave the family farm and to pursue a different life.

Rigney respects Billy Wilson. Rigney had little contact with Billy outside the classroom. They ate lunch together a few times. During those lunches, Rigney learned about Billy's background. He admitted that the course material did not come easy to him. Billy had to study long hours to get good grades. He also told Rigney that he must be successful in the navy because he did not want to go back to the family farm.

One night early in the course at a class gathering at the enlisted club, Celeste Wilson told Rigney that her husband admired Rigney's

43

understanding of cryptographic electronics. "Billy also thinks that you are the coolest and most calm person he has ever met. Billy says that nothing upsets you, nothing ever sets you off." Celeste had warned Rigney, "Don't slack off on your studying because Billy will pass by you."

Rigney is envious of Celeste's love for her husband. Rigney hopes that someday a woman will love him as much. He also hopes that one day he will be capable of returning such love.

"We will now recognize another first here at Submarine Radioman Schools. A graduate of this course has completed all Submarine Radioman Courses in the shortest period-of-time ever. Additionally, he is the youngest to complete all the Radioman Courses. RM3 Page, please come to the podium."

Rigney walks to the podium. All eyes are on him. He hears a few unclear whispers from some of his classmates.

"Radioman Third Class Rigney Page, you have earned a special certificate in addition to your graduation certificate. The certificate reads *'In Recognition of Special Achievement for completion of All Submarine Radioman Courses in the shortest period.'* The certificate lists each course and your class standing in each. I point out that RM3 Page was first in his class for two of the courses."

The Director covers the microphone with his hand, leans close to Rigney, and whispers, "I know that your future in the submarine service is unclear. Regardless of the results of your medical exam, I wish you well. I wish you success in wherever the navy sends you."

"Thank, your, sir. I will always appreciate the opportunities you gave me."

The Director hands Rigney his two certificates. The navy photographer snaps a picture. The Director indicates that Rigney should take his seat.

Rigney walks back to his seat. His classmates are staring at him. When he senses that no one is watching him, he looks at his class standing on the Graduation Certificate: 4 of 23. *Not bad. Being with Sally was worth it.*

The Director calls the remainder of the class, one at a time, to the podium to receive their certificates. As he hands each of them a certificate, he congratulates them on their achievement.

As the last graduate returns to his seat, the Director announces the end of the ceremony, "This concludes the ceremony. The master chief will now hand out the orders."

The Director steps down from the podium and steps off the stage and walks out the door.

Master Chief Doyle casts an impressive and authoritarian image in his Dress Blue uniform. He stands as tall as Rigney, though twenty pounds heavier. His gray hair and lined face commands respect for his experience. Four rows of ribbons stack above his left breast pocket. Seven gold hash marks and a custom made chevron run the length of his left arm. The master chief announces, "When I say your name, come and get your envelope. Your envelope contains your service records, orders, and if you are departing the area, airline or train tickets to your destination."

The master chief steps down from the stage and walks to a table that has two stacks of large manila envelopes. He picks up one of the envelopes and calls out the name of one of the graduates. Eventually all the graduates hold a yellow envelope.

Rigney looks in the pocket on the side of his envelope. He pulls out his orders and reads them. The orders direct Rigney to report to Bethesda Naval Hospital on Tuesday Morning, December 5th. The pocket also includes train tickets to Washington DC.

Rigney starts for the door.

"Hey, Rig! Aren't ya gonna say goodbye?"

Rigney turns around and sees Billy Wilson walking toward him. Rigney looks beyond Billy and sees Billy's wife talking with the other wives. Rigney walks toward Billy and takes Billy's outstretched hand.

"Yes, Billy. I want to say goodbye. I wish you success. You deserve it. What submarine are you going to?"

"The Scorpion SSN 589—home-ported in Norfolk."

Rigney nods acceptance of the information.

Billy asks, "I heard you've been medically disqualified from subs. Is that right?"

"Well, it's not final. I'm going to Bethesda Naval Hospital for evaluation. They may reverse what the local doctors have said."

"Where's Bethesda?"

"It's near DC. I've got train tickets for Sunday. I should be there about two weeks. Then, I come back here and wait for orders."

"I'm truly sorry about that, Rig. I know how much and how long you've worked to get a submarine."

Rigney puts his left hand on Billy's elbow and guides the two of them away from the crowd. They walk to where Billy's wife stands.

"Well, Rig, we must be on our way. I've got thirty days leave, and we're going to spend it with family in Pennsylvania. I report to my boat on the third of January."

Rigney extends his hand to Billy. They shake hands firmly.

"Goodbye, Rig."

45

"Goodbye, Billy. Good Luck." Rigney looks at Celeste Wilson and says sincerely, "Goodbye, Celeste. I wish you both well."

Celeste smiles and says, "Goodbye, Rigney."

The Wilsons turn and walk over to the coat rack. They find their coats and hats. Then, they walk out the auditorium door.

Rigney decides not to go out the door commonly used by students. Instead, he decides to exit the school through the quarterdeck door.

A navy quarterdeck represents naval traditions and customs. All crossings of the quarterdeck must be accomplished in a smart and military manner. All VIP's that enter and exit through the quarterdeck are rendered full honors. Students are not required to come and go through the school building's quarterdeck but are encouraged to do so. At the outer edge of the quarterdeck, he checks his appearance in the full-length mirror provided for that purpose. Satisfied with his appearance, Rigney turns to the quarterdeck watch and says, "Request permission to cross the quarterdeck!"

"Permission granted," announces the quarterdeck watch.

Rigney steps smartly across the quarterdeck and exits the building.

He had checked into the transient barracks before the graduation ceremony. The transient barracks has different regulations. Residents may come and go as they please. Security and fire watches roam on each floor. The open bay barracks is on the top floor—the third floor. Two-man rooms are on the first and second floor. The transient barracks is sparsely occupied this time of year.

Because of the low occupancy, the master-at-arms assigned Rigney to a two-man room, normally reserved for second class and first class petty officers. He has the room to himself. His room is on the first floor and conveniently close to the head and recreation room.

He enters the barracks through the resident's entrance. He goes to his room and changes into civvies. He puts his gym wear into his gym bag. He departs the barracks and walks to the base gym.

Chapter 9

Rigney's train arrives at Washington DC Union Station at 1930. After the train comes to a stop, he stands and puts on this white hat. He slips on his peacoat and gloves. He retrieves his gym-bag sized liberty-bag and departs the train. He follows the crowd to the cavernous main concourse.

Sailors, marines, soldiers, and airman move about all over the station. Hundreds of people coming and going and crisscrossing. The concourse is a field of contrasting colors—navy blue, marine green, army green, air force blue, and various civilian colors mixing, separating, coming together, and separating again.

Rigney estimates 75 percent of the travelers are in uniform. He wonders how he will find is ONI contact.

"Are you Page?" a voice asks from his left.

Rigney turns and sees a sailor of his own height, weight, and build. The sailor wears a peacoat and white hat and has a RM3 crow on his left sleeve. Rigney doubts the ONI contact is a RM3 because the ONI contact appears thirtyish.

"Yes, I'm Page."

"Okay, Page. Come with me."

They exit the doors of the main concourse. The thirty-one degree air coerces the two sailors to raise their peacoat collars to protect their necks from the cold. They cross a dimly lit parking lot. High piles of shoveled snow are evenly space across the parking lot. The ONI contact leads them to a U.S. Navy sedan.

After they have driven a few blocks through Washington DC, Rigney asks the ONI contact, "What's your name?"

"Smith. John Smith," the ONI contact answers in an amused tone. Then, he chuckles lightly.

Rigney casts a curious stare at the man named Smith.

Several minutes later, they are moving along a four-lane interstate. The road surface is clear. Dirty snow fills the shoulders.

Rigney sits quietly for fifteen minutes. He notices that they do exit the interstate at the Suitland ramp. "We're not going to Suitland?"

"No."

"Well," Rigney presses, "I will find out eventually, anyway. How about revealing this ultra-secret destination?"

"We're going to a small navy installation in the Maryland countryside. It's to the southeast of DC. ONI has some office space and some quarters there. It's a nice and quiet place. I'm sure you'll like it."

Rigney stares at Smith for a few moments. His curiosity needs satisfied. "Are you really a sailor? Are you really a RM3?"

"Do I look like a RM3?" Smith challenges.

"No," Rigney responds. "You look like me but ten years older. You're too old to be only a third class."

"Extremely observant," Smith responds sarcastically.

Smith drives the car down an exit ramp. Rigney sees several signs with directions to Andrews Air Force Base. They drive south along a road with signs that identify it as Route 5. Then, they drive through a small town named Clinton. After Clinton, they turn off Route 5 and onto a narrow country road.

After 20 minutes of driving along the country road, they arrive at a military base gate. Two petty officers with white colored helmets and *Shore Patrol* armbands stand guard. Each shore patrolman wears a white guard belt with a holstered .45 automatic pistol. One of the shore patrolmen holds up his hand with palm facing forward as an order for the car to a stop. The shore patrolman walks over to the driver's side of the car. Smith opens the window. Cold air blasts into the car. Smith shows his I.D. card to the shore patrolman.

Rigney pays little attention to their conversation. He concentrates on the sign at the gate, which announces that they are about to enter NAVAL COMMUNICATIONS STATION WASHINGTON DC. In smaller letters, the location is listed as Cheltenham, Maryland.

Smith orders, "Page, show the shore patrol your I.D. card."

Rigney reaches into his breast pocket and pulls out his I.D. card. He stretches his arm in front of Smith's face and displays his I.D. card to the shore patrol sailor.

"Okay. You may proceed."

Smith drives the vehicle through the gate. He comments, "Nothing unusual about a couple of radiomen passing through this gate."

Rigney does not feel the need to confirm his understanding.

Smith drives along the main road for a few blocks. Then, he makes a couple of turns and pulls into a small ten-space parking lot in front of a small two-story red brick building. Except for their sedan, the parking lot is empty.

After parking the car, they walk up a few concrete steps to the building's entrance. The door looks normal, except for a ten-button cipher lock to the right of the door. Smith enters the security code. A soft buzzing sound announces that the electromagnetic door lock disengages.

They walk through the doorway and enter a foyer that measures ten feet by feet. A heavy steel door stands opposite the outdoor entrance. Surveillance cameras are mounted near the ceiling in two corners. Another ten-button cipher lock is installed to the right of the steel door.

Smith takes off his hat, looks up at one of the cameras. He punches the security code into the cipher lock.

Rigney hears a motor . . . then a clunk.

Smith pulls the steel door open, and they walk through. The door closes with a clunk behind them.

Rigney hears the motor of the door's locking bars.

"This way," Smith directs as points down the hall.

The hall is not the usual green or blue colors seen in other navy buildings. Light and dark browns decorate this hallway.

They pass a dozen closed doors with numbers on them. At the end of the hall, Smith stops at a door with the number 15 on its face. Smith pulls a key out of his pocket and unlocks the door. The two sailors enter the room.

Smith turns on a light.

The size and décor of the two-room suite astonishes Rigney. The sitting room has a small couch, coffee table, and television set. A small refrigerator and a wet bar occupy the far corner. Dark blue carpet covers the sitting room floor, and matching dark blue curtains cover the only window in the room.

Rigney enters the bedroom. A comfortable looking double size bed stands against one wall. The bed's dark blue bedspread has the navy emblem embroidered squarely into the center. Two nightstands and lamps sit on both sides of the bed. The bedroom carpet duplicates the carpet in the living room. The bathroom is luxurious by barracks standards, with a tiled floor and a large combination bathtub and shower. The toilet porcelain shines brilliantly.

Rigney returns to the bedroom. John Smith opens the top drawer of the nightstand. The drawer is stocked with underwear, t-shirts, and socks. "These are for you," John advises.

Rigney looks toward the drawer and nods once. Then, he walks back into the living room area. "Nice quarters," Rigney comments to Smith.

"This building has five other rooms like this. All are built to Bachelor Officer Quarters standards, plus a few extras. The remaining rooms in this building are offices."

Smith opens a drawer and pulls out a piece of paper. "These are the combinations to the doors we just came through. Memorize them; then burn the paper in the ashtray. For the inside door, you need to take off your cover and look up at the camera. The security agent on the other end of the camera verifies that you entered the correct code. Then, he must identify you before activating the security door."

Smith pulls out another piece of paper. "This is a map of this base. Here's the dining facility and here's the exchange. Here's the enlisted club. Well, you can read it for yourself." After a short pause, Smith continues, "Eat your meals in the base dining facility, or you can eat the food in the refrigerator."

Smith walks over to a closet door and opens it.

Rigney peers inside the closet. Three sets of Service Dress Blue with RM3 crows hang from the rod. Also hanging from the rod are three sets of navy-blue jumpsuits. One dark blue, civilian style winter jacket hangs next to the jumpsuits. Three immaculate white hats sit on the closet's upper shelf. Next to the white hats are three navy blue ball caps. Two pair of highly polished civilian style boots stand on the closet floor.

Smith explains, "You wear a jumpsuit, boots, and ball cap inside this building and when leaving this building with an instructor. Whenever you leave this building by yourself, you must wear Service Dress Blues.

"In the morning, go to chow at 0700. Then, come back here and change into a jumpsuit. Report to room 4 at 0800.

"When you are outside this building and anyone in authority asks you to identify yourself, show them your I.D. card. If asked why you are here, say you are here for a medical evaluation. That is what your orders say. For show, I will drive you over to Bethesda a few times, just in case someone is tracking you."

"Who would be tracking me?"

"You will be briefed on all that while you are here."

Smith stops talking and hands Rigney the key to the room.

"Give me your orders. I will deliver them to the Admin Office in the morning, and they will take care of checking you into Bethesda Medical Center."

Rigney digs into his liberty bag, pulls out his orders, and hands them to Smith.

"Well, good luck to you, Page. If that's really your name."

Smith studies Rigney for a few minutes and asks, "Are you really an enlisted man? Are you really a RM3, or are you a GS or civilian contractor?"

Rigney does not answer Smith's question. He understands that he should not answer questions that he has not been briefed to answer.

Smith says, "Well, never mind. I know you're not supposed to answer. I often wonder about the guys I bring here. I wonder where they're from and where they're going and what mission they have. You're the youngest I've brought here. I'm curious. Please excuse my asking."

Smith walks out the door and closes the door behind him.

Rigney stares at the closed door for a few moments. He understands that he has entered a secret realm within the United States Navy.

After stowing his white hat, peacoat, and gloves in the closet, he walks to the refrigerator and opens the door. The top shelf is stocked with beer, soft drinks, and milk. He does not recognize the beer brand names. The brand names look European. The second shelf is stocked with sandwiches and baked chicken breasts. On the door shelf are several small bottles of wine. Rigney wonders if they know he is under twenty-one.

He reaches into the refrigerator and removes a bottle of beer with the name *Guinness* on the label. He inspects the sandwiches and decides on roast beef and cheddar on whole wheat. He sipped beer only a few times at family dinners. He never drank a whole bottle.

Using a bottle opener that he finds in a drawer near the wet bar, he opens the bottle and smells the top. *Smells like beer.* He takes a drink. *Okay, this is good!*

He turns on the television and finds only four channels. He hopes he can catch the news and searches the channels, but he finds only comedies. Rigney seldom watches television. The only time he searches for a television is when he wants to watch news.

He stops on a channel where the show's theme appears to be nautical. The comedic plot centers on a group of people who are marooned on a tropical island and who place their trust and confidence in characters named *Skipper, Gilligan, and Professor.* After ten minutes of watching the comedy, he turns off the television.

Next, he unpacks his gym bag. The only items are his shaving kit and a copy of the novel *Exodus* by Leon Uris.

Rigney finishes the beer and the sandwich while reading a few pages of *Exodus*.

Then, he walks to the bedroom and strips off his uniform, underwear, and socks and throws them all into a chair in the corner. Naked, he walks into the bathroom. He thoroughly brushes and flosses his teeth, followed with a long hot shower.

After the shower, he slips on a fresh pair of the ONI provided boxer shorts. He pulls back the covers of the bed and slides between the sheets.

What will tomorrow bring? He seriously wonders if this detour will be right for him or will it be a total mistake. *However, if the barracks are all like this, I can manage to survive!*

Chapter 10

Monday - December 4, 1967

Rigney awakes at 0620. He follows his normal bathroom routine. Then, he selects one of the ONI provided Service Dress Blue uniforms from the closet. The uniform fits perfectly.

He spends a few minutes memorizing the cipher lock combinations. Then, he burns the paper in the ashtray as instructed by John Smith.

At 0703, he departs his room. As he walks the hall toward the steel door, he thinks he must be the only person in this building. No one else moves about. He walks to the steel door. There are no handles and no visible unlocking mechanism. Rigney looks around for help. Then, he notices the surveillance camera mounted above the door. He removes his hat and looks up and the camera. Rigney hears a motor starting up. Then, he hears a clunk. The door does not open. He puts his hand on the door and pushes. The door opens outward. As he passes through the doorway, he glances at the door edge. The door is five inches thick and has three retracted locking rods.

The door to the outside opens when Rigney presses on the bar across the middle of the door. He steps into a cold and brisk morning. The trees in all directions are bare of leaves. He sees the frost of his own breath. In the distance, through the leafless trees, antenna arrays are visible.

As he walks the three blocks to the base dining facility, he scrutinizes every building he passes. He looks for some markings that tell the purpose of each building. Most of the buildings are two and three stories and rectangular in shaped. *This place looks more like a college campus than a navy base.*

Rigney enters the dining facility behind two WAVES. They both have seaman apprentice stripes with no specialty designator. They both look to be seventeen or eighteen. *They cannot be any older than that.* Rigney and the two WAVES stand in the foyer as they remove their gloves, hats, and coats. The taller one of the two women is a beauty with raven black hair and a rice-powder complexion. The other, the one with light brown hair, is kind of cute in a tomboyish sort of way. Rigney notices that the two WAVES are staring at him.

Raven hair gives him a sexy smile.

Rigney nods toward the two women and says, "Good morning." He motions for them to go first through the chow line.

As he follows them through the chow line, he notices that the two women whisper to each other and steal glances at him.

It's a curse! Rigney declares egotistically to himself.

Rigney sets a small bowl of sliced bananas and strawberries on his tray then continues along the chow line. He observes the cook frying some eggs. The sign on the glass shelf says *Eggs to Order*.

The cook asks Rigney, "What do ya want, sparks?"

"How about a couple of poached eggs?"

The cook looks at him strangely, "Well, it's supposed to be fried eggs to order. No one ever orders poached; give me a few minutes to boil some water."

Rigney asks, "Can you put them over dry whole-wheat toast?"

"Sure," the cook responds as he grabs two slices of whole wheat bread and slips them into the toaster.

While Rigney waits, a couple of radiomen in Undress Blues order eggs over easy and pass Rigney in the line.

Steam rises from the pot of boiling water. The cook checks the water and then cracks three eggs into the water. The cook gets a plate and puts the two pieces of toast on it.

"Only about 45 seconds," Rigney tells the cook.

The cook replies, "No problem."

Rigney had never experienced a navy cook this willing to please.

At about 45 seconds, the cook uses a straining spoon and lifts the three eggs out of the boiling water and lays them over the toast. The cook hands the plate to Rigney with a smile.

"Thank you very much," Rigney says sincerely.

"You're welcome," replies the cook with another smile.

Rigney exits the chow line and looks for a place to sit. The dining room is crowded. Most of the sailors are in dungarees—a few are in Undress Blue. Mostly, men occupy the tables. A few WAVES sit at various tables throughout the dining room. The dining room seats about one hundred people. Dark paneling adorns the walls. Light blue tile covers the floor. Four chairs sit around each table. The only available seat is at a table occupied by the two WAVES he had met at the door. He sits down at their table.

Both women cast curious stares at him.

"Did you just report aboard?" the tomboyish one asks.

"Report aboard where?" Rigney asks without much thought.

"COMMSTA. Did you just report aboard COMMSTA?"

"No, not COMMSTA. I am here for just a couple of weeks."

Tomboy presses, "Well, what command are you with?"

"I'm actually attached to Submarine Schools Command in New London."

"What brings you here?" asks the raven-haired beauty.

Rigney becomes suspicious of their questioning.

"I'm here for a medical examination," Rigney replies as he looks around the nearby tables. Some sailors from nearby tables are watching and listening to him and the two WAVES.

Rigney decides to provide no more information. He pretends to be preoccupied with cutting up his food and eating.

Tomboy asks, "Why would ya be sent to NAVCOMMSTA WASH for a medical exam?"

Rigney looks at tomboy for a moment while chewing his food and formulating an answer. He swallows the bite of food and answers, "Don't know. I was ordered here. I have an appointment tomorrow at Bethesda Naval Hospital."

"Bethesda!" tomboy exclaims in a surprised voice. "That's way over on the other side of DC! Don't those people in New London know how far away they sent you? They've got barracks at Bethesda. I spent three weeks there once. That's the navy for ya. One hand not knowing what the other hand is doing."

Rigney continues to cut and eat his food.

Raven hair says appreciatively, "I don't care why or how the navy made the mistake. I'm just glad you ended up here."

Rigney understands her meaning. *This lady is interested.* He looks across the table and stares into her dark brown eyes.

Raven hair responds with a sensual smile.

Tomboy cannot let it go. "How are ya gonna get over to Bethesda? That's an hour-and-a-half drive from here."

Raven hair's big brown eyes hypnotize him. He does not think before he speaks. "A navy driver will take me there and bring me back."

Tomboy praises with mock admiration, "Well! You submariners must be something for a third class to get his own driver!"

Tomboy's comment snaps him back to his senses.

"I don't know about that. It's just the way I was told it would happen."

Rigney looks at his watch—0743. "I must go."

The other sailors in the room, including tomboy, observed the eye-lock between raven hair and Rigney.

Tomboy glances back and forth between raven hair and Rigney. "Cathy, you're not gonna just let him walk out of here, are ya?"

Rigney stands to leave. Raven hair—Cathy—walks around the table and stands very close to Rigney. She stands on her toes and brings her lips as close to his ear as possible without appearing too intimate and whispers, "I am on watch till 1700. I will be in the enlisted club at 1900."

Rigney feels her body heat and inhales her scent. He becomes aroused.

"Are you asking me on a date?" Rigney whispers back. "If you are, I'm not sure that I can be there. I won't know until later today what my schedule will be."

"I'll be at the club anyway. If you make it, yes, it's a date." She is smiling as she lowers herself back down on her heels. She turns, picks up her tray, and, walks with tomboy toward the scullery.

As she walks away, Rigney stares at Cathy's swaying hips. He thinks her sway is somewhat exaggerated. *She must know I am watching. Nice butt, though!*

Halfway across the dining room Cathy looks back over her shoulder and smiles sensually at Rigney.

Rigney senses silence in the room. He looks around. Many of the sailors are staring at him. *Why are these people staring at me?*

He does not realize what just happened. Many of these sailors attempted, more than once, to get that close to Cathy. Many had asked her for a date. They never succeeded. Then, in walks this outsider and within fifteen minutes the two of them are standing close and whispering.

Chapter 11

Rigney walks along the street toward the direction of the ONI building. More cars are on the street and more sailors walk about. As he comes closer to the ONI building, he notices cars are now in the parking lot. As he approaches, he scans the building for signs that describe the purpose of the building. None are displayed.

As he crosses the parking lot, he notices the same navy sedan from last night. Rigney looks at his watch—0801. *I'm late!* He quickens his step.

He enters the code into the cipher lock. Then, he enters, crosses the foyer, takes off his hat, punches in the code, and looks at one of the cameras. The door opens. As he steps into the hallway, he hears typewriters and the buzz of people talking and working. He also smells fresh coffee brewing.

He passes the first door, which is open and exposes the contents of the room. *Looks like a sitting room or a waiting room.* RM3 Smith, the sailor who met Rigney last night at the train station, sits in the middle of the room reading a rating manual.

Smith looks up as he hears footsteps stop in front of the door. He sees Page smiling and nodding at him. Smith looks surprised and looks at his watch. He looks back at Page, points to his watch, and waves his hand in the direction of the other rooms.

Rigney nods understanding and hurries to his room.

Inside his room, he throws off his peacoat and gloves and the remainder of his uniform. He rapidly dresses in a jumpsuit from the closet. *Another great fit.*

Several minutes later, He complies with the instructions Smith gave him last night and knocks on the door for room 4.

"Come in," a voice says from the other side of the door.

Rigney enters the room. A man sitting behind a desk on the far side of the room waves Rigney to a chair in front of the desk. Rigney lowers himself into the chair as normal; he uses his arm muscles to control his decent into the chair.

The man behind the desk appears fiftyish. Curly salt and pepper colored hair falls to his shoulders. He sports a closely cropped beard—also salt and pepper colored. His reading glasses perch on the tip of his nose. His brown tweed jacket has patches at the elbows. In all, the man casts a scholarly image.

"Welcome, Rigney. I am Dr. Williamson. I am a Psychiatrist. I will determine if you are crazy enough to join this outfit." The doctor smiles and chuckles lightly.

56

Rigney does not know how he should respond. He just sits and listens.

"This morning, you will complete some questionnaires, which should take about two hours. After you are finished with the questionnaires, you should return to your room. Eat lunch in your room. It will take me an hour to analyze your answers. Then, most of the afternoon will be spent with you and me talking. Any questions?"

"No, sir," Rigney replies simply.

Dr. Williamson smiles. "I am not a military officer. The appropriate manner to address me is *Doctor*.

Rigney nods with understanding. "Okay, Doctor. Will doer."

"In the next room," the doctor points to his left, "You will find the questionnaires on the desk, fresh coffee, and a water cooler—a small head attached also. You should not leave that room until you have finished all questionnaire booklets. Do you have any questions?"

Rigney shakes his head.

"Answer the questions truthfully. Do not answer as you believe I, or the navy, or Brad Watson would want you to answer."

"I understand, Doctor."

"Okay. Get started."

Rigney enters the small room. Doctor Williamson shuts the door.

Rigney sits down at the desk. He reads the questionnaire instructions and then begins writing his answers.

Nearly three hours later, Rigney completes all the questionnaires. He looks at his watch—1115. He opens the door to tell the doctor he is done, but the doctor is not there.

Rigney goes to his room. As he enters the room, he notices that the room has been cleaned. The bed is made. Fresh towels hang in the bathroom. A bowl of fresh fruit, which was not there the night before, sits on the counter beside the wet bar. The latest edition of *The Washington Post* lies on the coffee table.

He sits on the couch and reads the paper. Headlines reporting Vietnam battles and NVA body counts fill the front page. On the second page, he finds an engrossing article that analyses the progress and power of the new military junta in Greece.

At 1145, he searches the refrigerator for some lunch. A few fresh sandwiches and some salads occupy the second shelf. He removes a bottle of *Perrier* and reads the label. *Okay, I will try this.* Then, he selects one of the salads that have a scoop of chicken salad in the center.

He likes the Perrier. It would be such much better with a slice of lemon or lime. He searches the fruit bowl and finds two lemons. He slices a lemon; then, squeezes several slices into a glass He pours the contents of the Perrier bottle into the glass. He takes a few sips. *Yes, I am addicted to this.*

While eating, Rigney thinks of Sally. He remembers their last conversation. They agreed that no commitment exists between them. Rigney will depart for places unknown for an undermined period. Sally will go to Europe to pursue completion of or doctoral degree. They both want to discover life's adventures. They did not want to make some juvenile commitment to each other. It would be too restrictive. They decided to keep in touch. When their paths cross again, they will consider rekindling their relationship.

He thinks about Cathy, the WAVE he met this morning. He has not decided if he will be at the Enlisted Club at 1900, even if he is available at that time.

Rigney feels that Sally is one of kind. He almost feels that relationships with other women would be futile. *How could any other woman match Sally?*

Fifteen minutes later, Rigney finishes lunch. *Now what?* He picks up *The Washington Post* and continues reading where he left off.

The phone rings. Rigney looks at his watch—1:08 p.m.

"Rigney, this is Doctor Williamson. Please come to room 4."

Three minutes later, Rigney sits in front of the doctor's desk.

"Rigney, our talk this afternoon will take several hours. Maybe you would be more comfortable lying on the couch over there." Dr. Williams points to the couch.

Rigney moves to the couch and lies down, positioning his head on the pillows provided.

Dr. Williamson moves to a chair facing the couch. A small coffee table separates them.

"Rigney, I must record our conversation. The medical assistants must transcribe it for the records."

Several hours later, Dr. Williamson concludes their talk. "That's all for today. We are not finished. We need another session tomorrow."

Rigney looks at his watch—1615. "What am I supposed to do now? Is there anything else on my schedule for today?"

"Hold on. Let me look at your schedule." The doctor walks to his desk and looks down at Rigney's schedule. "No, nothing more for today. You have an appointment at Bethesda Naval Hospital tomorrow morning at 0900. A driver will pick you up here at 0630. I want you back here at 1300."

"Okay. I am going back to my room."

Rigney exits room 4 and starts for his room. He stops and performs an about face and walks to the waiting room where RM3 Smith sits reading a rating manual.

"Hi, John," Rigney greets as he enters the room. "Are you driving me to Bethesda tomorrow?"

"Yes. I will pick you up at 0630," John Replies. "Your appointment is for 0900. We should be back here by 1300."

"Is there a gym on this base?" Rigney asks in a hopeful tone.

"Yes, it's not much of one. Just has some weight machines and some treadmills. There's a steam room and a whirlpool and some lockers. Oh yeah, some shower stalls."

"It's not on the map you gave me. Where is it?"

Smith explains how to get to the gym.

"Do ya know where I can get some gym clothes? I did not bring any with me."

"Let me check down in the basement. ONI keeps all sorts of clothes and uniforms down there. What size shoe do ya wear?"

"11D."

"Okay. Give me about fifteen minutes. Where will ya be—your room?"

"Yes, in my room."

Fifteen minutes later, Smith arrives at Rigney's room with gym shoes and several pairs of white socks, navy blue gym shorts, and navy blue t-shirts. Then, he departs.

Rigney changes into Service Dress Blues. He packs his liberty bag with one set of everything. He dons his peacoat, white hat, and gloves. Then, he exits his room.

As he walks the hallway toward the heavy steel door, he glances through the open door of some of the offices. He notices some sailors, all yeomen, and a few civilian women pounding away on typewriters. He walks by the waiting room. Smith is back to reading that rating manual.

Outside, the cold air bites at Rigney's face. Snow crunches under his feet.

Rigney returns to his room at 6:30 p.m. He thinks about meeting raven hair—Cathy—at the enlisted club. He considers the value of a short-term romance. His consideration leads him to visualizing her naked, which leads him to visualizing the two of them naked in his bed.

I wonder if she gives blowjobs. The fantasy causes his penis to gorge with blood. He closes his eyes and fantasizes raven hair on her knees and sucking on his hard, erect penis.

He walks into the bedroom and strips down naked. He stretches out on the bed and masturbates. He takes his time as he fantasizes Cathy naked and bent over him and sucking on his penis.

After he satisfies himself, the desire to meet Cathy diminishes. He finally decides to just stay in, eat some dinner, and read the newspaper. *No reason to start a short-term romance. I will only be here for two weeks. I should concentrate on my training.*

Chapter 12

Tuesday - December 5, 1967

Brad Watson enters room 4 and faces Dr. Williamson. "Okay, doc, what's the verdict on Page?"

"Brad, Rigney Page's psychological makeup falls within the scope of what ONI specifies for its field agents."

"I expected he would. As you know, my ONI peers want me to fail at this. If my plan is successful, the old school theories are out the window, and we change the rules. The intelligence world does not evolve easily. While our mission progresses, any problems resulting from Page's lack of training or experience will be added to the list of negatives. Even if the mission is successful, the list of negatives might still kill the long-term plan.

"I need to know Page's strengths and his weaknesses. In other words, I need to know what could end up on the negative list and what could end up on the positive list."

"Brad, I am a doctor. I loathe interagency politics. Over the last two days, I have come to like and respect Rigney Page. I just hope that he does not become a pawn and an innocent victim of interagency politics."

"I will protect him," Brad promises.

"Okay, his strengths . . . integrity tops the list. Rigney must be the most honest person I have ever encountered. Lying and deception and manipulative behavior are alien to his character. When he encounters it in others, he is total bewildered by it. He does not understand why people feel it necessary to be deceptive and manipulative."

Brad Watson interrupts, "Do you think that he can hide his true purpose during the mission?"

"Oh, he will be okay with that," the doctor replies. "This boy's intelligence is also one of his strengths. He's a quick thinker. I have no doubt that he can execute mission deception."

"What else?" Watson asks.

"Rigney clearly understands his commitments and responsibilities. When he makes a commitment, he will overcome all obstacles to fulfill that commitment. I believe he will do everything in his power, physically and mentally, to meet his commitments. He's the textbook example of *my word is my bond*. He readily accepts responsibility for any commitment he makes. Therefore, he takes extreme care to what he commits. He does not believe in such things as *inferred responsibility*. If you attempt to hold him accountable for anything that he has not agreed to, be ready for him to refuse any more contact with you and for

61

him to hold you in contempt."

Brad Watson considers the doctor's evaluation of Page. He asks, "What about his commitment to the navy and his agreement with me to accept this mission?"

"No problem there," the doctor replies with a smile and a wave of the hand. "When Rigney signed up, he knowingly made a commitment. He obligated himself and he willingly accepts responsibility for that obligation. Rigney totally understands that you expect him to go on the mission should he make it through this indoctrination. Rigney is trustworthy. You can count on him to do what you ask, and you can count on him to perform to the best of his ability."

"Any other strengths?"

"Yes, when adversely confronted by others, he will remain calm. He ignores those who try to manipulate him. When others berate him, he does not react in kind. He will not oblige others who want him to react. Rigney disrespects those who find it necessary to verbally abuse and bully others."

Brad Watson mentally scrutinizes the doctor's words. He considers that under normal circumstances, this characteristic would be strength. However, this trait is not common among young sailors. If Rigney continues to react this way, he may look too mature for his age.

Brad Watson asks, "What if someone threatens him with violence and he has no way out? How would he react to that?"

The doctor expends a few moments to ponder the question. Then, he answers, "Rigney would face the threat and fight his way out."

"How does he feel about the weapons training?"

"Rigney does not understand this part of his training. He tells me that you have promised him that this mission is not dangerous. So, he wonders why he needs to learn about guns. He thinks that you are hiding something from him. Brad, you need to talk to him about that."

"Okay, doc. I will. Did he object to the small arms training?"

"On the contrary. He is looking forward to it. Rigney says he has always like shooting guns. When he was a teenager, his uncle had a forty-foot boat. They would go offshore several miles, toss bottles and cans into the water, and use handguns and rifles to sink them."

"Okay, Doc, what about his weaknesses?"

"Rigney is a loner. Physically, Rigney exists in his chosen environment, the navy. Mentally, he does not fit. He has little in common with other sailors. He believes that his peers waste too much time talking about insignificant subjects like fast cars, sports, and casual sexual conquests. He becomes annoyed when others attempt to engage him in conversations about such things. He says that others are not interested in what he finds interesting. He quests to understand why the countries of this earth are in constant conflict. According to him, he studies the subject. According to him, he spends more time in libraries than most. He suspects that all cultural, social, and economic conflict has its roots in the differences in religious beliefs. Rigney is some sort of agnostic or atheist, I think. Did you know that? Anyway, all of this is rather deep and complex for a twenty-year-old sailor, and it makes him incompatible with his peers. I worry that his intelligence and his zeal for electronics will give him away. Brad, you need to do something about that."

"Yes, doc. I still believe Page is the best man for this mission. What about this '*I'm not sorry for my actions attitude*'? Remember, I asked you to look into that."

Doctor Williamson pauses as he recollects his evaluation. Then, he informs, "Rigney's self-confidence guides most of his actions. He's sure that his actions are based on logical reasoning, so he believes his actions are always justified. If others are offended or angered by his actions, he does not apologize. He believes that in no way is he responsible for how others react to him."

"I have heard that before. Anything else that I need to know?"

"Yes, there is an area of his character that I do not fully understand. I suspect that under certain conditions, Rigney will become coldly brutal."

"For example?" Watson asks.

Doctor Williamson's manner expresses concern; he responds, "Rigney appears to be the epitome of mature calm and cool. He wants you to believe that he will not *lose it* under any circumstance. However, several times during our talks, he came close to rage when talking about some of the conflicts and confrontations in his past."

The doctor's expression becomes reflective as he continues. "Brad, you need to ask Rigney about the boxing ring incident when he was a senior in high school. Insist that he tell you all about it. The significance of that incident is better felt when you hear it directly from him."

Brad responds, "Okay. I'll ask him."

"Please do because I think under specific circumstances Rigney will become violently ruthless."

Rigney sits in his quarters. Then, he occupies his time with reading *The Washington Post*.

The phone rings.

Rigney looks at his watch—1845.

"Hello."

"Rig, it's Brad Watson. I want you to meet me in front of the building tomorrow morning at 0800."

"Aye, aye sir," Rigney responds.

"How did your appointment at Bethesda go this morning?"

"I wasn't there long. The doctor looked in my ear and wrote some notes. Then, it was over."

"Okay. That sounds right." Then, Brad orders, "Tomorrow, wear a blue jumpsuit, blue coat, and blue ball cap. Remember the boots."

"No problem. Will do."

"Rig, do you have any gym gear, including gym shoes?"

"Yes."

"Good. Bring it with you tomorrow."

Brad hangs up.

Chapter 13

Wednesday - December 6, 1967

Rigney stands on the steps of the ONI building. He looks at his watch—0759.

The cold air penetrates the civilian style blue coat he wears. He stomps his feet.

He watches an approaching car, a 1965 olive green Mustang.

The Mustang enters the parking lot and stops in front of the steps.

Rigney moves down the steps, gets into the passenger side, and tosses his gym bag into the backseat.

Brad Watson offers his hand to Rigney. They shake hands firmly.

Brad drives off the base. They make small talk about the weather and about the changing seasons. They compare DC weather to Southern California weather. They both prefer Southern California. Rigney speaks about surfing Huntington Beach in the wintertime. They pass the turn-offs to Andrews Air Force Base. A few minutes later, Brad turns the car onto the four-lane road named Suitland Parkway.

Several minutes later, they come upon a complex of large government buildings. Brad maneuvers his car into an ONI employee parking lot. All the parking spaces are numbered. Brad passes several open spots before parking in his reserved parking spot.

Brad leads the way. They enter a building with the ONI emblem on the glass door. Access to the building is restricted and guards are posted inside the entrance. Brad pulls out his ONI Pass. He signs the visitor log to authorize Rigney's access to the building.

After walking a hallway that is the length of the building, they enter a door marked *Gymnasium*. The gymnasium is the size of a football field. Closest to them are two basketball courts. A weight area is located on the other side of the basketball courts. On the other side of the weight area is a large area covered with padded mats. About twenty men practice martial arts on the mats. Four boxing rings stand on the other side of the mats.

Rigney looks questioningly at Brad. "What's up here, Brad?"

"I'm your physical education instructor."

"Brad. I may be lacking knowledge and experience as an ONI agent, but   physical fitness is not one of them."

"More specifically, I am your hand-to-hand combat instructor. Whether or not you are physically fit has not yet been determined."

Rigney becomes apprehensive. *What's this all about? Being able to fight is not something I thought I would need. Did Brad lie to me about*

65

this mission not being dangerous?

"Let's get changed," Brad Watson says as he points to the locker room door.

In the locker room while they change clothes, Rigney cannot help but notice that Brad has bodybuilder muscles. Each muscle swells with definition and standout blood vessels and veins. Brad has broad shoulders and a narrow waist.

Rigney glances at himself in the full-length wall mirror. He does not have Brad's muscle definition, but he does have broad shoulders and stands a few inches taller than Brad. Rigney's waist is not as narrow as Brad's, but he is hard and lean with biceps larger than Brad's. Rigney considers why this is important to him. *Why do I find the comparison necessary?*

Ten minutes later, they are in the weight area. Brad leads them with limbering and stretching exercises. Then, they perform reps with barbells and dumbbells. They both use the same amount of weight. Rigney easily keeps pace with Brad.

"Now, we will run some laps around the perimeter of the gym," Brad announces; then, he asks Rigney, "How many do you think you can do?"

"I will not have any problem with laps. I will follow your lead. When you stop, I will stop."

"Okay," Brad agrees. "We will start with one hundred laps."

Brad starts jogging around the perimeter of the gym. Rigney follows a few steps behind and counts the laps. They reach one hundred, but Brad keeps going. After 140 laps, Brad stops by one of the boxing rings.

"I run 200 laps in here every day," Brad tells Rigney. "Do you jog? You appear to be conditioned for endurance."

"Not regularly, but I do play basketball almost every day. It keeps me in shape."

"Let's get into the ring," Brad commands. Then, he climbs into the nearest ring.

Rigney does not like this idea, but he will not show fear to Brad.

Brad slips on some boxing gloves. Rigney picks up a pair of boxing gloves and fumbles with putting them on. Brad helps.

"Are you ready for a few rounds?" Brad Watson challenges.

"No, Brad. I am not ready. I do not know how to box. You told me this mission would not be dangerous. So why are we doing this?"

Brad Watson expresses understanding. "Rig, I only have a few weeks to indoctrinate you. I cannot make you a hand-to-hand expert in two weeks. A slim possibility exists that you will need to fight. I need to understand your capabilities. By understanding your abilities, I can better judge how to maneuver you in the field. I only have enough time to teach you a few moves. You need to tell me about the boxing ring incident in high school."

Rigney now frets that he will be found out. This big, tough-looking surfer and weightlifter from the beaches of Southern California is a phony. *I am not tough. I never was and never had to be. I'm not even a reasonable facsimile.*

"You must tell me about the boxing ring incident," Brad orders.

"Okay." Rigney pauses to formulate his words.

"Well, go on!" Brad Watson demands.

"During my senior year in high school, I took two hours of gym every day. One day early in the year this guy comes up to me, another senior, and gets into my face about trying to take his girlfriend away.

"I vaguely knew this guy, but I did know that he had a reputation for being a fighter and a bully. I don't even remember his name. I never saw him fight, but others had told me he was *one mean motherfucker*. I didn't believe it, though. I mean he had the greaser tough guy image. He looked the type. You know—jeans and black leather jacket with greased back hair. All I saw was a thin and pale person with no muscle tone. He reeked of cigarette smoke. I just could not believe he was as tough as people said.

"Anyway, he challenged me to a fight after school. He mentioned the girl's name, and she was a girl that I had recently dated. I did not know this guy was her steady boyfriend. I wasn't really afraid of this guy, but I saw no reason to fight over such nonsense. The girl and I did not click. During our date, I discovered she wasn't my type. I had already decided not to ask her out again. I told this guy that we did not need to fight because I would not ask her out again. I told him that I would stay away from her because I did not want to be on his bad side. I also told him that nothing happened during the date. I told him that if I had known she was his girlfriend, I would never have asked her out.

"Well, that seemed to satisfy him. He didn't know how to react. A crowd had formed around us. He was acting tough, and he felt the need to do something tough. He said to me, 'that's right Page, you need to be fuckin' scared about this.' Then, he places both his hands on my chest and shoves me back about five feet. He was satisfied and he was done with it and started to walk away. I was done with it. He shoved me. I was not hurt. No damage done. I was glad it was over.

"But it was not over. The gym teacher saw none of what had transpired except when the guy shoved me. The gym teacher grabs the guy by the arm and brings him back over to where I was standing. The gym teacher wants to know what happened. Neither I nor the other guy was about to tell.

"The gym teacher announces that all conflicts are settled with gloves in the ring. I told the gym teacher that we had already settled our differences and that fighting in the ring was not necessary. When the gym teacher asked the other guy if he wanted to settle in the ring, he said, '*okay, sure, why not?*' I, on the other hand, told the gym teacher that there was no conflict between me and the other guy. I told the gym teacher that we'd talked it over and we settled it already, but the gym teacher insisted.

"We all climbed into the boxing ring. The gym teacher helped both of us put on the gloves.

"The school didn't own this boxing ring. The ring belonged to the local Golden Gloves club. They used the gym at night and on weekends.

"Then, it occurred to me that it was the gym teacher who wanted the fight. This gym teacher, Mister Thompson, was the basketball coach and was an assistant football coach. He was one of the teachers from the football thing I told you about. He was one of the teachers that found it necessary to try and embarrass me in class about me quitting the football team two years previous.

"Well, anyway, me and the other guy were standing in the middle of the ring with the gym teacher between us. I knew that no one else would hear. So, I asked the other guy if he was still mad at me. He said he was not. I asked him if he still wanted to fight. With no one other the gym teacher in hearing range, he said that he did not want to fight. He said that he got done what he wanted to get done and he was willing to let it go at that. He had proven his toughness already. Fighting was not necessary, but the gym teacher would not listen.

"I asked the teacher about mouth protection and headgear. He told us to '*start the fight and let the better man win.*' Well, in my opinion, better men are not defined by whether they can beat someone in the boxing ring. So, I said to the gym teacher, '*look, I do not want to fight. He says that he doesn't want to fight. Why can't we just forget this absurdity?*' The gym teacher obviously wanted to see a fight. He said to me, '*are you a coward? Are you afraid to defend yourself in the gentleman's way?*'

"For some reason the other guy felt that it's time to get tough again. So, he says to me, '*yeah Page, are you afraid how bad I'll kick your ass?*'

"The whole situation was crazy, and I turned to walk out of the ring. Then, the other guy grabs me violently by the shoulders and spins me around. Well, grabbing me like that made me see red. As I spun around, I swung as hard as I could with my right arm level. I caught him squarely on the left side of his chin. He spun around twice and fell flat on his back. I was mad as hell.

"This gym teacher had manipulated me, and I decided right then and there that the gym teacher was not going to get away with it. I walked over to the opposite corner where there was a stash of boxing gloves. I grabbed a set and brought it back to the gym teacher. I slammed them into his chest and yelled for him to put them on because what he just saw wasn't much of a fight, and if he wanted to see I fight, he had to fight me.

"The gym teacher was around thirty years of age and three inches taller than me, but he was not physically fit. I wanted to scare him into never doing this again. I yelled at him, 'put the fuckin' gloves on!' He just looked at me with a stunned face. Then, he looked at the other guy who was laid out on the mat; who was not moving. I shouted at him again. I don't know how many times I shouted at him. I was angry. I don't remember all of what I said. Most of what I tell you now is what other people said happened.

"I remember that the gym teacher threw the gloves to the mat and started to climb out of the ring. He was between the ropes when I grabbed him and pulled him back to the center of the ring. *'No! No!'* I said. *'You wanted a fight and now you are going to get one.'* I started by lightly jabbing him in the arm. He told me to stop and get back with the class. Then, I hit him lightly in the stomach a few times. He didn't hit back. *'Are you a coward?'* I shouted at him. He tried to gain control by grabbing me around the neck. I shook him loose and I hit him lightly on the jaw, which knocked him back a few feet.

"I remember calling him by his name and asking him why he was motivated to make others fight but not willing to fight himself. He tried to get control though authority and ordering me to the locker room, but I would not have any of that. I shouted that he was not going to get out of this ring until either he or I was laid out on the mat.

"I backed him into one of the corners. I screamed at him that he was the one who was a coward and an asshole and that he got his jollies by making his students fight each other. He tried to shove his way past me, but I placed one forearm on his chest and the other on his neck, and I slammed him against the corner post. He dropped to the mat and started gasping for air.

"When I realized he would not get up anytime soon, I climbed out of the ring. I calmly asked one of my classmates to help me off with the gloves. Then, I went to the locker room, changed my clothes, and left school for the day.

"The gym teacher was not hurt. I had just knocked the wind out of him. The other guy spent several weeks in the hospital with a broken jaw. They had to wire his jaw shut.

"The school principle investigated what happened. The gym teacher was fired, and I was suspended from school for a month."

Rigney pauses to see if Brad asks any questions. Brad does not say anything.

"That's it," Rigney says with finality. "No big deal. They got what was coming to them."

Brad Watson now knows why the doctor suggested he hear it firsthand. The incident shows that Rigney is capable of calculated violence.

"Rig, Doctor Williamson said that you did not think you are much of a fighter. The story you just told me sounds like you can fight when you want to."

"I don't think so. That time it was just another one of those occasions when I threw a few punches and knocked the fight out of the other guy. I know that I cannot do well in the boxing ring with someone who is a trained boxer. I would get my ass whipped in a street fight with an experienced street fighter. I just have no skill at it. I never wanted to be skillful at it."

"What about your parents? How did they feel about the boxing ring incident?"

"My mother said she was ashamed of me. She thought that I should have walked away. She said that only barbarians and lowlifes settle problems with violence.

"My father basically felt the same way, except that he understands that there are times when you must defend yourself. My father did tell me something that absolutely came true. He said because I knocked out *what's-his-name* and knocked out a teacher I earned a reputation as a fighter. Meaning other bullies and tough guys would challenge me to fight. He was right. I was challenged many times after that."

"What did you do?"

"My father said that if I fought, there would be no end to it, especially if I won the fights. When these guys challenged me to fight, I would tell them no. I would tell them that I had no desire to fulfill their moronic quest to be the number one tough guy. I told them that I would not meet them after school or any other time. I told them that if they wanted me to fight, they must attack me in a place where I just happened to be. Then, I would defend myself."

"Did any of them attack you?"

"No," Rigney replies with a frown.

"You sound disappointed that they didn't."

Rigney appears thoughtful for a few moments; then, responds, "I have often wondered about that. I was disappointed and I don't know why."

"Could have been that deep down you wanted to certify that you were the tough guy."

"But that was never important to me."

"Rig, you just wanted to think it wasn't important to you. You knew that fighting is an immature act, and you wanted to prove to everyone that you were not immature. You wanted to comply with your parent's wishes. On one hand, you want to be the essence of cool. On the other hand, sometimes you become enraged. You want to smash the object of your rage. Except for a few rare occasions, you have been successful. I think that if you ever faced a life or death situation, you would become fiercely brutal."

"Brad, my father was in street gangs when he was young. One of my uncles told me about many of the street fights my Dad was in when he was a kid. My uncles told me that my Dad was a fast and merciless fighter. My Dad taught hand-to-hand combat in the Army Reserves. In World War II, he was a combat engineer. He was awarded the Bronze Star and Purple Heart.

"One time when I was about seven, I saw him knock down two guys in just a few seconds. We went to the movies one night. There was a long line. We finally got to the ticket window when two mean looking guys walked up to the window and jumped in front of us. My father politely told them where the end of the line was. They told him to *fuck off*. Then, my Dad led us in front of these two. Well, one of them pushes us out of line, which knocked me down at the same time.

"I must tell ya, Brad, I've never since seen anyone move as fast as my Dad did against that guy. I mean his arms and feet were a blur of movement. He kicked the guy in the shins, followed by three or four punches to the face. When the guy puts his hands up to protect his face, my Dad hit him hard in the stomach. When the guy doubled over, my Dad hit him with an uppercut, which laid the guy out flat on the sidewalk. That guy hit the sidewalk so hard that you could hear his head crack on the pavement. The other guy tried to punch my Dad, but my Dad just kicked him in the balls. The guy bent over in agony. Then, in a swirling turn, Dad kicked him in the head. The guy fell to the ground screaming in pain. Blood flowed from the guy's mouth. The people in line applauded. We left and didn't stay for the movie. My Dad said that he did not want to be there when the cops came.

"Anyway, I was always getting beat up by bullies when I was little. They would take my lunch money or destroy my homework. Bullies saw me as an easy mark. There was no end to them. Then, one day when I was eight or nine years old, some bullies beat on me after school. I came home crying with black eyes and a bloody nose. My Dad cleaned me up. He cleaned my cuts and applied Band-Aids. He put ice in a towel and told me to hold it to my face. At that point, he just helped me feel better.

"About an hour later, he sat me down and talked to me about it. He wanted to know if I tried to fight them off. I told him I took a couple of swings, but they were all over me. They were bigger and older than me.

"My father wanted to know why they beat me up. I didn't know. My father told me that bullies have an inferiority complex. Beating on people gives the bully the sense that he is superior to someone.

"Anyway, getting to the point. My Dad told me that if you have no choice but to protect yourself, you should fight as dirty as you can and try to knock the fight out of the other guy."

Brad Watson smiles and says, "Your Dad and I agree. Did you ever do what he said?"

"My Dad told me to kick them in balls as fast as I can. Or kick them the shins or kick them in the back of the thigh with the point of my foot. Then, when they are bent over, kick them in the head. He said don't waste time trying to beat the guy with punches, unless it's a punch to the throat or stomach. My Dad said that I would need to inflict pain as fast as I could and balled fists to the head normally didn't do that. My Dad showed me how to do those things. But ya know, Brad, I never really had to do those things. I did not want to do them. Anyway, as I got older and bigger, I never had to use those moves. The few times after that when I needed to fight, I ended it with a power punch to the face or slamming the guy to the ground was all that was needed. A fighter I am not. I never had enough interest to become good at it. It's just not important to me."

"Do you think you could use what your father taught you if you were cornered?"

"Brad, you're scaring me with all this attention on fighting. It makes me doubt that ONI is for me."

"Rigney, I do not really think you will need it. Hand-to-hand combat training is more for confidence building than a skill you will need. Now, show me some of the moves your father taught you."

"It's been a long time. I don't remember them well. Kicking a guy in the balls takes little finesse. Basically, don't stand facing the guy. Be turned sideways at least at a forty-five degree angle. Don't give him an easy target to kick you in the balls. When a guy moves at you, you quickly turn to face him. Then, you take a bouncing step forward on your left foot and swing your right foot into the guy's crotch. My father said that will disable the son-of-a-bitch long enough for you to get away."

"Your Dad is right about that one. What if the guy is too close for that? What if he is within arm's reach, and he swings at you?"

"Dad says to step inside the swing and go for his throat. He showed me how to do it.

My Dad explained: "You might get hit with his forearm but not much damage there. Put both hands around his throat and squeeze your thumbs hard against his Adam's apple and push backward to take him off balance. The guy will become defensive and grab your arms. As soon as he grabs your arms, you kick him the balls."

"Those sound like good moves," Brad states. "What if the guy is obviously stronger and tougher than you, or he won't let you position yourself correctly."

"Then, he probably is not in a position to attack," Rigney replies.

"Maybe," Brad responds. "What if you think the guy is just too tough for you. What do you do then?"

"That's easy. I grab a heavy object and slam it against his head."

"And if no heavy objects are available?"

"Run!" Rigney replies with fake fear.

"What about eye gouging and nose smashing for close in work? Did your father ever show you that? Do you understand how to do that?"

Rigney responds with apprehension in his voice. "What I understand, Brad, is that you're scaring the hell out of me!"

"Rigney, you must understand that should you be discovered, unlikely as it may be, you will not be in danger. Like I said before, harming you verifies that they know that we know they are there. It would be to their benefit to do nothing, especially if you haven't discovered anything. If they do find out that you have discovered them, they must presume that you have already reported them. If the ship is at sea, they have no place to run. They must accept being arrested. Harming you has no benefit. Harming you would add to the charges against them. If the ship is in port, they can walk off the ship and disappear.

"Look, Rig, we at ONI are experts at how espionage agents think and how they are trained and how they operate. Our best minds have concluded that the espionage agent or agents on that ship are not Russians, but U.S. Navy personnel who have turned against their own country for money. This means that they are not highly trained fighters or killers. Experience with these types tells us that when we move in on them, they crumble and cry. But we cannot guarantee that a sailor turned traitor will not panic. And in the remote chance that you are attacked, you need to know how to stop the attacker stone cold. If you are faced with such a situation and you are attacked, you cannot think about just knocking your attacker down. You must do your best to put him down so that he never gets up. For your own safety, don't give him a chance to get back up. You must be brutal and show no mercy."

"Do you mean . . . do you mean kill him?" Rigney stutters with a shocked tone.

"Yes, if you are attacked, you must do that," Brad Watson says brashly while looking straight into Rigney's eyes.

"I don't know how to kill someone!" Rigney responds emotionally with a look of horror on his face.

"During your training these two weeks, I will show you how to disable an attacker. I will show you several ways to kill with your hands and your feet. If you are attacked you must assume the other person is trying to kill you. You cannot hesitate."

"Like judo?" Rigney responds while expressing intense curiosity.

"Some judo moves and some close-in maneuvering that will throw an opponent off balance. Take off your gloves and move to the middle of the ring. I will show you some moves.

Rig complies and tosses his gloves to the corner of the ring.

Brad explains: "I will slam you to the mat many times. If you lose your cool, you will discover it is easier for me to throw you to the mat."

For the next two hours, Brad Watson instructs Rigney in judo moves, karate techniques, and other hand-to-hand actions that quickly disable and kill an attacker.

Later, after taking a long hot shower, Rigney and Brad dress in the locker room. They are alone.

Brad speaks in a serious tone. "Rig, you have passed the mental and physical indoctrination. I want you to work for us. Do you still want to be assigned to this mission?"

"No problem, Brad. I will do it. If I appear to hesitate, it is only because I have not yet become comfortable with the possibility of danger. I think that will come with time. I'm anxious to get on with it. What's next?"

Brad appears thoughtful for a few moments as he stuffs his sweaty gym clothes into his gym bag. Then, he responds, "How do you feel about the moves you learned today?"

"Easy to learn," Rigney says flippantly, "but as I told you, I do not move fast, and I cannot run fast."

"Actually, you do move fast. You think because you do not run fast that you do not move fast. You are quicker with your hands and feet than you think. You're strong and have plenty of endurance. You have a viselike grip. We will have more sessions like this. Before you know it, you will react instinctively.

"Now for the other things we need to do. We need to put you through

74

some behavior control training. Additionally, we need to brief you on what we know about what's happening aboard that ship. And you will need several training sessions with small arms."

"Small arms? Like what kind?"

"You will learn to use the Colt .45 caliber automatic, the Smith and Wesson .357 Magnum, and a 9mm Beretta automatic."

"Brad, I am concerned that you have not told me all that you can. I hope you have been completely honest with me."

Lieutenant Commander Brad Watson shakes his head slightly, "More than honest. I just need to cram as much training into two weeks as possible."

"Huh, huh . . . and with only two weeks available, you think it necessary to cram in hand-to-hand combat and small arms."

"You don't trust me, Rig?"

"Yes, I trust you. If I stop trusting you, I will tell you."

Rigney and Brad enter the cafeteria inside the Suitland ONI Headquarters building. The cafeteria is 90 percent full. Rigney notices that he and Brad are the only two in blue jumpsuits. All the other men in the cafeteria wear dress shirts and ties or are in navy uniforms. Rigney notices that many people follow he and Brad with their eyes. They find a table and sit down.

Rigney queries, "Brad, why are people staring at us?"

"It's because we are in blue jumpsuits. It always draws stares. ONI employees know that only those in Field OPS wear blue jumpsuits. They are curious as to whom and what we are. It's the mystery and scent of danger that makes them curious. They've seen me before. They wonder about you."

"Isn't there a problem with them knowing that we are with Field Operations?"

"We are on a military installation. Everyone in this building has a top secret clearance. Nothing they see or hear may be discussed outside this building and they know that."

Brad and Rigney enter the firing range and close the door behind them. They proceed to the registration desk. A GM2, gunner's mate second class, wearing Undress Blue uniform pushes the registration book toward Brad and advises, "Your firing stall is ready, Commander—number thirteen."

As they walk along the firing line, Rigney observes six men at different stalls firing different types of handguns. Some of the men wear civilian clothes; all others wear blue jumpsuits.

At stall thirteen, three handguns and five boxes of ammunition sit on the stall's countertop. Brad picks up the Colt .45. He carefully points it down range. "Rig, have you ever fired one of these?"

"Yes, in boot camp."

"Explain the safeties to me."

Rigney explains the safeties and points to them, "The half-cocked safety, the grip safety, and the thumb safety."

Brad places the Colt .45 on the countertop.

"Do you recognize the other two pistols?"

"I have never seen these types before. I assume the revolver is the .357 Magnum, and the automatic is the 9mm Beretta."

"That's correct," Brad responds. "I will instruct you on the safeties of the two other weapons and how to fire them."

Brad spends the rest of the afternoon teaching Rigney how to fire the handguns. Rigney's proficiency with 9mm Beretta becomes obvious and he tells Brad that the Beretta feels the best in his hands. Rigney's shooting accuracy is best with the Beretta.

Chapter 14

Thursday - December 7, 1967

Rigney knocks on the door of room 4.

"Enter."

Rigney recognizes Lieutenant Commander Brad Watson's voice from the other side of the door. He enters the room and sees Brad Watson sitting on the couch and Doctor Williamson sitting behind the desk. With a wave of his hand, the doctor indicates that Rigney should sit in the chair in front of the desk. Rigney lowers himself into the chair in his normal manner. The doctor smiles as he observes Rigney perform his sitting ritual.

Rigney observes that Brad Watson wears his Service Dress Blue uniform.

Brad informs, "Rig, so that you are not conspicuous aboard ship, the doctor and I shall instruct you how to act more normal."

"Are you saying that I am abnormal?" Rigney responds with a chuckle while looking devilishly toward Brad.

"Not abnormal," Doctor Williamson answers. "You're just different. Your GCT and ARI scores are the highest I have ever seen. In some areas you're extremely mature for your age. In other areas you need to grow up. For the work you are going to perform, your behavior must be less mature. You must act less intelligent."

Rigney chuckles as he says, "Thank you. I think."

Brad Watson states with authority, "You must take this behavior modification seriously. When you go aboard that ship, you must act like an ordinary sailor. You must sometimes act in an immature way that everyone notices. The sum of your actions must make you appear unlikely to be a counterintelligence agent."

"What must I do?" Rigney submits with a shrug.

The doctor emphasizes, "You must react more emotionally. From time to time, you must be openly angry or least irritated when someone insults you. When someone mouths off at you, mouth off back.

"You must also demonstrate less intelligence. Do not engage in deep conversations regarding politics, religion, or current events. Do not reveal how *well read* you are. You must not brag or show off regarding your electronics knowledge. We do not want others to know your level of electronics knowledge and skill."

"I understand, Doctor. I will do my best to follow your instructions."

For the rest of the day, Doctor Williamson and Lieutenant Commander Brad Watson educate Rigney on how to act under various conditions. They do some role-playing.

After a full day of behavior modification training, Rigney feels wound tight. He needs exercise. He delays reading an article in *The Washington Post* regarding the thirty-sixth anniversary of the Japanese attack on Pearl Harbor. After a light dinner, he walks to the base gym.

Rigney exercises alone in the base gym. The gym operates on the honor system. The one door is always unlocked. He performs repetitions with the twenty-five pound weights. After one hour into his workout, he is drenched in sweat. He looks at the clock on the wall—7:45 p.m.

As he pumps iron, he thinks about the behavioral training he went through earlier in the day. He believes that he will have no trouble acting the way they want.

The gym door opens. Raven-hair enters. She wears a thick winter coat with a fur collar turned up around her neck. An inviting smile spreads across her face as she walks toward him.

He smiles back.

"I was about to go into the EM club across the street. Then, I saw you through the window. I thought I would come over and say hello. My name is Cathy Gillard. What's your name?"

"Rigney Page," he responds cheerfully. "Glad you came in. I was hoping to see you in the chow hall the last couple of mornings so that I could explain why I didn't show up at the club on Monday night."

"I haven't been on base," she explains. "I've been on my 96."

"96?"

"Yeah. The 96 hours off between watch strings."

As Cathy talks, her eyes roam over Rigney's body, and she is not subtle about it. Her breathing becomes heavy as she visualizes his muscled upper torso through the sweat-soaked, clinging t-shirt. Her eyes linger on his bulging biceps, and her eyes linger even longer at the bulge in the crotch of his tight gym shorts. She expresses craving.

Cathy's lustful stare causes Rigney to blush.

When Cathy sees Rigney blushing, she realizes what she is doing. She changes her expression and looks at his face and says, "I have gym clothes in my car. Mind if I join you?"

Rigney studies her face for a moment and wonders what she is planning. *What beautiful brown eyes!*

"I don't mind at all," he responds while exhibiting a pleasurable smile.

"I'll be right back," she says. Then, she darts out the door.

A few minutes later, Cathy returns with a large, red leather bag. "I'll change in the locker room."

Rigney wonders why she announced where she would change. The gym facility is small and coed with one locker room and two shower stalls, one head, and one steam room. The gym area itself is only sixty feet by sixty feet.

Maybe she wants me to follower her.

Rigney considers going into the locker room with her; then, he dismisses it. *What if someone else comes in? What if I'm wrong about her intentions? I will be embarrassed and so will she.*

Five minutes later Cathy comes out of the locker room.

Rigney gawks at her.

Cathy's gym clothes are more for showing off her body than functional for exercise. Her white and tight spandex shorts accentuate every curve of her perfectly sized and perfectly shaped hips, butt, and pubic area. Her shapely legs are long and slender. She wears a light blue, skintight tank top that leaves nothing to the imagination regarding the size and shape of her breasts and nipples.

Cathy knows Rigney is drooling, and that is exactly the reaction she wants.

Rigney refocuses on his workout. He gets a weight bar and performs arm curls.

Cathy works out on a ski machine.

Over the next hour, they become acquainted and tell each other about their background.

Cathy is from Georgia. Last June, she graduated from a private girl's prep school. While at the prep school, she was on the swim team and track team. She tells him that she purposely did not achieve academically because she was rebelling against her parents. Cathy explains that her parents had already picked her college and planned her life for the next ten years. She punished her parents by not studying and not getting good grades. She purposely instigated trouble at school.

When her parents ridiculed her for not behaving as a proper young lady, she signed with the navy and departed for boot camp the day after she graduated from prep school. She went to boot camp at Bainbridge, Maryland, followed by her current duty assignment at Cheltenham. She works shifts in the NAVCOMMSTA Copy and Distribution Center.

Her navy pay and a monthly distribution from her grandfather's trust fund provides her with enough money to share an off-base apartment and to own a decent used car.

Rigney tells her that he is from Southern California. He tells her about attending submarine schools in New London and the recently discovered ear problem that could disqualify him. That is why he is in

DC for two weeks—to see a specialist.

They chat casually about the navy and current events. Cathy becomes impressed with Rigney's knowledge of current events. Rigney discovers Cathy's limited understanding of the world situation. Cathy is ignorant of current world events. Rigney concludes that Cathy discontinued learning when she graduated from high school.

At 9:30 p.m., Rigney completes his workout. He says to Cathy, "I'm done with my workout. I'm going to the steam room to do my post workout stretching exercises."

"I'll join you in a few minutes," she advises.

All sorts of sexual pictures flash through Rigney's mind.

Rigney goes to the locker room and retrieves his shower shoes. He removes his sweat soaked t-shirt and he removes his sneakers and socks. He does not take off his gym shorts. He slips on his shower shoes, grabs six towels, and enters the steam room.

The steam room is twelve feet by twelve feet. The floor is ceramic tile. Three levels of wide, tiled-covered sitting-steps stand against two walls. Rigney pours cold water over the thermostat to turn on the steam. He lays towels on one of the steps and starts his stretching exercises. Sixty seconds later, the room is full of steam.

He sits on a bottom step. The steam room door opens, and Cathy walks in. She is naked.

"I like to be naked in steam rooms. Don't you?"

Before he can answer, she stands in front of him with her legs slightly apart and her hands on her hips. Rigney's penis becomes hard and aches as it is forced sideways by his jockstrap.

Rigney gulps and stares wide-eyed at Cathy. He runs his eyes up and down her naked body. His heart pumps faster as he stares at her raven-black pubic hair.

She leans toward him, puts her hands around his wrists, and pulls him to a standing position.

"How about shucking the shorts?" she asks. "I feel uncomfortable being the only naked person in here."

"But what if someone comes in?"

"No one comes here this time of night. Besides I locked the only door."

Rigney pauses. He is not sure. Then, Cathy puts her hands on the waist of his shorts and pushes a few inches.

"Make up your mind, Rigney. Can I take off your shorts?"

Rigney decides to relax and enjoy this experience. "Yes, you can take them off."

Cathy pushes down on his shorts and jock strap at the same time.

She stoops as she guides the shorts and jock strap down. When his penis becomes free of the jock strap, it snaps forward and hits Cathy in the nose. She jerks her head back a few inches and says sexily, "naughty boy."

She stoops lower as she pushes his shorts and jockstrap to his ankles. As Rigney steps out of the shorts and jock strap, Cathy is still stooping, her face just inches from his hard penis.

Rigney remembers his first sexual experience with Sally Macfurson. As he did then, he cannot help fantasizing that Cathy will start sucking his penis.

But she does not.

She stands and runs her hands softly over Rigney's sweaty biceps, shoulders, and chest. She runs her fingers like a comb through his thick chest hair.

Cathy stands just a few inches shorter than Rigney, and she easily slides her hands lightly around the back of his head. She guides him to kiss her. Rigney slides his arms around her and pulls her close. Their sweaty bodies come together. Rigney's penis presses against her lower belly.

They kiss softly at first. After a few moments they ache for more. The kissing becomes deep and open mouthed with tongues dancing. Their hands roam each other's body in search of pleasure zones.

Rigney guides them to sit on the bottom step where he laid some towels.

Cathy runs her hand up Rigney's thigh and wraps her hand around his penis. She stokes him softly and slowly. Rigney breathes heavier as he becomes more aroused.

He moves his right hand from her lower belly to her pubic area. She opens her legs to allow him access. Rigney uses his index finger to search out and discover the location of her clitoris. He finds it and massages it softly.

Cathy squirms with pleasure. Then, suddenly, she pulls her face away from his. She stops stroking him but does not remove her hand.

Thinking that he is doing something incorrectly, he stops massaging her clitoris; but keeps his finger in place.

"We can't have sex in here," Cathy says apologetically. It's too uncomfortable, and we do not have any condoms. The last thing I want is to get pregnant."

Rigney is about to say that he understands and that she can keep stroking him without concern of getting pregnant; but she starts stoking him again.

She looks into his eyes and says, "So would it be okay if tonight we satisfy each other with oral sex? Tomorrow night we can have sex in my apartment . . . in my bed. I will get some condoms. Is that okay?"

"Yes, I am okay with that." He attempts not to sound eager

She raises one eyebrow and asks, "Do you know how to give a girl oral sex? You know, cunnilingus?"

"Yes, I know how."

She stops stroking Rigney and says, "Okay, you do me first. Then, I'll give you a blowjob."

Must be the standard routine! Rigney's sighs deeply and becomes more aroused at the promise of sexual pleasure.

Cathy stands up and walks out of the steam room. She is back in a few seconds with a large stack of folded towels. She lays a couple of the towels, still folded, on the first step. Then, she creates a type of lounge chair with the folded towels. She sits down on the folded towels and leans back. She is comfortable.

"Can you get the steam back on in here?"

"Sure."

Rigney sets the temperature. Less than a minute later, steam fills the room.

Rigney kneels on the towels in front of her.

Cathy spreads and lifts her legs; then, she lowers her legs to bring her thighs to rest on Rigney's shoulders. She tells him, "If you do this right, it takes about fifteen minutes for me to come three or four times. I'm usually satisfied after that. Are you up to it?"

"Absolutely!" Rigney assures her.

Five minutes later, Cathy experiences orgasm; she stiffens, arches her back, giggles, and rasps repeatedly: "Yes, yes. That's it! Yes, yes. That's it!" The flowing waves of carnal pleasure block her mind from anything else. She responds the same during the second and third orgasm.

After twenty minutes, she feels totally satisfied. She lifts her legs off Rigney's shoulders. Rigney moves back and stands up. As he stands, he feels a pleasurable ache in his penis as it stretches and expands to its limit.

Cathy's head is lying back, and her eyes are closed. She breathes deeply. Her body is totally limp, and her arms are at her side. Her legs are still spread apart. She does not have the energy to close them.

Rigney waits patiently for Cathy to come back around. He rubs his jaw, which has become sore from twenty minutes of continuous activity.

After a full minute, Cathy sits up and leans forward. Her face expresses a look of total sexual satisfaction. She says to him, "You said you knew how. You didn't mention that you were expert! Until now only girls have made me come like that. You've had some good teachers."

Rigney does not understand her *only girls* comment. He decides not to ask about it now.

She stares appreciatively at Rigney. The sweat from his body mats down the reddish brown body hair that covers him from his shoulders to his ankles. Her breasts heave with desire as she looks up and down his hard and muscular body. Finally, her eyes stop their roaming at his erect penis.

"Please turn on the steam," she requests. "I think it makes the sensation better."

Rigney turns on the steam. He turns toward her. She still sits on the lower step.

"Come here," Cathy commands with a sexy smile as she licks her lips.

Rigney walks over and stands in front of her. She wraps her right hand around his penis and strokes it softly and slowly.

Steam fills the room.

"Do you mind if I do this with me sitting here and with you standing up. I think I am too weak to move from this spot."

"No objections," Rigney says huskily in between rapid breaths.

Cathy removes her hand from his penis. Then, she reaches around him and places her hands on his buttocks.

She pulls him forward and at the same time moves her head forward.

Rigney inhales sharply when he feels Cathy's warm and wet mouth move rapidly back and forth around his penis.

Cathy sucks loudly as she gives the blow job.

Four minutes later, Rigney closes his eyes and breathes rapidly as ejaculation begins. His whole body shudders. His mind is focused on the sexual ecstasy of his penis being sucked during pulsating ejaculation. The sucking continues until he is completely spent.

When he feels Cathy release his penis from her mouth, he opens his eyes just in time to see Cathy rise to her feet and dash from the steam room.

Rigney continues to breathe heavily. He sits on the first step. After a few moments, he lies down on the towels that are scattered along the steam room's first step. He feels totally spent and exhausted. The pleasure of the blow job lingers.

Several minutes later when his breathing and senses return to normal, he opens his eyes. He sits up. Then, he stands and starts toward the door. Dizziness causes him to wobble and become unsteady. He leans against the wall for a few moments to regain his balance. When he finally exits the steam room, he asks himself aloud, "Why does anyone bother with traditional, missionary-style sex?!"

Two minutes later, Cathy and Rigney are in the shower soaping each other down. When Cathy washes his scrotum and penis, he becomes erect.

"I can't do anymore tonight," she pleads. "I am too weak and tired. Tomorrow night at my place, okay?"

Rigney is disappointed, but he does not push it. He nods agreement.

After the shower, they towel each other dry and; then they get dressed. His penis stands erect as he slips into his uniform trousers.

As they walk out of the locker room, Cathy offers, "I will drive you to the barracks. No reason for you to be walking around in this cold."

Rigney does not pay attention to the direction that Cathy drives. His mind focuses on tomorrow night. When he feels the car come to stop, he surveys the area and finds they are parked in front of a large three-story brick building that he does not recognize.

"I will pick you up here at six tomorrow night. Is that okay?"

"This is not my barracks."

Confusion appears on Cathy's face as she responds, "This is the men's barracks. You're not staying here?"

Rigney looks around. He does not recognize this area of the Cheltenham base.

"I don't know how to get to my barracks from here. Drive back to the gym. Then, I can direct you from there."

Several minutes later, Rigney directs Cathy to pull into the ONI building parking lot.

"This is the spook's building," Cathy remarks calmly. "You're staying here?"

"Spook's building?"

"Yeah. Well, that's what everyone calls it. They say navy spies work in there."

Rigney takes a few moments to think how to respond. Then, he says, "No, it's just a barracks."

"Small barracks," Cathy observes. "Many guys staying there?"

"I don't know how many," Rigney replies; then he changes the subject. "You will pick me up here tomorrow night at six?"

"Uh huh. And I will make us dinner at my place." Cathy beams a smile and leans toward him for a kiss.

They kiss lightly on the lips.

Rigney exits the car and walks up the steps. He waits until Cathy drives away before entering the cipher lock code.

Chapter 15

Friday - December 8, 1967

At 0800, Rigney departs his room. He wears Service Dress Blues and his peacoat. He holds his white hat and gloves in his right hand and holds his gym bag in his left hand. When he enters the waiting room, he sees RM3 John Smith reading a navy manual.

Smith wears Service Dress Blues also.

As he approaches Smith, Rigney gets a closer look at the rating manual. The title reads Radioman 3 & 2 Advancement Course Book.

"Hi, John. Brushing up on your radioman skills?" Rigney asks.

"Oh, yeah," John replies. "I need to complete this course before I take the RM2 Exam."

Rigney stands quietly for a few moments and studies John's face. John's response does not make sense. The course must be completed prior to taking the RM3 Exam. John wears a RM3 crow on his uniform. Rigney is now convinced that John Smith is not in the navy.

John advises, "After your appointment at Bethesda, I am taking you to the ONI headquarters building in Suitland."

John Smith drives the navy vehicle into Captain Willcroft's reserved parking space next to the ONI headquarters building in Suitland. They exit the vehicle. John Smith opens the trunk.

"I don't know how long I'll be," Rigney tells John.

"That's okay. I've come to watch." John pulls a gym bag from the trunk.

"Watch what?"

"Your training," John snaps back.

Lieutenant Commander Brad Watson meets Rigney and John in the Locker Room of the ONI Headquarters gymnasium. Brad already wears his gym clothes. Rigney and John change. Then, the three men jog into the gym and start laps around the gym floor, after 80 laps, John Smith drops out and jogs to the weight area. Brad and Rigney jog 150 laps. At the end of the jog, they are both sweating heavily; but neither is out of breath. Brad leads the stretching exercises.

After the stretching exercises, Brad leads Rigney to the martial arts training area. As the two of them approach the martial arts training mats, the four men who practice on the mats stop and walk off the mats. The four men sit down on the floor at the edge of the mats.

Brad walks to a locker that stands against the wall. Rigney follows close behind. Brad opens the locker door and removes what looks like a quilted jumpsuit. Brad inspects the inside of the suit.

Brad explains the jumpsuit to Rigney. "This jumpsuit is specially made for martial arts training. Inside the suit are pouches that hold one-quarter-inch plastic plates. One-half-inch padding insulates both sides of the plates. The plates are positioned to protect the legs, crotch, and torso from hard blows. The crotch has the most padding with five inches of quilted pads and a full inch of plastic. Sufficient spacing exists at the body joints to allow freedom of movement."

Rigney stands quietly while Brad steps into the jumpsuit.

Rigney asks with an annoyed tone, "Is this another secret, or are you going to tell me what this is all about?"

"I'll explain shortly. Now zip me up," Brad orders as he turns his back to Rigney. The zipper runs up the middle of the back.

Rigney does as ordered.

"Should I put this stuff on too?"

"No."

The last item is padded headgear with a flap attachment that covers completely around the neck. The headgear covers the forehead, nose, and mouth. Only Brad's eyes are visible. The joints of the headgear at the neck are large enough to allow total freedom of movement of the head.

Brad performs a few jumping jacks and squats to verify free movement at all joints. Then, he declares, "Okay, we are ready."

Rigney follows Brad to the center of the mat. With a slightly exasperated tone, Rigney inquires, "Ready for what?"

Brad turns and faces Rigney, "Today, I play the attacker. Your job is to put me on the mat anyway you can. You can use any force that you want to put me down. Use the moves I taught you the other day. I will charge at you, but I will not punch or kick you. Don't go on the defensive and try to protect yourself. The first fighter to go on the defensive loses. You must be aggressive to put me down. At first, I will not resist your attempts to put me down. As you become more successful with the put-downs, I will start to resist slightly. As you do better, I will resist even more. I will not tell you when I start resisting or when I increase my resistance. You must be ready for me to start resisting at any time. Then, without warning, I will start to fight back. Not enough to hurt you but enough to challenge you. I will not kick you or punch you. When I think you have progressed far enough, I will start using leverage to lay you out. Are you ready?"

"No! I am not ready!" Rigney protests with irritation.

"Perfect!" Brad snaps. "Let's get started."

"I told you before—I am no good at this!"

"You're better than you think."

Doubts about his own abilities reflect in Rigney's face.

"Rig, when an attacker comes at you, he won't give you time to prepare. You must be ready. Remember, an attack on you will be spontaneous. Most likely you have surprised your attacker. You will probably be surprised also. Because it's a surprise, the attacker will act without thinking. That will be your advantage. Now, let's get started."

Rigney shakes his head as he says, "How can I do this when I lack confidence?"

"No one is born with the ability," Brad counsels. "It's a learned skill. I think you will surprise yourself."

Rigney looks around the perimeter of the mats. John Smith now sits with the onlookers.

The onlookers listen to Brad and Rigney's conversation. Each man has a knowing smile on his face.

"Who are those guys?" Rigney asks as he nods toward the onlookers.

"They were once where you are now. They, too, lacked confidence. Now, I would put them up against the best in the world."

"John Smith too?" Rigney asks.

"Yes, especially him."

"Okay," Rigney relents with a big sigh. "Let's do it."

The words are no sooner out of Rigney's mouth when Brad bends down and jumps forward with arms folded in front of him, like a football offensive lineman. Brad hits Rigney in the chest. Rigney lands hard on his butt.

Brad stands over and looks down at Rigney. He shakes his head slightly.

Rigney glares up at Brad. The suddenness and force of the attack angers him. Rigney puts his left hand on the mat with a move that looks like he is balancing himself to get up. Instead, Rigney swings his right leg as hard as he can against the back of Brad's ankles. Brad's feet fly from underneath him, and he lands on his back.

Rigney jumps to his feet and steps back six feet. He feels avenged.

Light applause comes from the onlookers.

Both Rigney and Brad look over at the perimeter. The crowd of onlookers is expanding.

"No applause and no booing!" Brad orders toward the crowd

The crowd becomes silent.

Brad stands. He looks Rigney in the eye and comments, "Very good. Where did you learn that? I didn't teach you that one."

"I saw a friend of mine do it once. Situation seemed right to do it."

Brad smiles at Rigney for a few moments. Then, Brad runs toward Rigney with arms raised, conveying he plans to grab Rigney.

Remembering Brad's instructions to be aggressive and not defensive, Rigney charges toward Brad. Rigney judges the distance correctly. After he comes down on his left foot, he kicks his right foot into the crotch of Brad's padded suit.

The kick stops Brad cold.

Rigney backs off about six feet.

Brad stands still for a full minute. The kick was so powerful that Brad felt a mild level of pain, despite all the padding and shielding.

Then, Brad walks slowly toward Rigney.

Rigney readies himself for another attack.

Brad stops about three feet away and says, "I think you have mastered the kick to the balls. I do not think it necessary for you to use it again."

"Can't I—"

"That's an order," Brad whispers through tight lips.

"Okay," Rigney whispers back.

Brad instructs and advises, "Turn around. I will attack you from the rear."

Brad slowly approaches Rigney. He holds his right hand above his head as if he has some sort of object to hit Rigney in the head.

When Brad is about two feet away and ready to swing down, Rigney spins around, leans forward, and places both hands around Brad's throat; he pushes Brad backward. Brad reacts like an unskilled attacker would react. Brad pretends to drop the object in his hand and grabs Rigney's forearms; he tries to force Rig's hands off his throat. When Brad grabs Rigney's forearms, Rigney uses Brad's off balance position to push him down. Brad lands on the mat with a smile on his face.

"Very good, Rig. You're a fast learner."

On the next frontal attack, Brad moves in slowly with fists rotating like a boxer. As Brad had taught, Rigney evaluates the position of Brad's fists and feet. Brad's left arm is extended out halfway and his left fist is chin high. Brad's right arm is tucked into his body and his right fist at shoulder height. Rigney looks at the position of Brad's feet. Brad's left foot is out front and pointed straight at Rigney. Brad's right foot is back about twelve inches and points to the right at a forty-five degree angle. All of this tells Rigney that the attacker is right handed, and his left arm is protecting against a punch to his head, and his right fist will be used for the first punch. According to Brad, Rigney has two options. First option: Rigney can just turn and walk away from the fight, but this option can only be used if Rigney believes the attacker will not return for another fight. Second option: Stay and fight. If Rigney chooses the second option, he cannot be on the defense. He must deceive the attacker and become the attacker himself. Rigney decides to stay and fight.

Following Brad's instructions for option two, Rigney pretends to be defensive by not moving forward or backward and by positioning arms, fists, and feet the same as the attacker. However, the difference in Rigney's stance is that he exposes his left side to the attacker. By doing this, Rigney protects his crotch and at the same time gives himself more leverage. Brad does what an amateur would do. He swings with his right fist. Rigney easily blocks the punch with his left arm. Then, he quickly steps inside Brad's left reach. At the same time Rigney swings up his right fist and forcefully hits Brad in the throat protector. The force of the punch would crush the windpipe, if Brad were not wearing the protector. Brad, playing the wounded attacker, falls to the mat, puts his hands at his throat and pretends to grasp for air. Then, Rigney says, "Kick to the head; kick to the head; kick to the head."

Brad springs to his feet and says, "Good! Exactly as instructed!"

Three staged attacks later, Brad starts to resist.

Rigney takes this as a compliment. Brad said he would not start resisting unless he thought Rigney was being successful.

Occasionally, Brad stops and reviews the previous action. Brad shows Rigney how his counterattack could have been more deadly or more disabling.

During one attack, Brad and Rigney find themselves face to face with only twelve inches between them. Both have their feet flat. This position would last one second. Neither have the advantage. Rigney reacts instinctively. Without moving his feet to get balanced, he thrusts both his fists into Brad's chest. Brad is knocked back six feet before he loses balance and lands on his butt.

The growing audience discusses in whispers the moves of each attack and counterattack. The power of Rigney's punch causes a temporary silence.

After a dozen more attacks, Brad starts using his skill at leverage to put Rigney to the mat. As he had promised, Brad does not use any punches or kicks. Brad is not successful with every attempt to put Rigney to the mat. During some maneuvers, Rigney's Herculean strength stops Brad cold.

During one maneuver, Brad has Rigney in a full nelson headlock and is ready to flip Rigney to the mat. Rigney, following Brad's instructions to be aggressive instead of defensive, throws his feet forward. Brad cannot hold up Rigney's 185 pounds. Rigney's weight forces Brad to lean forward and lose his balance. Rigney reaches over his head with both arms, grabs the material around Brad's shoulders, and pulls forward. The end result is that Rigney flips Brad over his head and onto the mat.

Brad feels that Rigney is progressing well. *Rig needs a lot of work, but he should not encounter any experts on his mission.*

After a few more attacks and counter attacks, Brad announces the session over.

Brad Watson, Rigney Page, and John Smith go to the locker room. They strip naked and head for the showers.

In the shower room, they chat about the hand-to-hand combat training. Rigney gets a good look at John Smith's build. Except for some slight flabbiness around the love handle area, John Smith's build duplicates of Rigney's. John stands tall at six feet and one inch, and, like Rigney, has wide shoulders, large biceps, and narrow hips and buttocks. Their facial features are similar. John does not have the amount of body hair that Rigney has.

"What the hell you are staring at, Rig?" John Smith says shaking his head.

"Yes, I am staring. Please excuse me if it bothers you. I just can't get over how much you and I look alike."

Back at their lockers, the conversation turns to the earlier hand-to-hand combat training.

John Smith says to Rigney, "You were impressive out there. You did well for an amateur. You're quick on your feet. You pack a powerful punch without having to put your whole body into it."

"Brad kicked my ass, and he was restricted from using punches and kicks."

John Smith smiles knowingly at Rigney. "No winning or losing here. The purpose is to expose you to possibilities and measure your capabilities. I think you will become an expert at hand-to-hand. Too bad there's not enough time to put you through the entire course . . . maybe next year."

"Next year? What are you talking about?" Rigney asks.

John glances at Brad Watson. Brad shakes his head.

Rigney looks back and forth between John and Brad.

Rigney looks around the locker room. Except for the three of them, the locker room is empty. Rigney looks directly at John Smith and asks, "Who are you? What are you? John Smith—a thirty-year-old RM3— give me a break! You are no more a RM3 than my little sister. You're Brad's age. Are you the same as what Brad is? Why are you a secret? Or are you just a secret to me?"

Brad Watson replies, "Rigney, you do not need to know."

Rigney asks John Smith, "So those questions the first night in my quarters. You were testing me—to see if I would tell you who I am, right?"

"That's right," John responds with a knowing smile.

Rigney looks at his watch–1410. He asks, "You guys hungry? I need to eat lunch."

Brad replies, "Sure. Let's go to the cafeteria."

After lunch, John Smith drives Rigney back to Cheltenham. John stops the vehicle at the *spook building* steps. He advises, "Brad will pick you up tomorrow morning at 0800."

"What's on the schedule for tomorrow," Rigney asks.

"More pistol training and more physical conditioning. Do you have a bathing suit?"

"No, I don't."

"That's okay. You can checkout one at the pool tomorrow."

"The pool?" Rigney questions.

"Brad will explain it to ya tomorrow. Oh, yeah, wear blue jumpsuit tomorrow."

Rigney exits the navy sedan. He enters the building and goes directly to his quarters. He is still *pumped* from today's activities. He decides to go to the base gym for a workout before Cathy picks him up at 6:00 p.m.

Cathy arrives at the ONI building at 6:00 p.m.

"Dinner's in the oven," Cathy tells Rigney as he enters the car.

"What are we having?"

"Roast duck."

"Sounds great. Then what?" Rigney asks while expressing a knowing smile.

"I was hoping we could work on improving our techniques from last night," Cathy responds with raised eyebrows.

Rigney says with a chuckle, "I'm not sure. I think you'll need to talk me into it."

"Okay, smartass. For that remark, I will have you begging like a puppy before the night is over."

"And I will have you purring like a kitten," Rigney promises confidently.

Cathy thinks about that and responds, "Maybe we will have dinner after."

Chapter 16

Saturday - December 9, 1967

Lieutenant Commander Brad Watson and RM3 Rigney Page walk the basement at ONI Headquarters. They both wear blue jumpsuits, and each carries a gym bag. Their footsteps echo along the basement hallway. No one else is around. Being Saturday, the building is empty except for duty personnel.

They enter the firing range. The range is mostly dark with only a few dim lights. The same Gunners Mate from the previous visit walks up to Brad Watson and advises, "Sir, the weapons and blackout range are ready."

Brad just nods and continues to walk past all the firing stalls. Rigney is in step beside him. They come to another door, and Brad opens it. They step into a room illuminated with red light. The room has only three firing stalls.

Brad walks to a bench that sits five feet back from the center firing stall and sets his gym bag on the bench. He takes off his coat and places it on the bench. Rigney does the same. Then, Brad leads them to the center firing stall.

Three 9mm Berettas lie on the stall counter. Six ten-round ammo magazines and five boxes of ammunition lie next to the Berettas. Three four-inch-long cylindrical objects that Rigney does not recognize lie next to the magazines.

Brad picks up one of the Berettas, points it down range, and presses on the magazine release as a safety measure to ensure no magazine is locked in. Then, he pulls back the slide and ensures no round is in the chamber. Then, Brad takes one of the cylindrical objects and screws it onto the front of the Beretta's barrel.

Rigney now recognizes the cylindrical object as a suppressor.

"I could never shoot anyone," Rigney states firmly.

Brad responds, "I need to understand your ability at using this weapon. The current plan does not include equipping you with such a weapon. There are no absolutes as to what situations you may find yourself. You may find yourself in a desperate situation where you will want to know how to use one of these."

Rigney does not understand. "If the plan is not to give me one of these, how will I have one if a desperate situation arises?"

"You will be told where you can find one."

"Aboard the ship!" Rigney responds, astonished.

"Yes, aboard the ship. There will be several hidden around the ship.

You will be told where. But, if you do not demonstrate proficiency with these weapons, we will not make them available to you. Now, let's get started."

Doubt about going on this mission returns to Rigney's thoughts. First, the hand-to-hand combat instruction and, now, training with weapons designed to kill. He worries about getting hurt or being killed. He now realizes that he might be expected to kill with a gun. Rigney decides that he must consider quitting this. For now, he will cooperate with today's training. *I have never fired a pistol with a suppressor—another thing to experience.*

Brad Watson senses Rigney's doubts.

Rigney obliges, "Okay. Let's get started."

The spend the entire morning in the firing range.

Rigney and Brad are standing poolside at the Suitland Olympic size swimming pool. Rigney checked out swimming trunks and swimming goggles. Although Rigney is wearing swimming trunks, Brad is still dressed in his blue jumpsuit. The pool is roped for eight lap lanes.

"This afternoon, you must pass the minimum swimming distance for an ONI field agent."

"What's the minimum distance?"

"Not telling you," Brad responds flippantly. "You just start swimming laps, and I will count them. You just keep swimming until you can't swim anymore. I will let you know whether or not you qualify."

"And if I don't qualify?" Rigney replies, equally flippant.

"It goes in your record, and you are given six months to meet the minimum requirement."

"You realize that swimming is something that I do very well," Rigney says confidently. "Is there a time limit?"

"No time limits. Now get in the water and get going."

Rigney spends five minutes performing stretching exercises. Then, he jumps into a center lane and starts swimming laps.

Brad finds a bench. He takes out a piece of paper and a pencil and writes a tic mark for each lap.

Eighty-five laps later, Rigney has slowed. However, his stokes and kicks are still smooth and synchronized.

"Okay, Rig. You can stop," Brad Watson says loudly from the side of the pool as Rigney finishes his eighty-sixth lap.

With one fluid motion, Rigney completes his last stroke and boosts himself out of the pool.

"Did I qualify?" Rigney knows he did.

"Yes."

"Good! I was worried," Rigney responds sarcastically.

Brad drives his 1965 mustang to the front steps of the Cheltenham ONI building.

Rigney looks at his watch—1530.

"Do you have any plans for tonight?" Brad asks.

"Yes, I'm going to the movies with a friend."

"Tomorrow is an off day. Do you have anything planned?"

Rigney replies, "Yes, I am going to tour the Smithsonian."

"By yourself?"

"No, I have a date with the same friend."

"Have a good time. I'll see you Monday morning at 0800—room 4."

Chapter 17

Monday - December 11, 1967

Rigney glances at his watch—0815. He sits on the couch in room 4 of the ONI building at Cheltenham, Maryland. He wears a blue jumpsuit. He studies his Indoctrination Schedule, which is now posted on the wall.

Lieutenant Commander Brad Watson sits at the desk, shuffling papers. Brad also wears a blue jumpsuit with no rank displayed.

Rigney says, "Brad, I have a question for which I need an answer."

"Don't you always. What is it?"

"Do I ask too many questions?" Rigney wonders if he is out of line.

Brad stops shuffling papers and stares at Rigney for a few moments. Then, he responds, "No, not really. You are not the usual field agent going through the normal training. We are blazing new trails here. We are learning this process as we go. What's your question?"

"The first night I was here, Smith told me that someone could be tracking my movements. He said someone would explain it to me. I have been here a week, and no one has said anything about it."

"Oh, that. It's possible that your movements are being tracked but highly improbable. Foreign agents constantly watch the major transportation centers to see if they can discover anything. Primarily, they look for high-ranking government officials and high-ranking military officers. They would not view a traveling junior enlisted man as a target of interest. There would need to be something unusual about your actions for them to take an interest. Remember, one of the reasons I selected you is that you would not be suspected as an intelligence field agent."

Rigney nods his understanding.

Brad hands Rigney a sheet of paper and asks, "This is a list of all the radiomen currently assigned to the ship you're going to. Do you recognize any of these names?"

Rigney studies the list.

"Well, I'll be!" Rigney exclaims. "Yes, I think I know this RM3 Larry Johnson. I went to Radioman 'A' School in San Diego with a Larry Johnson. We were friends. I remember that he had orders to a ship home-ported in Norfolk."

"You recognize any of the other names?"

"No."

"Thirty other radiomen are assigned. I think we better check them all out. Give me a list of every place you've been stationed and the dates."

Rigney takes about ten minutes to write the list.

Brad uses the intercom to call a yeoman from the office across the hall.

A second class yeoman, YN2, with one hash mark on this Undress Blue uniform comes into the room. Brad explains, "Randson, go to BUPERS and pull the service records on these radiomen. Then, determine if any of the radiomen were assigned to the same commands at the same time as RM3 Page."

"Aye, aye, sir. I will leave immediately."

Brad asks Randson, "How long do you think that will take you?"

"I can leave now and be back by late this afternoon."

"Okay. Do it."

"Aye, aye, sir." Randson turns and departs the room.

Rigney asks, "My schedule for today says *RM 'A' School, Bainbridge, Maryland.* What's that all about?"

"We're driving up to Bainbridge Naval Training Center. The radioman school there has what they call a *Practical Deck* or PRAC DECK. The PRAC DECK simulates a shipboard radio room and communications center. We have the PRAC DECK to ourselves this afternoon. Some ONI intelligence analysts well meet us there. The radioman school is also lending us their most qualified instructors for any technical questions that we have.

"When we first get there, ONI analysts will brief us. Then, we go to the PRAC DECK for a detailed explanation of communication systems operation." Brad pauses and stares at Rigney for a few moments. Then, he asks, "Did the San Diego radioman school have a PRAC DECK?"

"Yes—the last week of school. I sat the CW circuits for a few nights. Two nights, I was tape cutter. Two other nights, I sat the broadcast guard. They didn't teach us about how the systems and equipment were integrated. Most of what I know about systems operation and integration is what I learned at the submarine radioman schools."

"Refresh my memory on *CW circuits.*"

Rigney explains, "CW stands for continuous wave. It's a type of radio frequency modulation used for Morse Code—you know—dits and dahs."

Brad nods, conveying his understanding.

"And *broadcast*, what is that?"

Rigney explains, "Prior to a ship departing port, the ship must send a Communications Guard Shift message and list which teletype fleet broadcast the ship will copy. All the Naval Communications Stations get this guard message. When a commander wants to send a message to the ship, the message is routed over navy communications circuits to the

NAVCOMMSTA that generates the applicable broadcast. Many ships copy the same broadcast. The broadcast is encrypted radio teletype. The ship receives the broadcast signal, decrypts the signal through online decryption equipment, and prints the message to a teletype machine. The shipboard fleet broadcast operator is responsible for checking each message on the broadcast and *pulls* those addressed to his ship."

"And what is a tape cutter?"

Rigney responds, "Messages that must be relayed from one station to another to get to the distant addressee must be put on paper tape. The tape cutter is an operator that types the message on a teletype machine that produces both a paper page copy and a paper tape copy. As the tape cutter types each character, the character prints on the teletype paper and cuts holes in the paper tape. You've probably seen it. It's yellow paper tape about one inch wide with holes punched in it. The holes are in the Baudot Code. The paper tape is fed through a tape reader. The tape reader creates the electrical direct-current pulses equivalent of the Baudot Code."

Brad Watson observes, "For someone who has never been aboard ship, you seem to know a lot about shipboard communications."

Rigney praises, "Must be my navy training. It's been thorough so far."

Brad Watson drives a navy gray pickup truck. Rigney sits in the passenger seat. This navy pickup truck has no military rank markings. Brad drives north on Route 5 from Clinton Maryland and enters the Washington Beltway outer loop just north of Andrews Air Force Base. They drive northeast and exit the beltway onto Interstate 95 North. The drive along Interstate 95 takes them around the east side of the Baltimore Beltway.

Although the roads are clear, snow lies everywhere else.

About thirty minutes north of Baltimore, past the Aberdeen Proving Grounds, and just west of Havre De Grace, Brad takes the Port Deposit exit and drives north on Maryland Route 222, also known as Bainbridge Road. After a few miles they approach the Main Gate of Naval Training Center Bainbridge Maryland.

The navy security guard at the main gate checks Brad Watson's I.D. card. Rigney notices that when they are waved through, they are not waved through with a salute. Whatever I.D. card Brad showed the guard, it did not indicate that he was an officer.

As they proceed along the Training Center's main road, Rigney notices the large enlisted club on the left. The name of the club, *Fiddler's*

Green, displays on the side of the building. Most of the other buildings look like World War II vintage barracks. All the roads, sidewalks, and parking lots are clear of snow. I thick snow layer remains in the grassy areas and on rooftops. They find the radioman school, and Brad drives around to the back of the building and parks in a visitor spot.

As they exit the truck, Rigney notices that four men dressed in the same style blue jumpsuits, blue ball cap, and blue winter jacket exit a navy sedan. All the men, including Brad, address each other by first name. Brad Watson does not introduce Rigney, and the other men do not introduce themselves to Rigney.

They enter the building and find themselves in the quarterdeck area. A tall woman wearing a Service Dress Blue uniform walks toward them. She wears the chevron and one star of a senior chief radioman. Five gold hash marks run up her left sleeve. Her nametag advises that she is RMCS Rodan. Brad Watson introduces himself as the leader of the group. He does not give his name or rank.

"The OIC told me to expect you," the senior chief explains. "The conference room is prepared as instructed. Please follow me."

The senior chief escorts them down the hall and to the conference room. She does not enter.

Each man chooses his own seat around the conference table. Brad Watson closes the door and motions Rigney to sit next to him.

Rigney assumes that these four men are analysts from ONI headquarters. Three of the analysts look Brad's age. He assumes they are navy officers. The fourth analyst, who is obviously the oldest and a civilian, is heavyset and has white hair and a neatly trimmed white beard.

Brad looks at the older, bearded analyst and says, "Show us what you got, Bob."

The older man stands and lifts his document case onto the table and opens the latches. He pulls out three teletype paper rolls and sets them on the table; then, he pushes all three rolls toward Brad Watson. Bob advises, "These are the message files that were found with the Russian courier in Madrid."

Brad removes the rubber band from one of the rolls, lays the roll on the table, and unrolls about three feet.

Rigney recognizes the lines of print as military message format. Rigney moves closer to get a better look.

Brad looks at Rigney and asks, "Do you recognize what this is?"

Rigney responds, "It's teletype paper with navy messages printed on it." He studies the roll for another 30 seconds and reports, "I would say this roll came off a fleet broadcast printer."

Brad says, "Take a few minutes and look over the whole roll. Look over other rolls if you wish. Then, tell us what else you see there."

Rigney unravels the whole roll, which is thirty feet long. He reviews each message. He concentrates on the addressees, classification markings, and subject lines. He scans the text of some message and reads in detail the text of other messages. Occasionally, he writes on a notepad.

As Rigney reviews the teletype roll, Brad watches the body language of the four analysts. Bob Mater, a senior analyst, has been with ONI for twenty-five years. His first three years were as a Naval Reserve Officer during World War II. When the war ended, the Director of Naval Intelligence asked Bob to come back as a civilian analyst. The other three men are navy officers assigned to ONI. Their specialties range from signal intelligence to field operations.

All four of these men are critics of Brad Watson's revolutionary approach to train young enlisted sailors as counterintelligence agents. All four of these men believe it takes years of training and experience to become a valuable field agent. All of them consider experience as a military officer to be essential to becoming a successful field agent.

Brad Watson knows that only Bob Mater's presence is required at this meeting. Brad asked the three naval officers to join as observers. Brad wants them to observe Rigney this afternoon and later provide their opinion of Rigney's actions.

Rigney analyses all three teletype broadcast rolls.

A side conversation starts up between the analysts. They are discussing the upcoming Super Bowl. Rigney ignores them. He focuses on the broadcast rolls. He continues to write notes.

It takes Rigney 30 minutes to examine all rolls. After he finishes, he sits quietly.

After the side conversions die down, Brad Watson directs Rigney, "Give us your report."

Rigney takes in a deep breath. He senses he is being tested. He says to Brad Watson, "I think some of what I'll say is classified. Can I say it in here?"

"Yes," Brad replies. "This room was checked for listening devices earlier this morning."

Rigney provides his analysis. "I believe these teletype rolls came from a teletype machine used to copy a fleet broadcast. All rolls are from the same broadcast. The Channel Identification Designator at the top of every message is the same . . . *NGR*. All messages have Date Time Groups of late March 1967. The classification lines of the messages range from *unclassified* to *secret*. Most of the messages are marked *confidential*. Most of the precedence levels are *priority* and *operational immediate*. There are a few *routine precedence* messages that are *unclassified.* Most of the messages regard ship and task group movement and operations. A few messages have NATO classification markings. The most noticeable item is that there are three command addresses that appear common to the messages. All the non-NATO messages have the at least one or more of the addresses USS *Columbus*, COMCRUDESFLOT EIGHT, and CTG SIX TWO PT TWO. The most common addresses on the NATO messages are CTG FIVE ZERO TWO PT TWO and CTE FIVE ZERO TWO PT TWO PT TWO PT ONE."

Rigney pauses for comments and questions.

One of the officer analysts asks, "What do you conclude from the data you gathered?"

Rigney looks furtively from man to man in the room. *No doubt that I am being tested.*

Rigney glances at his notes and says, "I conclude that these are broadcast messages copied aboard the USS *Columbus* or COMCRUDESFLOT EIGHT. I think that this CTG FIVE ZERO TWO PT TWO is just another name for the USS *Columbus* or COMCRUDESFLOT EIGHT."

Bob Mater stares at Rigney. Rigney stares back.

Brad Watson also stares at Rigney.

In Rigney's opinion, Brad Watson's stare at Bob Mater looks like *I told you so.*

Bob Mater asks, "What questions do you have that need answered?"

Rigney understands that he is still under test. He clears his throat and says, "I would want to know the relationship between the USS *Columbus* and all these other common addresses. Also, I would want to know why the teletype paper is white. All the teletype paper that I've seen since I've been in the navy is yellow in color. I think that the most significant question that I have is how did these teletype broadcast rolls get in the hands of a Russian courier—I think that's what you called him?"

Rigney pauses.

"Any other questions?" Brad asks Rigney.

"Well, yes," Rigney responds with a puzzled look. "If all these addressees are the same ship, then that ship was the only one copying the broadcast. If it's a fleet broadcast, why are there not more ships as addressees?"

"I can give you a few answers," Bob Mater says looking directly at Rigney. "All the addresses you call common are in fact the USS *Columbus* or flag officers aboard the *Columbus*. For example, COMCRUDESFLOT EIGHT is a rear admiral. At the time those messages were sent, that rear admiral's flagship was the USS *Columbus*.

That rear admiral was also the commander of those task groups that you found commonly addressed. During the last week of March 1967, the *Columbus* was the only ship copying the NGR broadcast. That's an odd happening . . . just a fluke. Fortunately for us, it helped us identify which ship these teletype rolls came from.

"White colored teletype paper rolls are commonly sold in Europe. Olivetti Italia manufactured these rolls. The paper is lower quality than what we use in the U.S. Armed Forces. We checked the *Columbus* supply requisitions. The *Columbus* never ordered this type of teletype paper. As a matter of fact, this type of teletype paper is not in the Department of Defense supply system.

"Soviet warships in the Mediterranean always seemed to know where to find the *Columbus*. Several times during the *Columbus* Mediterranean deployment, *Columbus* changed its movement schedule while at sea. There was no in-port time when someone could get off the ship and pass the changes to the Soviets. The *Columbus* departed the MED last April. The USS *Albany* took her place. The Soviets did not always know where to find the *Albany*. Since then, we have suspected a Soviet agent is aboard *Columbus*."

Rigney expresses thoughtfulness. He attempts to think of ways that a Soviet agent could get information off the ship while still at sea. *I have never been to sea. How could I know? I guess I will find out.*

Rigney asks Bob Mater, "Sir, who or what is NGR?"

"NGR is the international call sign for U.S. Naval Communications Station Greece. It's located next to a small Greek town named Nea Makri. It's on the Greek coast facing the Aegean Sea, about fifteen miles from Athens." Bob Mater smiles patronizingly as he makes his final comment. "As for how all these fleet broadcast rolls got into the hands of a Russian courier while the *Columbus* was still at sea . . . I believe you are going to help us find out."

Rigney asks, "What happens if we never find out?"

Bob Mater answers, "Should war or hostilities break out the Soviets will already know the location of the task force. The enemy does not need to go looking. *Columbus* and the rest of the task force are always targeted by Soviet missiles and torpedoes. The lives of thousands of American sailors are in danger, along with billions of dollars of navy hardware."

Rigney had not previously considered the potential danger to all those sailors. So far, he had only considered how this situation affected him. He had thought only about adventure and his own safety. *How could I have been so self-centered? I should have understood this. Am I out of touch with the purpose of my service? My navy training so far never covered why the navy does what it does, nor explained my integral part in it. Yeah, there was all that training about teamwork and my responsibilities as a member of the team. But no one had ever explained what the team did and why; at least not in these terms.*

Rigney has more questions, but he holds off because he sees Brad Watson looking at his watch.

Brad Watson announces, "It's time to tour the PRAC DECK."

Brad stands, walks to the door, and opens it. He says, "Senior Chief, we want to tour the PRAC DECK now."

Senior Chief Rodan guides the group to the other end of the building. They come to a wide double door. A sign on the door announces: EXCLUSION AREA – AUTHORIZED PERSONNEL ONLY. A pushbutton cipher lock is located on the right side of the door. The senior chief enters a code and opens the door.

The ONI group enters a room filled with teletype machines along three walls and three CW stations along the fourth wall. Several desks sit in the center of the room. A sign above the CW stations advises that they are in NAVCOMMSTA PRAC DECK. Three of the PRAC DECK chiefs, dressed in khakis, stand next to the desks in the center of the room.

Senior Chief Rodan introduces the chiefs, "Chief Bullock, Chief Wells, and Chief Sincavage are senior instructors for the three areas of the PRAC DECK."

The senior chief explains, "This room simulates a shore communications station. The room through the door on the right simulates a shipboard radio room and communications center. Is there any particular area of our PRAC DECK that you want explained?"

Brad Watson speaks up, "Yes, please explain the *fleet broadcast* configuration."

"Chief Wells is our Broadcast Chief. He will take you through the process."

Chief Wells, a thin and balding man in his mid-thirties, explains, "On the wall over there is a flow diagram of message processing through the *Message Center*. Please follow the diagram as I explain the process."

Chief Wells pauses for about 30 seconds to give everyone a chance to digest the flow diagram.

Then, Chief Wells continues, "The *Message Originator* delivers the *Released Message* to a shore based *Message Center*. Then, the message is given to the *Router*. The *Router* has listings of all commands throughout the world and their individual *Routing Indicators*. The Router writes the applicable *Routing Indicator* next to each *addressee* on the message. All ships at sea must copy a fleet broadcast. Various

Naval Communications Stations throughout the world transmit a fleet broadcast.

"Let's say that our ship has stated in its Communications Guard message that it will copy the *NAVCOMMSTA Rota Spain Fleet Broadcast*. The *Router* will have this information and will assign the *Routing Indicator* for the *NAVCOMMSTA Rota Spain Fleet Broadcast*.

"The message is transmitted through teletype networks throughout the world until it arrives at *NAVCOMMSTA Rota Spain*. Then, Rota personnel will transmit the message over their *fleet broadcast*. The ship is required to copy the *fleet broadcast* and will receive the message."

One of the ONI analysts asks, "What prevents everyone with a radio receiver and teletype machine from copying classified messages?"

"Both the NAVCOMMSTA and the ship have online Jason cryptographic equipment in the teletype signal path. Text characters are encrypted electronically before being transmitted over the fleet broadcast. The ship must electronically decrypt the text characters before printing to a teletype machine."

"What do you mean by *Jason*?" The same ONI analyst asks.

"All cryptographic systems have a mythological designator. Fleet broadcasts use the KW-37 suite of crypto equipment—officially assigned the name of Jason, as in *Jason and the Argonauts*."

Brad Watson asks, "Chief, are you saying that anyone with Jason cryptographic equipment can decrypt the teletype signal?"

"No," Chief Wells responds. "The Jason equipment at both the NAVCOMMSTA side and on the ship side must have identical Jason keycards. The keycard is changed in both the NAVCOMMSTA's Jason and the ship's Jason equipment every 24 hours at midnight, Greenwich Mean Time."

Bob Mater asks, "Can you show us what the keycard looks like?"

Chief Wells looks to Senior Chief Rodan for permission. She nods her head in approval.

Chief Wells walks to a dark gray colored electronic device the size of a footlocker. He opens a drawer on the front panel of the Jason device. He removes a paper card the size of an IBM punch card. He holds up the card for everyone to see and explains, "As you can see, small holes are punched into the card."

"How are keycards distributed and safeguarded?" asks one of the ONI analysts.

"The National Security Agency produces and distributes all crypto material," Chief Wells replies.

"Anyone else have any questions?" Brad Watson asks the group.

No responses.

Brad Watson says, "Okay. We are done." Brad turns to Senior Chief Rodan and says, "Senior Chief, thank you for your cooperation. Chief Wells, thank you for your thorough explanations. This has been most educational."

Senior Chief Radon escorts the ONI group out of the PRAC DECK area.

Chief Wells and the other two chiefs stare after the ONI group as it departs.

"What was that all about?" asks Chief Sincavage to no one in particular.

"I have no idea," says Chief Bullock.

"Any idea who they are?" Chief Wells asks the two other chiefs.

"I have no idea," Chief Bullock replies.

"What's with the blue jumpsuits?" Chief Sincavage asks.

Chief Wells surmises, "Obviously, they wanted to hide their true identity."

Rigney stays a few steps behind Brad Watson as they depart the radioman school building and enter the parking lot.

"Wait in the car," Brad says to Rigney.

Then, Brad Watson walks over to Bob Mater and pulls him aside about twenty feet from all the others.

"Let's meet tomorrow morning at Cheltenham," Brad Watson says to Bob Mater. "I would like you to talk with Rigney and me. I think it would be beneficial if you share your thoughts about all this. Especially what Rigney needs to focus on once he is aboard ship."

"Will do, Brad. What time?"

"0830."

"Okay. I will be there," Bob Mater responds as he turns to walk away. Then, he stops and turns back toward Brad Watson and comments, "That Page is a smart boy. You say he has never been to sea?"

"That's right."

"Within 30 minutes, he came up with the same analysis and same questions that we came up with but took us three days and four analysts." An approving expression spreads across Bob's face as he informs, "Brad, I am more positive about your new program." Bob Mater turns and walks back to his group and slips into one of the navy sedans.

Brad Watson remains quiet as he drives the navy pickup truck off the Bainbridge Naval Training Center. At 4:30 p.m., the oncoming night darkens the woods along Maryland Route 222. Dirty snow outlines the road. Deeper white snow rises into the woods on both sides of Bainbridge Road. Brad turns on the pickup's headlights. Occasionally, they pass a small neighborhood of houses. Both men are quiet. Both men contemplate the events of the afternoon.

As they move south on Interstate 95, Rigney finally asks the question that formed in his mind back in the radioman-school conference room. "I'm going to the USS *Columbus*, right?"

"That's right," Brad responds with a smile. "If you didn't come up with the *Columbus* on your own, I would have been disappointed. You passed today's test. You even impressed Bob Mater."

"Who?"

"Bob Mater—senior analyst—the gray-haired gentleman with the beard."

Rigney nods.

Before getting on the Baltimore Beltway, Brad announces that he must stop and make a telephone call. They stop at a McDonalds Hamburger Shoppe. Both take a pee break. Brad makes his phone call.

For the remainder of the trip back to Cheltenham, they do not discuss the mission. They converse about their lives. Brad Watson opens up. Brad has been in the navy for nine years. He holds a bachelor's degree in engineering from the Naval Academy. Brad also earned a master's degree in International Relations at the Naval Post Graduate School. Brad was married for eighteen months. His wife did not like the hours and the travel. Brad has not seriously considered marriage since. After graduating from Annapolis, Brad was assigned to a destroyer home-ported at Pearl Harbor. During his second deployment to the Western Pacific aboard that destroyer, Brad was appointed as the ship's Intelligence Officer. Several of his reports landed on the desk of the Director of ONI. When the destroyer returned to Pearl Harbor, the Director ONI sent a recruiter to Pearl to meet with Brad. Brad agreed to come to work with ONI. Several weeks later, he had orders to ONI. Brad would not go into any detail regarding his work since joining ONI.

Rigney also opens up to Brad. He tells him about Sally and their parting before he came to Washington.

Brad stops in the parking lot of the ONI building in Cheltenham. He orders Rigney to report to room 4 at 0830 tomorrow morning.

Rigney exits the pickup.

Brad drives off.

The biting night air causes Rigney's breath to frost as he exhales. He looks at his watch—6:05 p.m.

He enters the building. All the office doors are closed, including the waiting room door. He enters his room and strips down to underwear and undershirt. He drops his jumpsuit in the laundry basket. He looks in the closet. As usual, three clean and pressed jumpsuits hang next to three clean and pressed Service Dress Blue uniforms. Rigney stares at his gym clothes, also clean and folded. He decides that he is not in the mood for a workout tonight.

Cathy works tonight. She told him to call her tomorrow so they can make another date.

He walks to the refrigerator and opens the door. As usual, the fridge is stocked with bottled water, wine, and beer with brand names he has never seen prior to occupying this room. On the bottom shelf sits a plate with sliced roasted turkey, sliced roast beef, and sliced fresh raw vegetables. He removes a beer with the brand name of Amstel. He also removes the plate of cold meats and vegetables.

Rigney turns on the television but does not watch it.

As he slowly eats turkey and vegetables and drinks the Amstel. He ponders the significance of the day's events. He knows that today he got a taste of ONI work. *What did they mean 'found with the Russian courier?' Was the courier dead when the fleet broadcast rolls were found? The messages on those teletype rolls have classified information about U.S. Navy operations.*

Rigney begins to grasp the importance of his mission. He begins to understand the enormous responsibility that he will accept. *A sailor or sailors aboard that ship are giving the Russians our nation's secrets. This thing is bigger than me. It's bigger than Brad. I've been worried about my own safety when the safety of thousands of other sailors is at stake!*

Rigney feels somewhat ashamed of the uncertainty and apprehension he has exhibited in front of Brad Watson.

Shit! I am only twenty. What do I know about espionage? Why does Brad think I can do this? Hell, two months ago the most important thing to me was where I was going to get my next piece of ass! Now, I am being asked to expose the activities of American traitors!

Rigney makes three more trips to the refrigerator for more bottles of Amstel.

He comes to understand that today's events are some sort of milestone. No one said anything, but he feels that he qualified for something today; that something being more significant than operating and fixing radios on a submarine.

Am I worthy of this trust? Can I even do this? The success of discovering those traitors is totally up to me!

Rigney no longer fears being disabled or killed. He now fears failing at his mission.

He remembers that as a young teenager he wondered what type of man he would become. He had looked to the gown men he knew for a model of what he may want to become. His father and uncles were all strong-willed, independent, self-reliant men. The medals awarded to them during World War II and during the Korean War spoke of their physical courage and bravery. But Rigney felt there was something missing in them that he himself wanted to possess. He could not identify it.

Then, he remembers a conversation with his mother some years back. When Rigney explained to his mother that he was looking for a model for which he would mold his manhood, his mother nodded understanding.

"You must mold your own manhood," she told him. "Do not let life's random events mold you. Identify the characteristics of the man you want to be then diligently and aggressively pursue to become such a man."

"But how do I discover what those characteristics are?" he had asked his mother.

She responded, "Start searching by reading the biographies and histories of great men." His mother handed him a book of poetry. She told him, "Start with this."

The book of poetry focused on events that challenged the human spirit and how some met that challenge. Thirty poems into the book, Rigney read the poem "Unconquerable" by nineteenth century Victorian poet William Ernest Henley. The verse emotionally moved Rigney.

Out of the night that covers me,
  Black as the pit from pole to pole,
I thank whatever gods may be
  For my unconquerable soul.

In the fell clutch of circumstance
  I have not winced nor cried aloud.
Under the bludgeonings of chance
  My head is bloody, but unbowed.

Beyond this place of wrath and tears
  Looms but the Horror of the shade,
And yet the menace of the years
  Finds and shall find me unafraid.

It matters not how strait the gate,
How charged with punishment the scroll,
I am the master of my fate:
I am the captain of my soul.

The poem startled and astonished Rigney as to its concise, simple, and powerful conveyance of courage, determination, independence, and self-accountability. After he read the poem three more times, he laid down the book and went directly to the Orange County library. He was determined to discover the life of a man who could write such moving, enlightening words. Rigney found several books on the life of Henley. He read all of Henley's works. He slowly savored every word that detailed the man's life. Henley's challenging life inspired Rigney to model his life, his manhood, to the poem "Unconquerable."

His quest to be *unconquerable* led him to becoming a loner. Few understood his fierce independent manner, his self-accountability, and his acceptance of self-actualization. By the time he reached the age of sixteen, most males his age avoided associating with him and avoided conversations with him. Girls, on the other hand, found his lone-wolf manner intriguing and sexy.

Rigney thought he had mastered the characteristics of the man he wanted to be. But, today, he had discovered the characteristic he is lacking. The motivating words spoken by President John F. Kennedy's at his Inaugural resound in Rigney's head.

"And so my fellow Americans: Ask not what your country can do for you - ask what you can do for your country. My fellow citizens of the world: ask not what America will do for you, but what together we can do for the freedom of man."

Rigney feels guilty. Everything he had done regarding his life so far was for his own self-interest to satisfy his own ego. He had not considered himself a selfish person, but that is what he had been. He had only thought of what the navy could do for him. He always considered his six-year navy obligation as a bargain when considering all of what he was getting in return.

He knows that motivational changes are occurring within him. He cannot define it because he never experienced these feelings before. Rigney changes from a person who previously acted in his own self-interest to a person who wants to serve his fellow Americans. He gains a sense of duty toward his country and his fellow servicemen. He thinks that he finally understands patriotism.

Rigney's eyes wander around the room. He looks through the doorway into the dark bedroom and sees the shadow of two objects on the nightstand. He goes into the bedroom and turns on the light. Sitting on the nightstand is a bottle of CAMUS Cognac and a box of Hauser Chocolates. These are two more items that he has never seen before. An envelope with his name on it lies next to the cognac. He opens the envelope and reads the note.

Rig, congratulations on passing today's test. Welcome to the ONI team.

Brad's signature is at the bottom of the note. On the back of the note, Brad wrote instructions on how to open the bottle of cognac. Rigney chuckles.

Several hours later, Rigney sits slouched and deeply asleep on the couch. The shifting shades of light from the television flash across him. The box of chocolates, now empty, sits on the coffee table next to the two-thirds empty bottle of CAMUS Cognac. What remains of the cold meats and vegetables lie drying on the exposed plate.

At four in the morning, Rigney awakes on the couch with a pounding headache. He goes into the bathroom and downs three aspirins. Then, he enters the bedroom and dives headfirst into bed.

The television continues to flash varying shades of light.

Chapter 18

Tuesday - December 12, 1967

Rigney feels a powerful hand shaking him. Someone calls his name. He falls back into unconsciousness.

A powerful hand grips his shoulder and shakes him violently. Someone shouts his name.

Rigney opens his eyes. He sees John Smith, who is dressed in Service Dress Blue uniform, standing over him. John grips Rigney's shoulder and shakes him vigorously.

"Rig, wake the fuck up! You're late!"

Rigney, annoyed by the rough treatment, forcefully knocks John Smith's hand off his shoulder. He opens his eyes slowly and scans the room.

"Christ, Rig! This room is a mess and smells of booze and farts. Did you have a party in here last night?"

Rigney tries to understand his surroundings. He slowly becomes conscious. He no longer has a headache, but his senses are dulled. *I am in bed . . . in my quarters at the ONI building.* He now recognizes John Smith. *Oh, yeah, the guy who pretends to be a third class radioman.*

"Late for what?" Rigney mutters as he looks at his watch—0915.

"Brad Watson and Bob Mater are waiting for you in room 4."

Rigney looks bewildered for a moment. Then, his eyes go wide. He sits up. "Shit! I was supposed to meet them at 0830. Give me about ten minutes to throw some clothes on, and I will be right there."

"Take it easy, Rig. Brad said that I might find you in this condition. He told me to wake you and tell you that the meeting is rescheduled for 1000. That gives you 40 minutes. Now, take your time and make yourself presentable. After you're on your feet, I will leave you in privacy."

Rigney slowly places his feet on the floor and pushes himself up from the bed.

"I will tell Brad you're up." John Smith smiles, looks around the room, shakes his head slightly, and departs.

Rigney wants to dive back into the bed but forces himself to the bathroom. He strips off his underwear and socks and lets them fall to the bathroom floor.

He needs to use the toilet. He continues to sit even after he's done. He falls asleep. Nearly falling off the toilet wakes him.

After stepping into the shower, he turns the water to hot. He braces himself by placing both hands in front of him against the shower wall.

He positions himself so that the water stream hits his head and runs down his back. After five minutes of hot water, Rigney turns the water on full cold. He becomes more awake and less groggy. His thought processes sharpen. He grabs the soap and bathes himself thoroughly. Using his favorite shampoo, he washes his hair twice.

He steps out of the shower and grabs one of the three large and fluffy white towels. He wraps the towel around his waist and uses another towel to dry himself.

After shaving and brushing his teeth, he steps into the bedroom. The odor causes shudder. Smith was right. This room smells. He opens the bedroom window. As he opens the window, ice cold air blast through the opening. He notices for the first time that thick metal bars are molded into the outside window frame. He goes to the living room area and opens that window also which has the same molded bars.

His rooms look like there was a party and no one cleaned up. The foul odor dissipates. *Room Service will have a challenge today.* Rigney has not seen those who cleans his quarters, provides the fresh uniforms, and stocks the refrigerator.

Rigney, now fully clean and dressed in a blue jump suit, looks at his watch—0955. He departs his quarters and walks toward room 4.

At the end of the hall, John Smith steps out of the waiting room, looks at his watch, looks at Rigney, and gives the *okay* sign.

At 0956, Rigney knocks on the room 4 door.

"Enter!" Brad Watson orders loudly from inside the room.

Rigney takes a deep breath then enters the room.

Brad Watson sits behind the desk; he wears his Service Dress Blue uniform. Bob Mater sits at the side of the desk.

Lieutenant Commander Watson waves his hand, "Sit wherever you want."

Rigney selects a hardwood captain's chair in front of the desk.

"Good morning, Rigney," Bob Mater greets in an annoyed tone.

"Good morning, Rig," Lieutenant Commander Brad Watson greets with an understanding tone.

"Good morning," Rigney responds in an embarrassed tone and with his eyes looking at the floor.

Brad Watson understands what happened to Rigney last night. Yesterday, Rigney tasted ONI work and received a heavy dose of the burden of responsibility that goes with it. Brad knows that Rigney, sometime yesterday, began to understand the importance of his mission. Brad also knows that Rigney has become more afraid of failing at his mission than afraid of being physically hurt. Brad has seen it before—many times. He provided Rigney with liquor that would ease the weight

111

of responsibility, at least temporary. He knew that Rigney would need help. Brad also knows that last night was the first and only time that Rigney can use liquor as a crutch. Brad will talk to Rigney about that but not now.

Brad Watson begins, "This morning, Bob and I will discuss with you what to search for onboard the *Columbus*—what to concentrate on— what behaviors in others may provide clues." He nods toward Bob Mater as an indication to start the discussion.

Bob Mater looks at Rigney over the top of his reading glasses. "Rigney, first and foremost, you must understand the scope of your mission. We want you to discover the identity of that Soviet agent aboard *Columbus* and how he gets those broadcast rolls off the ship. I emphasize that your mission is not to capture or expose the traitor. ONI and other U.S. organizations want to use that Soviet agent's delivery path to pass disinformation. When we have the delivery path under our control, we can instigate all sorts of chaos. We want to turn that American traitor to cooperate with us. The longer we have control of that path, the longer we can confuse the Soviets. Do you understand, Rigney?"

"Yes, Bob. I understand. Oh, may I call you Bob?" Rigney asks humbly and respectfully.

"Yes, of course. Call me Bob." Bob Mater appreciates the respect.

Bob Mater continues, "The white Olivetti teletype paper tells us that the fleet broadcast is being reproduced or captured somehow. You must discover how it is duplicated or how it is captured and stored. As soon as you discover how, you must report to us."

"How will I report to you?" Rigney interrupts.

Brad Watson answers, "I will explain that to you later. Right now, we need to concentrate on discovery."

Bob Mater continues, "You must always be alert to unusual technical configurations. Also be alert to people in locations that they normally should not be. Be alert to people involved in activities that they are normally not involved. Report even a single event of such activity."

"Excuse me," Rigney interrupts, "Should I write these events down?"

"Absolutely not!" Brad blurts.

"What if I forget?" Rigney replies calmly. He is truly concerned that he will forget—fail. "I might forget something important."

"Don't worry about that," Brad Watson counsels. "You won't forget. It will be too important to you."

Rigney just nods his understanding, but he is not sure that he agrees.

Bob Mater clears his throat, an indication that he wants to continue.

Rigney and Brad look at Bob Mater. Their expression says they are listening.

"This traitor will follow a certain behavioral pattern. He will think himself important. He makes up things about himself or his past experiences to make himself look important to others. Remember, this traitor is not a trained and experienced espionage agent. This person turned traitor because of an inferiority complex and desire to be someone he is not. Becoming an agent for a foreign power makes him feel important. Accepting money for espionage activities allows him the delusion he is just performing a job. He views the money he receives from his soviet controller as payment for unique talent. He perceives his activities as payback to those in authority who do not recognize him as a unique and talented individual." Bob pauses for questions.

Rigney asks, "What do I do if I think someone fits the description?"

"If you do not believe what someone tells you about himself, report him to us."

Rigney chuckles as he advises, "Uh, Bob. I don't believe what most sailors tell me about themselves. They tend to exaggerate about their abilities and backgrounds."

Bob glances at Brad.

Brad nods concurrence of Rigney's description of young sailors.

Bob nods understanding; then, clarifies, "This traitor will have been aboard for eighteen months or more."

Rigney expresses doubt that he can detect such a person. In a concerned tone, he states, "I worry that I will accuse the wrong person."

Bob Mater responds, "If a person fits the description, report him to us. We will determine further actions for you. We will tell you how to proceed." Bob pauses; then, he adds, "You must understand that intelligence work involves shifting through and filtering tons of data. We don't want you to judge what data qualifies for reporting. If it fits the descriptions we provide, report it; even if you think it not important or relevant."

"Well, that makes it easier," Rigney reasons. "It kind of relieves me from the responsibility of reporting irrelevant events."

"That's the point," Brad Watson emphasizes. "You do not have the training nor the experience to judge what should or should not be reported, and we do not expect you to."

"Okay. I am getting a better understanding of what you want me to report. It's like I load a machine gun with whatever ammo I can find. Then, I shoot, and the ONI analysts decide which bullets are harmful."

"Excellent analogy," Brad Watson declares with a smile.

Bob Mater nods his agreement with the analogy.

Rigney states, "I do not understand something about this situation."

"What's that?" Bob asks.

"This traitor has been releasing classified information to the Soviets for at least a year. Like you said yesterday, Bob, this puts many lives in danger. I understand ONI's desired option to turn the traitor's operation into a path for disinformation, but are not the lives of all those sailors who are placed in harm's way more important?"

Bob responds, "You have not been told all we know. You only know part of it. The navy is taking the risk so that we can discover the whole network that poses grave danger to the United States. The CO of the *Columbus* and the admiral above the CO know what you know and more. They are willing to take these risks for a few more months. Then, their responsibility for the safety of their people will become paramount. We have agreed with CO *Columbus* that if this mission is not successful by the end of March, we will take actions that will make it clear to the traitor that we know about him. We will send in a team and bulldoze the problem away. We hope we do not need to do that."

Bob pauses and expresses that he collects his thoughts; then, he continues, "Anyway, for the time being, all important high-precedence *Columbus* message traffic is being offline encrypted before transmission. Important, lower-precedence *Columbus* message traffic is routed to *Columbus* via ARFCOS. The actions of the Soviets indicate they did not know the contents of the offline encrypted messages or the contents of messages sent to the ship via ARFCOS."

"ARFCOS?" Rigney questions.

"Armed Forces Courier Service," Bob explains.

Rigney spends a few moments considering Bob Mater's words. Then, he asks, "Bob, will this sailor—this traitor—be dangerous? I mean, I know what he does puts sailors and ships in danger. What I mean is . . . well, is he, or they, likely to become violent. Especially toward me if they know that I have discovered him?"

Bob Mater responds, "I don't think so, but their Soviet controller could be a problem."

Bob's comment regarding the Soviet controller causes Brad Watson to sit up straight and shoot a disapproving look at Bob Mater.

Rigney notices Brad's response. He looks at Brad and waves his hand and shakes his head, conveying nonchalance. "It's okay, Brad. I have accepted that his mission has a degree of danger. You do not need to protect me from this knowledge. I know, now, that this mission is more important than my personal safety and that motivates me more than ever to succeed. I am outraged that a fellow sailor—another American— so willingly discards his citizenship and endangers his shipmates and other Americans. Ya know, I can understand why Soviets spy on us.

They do it for their country. They do it for what they believe in. This asshole bastard traitor on the *Columbus* has turned on his own country, probably for money. It's disgusting. It's an insulting slap in the face to those who willingly serve and willingly do their duty."

Brad detects anger and venom in Rigney's words.

Rigney turns back to Bob and says, "Okay, Bob. What about the Soviet controller?"

Bob looks at Brad Watson. Brad nods his head that it is okay to answer.

"You might be in physical danger during the period-of-time between when you discover the traitor and the time you report him to us. Once you have reported, they would have no reason to harm you."

"You mean kill me, don't you?"

Bob looks directly into Rigney's eyes and replies, "Killing you has no value. If they do that, they affirm that you have discovered something. The result, whether you report to us or you disappear, is that their operation has ended. They are not going to take life unnecessarily and strengthen our resolve to destroy them.

"The danger with the Soviet controller is if he thinks that his only way out is to kill you, but you would need to be physically in his escape path. The scope of your mission should never put you in his escape path. I have only seen it happen once in twenty-five years. In that case, the ONI agent, who was more experienced and more trained than you, violated his orders and went after the Soviet controller."

Rigney expresses curiosity and asks, "Why did he do that?"

"Please understand that the ONI agent extended his activities way beyond the scope of his mission. He was ambitious. He wanted to make his mark in the intelligence community. He was not supposed to discover the Soviet controller, but he did so anyway. The Soviet controller threatened the ONI agent's family. The ONI agent got in so deep that he felt that the only way his family would ever be safe was for him to kill the Soviet controller. He succeeded in killing the Soviet Controller; but he died from wounds that the Soviet controller inflicted on him."

"Okay," Rigney resolves with a sigh. "I am satisfied with your answers regarding mission danger. I think that I have covered my concerns. I will no longer express concern about it or request assurances. We can get back to the important stuff now."

Bob Mater continues. "Highly unlikely more than one traitor operates on that ship. The espionage operation is too vulnerable for a team of agents who are sailors turned traitor. Remember, these traitor types are weak in character. A Soviet controller would not take the chance of teaming up such weak and unreliable win. Too much chance they would turn on each other. It will only be one person."

Rigney nods his understanding.

Bob Mater continues. "Consider that this traitor made the last Mediterranean cruise on *Columbus*. So, you should focus on those who made the last Mediterranean cruise."

"When was that cruise?" Rigney queries.

"The *Columbus* returned to Norfolk last April after a six month deployment to the MED. She is scheduled to depart for the MED again on January 3rd and return in July. You will be aboard when *Columbus* departs Norfolk on January 3rd."

Rigney asks, "Will the captain and admiral know about me?"

"We told them that we would put a man aboard for the upcoming cruise. They will not know who. We can't tell them for security and safety reasons.

"The captain is a veteran cruiser-destroyer man. He made many MED cruises over the years. He said that too many Soviet surface ships and too many Soviet submarines were always in the vicinity of the *Columbus* to be coincidence last MED cruise. The captain kept reporting his suspicions even after the MED cruise was over.

"About a week after the *Columbus* returned from the MED cruise last April, the Spanish police found a crashed and burned car at the bottom of a ravine near Madrid. They found the courier dead and burned in the car. Looks like the accident had occurred several days previous. They found a leather case with all the fleet broadcast teletype rolls about thirty feet from the car. The Spanish police delivered the teletype rolls to our Embassy in Madrid. The Embassy passed the information to the Defense Intelligence Agency. At U.S. diplomatic request, the Spanish Government dumped the leather case and teletype rolls, burned beyond recognition, to the crash site—just in case someone came looking.

"The DIA contacted ONI and gave us the teletype rolls. We analyzed the rolls and gained all the information we talked about yesterday. We didn't have an agent available. So, the DIA volunteered one of theirs and had him placed undercover on the *Columbus* last May."

"What did he find out?" Rigney asked, eager to gain some information.

"Nothing. He was aboard three weeks. His cover was a first class electronics technician. He was supposed to be an administrator only—a Department 3M Coordinator. One day when the *Columbus* was cruising near Puerto Rico, the chief ET ordered our DIA agent to repair a radar system. The DIA man knows little about electronics. He ends up getting a high voltage jolt up his arm. It put him out cold for ten hours. They airlifted him to the Naval Hospital in Puerto Rico . . . took him five weeks to recover. We found out later that all the ETs picked up on his lack of electronics knowledge in the first week.

"After returning from her last MED cruise, *Columbus* has been conducting operations off the East Coast and in the Caribbean. The *Columbus*'s captain reports that Soviet surface ships and submarines continue to stalk his ship. He emphasizes that some of the other ships' captains are now reporting the same thing."

Brad Watson adds, "We changed the Jason crypto keycards to a different series to see if there was any affect. Changing the keycard series had no effect. The same level of stalking continued.

"So, in case someone was providing the Soviets with a continuous flow of crypto keycards of all series, we went to NSA and had special keycards made. Those keycards were hand delivered to both NAVCOMMSTA Norfolk and to *Columbus* and to the other ships while they were at sea. Again, the same level of stalking occurred. Therefore, for now, we are discarding the theory that we have someone providing the Soviets with crypto keycards. All the evidence points to someone on *Columbus* passing classified messages to the Soviets."

Rigney requests confirmation. "Then, there has not been anyone from DIA or ONI on *Columbus* since last May?"

"Actually," Brad replies, "I placed an ONI agent on *Columbus* several months ago—September. Because of his age, his cover was as a chief radioman. Again, we ran into the problem where he did not know enough about naval communications systems. He poked around for several weeks and discovered nothing. Then, he reported to me that his department head began questioning his competence as a radioman. I had to yank him. We faked a fall down a ladder. He was transferred to the Naval Hospital at Portsmouth."

"How did you stumble on me?" Rigney asks.

"We sent out inquires to all of our field offices to be on the lookout for a young radioman that had extraordinary knowledge and skill in his rate. One of our people in the New London office had heard about you from the Director of Submarine Radioman Schools."

Rigney nods and expresses understanding.

Bob Mater says, "Your Radioman 'A' School classmate, Larry Johnson, is aboard *Columbus*. We've investigated all the radiomen. Johnson is the only one who could know you from before. When you first see him, find an opportunity to get him alone. Ask him not to volunteer any information about you to any of your shipmates. Tell him that you are sensitive about being disqualified from submarines, and you don't want anyone to know about it."

"Okay. I will do that."

"That covers it," announces Bob Mater as he stands up and walks toward the door. When he opens the door, he turns and looks back and forth between Brad and Rigney. "I wish each of you success," he says with a smile. Then, he walks out the door and closes it behind him.

Rigney stares across the desk at Brad Watson and asks, "What's this *Communications Brief* that is next on my schedule?"

"That can wait until after lunch," Brad Watson replies. "I need to make some phone calls. Come back at 1330."

Rigney exists the room. He goes to his quarters in room 15.

Brad pulls out a red colored phone from the bottom desk drawer. He enters a number. A sequence of varying tones sound in his ear. Then, the SYNCH light illuminates on the phone unit.

"Captain Willcroft," answers the Chief of ONI Counterespionage on the other end.

"Brad Watson here, sir."

"How's Page coming along?" Captain Willcroft spends no time on small talk.

"Page willingly accepts his assignment. Actually, he appears dedicated to it."

"He's aware of the dangers, then?" Captain Willcroft questions.

"Yes, sir."

"Does Page know that our mission objective is to for him to lead us to Lucifer?"

"No, sir. I do not think it necessary to give him that much information. I do not want him to know the importance of Python's controller. I have told him that we will use the information paths he discovers to either terminate the operations on *Columbus* and other ships, or we will turn that path in our favor as a means of misinformation."

Captain Willcroft considers Brad's words. Then, he responds, "Well, those might be other alternatives should we fail at finding Lucifer." The captain pauses. Then, he inquires, "Does Page understand that once he discovers who and how on the *Columbus* he is to step aside, and we send in experienced and skilled operatives to take over?"

"Yes, sir. I have emphasized that to him, and he understands?"

"Whom will you send?"

"Galahad."

"Okay, Brad. I hope this novel approach of yours pays off. We are taking a big chance here. DIA and CIA have been after Lucifer for more than ten years. Both agencies have agreed to this approach, only because everything else has failed so far. When does Page report aboard *Columbus?*"

"December 28th. I promised him Christmas leave."

"Very well. Keep me updated."

Brad Watson stows the secure phone into the bottom drawer. He goes to the metal filing cabinet in the corner. The top drawer has a combination lock that controls all four drawers of the cabinet. He dials the combination and opens the second drawer. His fingers flick the folder tabs until he finds the one marked *Lucifer*. He removes the folder and takes it back to the desk. TOP SECRET SPECAT NOFORN is stamped on the folder. Brad sits down then opens the folder. The folder contains all the information collected so far on the Soviet Agent whose codename is Lucifer.

Brad browses the contents of the folder to refresh his knowledge of Lucifer. The identity of Lucifer is not known. The first reports on Lucifer and his activities date back ten years. Intelligence analysts speculate that Lucifer is not Russian, nor from a Soviet-Bloc country. Analysts think Lucifer is of Mediterranean origin. They know he is a paid agent of the Soviets.

Lucifer does not play by the rules. Unwritten rules between the espionage and counterespionage agencies of the West and of the Soviet-Bloc are that agents will not kill each other. When possible, agents are to be arrested and held for possible negotiations and trades later. Lucifer does not comply with these rules. He kills and tortures without mercy when it best suits him. The Soviets look the other way because Lucifer provides large volumes of U.S. classified material. When the U.S. diplomats protest Lucifer's actions via backchannels, the Soviets claim no knowledge of such an agent.

Several NATO and U.S. intelligence agencies reported that Lucifer personally killed three CIA field agents and a few NATO agents who got too close. Lucifer is known to use Spain as his base of operations. Therefore, the discovery of the teletype rolls near Madrid strongly indicates Lucifer's involvement.

Rigney returns to room 4 at 1330.

Lieutenant Commander Brad Watson still sits behind the desk. He is in shirtsleeves, now. He tells Rigney, "Sit anywhere."

Rigney sits on the couch.

"This afternoon, I will explain how you will make reports to ONI. You cannot take notes. You must memorize all of what I explain to you. Before we're finished, you must recite it all back to me. If necessary, we will continue into the night and into the following days. Are you ready?"

"Sure, Brad. Go ahead. Memorizing detail is one of the things that I am very good at."

"I do not expect you to memorize the codewords for report text." Brad hands Rigney an index card with typing on both sides. He explains, "Codewords and translations on this card are extracted from a SECRET document. However, the card is not stamped SECRET because it would be too noticeable. The codewords only apply to this operation. The card is meaningless to anyone else. Carry the card with you only when you expect to make reports. Any questions about the card?"

Rigney gives the card a quick look over. Then, he responds, "No questions."

Brad lifts a sheet of paper from the desktop and scans it. Then, he says, "The name of your mission is Operation Jupiter and is classified TOP SECRET SPECAT. You will find yourself in a number of situations where . . ."

Rigney listens carefully to everything Lieutenant Commander Brad Watson tells him. Occasionally, Brad stops and gives Rigney a chance to memorize some of the details. Brad also provides Rigney with memorizing techniques for easy recall of the information.

". . . and one final item." Brad emphasizes, "Should anyone ask you about this operation, you are not to provide any discussion or answers unless the person asking has stated the mission as *Operation Jupiter* and has properly addressed you by your codename and has properly authenticated."

"My codename?"

"Your codename is *Apollo*. My codename is *Triton*. The codename for our traitor on *Columbus* is *Python*. Those codenames are unclassified when used by themselves. To whom those codenames are linked is classified TOP SECRET SPECAT."

"Interesting," Rigney responds. "The name of the operation comes from Roman mythology, but our codenames come from Greek mythology."

"I don't know the difference," admits Brad Watson. "Bob Mater comes up with the codenames."

Rigney adds, "I have read a lot about mythology. I've always been interested in the source of religious beliefs."

"Please," Brad Watson pleads, "Don't let anyone know that you have educated yourself on these things. Remember, you're a dumb and emotional kid."

"I understand, sir."

Brad sighs deeply; then continues. "If the person has given you the correct operation name of Jupiter and your codename of Apollo and the correct authentication numbers, you are to answer every question asked of you. You are to follow any orders given to you by that person. Do you understand?"

"Yes, sir."

"If someone approaches you and does not give all three, you are to play dumb, as if you do not know what they are talking about. If someone is a fraud, they usually get the authentication wrong. Never prompt anyone for any of the three requirements. If they don't give all three requirements up front, they are a fraud. If that fraud tries to detain you, you are to attack and disable that person. Do you understand?"

"Disable?"

"Yes, disable. We have fully discussed what that means. If someone does not provide all three items and that person attempts to detain you, you are in danger."

"Yes, sir. Disable. No matter who that person is?"

"That's correct," Brad Watson answers with cold finality.

"Why would someone know the codenames, but not know the authentication numbers?" Rigney asks.

"Because the codenames are known by many, even if they do not know to whom the codenames refer. Currently, only two people, you and I, know the authentication formula. I design the authentication formula for each mission. Only one written copy of the formula is allowed to exist. The formula is kept in the top secret SPECAT file at ONI. Should something happen to me, only my direct superiors in the chain of command can get access to the file."

"Okay. I understand."

"That's it, Rig. You have it down pat. Six hours . . . not bad."

Rigney looks at his watch—1737 hours.

Brad advises, "We will finish up on Thursday. I have all your records, and I have your written orders to the *Columbus*. Do you want to go back to New London, or would you rather just go straight on leave to California from here?"

Rigney thinks for a few moments. He and Sally already said their goodbyes. She is on Cape Cod with family for the holidays. The only plan was that Rigney would write and tell her where he would be stationed. The only reason for going back to New London would be to clean out his locker and pack his seabag. "I have the rest of my uniforms and some civvies in my room in the barracks in New London."

"I can arrange for your stuff in New London to be packed up and sent to your home in Seal Beach. Would you like me to do that?"

Rigney ponders Brad's offer for a few moments; then, he says, "Yes, I have no reason to go back to New London."

"Consider it done. I will also have the yeoman take care of plane reservations to Los Angeles and to Norfolk. You can fly out on Friday morning."

Rigney looks up at the bulletin board that holds his schedule in large scale. "Back to the firing range, tomorrow? We've done two sessions already. I thought we decided that I am expert with the 9mm Beretta."

"I will introduce you to different weapons tomorrow."

"And on Thursday—*Telecommunications Training*—what is that?"

"Rig, it's late. We'll talk about it tomorrow. Let us both get a good night's sleep. You will need to focus tomorrow. No alcohol tonight. I recommend that you do not go anywhere tonight. Don't be up late. Get to bed early. Be here at 0745 tomorrow morning and be dressed in blue jumpsuit. One other thing. Keep going over the communications scenarios and codewords. I will test you '*at will*' over the next two days. Get any of them wrong, and you risk not being on that plane Friday morning."

Rigney responds, "Okay. I will see you tomorrow morning."

Lieutenant Commander Brad Watson sits at the desk in room 4. He rubs the back of his neck where a dull pain will shortly turn into a headache. He sat in this chair all day. He did not have his normal workout. *Today was important, and it turned out better than I expected.*

Brad feels good about Rigney being successful. Brad does have a few concerns. He saw several emotional sides to Rigney today. The first was his expressed anger, almost hate, toward the traitor on *Columbus*. *Rigney's patriotism has an emotional edge. He appeared to take it personal. Taking it personal leads to unwise actions.*

Brad is concerned about Rigney's feelings toward Sally Macfurson. Brad writes a note to track Sally Macfurson whereabouts for the next six months.

Chapter 19

Wednesday - December 13, 1967

Rigney stands on the steps of the Cheltenham ONI building. He looks at his watch—0744. He is bundled in the thick blue coat that covers his blue jumpsuit. His ears, face, and neck feel the biting cold. *It must be below freezing!* Fortunately, his thick gloves protect his hands.

At 0745, Brad drives a navy pickup truck with a cap over the bed into the parking lot. Rigney enters the vehicle; then, Brad guns the pickup out of the parking lot.

Brad glances over at Rigney and says, "You look pale and tired."

"I didn't sleep well. I lay awake most of the night."

Brad nods his understanding. "Feel like the weight of the world is on your shoulders?"

"Yeah."

"Don't be concerned. Every new agent goes through it. The responsibility of your first mission burdens and surrounds you like a suffocating cloud. You know you will be isolated from ONI most of the time. It's a lonely feeling. Believe me when I say it gets easier."

Rigney responds with a worried tone. "Brad, sometimes you talk like I will be going on more missions. Do you think I will do that? I don't know if I will. You must think I will."

Brad nods and expresses understanding. "I don't know if you will. Maybe after we see you in action, we won't want you. I have promised you submarine duty when this mission is over, if you still want it. Who knows? Maybe when this mission is over, you will want to stay with ONI. You could be one of those people who quest for dangerous situations. I have known men that the mere sniff of danger acts like an aphrodisiac. They can't stay away from it. Some become obsessed by it." Brad pauses for a moment; then, he continues, "But most agents stay in the game because they feel it their duty. These men have dedicated their lives to protecting their country in the manner they know best."

Rigney does not respond. He just listens. He speculates from Brad's tone that Brad is one of those who are duty bound.

After exiting the Cheltenham main gate, Brad turns south on route 301, instead of driving north toward Clinton.

Rigney looks at Brad and asks, "Where we going?"

"We are going to the Naval Surface Warfare Center at Indian Head. It sits on the Potomac—twenty miles south of DC—about an hour drive from here. The spook community has a joint facility there. We will have the place to ourselves today."

"Joint facility?" Rigney asks.

"*Joint* . . . that means it's used by all the military services, but the navy runs it."

The journey to Indian Head runs along narrow two-lane country roads. Random patches of snow mark the road shoulder. Snow is more plentiful off the road and up in the forested areas. Route 301 connects to Route 5 and they continue south through the small towns of Waldorf and La Plata. In La Plata, Brad makes a right turn.

Occasionally, Brad asks Rigney a question about communications from the previous day's training. Rigney answers every question correctly.

Finally, they come to the Indian Head Main Gate. The two Marine guards wear side arms. While the guards check I.D. cards, Rigney has a chance to see inside the guard shack. He sees a locked gun case with several shotguns and automatic rifles. He also sees another Marine watching several surveillance monitors.

The Marine guard who checks Brad's I.D. card salutes them through the gate.

He must have his real I.D. card today, Rigney says to himself.

About one-quarter of a mile from the Main Gate, Brad turns onto a narrow, dirt road in a heavily wooded area. After going one mile, they come to a large Quonset hut building with a dirt parking lot.

They step out of the pickup. The frozen dirt crunches beneath their boots.

Brad takes the lead through the door. They step into a room that measures forty feet by forty feet. The room is warm. They both take off their gloves and hats and unzip their jackets.

The inside of the Quonset hut looks like a rich man's den. Dark wood paneling covers the walls. Large bookcases stand along the right wall. Photographs and paintings of naval battles from the Revolutionary War through World War II hang on the left wall. Also hanging on the left wall are plaques and memorabilia from the navy, Marines, Army, and Air Force. A four-foot-high counter runs from wall-to-wall. Desks and filing cabinets fill the back half of the room behind the counter. The song, *The Beat Goes On,* sung by Sonny & Cher blasts from a radio on a desk behind the counter.

Brad and Rigney's entry into the room is not noticed by a second class petty officer and a third class petty officer who sit at desks reading novels. The two sailors are in dungarees. The nameplates on their desks advise that they are gunner's mates.

When Brad walks closer to the counter, the second class looks up, startled. "Oh. Hello, Commander. You're early—didn't expect you until

1000."

"Obviously," Brad remarks. "I want to verify the range schedule."

"Yes, sir. It's right here." The GM2 picks up a clipboard from his desk and brings it to the counter.

The third class, now noticing the two arrivals, walks quickly to the radio and turns it off.

Brad studies the schedule.

Rigney walks to the bookshelves. All the books are about guns. Some of the books are military manuals, and the other books are civilian published. *There must be a thousand books here.* When he looks closer, he notices some of the books are in foreign languages.

"I want to ensure that no one else is on the range today. I want you to raise the barricade and block the entrance road."

"Aye, aye, sir. It will be done."

"Are the mechanical targets set per my request?"

"Yes, sir. They're all set."

"Very well. We will proceed to the range."

The finality tone in Brad's voice tells Rigney that they are about to leave. Rigney walks to the counter and stands next to Brad.

The two Gunners mates get their first good look at Rigney. They are surprise at how young he appears.

"Let's go," Brad orders.

After exiting the building to the parking lot, they bundle up.

Rigney says, "They were looking at me like those people did back in the ONI cafeteria."

Brad does not comment.

They get into the pickup.

"The firing range is down this road one-half mile."

Brad drives the pickup into a small dirt parking lot. At the far end of the parking lot are four firing stalls. Several wooden stools stand around the firing stall areas. They exit the pickup.

Rigney looks around. Evergreens sparsely mix with the leafless trees. The sky is totally overcast. Two inches of snow lie in the wooded areas.

Brad walks to the rear of the vehicle. Rigney stands at Brad's side. Brad lowers the tailgate and lifts the cap door.

Rigney, surprised at what he sees, remains silent. Two rifles, each with a telescopic sight and foot-long suppressor, lie on a quilt. He has only seen such weapons on television and in the movies.

He promised, yesterday, no more objections regarding his training. Rigney has resigned himself to accept whatever tasks are assigned to him. He doubts that he is capable of killing anyone with a sniper rifle.

Brad advises, "The rifle on the left is a Winchester model 70, 30.06, bolt action. The rifle on the right is an XM21 automatic, which is a modified M14. Both rifles, except for the suppressor attachment, are the most common sniper rifles being used in Vietnam. These two weapons were modified under navy contracts to attach a suppressor. The scopes of both weapons are zeroed. The Winchester is accurate to 1000 meters. The XM21 is accurate to 700 meters. Any questions?"

"Not yet."

"Today, I evaluate your ability to use these weapons and your ability to be a spotter."

"A spotter?" Rigney asks.

"Snipers do not always work alone; sometimes, they work in teams. Most sniper teams have a sniper and a spotter. The spotter's job is to find the target and to advise the sniper of target direction, distance, wind direction, and wind velocity. The spotter uses high-powered binoculars. After receiving direction and distance instructions from the spotter, the sniper finds the target through the scope of the rifle. The spotter advises the sniper of happenings around the target. Sometimes, a sniper team will include a security lookout. If necessary, the security lookout eliminates anyone who gets too close to the team.

"Our goal today is to determine if you are *technically* sniper and spotter material. I say technically because a qualified sniper is more than a good shot. You must also be mentally capable of killing someone at a distance without anger. Few men are capable of this. This training is not standard for ONI agents. My superiors insisted that I conduct this training. They insisted after reviewing your service record, which shows that during your boot camp training you shot expert with a rifle at 100 yards. You did this without a scope."

"Yes, Brad. That's correct."

"Did anyone approach you about the possibility of specialized training and becoming a—"

"Yes, Brad," Rigney interrupts. "I told them that I wanted to be a radioman on submarines. That's why I joined the navy."

"Where did you learn to shoot a rifle so well?"

"When I was a boy, my uncle took us out on his boat for fishing trips. We would go off Seal Beach about four miles. After we got tired of fishing, we would throw old bottles and coffee cans into the water. Then, we would use handguns and rifles to sink 'em. My uncle had some war surplus rifles. He was in the infantry during World War II. He taught me how to shoot a rifle."

Rigney looks curiously at Brad and asks, "How about you? Are you capable? Have you—"

"Never mind that!" Brad snaps.

Rigney flinches and expresses surprise.

Brad reaches into the truck bed and pulls out the cardboard box. He puts his hand into the box and pulls out several pairs of navy-blue colored wool socks and two navy-blue colored ski masks.

Brad directs, "Put on this pair of wool socks over the socks you are wearing. Also put on this ski mask and put your hat back on. The ski mask and hat will preserve body heat. We will be outside in the cold all day. These items will protect you."

They both don the protective gear.

Brad pulls two pair of leather gloves from the box.

Brad hands the right hand glove to Rigney and says, "The trigger finger snaps on and off. When you are ready to fire, you need the feel of the trigger against your bare finger. Ensure your trigger finger is gloved the rest of the time."

Rigney nods his understanding.

"We will start with the Winchester."

At 1700, they are back at the truck and stowing the weapons. Brad shuts and locks both the trunk bed tailgate and the cap door.

As they stand behind the truck, Brad studies Rigney for a few moments. Then, he comments, "You're a natural, Rig. If you went through the whole course and could kill without passion, you would become one of the best."

"No thanks!" Rigney responds firmly.

"I don't blame you?" Brad says as he stares into space as if remembering experiences from his past.

"Will one of these sniper rifles be hidden on the *Columbus*?"

"No."

Rigney and Brad enter the truck. Brad drives back to the range office. Brad tells Rigney to stay in the truck while he goes into the Quonset hut and signs out.

An hour and twenty minutes later, Rigney is back in his quarters at Cheltenham. He strips off his clothes and throws them in the hamper. He decides not to go to the gym. *I must have walked twenty miles through those woods today.* He takes a long hot shower.

Twenty minutes later, he slips into a clean jumpsuit. He hasn't eaten since breakfast and his stomach growls loudly. He removes a plate of sliced turkey and sliced roast beef from the refrigerator. He also takes

127

the plate of sliced tomatoes and cucumbers. *Oh yeah, don't forget two bottles of Heineken!*

Rigney turns on the television and searches for a news broadcast. Because 7:00 p.m. as passed, all newscasts are over.

He reaches for the newspaper. One article says that the Department of Defense reports that the number of U.S. troops in South Vietnam is now close to 500,000. *The numbers continue to climb.*

Rigney finds the newspaper articles depressing, and the television programming lacking in entertainment. He decides to just sit and eat.

As he chews his food, his mind wanders. He thinks about Sally Macfurson. *I must write her a letter and tell her where I am going.* He wonders if working with ONI will become a long-term arrangement. He now has orders to the Guided Missile Cruiser USS *Columbus*. Assignment to a submarine appears more distant. Rigney wonders if he will have opportunity to use his electronics training while on the *Columbus*.

The phone rings. He picks up the handset and puts it to his ear.

"Page, this is Barry in the ONI security center. I thought you would want to know that the woman who dropped you at your building a couple of times is outside in the parking lot trying to find a way to get in. I recommend that you go out and see her before Cheltenham Base Security picks her up."

"Okay, Barry. Thanks. I will go out and meet her."

Rigney hangs up the phone. He grabs his coat; he hurries through the unoccupied office area to the security door and opens it. Then, he rushes through the foyer and opens the front door. He moves out to the steps. He sees Cathy at the corner of the building looking up. He waves. She notices him and starts walking toward him. She is bundled in her uniform overcoat with a scarf around her neck.

The twenty-two degree temperature and falling snow causes Rigney to zip his jacket to the neck and pull the jacket hood over his head.

Cathy smiles appreciatively. "I am glad you're here. I wanted to see you before you leave on Friday. Can we go inside and get out of this cold?" Cathy shivers.

Rigney hesitates. Brad had told him *no guests* for security reasons.

"Come on, Rig. It's cold out here."

Rigney decides that they can talk in the foyer. *Brad shouldn't object to that.* He enters the cipher lock code and pushes the door open for her. Cathy looks around the small foyer. She looks curiously at the steel door. Then, she looks up at the security cameras.

"What kinda barracks is this? Where's the quarterdeck watch? For that matter, where's the quarterdeck?"

Rigney explains, "No watch in this barracks. That's why the security is so tight."

"Not even a fire watch?" Suspicion edges her voice.

"Security cameras take care of that, and Base Security patrols past the building every hour."

"What's behind that door?" she asks.

"The barracks rooms," Rigney replies lightly.

Cathy cocks her head to the side and stares dubiously at Rigney. She challenges, "Rigney, you're not what you say you are . . . are you?"

Rigney does not respond immediately. He does not have a prepared response. He knows she will be offended if he tells her another lie.

Cathy expresses understanding, "It's okay. You don't need to answer, 'cause I think you are part of what everyone says this building is all about. I understand why you've not told me the truth. I can accept that, but I must know the truth about one thing. You're not married or engaged, are you? I would feel so cheap if you are."

"No, I am not married or engaged," he responds while looking her straight in the eyes.

Cathy studies his face for a few moments before responding. "I believe you." She pauses for a few moments; then, she says, "I know that you cannot be truthful about everything. But I don't think you are a deceitful person. I just don't think deceit is in your nature."

"You are correct about that," Rigney responds with an appreciative smile.

Cathy smiles in return and says, "They changed my watch schedule. I have the midwatch tonight, but I have tomorrow night off. Can we spend your last night at my place? Will you stay the night?"

"Yes, I will. Thank you."

"What time can I pick you up?"

"Six-thirty."

She snuggles up to him and lifts her face to be kissed. Rigney wraps his arms around her and lowers his lips to hers. He lifts one eye toward the security camera. He wonders what the security men on the other end are thinking.

After Rigney walks Cathy back to her car, he goes back to his room and writes a letter to Sally. He tells her that he is well, and the navy doctors found him medically unqualified for submarines—*nothing serious, a scarred eardrum*. He writes that he will be reevaluated in six months. He tells her about his orders to USS *Columbus*. He writes that he remains cheerful and optimistic. He ends the letter by promising to send his new address as soon as he knows it.

Rigney wonders about his feelings toward Sally. Truly, she is an attractive and accomplished woman, which is what initially attracted him to her. When he got to know her better and when the great sex became plentiful, he had to assess his continuing desire to be with her. *Is it the sex, or do I love her? I don't know what love is. Maybe when I understand the essence of love, I will know. But love and commitment are not something I want now. I want to experience life. Love and commitment can come later.*

He also wonders about Sally's interest in him. She had told him that her initial attraction was purely sexual. She said her attraction became more intense as she came to know his unassuming and truthful nature, which is rare in men according to her.

Rigney looks at the clock—9:05 p.m.—bedtime. He must meet John Smith tomorrow morning at 0800. His last day at of training will be spent at the ONI Telecommunications School.

Chapter 20

Thursday - December 14, 1967

At 0802, John Smith drives a navy sedan up to the steps of the Cheltenham ONI building. Rigney notices the O6 eagle insignia on the front license plate. Smith is also dressed in blue jumpsuit.

On the drive to ONI Headquarters at Suitland, Rigney asks Smith, "What is this telecommunications training on the schedule for today?"

"Brad didn't tell me too much. He said that you and I are to meet him in the cafeteria at 0930."

"Have you been through this training?" Rigney asks Smith.

"Nope."

Rigney considers Smith words. He takes a long look a Smith. "John, I hope that someday I will be told who you really are and why ONI thinks it necessary to hide your true identity from me."

"Rig, I bet that someday you will."

At 0930, Lieutenant Commander Brad Watson walks into the ONI building cafeteria. He wears his service dress blues. He motions for Rigney and John to follow him. They all get into the elevator. Brad pushes the button for the desired floor. They exit the elevator, walk down a long corridor, and come to a large metal door with a cipher lock. The sign on the door displays advises, *"Communications Center—Exclusion Area—Authorized Personnel Only."*

Brad enters the code into the cipher lock. They enter the communications center main passageway. As they walk the hallway, they pass a door marked Message Center and a door marked Communications Officer.

Then, they come to a door marked *Field Communications*, which they enter. Inside, a dozen radio operators wearing headsets work radio circuits. Rigney recognizes various transmitters, receivers, and encryption systems. Teletype machines are clacking away in the far corner. Rigney also notices two operators sitting at CW—Morse Code—positions. At the other end of the Field Communications Center, they enter a door marked *Training Room.*

The Training Room contains more of the same types of equipment as in the Field Communications Center. Communications equipment stands against two of the walls. Chalkboards cover the other two walls. Student chairs and tables sit in the center room. The room has no windows.

A first class radioman, dressed in Service Dress Blues, stands at the podium. Three gold colored service stripes and a gold colored chevron on his left arm represent twelve consecutive years of good conduct. Three rows of service ribbons adorn the area above his breast pocket. Included in the cluster of ribbons are a Vietnam Service Ribbon and a Purple Heart Ribbon. His uniform is impeccable. His leather shoes reflect a perfect shine. His five-foot nine-inch frame stands lean and broad shouldered. His pepper gray crew cut is perfectly trimmed around the sides and the back. The cut of this sailor belongs on a recruiting poster.

RM1 Crane is happier than usual today. This morning, he was informed that he has been selected for promotion to chief radioman. His official advancement date is the middle of next month; however, he will be frocked three days from now.

"Good morning, Commander," the RM1 says cheerfully and with a smile.

"Good morning, Crane," Brad Watson responds.

Brad introduces Rigney and John.

"RM1 Crane, this is Page."

Crane extends his hand to Rigney and the two men shake hands. Rigney feels a strong grip by Crane's calloused and leathery hand.

"And this is Smith."

While Crane shakes Smith's hand he says, "I've seen you around the building. Nice to meet you."

Smith does not say anything. He just nods and smiles.

"Okay, Crane. I leave these two in your capable hands. I will check back with you this afternoon."

Brad Watson exits the room.

Rigney scans the Training Room. In Submarine Radioman School, he learned to operate and repair most of the equipment in this room.

An easel with a pad of chart paper stands next to the podium. The front page of the pad reads, *"ONI Field Communications, Condensed Course."*

Rigney observes Smith looking around the room. Smith's manner neither confirms nor denies familiarity with the equipment.

Crane says, "You can hang your hats and coats over there on that coat stand. Then, take a seat."

Rigney and John take a seat at the same two-man table facing the podium.

RM1 Crane walks behind the podium and turns some pages in a three-ring binder. Then, he begins the lesson. "I have been told that both of you have gone through the code word and authentication training. That training prepared you for how to make your verbal reports in the field face to face. Today, you will learn how to make your verbal reports via telephone and via radio communications. You will learn to operate the radio equipment commonly used in ONI Field Operations. You will also learn high-frequency theory so that you can best select the frequencies necessary for successful communications. By the end of today, you must memorize the frequencies that are available for communicating with the ONI Field Communications Center."

Crane pauses; then, he asks, "Any questions?"

Rigney would like to ask where he would find such equipment in the field, but he realizes that he will be told that when and if he needs to know.

Rigney and John shake their heads to indicate they have no questions.

RM1 Crane hands pads of paper and several pens to his two students. "You may take notes if you wish, but you cannot take them with you. I must destroy your notes when the day's training is over."

Rigney and John nod their understanding.

Crane continues, "The first lesson is the format of your reports. The format of your reports will be the same whether you make them over the phone, over voice radio, or via Morse Code in radio CW mode. You will be required . . ."

Forty minutes later, Crane asks, "Are there any questions regarding the format of your reports?"

Rigney and John shake their heads.

As he flips a page of chart paper, Crane announces, "The next lesson is *High-Frequency Theory*." The chart paper displays a diagram depicting the radio frequency spectrum.

"The high-frequency range, or HF range, is three to thirty megacycles. However, U.S. Navy HF transmitters and receivers cover two to thirty-two megacycles. A general rule to follow is that lower frequencies are best at night and higher frequencies are best during the day. When deciding which frequency. . ."

Rigney already knows HF theory, and his mind wanders. He stares at the radio equipment along the wall. He attempts to visualize when and where he would use such equipment. An optimum antenna to cover the range of two to thirty-two megacycles would need to be conspicuously long. *I wonder how such an antenna would be hid from view so as not to reveal the location of an ONI Field Office.*

Crane lectures, "ONI sends a continuous vocal broadcast on these frequencies. The broadcast content is the same on all frequencies. ONI uses these broadcast frequencies to send emergency instructions to field agents and to acknowledge receipt of reports from field agents." RM1 Crane points to a chart with a list of the ONI broadcast frequencies. He pauses to allow time for his two students to write down the frequencies.

Rigney and Smith quickly write down the frequencies.

Rigney looks over at Smith and wonders why Smith is in this training with him. *I guess if I were supposed to know, I would be told.*

RM1 Crane continues the lesson. "These broadcast frequencies are not the normal method to deliver instructions to field agents. Emergency instructions are sent via ONI broadcast only when the field agent has been instructed to listen, or when all contact has been lost with the field agent.

"If an *Emergency Instruction Transmission* is sent to you, the first word will be your codename, the second word will be the transmission identification, followed by the coded instructions in the middle, and the last item will be an authentication number.

"Any questions?" Crane asks.

Rigney and John shake their head.

"The next lesson covers procedures for sending reports from the field. When you. . ."

One hour later, Crane summarizes the lesson. "To recap, the first word of your transmission must be your codename, the second word must be the transmission identification number, the middle of your transmission is your coded report, and the last item in your transmission must be the calculated authentication number. You learned how to calculate the authentication number during previous training." Crane pauses while his students write notes; then, he queries, "Any questions?"

Page and Smith shake their heads.

RM1 Crane hands a small booklet to each of his students. "At the end of this lesson, you will know how to tune radio receivers to the desired frequency. Turn to page three of the booklet where you will find pictures of the receiver front panel and explanations of all the front panel controls.

"The first front panel control we will cover is the mode switch. With this switch, you select the mode in which you will receive. Always set this to LSB—lower side band. All ONI HF transmissions are lower side band. To achieve LSB reception you must set the frequency as follows . . ."

By 1300, Rigney and Smith have completed the training on radio receivers. They tuned in every ONI broadcast frequency and every field office transmit frequency. They heard a few coded reports from the field. The codewords for those reports are unique to the applicable operation and not translatable by Rigney or John.

RM1 Crane calls a break for lunch. They are to reconvene at 1400.

At 1400 RM1 Crane and his two students are back in the classroom. Crane begins the next lesson. "During the remainder of the afternoon, you will learn how to operate the HF transmitters and tune antennas for maximum power output."

Crane hands a booklet of transmitter operating procedures to both Rigney and Smith.

"Setting up the transmitter is the easy part," RM1 Crane explains. "Tuning the antenna for maximum output is more difficult. The goal is to tune the transmitter output to the antenna's electrical characteristics to achieve the lowest SWR—standing wave ratio. You should always attempt to get this ratio down by . . ."

At 1600, Lieutenant Commander Brad Watson enters the training room.

"How are my men doing?"

"We are on the last lesson, now," Crane replies.

"Okay. I will stick around and observe."

By 1645, Rigney and Smith are proficient with the radio equipment. The last exercise is for each student to recite all frequencies from memory. Both Rigney and Smith have no problem with the last exercise.

Crane says, "Okay. We're done. Give me your notes and you can go."

John and Rigney gather their coats and hats and head for the door.

Crane requests, "Mister Watson, may I speak to you?"

Watson orders, "Page, Smith, I will meet you out in the corridor."

John and Rigney exit the room and close the door behind them.

"What is it, Crane?"

"Sir, I just wanted to tell you that Page picked this up really quick. He would be an excellent candidate to run a Remote Field Communications Office."

"How about Smith?"

"Smith has it down pat. No problem there. It's just that I thought I should mention that Page seems to have a complete understanding of this subject."

"Did Page tell you about his background?"

"No, sir. He did not. Wouldn't that be inappropriate?"

"Yes, it would. I'm pleased that he did not. Thanks again for preparing this condensed course. I know it is out of the ordinary, but we are dealing with extraordinary circumstances."

"No problem, sir. Anytime."

Brad turns to leave. Then, he remembers something. He turns back toward Crane and says, "Congratulations on making chief. It's well deserved."

"Thank you, sir."

Brad Watson nods his goodbye and departs the training room.

Brad Watson, Rigney Page, and John Smith stand in the lobby of the ONI headquarters building. Rigney looks at his watch—1705. Traffic is heavy in the lobby as civilians and military finish their workday and depart the building.

Brad says, "Rigney, your indoctrination is complete. Tomorrow morning you are to wear the uniform you wore when you traveled to D.C. and take only those other items you brought with you. You must checkout with the yeoman in the admin office at the ONI building at Cheltenham. The yeoman will give you all your records and travel orders. The yeoman will make arrangements for transportation to the airport."

"Yes, sir. Will do. Does that mean I will not be seeing you again before I leave?"

"That's correct," Brad confirms. "I will be waiting anxiously for your reports from the MED." Brad extends his hand to Rigney. The two men shake hands firmly. "Good luck to you, Rigney. I am sure you will be successful."

Brad Watson walks away from the lobby and back to the ONI offices.

Rigney's eyes follow Brad Watson down the hall until he disappears around a corner. Rigney is surprised at himself for feeling somewhat emotional about their sudden parting. Rigney and Brad had been a team for the last two weeks. Rigney felt comfortable in Brad's presence, especially when they were away from Suitland. Rigney considers Brad as his guardian and mentor.

The realization that he is released to *go it alone* hits him like a ton of bricks. He expresses a trance-like state as the burden of responsibility sets on his shoulders.

"Hey, Rig, come back to earth," John Smith snaps.

Rigney turns and faces John Smith and asks, "John, how long have you known Brad Watson? Can I trust him to tell me the truth? He seems honest and trustworthy. I have come to like him. You know, he comes across as one of those officers who are truly interested in the wellbeing of others and not just his own career."

"Rig, I have known Brad for eight years. I have never known him to lie about anything. You can bank anything he tells you. However, please remember he cannot tell you everything for security reasons. You are right about him being one of those rare officers that are more interested in the wellbeing of others than his own career. That does not mean he ignores his own advancement. He just puts a higher priority on the morale of his people. He is eligible for advancement to full commander in a few months. I hope he gets it."

"Yeah. Me too," Rigney affirms sincerely.

Chapter 21

Rigney's father meets Rigney at Los Angeles Airport. His father is a big man. He stands four inches taller than Rigney. His facial features are rugged. His light brown hair is cut short. His nose is pushed to the side as a result of broken nose from a teenage fistfight. Although his father has grown a beer belly, his father is still one of the strongest men that Rigney knows, as he is reminded when his father hugs him.

James Page retains the large and rock-solid biceps and forearms of his youth. Rigney remembers the many pictures from the 1940s of his father flexing his muscles on the beach. The pictures show that he had a thin waist, was broad shouldered, and was solid muscle. Rigney always wondered how his father kept those rock-hard muscles. *Dad is a salesman, and his lifestyle is sedentary. He never exercises.*

As Rigney releases his father from the hug, he looks around for the other members of his family.

"Your mother and sisters are still preparing for your coming home party tomorrow night. They've been cooking and cleaning for a week. Your uncles will be there, and your mother invited some of your friends. But tonight, it's just your mother and I and your sisters."

What friends, Rigney wonders. They must be from his high school days. Rigney never kept in touch with them.

"You really look good in that uniform, son. I am proud of you and what you're doing."

"Thanks, Dad. I thought you wanted me to go to college instead of going in the service."

"Not really. I think that what's best for you is to do what you want. I can tell you from experience that many people are miserable because they didn't follow their own dreams. If you want to go to college after the navy, well, that's up to you. By the way, you will have to pay for it, I don't have the money."

"I have the GI Bill to help me with college, if I decide to go."

"What happened to the submarine duty you wanted so bad?"

"I was medically disqualified."

"What's wrong with you? Will you be okay?"

"It's nothing serious. I have a scarred eardrum. The condition is not serious. Onboard submarines, pressures and vacuums occur. It could bust my eardrum."

Rigney's father thinks about that for moment. "Wonder why the doctors didn't find that when you were qualifying for your Master Scuba Diver Certificate several years back?"

Rigney just shrugs and does not comment.

"You're okay with that . . . not going to a submarine?" his father asks with genuine concern for his son's wants.

"Yeah, Dad. I'm fine with it."

"Couldn't you get out of the navy because they can't give you what they promised?"

"Dad, I still must do military service. The Draft, remember?"

"Just wondering because your cousins, Bob and Davy, just did two years active duty and need only serve four years in the active reserve."

"Dad, they were ground-pounders—infantrymen. For the training that I have received, I must serve at least six years active."

"Well, they both survived a year in Vietnam. Everyone is so happy they are home safe and sound."

"What are Bob and Davy doing these days?"

"Davy works with his Dad in the roofing business, and Bob is pre-med at UCLA. Bob wants to be a dentist."

"Their lives sound exiting," Rigney comments cynically.

"Nothing wrong with being a roofer or a dentist," James Page defends.

"Boring, Dad, just plain boring."

"And how about you, Rig? How do you see your life on a cruiser . . . exciting and adventurous?"

"I'm sure it will be boring. What I desire is visiting foreign ports, like in Europe. My ship leaves for the Mediterranean the first week of January."

"Why Norfolk? Couldn't you have gotten a ship in Long Beach or San Diego?"

"Just didn't work out that way."

"I promised your mother I would talk to you about Vietnam. We don't want you going there. We don't want you getting killed in some no-account country where who rules makes no difference. World War II was worth fighting because the safety of our country was at stake. The North Koreans were no threat to us, and neither are the North Vietnamese. I don't understand why our government keeps getting us involved in the rebellions and civil wars of other countries. The ruler of South Vietnam is a dictator who the American Government put in power. We didn't care about his country until the communists started a civil war. Murderous governments rule half the countries of this world, and they are only a threat to the people they rule. The only reason our government cares about Vietnam is to save face with all those other countries that we have promised to keep safe from communism. The only time the Russians threatened us directly was with Cuba. President Kennedy was right when he put a blockade around Cuba. The Russians backed down, and they will always back down. But we cannot underestimate the Russians. They have their sights on Europe, and that is where we need our troops."

Rigney responds, "Dad, I don't know if we are right in being in Vietnam. I haven't experienced as much of life as you have. You fought in the big one. When men of your generation were being killed by the thousands in the Pacific and on the battlefields of Europe, there were few American dissenters. Americans sacrificed together to win that war. Dissenters to the Vietnam War are glorified on television every night. That must be totally demoralizing to our military men. I know that it affects my morale. On one hand, I understand the need to stop the spread of communism. On the other hand, I am concerned about thousands of men my age that are being killed each year in Vietnam. If I were ordered to go to Vietnam, I would go without question. Following orders is my duty."

"Please don't get me wrong, son. I totally support our troops. They are duty bound. It's the politicians. They have sent these boys to war. If we had no troops in South Vietnam, we wouldn't have an enemy there."

Rigney argues, "But if America was not there, the communists would take it."

"So what? Whether Vietnam is ruled by a murderous dictator or by communists will make no difference to our way of life."

"Dad, you don't believe in the Domino Theory?"

"Oh, yes, son. I'm a big believer in it. I just don't think Vietnam is part of it. The communists will win Vietnam eventually, anyway," James Page states with finality.

"Why do you say that?"

"Because we are not fighting an invading army in Vietnam. We are fighting the residents of a country who want change. First, they had to fight the French for it, and they beat the French. Now, they are fighting Americans for the same reason."

James Page turns right at the intersection of Pacific Coast Highway and Seal Beach Boulevard.

Rigney looks at his watch—5:30 p.m.

The Seal Beach Naval Weapons Station lies to their left. Night has fallen. Rigney looks through the chain link fence of the Naval Station and sees the outline of a ship at the pier.

James Page drives a short distance along Seal Way; then, he stops the car. Rigney exits the car and opens the door to the one car garage. James Page drives the car into the garage, and Rigney shuts the garage door. The garage is not attached to the house. A small backyard spreads between the house and the garage.

The Page home on Seal Way faces the fence of the Naval Station. A twenty-foot-wide concrete walkway separates the front of the Page home from the chain link fence of the Naval Station. The beach is a short walk southward on the concrete walkway. The Page home is a small three-story structure. Even with the attic family room, the house is only eighteen-hundred square feet. The exterior is stucco. A small courtyard outside the front door separates the house from the concrete walkway that borders the beach. The interior of the house is a mismatch of furniture styles that Rigney's parents purchased at auctions and yard sales. All the floors are polished hardwood. Area rugs of different colors cover most of the hardwood floors throughout the three-story house.

Rigney's parents bought the house in 1948 when Seal Beach still had the remnants of a bad reputation. In the past, Seal Beach was called *Sin City*, and real estate prices were not outrageous at the time. Rigney's father borrowed the down payment from his brothers. It takes all of James Page's effort and income to make mortgage payments and maintain the house. Rigney's mother, Margaret Page, works part time at an employment agency to help with the cost of living. All their wealth is in their house. They have no savings.

All family gatherings, celebrations, and all entertaining occur in the third floor family room. The family room is the most comfortable room in the house. The rug is thicker and softer. Overstuffed chairs and sofas are strategically positioned throughout the room. The room has a wet bar, which is well stocked with scotch and bourbon. The Page's navy friends purchase the liquor at very low prices at the Naval Weapons Station. Two walls have custom-installed bay windows, which provide a spectacular view of the Naval Weapons Station and the Pacific Ocean.

As a teenager, Rigney spent many hours at the bay windows with binoculars and scrutinized the ships and submarines that visited the Seal Beach Naval Weapons Station. Often, navy friends of his parents would describe the features of the vessels as Rigney analyzed them through the binoculars. Rigney would ask the sailors many questions. Most of the time, they answered. Sometimes they would say, "Sorry, Rig, that's classified."

Chapter 22

Rigney's reunion with family and family friends on the second night home includes lots of hugs and many *"we are proud of you"* declarations. But Rigney detects a change in his relationship with friends and family. They are not aware of it, but he is. What they deem important and interesting he no longer believes important and interesting. During previous visits home, he would revel in the stories about his teenage exploits and accomplishments. Now, he no longer values his teenage activities to be relevant or important.

His family tells him of high school friends that are either in college or in military service. He never hears from those friends, nor has he tried to contact them. Some of his schoolmates were killed in Vietnam. He did not know them well; but when he hears of their deaths, he feels sympathy for them and their families. Girls he knew in high school are married, working at minimum wage jobs, or are in college.

On several occasions, Rigney asks his cousins, Bob and Davey, about their year in Vietnam. Neither wants to talk about it. After a few failed attempts, Rigney discontinues his queries into their experiences.

Rigney has plenty of free time while his family goes about their work and their lives. He completes all his Christmas shopping in two days. So, he exercises a lot. He dusts off his weight equipment in the garage and spends hours lifting weights. He runs on the beach two or three times a day. Sometimes on his run, he stops and watches the surfers. He recognizes fewer of them each time he comes home. He knows a few and talks with them. He hears about more people he knew being killed in Vietnam.

During one of his runs along the beach, he stops and faces the ocean. Then, he wades ankle deep into the surf. He closes his eyes. The cawing seagulls, the smell of the ocean, and the sounds of the waves bring back memories of his youth on the beach. He recalls the early years of fumbling with his homemade surfboard. He remembers the experienced, older surfers who taught him. He recollects the fears of his mother and father when he taught himself scuba diving. He reminisces that summer night when he was fourteen on a blanket behind some sand dunes and rocks when he engaged in his first sexual acts.

He opens his eyes and comes back to the present. He understands that life is much more complicated now. He comprehends that evil people commit evil acts that place innocent people in danger. The responsibility of his mission weighs heavily upon him.

Rigney extends his exercise routine to include running around the entire community of Seal Beach. He starts at his home on the southeast end of Seal Way. He runs along the sidewalk that borders the sand of the beach. He runs west to 1st Street; then, runs north on 1st street. Then, he turns east at Pacific Coast Highway and runs until he reaches Seal Beach Boulevard. Then, he turns south until he meets again with Seal Way. The entire run stretches three and half miles and takes forty-five minutes.

During one very cold morning on one of his runs, he stops to watch some die-hard surfers in wet suits near the Seal Beach pier. They are young teenagers that Rigney does not recognize. As he looks around the beach near the pier, memories come to him of the first time he met his best friend, Thom Mundey.

He remembers that sunny afternoon in August of 1963. He was on the beach with friends near the Seal Beach pier. At sixteen, he looked the typical surfer of the early 1960s. He wore bright orange surfer baggies. His skin, bronzed from the summer sun, always glistened with sweat and sun block. While on the beach he always applied a thick coating of sun block to his nose. His nose looked like a white splotch in the middle of his suntanned face.

On that afternoon, he decided to do some surfing on the west side of the pier. He picked up his surfboard and carried it under his right arm. When crossing underneath the base of the Seal Beach pier, he saw a crowd gathering. Beyond the crowd, he saw three men pushing and punching a fourth man. Rigney knew all the people in the crowd. He did not know the three attackers or the victim. Rigney wondered why no one in the crowd went to the aid of the victim.

The victim had stringy long black hair and a stringy black beard. He was thin and frail and had pale skin. The victim wore faded denim trousers and a bright yellow t-shirt with a large *peace symbol* printed on the front and back. He appeared to be a young man, but it was hard to tell from all his hair and beard. To Rigney, this man had the typical look of a those who were later referred to as hippies.

Because of the attackers' words and appearance, Rigney determined the three attackers were obnoxious bullies. All three appeared to be in their mid-twenties. They were clean-shaven and had closely cropped hair. Two of them wore faded and threadbare, sleeveless fatigue shirts with US ARMY embroidered over one of the breast pockets. All three had beer bottles in their hands. They were drunk.

The frail victim fell to the sand.

The three drunken bullies shouted at the man and called him a *draft*

143

dodger and a *coward*.

Acting instinctively, Rigney dropped his surfboard, broke through the crowd, and rushed to help the man who lay on the sand. Rigney knelt beside him. The man bled from the nose and mouth, and he had cuts on his forehead and cheeks.

One of the bullies walked quickly and menacingly toward Rigney and shouted, "Stay away from him, boy! This is none of your business!" Then, the drunk took a step closer. The drunk's friends, encouraged by the boldness of their buddy, took a few steps closer.

Rigney was kneeled over the victim and thought the bully was going to hit him. Rigney reacted instinctively. From his kneeling position, he clenched his right fist, made a 90-degree swing, and punched the attacker squarely in the chest. The attacker back-stepped about ten feet and fell firmly on his butt. The attacker fought for breath. Rigney had knocked the wind out of him.

Rigney eyed the three attackers and said loudly and confidently, "The only ass kicking to be done here will be done by me!"

Some of the crowd applauded, and someone said loudly and excitedly, "Way to go, Rig!"

The other two bullies went to the aid of their friend. They lifted him to his feet. He was still gasping for breath. They exchanged a few words.

The three men poured the remaining beer from their bottles. Holding the bottles by the necks like clubs, they raised the bottles over their heads. They moved toward Rigney and the still prone victim.

Rigney rose to his feet.

One of the attackers ran toward Rigney.

Rigney readied himself to deflect the blow.

Just as the attacker was about to swing down on Rigney, the prone man—the victim—kicked his right leg fast and hard and caught the attacker in the back of his ankles.

The attacker collapsed backward. He landed solidly on his back. Fortunately, the sand absorbed the impact. The bully got right back up.

The attackers stared at Rigney.

Rigney stood tall and with his muscles flexed. His hairy, athletic body complemented his image of powerful toughness.

Rigney's actions encouraged four older surfers in the crowd to stand beside him. These friends were surfing acquaintances that Rigney had known half his life. When he was eight and first started surfing, they adopted him and showed him how to surf. They were three-to-four years older than Rigney, and all of them were in college.

"This should even things up!" declares one of the older surfers.

The three bullies stopped and looked at the teenagers standing over the frail man on the sand, who was now sitting up and smiling. The three bullies reconsidered. They made some nasty remarks about *fucking draft dodgers* and *young fucking punks*; then, they wandered off.

The crowd dispersed.

Rigney helped the victim rise to his feet.

"Thank you so much. What's your name?" the frail man asked.

"Rigney."

"Hi, Rigney. My name is Thom Mundey."

Thom took Rigney's hand and shook it up and down with enthusiastic fervor. Thom nodded his appreciation to the other teenagers who came to his aid.

One of the older surfers said to Rigney, "That was really bitch'n, Rig. When did you get so physical?"

"Yeah, Rig, and when did you get so tall?" asks another, more of a statement than a question.

"Gentleman," announced another of the older surfers, "Rig has grown up, and we all are getting old."

They all chuckled.

"Thanks, guys," Rigney said shyly.

"Anytime, Rig," said one of the other older surfers.

Another surfer says, "Please don't ever get mad at me, Rig."

They all chuckled again.

Rigney turned to Thom and asked, "Are you're okay?"

Thom felt his nose and jaw. "Nothing broken. I'm okay."

Rigney offered, "If you want, I will help you clean the blood off your face. There is an outside shower close to the pier."

"Okay. Thanks."

Rigney retrieved his surfboard and led the way to the shower.

At the outside shower, Thom explained that the three men had followed him from the bar on the corner across the street. Thom advised that he was twenty-one and a sophomore at USC.

Then, their conversation wandered. They talked all afternoon and into the night. They both strongly believed in one's right to be different and to be unconventional. They both found it interesting that their other philosophies were so different. Thom's philosophies were extreme left-wing. Rigney was mostly a right-winger.

In Rigney's mind, Thom is an intellectual and a crusading atheist. Rigney found Thom's atheistic arguments to be logical. Prior to meeting Thom, Rigney already had growing doubts regarding the existence of a supreme being. Thom's eloquent logic clarified Rigney's doubts but did not convince Rigney that God does not exist.

Chapter 23

Rigney is bored with his vacation routine. He thinks mostly about his upcoming mission onboard the USS *Columbus*. He goes to the Seal Beach City Library and checks out books on Europe. He does not know which Mediterranean ports the *Columbus* will visit, but he spends some time planning possible two-week trips around the Mediterranean.

At gatherings of family and friends, he is the focus of attention. He tends to gather with the older navy men that are friends of his parents. He remains quiet when stories are told about his teenage years. He does not want to offend anyone by claiming the irrelevance of his past. They tell stories about his surfing skills and how proud they all were when he earned his Master Scuba Diver Certificate. His parents remind everyone about his straight 'A' average in high school. His sisters tell stories about admiring girls that Rigney mostly ignored.

His uncles, who served in World War II, comment that he should have gone to college first, so that he could do his military obligation as an officer. "The military treats a dogface like garbage," they would say.

On the morning two days prior to Christmas, Rigney awakes at 0600. At 0610, he starts his first run of the day around Seal Beach. By 0745, he has shaved, showered and dressed. He wears clean and pressed faded jeans and a navy-blue colored t-shirt with SUBMARINE BASE NEW LONDON printed in white across the front.

Rigney and his mother sit at the kitchen table having coffee. His mother is still in her bathrobe. He explains why he is not going to a submarine. He lies, of course. He tells his mother about this eardrum problem.

"I just don't understand it," his mother emphasizes. "You joined the navy for six years because they guaranteed you submarine duty. That's what you always said you were going to do. Now, they won't let you, and you still must spend six years in the navy? Why do you want to do that?"

"Mother, would you believe that I want to serve and protect my country from the evil that exists in this world?"

"No," says his mother emphatically. "You have always been too self-centered for that. This quest to be in submarines has never been for anyone's benefit other than your own. You are doing it because it's what you want and not what is good for anyone else."

Rigney responds, "That's the way it was in the beginning, but recent events have changed my mind about my navy service."

"What events?"

"Well, I can't really—"

Rigney's youngest sister enters the kitchen and interrupts their conversation. "Hey, Rig, there's a hippie at the door to see you."

"Hippie?" Rigney questions. The only hippie that Rigney knows is his friend, Thom Mundey.

Rigney goes to the front door.

Diane Love, his high school girlfriend, stands just inside the door. He has not seen her since the morning after their senior prom, which was two and a half years ago. She wears a rawhide Indian dress and a light-blue headband. On her feet, she wears rawhide moccasins. A silver *peace symbol* hangs around her neck on a leather strap. A multicolored, Indian blanket drapes like a shawl over her shoulders. She wears no makeup. Her flaming red hair hangs straight and uncombed over her shoulders and down to the middle of her back. Granny glasses sit perched on the end of her nose.

His memory and feelings of Diane come flooding back to him.

Chapter 24

Diane Love and Rigney Page attended the same junior high school and the same high school; they shared some of the same classes. During junior high school, Rigney paid little attention to her. He knew her family was rich. A chauffer driven car delivered her to school each day. He had heard that her father was the president of a stock brokerage company.

Then, one day in the early fall of 1962 during his high school sophomore year and shortly after the football incident when he quit the team, Diane came up to him while he was at his locker. She said to him, "Rigney, I heard about the football thing. It's about time someone put the coach in his place. He's my history teacher, and he is no good at it. Football is the only thing he cares about, and he always gives preference to his players. It took a lot of courage for you to do what you did, and many others think what you did is okay."

Rigney was quite surprised by her words and even more surprised by her appearance. She had developed curves and breasts, and her smile was inviting and sexy. She wore her flaming red hair long and teased. She wore her makeup to best accentuate her features. Her most noticeable facial feature was her dark green eyes. Later that same week and to his surprise, he discovered that she was on the high school cheerleading squad. During last period on the following Friday, all students were required to attend a football rally in the gym. There she was—standing taller than the others—her long legs gracefully going through the cheer routines. Diane did not have the pretty and perky looks of the other cheerleaders, but her whole manner radiated sex appeal.

During their sophomore and junior years, he found himself staring at her while they were in class. Her facial features were plain—*but what a body!* She stood five feet and nine inches tall. She had long legs and her body became perfectly shaped. Her tight clothes barely passed the school's dress code. The only occasions when Rigney saw her in loose fitting clothes was when she was in her cheerleader outfit.

Diane ran with a different crowd. Their paths never crossed outside of school. She dated jocks and associated only with other cheerleaders.

Rigney spent most of his after school hours playing basketball, lifting weights, or surfing. During the school year, surfing was only practical on the weekends.

Their relationship drastically changed on a mid-August afternoon in 1964. Diane seldom went to the beach, but she came to Seal Beach that day with three girlfriends. They wanted to become tanned before school started. They laid out their blankets, removed their outer beachwear, and

148

sat down on their blankets.

Rigney was surfing near the Seal Beach Pier.

Diane and her friends were applying sun block and checking out the male populace when one of her friends pointed toward the water and said, "My God, is that Rigney Page?" They all looked toward the surf and saw Rigney riding a wave. He wore his favorite orange Baggies. When he finished the ride, Rigney decided to rest for a while. He pulled his surfboard up to the sand just beyond the surf's edge. He contemplated whether to go to his blanket or just rest where he stood.

One of the girls exclaimed with astonishment in her tone, "He looks like a bronzed Greek statue. Look at all that hair . . . and those muscles!"

"For sure!" exclaimed another.

Rigney was unaware that he was being appraised. He was just one of many surfers standing on the beach at that time. He did have a thicker than normal coating of body hair that covered him from his neck to his ankles. During the summer when exposed continuously to the sun, his body hair changed color from reddish brown to blond. Also, during the summer, Rigney let his hair grow long and often let his beard grow for several days. His hair, normally reddish brown, was also bleached blond from the sun.

"He looks much older without clothes on," one of the other girls declared admiringly.

They all giggled.

"I wonder how he looks totally naked?" asked another.

More giggling.

"Hair all over his butt, I bet!"

More giggling.

"Those shoulders are as wide as the Grand Canyon!"

More giggling.

Diane evaluated Rigney's image. "It's not just that he looks older; he also looks . . . Oh, I can't think of the word. You know, rough looking." Diane searched for the right word.

"*Rugged* is the word," said another girl with a panting sigh.

"Yeah! That's the word!" Diane agreed.

"Totally sexy!" sighed another.

Diane became aroused just watching Rigney. She had always thought him to be good looking, but this is the first time she had ever seriously considered having sex with him.

"So why does everyone think him weird?" asked one of Diane's friends.

Diane replied, "People think him weird because he is different— unconventional. He does his own thing. He does what he wants, not what other people want him to do. He is totally self-confident. He truly does not care what others think or say about him."

"But he's not jock. He's just not with it," said one of the girls.

"So what?" Diane challenged. "No doubt he's athletic. Just look at him!"

One of the girls commented, "Well, there was that football thing a couple years ago. He became totally untouchable after that. They say that he spends his lunch period and study hall in the school library reading books on mythology and religion. My sister is a student librarian. She says he checks out books about physics and submarines. He also reads books about communism. Only nerds read that kind of stuff."

"I will make sure that your sister is not around the next time I check out books," Diane scolded.

Rigney went back into the water. The girls' eyes roamed the beach, but they always came back to Rigney when he rode a wave.

After another hour of surfing, Rigney decided to call it a day.

Diane rose from the blanket.

"Where ya going?" asked one of the girls.

"To break with convention," Diane replied.

As Rigney came out of the water carrying his surfboard, Diane walked up to him and said, "Hello, Rigney."

At first, he didn't recognize her. She wasn't wearing makeup, and her hair was pulled back. Then, she gave him that sexy and inviting smile that always put him in a trance of sexual fantasy.

Rigney stared lustily at Diane's body. She wore a skimpy two-piece black bathing suit, which offset her blemish free white skin. Her long, slender, and sexy body caused Rigney's heart to beat faster.

"Stop staring at my breasts, Rigney. You're embarrassing me."

Rigney shifted his eyes to her face and it was blushing. Then, he said something stupid like, "Don't wear that bathing suit, then."

Diane ignored the comment.

"I hope you are wearing sun block," Rigney cautioned. "Looks like this is your first day at the beach."

They stood at the water's edge for several minutes and chatted about surfing and swimming. Rigney told her that he had been at the beach all day and asked her if she would like to go somewhere and have some food and a coke. Diane agreed.

Diane stopped by the blanket and put on her outerwear.

She told her friends, "Don't wait for me. Rigney will take me home."

Rigney's 1951 Ford pickup truck was parked at the corner of Ocean Avenue and 8th Street, which is just a block away from the pier.

During the previous summer, the summer of 1963 when Rigney turned 16, his uncle gave him the pickup truck. During the last year, Rigney had sanded out all the rust, pounded out all the dents, and primed the entire surface of the truck. He had not decided on the color, yet.

He tossed his surfboard and other beach articles into the pickup bed. He unlocked and opened the passenger side door for Diane. He walked over to the driver's side, unlocked the door, and opened it. He removed a flowered print shirt from the driver's side and put it on. He grabbed his leather sandals from the floorboard and slipped them on.

Rigney and Diane began dating. They became good friends, but they were not a steady couple in the beginning. That was okay with Rigney because he did not need to consider her when planning his activities. When he wanted to date someone else, he had no obligation toward Diane. That was okay with Diane. She was a cheerleader and liked being seen with jocks. She thought of Rigney as her secret rebel boyfriend.

Rigney taught Diane how to surf and how to scuba dive. He even allowed her to watch him exercise with weights a few times; he did not want that, but she insisted.

To keep his pickup running, Rigney had to work after school three days a week and on Saturdays. He had to give up playing basketball outside of school. So, Saturday nights and Sundays were the only time he had for dates.

After they had sex a couple of times, Diane wanted to see Rigney more often and have sex more often. They would go to Diane's house when they wanted to have sex. Diane was an only child. Her parents went to their house in Palm Springs every weekend. Sometimes her parents would stay in Palm Springs for weeks at a time.

Diane always insisted that Rigney wear a condom. Their sexual act was always the same with Rigney on the bottom and Diane sitting straddled across him. Rigney enjoyed it immensely.

Diane asked Rigney to quit his part-time job so they could see each other more often. Rigney told Diane that his job was his only source of money. He would not quit. Diane said that she had plenty money for both of them. She could easily pay for their dates and keep Rigney's pickup running. Rigney declined.

They enjoyed each other's company and conversation. She told Rigney of her wish to graduate from UCLA with a Business Degree and become a stockbroker. She told him, "Rigney, you can make a fortune in three ways in this country. One way is to start your own business and sell it for megabucks. Another way is investing in real estate. The easiest

151

way is being successful in the stock market. You must be ruthless and never give the other guy a break."

Money was always on her mind. "To misquote *The Beatles*," she would say, "Money can't buy me love, but it will buy me everything else."

Diane could not understand Rigney's decision to join the navy after high school. "There's no money it that," she advised.

He attempted to make her understand, "Look, by law I must perform military service. Instead of being drafted into some line of work that I don't want, I pick my line of work before I enlist."

She would argue, "But why not go to college first?"

"Because I want to experience the world now. I don't want to spend the next four years in college. I don't want to spend four more years listening to people, teachers, who never work in the disciplines they teach. All my life I have read about exotic and exciting places. When the sailors from the navy base talk about where they have been and what they have done, I visualize myself standing on some tropical palm-laden beach or walking the ruins of ancient Athens. I want to see those places, and the navy can get me there! If I want to learn about how to earn money in the stock market, I would listen to a successful investor—not some college professor. If I want to learn about the Acropolis, I want to go there and see it, not listen to some teacher who has never been there. We graduate from high school on June 4th. I leave for boot camp the following week. I will learn about the navy from people who have been successful in it."

On several occasions, Rigney asked Diane to sit at the third floor bay windows of his home and watch the ships and submarines arrive and depart the Naval Weapons Station. While watching the ships, Rigney asked Diane, "Doesn't seeing those ships come and go make you wonder about where they are going and what they will do when they get there? I wish you understood how it excites me."

During the last half of their senior year in 1965, Diane distanced herself from the norms of high school life. She quit the cheerleading squad. She stopped caring if others saw the two of them together. She took Rigney to parties hosted by the in-crowd. However, after she quit the cheerleading squad, the invitations to parties became infrequent. What she knew as her social circle faded away. She realized that she was on her own. That circle of friends existed only if she conformed to their standards. Diane adopted Rigney's loner attitude. She learned and practiced Rigney's philosophy that you should only try to please yourself because you would never be happy trying to please others.

Rigney had no circles. No one, except his parents and sisters, cared much about what he did. The beach culture existed in a pool of casualness, permissiveness, and laissez-faire. Around the beach, the unexpected was expected and the unconventional was conventional. Judging others was not part of the beach lifestyle philosophy.

Diane asked Rigney to start picking her up in front of her house in his pickup truck. Her parents disapproved. Her parents threatened her with loss of college tuition if she did not stay away from him. Her parents judged others by their appearance and their social and economic standing.

"Rigney, you and I are conservative types," Diane would say. "We believe in accountability of the individual. We don't believe that society is accountable for the illegal and evil actions of the individual. But our desires to acquire wealth differ. What you must understand is that money controls this world, and those with money cause the world to go around. If you don't have money, you will be pushed around.

"Instead of discovering the world, Rig, you need to learn how to control it. You need to get a head start on earning that money. You need to get a million bucks in the bank, first. Then, you can tell the rest of the world to fuck off. As an enlisted man, you will be a poor man living a poor man's life."

Rigney responded, "I will probably never have a million dollars, but I will have a million dollars' worth of experiences."

"Rigney, your reasoning is just like mine. You want something . . . passionately . . . for yourself. It's just that we want different things. Hopefully when you are done with this navy thing, you will come back and find a way to make something of yourself."

"Make something of myself by whose standards?" Rigney challenged.

They finally agreed to disagree.

They decided to be each other's date to the Senior Prom. Rigney's parents were exuberant. However, Diane's family, friends, and acquaintances gasped with disgust at Diane's prom date choice. Among Diane's family, Rigney was known as that *Irish beach bum*.

On Senior Prom night, they departed the prom early. They checked into a motel on Pacific Coast highway. At 4:00 p.m. they left the motel and went to the Seal Beach Pier. Diane brought bourbon from her father's bar. They sat on a wooden bench facing Main Street. Rigney sat in his rented tuxedo, and Diane sat next to him in her prom dress.

As the sun rose, they toasted the end and they toasted the beginning. They toasted their time together, knowing that it was at an end. They held each other, and they wept in each other's arms. They wept because they knew their safe and comfortable youth was at an end. They also understood that they had come to a beginning. They kissed their last kiss, and they put everything they had into that kiss. That kiss was deep and passionate, and that kiss was final.

And that is Rigney's remembrances of Diane Love.

Chapter 25

"Hello, Rigney. I heard you were home." Diane steps forward with arms outstretched. They hug each other strongly and emotionally.

Rigney cannot help noticing that Diane smells of acrid cigarette smoke. With his arms still around her, he leans back and looks at her questioningly.

"What?" she asks.

"When did you start smoking?"

"Damn it, Rigney! We haven't seen each other for over two years, and that's the first thing you want to ask me?"

"Well, except for your hippie appearance, it is the next thing I noticed?" A wide smile spreads across his face.

Diane stares at him for a few moments; then, she says, "Oh, yeah! Well . . . uh . . . your hair is too short. Your muscles are bigger, and you're better looking than ever. You look squeaky clean. You're disgusting!" A large smile spreads across her face.

They are still holding each other. They both chuckle.

Diane tilts her head up, inviting Rigney to kiss her.

Rigney pulls her closer and kisses her. Their lips do not open. Purposely, he does not kiss her passionately. However, the kiss is warm, solid, and lingering. The kiss is powerful enough to remind them of their previous passions for each other. They both want to kiss more, but they both sense Rigney's mother and sister in the room.

Diane pulls back. "Hello, Mrs. Page . . . nice to see you again."

"Hello, Diane," Margaret Page responds slowly. "I didn't recognize you at first."

"That's okay. I heard Rigney was home and I wanted to see him."

"Why don't you two go up to the family room? You'll have privacy up there. I will bring you coffee and coffeecake."

"Thanks, Mom."

Rigney leads Diane up the two flights of stairs that lead to the attic family room. They pick two overstuffed chairs that face each other, just a few feet apart.

Diane says, "Tell me about your travels."

"Oh, not much traveling yet. I just finish my technical schools."

"You've been in navy schools for the last two and half years?" Diane is surprised.

"Yes."

"I thought your plans were to be a world traveler by now. Whenever I thought of you, I imagined you in some foreign land, winning the hearts of all those sultry foreign women."

"It didn't work out that way. I did so well in the initial schools, I was allowed to take all the courses available to me. In January, I will depart for the Mediterranean."

"Will you be stationed over there?"

"No, I will be on a cruiser making a six month deployment to the Mediterranean."

Diane looks puzzled for a moment. "Cruiser? That's not a submarine, is it?"

Rigney tells her the cover story about his eardrum.

"I feel for you, Rig. I know how much you wanted submarines. Tell me where you've been and what you've been doing."

Rigney explains the schools he attended and where the schools are located. He did not tell her anything about ONI, of course. "And that's it. Not much to tell."

Diane informs, "A lot has changed in my life. I am still going to UCLA. I'm in my junior year. Last year I changed my major from economics to political science."

"Why did you do that? I thought you wanted to be a stockbroker in your father's firm."

"That's in the past," Diane explains contemptuously. "I now know the harm that people like my farther have caused. My father and others like him are part of the Military Industrial Complex that oppresses the working class, rages war on poor countries, and pollutes the air and oceans. My father is part of that integrated conspiracy that has been formed between government and industry. My father and other rich people like him are getting richer from the Vietnam War. They use poor people to fight the war while they protect their own children from it. They plot to prevent common people from ascending to political office so that the needed social, economic, and environmental changes are not made."

Rigney stares at Diane with astonishment. His eyes are wide, and his mouth is open.

"What's the matter, Rigney? Do you feel guilty because you are part of that conspiracy?"

Rigney closes his mouth and focuses his eyes on Diane. "Diane, I am not part of any conspiracy."

"Oh, but you are! By blindly volunteering yourself to military service, you have enslaved yourself to serve the masters of the vast right-wing conspiracy. Everyone I know thinks that people like you are surrendering to the status quo by enlisting or by letting themselves be drafted."

Rigney hears Diane speak words that he has only read in newspapers and magazines. Occasionally, Thom Mundey says things like this in his letters but never in the contemptuous manner that he hears from Diane.

"Why did you come here today, Diane? Is it your plan to become confrontational and argumentative? Did you come here to convert me to some cause?"

"I'm sorry, Rig. I am always preaching, lately. I am always arguing with my parents about these things. Whenever I visit them, we always get into the same argument. They do not understand the damage they have done. Those arguments are so frustrating!"

"You're not living at home, then?" Rigney asks.

"No, I live in a commune in Huntington Beach."

"How do you pay your tuition at UCLA?"

"My parents still pay my tuition, and they give me money. They say that I am just going through another phase. They say they love me and will not allow me to fail in life. I often feel guilty about it because others in my commune have totally broken their ties with their families to prove their dedication to the protest movement."

"You don't think you are dedicated to *the protest movement*?"

"Well . . . yes . . . mostly. I want so hard for the protest movement of our generation to succeed. I just can't survive with the poverty that comes with living in a commune."

"This protest movement you talk about is not my movement, and I am part of our generation. Does not sound to me like you are living the life you really want to live."

"Yes I am. When I moved into the commune, I sent a message to the capitalist that raised me and brainwashed me."

"Capitalists? Diane, you sound like a communist. The words you speak sound like words from a communist pamphlet."

"No, Rigney, not a communist. I see myself as a democratic socialist. We seek change though democratic processes. I wish you could meet the leader of our commune. He makes so much sense. He helped me understand how I had been corrupted by the capitalist lies of my childhood."

"No thanks. Remember, I have little use for people who try to convert others to a cause. They are more interested in manipulating and controlling others than they are in crusading for some cause."

Diane studies Rigney for a few moments; then, she says, "I hoped you would understand. I thought our relationship would give you insight into what I believe."

"What relationship! You stopped answering my letters two years ago. If you remember our long talks, you would remember that leaders of causes repulse me. They convert by preying on the weaknesses of others."

"Is that what you think of me . . . that I am weak?"

"Diane, I have not seen you for two and a half years. I can see that your philosophy of life has completely changed. I want to accept you and everyone else I know for what they are. I don't want to openly criticize anyone. There will always be causes, and there will always be differences in opinion. Our constitutional values allow us to be different and believe in different things. It allows us all to coexist, despite our differences. If you came here today to convert me to some cause, you can leave now. If you came here to visit and talk with an old friend, you are welcome to stay. I want you to stay. So, which is it?"

Tears come to Diane's eyes. Within a few moments she is sobbing. Rigney finds some tissues and hands them to her. Rigney returns to his chair.

In between sobs she explains, "I get so frustrated sometimes. I feel guilty about my family, and I want you to understand why I changed. But talk about change! You were never the type of person who issued ultimatums. You would never have scolded me like that when we were dating."

Rigney smiles understandingly. "I have never been confronted with such a change in a person before. I don't have much use for those who consider it their quest in life to change my beliefs. I don't try to change other people, and I reject those who try to change me."

"David, our commune leader, says that everyone will eventually change toward the common good."

"Did your David ever serve in the military?"

"Yes, he was in the navy for three years. He says he learned firsthand how the military brainwash their people. He says they are all corrupt."

Rigney shakes his head in disapproval. "Diane, you disappoint me. I remember you as a person who expounded her own beliefs, not the beliefs of others. What has happened to you? You have become a follower. I remember you as someone who was in charge of her own destiny."

Diane replies stubbornly, "Haven't you become a follower. Aren't you following the orders of others? You're an enlisted man, you must follow everyone's orders."

Rigney responds, "Following orders is the essence of the military, but no one in the military expects me to believe in what they believe. I do not quote the beliefs of some officer as my own beliefs, and I am not required to. I am only required to support and defend the constitution and to follow lawful orders of the officers appointed over me. Strict rules and strict punishments exist for those who attempt to convert others to a cause or beliefs. I am not required to adopt the philosophies of others."

Diane shakes her head with frustration; she queries, "So where does that leave us?"

Rigney studies Diane and considers her behavior. *What a change. She has lost her confidence. She permits others to manipulate her.*

Rigney smiles compassionately. "Remember our disagreement about the essence of God? We amicably agreed to disagree because we agreed on so many other things. It appears, of course, that we are disagreeing on more. Is it possible for two people who were once lovers to become enemies? We had a bond. Can't what bonded us once, keep us friends now?"

Diane reminisces. She remembers the good times. She still wants to call him friend, despite their differences.

Diane reveals, "Like you, I no longer believe in God."

Rigney looks quizzically at Diane and says, "I never claimed not to believe in God. If you remember, I questioned the teachings of others who proclaimed the power of God. I doubt that any being, supernatural or otherwise, is all knowing and all powerful."

"Hmmm," Diane utters. "I always concluded from our discussions that you were an atheist. But you're right. You never declared that God does not exist. So, you believe in God, then?"

"I have doubts," Rigney responds. "I doubt that any being, God or otherwise, has the power at whim to create or destroy mankind or the world. I don't believe there is any supernatural being that controls or guides people's actions. I mean, if there were, why would such a being allow evil to victimize the innocent."

Diane smiles and looks bewildered; then, she states, "Well, if you strip all that power from a being, that being cannot be a God."

"Exactly!"

Diane nods confidently and states, "You will cross that line, eventually. Like I did."

Rigney responds, "I keep searching libraries for a reference that will lead me to physical evidence of God. Instead of answers, I just develop more doubts and more questions. All my research so far leads to the concept that man created God."

Diane studies Rigney and his behavior. *His appearance is more rugged. He has become stronger, not just physically; his manner is more mature. He has become a man—an extremely sexy man!*

Diane stands and walks over to Rigney; then, sits in his lap. She puts her arms around his neck and kisses him passionately. Rigney responds with equal passion. This time their mouths are open and their tongues touch. The smell of acrid tobacco smoke still bothers him.

When they pull away from the kiss, Rigney asks, "When did you start smoking?"

"It's not cigarettes. It's pot."

Rigney is alarmed. "You don't have any on you now, do you?"

"No, I smoked the last one several hours ago."

Rigney relaxes. "Diane, I ask you as a friend. Please do not have any illegal drugs with you when you and I are together. Will you do that for me?"

"Yes, I will do that," Diane agrees with a smile. "We can be together again, then?"

"Yes, I would like that, but I depart for Norfolk in five days. We should not get involved again. I don't want to commit to anything."

"We can just enjoy each other," Diane says with a pleasurable smile. "We can be sex partners, again. I would like to feel what you have learned from all those other women. You must tell me about them."

Rigney's heart skips a beat at the promise of enjoying sex with his high school sweetheart. "Yes, I would like to be lovers again, but I will not tell you about other women in my life; and I don't want to hear about the men that you have been with. Is that okay?"

"Agreed!" Diane says with enthusiasm and her sexy smile.

"One more thing, you must take me on a tour of your commune and with me in my dress uniform."

"Absolutely not!"

"Just kidding."

"Hey! You kids ready for some lunch?" Rigney's mother shouts from the bottom of the stairs. "I have a tray with coffee and cake."

"I'll get it," Rigney answers.

Diane slips off Rigney's lap.

Rigney darts down the stairs.

His mother hands him the tray and says, "Your sisters and I are going shopping. We'll be back in a few hours."

Perfect timing!

Rigney returns to the attic family room with the tray and sets it on a table.

As they eat, Rigney and Diane make small talk. Diane updates Rigney on people they knew in high school. Diane adds to the list of names of guys he knew that were killed in Vietnam. Rigney tells Diane about life in the navy. He tells her what he likes and dislikes, especially his dislike of living in a barracks.

The front door to the house slams shut.

"What's that?" Diane asks.

"Everyone has gone shopping. They won't be back for several

hours."

Diane smiles devilishly at Rigney.

Rigney returns the same devilish smile. Then, he says, "I don't have any condoms. I was not expecting this."

"Not to worry. I have been on birth control pills for more than a year."

Diane walks to the far end of the room where a large sofa sits under a large bay window. She removes the peace symbol from around her neck and places it on a coffee table. She kicks off her moccasins. Then, she stretches her arms straight up.

Rigney walks over to her and looks questioningly into her eyes.

"The dress comes off over the shoulders."

Rigney grabs the dress around her hips and pulls the dress off her body. As soon as the dress clears her shoulders, he sees that she is not wearing any underwear. He turns and drapes the dress over the back of a chair; then, he turns back to face her. Her body is thinner than her senior year of high school. Her milk-white skin is firm and taught. Her flaming red hair falls over her shoulders and covers the top half of her well-proportioned breasts. Her waist narrows to flared and rounded hips. Her legs are long and perfectly shaped. Her pubic hair is the same flaming red color as her hair.

Diane grabs the bottom of his t-shirt and pulls it over his head. He wears no belt. She unbuttons his jeans, pulls down the zipper. She stoops as she pushes the jeans to his ankles. Rigney, who is not wearing shoes and socks, easily kicks off the jeans. He lets them lie where they fall.

Diane giggles. "Boxer shorts?"

"Navy issue!" Rigney flippantly remarks.

"Well," she says.

"Well, what?"

"Take off your shorts."

"You take them off," Rigney smiles.

"Why do you want me to take them off?"

"Because I want to see your reaction when you come face to face with Johnny Hot Rod."

The both laugh at the mention of the familiar nickname.

Diane pulls down Rigney's boxer shorts and faces and old acquaintance. She stands and faces Rigney. They wrap their arms around each other and kiss passionately; their mouths open and their tongues intertwine.

They move to the sofa.

Their foreplay is awkward as they rediscover each other. After a few minutes, Rigney begins to caress her breasts. Diane pushes down on his shoulders. This was always Sally's signal for Rigney to go south.

"Do you want me to go down on you?"

"Oh, yes! Please! Then, I will do you!" Diane moans.

There's something to look forward to! Rigney says to himself.

When they dated in high school Diane never put her mouth around Johnny Hot Rod. She had said, "The thought of semen shooting into my mouth revolts me. It's degrading. Only tramps and sluts give blowjobs. It's the only way they can get boys to go out with them." At the time Rigney did not know what he was missing; so, he never pushed it.

When they dated in high school, Rigney did not know about cunnilingus. The thought never entered his mind. Diane knew about it, though. She never asked Rigney to do it for concern that he would want oral sex in return.

Rigney gets on his knees in front of Diane. She slides forward on the sofa as Rigney gets his head between her thighs. He lifts her legs so that the bottom of her thighs rests against the top of his shoulders.

Several minutes later, Diane is moaning and puffing, "Yes! Yes! Yes!"

Rigney continues. He will continue until she tells him to stop.

Several minutes later, Diane again feels release. The "Yes, Yes, Yes," is much softer this time.

Rigney continues.

"Stop Rigney! You're driving me crazy!"

Rigney pulls his head from between Diane's thighs. Then, he sits beside her on the sofa. They sit there totally naked. Diane pants deeply and rapidly. Her body still sits low on the couch, and her legs are spread apart.

"When did you learn how to do that? Did you do that with girls when we were in high school?"

"No, I didn't know about it then."

"Whoever taught you must be some woman!"

"Yes, she is," Rigney says fondly, thinking of Sally.

"Tell me about her."

"No, Diane. I don't want to talk about other women while I am with you. While I am with you, I want to be totally with you." But Rigney cannot block Sally from his mind.

Diane pulls herself up to sit higher on the sofa, sideways, facing Rigney.

"I think that is the nicest thing you ever said to me. You're becoming a sensitive male. Anyway, you cannot go back to the navy. You will live in my closet. When I want more of that, I'll let you out of the closet."

They chuckle.

As they talk, Diane continually moves her eyes up and down Rigney's body. Rigney is doing the same to Diane.

"Rig, you are more in shape now than when I last saw you."

"I workout regularly," Rigney explains. Then, he says to Diane, "I would say that you are leaner. You have a perfect body."

"Thank you for the compliment."

Diane reaches over and puts her hand lightly around his penis, which is rock hard.

"Johnny Hot Rod looks the same," she says—staring at it—almost in a trance.

Rigney inhales sharply as he feels the pleasure of her hand around him.

"Looks like Johnny Hot Rod is ready to race," Diane says with a giggle as she moves her hand up and down a few times.

Rigney inhales sharply—twice.

Diane slides off the sofa and onto her knees. She moves in front of Rigney, places her hands on his knees, and spreads his legs apart. She maneuvers herself between Rigney's thighs.

Rigney sits reclined on the sofa with his legs apart. Diane is kneeling between his legs. She moves her mouth closer. The image is the same as what Sally had done many times. Both women have flowing red hair and green eyes. *Will it be the same?*

Diane lowers her head and puts her mouth around Johnny Hot Rod.

Ten minutes later, Rigney lies back against the sofa, alone and panting. Diane has dashed down to the second floor bathroom. Rigney looks down at Johnny Hot Rod, who lies sideways and is limp and wet. *That was the best ever!* Diane's technique took ten pleasurable minutes before Johnny Hot Rod crossed the finish line.

He hears Diane come back up the stairs.

Rigney is lying back, limply, against the sofa. His legs are still spread apart. He watches Diane as she walks across the room. Her hair and breasts sway as she walks.

Diane holds a steaming hot washcloth and dry towel. She again kneels between Rigney's thighs.

"Well, I guess you liked that, huh?" Diane queries with a perky smile.

Rigney responds weakly, "On a scale of one to ten, I would say—"

"Oh, be quiet. You know it's the best blowjob you ever had." Diane giggles.

She wraps the steaming washcloth around Johnny Hot Rod and lets it sit for a minute.

More pleasure.

163

She thoroughly washes the expended Johnny Hot Rod. Then, she towels him dry.

"Diane?"

"Yes?"

"Will you live in that closet with me?"

They both laugh.

"Why didn't we do this in high school?" Rigney says with disappointment. "We missed out on a lot!"

Diane informs with equal disappointment in her tone, "We didn't do it because we were victims of convention and other people's values."

They sit on the sofa. They are still naked. They sit close. Rigney has his arm around her shoulders. They engage in more small talk. They kiss and snuggle and fondle each other. As the fondling and kissing continues, they start to pant softly. Rigney places his hand on Diane's breasts. He feels Diane's nipples become hard and extended. Diane reaches for Johnny Hot Rod. Yes, Johnny is ready for another race.

"This sofa rolls out to a bed. Do you want to stretch out?"

"Yes, I would like that."

A few moments later they are lying side by side with their arms around each other. Their kisses are soft and tender. They do not want to rush.

Then, Diane rolls over on her back and spreads her legs. She guides Rigney to lie on top of her. She reaches between Rigney's legs and guides him into her.

Rigney gyrates his hips slowly in the same manner as Sally had taught him. He hopes Diane enjoys the same.

Rigney and Diane want to share each other. They lock their bodies together.

"We didn't usually do it this way," Diane rasps between deep breathes.

"Do you want to get on top?" asks Rigney.

"No, I like this. I can relax this way. Feeling you move around inside me is comforting and makes me feel warm. Hold me tight, Rigney. I need to forget the outside world right now. Oh, Rigney, why did our world change? Why couldn't it stay the same? Why couldn't we have stayed the same?" Diane's questions are spoken in a soft and sad tone.

"The world didn't change," Rigney whispers calmly. "We're just beginning to discover it."

"Hold me, Rigney! Hold me tight! For this moment, we can feel that we are the whole world!"

"Yes, that's the way I want to feel right now . . . you and I holding each other against the outside. Oh, Diane, I wish we had shared these

164

feelings before."

"I love you, Rigney. You know what I mean—this moment—this experience—what we once felt."

"Yes, I understand," Rigney responds. "I love you the same way."

Tears come to Diane's eyes. She brushes her face against his so that he feels the tears. Rigney eyes moisten.

Their lips come together. They kiss harder.

Diane starts to move her hips. Rigney matches her motion.

After a few minutes, Rigney stiffens as he ejaculates.

Diane pleads, "Hold me tight, Rigney! Use your strength to protect me from the world!"

Twenty minutes later, Rigney pours shots of bourbon for them. They sit on the sofa, now dressed. They sip the bourbon as a toast to their reunion. Diane reminds Rigney of their senior prom night and of the next morning at the Seal Beach pier. "Remember when we toasted to a new beginning?"

"Yes, I think of it often."

Rigney sits in thought for a few moments; then, he asks, "Diane, would you like to come to my parent's Christmas party tomorrow night?"

"They won't mind?"

"Of course not. They always liked you."

"I have changed, and I will wear the same style clothes. I will not compromise the cause to which I now belong."

"My parents have always been tolerant toward the differences in people. They have always respected other people, no matter how different."

Diane response, "I'll come, but I will not lie to anyone. If anyone asks me how I feel about anything, I will tell them the truth."

Rigney considers her words. *Diane is a true convert. She suffers from the common misperception of cause champions, which is that they must convert the world to the so-called truth.* Rigney does not care about this flaw in Diane. He accepts her as she is, and he hopes she will accept him as he is. They have enough in common to be friends. *Hell, twenty years from now both of us will probably look back on this time in our lives and laugh at how naive we both were.* He counsels, "Say what you want. I just ask that you not get into arguments with people. Please don't challenge anyone on what they believe. If you are challenged, just respond that you are not here to argue with anyone."

Diane smiles. "Then, I should not call anyone a war-mongering fascist pig or a heartless bourgeois capitalist, right?"

"Right."

Diane and Rigney hug and say goodbye at the front door.

Rigney's mother and sisters have not returned. Rigney goes back to the third floor family room. The room smells like sex. He opens the windows at both ends of the room. Cold, fresh ocean air floods the room.

Chapter 26

Rigney stands at the open bay window facing the Seal Beach Naval Weapons Station. He retrieves binoculars from the closet and surveys the base. A navy destroyer is moored to the pier. Cranes place weapons and ammunition on the fantail.

I wonder where they are going two days before Christmas. WESTPAC? Vietnam? Does the American public appreciate their sacrifice? I wonder how the American public, including Diane's commune, would react if they knew that American citizens are endangering servicemen by selling national secrets to the Soviets? Would they care?

Diane is a sensitive person. I'm sure that when not influenced by her commune leader, she would be appreciative. I'm sure that she understands her right to be different—her right to protest—is guaranteed by the sacrifice of the American serviceman. Does she really believe that those who agree to serve are surrendering? I wonder what she would think about my mission onboard Columbus.

Rigney scans the destroyer from bow to stern. He watches white-hats move weapons and ammunition forward and into the superstructure. He sees officers directing operations from the bridge wings. Then, the lines are taken in. A tug approaches and pushes the destroyer's bow to face the channel—southward toward the Pacific Ocean. Rigney sees white water churning at the destroyer's stern. The destroyer moves forward. The tug backs away. He sees a lookout on the destroyer's starboard bridge wing talking into a sound powered phone. The lookout shouts something toward the bridge.

As the destroyer steams south through the channel, Rigney stands at attention. When the destroyer is 180 degrees relative from his window, he salutes.

On the signal bridge of the destroyer, the *signalman of the watch* inspects the western fence of the base through deck mounted, fifty-power *big-eye* binoculars. He sees a man standing in a third floor window of a house bordering the fence. The man stands at attention and holds a salute.

The Signalman calls to his superior, "Hey, Chief. I think there's a sand-crab in one of those houses rendering us honors."

"What's he doing?" asks the chief.

"He's standing at attention and saluting. He's saying something, but I don't see anyone next to him."

The chief signalman comments, "Saluting us? That's something you don't see these days from civilians." The chief pauses, then he orders,

"Return the salute."

"What?"

"You heard me."

The *signalman of the watch* removes his eyes from the binoculars, stands at attention, and returns the salute.

"I will do my best to keep you guys safe," Rigney declares aloud as he renders honors. "I will catch that traitorous son-of-a-bitch. That's my promise to you. He will not be a threat much longer."

When the destroyer clears the channel, Rigney lowers his hand and stands easy.

The Next morning, Rigney goes shopping to purchase Diane a Christmas gift. He shops the gift stores on Main Street. He finds the perfect gift—a silver plated *peace symbol* on a silver plated bracelet.

168

Chapter 27

Rigney walks north on Main Street. The buildings and businesses on this narrow street still project the lazy beach-town atmosphere of Seal Beach, California. As a boy, he had frequented all the ice cream and hotdog stands that line the street. As a teenager, his favorite spot was the Main Street Café where he and his surfer friends would have sandwiches and soda pop. He and Diane often met at the café before departing on their dates.

Rigney enters the door of the Main Street Café. The Café has not change since the last time he was here, which was his last week in high school. He feels the old beach town décor. The wooden plank floor is worn with age. 1930s style cabinets and counters line the walls. Old and worn wooden tables and chairs are in no organized manner around the café. Six belt-driven ceiling fans stir the air. Nautical objects hang on the walls.

Like a city landmark, Fat Chad stands at the grill, cooking. He wears the same old, grease-splattered white apron. Chad has owned the café since before Rigney can remember.

The best hamburgers in Seal Beach fry on the old grill. The smell of frying onions permeates the air. Greasy French fries drain in a wire basket over the deep fry.

"Hey, Chad, good to see ya," Rigney says sincerely as he walks by the counter. Chad and the café are part of the best years of his life.

"Hello Rig!" responds a surprised Chad. "Ya look good in that uniform!"

"Thanks, Chad. I'm proud to wear it."

"Glad to hear that. I was in the navy during World War Two, ya know."

Rigney stops and turns toward Chad. "No, I didn't know that. All those years in high school when I came in here you never said anything."

"Why would you be interested? Anyway, most WWII vets don't want to talk about those time—witnesses to so much death. Anyway, I spent three years on a submarine in the pacific."

"No kidding!" Rigney becomes fascinated about this interesting part of Fat Chad's life.

Chad responds by raising his right hand and says seriously, "I swear, and I have a picture of me in my uniform. Would you like to see it?"

"Sure would," Rigney responds with genuine enthusiasm.

Chad pulls a worn, black and white picture from his wallet and hands it to Rigney.

Rigney looks at the picture and is astonished by what he sees. Two people are in the picture. One is a thin and lanky sailor in Dress Whites with a second class torpedoman's chevron on his sleeve and the coveted dolphins pin above two rows of service ribbons. A stunning and voluptuous Hawaiian women stands next to the sailor. They stand on a pier with a WWII submarine in the background.

Rigney looks for similarities between the young and slim sailor in the picture and the 280-pound middle-aged man in front of him. Rigney looks back and forth between Chad and the picture. *Yes, the eyes and mouth and the ears are the same.*

Rigney's eyes fix on Fat Chad's face. He does not know what to say. *Who would have ever thought!*

"That was a long time ago," Chad reminisces. "The woman in the picture was my wife. She died in 1952, before I came to Seal Beach."

Rigney does not know what to say. *Who would have ever thought!*

"I can see that you're surprised. Bet ya never thought that old Fat Chad has an interesting story, did ya?"

"I must apologize, Chad. I just never thought of you anywhere else other than behind the counter and in front of that grill."

Rigney hands the picture back to Chad.

Chad stares lovingly at the picture for a few moments. Then, he sighs deeply, chokes back a sob, and puts the picture back in his wallet.

"Rigney, please do something for me, will ya?"

"Sure, Chad. Anything. What is it?"

"Always remember that everyone has something interesting and of value in their past. Never forget that. Don't be deceived by how they act now or how old they look or how slow they move. You've always been a polite and respectful boy. Please stay that way."

"You got it," Rigney promises as he reaches his hand across the counter and shakes Chad's hand for the first time.

Chad's face shows appreciation that Rigney values his counsel.

"Okay, now," Chad says with misty eyes and an enthusiastic smile. "Diane is in the back waiting for you. You don't need to stay and talk with this salty old fart."

"Okay, Chad. Nice seeing ya! Thanks!" *Who would have ever thought!*

As he enters the back area of the café, Rigney sees Diane sitting at a small table. She chats with four hippie types, two men and two women, who sit several tables away. Rigney thinks that he recognizes one of the two men.

When Diane sees Rigney in uniform, her eyes go wide and her mouth drops open. Obviously, she had not expected that he would show up for their date in uniform. The conversation at the hippies' table ceases when Rigney sits down beside Diane and kisses her on the cheek. Rigney sees his Christmas present to Diane around her wrist.

He reaches for a menu.

"I have already ordered for us," Diane says as her disapproving eyes look Rigney's uniform up and down. She glances at the hippie table as she whispers, "Why did you wear your uniform?"

"I felt like it. Anyway, why shouldn't I? It's what I am, Diane. I am proud to wear it."

"Because so many civilians hate military people," Diane says nervously, followed by a furtive glance at the hippies' table.

"Like who?"

Diane nods toward the hippies' table.

Rigney turns his head to appraise the two men and two women sitting several tables away. His first impression is that except for the beards on the men all four of them look alike. They all have shoulder length hair. They all wear headbands. They all wear the same style faded-denim clothing with *peace symbols* sewn into their denim jackets. They are Rigney's age. All four stare at Rigney. Rigney stares at them while trying to get a feel for their attitudes. The guy who Rigney thought he recognized nods at Rigney with a smile. Rigney nods and smiles back. The other three hippies have a look of disapproval on their faces.

Rigney spends a few moments looking intently at Diane. Then, he comments loudly enough for the hippies at the other table to hear, "Well, I have no problem with all of you wearing your uniforms. So why should any of you have a problem with me wearing mine?"

Diane looks quizzically at Rigney. Low volume chatter spurts from the hippies' table. Rigney hears his name spoken in a male voice at the other table. Rigney looks back at the hippies' table at the guy he recognizes. Rigney tries to remember who he is, but he cannot. Rigney turns his head and returns his eyes to Diane's face.

"What do you mean by saying I wear a uniform?" Diane challenges indignantly.

"The five of you are all dressed the same. Don't you groom yourself and dress yourself in a manner to align yourself with a specific group of people . . . to announce to the world who you are?"

Diane realizes that she never thought of it that way before, but she refuses to agree that her appearance and attire represent a uniform.

"Yes, I guess to some level that could be true," Diane admits. "But we dress like this as a statement of nonconformity. We try to look as much antiestablishment as we can. We want big business, the Military Industrial Complex, and the government in general to know that they cannot control our lives any longer and that we stand against Americans killing Asians in Vietnam. We do not—"

"Change the subject!" Rigney interrupts and orders in a sharp voice.

Diane, surprised by Rigney's abrupt manner, sits in thought for a full minute. Then, she says, "You would be surprised at the number of people who dress like hippies but are not hippies. They dress as hippies at night and on weekends and wear longhair wigs, but on weekday mornings they store their wigs and don their suits and ties and go to their capitalistic jobs."

"Why do they dress up like hippies when they are not hippies?" Rigney asks.

"Gosh, Rig! Where have you been? Does your navy insulate you from what's going on in the world?"

Rigney thinks about that for moment and responds, "For the last two and a half years, I have been buried in navy schools. I mean, I still read newspapers every day. I also read all the weekly news magazines. I think I am well educated on what's going on in the world. But I must admit that I have not keep current on what's going on with hippies, or with people who want to look like hippies."

"Don't you watch TV?" Diane queries.

"I don't watch much television. I can go weeks without watching television. When I do watch television, it's just for a few minutes while my belief is validated that television is just a source of make-believe and entertainment and not a source of truth and fact."

Diane shakes her head in disagreement as she asks, "You think the nightly news reports of death and destruction coming from Vietnam are make-believe and entertainment?"

"I thought we were changing the subject." Irritation edges Rigney's voice.

"No, Rig! I want to know what you think."

Rigney sighs deeply then answers Diane's question. "I think that the war in Vietnam causes death and destruction." He does not like the path this conversation is taking.

Diane shows her confusion with a shake of the head and another quizzical look. "I don't understand. You're not making sense."

"I'm saying that reality is one thing, and what you hear and see from the news media is another thing."

"Rig, the TV shows dead Vietnamese and dead American soldiers. You don't believe they are really dead?"

"I know they're dead!" Rigney's voice still reflects irritation.

"So what part is not truth?" Diane's voice becomes tight and frustrated.

"Why they're dead," Rigney responds in a troubled tone.

"I'll tell you why!" Diane exclaims. "Because our government is fighting an illegal and immoral war—because the Military Industrial Complex wants to fill its pockets with the income from military contracts—because our government has become too powerful and no longer represents the will of the people! That's why they are dead! For Christ sakes, Rig, you say you're educated on what's going on in the world! Why they are dead is obvious!"

Rigney does not respond.

Fat Chad delivers their coffee and sandwiches. He shakes his head sorrowfully at the differences that separate these two.

They are silent for a few moments while taking a few bites of sandwich and sipping coffee.

Rigney finally breaks their silence. "Diane, what you said about why people are dying in Vietnam . . . how do you know what you believe is the truth?"

Diane stares into Rigney's eyes. She does not comprehend why he does not understand the obvious.

"Why do you think it isn't?" she questions back.

Rigney smiles with satisfaction.

"What?" she questions.

"I didn't say I didn't believe the same as you. What makes you think that I don't believe the same as you?"

"Well, I . . . I thought that . . . well, the uniform . . . I mean, you did say . . . I mean you're a military man. Are you playing a game with me? What are you trying to say? Why do you think people are dying in Vietnam?" Diane's tone has become slightly angry.

Rigney does not respond immediately. He thinks about whether he should tell Diane what really bothers him, which is the constant barrage of others trying to convert him. *A constant barrage that has been going on all my life. So much of what I once believed to be the truth would later be shattered with fact and logic. What I had once believed to be sacrosanct and engraved in granite would turn out to be just someone else's faith or cause. The barrage comes from many directions—from my parents—from my uncles—from acquaintances—from teachers and priests. They all had me believing in their perceptions.*

As he grew, he began to question. He went to the library and researched answers on his own. During his teenage years, one belief after the other came under doubt as he reasoned the logic or illogic of it all. Now, he questions everything. He believes no one until he verifies. All the study and analysis that he has done regarding history, religion, and politics just lead to more shattered beliefs and more questions. As he discards the popular beliefs of others, he becomes more distant, more of a loner.

Rigney understands why technical subjects appeal to him so much. With electronics and digital circuitry, the truth is a simple matter of input and output. The truth is that specified input always results with a specified output. It cannot be otherwise. Maybe that's why he buries himself into it.

He finally responds to Diane. "A thousand years ago, governments executed those who professed that the world was round and not flat. Those who held the *round* belief were few and were considered demonic radicals. Royalty and clergy employed torture and death as punishment for such fiendish philosophies. Since about the sixteenth century, popular opinion changed to knowing that the world is *round* and not *flat*."

Diane has no clue as to what Rigney is attempting to convey. "Rig, I was a high school honor student, and I am a third year college student. Anyone with half an education knows about that. What's your point?"

"Ever consider why after it was proven that the world is round that governments did not execute those who still believed the world to be flat?"

"Rigney, please make your point!" Diane sounds exasperated.

Rigney responds confidently, "I conclude from this history lesson that when governments support and believe in lies, those governments violently force lies on its citizens. However, when governments support and believe in the truth, it is not necessary to force the truth on citizens, and those who believe in lies are free to believe in lies."

Diane nods understanding and states, "I understand your conclusion and agree with it, but it doesn't tell me what you believe regarding American involvement in Vietnam."

"I don't have a firm opinion because I don't know what the truth is about us being there. For the time being, I keep my mind open. I stick with the belief that America is not perfect, and we haven't always done what is right. Overall, we have been successful with our republic."

"Rigney, you are missing the point. What difference does it make why we're there? People are being killed. If we pullout, the killing will stop."

"Not true, Diane. The reason we are involved is because one group of people, the communists, are killing non-communists to take over the government. If America pulls out, the killing will continue."

"Rig, why should the internal struggle of any other country be our business. What right does America have to interfere? Why should Americans die over the political differences within another country?"

"Diane, if America does not defend those who cannot defend

themselves, who will? If not America, who? If not now, when?"

"American boys have the right to choose whether or not they go to war," Diane chokes a sob.

"I see," Rigney responds. "You're not against people being killed, just against Americans being killed while defending those who can't defend themselves."

"No! God damn it! People will be killed whether Americans are there or not. It's not our war! Why can't you understand that?" Frustration overcomes Diane. She starts to sob.

The hippies at the other table turn and stare at Diane and Rigney. Except for the one man who Rigney recognizes, they stare with hostility at Rigney.

Rigney moves closer to Diane, and he puts his arm around her. He takes his napkin and pats the tears from her face. Softly and tenderly he whispers into her ear, "Diane, I understand your frustration. I must decide if the fight against communism in Vietnam is worth American lives. We need to fear the spread of communism. Communists have never been voted into power. They have never taken control of any government as a result of democratic vote. Communists always take power by force. I think that if we don't fight the communists overseas, eventually, we must fight them on our shores."

Rigney continues to pat away her tears. They are cuddling together. They feel the heat of each other's body.

Diane looks into Rigney's eyes and says, "I hope you go to college when you get out of the navy. College opened my eyes and helped me understand the corruption in the world. I think that what you learn in college will make you understand it all."

Rigney shakes his head in disbelief. He says to Diane, "I can't believe you said that. The people who got us into Vietnam and those who run our government have college degrees."

"Oh, Rigney. I promised myself that I would not get into the Vietnam argument with you. I want us to enjoy this short time we have."

"Let's drop it, then. I think we must understand that you have made up your mind about it, and I am still trying to make up my mind. We should not let it come between us."

Three of the four hippies from the other table stand and depart the café. The guy who Rigney recognizes walks over to their table. "Look at the two of you . . . together again. But this time you don't look like a pair. If I were to take a picture of you two right now, it would probably win some kind of award."

Rigney looks up at the guy. He searches his memory."

"Rigney, I'm Todd Moyer. We were in high school together. We had some classes together."

Now, Rigney remembers. They were just acquaintances in high school. They had surfed together a few times and had a few short conversations. He remembers Todd Moyer as one who dressed and groomed *ivy league*—letterman sweater and all. Now, he wears faded denim, flowing shoulder length hair, a long beard, headband, and a *peace symbol* on a leather string around his neck.

"Yes, Todd. Please excuse me. I thought I recognized you, but, well, you look so different, now."

"Except for the short hair, you look the same," Todd responds.

Rigney notices that Todd holds a cup of coffee.

"Todd, please sit with us," Rigney offers.

Diane has stopped sobbing and has regained composure. "Yes, Todd. Please sit down," Diane also offers.

Todd sits next to Diane. He looks over at Rigney and comments, "Who'd have ever thought you would end up in the navy."

"I had to join. Otherwise I would have been drafted into the Army."

"You were an honor student, Rig. Why didn't you to college? You would've had a deferment."

Rigney responds, "Going to college was not what I wanted."

Todd emphasizes, "But if you went to college, you could have stayed out of the military."

"I must serve sometime. Why not now?"

"Military service can be avoided in different ways," Todd states with a conspiring tone.

"Todd, I don't think you understand. I wanted to join the navy."

A doubtful expression appears on Todd's face. Todd's black and white view of the world holds that only two types of people walk the earth—those who believe as he does, and those who are wrong.

"Why?" Todd asks.

"Why not?" Rigney snaps back.

Todd has to think about that for a few moments; then, he says, "Because joining the military is a copout. It shows that you support the establishment and the Industrial Military Complex. It shows that you support the military actions in Vietnam."

Rigney shakes his head with annoyance. "*Nope!* I joined for the training and adventure."

"Training and adventure?" Todd questions.

"Yes."

Todd smiles and snorts contemptuously as he remarks, "Sounds like selfish motives. You will never change the world if you remain selfish."

Rigney responds pleasantly, "I never attempted to disguise my ambitions as anything else. I feel no obligation or inclination to follow any path other than what pleases me. It's my right to do so. It's guaranteed by The Constitution, which, by the way, is defended by those in uniform."

Todd becomes irritated at the inference that he is against defending The Constitution, and Rigney senses Todd's irritation.

"Todd, I am not saying that you do not support defending The Constitution. I think that you are doing that in a way in which you think best."

Todd's irritation subsides. Todd and Rigney just stare at each other.

Diane does not like the direction this confrontational conversation is taking. She takes advantage of the pause to say, "Todd, Rigney, please change the subject. Can't we just reminisce old times?"

Todd and Rigney nod with agreement.

An awkward silence falls upon them.

Todd speaks first, "When I get together with high school friends, one of the things that always comes up is the time you laid out Mister Thompson and Jimmy Carriano in the boxing ring."

Jimmy Carriano! Rigney repeats to himself. *Yes! That was his name!*

"I try to forget that day. It wasn't one of my best."

Todd laughs. "What are you talking about? They both deserved it. That punch you landed on Jimmy is the most powerful I ever saw. Even better than Cassius Clay, I bet."

"You were there?" Rigney asks.

"Yeah. We were in the same gym class."

Diane looks quizzically back and forth between Todd and Rigney. "When did that happen?"

"You don't remember?" Todd asks. "It was all over school for weeks."

"I never knew about it. What happened?" Diane asks, looking at Rigney.

"It was early in the school year, before we got serious."

"I'm surprised you never told me."

Rigney stares at Diane as he realizes that Diane does not understand anything about him.

Rigney shifts his eyes to Todd and says, "I sometimes wonder whatever happened to Mister Thompson."

"He teaches at USC now," Todd answers. "After he was fired by the school district, he went back to college and finished his doctorate. This is his first year as a professor at USC."

Rigney shakes his head in lack of understanding how Mister

Thompson could get another teaching job.

"As for Jimmy Carriano, he was killed in Vietnam last year."

Diane swings her head toward Rigney and states in an *I told you so* manner, "Now that is some hard fact and truth equal to proving that the world is round. Don't you think?"

Rigney's heart skips a beat as he sits stunned by the news. Sadness appears on his face. He feels sympathy for Jimmy and his family.

Todd, obviously confused by Rigney's reaction, comments, "I'm surprised that the news affects you that way. I'd think Jimmy meant nothing to you."

"His death affects me. I knew him, not well, but I knew him."

Todd studies Rigney for a moment; then, he says, "Rigney, I never realized how sensitive you are."

Diane smiles with appreciation at Todd's remark.

Todd looks at his watch. "I must go." Todd stands. He looks at Diane and asks, "Will you be at the protest rally tomorrow?"

Diane glances quickly at Rigney and says, "I haven't decided yet."

Todd extends his hand and says with appreciation and sincerity, "Rigney, great seeing you again."

Rigney stands and shakes Todd's hand.

"Another award winning photo—peacenik and war monger!" Todd jokes.

Rigney's eyes follow Todd out the café door.

Rigney shifts his gaze toward Diane and inquires, "Protest rally?"

"I thought we said we would drop the subject." Diane avoids Rigney's eyes.

"I'm not criticizing, Diane. I'm interested to know."

"I will tell you. Then, we drop it. Okay?"

"Okay."

"We will rally at the ROTC offices at UCLA. We will protest the university's support of the Vietnam War. Some of the guys will burn their draft cards."

Rigney decides not to argue the wisdom or purpose of such protests. His deepest concern is how such protests affect the morale of those who obey the laws of their country and are fighting and dying in Vietnam.

Chapter 28

RM3 Rigney Page looks at his watch—7:10 p.m. He spent the entire day traveling, starting with his departure from his hometown of Seal Beach, California. He looks out the airplane window. All he sees is black with occasional spotted lights indicating human life somewhere below. His plane will land in Norfolk, Virginia within the hour.

As he stares out the airplane window, the events of the last month dominate his thoughts. December started with two weeks of discovery as he went through ONI indoctrination. The condensed ONI training provided him with a glimpse of espionage and counterespionage. ONI trained him on weapons that he had only seen in books or in the movies. He learned how to cover his true intent with deceptions in behavior. He was taught how to use his hands and feet to kill another human being. He gained self-confidence in his ability to handle himself, physically.

After ONI indoctrination, he went home on leave to Seal Beach. He visited family and old friends. *Such drastic changes in people! What a change in Diane! What about Fat Chad! Who would have ever thought!*

Rigney disembarks the airplane and enters the Norfolk airport terminal. He goes to the men's room nearest his arrival gate. He stands in front of a urinal and unbuttons the thirteen buttons on the trousers of his Service Dress Blue uniform.

As he washes his hands, he looks in the mirror and appraises his rumpled appearance. His five o'clock shadow is well on its way to becoming tomorrow morning's beard. He spends a few minutes picking lint from his wrinkled, Melton cloth uniform. He re-ties his neckerchief. Then, he buffs his shoes with a paper towel. He worries about not looking sharp when he reports aboard *Columbus*. He becomes concerned that the *Columbus's* OOD will not permit boarding of such a rumpled and unshaven douche bag.

At baggage claim, he retrieves his seabag. He lifts the seabag onto his left shoulder and holds it in place with his left arm. A sign tells Rigney that newly reporting Naval personnel are to proceed to the navy desk at the end of the building. At the navy desk, a third class petty officer tells Rigney to wait for the naval station bus.

At 10:00 p.m., Rigney walks outside to the bus boarding area. The damp, foggy night chills his body. He stands on the concrete boarding pad with ten other sailors. Only five of the sailors have a seabag. Rigney buttons his peacoat at the collar and turns the collar up to keep his neck warm. The sign on the front of this bus announces it destination as *Naval*

Operations Base.

The bus driver directs, "Listen up! Carry your seabag on the bus with you."

As Rigney boards the bus, the bus driver asks, "What ship ya goin' to?"

"USS *Columbus.*"

The driver checks his list. "Get off at Pier 2."

The bus moves quickly through the dimly lit streets of Norfolk. All traffic lights along the bus's path flash yellow. Few cars and few people find it necessary to be on the streets at 10:00 p.m. on this Thursday night—four nights before the New Year.

Inside the bus, no one speaks. Most of the sailors appear familiar with this travel routine. Some of the sailors went to sleep as soon as they sat down. Those sailors not asleep just sit quietly.

Rigney stares out the bus window. The buildings and streets of Norfolk appear to be one-hundred years old and echo a bygone era. During his time in the navy, Rigney had heard many negative comments about Norfolk. The perennial label of Norfolk personality being '*Dogs and Sailors Keep off the Grass.*' Rigney wonders about the validity of such a saying.

Rigney sees an unending chain link fence on the right side of the bus. He sees military type buildings inside the fence. *Must be the Norfolk Naval Station.* He observes a sign announcing MAIN GATE. The bus moves briskly past the MAIN GATE. On the left side of the bus, Rigney sees a large sign advertising *The Home of Ole Bill* Uniform Store. Other signs advertise bars, stores, pawnshops, and locker clubs.

The bus stops at Gate 1. The spotlights around the guard shack cast a glare. Rigney looks past the gate and toward the piers. He sees the outline of ships. The mist and fog make it difficult to see detail.

The bus proceeds through the gate. Rigney looks out the window in the direction that he believes the water to be. He cannot see far. He does see a street sign that says the bus travels on Decatur Avenue. The fog does not allow a distant view. At the first pier, Rigney makes out the shadows of two ships. One ship is moored to port on the left side of the pier, and another ship is moored to starboard on the right side of the pier.

The bus stops. "Pier 2!" the driver announces. "USS *Columbus!*"

Rigney buttons his peacoat and slips his hands into his black navy issue gloves. He grabs his seabag from the overhead rack and walks to the front of the bus.

The bus door opens. Rigney steps down to the pavement, which is wet from a recent rain. Puddles of water accumulate on the uneven road surface. Around him at varying distances, steam shoots up from a dozen indiscernible sources. He notices many large buildings.

The bus drives away.

Rigney turns to face the pier. He holds his seabag in his left hand. He walks to the head of the pier where a barricade prevents unchecked entry and routes people past a guard shack. Rigney stops at the guard shack. A second class petty officer, bundled in his peacoat, holds up his hand as an indication for Rigney to stop. Rigney notes the Shore Patrol armband on the guard's right arm and the guard belt with nightstick around his waist.

Rigney looks at the petty officer and waits for further instruction.

"Show me your I.D. card and state your purpose for entering the pier."

Rigney is distracted as he looks down the pier. He sees a ship on his left and a ship on his right. The ship on the left cannot possibly be a cruiser—*too boxy*. The ship on the right, a tall two stacker must be the *Columbus*. He remembers the pictures from *Jane's Fighting Ships*. He squints his eyes as he tries to see the length of the ship.

"Come on, sailor; show me your I.D. card."

Rigney snaps out of it and obeys the shore patrol petty officer. He reaches inside his peacoat to the right breast pocket of his jumper and pulls out his I.D. card.

The guard yanks the card from Rigney's hand and holds it under the light and studies it. Then, he looks at Rigney's face. "Okay, so you're Petty Officer Page. State your purpose for entering the pier."

Rigney, still concentrating on the cruiser, states, "I am reporting aboard the *Columbus*."

The Shore Patrol Petty Officer responds, "Okay. You may proceed."

Rigney walks along the pier. He passes several sailors who wear dungarees and foul weather jackets and carry toolboxes. They pay no attention to him.

The long, towering, and intimidating USS *Columbus* fascinates him. The mighty cruiser, officially designated as a Heavy Guided Missile Cruiser, rises one-hundred-ninety feet from the water line to the top of the masts. Her length stretches six-hundred-seventy-five feet. He remembers the stats from *Jane's Fighting Ships*. The dark night and fog prevent Rigney from seeing the top of the masts.

As he approaches the *Columbus*, he shifts his seabag to his left shoulder. *I must keep my right hand free for salutes.*

The rounded bow towers high above him. On the bow, the number 12 displays bold and bright.

Rigney continues his journey down the pier along the *Columbus* starboard side. He hears the sounds of the harbor—whistles and foghorns in the distance. He feels a vibration under his feet—*some motor performing its duty*. Rigney also hears water lapping at the side of the *Columbus*.

His head stays turned toward the cruiser. He comes abreast of the forward TALOS missile launcher on the Main Deck. The Main Deck is about twenty feet above the pier. The missile launcher has two large white colored missiles attached. The missiles point forward and up at 45 degrees. Immediately aft of the TALOS missile launcher is a towering structure that has two large drum like fixtures on top of it; the aft drum stands higher than the forward drum. *Must be part of the TALOS missile guidance system*. Just aft of the missile guidance structure, the ships superstructure towers into the foggy night.

Rigney approaches a gangway. A sign at the gangway entrance states *Officer's Gangway*. He stops and looks up and finds where the gangway and Main Deck meet at the quarterdeck. A white canvas sign—announcing "USS *Columbus CG-12*"—connects to the Main Deck rail. A white canvas cover serves as the officers quarterdeck overhead.

Another missile launcher catches Rigney's attention. This launcher sits slightly aft and one deck up from the quarterdeck. Two TARTAR missiles are attached to the launcher. The TARTAR missiles are blue in color and are smaller than the TALOS missiles on the bow.

Then, Rigney notices an officer on the quarterdeck waving at him. Rigney focuses on the waving figure. *Looks like LTJG stripes on his shoulder boards.*

Rigney salutes the officer. The officer returns the salute.

"State your purpose, sailor?" the officer says loudly over the din of harbor noise.

"I am reporting aboard, sir," Rigney replies in a similar loud voice.

The officer points aft and says, "Board at the enlisted gangway."

"Aye, aye, sir."

Rigney looks down the pier and sees another gangway. He walks down the pier. He comes abreast of amidships. He sees two tall stacks. The tops of the stacks are not clearly visible through the dark and the fog. The starboard gun mount sits outboard of the second stack on what Rigney estimates to be 02 or 03 level.

A few seconds later, Rigney climbs the enlisted gangway. As he reaches the top of the gangway, he sees a chief petty officer with a JOOD armband. Standing adjacent to the JOOD is a second class petty officer who wears a guard belt around the waist of his peacoat.

Rigney salutes the JOOD and recites, "Request permission to come aboard, sir."

The chief returns the salute. Then, says, "Permission granted."

Rigney steps off the gangway and onto the ship's deck; then states, "RM3 Page reporting as ordered, sir."

"Okay, Page, let me have your orders?"

"My orders are in my seabag."

Rigney removes the clip that holds the top of his seabag closed. He reaches into the seabag and pulls out all the copies of his orders and the yellow envelope that contains his records. He hands the chief the original and all copies of his orders.

The chief scans the orders and says, "Orders were cut at Naval Medical Center Bethesda. Is that where you were stationed prior to coming here?"

Rigney does not understand the chief's question, but he responds, "Yes, Chief."

The chief writes the date and time on the ORIGINAL copy of Rigney's orders. Then, the chief records Rigney's arrival time into the Deck Log.

The chief takes one copy of Rigney's orders and hands the envelope back to Rigney. "Report to the personnel office at 0800 tomorrow."

"Aye, aye, Chief."

"Wait here for a few minutes. I'll have the *messenger of the watch* take you to the master-at-arms shack to get linens. Then, he will take you to CR Division's berthing compartment. There you can find a rack and unpack your gear."

"CR?" Rigney queries.

"Yeah, CR, Communications Radio."

Rigney nods his head in understanding; then, he asks, "Chief, how will I know what rack I can have?"

"Any rack that has no linens and an empty rack-locker under the mattress."

"Okay, Chief. Thanks."

"No problem . . . and welcome aboard *The Tall Lady*—the best ship in the Atlantic fleet. I hope your tour aboard is successful, rewarding, and satisfying."

"Thank you, Chief, I am pleased to be aboard," Rigney responds. Then, after a short pause, Rigney queries, "*The Tall Lady?*"

"Yeah, *The Tall Lady*. It's the *Columbus*'s nickname. All ships have one."

Rigney nods understanding; then, he stands quietly and waits.

A few minutes later, a seaman with a white guard belt around the waist of his peacoat arrives with two cups of steaming hot coffee. He hands one cup to the chief and the other cup to the *petty officer of the watch*.

Rigney stares at the seaman. He is about five and a half feet tall and looks like he is thirteen. *Well, I guess he could be seventeen. You can join the navy at seventeen. He looks so young!*

"Manson, take Page to the master-at-arms shack to get linens. Then, take him to the CR Division berthing compartment."

"Okay, Chief. Where's the CR Division berthing compartment?"

"How long you been onboard, Manson?" the chief asks tersely.

"Two months, Chief, right outta boot camp. I've spent all my time chipin' paint off the Foc'sle. I don't know where everything is yet."

The chief points to a hatch just aft of the gangway and says, "Go down the ladder there to the mess decks. Stop at the master-at-arms shack first. Then, go all the way forward until you cannot go any further. There will be a hatch that leads down to the CR Division berthing compartment."

"Aye, aye, Chief. Will do. I know where that is."

"Then immediately return to the quarterdeck. No slacking!" the chief orders.

"Aye, Chief!" Manson responds smartly.

Manson walks over to Rigney. "Come on, Page. I'll take care of ya."

Rigney grabs the handle of his seabag, pulls it up, and follows Manson through the hatch and down the ladder to the aft mess deck. Immediately, Rigney's nostrils fill with the smell of the ship, which is a combination of engine oil, cooking grease, floor wax, and cigarette smoke. They cross the aft mess deck from starboard to port. Rigney notices that the deck is covered with black and red tiles, and the deck is highly polished. The dining tables are welded to the deck. The tables are immaculate, not a speck anywhere. Rigney also notices a door at the aft end of the mess deck with a Marine Corps emblem. The sign under the emblem says MARINE DETACHMENT.

They stop at the master-at-arms shack where Rigney is issued two sheets, two pillowcases, and one thick wool blanket. He signs for the linen.

The duty master-at-arms is a short and heavyset first class signalman. He speaks tersely toward Rigney, "You are responsible for the linens and must return the same number when you transfer off the ship, or you must pay for them!" Then, he slams the door shut in Rigney's face.

As they walk aft, Rigney asks Mason, "Do you know why the master-at-arms was so angry at us."

"Most of the M.A.A. petty officers are mad at everybody. Don't take it personal. They're always yelling at people."

Manson leads Rigney forward along the port passageway. They step through several watertight doors. They come to the end of the port passageway. They are standing in a large berthing compartment that Rigney thinks must berth 100 men or more. A sign on the bulkhead states DECK DEPARTMENT BERTHING.

Manson stops and looks down a ladder to the compartment below.

Manson says, "That must be CR Division down there. I seen guys go down there all the time. I just didn't know who they are."

Rigney scans the deck department berthing compartment. No one moves about and no one lies in their rack. Rigney knows from *Jane's* that *Columbus's* complement numbers about one-thousand. He asks the messenger, "Where is everyone? I've only seen a few sailors."

"We're in stand-down for Christmas. Only the duty section must be onboard. Everyone will be back onboard before we depart for the MED on Wednesday."

Manson starts down the ladder toward CR Division Berthing compartment. Rigney follows.

As Rigney reaches the bottom of the ladder, he sees a small table and four chairs between the bottom of the ladder and the port bulkhead. The bunks—racks—are stacked three high. On the starboard side of the compartment, Manson talks to a sailor who lies in a middle rack with the bunk light on. Rigney recognizes Larry Johnson.

Larry jumps out of his rack. The lanky blond haired *navy brat,* as Larry always calls himself, wears a white t-shirt and white boxer shorts.

"Hey, Rig. What are you doing here?"

"It's a long story."

Manson looks at the two of them and states, "Okay, Page. This is CR Division. As the chief said, take any rack that you want. I've got to get back on deck. See ya."

Manson disappears up the ladder two rungs at a time.

"What are you doing here? I thought you went to submarine duty."

"I was medically disqualified. Some sort of ear problem that can't deal with the atmospheric pressures that sometimes happen in a sub."

Larry stares into Rigney's face. "Well, anyway, welcome aboard *The Tall Lady.*"

"Why *The Tall Lady?*"

"*The Tall Lady* has something to do with how tall the masts are. It's the *Columbus's* nickname; its handle. All ships have one, don't submarines?"

"I don't know."

"What submarine did you serve in?"

"Never served in a submarine," Rigney answers.

"You never served in a submarine? Where the hell have you been all this time?"

"Schools mostly. This is my first command."

"What school takes 20 months?" Larry expresses astonishment and he also expresses a realization. "Have been on this bucket for that long?!"

Rigney realizes he gave too much information. "Like I said, it's a long story and I am tired."

Larry nods understanding and says, "I must make a message run at 0600. Let's get some sleep. We can talk then."

"Message run?" Rigney inquires.

"NAVCOMMSTA Norfolk has our communications guard. The *duty radioman* makes several runs a day."

"That sounds good, Larry. I will find a rack."

Rigney scans the dimly illuminated berthing compartment. The only illumination in the compartment shines down from the upper compartment, from Larry's bunk light, and from light shining through an open door to the head. He estimates 30 racks in the compartment, with most of them made up. He checks a few racks with no bedding and with empty rack-lockers. "I will take this one," Rigney announces as he holds up the lid of an empty rack-locker. He has selected a middle rack in the forward starboard corner. The corner is concealed from most sources of light and provides the most privacy.

Rigney evaluates his new home, which is a space three feet high by three feet deep by six feet long. Rigney shakes his head in disappointment while comparing his new home to his quarters at ONI Cheltenham. He expels a deep sigh.

"I advise against that rack," Larry warns.

"Why's that?"

"That's a prime rack. It's off-limits until we get underway for the MED next Wednesday.

"What do you mean by off-limits?"

"That's Rouché's rack."

"Who is Rouché?"

"RM2 Philippe Rouché—the toughest man I have ever known. He's short and stocky, and he's hard as nails. He's always getting into fights on the beach. Last MED cruise, he took on two Spanish sailors in a Barcelona bar. Not only did he whip their asses, he nearly killed them with his bare hands. Those Spaniards beat on Rouché hard. They broke his nose and cracked a few ribs, but Rouché appeared not to even feel it. He outlasted those Spaniards. He wore them out. That's when he went to work on 'em. He kicked them and punched them. When they fell, he stomped on their backs and legs.

"Wasn't even his fight. The Spaniards were pushing around another sailor from the *Columbus*. Rouché butted in and dared those Spaniard to make it two against two.

"Rouché is sort of a legend around the ship. People stay out of his way. He's a real bully. He pushes his way around the division and usually gets what he wants."

Rigney finds this hard to believe. "How is it possible to have a bully in the navy? Isn't he put on report when he bullies people?"

Larry exhibits thoughtfulness for a few moments. Then, he answers, "He is careful not to bully anyone who is first class and above. You know—the lifers. He is very careful around the officers. Yeah. Rouché has the officers buffaloed."

Rigney's expresses doubt.

"Rig, you're in *the real navy*, now. One of the first things you will learn is that the navy is separated into two levels—second class and below and the lifers. Lifers are the first class and chiefs. Rouché usually bully's the second class and below. Everyone in that group is afraid of him, and they don't complain to the lifers."

Rigney responds with a doubtful frown on his face, "Doesn't seem to be the navy way. Not the navy I've known."

Larry explains, "You're in the fleet, now—*The Real Navy*. You can throw out what you learned in navy schools and from navy training manuals."

"I must see this to believe it," Rigney challenges.

"You're still the *prove it to me* skeptic that I knew from Radioman 'A' School."

"Yeah. I guess I am. Why has Rouché vacated his rack?"

"About four weeks ago, he got into a fight at the Purple Onion. That's a club over in Ocean View. He was hurt bad. A couple of the M.A.A. petty officers came down here, emptied his rack, and packed his sea bag. They said he was transferred to Portsmouth Naval Hospital and probably would not be back. Anyway, a couple of his buddies from First Division went over to see him. They came back and told us that no one was to take his rack. His buddies said that Rouché said he would heal quickly and would be back for the MED cruise. No one has the balls to take his rack. if Rouché isn't here when we get underway on Wednesday, I'm sure there will be rush to claim his rack."

"What if a lifer wants the rack?"

"The lifers already have the best racks. They won't want it."

"Well, if he does come back, I have no problem with giving up the rack. I don't want any trouble, especially after just reporting aboard. I will just move to the bottom rack."

Larry looks and Rigney and shakes his head. "Rig, believe me. If Rouché finds out you've taken his rack, it won't make any difference that you are willing to give it back. He will be angry just because you had the nerve to occupy it after he ordered people to stay out. He won't touch you aboard ship. He will find you on the beach. That's when he goes to work on ya. During last MED cruise, some sailors who crossed his path came back to the ship beaten and bleeding. They didn't say it was Rouché, but they had words with Rouché previously."

"Alright, Larry. Thanks for the warning. I will see you in the morning."

"Okay, Rig. See ya in the morning. By the way, the ship is in stand-down for the holidays, no reveille in the morning. If you're not awake when I come back from the message run, I will shake ya."

"Sounds good. Thanks."

Larry climbs into his rack and turns off the bunk light.

Rigney unpacks his seabag and puts the contents into the rack-locker, which is the locker space under the mattress. The mattress sits on the lid of the locker. He makes the rack. He undresses and goes to the head to brush his teeth and take a shower. Fifteen minutes later, he comes out of the head wearing only a towel around his waist. He puts on fresh boxer shorts. Then, he climbs between the sheets and quickly falls asleep.

Chapter 29

Rigney awakes and opens his eyes. The compartment is still dark. He looks at his watch—0625. He closes his eyes and goes back to sleep.

Rigney feels someone holding his hip and shaking it.

"Hey, Rig, wake up. It's 0650. Time for chow."

Rigney opens his eyes and sees his friend Larry Johnson smiling at him.

"I'm up, Larry."

Larry advises, "I'm going into the head. I will be ready in about five."

Rigney remains prone and ponders the best way to get out of this middle rack. He is on his back. He rolls to his left and lets the weight of his legs pull him over the edge. He lands on his feet facing the rack. *That works!*

He senses someone near him. He looks to his left and sees a sailor dressed in t-shirt and dungaree pants standing a few feet away. The sailor pulls a dungaree shirt out of his locker. The sailor looks surprised to see Rigney. They stare at each other for a few moments. Rigney notices that Larry is standing farther aft in the middle of the compartment and watches Rigney.

The sailor steps close to Rigney and puts out his hand. "Hi. I'm Frank Carter. When did you report aboard?"

Rigney shakes Frank's hand. "Last night. My name is Rigney Page. Nice to meet you."

Frank dons his dungaree shirt. Frank wears *second class* chevrons.

Rigney can see the contents of Frank's open locker. Rigney notices a Dress Blue jumper with one hash mark. *Frank is on his second hitch.*

Frank Carter looks at Rigney; then, he looks at the rack that Rigney just exited. He looks back at Rigney. "Rigney, you should move to a different rack."

"Thanks for the advice, Frank. Larry over there has already warned me about Rouché."

"He told you about Rouché, and you still took the rack!"

"Yeah. I'm hoping that Rouché does not come back; then; I have a prime rack."

Frank stares at Rigney with mock admiration on his face. "I guess you deserve the rack just for having the balls to take it."

Frank gives Rigney a thorough look over and says, "Maybe Rouché won't mess with you. I wish you luck."

189

Frank turns to Larry and says, "I'll see ya in MAIN COMM at 0745."

Frank goes up the ladder.

Rigney finds all this fuss about Rouché to be incomprehensible. *The man has transferred. Even if he comes back, I am willing to give up the rack, which shouldn't anger anyone. How can experienced navy men be so apprehensive over a person who is subject to military law and discipline? Maybe this Rouché is more than a bully and thug.*

Rigney looks at Larry and says, "Larry, give me 10 minutes to shave and get dressed. Then, we can go to chow. What uniform should I wear?"

"Dungarees and white hat." Larry responds. "And wear your blue working jacket. We'll be going on deck."

Rigney gets his shaving kit from his locker and proceeds to the head."

Larry walks over to the table, sits down, and grabs a magazine to read.

Ten minutes later, Rigney and Larry are walking aft along the port passageway. They reach the mess decks and spend a few minutes going through the steam line to get their food. Then, they walk to the aft mess deck and pick a table away from the few other sailors who are eating before going on watch.

Rigney does not want to start answering Larry's questions. So, he decides to ask a barrage of questions and not give Larry an opening for a question.

"What is stand-down?"

"Stand-down is a time period over the holidays or when just returning from a long deployment. Holiday routine is in effect—no reveille and no taps. Duty section personnel are the only people required onboard. The duty section takes care of all the in-port watches and working parties. By the way, were you told to report to the personnel office this morning?"

"Yes."

"You may find it difficult to check in. There'll be a duty personnelman, so you should be able to check in with the personnel office. I don't know about the other offices. You may need to wait until Tuesday. The senior chief is not back till Tuesday. So, you won't be assigned to a duty section until then. That means you won't have a liberty card. Without a liberty card, you can't leave the ship. You should go to the CDO, the Command Duty Officer. Explain your situation. He should give you some kind of special liberty chit. Hold on. Let me check the Plan of the Day."

Larry walks to the forward area of the mess decks and returns with a clipboard with a single sheet of paper attached.

"You're in luck. The CDO is the operations officer. CR Division works for him. Well, we work for him until *The Flag* comes aboard on Tuesday."

"*The Flag*?" Rigney queries.

"Yeah, COMCRUDESFLOT EIGHT—a rear admiral. When he and his staff come aboard, CR Division works for him. We're sort of detached from ship's company.

"Anyway, the new duty section takes over at 0800. After checking in with the personnel office, go to the CDO. He'll probably be in the wardroom. That's where he normally hangs out. I will be leaving the ship after my turnover to Carter. You want to go with me to MAIN COMM while I perform the turnover?"

"Yeah. I'll go."

"Before I leave the ship, I will help you find the CDO."

The conversation pauses while they eat a few bites of food. Rigney senses that Larry is about to ask a question. Rigney preempts Larry's question. "Tell me more about this Rouché. Has he been put on report for fighting?"

Larry takes a moment to chew and swallow his bite of food; then, he responds, "Rouché never throws the first punch. What he does is insult, taunt, and get in the face of the person he wants to fight. Ya know; he invades the guy's space. Rouché gets all over him, verbally. He makes his insults in a calm voice. He sneers and snickers. Rouché finds some flaw in your appearance or manner and he pushes you on it. If he senses you're sensitive about it, he pushes more. He pushes so the other guy throws the first punch. Even if the first punch hits Rouché, he doesn't seem to feel it. Then, Rouché throws a few punches, maybe two or three. He hits you in the face and stomach until he knocks you down—just enough punches to claim he used reasonable force against his attacker. He seems to get a *high* out of it and he gets away with it. He also borrows money from people and doesn't pay it back. I don't think it's because he wants or needs the money. I think he does it to hold power over people."

"Don't any of these guys tell him to back off or get lost? Why don't they just walk away?"

"Rig, you just have to see Rouché in action. He maneuvers you into a corner and won't let you go. Some guys have tried to push passed him. Rouché claims later that they guy put his hands on him first. Man, he just makes you feel like a pussy if you try to walk away. He wants you to stand up to him."

"Larry, he ever try this with you?"

"No."

"Why not?"

Larry considers the question for a few moments; then, he replies, "It might be because I am not a threat to him. I mean, he only gets into it with guys that are bigger than him, look tough, or stand out in some way. I never really thought about it before. I'm just an average guy that does his job. I never seem to cross his path."

"I assume he gets into more fights than anyone else. Doesn't the chain of command get suspicious?"

"No, most guys don't report it because they threw the first punch, and it usually happens on liberty. He will insult and taunt sometimes aboard ship but kind of careful like. He wants the fighting to wait until he's on liberty."

Rigney takes a few more bites of his breakfast before asking his next question. "You seem to know a lot about this. Have you been present when these things happen?"

"Oh, yeah! I have seen it down in the compartment. But like I said, he doesn't get too heavy with this while onboard. Most of the time, it happens in bars in the MED . . . when we're on liberty."

"Have you ever seen Rouché lose it? Ya know, get to the point where he gets angry enough to throw the first punch. Like, what's his sensitive spot?"

"Yeah, now that you mention it. Several times last MED cruise there were a couple of times when he insulted people and they just ignored him. Rouché can't stand that. If you ignore him when he's insulting you, he gets mad, even shouts. He will get angrier and angrier when he says things to people and they ignore him."

Rigney's eyes look distant as he considers Larry's explanation.

"Rig, why are you asking so many questions about Rouché?"

"I want to know the best way to stay out of his way. I don't want any trouble."

Larry snickers and shakes his head slowly. "You got yourself a whole lot of trouble if Rouché comes back and finds you have taken his rack."

Rigney considers that he should vacate the rack to avoid trouble. However, part of his cover is bringing negative attention to himself.

Larry stands up and says, "Come on. Let's go to MAIN COMM so I can get relieved."

They carry their trays over to the ports side and dump them into the scullery. Larry leads them along the port side passageway and up a ladder to the Main Deck. Larry opens a hatch, and they both step outside and onto the portside weather deck. The cold, damp, and foggy weather affirms the need to wear a blue working jacket. They walk forward

192

twenty feet. Then, Larry leads them up a ladder. They walk across a flat area between the two stacks.

Larry stops. He turns toward Rigney, then advises, "This is where CR Division musters and holds quarters on normal workdays."

Rigney scans the deck and observes a large rectangular structure affixed to the same deck level on which they are standing. "What is that," he asks Larry as he points to it.

"ASROC launcher—Anti Submarine Rocket. We use ASROC to kill enemy submarines."

The two sailors proceed across the ASROC deck. Then, they climb a series of outside ladders attached to the port side of the superstructure. At the top of the highest ladder, Larry leads them through a hatch to the inside of the superstructure.

"This is the 04 Level." Larry informs. "We must go up two more inside ladders to the 06 Level. MAIN COMM takes up most of the 06 Level."

When they are at the top of the ladder and standing on the 06 Level, Larry educates Rigney as to the layout. "That forward door is to Radio Central. Over there on the starboard side is the Signal Flags Locker. That's where they store and repair signal flags."

Larry nods toward the door at the top of the ladder. "This is the forward door to MAIN COMM."

Larry punches in the cipher lock code, and the door unlocks. They enter MAIN COMM and find Frank Carter sitting at a desk in the Message Center. Frank reviews copies of message traffic from the previous day.

Larry briefs Frank on the events of the previous day.

Rigney wanders into other rooms of MAIN COMM. He notes the positions of radio receivers, patch panels, crypto equipment, and teletype machines. Then, he steps back into the Message Center. Frank Carter looks up and notices that Rigney must have been roaming the other spaces.

Carter picks up the Visitor Log clipboard and hands it to Rigney. "You need to log in," Carter says. "You're not on the access list yet. You're not allowed to be alone in the communications spaces."

Rigney writes his name, rank, and the date in the log. Carter tells Johnson, "You should authorize since you brought him in here."

Larry Johnson signs the log and sets it back on the desk.

"I relieve you," Frank Carter announces to Larry Johnson.

"I stand relieved," Larry Johnson responds.

Rigney clears his throat.

Johnson and Carter look at Rigney.

193

Rigney asks, "There must be some transmitter rooms somewhere. What kind of transmitters do we have? What about offline crypto? Where is that?"

"Can you operate and tune transmitters?" Frank asks Rigney.

"Yes," Rigney replies. "Mostly HF transmitters in Single Sideband and FSK mode."

Frank looks dubiously at Rigney and says, "Larry says this is your first command. Where did you learn about Single Side Band and FSK? I don't remember it being taught in Radioman 'A' School."

Rigney lies. "Oh, when I was in high school, I had a friend who was a HAM operator. He'd let me tune his transmitter and receiver and operate his HAM station from time to time."

Frank remains doubtful. "You operated an FSK HAM station?"

"Well, yes, a little," Rigney lies again.

Frank looks doubtful, but Larry isn't. Larry understands that Rigney is quite capable of knowing these things.

Frank's face continues to display doubt and sarcasm. He asks, "How did you learn your rate? Are you a push-button third class?"

"No, I am not a push-button. I took and passed the RM3 test the first time. I am now eligible to take the RM2 exam. I have completed the courses and the practical factors."

Frank shakes his head in doubt. It took Frank two and a half years to make RM3 and four years to make RM2.

Rigney realizes again that he gives away too much information. His enthusiasm caused him to speak before thinking. *I must be careful. Frank is not easily deceived.*

Larry changes the subject. "I'll locate the CDO." Larry reaches for the phone and dials a number. "Sir, this is RM3 Johnson in MAIN COMM. Can you tell me where I can find the CDO? . . . Okay. Thank you, sir."

Larry looks at Rigney and says, "CDO is down in his stateroom. Let's go on down there."

Frank asks Larry, "Are you off 'til Monday, now?"

"Yes, I am," replies a smiling Larry. "The wife and I are going to use up six months of love making this weekend."

"Okay," Frank responds with a shake of his head. "I'm going to the mess decks for some coffee. I'll see ya two later." Frank departs MAIN COMM.

"When did you get married?" Rigney asks.

"After the last MED cruise."

Rigney smiles. "I thought you'd rather be off the ship now than help me with this liberty thing."

"I have to give my wife enough time to throw out the Marine."

"What?!" Rigney queries, bemused.

"Never mind. It's a saying."

They find the CDO.

The CDO advises, "All the appropriate security officers are gone until Tuesday. You can't get on the Radio Access Lists until then."

The CDO writes out a *request chit* for Rigney that grants special liberty through Tuesday morning. The CDO tells Rigney to check in with the duty personnelman and duty disbursing clerk within the hour. With both Rigney and Larry standing there, the CDO calls the duty personnelman and the duty disbursing clerk. He tells the personnelman that RM3 Page will be there shortly to deliver his record. The CDO tells the disbursing clerk to make sure Rigney is paid up to date this morning.

They step out of the CDO's stateroom and into the Officers' Country passageway.

"He's an understanding officer," Rigney tells Larry.

"Yeah. He's one of the best officers I've seen. Always lookin' out for his troops."

"Larry, I need to ask a favor of you."

"Sure, Rig, anything you want, man."

"Please don't tell anyone that you know me from the past or know where I have been for the last 20 months."

Rigney's request puzzles Larry. "Sure, Rig. I don't think I really know, anyway. You said something about school. Sure, I will keep quiet about it."

"Thanks," Rigney responds appreciatively.

"Can you find your way around? I need to get home."

"Sure, Larry. Go ahead. Thanks for all the help."

Chapter 30

One hour later Rigney has checked in with the Duty Personnelman and Duty Disbursing Clerk. Now, he sits alone in the CR Division berthing compartment. He looks at his watch—10:15 a.m. He wonders what he should do. He had checked in with the personnel office. They gave him a *Check-In Sheet* and told him to start checking in Tuesday morning when everyone would be back aboard. The disbursing clerk gave him $172.00 in back pay.

What do I do now?

Rigney walks over to his rack and considers catching up on some sleep. Instead, he begins to reorganize his rack-locker.

Ten minutes later, an announcement comes over the ship's announcing system, 1MC: *"NOW, MUSTER THE STANDARD TWENTY-MAN WORKING PARTY ON THE PIER!"*

Twenty minutes later and after completing reorganization of his rack-locker, Rigney stands at his rack and stares at the locker's contents. *What should I do now? Should I reorganize again?*

Rigney hears someone stomping down the ladder.

"Anyone down here?!" A loud voice booms.

Rigney's rack cannot be seen from the bottom of the ladder. He walks aft to the center of the compartment. Incredulous at what he sees, his eyes go wide with disbelief. The fattest sailor that Rigney has ever seen stands at the bottom of the ladder. The sailor wears Undress Blue uniform and has a first class boatswain mate chevron on his left sleeve. On his right sleeve, he wears a M.A.A. armband—Master-at-Arms—a ship's policeman.

The sailor's belly hangs so far over his trousers that his t-shirt is exposed for three inches all around. The sailor's jumper stretches to the bursting point over his belly. The flab on his chin hangs down at least four inches. He stands a few inches taller than Rigney. He has black, thinning hair and looks in his mid-thirties.

Rigney shakes his head in disbelief. *His waist must be six feet around!*

The master-at-arms steps closer and scrutinizes Rigney's name stencil, located above the left breast pocket of this dungaree shirt. "Are you on watch, Page?!" the master-at-arms sputters, almost a shout.

"No, I'm not in the duty section."

"Why didn't ya muster for the working party?" The master-at-arms' raised tone accuses more than questions.

"I didn't know that I was supposed to. I just came aboard—"

"Don't give me no shit, Page!" the BM1 booms with an angry voice. "If you're aboard, you're on duty. You fuckin' twidgets think you're exempt from everythin'. Now get your fuckin' white hat and your fuckin' foul weather jacket and report to the storekeeper on the pier."

"Excuse me. What's your name?" Rigney asks in a soft and calm voice.

The fat sailor answers tersely, "Genoa! BM1 Genoa!"

"Genoa, I don't understand why you are speaking to me in such a vulgar and angry manner. Have I done something wrong?"

"Shut up, Page! Don't give me no shit, and I won't put you on report for not reporting to the working party!" Genoa's body shakes with anger.

Rigney wonders why this sailor is so mad at him. Then, he advises, "I don't have a foul weather jacket."

"Jesus Christ! How long ya been aboard? Never Mind! Come up to the master-at-arms shack, and I'll check the records. If ya don't have one by the records, I'll issue you one! We won't let this be another fuckin' excuse for another fuckin' twidget to get out of another fuckin' working party!"

As they walk aft, the BM1 mumbles repeatedly, "I ain't gonna allow another pussy-ass twidget get out of another fuckin' working party. Vulgar, my fuckin' ass . . . sum-o-bitch'n twidgets . . . they all think they're prima donnas . . . not this fuckin' time and not this pussy twidget."

Rigney follows the fat BM1 to the master-at-arms shack.

Genoa checks the records. "Looks like ya don't have one. Haven't ya been on a working party before? *Never mind!* What's your jacket size?"

"I'm a 42 to 44 long—depends on the cut."

"That's an odd size," Genoa mumbles.

With his back to Rigney, Genoa bends over and digs through the pile of army-green colored, ragged and dirty foul weather jackets that lie in the corner of the master-at-arms shack. Five inches of his butt crack are showing. The scene reminds Rigney of a cartoon.

The man's butt is as big as the ass end of a truck!

"Everythin' here is too fuckin' small. Let me check in the back where the new ones are. *Stand fast* while I go back there. You know what *stand fast* means? Right?"

"Yes, I know what it means," Rigney replies. He is totally amused by this situation; he hopes it does not show.

Genoa is gone for a few minutes. He returns with a new foul weather jacket. He holds up the jacket to see the numbers on the back; then, he records the number on an index card with Rigney's name on it.

"Here's your jacket. When you transfer from *Columbus*, you must turn this back into the master-at-arms. Otherwise, you will be charged for it. Understand?"

"Yes, I understand."

Rigney puts on the foul weather jacket. The feel is soft and warm and comfortable.

"Do ya have work gloves?"

"No."

"God damn it, Page! Haven't you been on a working party before? Never mind! Hold on!"

Genoa disappears into the back room again. When he returns, he hands Rigney a pair of wool glove-liners and a pair of worn, heavy leather gloves. Genoa makes another note on the index card."

Rigney slips the glove liners over his hands; then, he slips on the leather gloves. *Warm and comfortable!*

Genoa looks at Rigney's shoes. "*Jesus Christ, Page! Don't you have any boondockers?*" The master-at-arms refers to the standard navy work shoes.

Rigney looks down at his shoes. He wears highly shined dress shoes.

"Yes, they're in my locker. Shall I go back and put them on?"

"Fuck no!" shouts the master-at-arms. "You've missed too much of this working party, already! Go to the pier—now! Report to the second class storekeeper. I'll check the roster sheet later. Your name better be on it. If not, I will find you and put you on report! Genoa pauses, stares and Page, and shouts louder, "Do you understand!"

"Yes, I understand," Rigney replies softly. *Why is Genoa so mad at me? Maybe he's mad because he has the duty or maybe he's mad because he's so fat.*

Rigney turns and walks across the aft mess deck. He climbs the ladder to the Main Deck. He renders the proper honors at the enlisted gangway then steps down the gangway to the pier. He sees a big truck and about twenty sailors stacking boxes. He sees a second class petty officer dressed in dungarees and white hat with a clipboard; the second class petty officer appears to be in charge.

Rigney approaches the second class and says, "RM3 Page reporting for the working party."

The SK2 shakes his head in disgust and says in a confrontational tone, "Jesus! Another twidget late for another working party!"

Rigney shrugs.

The SK2 directs, "Go over there and start taking boxes from the sailors in the back of the truck. Stack the boxes with the rest over there. When we're done unloading the truck, we'll carry the boxes aboard to the stores locker."

Rigney points to the clipboard. "Is that the roster? If it is, please put my name on it. The duty master-at-arms insists."

"Okay, Page, but I'm reporting that you are forty-five minutes late."

Reporting to whom? Rigney wonders to himself.

Rigney spends one-and-a-half hours on the working party. Each box weighs thirty pounds and contain various canned fruits. Rigney carries each box without much effort up the gangway and down the various ladders to the stores locker. Everyone else pants, grunts, and complains.

These guys are so out of shape.

Chapter 31

After the working party, Rigney goes directly back to the CR Division berthing compartment. He sheds his dungarees, folds them properly, and places them in his rack-locker. He slips into his Dress Blue uniform. He stuffs his I.D. card and Special Liberty Chit in the breast pocket of his jumper. Then, he puts on his peacoat and white hat.

At the Enlisted Gangway, the JOOD is the same chief that was there when he was on the working party.

Rigney salutes, "Request permission to leave the ship, sir."

The chief does not give permission. He stares at Rigney. Then, he asks, "You must show your liberty card and I.D. card."

"Oh, excuse me, Chief. I didn't know that."

Rigney reaches into his jumper breast pocket and pulls out the Special Liberty Chit and his I.D. card. He hands the chit to the chief. The chief studies the chit and Rigney's I.D. card. Then, he asks, "Didn't I just see you on the working party a while ago?"

"Yes, Chief."

"Aren't you in the duty section?"

"No, Chief. I am not."

The chief walks over to a phone mounted on the bulkhead; he dials a number. Rigney cannot hear. The chief has his back to him. The chief hangs up, walks back over to Rigney, and hands him back the chit.

"Everything's in order. OPS Boss says it's okay for you to go on liberty. You have permission to leave the ship."

"Okay, Chief. Great! Thanks!"

Rigney snaps to attention, raises his right hand in a salute, and recites, "Request permission to leave the ship, sir."

The chief smiles and returns the salute and replies, "Permission granted."

Rigney walks down the gangway toward the pier.

"Hey, Page!" the chief shouts after Rigney.

Rigney turns and looks at the chief.

The chief points aft. "You must salute the ensign."

Rigney nods understanding. He snaps to attention and salutes aft. Then, he proceeds down the gangway to the pier.

"What a boot camp," the chief mutters, amused.

Rigney walks off the pier and onto Decatur Avenue. He looks north along Decatur Avenue and sees Cruisers, Amphibious Landing Ships, and Aircraft Carriers.

Most of the buildings near the piers are large warehouse buildings. Some of the buildings cover an entire block. The appearance of area and loud machinery noise are typical of an industrial area. Sailors and civilian workers walk about. This may be the week between Christmas and the New Year, but naval ships still require constant attention and maintenance.

He turns east on Morris Street. The farther he walks from the piers, the less people he sees. After a few long blocks, he comes to Maryland Avenue, which looks like a major street. Rigney stops a sailor and asks him directions to the Navy Exchange.

Rigney finds the Navy Exchange. He purchases some good running shoes and some extra exercise shorts and t-shirts. He also purchases a larger gym bag.

After leaving the Navy Exchange, he finds the NAVSTA Library. This area of the NAVSTA is more modern than the pier area and has manicured landscaping. The buildings are two and three stories and made of brick.

Rigney spends several hours in the library reading newspapers and magazines. He decides to find the NAVSTA Gym for a workout. The Librarian tells him how to find it.

Only a few people exercise in the gym. He has the weight room to himself, and he spends an hour working through his weightlifting routine.

After his weight workout, he finds a half-court basketball game that is short on players. He gladly joins the game when invited. After another hour, he feels hungry. He looks up at the clock on the wall—4:10 p.m. One of the basketball players tells Rigney that the dining facility is just a short distance away.

At 5:50 p.m., Rigney enters the dining facility. Because he does not have a meal pass, he must pay 55 cents for dinner. He walks the stainless steel food line. He is pleased with the selection of vegetables, fruits, and lean meats. He passes on the mashed potatoes and desserts.

Most of the dining room is roped off from use. Only a few mess cooks are working. Rigney overhears some of them talking about the light workload during stand-down. Most tables are not occupied. Rigney assumes that most sailors have gone home for the holidays.

He feels lonely. He misses Sally's company. His only true male friend, Thom Mundey, lives in San Francisco. He hasn't seen Thom in two years. Rigney appreciates his renewed friendship with the unassuming and nonjudgmental Larry Johnson. Larry is truthful and lacks the ability to be deceitful. Larry accepts everyone as they are. When they attended Radioman 'A' School, Larry was the only one to standup for Rigney when Rigney was wrongly accused of misconduct by some of his envious and conniving classmates. Larry's testimony turned the situation around and the accusers were eventually punished for lying.

Rigney eats slowly. He is in no hurry to go . . . *where? Not back to the ship.* He decides to see a movie. He had noticed the base movie theater near the Navy Exchange.

The theater marquee announces that *The Dirty Dozen* is playing. He has not seen it. Fortunately, the movie is long. No more than twenty people occupy the theater. Rigney finds the movie's story to be unbelievable but excellent entertainment.

When he exits the theater, the cold, damp, and windy air slaps his exposed skin. He looks at his watch—9:45 p.m. He pulls his peacoat collar up to cover his neck. The long and dark walk along Morris Street toward the piers increases Rigney's loneliness. The stark lights cast dark shadows of the buildings. He is the only person walking these streets at this hour. The machinery noises from this morning are gone. Only distant foghorns break the silence between his footsteps. Steam shoots up from random locations along the piers.

At 10:15 p.m., Rigney steps down the ladder into the CR Division berthing compartment. He walks toward his rack. Frank Carter is asleep in the rack just aft of Rigney's rack.

After undressing and folding his uniform properly for storage in the rack-locker, he slips on his shower shoes and goes to the head. By 10:45 p.m., he is in his rack. He feels comfort in the warmth under his blanket. He decides to depart the ship tomorrow before 0800, before the new duty section comes aboard.

Chapter 32

Rigney opens his eyes. He hears movement in the darkened berthing compartment. He sees Frank Carter dressing in Service Dress Blues. Rigney looks at his watch—0645.

Rigney jumps out of his rack.

Frank Carter looks over at Rigney and nods hello.

Rigney responds politely, "Good morning, Frank. How was your duty day?"

"Routine. Just routine. Where were you all day? I was expecting to see you hanging around the compartment."

"I went ashore. I mostly walked around the naval station. Have you been relieved, already?"

"No, I'm going on the morning message run."

Rigney remembers seeing the NAVCOMMSTA Communications Center building when he was walking around the naval station the day before.

"How do you get there?" Rigney asks. "That's a good distance from here."

"The duty driver takes me."

Rigney lays his Dress Blues on his mattress.

Carter stares at Rigney's Dress blues for a moment. He asks, "Are you going ashore again, today?"

"Yeah."

"How are ya getting off the ship? You don't have a Liberty Card, do ya?"

"I got a Special Liberty Chit from the operations officer. He said I could come and go as I please, but I must be here by 0700 Tuesday morning."

Frank wonders why Rigney was not put into a duty section. *The boot comes aboard and immediately gets four days off. Shit, he could have cleaned the COMM spaces instead of me.*

Frank Carter frowns and shakes his head as he climbs the ladder.

What's wrong with him? Rigney wonders.

After shaving and showering, Rigney comes back to his rack and puts on his Services Dress Blue uniform. He places several sets of clean exercise clothes and his new running shoes into the gym bag.

By 0750, he has eaten breakfast and walks down the enlisted gangway.

Rigney exits the naval station through Gate 1. He walks east on

Admiral Taussig Boulevard. He passes some locker clubs and comes to the *Home of Ole Bill* Uniform Store. The Naval Station's Gate 2 is directly across the street.

He enters *Ole Bill's* and browses the racks of *crackerjack* style uniforms. He discovers a section of *crackerjacks* made of gabardine cloth. Rigney wears the navy standard wool fabric. He has seen many sailors in the gabardines, which are lighter weight and do not wrinkle as easy. He thinks it a good idea to buy a set. He plans on taking liberty as much as possible in the MED.

Rigney searches the racks of gabardine uniforms and finds his size jumper and trousers. He enters the dressing room. The uniform fits well and looks better on him than the wool uniform.

He removes the gabardine uniform and slips back into his wool uniform and proceeds to the sales counter. The salesclerk is a gray-haired middle-aged man with crossed anchor tattoos on his forearms. Rigney speculates that the clerk is a retired navy man. He asks the clerk, "How long to put a third class radioman crow on this uniform?"

"Only a few minutes. We have a seamstress on duty."

"Okay. I will take this set of gabs and wait for the crow to be sewn on."

"Sparks, did ya know we have a special on those *gabs*? Buy two and ya get the second one for half price, including the second crow and having it sewn on."

Rigney calculates the total price and decides to buy two sets of gabardines. He also buys two more white hats and two more neckerchiefs. And because he could be advanced to second class while on the MED cruise, he also purchases two additional gabardine radioman crows.

Thirty minutes later, Rigney exits the uniform shop and crosses the street. He enters the naval station through Gate 2. Loaded down with his gym bag in one hand a large shopping bag in the other hand, Rigney walks to the NAVSTA Library.

He spends most of the morning in the NAVSTA library and the NAVSTA gym.

At 1230, he enters the NAVSTA dining facility for some lunch. He makes a large salad and pours a bowl of hearty chicken vegetable soup. He walks over to a table near a window, sets his tray down, and removes his peacoat.

After several minutes of eating, he wonders what to do after lunch. He is bored and lonely. He wonders why Brad Watson wanted him to report to the ship so early. *I could have waited until after the New Year.*

As is his normal habit, he eats slowly. He decides to go on the prowl for women after lunch. He looks around the dining room and sees many open tables. Only one woman, a second class radioman, sits in the room. She sits with four other radiomen. Rigney considers that they are on lunch break from the Communications Center, which is just a short distance away. He wonders how one goes about finding female companionship in these surroundings. *I guess one must go off base . . . but where?*

Rigney decides that after he eats, he will drop off his bags at the ship then take a bus or a taxi into town.

"May I sit with you?" a female voice with a southern drawl asks.

Rigney looks up into the face of a tall, slim, and pretty woman with short brown hair and brown eyes. She looks late twenties. Her attractive face has a few lines around the eyes and mouth. She wears a first class yeoman crow with two hash marks on the left arm of her Service Dress Blue uniform. She holds a tray of food.

She smiles at him and asks again, "May I sit here with you?"

"Yes, please sit," Rigney responds as he points to a chair across from him.

She does not sit across the table as Rigney expects. She sits in the chair next to his. Her perfume envelops him.

I didn't think it would be this easy!

The first class WAVE organizes her plates and silverware. Then, she takes a few bites of food.

"What's your name?" Rigney asks.

"My name is Barbara Gaile."

She did not say YN1 Gaile. She does not want to be formal. This is good!

"Hello, Barbara, my name is—"

"I know who you are," she interrupts with a whisper. "You are Apollo from Operation Jupiter."

Rigney sits stunned—totally surprised. His mind races back to his ONI training as to what he is supposed to do next. Now he remembers. She did not provide an authentication. Rigney quickly calculates in his mind the authentication number—*four zero eight eight*. He decides to give her 60 seconds to give the authentication. If she does not give the authentication, he will pick up his things and walk straight for the door. His heart pounds, his face flushes, and he feels sweat on his neck and armpits. He fears what may come next.

"Take it easy, Apollo," she whispers as she smiles directly at him. "Authentication is four zero eight eight."

Rigney relaxes. For a moment, he considered what he would do if she tried to detain him.

"You look like I said something naughty to you," she says flirtatiously. "That's good. We need to look like a couple engaged in intimate conversation."

"In the chow hall?" Rigney questions as he looks around the room. No one seems to be looking at them. He questions, "Wouldn't people think that you're too old for me?"

Barbara responds with an exaggerated southern drawl and fake hurt feelings. "My! My! You must sweep women off their feet with such complimentary remarks."

"Oh! I didn't mean it offensively. You took me by surprise. I was not prepared. I never considered that I would be contacted in here."

"Actually, this place is perfect. After following you all day yesterday, I was hoping you would go somewhere that I could contact you. When I saw you come in here after the gym last evening, I figured you would be back here today."

"You followed me all day yesterday? I never noticed."

"I hope not," she responds casually. "Otherwise, I would not be doing my job correctly. By the way, how was *The Dirty Dozen*? I haven't seen it yet."

Rigney thinks back on yesterday. He does not remember seeing her anywhere.

"Uh, um . . . *The Dirty Dozen* was very entertaining. When did you start following me?"

"Yesterday morning. When you left the ship."

Rigney shakes his head slightly; he is amused with himself for not noticing an attractive woman following him.

Barbara watches Rigney closely. She is surprised by his youth.

After a short pause, Rigney asks, "Why did you contact me?"

Barbara opens her purse, retrieves a piece of paper, and hands it to Rigney. "I made contact for two reasons. The first is to give you that piece of paper. The second is to get a report from you on what you have observed so far."

Rigney retrieves the *ONI report codewords* from memory. "My report is ZULU BRAVO OSCAR ZERO." The codewords translate to *nothing to report*.

Barbara memorizes the words. "Any narrative?" she asks.

Rigney contemplates if he should provide a narrative to go along with the coded report. Brad Watson had told him to provide a narrative only when clarification is essential. "No, I have no narrative."

Barbara accepts the report with a smile. "Okay. I will relay your report."

Rigney looks at the paper she gave him. The paper contains written directions for two locations aboard *Columbus*. Rigney assumes the locations are where the Beretta handguns are hidden.

"You are to memorize the information on that paper before going back to *Columbus*. Once memorized, you must destroy it."

Rigney acknowledges with a nod and sticks the piece of paper in his breast pocket.

They both continue eating in silence. Then, Rigney starts an informal conversation with several questions regarding her life in Norfolk. As they talk, they both begin to feel an attraction to each other. They stare into each other's eyes as they talk. They listen intently when the other speaks. They move closer together so that their bodies touch.

Rigney looks at Barbara's hand to see if she is wearing an engagement ring or a wedding band. She does not.

Barbara already knows that Rigney is not married or engaged.

Rigney pulls the piece of paper from his breast pocket. He stares at the writing on the paper for about 30 seconds. Then, he looks up and into Barbara Gaile's eyes. He has a sly grin on his face when he says, "I think it will take several days for me to study and memorize this. I think I need a quiet place to study, probably off base. Do you have any suggestions?"

Barbara knows exactly what he means. "I thought you said I was too old for you?"

"Oh, no. I don't think that. I thought others would think that."

"I have an apartment in Virginia Beach. You can stay with me for the weekend."

"I'm agreeable," Rigney blurts quickly.

"Not so fast, Rigney. For now, you can plan on sleeping on the couch. I have been briefed on you, but I have only known you for thirty minutes. My physical being tells me to throw the rules to the wind and have a whirlwind weekend romance. My sensible being thinks that is the wrong thing to do. I am undecided about you, but I do not want you to leave and return to your ship."

"My friends call me Rig."

"My car is in the parking lot."

Chapter 33

Barbara drives her car out Gate 2 and waits at the red light at the intersection of Admiral Taussig Boulevard and Hampton Boulevard.

Rigney stares southward on Hampton Boulevard. He observes one pair of Shore Patrolman on the corner of every block.

The traffic light turns green, and Barbara turns left onto Admiral Taussig Boulevard. During the drive, they chat about small things. They both avoid talking about their ONI affiliations. Such talk is out of bounds. They discover their common interest in scuba diving, which they talk about in depth.

Barbara turns onto Virginia Beach Boulevard and drives east.

Rigney notices that most of the cars on the road have NAVSTA Norfolk stickers on their windshields.

"How far do you live from the base?"

"It takes about an hour and fifteen minutes during rush hour. It's not too bad today because it's Saturday. Is this your first time in the Norfolk area?"

"Yeah. I have heard a lot about it since I've been in the navy—lots of bad things."

Barbara chuckles. "I suppose you've heard a lot of '*shit city*' and '*dogs and sailors keep off the grass*' stories?"

"Yes, a lot of stories like that."

"I had heard them too. I have been here for over two years, and I can tell you with certainty that those stories are nonsense. I think people who don't know how to adapt and take interest in new surroundings tell those stories. The Norfolk area is a pleasant place to live. I just wish my navy job were more exciting."

Rigney stiffens with silence and looks straight ahead. They are not supposed to talk about ONI.

Barbara notices his silence and manner. "Oh, no. You don't understand. I am the Correspondence Supervisor in the Naval Station Administration Department. I work in the same building as the commander of the naval station. What I did today happens infrequently. My command does not know about what I did today."

Rigney turns and looks at her questioningly. He does not understand her explanation. *Does she not work for ONI? But then, of course, the commanding officer of* USS *Columbus does not know about my ONI affiliation either.* Rigney knows he should not ask any questions about ONI work. He says, "I don't think I totally understand, but I will not ask any questions regarding that area."

"Well, anyway, I dislike my job so much that I was leaving the navy.

I think those years in Europe really spoiled me. Then, the XO called me into his office and wanted to know why I was leaving the navy after ten years. I told him that I was bored with it."

"You're not getting out, now?"

"No, I'm staying."

"What changed your mind?" He often wonders what motivates people to make the navy a career.

"I was not looking forward to another two years here before my normal rotation is up. However, my enlistment is up in March. I want to do something different. I didn't know that I could transfer somewhere else as a reenlistment incentive. I thought they only did that for those reenlisting for the first time. You know, after you reenlist the first time, the navy thinks they got you for twenty."

"No, I didn't know that. I'm not knowledgeable on how this reenlistment stuff works."

"I agreed to reenlist for orders. I transfer to Naples, Italy next month."

"Looks like we are both leaving," Rigney states. "The *Columbus* sails for the MED on Wednesday."

Barbara smiles and says, "With both of us departing the area soon, it looks like this weekend is it."

"Barbara, from what I have learned about you in the last hour, I think that you and I could become real friends. I hope you feel the same. I totally understand that you would not want a romantic weekend knowing that we might not see each other again."

"Rigney, I'm thirty years old. I know my own mind, and I know what I am doing."

"The idea already has my heart pounding," Rigney admits.

"Me too," She also admits; then, she chuckles and says, "I just hope that I don't get arrested for statutory rape."

"Very funny," Rigney responds sarcastically.

Barbara pulls into an apartment complex. Her apartment is on the second floor.

Two minutes after entering the apartment, they are in her bed, they are both naked, their arms are wrapped around each other, and their lips are locked.

Chapter 34

Yeoman First Class Barbara Gaile, codename Magnolia, performs occasional tasks for ONI. She is not permanently assigned to ONI, and ONI does not control her duty assignments. ONI recruited her to perform short-duration, low-risk tasks in the geographical areas where she just happens to be stationed at the time. Her commanding officers are not advised that she occasionally serves an ONI purpose.

ONI started the program of recruiting these *napping* agents in the early 1960s. Their identities are classified top secret. Brad Watson's predecessor at ONI created and implemented the program. The program provides a means of added secrecy, compartmentalization, and an ability to get tasks done quickly. ONI Headquarters asks its field agents to be watchful for possible recruits. Only E5 and above and those who are on their second or later enlistment are eligible for recruitment. Only those who exhibit mature behavior and high intelligence are recruited. These *napping* agents have only one ONI contact—an ONI Controller. Contact and coordination between the ONI Controller and the ONI *napper* is accomplished through personal contact and with the use of unique codenames, codewords, and authentication procedures. The ONI Controllers that fulfill these roles are full-time ONI Field Agents, usually an O3 or O4. Some of these ONI Controllers are civilians of grade GS14 or GS15.

ONI Controllers exercise extreme caution to ensure that tasks do not interfere with the *napping* agent's normally assigned duties. ONI does not want the commanding officers of these personnel asking compromising questions.

ONI recruited Barbara Gaile in 1963. She was a second class yeoman, YN2, assigned to Headquarters Allied Forces Europe in Paris France. She was noticed after she assisted an ONI field agent. The ONI field agent was posing as an allied military policeman who was investigating the theft of office furniture. His ONI mission was tracking the theft of NATO classified material. There were three suspects. Barbara was asked to plant three separate files of fake classified documents. Each file had unique details that if compromised would identify the traitor. Barbara's additional task was to keep the undercover ONI agent informed as to whom checked out which files. The traitor was caught, and Barbara was an unsung hero.

Barbara was raised in Pensacola, Florida. Both her parents were teachers, and they lived an upper-middle class lifestyle. After graduating from high school, she attended college for a few years. She did not return for her junior year. Instead, she joined the navy in 1958. When family and friends asked her why, she said college was boring. She announced she wanted adventure and wanted to see the world. She did not think a teaching degree from an insignificant teachers college was going to do that for her.

During 1960 while stationed in Charleston, North Carolina, she married a sailor she met in her command. Before they were married, his behavior imitated the amicable Dr. Jykel. After they married, he became the brutal Mister Hyde. The marriage lasted eighteen months.

After the divorce, she decided to reenlist with guaranteed orders to the NATO Headquarters in Paris, France. She took advantage of her European assignment and traveled often. Barbara received excellent evaluations. Her superiors held her in high regard for her competence and reliability. She had a few lovers while stationed in Paris but no one special. While in Paris, she enthusiastically agreed to become an ONI *napper* agent. She was disappointed that she had only performed a few tasks for ONI during the Paris tour.

Her tour in France ended in 1965, and she arrived in Norfolk shortly thereafter. Every few months she takes several days leave and goes scuba diving in the Bahamas. Every now and then, her ONI Controller tasks her to deliver notes and relay reports.

ONI has tasked Barbara seven times. She has gained a reputation as a competent and resourceful *napper*. About a year ago, she asked her controller about the possibility of joining ONI full-time as a field agent. Her controller advised her that she did not have the qualifications. The best he could do would be getting her assigned to the administrative offices at ONI Headquarters in Suitland, Maryland.

"No thanks," she responded. "I would just be doing the same thing there as I do here."

Her controller assured her that these tasks, although appearing insignificant, are vital to national security. "Without people like you," the controller had commented, "Operations could not be as compartmented as they are."

She had decided to leave navy at the end of her current enlistment, and she notified her chain of command of such. Then, several weeks ago, her commanding officer told her she could have her choice of three European assignments, if she reenlisted. Her choices were Rota Spain, Bremerhaven Germany, and Naples Italy. At first, she said no. Later, she went to the library and researched the three locations. She had been to Germany and other locations in Northern Europe many times when she was stationed in Paris. Rota was a possibility, but Naples was centrally located in the Mediterranean and would give her rapid access to other Southern European locations. She reenlisted and will transfer to Naples next month. She is excited about going back to Europe.

Last week, she was tasked to pass a piece of paper to Apollo and to relay a report from him. Her task with Apollo was the first time that she was tasked to follow someone and pick the most suitable place to meet. She was given four days to complete the task—the longest she had ever been given. She was excited about being assigned a more complex task. She was told to follow Apollo from the ship until he was in a place where a casual encounter between them would not be suspect. She was not briefed on what the piece of paper contained or the nature of Apollo's mission. She knew his report would be coded, and she would not know what it meant.

 She was given Apollo's photograph to study. *Good looking,* she thought, *but don't they have a more recent photo?*

She was also given a short list of details about him, which didn't tell her much. The details did advise of his age and marital status. *Twenty years old . . . must be an error?* The list stated that he is a weightlifter and basketball player. She speculated that there was a good chance he would go to the NAVSTA gym sometime in the first few days.

Yesterday, Magnolia sat in her car in a parking lot across from Pier 2. Navy Security had stopped once and asked her for her I.D. card and her purpose. She had told them she was waiting for her boyfriend, who should be off duty soon. At 1255, Apollo walked off Pier 2 and onto Decatur Avenue. She followed him all day. She considered contacting him in the dining facility. But as she was exiting her car, he departed. She stopped following him when he went into the NAVSTA theater.

Today, Magnolia knew she could not park across from Pier 2. Two days in row would draw too much attention to her. At 0800, she parked her car in the lot across from the NAVSTA gym. Apollo did not disappoint her. He went into the gym at 1015. He departed the gym at 1220 and entered the dining facility at 1230. Magnolia entered the dining facility a few minutes later.

Chapter 35

Rigney lies naked in Barbara Gaile's bed. He lifts his head off the pillow and looks over at the clock on the nightstand—11:43 a.m. He lowers his head back down on the pillow and sighs deeply.

Barbara Gaile lies naked and curled next to him. Her hand rests palm down on his stomach.

"More," Barbara purrs as her hand moves lower.

"Barb, we have been at this since yesterday afternoon! We've had sex in one form or another at least . . . I don't know. I lost count. Is it nine times? I am sore. I need medical attention."

"Barbara giggles and responds, "I would get the first aid kit, if I could walk."

They both chuckle.

Barbara expels a deep sigh; then says in an appreciative tone, "Now I know why older women fantasize about younger men,"

"I need sustenance," Rigney pleads. "We haven't eaten since lunch in the chow hall yesterday."

"Okay," she relents. "I'll make some bacon and eggs."

Rigney stands up slowly. He feels dizzy.

Barbara lifts herself off the bed. She groans. She walks slowly around the front of the bed. She puts her arms around Rigney's neck and looks wantonly into his face. "One more big kiss. Then, we eat."

They embrace in an arousing kiss; then, they draw apart and start walking toward the bedroom door.

"Where did I put my t-shirt and shorts?"

"Oh no you don't," insists Barbara as she slips into a robe. "If I only have you for the weekend, you will walk around here naked. So that we don't waste time when we feel the urge again."

"Then, you must too," demands Rigney.

Barbara lets the robe fall to the floor.

Rigney stares at her body.

She smiles.

He compares her to Diane Love, who is twenty, and to Sally Macfurson who is twenty-six, and to Cathy Gillard who is eighteen. *They have different bodies, and each are sexy and attractive in their own way. Barbara is thin with small rounded hips and small rounded buttocks. Her breasts are proportioned properly for the frame of her body. She has just a little flab around the love handles, but it is not distracting. She's in good shape.*

"What are you staring at?" she asks with her exaggerated southern drawl. *"I'm blushing!"*

213

Rigney thinks for a moment before responding. "Do you exercise regularly?"

"No exercise. I think that thin is in my genes. Everyone in my family is thin. I don't eat a lot, which is probably why I stay thin."

"I hope that I can be in as good shape as you are when I am thirty," Rigney states flatly.

"My! My! You have improved with your compliments in the last twenty-four hours." Her southern drawl is deeply exaggerated. "Now that you have said that, Rig, I hope when you're thirty you will be able to say the same thing about me again."

"I'm sure I will," Rigney compliments with a smile.

Barbara stares appreciatively at Rigney for a moment; then, she says, "I must say this, Rigney. You are the sexiest looking man undressed that I have ever seen. Where does all that body hair come from? It's like a fur coat from your shoulders to your ankles. It's really a turn on . . . like a big huggable bear."

Rigney just smiles, "Let's eat, now. Please!"

While they eat, they tell each other more about their lives.

Barbara tells him about her failed marriage and her physically abusive husband. "I haven't seen him since I hit him in the head with a frying pan and walked out. He had yelled at me and had punched me all night. The last time he came at me, I hit him with the frying pan. He fell to the floor. I grabbed my purse and ran out. I never returned. I left everything I had in that apartment—clothes, toothbrush, my car, everything. The Navy took care of me, though. I went to the WAVE barracks and asked the duty master-at-arms if I could stay there. I remember her well. She was a first class personnelman . . . big and fat . . . and as nice a person you could find anywhere. She scrounged up some bathroom items for me, including makeup. The next day, she took me to the exchange, and I bought some clothes. We still write. She is about to retire from the navy."

"You've never heard from him since?"

"He called me at work a couple of times. He said that if I didn't come back to him, he would hurt me bad. I told him I had a restraining order that said he was not allowed to come within one-hundred feet of me. I told him I would call the police if I saw him again."

"Whatever happened to him?"

"I don't know. We were both on our first enlistment at the time. He could still be in the navy or maybe back in his hometown. I just don't know."

"I hate bullies!" Rigney blurts. "Especially women beaters! The only thing they deserve is having their brains beat in!"

Barbara is taken back by Rigney's brutal burst of words. This side of him is totally unlike the gentle and caring lover she has come to know. She considers the manner of the young man before her. She sees two sides of him. On one side, he his calm and soft-spoken and he is caring and gentle. On the other side, he appears tough and brutal. *He is only twenty. What is his value to the ONI? It must have something to do with the Columbus.*

Rigney tells her a little bit about his home in Seal Beach. He speaks enthusiastically when talking about surfing and building his Heath Kits.

After a few moments of silence, Barbara suggests, "Rig, how 'bout we go out for dinner tonight to celebrate New Year's Eve. I have a favorite restaurant on the Virginia Beach Boardwalk.

"Boardwalk?"

"Yes, it's right on the beach. I can call and get us reservations."

The mention of a beach excites him.

"All I have is my uniform to wear. I have changes of underwear and socks in my gym bag, no civvies."

"Let's both wear our uniform," she urges enthusiastically.

"Okay! It's a date."

Fifteen minutes later, they are back in bed.

Chapter 36

Rigney and Barbara arrive at the boardwalk restaurant at 7:00 p.m. The New Year's Eve diners are festive. Laughter and chatter permeate the room. The restaurant employees know Barbara and call her by her first name. Rigney is impressed.

Rigney looks at the menu. The prices are high.

Barbara offers, "Dinner is on me. I will use my credit card."

"Credit Card? I've seen advertisements in magazines. I don't know how they work."

"You've never seen anyone use a credit card?" Barbara expresses surprise.

"No. How does it work?"

Barbara explains.

Rigney does not know what to order. They agree that Barbara will order both the food and the wine. She orders lamb for herself and the prime rib for Rigney. Barbara also orders a half carafe of merlot.

Diners occupy every table. Barbara and Rigney are the only two in military uniform.

Barbara's knowledge of restaurant protocol impresses Rigney. He does not know what merlot is; though later, he discovers he likes it. Since Barbara ordered the wine, the waiter did not ask Rigney for proof of age.

During dinner conversation, they expand their knowledge of each other. Rigney comes to realize that he really likes this woman. He finds her intelligent and worldly. He asks many questions about her experiences in Europe. Barbara discovers Rigney's immense knowledge of politics and religion. She has never known someone so young to have so much knowledge of these subjects. They finish dinner on the light side with a few jokes and rationalizations about their short-term relationship. They enjoy their dining experience. They take their time and are not rushed.

The waiter places the bill in front of Rigney.

"Shall we consider him a stereotyping Neanderthal," Rigney jokes as he hands the bill to Barbara.

Rigney watches the bill paying process with the credit card. He sees no money change hands. *I must discover more about this credit card stuff.*

They decide to walk along the boardwalk for a while before driving back to Barbara's apartment. They go to the checkroom and retrieve coats, hats, and gloves. At 9:25 p.m., they exit the restaurant and step onto the boardwalk. The air is cold and damp. A thick fog crept ashore while they were in the restaurant. They hear the waves lapping at the shore, but they cannot see the water.

As they raise their coat collars around their necks, they notice a disturbance on the boardwalk about thirty feet away. A broad-shouldered man who is at least six and half feet tall holds a small woman by her right arm. The man screams at her in a rage about her embarrassing him. He hits her in the head with his fist-clenched right hand. His language is base and foul.

The woman yells in a frightened voice, "Help me! Someone please help me!"

People on the boardwalk near the scene turn around and walk away to avoid becoming involved.

Rigney stops and watches the scene for a few seconds. Rage rises within him as he sees this helpless woman being beaten by a bully.

Barbara urges, "Rigney, let's go. We don't want to get involved."

"We can't walk away from this. We talked earlier about men beating women. If that were you being beaten by your ex-husband, wouldn't you want someone to help?"

"Yes, but he's so big. We can't—"

"Stay here," Rigney says calmly as he takes off his hat and hands it to her.

Rigney walks toward the couple and stands eight feet away. He calmly threatens in a cold, deadly tone. "Hey, asshole, let that woman go or regret the day your mother gave you birth."

Rigney's chilling threat stuns Barbara.

The man turns and looks angrily at Rigney. The overhead lights of the boardwalk are behind Rigney. The man cannot see Rigney's face. All he sees is the outline of someone in a sailor's uniform.

The man snarls a warning. "Fuck off, squid! This is not your goddamn business! Stay the fuck out of this!"

With the light behind him, Rigney sees the man clearly. Rigney judges the man's age to be mid-thirties. He is in civilian clothes and wears a thick red jacket with the words U.S. MARINES on the back. The man's short haircut indicates he is military. The man's shaved sidewalls haircut confirms that he is a marine.

"I'm making it my business you pathetic woman beating bastard," Rigney replies calmly and coldly.

The marine still has a grip on the woman's right arm. He steps a few feet closer to Rigney, and he drags the woman with him. Rigney and the marine are now four feet apart.

The marine still cannot see Rigney's face; he does see the third class crow on his sleeve. "You're not just a squid, you're a baby squid. You don't want to fuck with me, boy. Leave now and live!"

Rigney knows there will be a fight. He knows this marine is accustomed to being obeyed and has no fear of the younger sailor in front of him. Rigney is afraid, but not so afraid that he will not risk his own safety to save the woman from a beating. Rigney fears more what this man might do to the woman. He prepares his stance to go on the attack. The marine is right handed, so Rigney puts his left foot forward. He raises his gloved fists.

"You gettin' ready to fight me, squid? You don't want to test me! I am madder than hell, and I feel like killing someone! Now, get the fuck outta here!"

Rigney shouts, "I will not leave until you let the woman go!" Then, in a calmer voice, "Is this how you prove how tough you are, by beating up on women? You're big, but you're just a dumb fucking pussy."

The marine throws the woman to the ground and moves toward Rigney.

Barbara screams, "No! Please don't!" She fears terribly for Rigney's safety.

What happens next occurs in less than five seconds. The marine steps forward and swings his right fist toward Rigney's head. As the marine swings his right arm forward, Rigney springs the left side of his body forward and raises his left arm. He steps inside the circle of the marine's swinging fist. The marine's right forearm slams into Rigney's upraised left forearm—the punch is successfully blocked. As he blocks the punch, Rigney levers on his left foot and swings his right foot up with all his power and kicks the marine solidly in the testicles. The marine screams out in pain, doubles over, and grabs his crotch.

Rigney quickly moves to the left of the bent over man. When he is at the correct distance for his planned maneuver, he swings up his right foot again and kicks the marine in the face. The toe of Rigney's shoe hits the bridge of the marine's nose. Blood spurts from the marine's face and spatters over the boardwalk and over Rigney's shoes and trousers. The marine falls to the ground screaming in pain.

Rigney stands over the screaming marine. He says to himself, *Thanks, Brad! Just like you taught me!*

Barbara stands stunned, bewildered, and opened mouthed. One moment she fears that Rigney will be severely beaten. The next moment she sees a flurry of arms and legs, followed with the big man lying on the ground, screaming in pain. She sees Rigney standing over the marine, rubbing his left forearm.

Her relief turns to concern as she thinks about how badly Rigney hurt the man. She had watched men fight before, but she never saw one man put down another man so brutally with hardly any effort. The way she saw it, the whole thing was effortless execution on Rigney's part, as it were a natural part of his behavior.

Rigney approaches the women who lies on the ground. Barbara joins him immediately. The woman appears mid-thirties.

Rigney's words are calm and polite, "Are you okay? Can you stand up?" He helps her up and cradles her softly in his arms. Barbara puts a comforting arm around the woman also.

Rigney speaks softly to the woman, "There is a taxi stand in front of the restaurant. Can I help you with taking a cab home?"

"Yes, I should take a cab," the woman responds weakly. She weeps softly.

"Who is he?" Rigney asks.

"He's my ex-husband. He's been stalking me for weeks. I have a restraining order, but he just laughs at it."

Rigney continues to console the woman as they walk around her ex-husband who lies on the ground and moans loudly in pain.

A crowd gathers around the marine.

Rigney and Barbara guide the woman to the taxi stand and put her in a cab.

"Where do you want to go?" Rigney asks through the window.

The woman provides an address.

"Who's paying for this?" asks the cabbie.

Rigney notices that the woman does not have a purse.

"How much to the address she gave you?" Rigney asks the cabbie.

"That's quite a distance. I would say about thirty dollars."

Rigney looks at Barbara for confirmation.

Barbara says, "Yes, that's about right."

Rigney opens his wallet and hands the cabbie forty dollars. "This should take care of the whole thing. Right?"

The cabbie replies, "Sure thing, sailor. I'll get her there—not to worry."

"Sailor!" the battered woman calls from the backseat of the taxi. "Thank you so very much for stopping him." Tears flow from her eyes.

"What's your name?" Rigney asks.

"Mary."

"Take care, Mary," Rigney says sympathetically.

Then, the taxi speeds away.

Barbara pleads, "Let's go before any cops show up,"

"No, Barbara. I need to do one more thing."

Rigney walks back to the boardwalk. A crowd around the marine has grown larger. Rigney pushes his way through the crowd. Barbara follows close behind him.

The marine still lies on the ground and on his side and moans.

Rigney puts his right foot under the marine's knee and kicks him onto his back.

The marine still has both hands cupped around his crotch.

Rigney stoops near the marine's head.

The marine's eyes are closed. Blood flows from his nose and mouth. He whimpers and moans.

"Open your eyes!" Rigney demands.

The marine does not respond.

"Open your eyes you woman beating pussy, or I will kick you again!"

The marine forces his eyes open. He expresses wide-eyed fear. The light is still behind Rigney. The marine cannot make out the features of Rigney's face.

"I know who you are," Rigney says calmly, coldly, and brutally. "And I know Mary. If you stalk her or hit her again, I will come back and rip out your balls with my bare hands. Do you understand?"

The marine does not respond.

Rigney raises his right arm and slams his gloved fist into the marine's face. Blood spatters from the man's nose.

The crowd collectively gasps.

Rigney shouts, "Do you understand you pathetic pussy son-of-bitch?!"

The marine pleads, "Yes! Yes! I understand. Please don't kick me again! I will never go after her again. Please don't kick me again!"

Tears are steaming from the marine's eyes.

Rigney stands up. He feels an overwhelming urge to kick the marine in the side. Then, Rigney feels a rush of satisfaction. He feels that he has accomplished something. He relishes the idea that another bully has got his just due, and he was the one who did it. *I did it!*

Rigney feels Barbara pulling at his elbow. "We must go!"

"Okay, let's go," he agrees.

The crowd parts as they walk away.

They pass the restaurant as they walk to the parking lot.

"I must do one more thing," Rigney says as he guides Barbara back into the restaurant. They walk up to the coat check girl. Rigney says, "You should call an ambulance. Some guy is hurt out on the boardwalk. He looks in extreme pain."

They say nothing on the thirty-minute drive back to Barbara's apartment.

As they enter Barbara's apartment, Rigney throws off his peacoat and jumper. Then, he unbuttons the thirteen buttons on his navy trousers and steps out of them. He peels off his socks. He sits on the couch. His eyes glaze over. He stares blankly into space.

Barbara stands in front of Rigney. *Something is wrong with him. My god, what is it?* She inspects him closely. *He's not bleeding.*

Rigney's uniform lies in a pile on the floor. Barbara picks up the uniform items and sees the blood splatters on his peacoat, trousers, and gloves. Blood spots some of the white piping around the sleeves of his jumper.

"The bloodstains will never come out of the piping," Barbara tells Rigney.

Rigney does not respond.

She drops the uniform items to the floor. Then, she walks back to the couch and stands in front of him. He still stares into space.

Rigney realizes that he took pleasure in what he did. He enjoyed it, and that concerns him. He never thought he would enjoy inflicting pain on someone. *I have changed.*

What have I gotten myself into? Barbara worries. *The last two days have been wonderful. Now what I'm a supposed to do?* Barbara considers calling her controller. *No, I cannot do that. My orders are to contact him tomorrow.*

"Barb, what are you in deep thought about?"

"Well, you're back from outer space."

"Sorry. You must think I'm a brutal son-of-a-bitch."

"I don't know what to think, Rig. One minute you're gentle and charming, and the next minute you're kicking a man in the balls and face. Then, you show pure kindness and compassion toward that woman. Then, you go back to that man, hit him in the face, and threaten him. Then, you seem okay. Then, we come back here, and you are like in a trance.

"I'm okay. I'm just thinking about what I did."

"Do you get into fights often?"

"No, I am afraid that this time I . . . I . . ."

"This time, you what?" she prompts.

"I think I wanted to fight him." Rigney exhales the words with a burst of air. "I could have walked away, but I wanted to hurt him. I wanted to teach him a lesson."

"Weren't you afraid?"

"Yes . . . a little. He was beating that woman. I felt compelled to stop him. I knew that my first maneuver needed to be correct. If he had connected with that punch, I would be the one laid out. He made a big mistake by thinking me as just a boy and not someone who can handle himself. I knew he thought that, and I knew it gave me an advantage."

221

"Why did you kick him a second time? The first time was good enough. That stopped him." Barbara shakes her head slightly from side to side.

"Because I could," Rigney admits.

"What?!"

"Barbara, I've had conflicts with bullies all my life. The most I have ever done before was just enough to chase bullies away. This guy tonight . . . he's the king of bullies. He beats on women. I saw my chance to hurt him bad . . . really teach him a lesson. So, I did."

Barbara studies Rigney faces. She sees that he experiences some revelations about himself.

"If you've never done this kind of thing before, where did you learn to fight like that?"

"Think about it, Barb. I think you know."

Barbara's face expresses surprise. She mouths the question without saying them . . . *ONI?*

Rigney nods his head in the affirmative.

ONI teaches men to fight like that. Rigney could have killed that man, if he had kept kicking. Barbara's knowledge of ONI has just expanded. She now understands that for ONI to teach Rigney how to fight like that, Rigney must be capable of coping with dangerous situations.

They are silent for a minute.

"Barbara?"

She stares into his eyes.

"Will you report what happened tonight?"

"No." she replies softly and smiles. "I must only report that I passed you the note and the report you gave me."

Rigney follows Barbara into the bedroom.

Chapter 37

Rigney feels Barbara stirring beside him. He looks at the clock on the nightstand—9:39 a.m.

"I'm late with my report," Barbara says as she gets out of bed.

Rigney stays in the bed and closes his eyes. He is exhausted after another night of endless lovemaking.

A few minutes later, he hears Barbara talking on the phone. He looks at the nightstand clock again—9:41 a.m.

"Yes, I passed the note. Yes . . . ZULU BRAVO OSCAR ZERO."

Rigney hears the phone hit the cradle as Barbara hangs up.

Barbara enters the bedroom and climbs back into bed. Rigney turns on his side to face her. She moves closer, and Rigney moves to wrap his arms around her.

She comments, "That's a nasty bruise on your arm. Does it hurt?"

Rigney looks at the bruise on his forearm where he blocked the marine's punch. "Yeah. It feels tender," he admits.

"I'll get some ice," Barbara says as she gets out of bed.

She comes back with ice wrapped in a towel and holds it to his forearm. "Here, hold it in place."

Rigney uses his right hand to hold the towel in place and says, "I guess that's the end to the lovin' for a while. I don't have the use of my hands."

Barbara smiles sexily. "Not to worry, stud. I will do all the work."

Then, Barbara ducks under the blankets.

Rigney inhales sharply and moans softly as he feels pleasure from Barbara's sexual activity under the blanket.

Chapter 38

Lieutenant Commander Brad Watson sits in his office at ONI Headquarters in Suitland, Maryland and studies the Operation Jupiter folder. He looks at his watch—1630. *Cranston's late. Not a good sign.*

The Secure Telephone Unit, STU, on Brad's desk rings.

Brad picks up the handset from the red colored telephone unit. "Lieutenant Commander Watson," Brad says into the handset.

"Lieutenant Cranston, here, sir."

"How are things in Norfolk, Barry?"

"Magnolia made contact, and Apollo has the note."

"Good!" Brad responds as he raises his voice. "Are things going as planned?"

"Yes, sir. They're sleeping together."

"I need that confirmed," commands Brad.

"Well, like you directed, sir, I put tails on both of them. Magnolia made contact in the Naval Station chow hall on Saturday. From there, they went directly to her apartment. Except for going out to dinner last night, they have been in her apartment for the last two days. Both tails reported the same thing."

"That's what I figured would happen." Brad thinks about Sally Macfurson.

Lieutenant Cranston does not comment.

"When does Magnolia transfer to Naples?" Brad asks.

"Two weeks."

"And Magnolia has no idea that we plan to use her in Naples for contact with Apollo."

"Sir, I suspect she thinks she will be called by us, just like any other napper."

"Good. Anything else to report," asks Brad.

"Yes, sir. Apollo beat up a marine on the Virginia Beach Boardwalk last night."

"He did what?!" Brad responds incredulously.

"Again, both tails report the same thing. The tails were watching the restaurant, and both see this big guy beating up on a woman just a short distance from the restaurant. Then, Apollo and Magnolia exit the restaurant. A few moments later, Apollo is yelling at the marine. Then, the marine takes a swing at Apollo, and Apollo lays out the marine with two of the most powerful kicks they have ever seen. Then, Apollo and Magnolia escort the woman that the marine was beating to a taxi. Apollo pays the cabbie, and the taxi leaves." Lieutenant Cranston pauses.

"There's more to this incident, isn't there?" Brad queries

apprehensively.

"Yes, sir. A crowd gathered around the laid out marine. The tails joined the crowd. After sending the woman off in the taxi, Apollo comes back, breaks through the crowd, leans down and punches the marine in the face and threatens to castrate him if he goes near that woman again."

"Shit!" Brad blurts irritably. "Does Apollo know the woman?"

"I don't think so sir. One of the tails heard Apollo asking the woman her name."

"Anything more?" Brad asks.

"Yes, sir. It gets worse. Both the local police and the shore patrol are involved."

Brad sits back in his chair. He sees his operation disintegrating before it ever gets started.

"Go on," Brad directs in an exasperated tone.

"The police and an ambulance arrived about the same time. The police sent the marine to Portsmouth Naval Hospital and contacted the Shore Patrol. I read the Shore Patrol report just before I called you. The marine claims that he and his ex-wife were walking along the boardwalk when this sailor came out of nowhere and started kicking him. The good news is that the marine said he never got a good look at the attacker's face. He said that the light was always behind the sailor's head, and the sailor's face was always in shadows. He could only describe him as a young sailor who had a third class crow on his peacoat. The marine says he might be able to identify the sailor if he got close to him again, especially if he heard his voice. The police report is attached to the Shore Patrol report. The police report says the same thing.

"The police report also says that none of the witnesses could describe the sailor other than he looked young. However, the witnesses say the marine was beating up a woman. Then, the marine attacked the sailor. Comments by the police on the scene believe the witnesses are protecting the sailor, and the witnesses say that the marine got what he deserved."

Brad asks, "Do any of the police reports or shore patrol reports say that Apollo and Magnolia came out of the restaurant?"

"No, sir."

"Looks like Apollo will remain anonymous," Brad comments assuredly.

"Sorry, sir. It does get worse," Cranston advises in a serious tone.

"Damn! What is it?"

"The marine is assigned to the Marine Detachment onboard the USS *Columbus*."

"Hold on, Barry. Let me think about this for a few minutes."

The line goes silent for several minutes.

"Barry, any mention in the reports that the sailor's crow was a third class radioman's crow?"

"No, sir. Just says it was a *third class crow.*"

"What's this marine's name?"

"Gunnery Sergeant Christopher Bronston."

"Barry, do you know if Apollo and this marine crossed paths on the *Columbus*? He could have recognized Apollo and wants to get revenge and doesn't want police interference."

"I don't think so sir. Apollo was only aboard for two days. I called the *Columbus* and talked to the Sergeant of the Guard. I told him I was a relative, and I wanted to know when Gunny Bronston would be back. The SOG said Bronston would be back on Tuesday. The SOG volunteered that the Gunny was on leave and hadn't been aboard since December 20th."

"What's the prognosis for this Bronston?"

"The hospital will release him tomorrow and return him to *light* duty."

Brad Watson directs, "Send me everything you have on this Gunny Bronston."

"Will do, sir."

Brad asks, "What's the mission of this Marine Detachment aboard *Columbus*?"

"They run the brig and guard access to the weapons storage areas."

Their conversation pauses. Cranston, being the junior, waits for Brad Watson to speak.

"I'm curious, Barry. Did your tails add any off the record comments about what Apollo did to Bronston?"

"Yes, sir. They said they saw the marine beating this woman before Apollo came out of the restaurant. Apollo was like a knight in shining armor on a rescue mission. He baited the marine, and the marine fell for it. They said it was the smoothest putdown they had ever seen. They said Apollo's maneuvers were lightning fast and as graceful as a ballet dancer."

The male ego and machismo within Brad cause him to beam with pride for his protégé. The disciplinarian within him says that Apollo needs a reprimand.

"This should turn out okay," Brad speculates. "Even if Apollo were identified as the sailor in this incident, anyone evaluating it would dismiss Apollo as an undercover agent. Over one thousand men live and work aboard *Columbus*. No reason to believe that Bronston and Apollo should cross paths. As long as Apollo does not speak in Bronston's presence, he should remain anonymous."

"Apollo's voice is that unique, sir?"

"Yes, he has a uniquely deep and resonant voice, like an announcer."

"Should I warn him, sir?" Barry asks.

"No, I'll warn him. He does not know you. Apollo does not trust people easily. When did you last sweep Magnolia's apartment and phone?"

"Last week. Nothing has ever been found. No reason to believe she has been compromised."

Brad directs, "I want you to keep a tail on Magnolia until she departs for Naples."

"Yes, sir."

"Also have someone play NIS investigator and see just how easily someone can find out about our couple. Start with that restaurant. Interview anyone who is listed as a witness on the police report. Also have your man take actions to erase our couple's trail."

"Yes, sir."

"What's Magnolia's telephone number?"

Cranston provides the number.

"Oh, one more thing," Brad Watson states.

"Yes, sir."

"Put a tail on Gunny Bronston. I want to know all his movements up to the time *Columbus* gets underway."

"Yes, sir. Will do."

Chapter 39

Rigney stands in his underwear at Barbara's ironing board and irons one of his new gabardine uniforms. He previously decided to throw out his blood stained Melton Wool uniform and his peacoat. The bloodstains would not wash out.

"Fortunately, I purchased additional uniforms. I don't know what I am going to do about a peacoat."

Barbara suggests, "We can get you a peacoat tomorrow morning, before I take you to the ship. We will stop by one of those civilian uniform shops. They open early."

Barbara's phone rings. Rigney looks at his watch—7:48 p.m.

Barbara picks up the handset. "Hello." She listens for about five seconds.

Barbara turns toward Rigney with a surprised look on her face. "It's for you." She holds the handset toward him.

Rigney is equally surprised. He walks to the phone and takes the handset from Barbara.

"Hello."

"Hi, Rig. Do you recognize my voice?"

Lieutenant Commander Brad Watson's voice is unmistakable to Rigney. "Yes, it's nice to hear from you."

"Rig, that stunt you pulled on the boardwalk last night jeopardizes our operation. I understand why you did it, but you could have been arrested and missed ship's movement. Do you understand how that jeopardizes the operation?"

Stunned that Brad knows about the fight, Rigney takes several moments to formulate his response. "I understand, now. At the time, I just wanted to stop him from beating that woman."

"Don't bullshit me, Rig. You didn't do it for that reason. I mean that was your initial reason. After kicking him the first time, you could have stopped. You continued to hit him for different reasons, didn't you?"

Rigney is silent for a few moments; then, he admits, "Yes."

"Rig, that marine is not responsible for all the beatings you took from bullies when you were a boy. I did not teach you how to fight so that you can go on a revenge rampage. Do you understand?"

"Yes."

"You must reserve the moves I taught you for the circumstances that I taught you. Do you understand?"

"Yes."

"We taught you about compartmentalization of information. You must understand that for security reasons you have not been briefed on everything. You must follow orders to the letter for all the pieces to come together."

"Yes, I understand."

"That marine from last night says he cannot identify you. He says the light was always behind you. So, your face was always in the shadows. All he knows is that the attacker was a young sailor—a third class petty officer. But he said he can identify your voice."

"He attacked me. I didn't attack him. He had the choice to let the woman go."

"You baited him. You accurately judged his nature. You knew he would not back down, and you took advantage of that. You cannot do that again. Please don't prove me wrong about you and your ability to carry out this mission."

Rigney remains silent. He does not know what to say next.

"Here's the worst part. That marine is a Gunnery Sergeant assigned to the *Columbus's* Marine Detachment."

Rigney stiffens. Visualizations of future confrontations with the marine race through his mind.

"It should be okay. Just make sure that you avoid him and never speak in his presence. Can you do that?"

"I will avoid him."

"Good. I think we are back on track. As long as you follow orders, this incident should not affect the operation. I will be looking forward to your reports from the MED." Brad hangs up.

Rigney cradles the phone handset and asks, "Barb, do you have any whiskey? I need a couple shots."

"I have some Jack Daniels. I'll pour you some. I will have a couple of shots also."

Rigney walks to the couch and sits down. He thoroughly evaluates the events of the last few days.

Barbara hands him a glass with several shots of Jack Daniels. Her glass holds the same amount. She sits beside him.

He is in deep thought as he puts his arm around her shoulder and pulls her closer.

They both sip their drinks.

After several minutes, he says, "We're being followed. ONI has someone following us. Did you know that someone was following us?"

"I didn't know. We should not be talking about this."

"Why not? It doesn't make any difference. If Brad can call me on your phone, there is no reason why we cannot talk out loud. Besides, it's an obvious conclusion. How else could Brad know about it? He must know that I would conclude this."

"You're right. It's an obvious conclusion."

Rigney says, "It's okay; I think. I mean, I trust Brad. He would not have us followed if it weren't needed for the operation."

"Brad? What operation?" Barbara asks.

"You know I cannot tell you."

"Yes, of course you can't. It was an instinctive question."

They both sit silent. They sip their drinks.

All of sudden Barbara sits up straight and leans forward on the couch and says, "There could be another conclusion."

"What's that?" Rigney asks.

"Did you know that Naples is a frequent stop for ships on MED cruises?"

Rigney expresses revelation as he responds. "No, I did not know that."

Barbara turns toward Rigney, smiles slyly, and states, "And several weeks ago, I was offered orders to Naples. I wonder if it's a coincidence . . . or some design to it all."

Rigney responds, "I don't know, but I think we'll find out."

Rigney and Barbara are curled up together, naked, in bed. They have their arms wrapped around each other.

"This is our last night," she says. "I have duty tomorrow, and the next morning you leave for the MED."

Rigney smiles appreciatively at Barbara and says, "I really enjoyed being with you this weekend. I'm glad we met. You're a super person. I guess I put you through the test last night. Thanks for sticking with me. You could have told me to hit the road."

"I enjoyed this weekend too. Please come to see me when your ship pulls into Naples. You can find me at the Naval Support Activity Administrative Offices. I will give you the address in the morning. Promise that you will write and will come to see me in Naples."

"I will do that. However, I believe that our ONI bosses will insist on it."

Barbara reaches over Rigney and turns out the light.

Chapter 40

Barbara brakes her car to a stop just off to the side of the entrance to Pier 2. All the authorized parking spaces were taken hours ago. Rigney reaches into the backseat and retrieves his gym bag and the bag full of recently purchased uniform items. He looks at Barbara who is trying to smile, but her moist eyes betray her true feelings. Rigney's eyes mist over also. They kiss lightly and try the best hug they can in the car and while bundled in their peacoats.

Rigney conveys appreciation as he says, "Goodbye, Barbara. Thank you."

"Take care of yourself, Rigney Page. Whatever you're doing on that ship, please do it carefully. I will see you in Naples."

Rigney exits the car and walks toward the pier. Barbara steps out of the car and waves at Rigney as he stands in line at the pier security shack. He waves back.

"Hey, Rig. Who's your friend?"

Rigney turns and sees Larry Johnson behind him.

"She's someone I met a couple of days ago," Rigney answers.

Barbara enters her car and drives off.

"Well, she's a looker all right, but aren't you fraternizing? She's a first class."

Rigney glances sideways at Larry, smiles devilishly, and says, "When we're naked under the sheets, we're all the same rank."

Larry smiles approvingly and in his best W.C. Fields voice says, "Truer words were never spoken, Rigney, my boy, truer words were never spoken!"

They both chuckle.

They wait behind thirty people in line to get onto the pier. The shore patrolman at the checkpoint verifies all faces with associated I.D. card.

Rigney surveys the area. The parking lots are full. Sailors and civilian workers move about everywhere. Bursts of steam shoot up randomly. Everyone is bundled in heavy coats. Ships occupy most of the berths going all the way to Pier 12. Private cars are bumper to bumper going in both directions on Decatur Avenue. Several large navy trucks are lined up to enter Pier 2.

Rigney asks Larry, "Is it normally like this in the morning?"

"Yeah . . . most workday mornings . . . up until colors. By colors, 0800, everyone is aboard their ships and all civilians are in their buildings. It's always worse the first workday after a big holiday, like today."

Rigney looks at his watch—0718. "What time do we need to be

aboard?"

"We need to be in the compartment by 0730 so that we can change into working uniform for quarters and muster at 0745."

"Are we going to make it?" Rigney becomes concerned that he will be late on his first day.

"Oh, yeah. The line is like this every morning at this time."

"I guess there will not be time for chow before quarters," Rigney concludes.

"No time," Larry confirms.

Rigney and Larry pass through security and walk onto Pier 2. Cargo trucks sit everywhere. A continuous stream of sailors ascends both the officer gangway and enlisted gangway.

After crossing the quarterdeck, they descend the ladder to the aft mess deck. Sailors and marines are moving in all directions. Some sailors and marines sit at the tables eating breakfast. Rigney looks around quickly for Gunny Bronston. He does not see him. Larry leads the way across the mess decks to the port passageway. They walk quickly and must dodge sailors walking in the opposite direction. They step down the ladder into the CR Division berthing compartment.

The compartment is full of sailors who are changing from dress uniform into dungarees. Low-volume chatter covers the compartment. Some say hello to Larry as he enters the compartment. Some stare at the stranger who enters the compartment with Larry. Larry stops at his rack. Rigney weaves his way through sailors to get to his rack. The chatter in the compartment lowers to near silence when Rigney enters the lock combination for his rack locker.

The radioman who has the rack above Rigney stands on a bulkhead beam and has his head buried in his rack-locker.

Rigney props open the lid to his rack-locker and starts changing his clothes. He dresses in dungarees. Then, he pauses to see what others wear for hat and coat. All are wearing ball caps. Some wear blue working jacket, and some wear foul weather jacket. All are wearing their boondocker boots. Rigney puts on his newly acquired foul weather jacket and his ball cap.

The sailor who had his head buried in the rack above Rigney's lowers himself to the deck and stands next to Rigney. "Shit! I don't have any socks! My wife said she packed them! Fuck! I can't go to the MED without socks!"

Then, the sailor notices Rigney standing next to him. He looks at Rigney, glances at the middle rack, and looks back at Rigney.

The sailor is rail thin and stands about five feet and seven inches. He wears a third class crow on the sleeve of his dungarees. The name Spaulding is stenciled over his left breast pocket.

"That your rack?" he asks Rigney.

"Yes."

"Oh! When I saw the rack made up, I thought Rouché was back. Excuse me for staring. I guess no one told you about that rack."

"Yes," Rigney replies in an even tone. "I got the full briefing."

"And you still took the rack!" Spaulding responds, incredulous.

Other's standing in the immediate area turn to see why Spaulding raises his voice.

Rigney decides not to respond.

A lean and medium height first class petty officer stands four feet away. He turns toward Rigney and Spaulding; then, he weaves his way over to Rigney and sticks out his hand.

"I'm RM1 Dukes. I'm the LPO."

"Rigney Page." Rigney introduces himself as he shakes Dukes's hand.

"Anyone showing you around," Dukes asks.

"Yes, Larry Johnson."

"Follow Johnson up to the ASROC deck for quarters. I will give you more instructions after quarters."

Dukes takes a clipboard off his rack and exits the compartment.

Chapter 41

Rigney follows Larry Johnson up to the ASROC deck. The air is cold, and the sky is overcast.

RM1 Dukes directs formation of CR division personnel into ranks on the port side of the ASROC deck. Rigney is the tallest and RM1 Dukes directs Rigney to the first position in the first rank.

A senior chief stands behind Dukes to the outboard.

"ALL HANDS TO QUARTERS FOR MUSTER AND INSPECTION," blasts over the ship's 1MC interior communications system.

RM1 Dukes orders, "CR Division . . . fall-in!"

One minute later, Dukes orders, "CR Division . . . atten'hut!" the twenty-eight men in ranks snap to attention.

"CR Division . . . parade rest!"

"CR Division . . . attention to muster!" Dukes reads from a list in alphabetical order. Each man responds with *"here"* or *"yo"* when he hears his name called.

Dukes turns to the senior chief and reports, "All hands present or accounted for, Senior Chief."

"Very well," responds the senior chief.

A few minutes later, a lieutenant junior grade walks toward the senior chief. The senior chief snaps to attention; then, he salutes the officer. The officer returns the salute, and the senior chief reports, "All hands present or accounted for, sir."

"Very well, Senior Chief. Proceed with the reading of the Plan of the Day."

"Aye, aye, sir!"

The senior chief turns toward Dukes and orders, "Dukes, proceed with the reading of the Plan of the Day."

"Aye, aye, Senior Chief."

Dukes reads the Plan of the Day to the men in ranks. He has read one third of the Plan of the Day when a bugle sounds over the 1MC, followed by, "NOW, ON DECK, ATTENTION TO COLORS."

Dukes comes to attention and performs an about face so that he faces in the same direction as the men in ranks. Dukes orders, "CR Division . . . atten'hut!"

The Star Spangled Banner plays through the 1MC as all ships raise the American Flag at the same time.

As the Star Spangled Banner plays, Rigney wonders if Python is present and wonders if Python is feeling patriotic.

When the Star Spangled Banner completes, Dukes orders, "CR Division . . . stand easy!"

Everyone relaxes and stands in place.

Dukes takes another five minutes to finish reading the Plan of the Day.

Dukes, the senior chief, and the officer engage in conversation. During the conversation, all three of them glance over at Rigney. They continue their conversation for another two minutes.

The officer turns to the ranks and says, "Men, I would like to welcome RM3 Page to the Division. Page, please raise your hand."

Rigney raises his hand for a few seconds.

The officer continues, "Page reports to *Columbus* from Bethesda Medical Center, which is in the Washington DC area. All of you please introduce yourselves when suitable."

Rigney's new comrades in arms voice some welcoming phrases.

"Shore duty puke!"

"New foul weather jacket pussy!"

"Welcome aboard fresh meat!"

Everyone in the division, accept for Larry Johnson and Frank Carter, now believe that Rigney was stationed at the Bethesda Medical Center Communications Center and that the *Columbus* is Rigney's second duty station.

Python takes another look at the new man. To Python, Page looks like another young sailor of no consequence. However, he knows that he must notify Javier of all new men to the division. The notifications are a requirement to continue the monthly deposit of money into his Bahamas bank account.

The officer continues, "As was explained before we went into stand-down, CR Division shifts to the *underway watch bill* this morning. No one may leave the pier area without the permission of the senior chief. Section One will assume the watch immediately after quarters. We drop our communications guard from NAVCOMMSTA NORFOLK at 1600. Therefore, we need the entire Communications Plan in effect by that time, including the fleet broadcast and our primary ship-to-shore termination. At 1600, we assume the communications guard for Commander, Cruiser Destroyer Flotilla Eight. The admiral and his staff move aboard today. CR Division comes under the operational control of the admiral at 1600. The ship is scheduled to get underway tomorrow morning at 0900."

The officer pauses; then, he asks, "Are there any questions?"

No one asks any questions.

The officer orders, "Senior Chief, take charge of the division."

The senior chief salutes the officer; the officer returns the salute, then turns and walks forward.

The senior chief orders, "Those in Section One are dismissed to assume the watch."

A third of the men, including Dukes, break ranks and climb the ladders toward MAIN COMM.

The senior chief divides the remaining second class petty officers and below, except for Rigney and Larry Johnson, into five groups. Each group is assigned a radio space to clean and rig for sea.

Rigney and Larry Johnson remain on the ASROC Deck with the senior chief.

"Page, I am Senior Chief Bulldoone. Welcome aboard."

Bulldoone shakes Rigney's hand, and Rigney responds, "Thanks, Senior Chief. I'm pleased to be aboard."

RMCS Bulldoone is forty-two years old. He stands five feet and eight inches. He is fifty pounds overweight and his belly hangs over his belt. Bulldoone has twenty-four years in the navy. He has been passed over twice for master chief. He has decided that he will retire after the MED cruise.

Bulldoone asks Rigney, "What's left on your Check-In Sheet?"

Rigney pulls the Check-In Sheet out of his back pocket and looks it over. "I still have ten people to see."

"Check-in is your focus this morning. Get it done. Johnson, you are to take him around and see to it that he finishes the check-in process."

Larry responds, "Okay, Senior Chief. Will do."

Bulldoone orders, "At 1400, come and see me in Radio Central."

"Aye, aye, Senior Chief," Rigney and Larry reply in unison.

The senior chief inquires, "Page, how did you get that new foul weather jacket?"

"Well, that's a long story," Rigney responds. "Do you know BM1 Genoa?"

"Oh, shit!" Larry blurts.

Senior Chief Bulldoone responds, "Never mind, Page. If BM1 Genoa is involved, I'm sure it's a good story."

The senior chief walks forward and goes up the ladder toward MAIN COMM.

"Thanks, Rig!" Larry says appreciatively.

"Thanks for what?"

"For getting me out of a morning clean up and rigging for sea."

"Oh."

Chapter 42

At 1400, Rigney and Larry report to Radio Central. RMCS Bulldoone sits at his desk and talks with RM1 Dukes.

Radio Central is the switching center for radio communications. The entire port bulkhead contains *dial switch panels* that are seven feet high and twenty feet long. All the transmitters, receivers, operating positions come together on these switch panels. These switch panels provide the means to connect any transmitter and any receiver to any operating positions on the Bridge, Flag Bridge, CIC, and MAIN COMM. The aft end of Radio Central is where the Radio Central Operator stands his watch and maintains a large status board that lists the current patch status of all equipment. The senior chief has his desk in the forward end of Radio Central.

"Okay," the senior chief says to Dukes. "Let me know when we have two consecutive hours of no H.J. on the ship-to-shore termination crypto."

RM1 Dukes departs Radio Central and returns to MAIN COMM where he supervises establishment of communications circuits.

Rigney walks over to the senior chief and says, "Except for the Commanding Officer, I'm checked in."

"Why not the CO?"

"The CO's yeoman scheduled me for an interview at 1530 tomorrow."

The senior chief looks at Larry Johnson and says, "You can knock off. Get some rest before reporting for watch."

"Thanks, Senior Chief. See ya, Rig."

Larry Johnson walks out of Radio Central.

"Page, pull up a chair."

Rigney pulls up a chair to the senior chief's desk and sits.

"Here's your liberty card." RMCS Bulldoone hands Rigney a three-by-two-inch laminated card.

Rigney sees his name typed on the card. The words *Watch Stander* are typed over the line for DUTY SECTION. The card has the Operations Officer signature.

The senior chief explains, "CR Division personnel have *Watch Standers Liberty Cards*. It means that whenever liberty is authorized you can come and go as you please, regardless of which ship's section has the duty."

Rigney nods understanding.

Senior Chief Bulldoone points to a grid chart titled *Watch, Quarter, and Station Bill*. "I need to explain the watch bills to you."

237

Rigney sees his name with *PPO* listed on the *Watch* column; his General Quarters station is Radio Central. All other *Stations* for Rigney are listed as CR DIV BERTHING."

"Initially, you are assigned as the Division Police Petty Officer. If General Quarters sounds, you are to come here to Radio Central. For all other situations, your station is the CR Division berthing compartment. Do you understand so far?"

"What is a PPO, Senior Chief?"

RMCS Bulldoone jerks back in surprise and asks, "You don't know what a Police Petty Officer is?"

"No."

"The PPO is in charge of the berthing compartment. You will have the two junior seaman assigned to you. You will report directly to RM1 Dukes. You will be responsible for ensuring that the berthing compartment and head are cleaned every day. You are the point of contact for any maintenance items that need completed in the berthing compartment. You will have your seaman collect the laundry twice a week and ensure it is delivered to and picked up from the ship's laundry."

"I won't be working in Radio?" Rigney questions. Disappointment edges his voice.

"Not at first. You will be the PPO for three months."

"Three months!" Rigney responds objectionably. "I don't understand. Why am I being assigned to PPO instead of radio watches." *How can I find Python if I am not working in Radio?!*

Bulldoone responds, "The junior third class who has not previously served as PPO is the one assigned. It's an essential position for the good morale of the division. Some consider the assignment as a boondoggle. Most of the *thirds* would take it if I offered it to them. It's short hours and no watch standing, and you have *Watch Standers Liberty* when in port. You can go on liberty every night if you wish. However, some *thirds* consider PPO a shit job. They have too much pride to be a compartment cleaner."

"Senior Chief, I have been a third class for a year. I am qualified for advancement to *second class*. The only remaining item is to take the RM2 Exam. My last two performance evaluations include recommendations for advancement to RM2. I think if you check, you will find that I am probably not the junior third class. I would rather work in Radio."

Bulldoone studies Rigney's face for a few moments; then, he responds, "You're the junior in time aboard, and that makes you the PPO. Besides, CR Division is shorthanded. We're not scheduled to get any more radiomen until March. All the RM3s are already qualified in two or more watch stations. I cannot short the radio watch, when I have a less qualified *third* to serve as PPO."

Bulldoone is impressed with Rigney's desire to work and qualify in radio, instead of quickly accepting an easy job. Privately, Bulldoone objects to the PPO position because it takes radiomen away from an already undermanned division.

Rigney worries. *What do I do now? The senior chief has made up his mind, and his reasoning is correct. I would do the same thing if I was in his shoes. I must find a way to change this. I have no way of contacting Brad, unless I can get off the ship and make a phone call . . . a report.*

"Don't worry, Page. I see no reason why you should not take the RM2 Exam."

Rigney scans the *Watch, Quarter, and Station Bill*. He looks at the various Radio Watch Stations. *Fleet Broadcast Operator* seems to be the Watch Station best suited to discover Python.

"What should I do now, Senior Chief?"

"Nothing more for today. Tomorrow morning, RM1 Dukes will get with you and the two junior seamen and explain all your duties."

"Senior Chief, I need to make a phone call. Where I can do that?"

"There is a bank of public phone booths near the front of the pier. Come right back to the ship after making your call."

"Thanks, Senior Chief."

Rigney stands and exits Radio Central.

Rigney makes his way to the enlisted gangway and onto the pier. As he walks toward the head of the pier, he forms the report in his mind. No codewords exist to cover this situation. Rigney decides that he must make a narrative report.

The lines are four deep at each phone booth. Rigney gets in line. An hour later, he dials the 800 number that he has memorized. A recorded voice answers. *"Press one if a push button phone. Dial two if a rotary phone."*

Rigney dials the number two.

"Enter your user code."

Rigney dials his user code.

"Enter your password code."

Rigney dials his password code.

Fifteen seconds later a recorded voice says, *"Dial one to record a message. Dial two to listen to messages."*

Rigney dials the number one.

"Record your message."

Rigney cups his hand over his mouth and handset and speaks softly. "Apollo . . . 010268-01 . . . I have been assigned as PPO, which means I do not work in the radio spaces for the next 90 days. Request instructions. Authentication is 8795."

The phone line stays silent for fifteen seconds. Then, a mechanical sounding voice on the other end says. *"Apollo 010268-01 acknowledged."*

Rigney hangs up.

The berthing compartment lights are off. Rigney looks at his watch—1620. He sees a number of men asleep in their racks. Larry Johnson lies in his rack—reading.

"Larry, what's going on down here?"

"CR Division is in underway watches. We are watch standers. The compartment is always dark when underway and in foreign ports. We don't follow the ships daily routine. We are assigned to The Flag. No one fucks with us."

Larry pauses for a few moments; then, he asks, "What watch section are you assigned?"

"I'm not," Rigney replies. "I'm the PPO for ninety days."

Larry jerks with surprise and asks, "Whose dick did you suck? How did you swing that?"

"Believe me Larry, I don't want it, and the senior chief is firm on this."

"Quiet you two!" a voice orders from the darkness.

Larry lowers his voice. "Climb into your rack. Sleep or read a book. I'll talk to you at chow."

Rigney retrieves the book *Exodus* from his rack-locker. He undresses, folds his dungarees, and stows his dungarees in his rack-locker. He climbs into his rack and turns on his bunk light.

He cannot concentrate on the novel. He can only think about this new obstacle to his mission. He decides to wait until 0600 tomorrow to call ONI and get the reply. At that time of morning, there should be no lines at the phones.

Lieutenant Commander Brad Watson sits in his office at ONI Headquarters in Suitland, Maryland. He just added another report to the *Operation Jupiter* file. The CO of an aircraft carrier in the MED reports that Soviet trawlers and submarines always seem to know the location

240

of the carrier task force.

Lucifer must have expanded his number of paid American traitors.

Brad knows the solution to this problem is to discover and stop Lucifer. In addition to Rigney, Brad has two other field agents on ships in the MED. They are both assigned as radio officer and have been in the MED and aboard those ships for three months. They have not discovered anything.

The message light on his field communications phone starts flashing. The flashing light indicates that the Field Communications Center has queued a message from one of his agents.

Brad picks up the handset, enters his access code, and listens. His face turns grim. Apollo reports that he will not have access to the radio spaces for three months, and he wants instructions on what to do.

Brad places the handset back on the cradle.

What the hell is a PPO? Brad dials a number on his unclassified office phone.

"Field Communications—Chief Crane speaking."

"Mister Watson here. How much sea time you got, Chief?"

"Eight and half years, sir."

"What is a PPO?" Brad asks.

RMC Crane explains. Brad nods a few times and asks some clarifying questions.

"Thank you, Chief, very enlightening."

Brad Watson hangs up the phone and sits back in his chair. He contemplates what to do. He must provide instructions to Apollo today because the *Columbus* sails tomorrow morning.

Chapter 43

Rigney awakens. He hears movement in the berthing compartment. The *communications messenger of the watch* wakes the ongoing watch section. Rigney turns on his bunk light and looks at his watch—0615. *Shit!*

He jumps out of his rack and dresses quickly into dungarees, foul weather jacket, and ball cap. He hears some good-natured comments about the PPO being up so early. Rigney smiles at those making the comments. He dashes up the ladder and walks quickly to the enlisted gangway.

Rigney approaches the first class that stands watch as the JOOD. Rigney salutes and recites, "Request permission to go on the pier?" The first class does not return the salute and does not give permission. The JOOD is BM1 Genoa.

Shit!

Rigney stands at attention with his hand raised still in salute, waiting for Genoa to reply.

Genoa's peacoat stretches tight across his chest and belly. Genoa's tight fitting uniform reminds Rigney of a straitjacket.

Genoa waddles toward Rigney and puts his face about six inches from Rigney's face, and asks, "You got permission from your division officer to go on the pier."

Genoa's rotting teeth and garlic-laden breath repulse Rigney.

"Senior Chief Bulldoone gave me permission."

"Let me see your Liberty Card."

"I'm not going on liberty."

"I didn't ask you that!" Genoa growls. "Now show me your Liberty Card and your I.D. card."

Rigney lowers his hand from the salute, removes his wallet from his back pocket, picks out the items, and hands them to Genoa.

Genoa looks at both cards. "Why ya going to the pier?"

"To make a phone call."

"Aren't you the twidget that gave me a hard time about going on the working party last week?"

"No, I'm not."

"Don't lie to me, Page. I know you're the twidget I sent on that working party. You got that new foul weather jacket out of it."

"Well . . . yes . . . you sent me on the working party. No, I did not give you a hard time about it."

"Another smartass, boot camp twidget!" Genoa responds in a disgusted tone.

242

Genoa walks to the bulkhead mounted phone. He looks up the number to the chiefs mess and dials the number.

Rigney worries that Genoa will deny him permission to go to the pier. *How does the navy tolerate such people in leadership positions?* Discouragement clouds Rigney's mind as he thinks about why the navy permits this.

Genoa speaks into the phone, "This is the JOOD. Is Senior Chief Bulldoone there."

Thirty seconds pass.

"Senior Chief, this is BM1 Genoa, the JOOD, at the enlisted gangway. Did you give RM3 Page permission to go to the pier and make a phone call?"

"Thank you, Senior Chief."

"Okay. You're authorized." Genoa returns Rigney's Liberty Card and I.D. card.

"Rigney stands at attention, salutes, and recites, "Request permission to go to the pier?"

Genoa returns the salute and says, "Permission granted."

Rigney proceeds down the gangway. He looks at his watch—0638.

As he steps off the gangway and onto the pier, he looks toward the head of the pier. No one stands around the phone booths. *Much better!*

After entering the phone booth, he dials the telephone number. He dials all the codes when prompted. He selects the option to get messages.

Rigney recognizes Brad's voice. "Reference Apollo 010268-01: Contact the ship's commanding officer. Tell him that you are part of the Operation Jupiter. He will recognize the operation name. He will already suspect that someone like you is aboard. Do not provide him any codenames or codewords other than the operation codeword. Tell him that you need assistance with getting assigned to the required watch stations. Under no circumstances are you to tell him any of the operation details. Authentication is 1529."

Rigney decodes the authentication and is satisfied the message is valid.

As he walks along the pier toward the Enlisted Gangway, he considers how he will reveal himself to the CO. He has his check-in interview this afternoon. *I will do it at that time.*

Rigney returns to the CR Division berthing compartment just as Larry Johnson starts up the ladder.

"You had chow?" Larry asks. "If not, let's go. My treat."

The long chow line wraps around the passageway and up the ladder to the Main Deck. A short and stocky first class gunners mate, who sailors are calling *Gunner*, controls the chow line. The gunners mate is the *mess deck master-at-arms*. Although disgruntled at being assigned the 90-day shit detail, he remains mild mannered, jokes with the sailors in the chow line, and efficiently manages the chow line.

Fifteen minutes later, Larry and Rigney have gone through the steam line and are looking for a place to sit. They move to the aft mess deck and find two seats together.

Marines fill the table next to them. Rigney looks around for Gunny Bronston; he does not see him.

Rigney looks at his watch—0723. "We have twenty-two minutes before quarters," Rigney comments with concern.

"Jesus, Rig. You're such a boot camp. CR Division is in underway watch bill, no quarters."

"Oh."

Rigney and Larry engage in casual conversation.

"Damn, Gunny! What happened to you?" says one of the marines at the next table, loudly enough for everyone on the aft mess deck to hear. The loud voice causes everyone in the aft mess deck to turn and look in the same direction. Rigney turns and looks with everyone else.

Gunny Bronston, dressed in Service 'A' uniform, walks with a limp across the mess deck. His uniform fits perfectly to his intimidatingly tall, broad-shouldered frame. Thick white gauze bandages cover his nose and left jaw. Black and blue marks surround both of his eyes. Patches of dried blood reveal a number of cuts on his face. Several cuts are closed with stitches His lips are bruised and swollen.

One of the other marines at the next table asks loudly, "I hope the other guy is lying dead somewhere?"

"He is! Don't worry about that!" the Gunny lies to his men with a smile and casual wave of his hand. The Gunny walks through the door marked MARINE DETACHMENT.

The murmur of conversation rises. Rigney hears one of the marines comment, "The Gunny is one mean motherfucker. I have always been afraid of him. Now, I am more afraid of the guy who did that to him."

Rigney returns to his meal. After a few moments, he looks at Larry Johnson and asks, "What's the story on the Gunny?"

"He came aboard right after I did. All the grunts are afraid of him. He runs the Marine Detachment with an iron fist. They say he leads by intimidation. None of them like him. They say he's a real asshole."

Rigney remarks, "Looks like someone did a number on him."

"Yeah. Maybe he's not as tough as we all thought."

"Maybe not," Rigney responds as he raises his coffee cup to his lips.

Chapter 44

After Gunny Bronston checks in with his lieutenant, he goes to the chiefs mess. Because he is an E-7, he sleeps in the chiefs quarters and belongs to the chiefs mess. Bronston goes to his locker and changes into his camouflage utilities, which is his underway uniform. He stands no watches and is not assigned to any duty section. As long as his marines do their jobs well, the lieutenant stays off his back.

Bronston enters the dining area of the chiefs mess and draws a cup of coffee. He sits down at a table with several chiefs. The chiefs stare in disbelief at the Gunny's appearance. They do not say hello or acknowledge him. Gunny Bronston is not respected by anyone in the chiefs mess. They find his leadership style disgusting and his manner arrogant.

Gunny looks up to see the chiefs staring at him. "What the fuck you squids staring at?" Bronston growls.

"Why nothing," says the chief boatswain mate, "nothing at all. I was just commenting that it looks like someone finally gave you what you deserve." The chief boatswain mate is just as big and just as tough as Gunny Bronston and has never been afraid or intimated by him.

"Fucking squids! You're just taxi drivers for real warriors. You know nothing about what it takes to be a marine."

The chief boatswain mate shakes his head in disgust. He has known many good marine NCOs. The chief boatswain mate views Bronston as another one of those military conundrums as to why Bronston is permitted to practice his perverted style of leadership.

Christopher Bronston suffered a violent childhood. All of the men in his family are child beaters and women beaters. When his father was not drunk and beating up on his mother, he was drunk and beating up on Christopher.

Christopher Bronston learned from his father to disrespect women. His father taught him that women are stupid and of little value outside the bedroom. His father educated him to the concept that *women are subservient to men, and a woman's only purpose is to serve her man and have children. They are so stupid that you must punch them to make them understand. Never allow a woman to get away with disrespecting you. If she shows disrespect, punch her in the mouth. That will teach her.*

Christopher was always bigger and stronger than others his age. In school, he was the ultimate bully. He stole kid's lunches and stole their money. If they objected, he would beat them. If classmates disrespected him, or he perceived disrespect, he would beat them.

One day when Christopher was fourteen, some schoolmates brutally beat Christopher. When he arrived home, his father beat him for not winning the fight. Christopher's father advised, "Never let anyone get away with beating you. Find a time to get revenge and make that revenge permanent."

Christopher Bronston learned well from his father. Just after Christopher turned eighteen, his father came home drunk one night and started punching Christopher. To protect himself, Christopher grabbed a baseball bat and brutally beat his father. His father spent six weeks in the hospital and had to have his spleen removed. Christopher joined the marines to avoid going to jail. One year later, Christopher's father died after catching the flu. The removal of his spleen drastically reduced the capability of his immune system.

Christopher reaped permanent revenge on his father. *Thanks, Dad, you taught me well.*

Since being in the Marine Corps and except for hand-to-hand combat in Vietnam, no one had ever attacked him. He was too big and too tough looking. He always took great care to avoid exposing his true nature to his seniors.

Everyone respects me. Everyone is afraid of me. After this MED cruise, that bitch cunt ex-wife of mine will get her punishment. I was humiliated on New Year's Eve. I must have looked pathetic pleading to that the fuckin' squid not to hit me again. All those people standing around and staring at me on the ground. I will find that squid and kill him. That will be his punishment for what he did to me. No matter how long it takes. That's what you're supposed to do. Everyone knows that. It's a matter of honor and respect.

Chapter 45

"NOW SET THE SPECIAL SEA AND ANCHOR DETAIL! THE OFFICER OF THE DECK IS SHIFTING HIS WATCH TO THE BRIDGE!"

Rigney has no assigned station for the SPECIAL SEA AND ANCHOR DETAIL. He climbs the ladders to the Signal Bridge to watch the ship get underway. The Signal Bridge is on the 07 level, one level above the MAIN COMM level.

Rigney exits the hatch on the starboard of the Signal Bridge, the side facing the pier. He walks outboard and stands at the rail, just in time to see the mooring lines pulled aboard the ship. He hears tugs *tooting* on the port side.

Women and children crowd the pier; all of them wave small American flags. He sees several senior officers on the pier waving their hands and looking toward the bridge.

Rigney looks toward the bridge wing. He sees an officer with four gold strips—the captain. The captain waves back to the senior officers on the pier.

A band on the pier plays *Anchors Away* as the ship moves away from the pier.

Rigney's eye catches a woman in uniform at the back of the crowd waving frantically in his direction. His face breaks into a smile as he recognizes Barbara Gaile. He waves back.

A look of gratification that she finally got his attention flows over her face. She came to the pier hoping to see Rigney but doubting she would. She smiles widely and blows him a kiss.

Rigney mouths the words *thank you*. He knows she would never hear him, even if he shouts.

The ship's movement away from the pier becomes rapid. The people on the pier become smaller. As the *Columbus* backs into the channel, individuals on the pier become indistinguishable. The band stops playing.

The ship sits still in the channel. Then, Rigney sees two tugs. One tug rounded the bow from the port side, and the other tug rounded the stern from the port side. Each tug proceeds to the tug piers.

The *Columbus* moves under her own power. Slow at first; then, she increases speed. The *Columbus* proceeds north through the marked channel. A spectacular view of ships at the NAVSTA piers presents itself. Destroyers, cruisers, and a couple of amphibs are moored to piers. Two aircraft carriers are berthed at Pier 12.

After twenty minutes, the *Columbus* turns to starboard and steams northeast. The *Columbus* passes over the Hampton Roads Tunnel. Thirty minutes later, *Columbus* turns to starboard and proceeds east. She passes over the Chesapeake Bay Tunnel and steams east toward the open sea— The Atlantic Ocean.

All that Rigney sees and all that he senses awe him. He has never experienced such events before. *What it must take to get this massive ship—this massive machine—underway. All those other ships at the NAVSTA. What it must take to engineer and build them. What about those bridges and tunnels!*

Rigney proudly revels that he is a citizen of a country capable of such engineering marvels. He is equally proud of his contribution to serve and protect his country.

"NOW SECURE THE SPECIAL SEA AND ANCHOR DETAIL. SET UNDERWAY WATCH, SECTION ONE!"

Rigney stays on the Signal Bridge. To the west, the City of Virginia Beach becomes increasingly distant. He feels the swell of the ocean under his feet. *The Tall Lady* rises and falls and moves from side to side. He remains on the Signal Bridge until all land disappears from the horizon.

Rigney spends the rest of the morning and the early part of the afternoon supervising the cleaning of the CR Division berthing compartment. Fortunately, the two seaman assigned to him are agreeable types. The senior chief had given each seaman the choice of compartment cleaning or mess cooking. They perform every task that Rigney assigns to them without question. They know that if they object or are disrespectful, the senior chief will send them back to the Deck Department from where they came.

Rigney glances at his watch every few minutes. He awaits his meeting with the Commanding Officer with both anticipation and trepidation.

Chapter 46

At 1515, Rigney departs the berthing compartment. He climbs the inside ladders to Officers Country. Then, he enters the small office just outside of the captain's stateroom. Rigney advises the yeoman of his 1530 appointment with the CO. The yeoman checks the CO's calendar for confirmation.

At exactly1530, the yeoman escorts Rigney into the captain's stateroom. The stateroom is large and luxurious when compared to other compartments on the ship. The compartment combines office and meeting room. A conference table sits in the middle. Rigney notes that his service record lies at the head position of the conference table. Paintings of historical sea battles hang randomly on the dark-wood paneled bulkheads. Dark blue carpet covers the deck.

Captain William F. Saunders, Commanding Officer of USS *Columbus*, comes around to the front of his desk and extends his hand to Rigney. At six feet and four inches tall and with a trim and athletic build, the CO presents a distinguished and powerful image. "RM3 Page, welcome aboard," the captain greets cordially.

"Thank you, sir. It's a pleasure to be aboard."

The captain directs, "Let's sit here at the conference table." Then, he orders the yeoman to have the mess cook bring them some coffee.

After he is seated, Captain Saunders opens Rigney's service record to a tabbed location. "Page, I make it a practice to meet all my petty officers when they first report aboard. I think it important that we meet, talk, and come to agreement on leadership principles. I also want to know about your background. Where is your hometown?"

"Seal Beach, California, sir. It's in Orange County."

"Well, we're practically neighbors. My home is Santa Barbara. I have been to Seal Beach a number of times when my ship was loading weapons. Seal Beach is a nice and quaint town. I enjoyed it immensely. You should be proud of it."

"I am proud. Thank you for saying so Captain."

Captain Saunders nods.

A Filipino mess cook places a silver serving set of coffee on the conference table. He pours a cup for the captain and a cup for Rigney. Because of the ship's pitch and roll, the mess cook exercises extra care not to spill coffee and cream.

The captain peruses a page of Rigney's record.

The mess cook departs the compartment.

Rigney busies himself with adding cream to his coffee and stirring it.

"We have something in common, Page. We are both surfers. Actually, I have done little surfing since my college days. I did get a couple of chances in Hawaii, but that was twenty years ago. Do you still engage the sport?"

"No, sir. Unfortunately, surfing is only worth it in limited places. The navy hasn't sent me to any of those places, and the navy takes a lot of my time."

"Those were some good times," Captain Saunders reminisces.

"Yes, sir. They were."

"I see that your other interests include scuba diving and weightlifting. We do have a small weight room onboard, and it's open to all hands. However, on days like today when the ship is pitching and rolling, the weight room must be secured for safety reasons."

"I didn't know about the weight room, Captain. I will find it and use it as much as possible."

They both take a sip of coffee.

"I see here that you were attached to Submarine Schools Command in New London as a student for two years. Then, last month you were transferred to Bethesda Medical Center. You were there for two weeks. Then, you came here. What were these assignments all about? Were you in training for submarine duty?"

Rigney judges each of Captain Saunders's questions as an opportunity to bring up the subject of his mission. He does not feel the correct time has yet arrived.

"Sir, I was medically disqualified from submarines."

"I see." Captain Saunders closes Rigney's service record and starts on the subject of leadership. "Page, I believe in leadership by integrity and by example. Do you understand what I meant by that?"

"I think so sir. It means that I should be able to accomplish anything that I direct anyone else to do. I should always be honest and fair with assignments. Never show favoritism."

"You are correct. I believe that good morale is based on good leadership. I want all my petty officers to exercise such leadership skills. Do you agree with that?"

"Yes sir. I do." Rigney thinks about Genoa and Bronston. *Why do those two get away with what they do?*

They both take another sip of coffee.

"Good. I am glad you and I agree. Now, while you're in my command, I want you to progress in your rating and become as good as you can be at your job. If you feel that you are being denied this opportunity, do not hesitate to bring up the issue with your chain of command." The captain stands up to indicate the meeting is over.

Rigney remains seated.

Captain Saunders looks down at Rigney and says, "Thank you, Page. You may return to your duties now."

"Sir, I am having a problem with progressing with my assigned duties. I must discuss this situation with you."

"As I said, Page, you must take the issue to your immediate superior and properly use the chain of command."

"Sir, my immediate chain of command cannot help with this one. Only you can."

The captain studies Rigney for a moment. Then, he sits back down.

"Okay, Page. What is it?"

"Captain, I have just reported aboard, and I have been assigned as the division Police Petty Officer, which basically does not allow me to work in Radio."

"Page, the assignment is typical. I'm sure that Senior Chief Bulldoone and your division officer make assignments based on what's best for the division at the time."

The captain looks at his watch. Then, he picks up the coffee cup to take another sip.

"Oh, don't get me wrong, Captain. I don't fault the senior chief for assigning me to PPO. It probably is the best for CR Division operations, but it is not the best for Operation Jupiter."

The captain flinches with surprise and spills some of the coffee on the conference table. He uses a napkin to clean up the spills. Then, with a dubious tone, he queries for confirmation, "You are part of Operation Jupiter?"

"Yes, sir," Rigney replies while looking directly into the captain's eyes.

The captain looks at his watch. Then, he stands and walks to his stateroom door, opens it, and says, "Yeoman, reschedule my next appointment." The captain locks the door. Then, he walks to the door that leads to his galley and locks that door. He returns to the table and sits down.

"What's your mission?" Captain Saunders asks in a demanding voice.

"Sir, I have been specifically directed not to discuss my mission with anyone. I was instructed to solicit your influence to get me assigned to communications watches."

"I know these cloak-and-dagger missions are necessary. I spent a few years as an intelligence officer, but I need to know all of what's going on in my ship." The captain's frustrated voice is strained.

Rigney worries that the captain will try to force him to tell all he knows.

"Page, did your superiors tell you that you have only three months to complete your mission. After that, the Admiral and I will take our own actions to ensure the security and safety of *Columbus* and its crew."

"Yes, sir. ONI briefed me. That is why I need access to Radio, now. You need to get me that access, but you can't tell anyone why, of course."

"I must be honest with you, Page. ONI has not impressed me so far. Ten months have passed since I first reported my suspicions. My bosses tell me larger issues exist that I need not know about. For now, the admiral and I go along with this ONI operation. Now, I look at you. You cannot be experienced in these operations. You're too young. My doubts deepen. Anyway, I must inform you that I will make the admiral aware of your presence."

"I understand, sir."

"Do you, Page? How can you possibly understand the role this ship, and the admiral's task group plays in our National Security Program? Do you really understand? I'm doubtful."

Captain Saunders scrutinizes Rigney's face and build. Then, he opens Rigney's service record. "Is this you? Are you really a surfer from Seal Beach? Did you really spend two years attending radio schools in New London?"

Rigney knows that he must give a little to gain the captain's confidence.

"Yes, sir. My real name is Rigney Page, and I am a surfer from Seal Beach. I did attend all those schools."

Captain Saunders still looks doubtful.

"Sir, I can make you this promise. I cannot tell you much about my mission. However, if I do tell you something, it will be the truth."

The captain nods slightly to indicate his acceptance of Rigney's promise. Then, he says, "Page, if you become aware of any situation that puts any member of my crew or this ship in danger, you are to report it to me directly and immediately."

"Yes, Captain," Rigney replies automatically, although he is not sure that he would recognize such a situation—even if it slapped him in the face.

Captain Saunders is not satisfied with Rigney's answer, and frustration overcomes his manner. Then, he stands to indicate the meeting is over.

Rigney stands.

Captain Saunders extends his hand, and Rigney takes it. "I will take care of getting you assigned to communications watches."

The captain escorts Rigney to the door. Before opening the door, Captain Saunders says sincerely, "Good hunting, Page."

Rigney departs Officers Country and proceeds back to the CR Division berthing compartment. He walks slowly down the CR Division ladder into the darkened space. He takes a seat at the small card table at the bottom of the ladder. He looks at his radium-illuminated watch—1618. *I wonder how long it will take the CO's orders to flow down to the senior chief.*

Chapter 47

Brad Watson answers his secure telephone, "Lieutenant Commander Watson."

"Lieutenant Cranston here, sir."

"Anything significant to report?"

"I think so sir. Gunny Bronston was released from the hospital yesterday afternoon. He went straight to a private detective's office in Norfolk. He stayed one hour. Then, he went to his apartment. He spent the rest of the day there. This morning, he took a taxi to NOB and went aboard the *Columbus*."

"Private detective!" Brad Watson states with concern. "Bronston isn't going to let this go!"

"Doesn't look like it, sir."

"Did you put a tail on the private detective?"

"Yes, sir. It doesn't look like he has started an investigation yet."

"Well, that's a bright light," Brad Watson declares with mock enthusiasm.

"More bad news," Cranston adds.

"Lay it on me." Brad sighs with resignation.

"Only took me one hour posing as a NIS investigator to discover Magnolia's true name. She paid the restaurant bill with a *Diners Club* credit card. She dines frequently at that restaurant. Many of the staff know her by her first name. However, the staff at the restaurant did not know she is in the navy until they saw her in uniform on New Year's Eve. The bright side is that none of the restaurant staff know where she is stationed, nor do they know her rank. A couple of the waiters thought she wore an officer's uniform."

"Anyone say anything about Apollo?"

"Good news there, sir. No one knows him or saw him before. All the restaurant people and the witnesses to the fight cannot describe him other than to say he is a young sailor."

"Did you get the credit card receipt and all copies of it?"

"Yes, sir. The restaurant hadn't submitted it for payment. I paid for the dinner in exchange for all copies of the credit card receipt, and I gave the accounting clerk another one-hundred dollars not to tell anyone else. The accounting clerk also agreed to let us know if anyone else comes around asking about Magnolia."

"That should run our private detective into a dead end," Brad responds with a sigh of relief.

"Yes, sir. Looks like it will."

"What's your report on Magnolia?"

"She had duty yesterday. This morning she went to Pier 2 and watched the *Columbus* get underway."

"Did she have any contact with Apollo?"

"No close contact, sir. The tail believes she waved to him."

"What day does Magnolia depart for Naples?"

"End of next week, sir."

Brad responds with a concerned tone, "I'm not comfortable with that. A lot can happen in ten days. I will get BUPERS to issue a message that she is needed in Naples now. The BUPERS message will tell her to leave in two days—that's Saturday at the latest."

After a short pause, Brad continues. "Barry, does she own the furniture in her apartment or rent it?"

"She rents everything."

"Good. Have her pack her belongings, and you take care of getting it shipped to Naples for her. That will get her to Naples faster."

"She'll ask questions. She's smart, sir. She will know this is related to Apollo."

"That's okay. Tell her about the private eye. She needs to know about that. You told me that she wanted to expand her work with ONI. Tell her that this is her chance. Tell her that we plan to use her as a contact with Apollo in the MED. Her cover is that she and Apollo are a couple."

"Sir?"

"Yes, Barry."

"Seems to me that we are giving away a lot of compartmented information to recover from Apollo's irresponsible actions."

"Yes, we are. However, if Apollo strikes pay dirt, the payoff will be immense."

Chapter 48

"Sir, you gotta be shittin' me!" protests RMCS Sean Bulldoone to his division officer, LTJG Rowing. "You never interfered before. I sweated bullets getting the Watch Bill balanced with the available talent. Now, you want me to pull Page from PPO and put him on the watch bill. You know the XO insists on every division having a PPO to take care of the berthing compartments. Your predecessor caught hell from the XO when he did what you want me to do. If I put Page on the Watch Bill, then I must put a Radio qualified petty officer in the compartment. It just doesn't make sense."

"Yes, I know, Senior Chief. Put the senior seaman currently on compartment cleaning as the lead until we get to Spain. We got a message from Portsmouth telling us that Rouché will meet *Columbus* in Rota. That's only six days away. I've already cleared it with the Communications Officer. He will clear it with the XO. Rouché will be on the light duty list for a month. So Rouché can be the PPO."

"Sir, Rouché is qualified in five MAIN COMM watch stations," Bulldoone protests more. "Tape Cutter and Message Router are light duty."

"Senior Chief, the decision has already been made. Now proceed with getting Page on the Radio Watch Bill."

"What do you mean the decision has already been made? Are you saying that this wasn't your doing? How high up does this go? Sir, I have never seen anything like this before. Is my judgment in question?" The senior chief becomes agitated.

"Calm down, Senior Chief. Your judgment is not in question."

Bulldoone droops his shoulders and shakes his head in resignation. "Okay, sir. I will get it done."

Rigney lies in his rack reading. He attempts to concentrate on the novel *Exodus*.

The calm, slow pitch and roll of the ship acts like a rocking cradle. Rigney fights sleep.

The *communications messenger of the watch* approaches Rigney's rack and says, "Hey, Page. Senior chief wants to see you in Radio Central."

"Okay. I'll be right there." Rigney looks at his watch—1948.

Rigney jumps out of his rack and dresses in dungarees and the foul weather jacket.

In order to maintain his balance against the pitch and roll of the ship, he outstretches his arms and lightly bounces himself off the rack frames as he walks toward the ladder. As he climbs the ladder out of the berthing compartment, he finds it necessary to hold onto both rails.

He finds his way through a hatch and onto the Main Deck. The night is pitch-black. He must wait a few minutes until his eyes adjust. He hears the sea rushing along the hull only a few feet away.

After his eyes adjust and he can discern shapes and shadows, he climbs the outside ladders all the way to the 04 level where he enters the superstructure. He climbs the inside ladders to Radio Central on the 06 level.

As Rigney enters Radio Central, RMCS Bulldoone motions Rigney to a chair.

"Page, I am putting you on the Radio Watch Bill effective immediately. You are relieved of your PPO duties."

"Great, Senior Chief. When do I start?"

"We need qualified Fleet Broadcast Operators. Most watch standers don't like this position because the fleet broadcast requires a lot of attention. Normally, no slack time. The pace is rapid and frantic for the eight hours you're on watch."

"Great!" Rigney exclaims enthusiastically and with a smile.

Bulldoone stares at Page. He wonders if this kid jumped the chain of command. *But why would my superiors overrule me on such a minor assignment?* He decides to fish around a little. "What else could I do after you went to the Communications Officer and whined about it?"

Rigney knows the senior chief is guessing. "I didn't say anything to anyone."

"Well, anyway, you can start with the current watch. Come on, I'll introduce you to the on-watch Fleet Broadcast Operator. He will teach you."

Two days later, Rigney qualifies as Fleet Broadcast Operator. He passes the senior chief's oral test and performance test on the first try. Rigney now serves as Fleet Broadcast Operator for his watch section.

The veteran RM3 Broadcast Operator who taught Rigney is pleased because now he has moved to Ship-to Shore-Operator Under Instruction.

Having one additional qualified Fleet Broadcast Operator also pleases the senior chief because he has more flexibility within in his division. He would be more pleased if those *damn laxatives would start working!*

Chapter 49

The CR Division berthing compartment is dark. The pitch and roll of the ship increase with every passing hour. The CR Division berthing compartment is the most forward berthing compartment in the ship, and it feels the pitch and roll more severely than any other berthing compartment.

Rigney lies in his rack. He just came off the midnight shift. He glances at his watch—0720. He must go back on watch in six hours. He feels the bow rise high and then come slamming down. He can hear the seawater crashing against the ship's hull.

"STAND CLEAR OF ALL WEATHER DECKS DUE TO HIGH WINDS AND HEAVY SEAS."

Rigney attempts to sleep. However, the rest of the ship conducts normal daytime routine. At least once an hour some message blasts over the 1MC. Rigney sleeps only thirty minutes at a time.

The most annoying ship-wide announcement comes at 1045. Over the 1MC, a bugle plays a tune for thirty seconds, followed immediately with the words, "CLEAR THE MESS DECKS." Rigney wonders about the necessary and unwavering operational reason for the bugle. *Why else would they do it, knowing that I am trying to sleep!*

Two hours later: "CLEAR THE MESS DECKS!"

One hour later, another equally important message blasts over the 1MC: "AIR BEDDING DAY IS CANCELLED DUE TO HIGH WINDS AND HEAVY SEAS."

At 1630, the *communications messenger of the watch* passes through the compartment to wake the ongoing watch. Everyone in the ongoing watch is already awake.

Rigney jumps out of his rack. Because of the ship's heavy pitch and roll, he must balance himself by leaning against his rack. His body does not feel rested. He is not alert, and this concerns him. During tonight's watch, the *Columbus* shifts radio connectivity from NAVCOMMSTA NORFOLK to NAVCOMMSTA ROTA SPAIN. New crypto key lists will be distributed, and new radio frequencies utilized. Rigney hopes that tonight's radio connectivity changes will cause Python to perform some obvious actions.

Rigney goes to chow with members of his watch section. They walk aft toward the mess decks. They must walk with their legs wide apart to allow for the continually shifting deck beneath their feet. They pass up the long chow line because they are ongoing watch. They advise Gunner, the mess decks master-at-arms, that they are going on watch.

Gunner yells to the sailors at the head of the chow line, "Hey, you douche bags at the beginning of the line! Let the twidget pussies go to the head of the line!"

One of Rigney's watch mates says to Gunner, "Thanks, Gunner. You're not bad for muzzle fucker!"

Gunner and the sailors in the chow line smile and chuckle. These good natured, irreverent exchanges are common aboard ship. These exchanges add some humor to the dull routine of shipboard life.

Thirty minutes later, Rigney and his watch-mates climb their way to MAIN COMM using inside ladders. The route inside requires they pass through Officers Country, which is permissible because they are not allowed on weather decks. They hold firmly to ladder rails and carefully select where they put each step.

"NOW DARKEN SHIP. THE SMOKING LAMP IS OUT ON ALL WEATHER DECKS."

Rigney proceeds to the Fleet Broadcast Watch Station to relieve Larry Johnson.

Larry points to a list of frequencies for the NAVCOMMSTA ROTA SPAIN Fleet Broadcast and explains, "You must start copying the Rota Fleet Broadcast two hours prior to shift time, and you must continue copying the Norfolk Fleet Broadcast until two hours after the communications shift time."

Larry opens the small crypto safe mounted to the bulkhead above the Jason cryptographic equipment. He reaches into the safe and pulls out a keycard pad wrapped in cellophane. "These are the crypto keycards to be used for the Rota Fleet Broadcast."

Rigney nods his head with understanding and states, "I relieve you."

"I stand relieved," Larry says with a sigh, conveying his pleasure at finally being off watch. He asks, "What's for chow?"

Rigney responds, "Mystery meat, soft and soggy veggies, tasteless mash potatoes, and bug juice."

Larry smiles and expresses enthusiasm as he declares, "Outstanding! Nothing like chow at sea to raise your morale."

Before departing, Larry says to Rigney, "I heard the Division Officer telling the senior chief that Rouché will meet the ship in Rota."

"Should that be of interest to me?" Rigney questions nonchalantly as he pretends to busy himself with screening broadcast messages.

"Just thought you would like to know," Larry responds sarcastically.

Rigney turns and looks into Larry's face and says sincerely, "Larry, you have always been a good friend. Thanks for the info. I appreciate it."

"No problem, Rig. See ya later."

Rigney sits at his watch position. As messages print on the teletype machine, he compares the addresses on the messages to the list of address for which the *Columbus* guards. When he finds a match, he writes the Time of Receipt, TOR, on the message. Then, he removes the top ply copy and gives it to the Message Center Supervisor for ship's internal routing.

At 1900, he goes about setting up all the equipment necessary for copying the Rota Fleet Broadcast. Except for the radio frequencies and crypto keycards, he must configure a system identical to the one currently used to copy the Norfolk Fleet Broadcast. He follows the procedures to synchronize the NAVCOMMSTA ROTA transmit Jason cryptographic equipment to the *Columbus* receive Jason cryptographic equipment. Synchronization occurs and messages from the Rota Fleet Broadcast print on the teletype machine.

Rigney must now check both broadcast printers for messages under the *Columbus* guard. Most of the messages that Rigney *pulls* regard scheduled exercises after entering the Mediterranean.

From his watch position, Rigney can see other watch standers preparing for the radio communications shift. He concentrates on everyone's movements and mannerisms. He looks for actions that are out of the ordinary.

More people than normal crowd the MAIN COMM spaces. The Division Officer, the Radio Officer, and RMCS Bulldoone arrive and roam around MAIN COMM and verify that the correct actions are taken for the communications shift.

As Fleet Broadcast Operator, Rigney must also ensure that the Associated Press and Reuters teletypes continuously print news. During a routine check of the Associated Press teletype, he notes that the teletype prints garble. He tunes the radio receiver to a different Associated Press broadcast frequency. The teletype again prints news. Rigney glances at the first story. AP reports that U.S. troop strength in Vietnam is now at 486,000.

"NOW ON DECK ALL EIGHT O'CLOCK REPORTS!"

Rigney looks at his watch—7:30 p.m.

Rigney concentrates on the senior chief's movements. In the last several days, Rigney has come to admire Senior Chief Bulldoone's technical expertise. There were no questions Bulldoone could not answer, and there were no problems he could not solve. When necessary, he steps in and instructs watch standers on how to work a particular piece of equipment for optimum performance. From what Rigney has observed, no one knows these communications systems better than the senior chief.

"STAND CLEAR OF ALL WEATHER DECKS DUE TO HIGH WINDS AND HEAVY SEAS."

RMCS Bulldoone enters the Fleet Broadcast Room. He reviews the equipment setups, evaluates the quality of the radio signals, and reviews the most recent broadcast messages. He says to Rigney, "Looks like both broadcasts are taking some interference bursts which are causing some garbled text. Any of our messages too garbled to fix?"

"I've been able to fix all of the garbles so far. The other broadcast frequencies are much worse. We aren't getting too many messages, maybe four or five per hour between both broadcasts."

"Expect more interference problems. This storm we are steaming through is really churning up the atmospherics. Severe lightning storms predicted later tonight."

"Okay, Senior Chief."

RMCS Bulldoone watches Rigney perform his duties for about fifteen minutes. Then, he says, "Page, after we enter the MED, you can expect to pull thirty to forty messages every hour. In the MED, radio communication conditions are worse. Expect a third of the messages to have garbles. You will constantly search for better quality frequencies. Do you think you will be able to keep up with all that?"

"Yes!" Rigney blurts, somewhat offended that his ability could be in question.

"Page, never be so proud as not to ask for help. What we do here is too important for pride. If the volume gets too much to handle, never hesitate to ask for someone else to search for better frequencies or help synch the broadcast."

"I understand, Senior Chief. Thanks for the advice." Rigney sincerely appreciates the senior chief's guidance.

RMCS Bulldoone nods acknowledgement. Then, he turns and walks into the Technical Control Room.

RM1 Dukes stands watch as the Technical Controller. Dukes

struggles to establish the ship-to-shore circuit with NAVCOMMSTA Rota Spain.

Rigney hears the conversation between Dukes and the senior chief.

"The Norfolk frequencies are shit," Dukes reports. "I lost synch on the Norfolk traffic channel and coordination channel an hour ago. I've been coordinating restoration with Norfolk on CinCLANTFLT HICOMM Voice Net. Every frequency Norfolk gives me is trashed with interference or static. I've gone through a bucket full of keycards. And to top of all that, I keep finding the spare channels on the UCC-1 plugged in. I come on watch, and I find them plugged in. I call Bollier up here to unplug them. Later in the watch, I find them plugged in again. Technical Controllers on the other watches are saying the same thing."

Bulldoone responds, "Forget about the UCC-1 spare channels for now. Tell the Radio Central Watch to take down CinCLANTFLT HICOMM Voice Net and bring up the CinCUSNAVEUR HICOMM Voice Net. Then, contact Rota and pass them our position and ask them for our transmit frequencies. At the same time, give Rota frequencies we want them to transmit to us."

"Okay, Senior Chief, will do."

RMCS Bulldoone adds, "Remember that the CinCUSNAVEUR HICOMM uses different *numerical codes* and different *authentication tables*. Both of which are in the Radio Central safe and marked *MED ONLY*. Make sure that the Radio Central watch knows that."

"Okay, Senior Chief. I will tell him."

Rigney focuses on the comments regarding the UCC-1. *Wouldn't you know it! The only unusual thing mentioned, and It's about a piece of equipment that I have never seen before!* Submarines don't use UCC-1 equipment. Rigney never trained on it. Rigney knows he must learn as much as he can about it.

"SWEEPERS, SWEEPERS, MAN YOUR BROOMS! GIVE THE SHIP A CLEAN SWEEP DOWN FORE AND AFT! HOLD ALL TRASH AND GARBAGE ON STATION! NOW SWEEPERS!"

Rigney watches Dukes and the Assistant Technical Controller, RM2 Frank Carter, work frantically to establish the Ship-to-Shore circuit with Rota, Spain. Occasionally, Dukes gives orders to the Radio II Watch to setup transmitters that radiate on specified frequencies. Rigney recognizes that this is not a good time to ask a lot of questions. He decides to wait until Dukes is not so busy.

"TAPS. LIGHTS OUT. THE SMOKING LAMP IS OUT IN ALL

BERTHING SPACES."

RM2 Carter reports to Dukes, "We're *in synch* on the UCC-1 coordination channel, and I am reading Rota."

A few minutes later Carter reports, "Hey, Dukes, we are now communicating transmit and receive with Rota on the UCC-1 coordination channel."

"Great!" Dukes responds with a smile on his face. "We can use the UCC-1 coordination channel instead of HICOMM to coordinate establishing the traffic channel."

About twenty minutes later, the ship-to-shore Traffic Operator reports to Dukes, "I'm talking with Rota on the UCC-1 traffic channel. I told them I have a backlog of nine messages. Rota says that I can start transmitting messages."

Dukes responds, "Send your messages. I will notify Senior Chief Bulldoone."

Rigney senses the relief in Dukes's voice. Rigney sees Dukes pick up a phone handset and dial a number. So that he can hear Dukes, Rigney steps closer to Dukes.

"... and the signals on those frequencies are solid . . . just an occasional hit now and then, not hard enough hits to drop crypto synch on the Romulus."

Dukes listens for a few moments; then, he replies, "Yes, Senior Chief. We are sending our traffic now."

Dukes listens for a few moments; then, he says into the phone, "Okay. I will call you when all our messages have been sent."

Dukes cradles the phone. He looks around the room. He smiles and says gleefully to anyone listening, "Well, that wasn't so tough. This Tech Control shit is fun."

"Yeah. Real fun," RM2 Carter responds cynically.

A few minutes later, the Ship-to-shore Operator reports all messages transmitted and accepted by Rota. Dukes acknowledges with a nod. Then, Dukes looks around the room and spots Rigney standing close by.

"Page, how's the broadcast? Are we copying Rota?"

"Yes," Rigney replies. "We're copying Rota with occasional hits. I dropped the Norfolk Fleet Broadcast about thirty minutes ago."

Dukes smiles and looks at his wristwatch—2325. He puts his hands out, palms up, turns slowly around to cover the whole room and says, "Hey! Watch relief time. We shifted our communications guard and no backlog! Are we the power section or what?!"

The watch section lightly applauds itself. Then, they all return to their watch stations to prepare for watch relief.

263

Rigney checks the Associated Press teletype. One news story catches his attention. France has confirmed that it will withdraw its troops from West Germany. France plans to distance itself from the military arm of NATO.

After being relieved, Rigney quickly descends all ladders and goes directly to the CR Division berthing compartment. Before undressing, he stretches and exercises. He grabs hold of an overhead pipe and performs 40 chin-ups. Then, the gets down on the floor and performs 50 pushups, followed by 200 sit-ups. Afterwards, he works through a number of stretching exercises.

From his rack, Larry Johnson watches Rigney exercise and stretch. When Rigney finishes, Larry inquires, "I've watched you do those exercises every day. Do you really gain anything from them?"

"Of course," Rigney responds. "Keeps you muscles toned and ready for rapid movement. So that you don't injure yourself if you must make a sudden, forceful movement."

"I don't understand," Larry admits.

Rigney expresses thoughtfulness for a few moments, then he asks Larry, "Have you ever thrown a baseball a distance after not having thrown one for a long time?"

"Yes."

"Remember how your whole arm felt."

"Yes . . . felt like I threw it out of its socket—all the muscles burned. The whole arm ached for hours, and I couldn't play ball for hours."

Rigney says, "That's why I exercise . . . in case I must suddenly, without preparation, thrust out my arms or legs . . . so that the sudden action does not disable me."

Larry responds in a dismissive tone, "Not a problem in this living environment. Never had a problem with that."

Rigney smiles. Then, he says, "Time to take a shower then go to bed."

"Goodnight, Rig."

"Goodnight, Larry."

Rigney grabs his towel and soap; then enters the head.

Twenty minutes later, Rigney lies in his rack. He decides not to read, and he does not turn on his bunk light. Instead, he thinks about what he saw and heard during his last watch. He thinks about all the people who were in MAIN COMM during the watch. Other than the assigned watch standers, the Communications Officer, Radio Officer, and Division Officer were present. Others not part of the assigned watch were the senior chief and RM1 Bollier, the teletype repairman. He considers each one of them as a possible candidate to be Python. He saw no one involved in unusual activity. *Dukes was concerned about the spare channels of the UCC-1 being plugged- in.*

Tomorrow is Sunday, and Rigney has the afternoon watch. He decides that in the morning he will go to MAIN COMM and see what he can learn about that UCC-1.

Chapter 50

A bugle tune sounds loudly over the 1MC, followed by, "NOW REVEILLE! ALL HANDS HEAVE TO AND THRICE UP! . . . NOW REVEILLE! . . . THE SMOKING LAMP IS LIT IN ALL AUTHORIZED SPACES! . . . SWEEPERS, SWEEPERS, MAN YOUR BROOMS! GIVE THE SHIP A CLEAN SWEEP DOWN FORE AND AFT! DUMP ALL TRASH AND GARBAGE OVER THE FANTAIL! NOW SWEEPERS!"

Down in the CR Division berthing compartment, the twidget pussy radiomen moan in unison, turn in their bunks, and go back to sleep.

Rigney opens his eyes. The compartment is dark, except for some light shining down the ladder from the Deck Department berthing spaces above. Rigney glances at the luminous face of his watch—0630. The pitch and roll of the ship lessened over the night. The ship now moves with a slightly noticeable and shallow pitch and roll.

Rigney sees others dressing for the on-going watch, including Larry Johnson. Rigney jumps out of his rack and walks over to Larry.

"Larry, you going to chow before going on watch?"

"Yes I am."

"Mind if I go with you?" Rigney asks.

"Of course not."

Rigney and Larry Johnson sit at a table on the aft mess deck. Other members of CR Division fill all seats at the table. Casual conversations include discussions about sex, women, cars, and professional sports. Rigney knows little about cars and professional sports. The subject of women interests him, but he considers it improper to discuss one's sexual activities.

He would rather not participate in their conversations. However, his ONI indoctrination taught him to take actions to fit in. Listening to these guys, they all have expensive sports cars back home and have plenty of women just yearning for their sailor to come back from the sea and satisfy them.

When asked about his vehicle, Rigney tells the group about his 1951 pickup truck.

His shipmates exchange glances and chuckle.

"What kind of chicks do you *pick up* with a 1951 pickup truck?" one of the chucklers asks sarcastically.

"Beach bunnies," Rigney responds casually.

266

"What are beach bunnies?" another asks with a distinct southeastern drawl.

Rigney seizes the opportunity to do some role-playing as taught to him by Brad Watson and Dr. Williamson. "Beach bunnies are mammals of the female human variety. They usually stand about five and a half feet and weigh one-hundred-fifteen pounds. Their measurements average 36-24-34. Their flowing long hair is bleached-blond from the summer sun. When clothed, they wear only bikinis. When naked, two narrow strips of white flesh border their tanned skin. One narrow strip of white flesh bands their large and firm breasts. The other bands their pussy and ass. Their bellies are flat, and their waists narrow."

Rigney smiles, takes a sip of coffee, and continues, "Their favorite time and place is a dark summer night in a deserted beach cove. Their favorite position is on their back on the oversized air mattress in the bed of my pickup truck with me between their long, shapely legs and with me pumping my cock in long, deep, and fluid strokes in and out of their pussies. They like it with their legs straight up and with their toes pointing at the stars. In between passionate and deep moans of carnal ecstasy, they pant out their favorite words in hot, wet whispers in my ear *'fuck me harder—fuck me faster—make me come again!'*"

Rigney pauses to take a sip of coffee. Everyone at the table stare mesmerized and slacked jawed at Rigney's words. He notices that some of the sailors and marines within hearing range at close by tables are in the same mesmerized state and are breathing hard.

"Sometimes they would rather give me a blowjob than fuck me. I would lie naked on that air mattress with my feet dangling over the tailgate. If she were really good, she would take her time and would bathe me with her tongue and tease me with occasion sucks on my cock. Then, when I was rock hard, she would suck my cock in such a way that it took thirty minutes for me to come. At the end of thirty minutes I would be screaming at her to finish it. Then, she would suck me tight and fast as I shot my load. My beach bunnies were best at that because they would keep sucking until you could no longer tolerate the ecstasy, and you would beg her to stop."

Rigney's deep and resonant voice carries for thirty feet in all directions. Rigney looks around. Most of the sailors and marines stare at him. No one speaks. Many are breathing hard.

After a few moments, many leave their table—their meals not finished. Rigney assumes it is a mad dash for the heads. A few of his division mates excuse themselves with soft remarks that they must go on watch.

Larry Johnson lets his fork fall to his tray. "Christ, Rigney, must you be so graphic? Most of us won't be with our wives for six months."

"They wanted to talk about sex, and I was asked!"

"And you said it well. Your words sounded like they came right off the page of some crotch novel. Sailors will be walking around here with stiff dicks for hours. Are all the girls you know in Southern California like that?"

"I made it up," Rigney admits.

"What!"

"Yeah. I made it up. Well, most of it. Look, those guys were telling some real whoppers about their cars and sex lives. I just fabricate better than they."

Larry Johnson smiles at Rigney and shakes his head. "You surprise me, Rig. You've changed. Back in radio school, you would not have played *I can top that*. You were too cool for that."

"I guess I am bored. I wanted to liven things up a little."

"Okay, Rig. See ya later. I must go on watch."

The remainder of the on-going watch section stand and leave the table. Within a few minutes, other members of CR Division sit at the table. Rigney observes that three of them lay Bibles on the table as they sit down. The conversation changes to discussions of religion and politics.

"Will you join us for chapel services?" the sailor sitting next to Rigney asks.

"No, I am going to MAIN COMM."

"But we don't go on watch until noon."

"I'm going up early for some training."

"Page, have you been saved?"

"Saved from what?"

"Saved by the Lord from Eternal Damnation."

"CLEAR THE MESS DECKS!"

Chapter 51

Rigney climbs an inside ladder to the Main Deck. Before exiting the hat to the weather deck, He puts on his watch cap, tucks his hair and ears under the wool cloth, and pulls up the collar of his foul weather jacket around his neck.

A strong wind fights him as he opens the hatch. He exits the skin of the ship on the port side. The same strong wind assists him with shutting and dogging the hatch. The wind causes seawater to spray the decks. The nonskid deck surface allows him to keep his footing as the ship pitches and rolls. The sea swells appear to raise above the Main Deck as the ship dips forward into a trough.

Rigney proceeds forward and climbs ladders to the to the 04 level. He enters the superstructure and dogs the hatch behind him. He stands facing the hatch to a fan room. To his left, a ladder inclines to the 05 Level. He looks around the passageway; he hears no one. He studies the small hatch, only four dog handles. He considers entering the fan room to verify the presence of one of the two 9mm Berettas that have been hidden onboard for him. Then, he hears someone coming down the ladder. He decides against entering the fan room.

He darts up the ladders to the 06 level. He starts to enter the cipher lock combination to the MAIN COMM door; then, he stops. He looks up the ladder to the 07 level. Rigney decides to go to the Signal Bridge for some sightseeing.

"DIVINE SERVICES ARE NOW BEING HELD IN THE AFT MESS DECK. MAINTAIN SILENCE ABOUT THE DECKS."

Rigney exits the 07 level hatch and steps onto the Signal Bridge, starboard side. He looks forward toward the ship's bridge. He observes a lookout standing watch on the ship's starboard bridge wing.

The lookout, all bundled up in foul weather gear, looks through his binoculars as he sweeps the horizon.

Rigney walks to the rail and places both hands on the top railing. He scans the same area of ocean as the lookout. Awe overcomes him as he comprehends how the vast ocean dwarfs the powerful *Columbus*. At the horizon, the gray color of the sea meets the lighter gray color of the overcast sky. The two meld together as if they are different shades of the same substance. He would like to view the horizon through the 50 power binoculars that mount to a five-foot pedestal on the deck, but the binoculars are covered with a canvas hood.

From the height of his position on the 07 Level, Rigney observes most of *Columbus*'s starboard side. The *Columbus* churns a wake that tails the stern. At this point in time, the sea allows the power of *Columbus* to steam easily at 22 knots across its surface. Today, the sea permits this intrusion without protest. The sea will not always be so accommodating.

Rigney walks to the aft side of the Signal Bridge. He waves to the *signalman of the watch* who sits snuggly in the heated Signal Shack. Rigney comes around to the port side of the Signal Bridge. The port side 50-power binoculars are also covered with a canvas hood. The port side bridge-wing lookout duplicates the actions of the starboard side lookout.

Rigney continuously roams both sides of the Signal Bridge. He wants to observe as much as he can of this ship maneuvering through the sea. The bridge wings would provide a better view of the ship, but the bridge wings are off limits unless you are on watch.

As he comprehends the immensity of the ocean, a sense of comfortable loneliness overcomes him. He thinks about the nature of the sea. He comes to understand that the sea is both friend and enemy to the sailors of all countries. Countries become enemies and countries become allies, but the relationship between man and the sea remains the same.

Rigney understands that citizens join the navy of their respective countries for any number of reasons. For Americans, some join to meet a legal obligation to serve in the military. Others are seeking adventure. Many just want a job or an education. Some join because they feel a sense of honor and duty to serve. Rigney enlisted looking for both adventure and an education. Now, he believes that he falls into the category of serving for honor and duty.

His thoughts turn to his romantic involvements. He wonders if he and Sally have a future. Sally's developed womanhood feeds Rigney's appetite for mature relationships. Sally's educated and cultured manner leaves him wondering what she sees in him. In addition to her helping him discover his hidden sensitivity, Sally opened the door to a whole new world of sexual experiences.

On the other hand, Rigney enjoyed sexual freedom for the last six weeks. *Four different women in six weeks!*

He knows his relationship with his high school girlfriend, Diane Love, is supported only by the past. They are different people, now. Rigney doubts any future romantic relationship. He appreciates what they shared at Christmas time.

Barbara Gaile comes to mind. He knows their relationship will extend beyond the intimate New Year's weekend they spent together. Barbara's life experiences interest him. He wants to learn from her. He understands that their ONI affiliation bonds them. *Will I really see her in Naples?* The ship's port visit schedule puts the *Columbus* in Naples the first week in February—three weeks from now.

His thoughts turn to Python. *What causes Americans to become traitors? Do they understand that acts of espionage constitute betrayal? Do they not care about the danger they cause? Do they rationalize their actions in their own minds as Brad Watson and Bob Mater say?*

Rigney looks at his watch—1010. He goes on watch in two hours.

Chapter 52

RM3 Page enters MAIN COMM, the sound of teletype machines, ventilation fans, equipment fans, and the low murmur of multiple conversations fill the space.

"You're two hours early," Larry Johnson says as Rigney walks through the Fleet Broadcast Room on his way to Technical Control Room. "I stand relieved, anyway."

"Not yet, Larry. I'm here for some training."

RM1 Turner stands watch as the Technical Controller. He types on the teletype keyboard for the Rota coordination channel. A lit cigarette dangles from his lips.

Rigney stands a few feet away and waits for Turner to stop typing. While waiting, Rigney stares at the UCC-1, which sits next to him on a shelf four feet high off the deck.

The UCC-1 is boxed shaped, two-feet high by two-feet wide by one-foot deep. The unit is divided into two sections. The top section has eight small drawers. Drawers three through eight are pulled out about one-half inch and are powered off. The bottom section has eight drawers also. All eight drawers on the bottom are pushed in and powered up.

Turner turns his head and looks over at Rigney. "What's up, Page?" As Turner talks, an ash from the cigarette falls onto the teletype keyboard.

"I was hoping that you could give a little training on the UCC-1."

"Wadda ya wanna know?"

"What does it do?" Rigney asks.

"It's a multiplexer. It allows more than one teletype signal to be transmitted on the same radio frequency. The top eight drawers are our transmit to Rota. The bottom eight drawers are our receive from Rota. For example, we use only two of the eight channels. Channel one, send and receive, is the traffic channel for sending and receiving messages. Channel two, send and receive, is the coordination channel for ordering frequency changes and crypto changes.

"The multiplexer takes the two channels which are digital and converts them to multiplexed analog. The analog signal is patched to a high-frequency single-sideband transmitter."

Rigney asks, "So those transmit drawers pulled out and powered off on the transmit side are not used?"

"Transmit channels three through eight are seldom used," Turner replies. "Sometimes during the MED cruise, we use channels three and four for message traffic overload. Our communications requirements normally do not need more than two channels. An aircraft carrier, for example, would use more all the time."

"Why are the six transmit unused channel drawers pulled out?"

"The more channel drawers in use, the less radiated power each channel gets."

"I see," Rigney comments. "The fewer channels in-use the more power each in-use channel gets, resulting in more stable communications."

"Yeah, something like that," Turner responds while nodding agreement.

Rigney explains, "During my last watch, Dukes was complaining about someone pushing in the unused drawers. Why would someone do that?"

Turner thinks for a few moments; then, replies, "Pushing the drawers in powers up that channel. Makes no sense to do that. I have found the same thing from time to time. It's frustrating, especially when we're having problems with staying in contact with the shore station."

Rigney studies the front of the UCC-1; then, he asks, "When you find the drawers pushed in, what do you do to fix it?"

"We must call RM1 Bollier up here to fix it. He's the only teletype repairman and the only UCC-1 repairman onboard. He works from the Teletype Repair Shop on the deck below us."

Rigney remembers seeing the rotund, fat, and balding teletype repairman hauling teletype machines in and out of MAIN COMM.

"Why must you call Bollier?"

"Bollier says that if you push in or pull out the drawers when the UCC-1 powered on, the UCC-1 will get damaged. If we power down the UCC-1, we lose crypto synch with Rota. Bollier made a special cable that he puts in place that allows the drawers to be pushed in or pulled out without damage."

Puzzlement clouds Rigney's face. "Why doesn't he just train you guys on how to do it and leave the cable up here?"

"Bollier won't allow it. He's a patronizing, know-it-all kind of person. He thinks the rest of us are nothing but stupid idiots. *The walking brain dead* is what he calls us. He convinced the senior chief that working on the UCC-1 is beyond the comprehension of mere mortals. Anyway, none of us like him. He has no friends on this ship. If you try to talk to him, he responds with some sort of philosophical quip in an attempt to piss you off."

Interesting. Rigney considers. *That behavior fits the profile described by Dr. Williamson back at ONI.*

Some of what Turner explained about the UCC-1 confuses Rigney. He asks Turner, "If the UCC-1 will be damaged by pushing in the

273

drawers while the UCC-1 is powered on, then whoever is pushing in the drawers must be doing it when the UCC-1 is powered down. When is it powered down?"

Turner's face shows that he never thought of that. "It's never turned off when the ship is at sea. It only gets turned off during preventive maintenance, and that can only be when we are in port and a local NAVCOMMSTA has our communications guard."

Rigney states, "That means that whoever is pushing in the drawers is doing it when the UCC-1 is powered up. Isn't the UCC-1 working now?"

"Yes," Turner replies as he looks quizzically at the UCC-1.

Rigney declares cynically, "Looks like Bollier does not know what he's talking about."

"None of this stuff about the UCC-1 and Bollier make sense to me," Turner states cynically.

Rigney decides not to say any more about Bollier—could bring too much attention to himself.

Rigney asks, "How are the digital inputs from the coordination teletype and traffic teletype patched into the channel one and channel two?"

"The patch panel is in the Fleet Broadcast Room. I'll show you."

The Fleet Broadcast Room is just aft of the Technical Control Room. As they step into the Fleet Broadcast Room, Larry Johnson perks up, "You here to relieve me now?"

"No, Larry. I will relieve you at the normal time."

"What's with you, Rig? No one ever comes up here in their off-time for training, unless they're ordered to."

"I'm setting a precedent," Rigney responds cheerfully.

Turner points out the UCC -1 patch panel, which is mounted to the right of the fleet broadcast equipment patch panel. The UCC-1 channels are labeled across the top. The traffic channel equipment is patched into *UCC-1 CH 1* and the coordination channel equipment is patched into *UCC-1 CH 2*. Nothing is patched into *UCC-1 CH 3* through *CH 8*.

"Anything else?" Turner asks.

Rigney thinks for a moment before he responds. "No more, now. Do you mind if I ask questions from time to time?"

"No problem. Anytime." Turner steps back into the Technical Control Room.

During the next few days, Rigney observes several occasions when one or more of UCC-1 transmit channel drawers three through eight were pushed in. Twice during his watches, Rigney watched RM1 Bollier working on the UCC-1. Bollier would pull a cable from his tool bag and rig it to the back of the UCC-1. After attaching the cable, Bollier would pull the desired channel drawer out. Sometimes Bollier would leave the cable attached and sometimes he would not.

Rigney sits at his watch position as Fleet Broadcast Operator. Tomorrow morning *Columbus* docks at Rota Naval Station. The number of messages for *Columbus* coming over the Rota Fleet Broadcast steadily increases. About one-third of the messages regard loading supplies while in Rota. The remaining two-thirds regard procedures and time schedules for USS *Columbus* to relieve USS *Albany* as flagship for Commander Task Group 62.2

The traffic load keeps Rigney busy. Comparing the guard list to addresses on messages requires intense concentration.

RM1 Bollier enters the Fleet Broadcast Room on his way to Technical Control. As he comes up to Rigney, Bollier orders, "Page, relocate 50 percent of your insignificant Cro-Magnon mass to starboard."

Rigney looks up and behind him. Several seconds pass before he comprehends the meaning of Bollier's words. Then, he understands. Bollier's obesity will not allow him to pass without Rigney moving out of the way.

"Sure. I'll go into the Tech Control Room," Rigney replies politely.

Rigney enters the Tech Control Room and stands to the side of the door.

Bollier enters. He carries the internal assembly of a teletype machine.

Rigney goes back to his watch station and sits down. He can see most of the Technical Control Room from his position. He pretends to busy himself with checking broadcast messages while keeping an eye on Bollier's actions.

RM1 Bollier, RM1 Dukes, and RM2 Carter are in the Technical Control Room. Bollier's immensity makes it difficult for all three to maneuver.

With frustrated sarcasm, Bollier quips loudly, "Would you two useless containers of carbon-based tissue please move to the forward end of the room? You're in my way, and I need to replace this teletype machine."

Rigney hears Bollier's comments and observes Dukes and Carter move toward the forward bulkhead.

275

The teletype machine that needs replaced sits on the same self and just forward of the UCC-1. Bollier places the replacement teletype unit on the deck. Then, using the equipment shelf in front of the UCC-1 to brace himself, Bollier kneels on one knee.

Bollier's back is toward Rigney, and his bulk blocks Dukes's and Carter's view of the UCC-1.

Then, Rigney sees the subtle action of Bollier's fingers pushing in two of the UCC-1 transmit channel drawers. Rigney was not prepared for what he saw. He takes a few moments to convince himself of what he saw. *No doubt about it!* Rigney can see that transmit channel drawers three and four are pushed in.

Rigney returns his attention to scanning broadcast messages, just in case Bollier looks over his shoulder to see if anyone is watching from behind.

A few moments later, Bollier looks back over his shoulder to see if anyone is watching him. The only person that Bollier sees is RM3 Page in the next room scanning fleet broadcast messages. Page appears to pay no attention to Bollier's actions.

Bollier replaces the teletype machine. With extreme physical effort, he stands. He sweats heavily. The MAIN COMM spaces are heavily air-conditioned. Most watch standers wear jackets. Bollier's totally out-of-shape condition causes him to sweat at the slightest exertion. Bollier pulls a large red handkerchief from his back pocket and wipes the sweat from his bloated face.

With Bollier back on his feet, Rigney feels safe to take his eyes off the fleet broadcast printer and look back into the Technical Control Room. Rigney sees Bollier tucking his shirt into his dungaree trousers and pulling up the waist of his trousers to the middle of his belly.

Bollier departs the Technical Control Room and steps into the Fleet Broadcast Room.

RM3 Page unconsciously stares at Bollier's liberty-bell-size belly.

"What are you staring at you muscle bound idiot?" Bollier snips as he sneers at Rigney. "Brainpower moves the world. Muscle power has no relevance. I suppose your pea-sized brain cannot comprehend that. Now, move out of my way so I can get by."

Rigney raises his eyes to meet Bollier's eyes. He stands; then, puts his back to the equipment rack so that Bollier can pass. As Bollier passes, Rigney cannot help but comment, "Bollier, you're stereotyping me, and stereotyping is the preoccupation of the unenlightened. I suppose you cannot comprehend that?"

That comment causes Bollier to turn and face Page. He stares intently into Page's eyes. Bollier considers that he may have misjudged this young sailor. Page's comment reveals more intelligence than what Bollier previously concluded Page to have. Bollier had noticed Page doing pushups and chin-ups in the berthing compartment. He assumed that Page was just another mindless boy who spends his spare time on bodybuilding, *much like that Rouché ape*. Bollier cannot devise a clever comeback; he turns and walks away.

After Bollier departs, Rigney walks to the UCC-1 patch panel. He looks around to ensure that no one is watching him. He puts the meter select switch to *CH-1*. The meter needle continually bounces from zero milliamperes to sixty milliamperes, which displays a teletype signal—keying—on the ship-to-shore traffic channel. Then, he switches the meter select switch to *CH-2* and the meter displays teletype keying, as it should for the coordination channel. He moves the meter switch in succession to *CH-3* and *CH-4*. The meter displays teletype keying on those channels also. *The meter should not display keying on channel three and channel four. No teletypes are patched to those channels.* Suspicion floods Rigney's thoughts.

Rigney wonders if he can get more information about Bollier from Dukes and Carter. He steps into the Technical Control Room. Dukes and Carter engage in conversation about Bollier. Neither Dukes nor Carter have noticed that the UCC-1 channel three and channel four drawers are pushed in and powered up.

As Rigney moves closer, Carter asks in an annoyed voice, "What do you want?"

Carter has become irritated at Rigney's unending barrage of questions regarding Technical Control operations. What really bothers Carter is how fast Rigney grasps the concepts and procedures of the Technical Control Watch Station.

Rigney ignores Carter's tone. He recognizes the behavior and knows that Carter feels threatened.

Rigney looks at Dukes and asks, "What's with Bollier? He appears angry at the world."

Dukes considers not responding to Rigney's question. After all, Bollier is a fellow first class petty officer. Even though Dukes despises Bollier, Page has no privilege to enter this fraternal area.

Dukes decides to avoid the question, "I don't know, Page. Why don't you go ask Bollier yourself?"

Dukes's response surprises Rigney. Usually, Dukes manner toward him is congenial and cooperative.

Dukes and Carter stare at Rigney and wonder how he will respond.

"Oh. Okay," Rigney responds mildly. "Just making conversation."

Rigney goes back to his watch position. He does not approach either

Dukes or Carter for the rest of the watch. Neither of them notices that the UCC-1 channel drawers three and four are pushed in.

As *Columbus* closes the distance to Rota, radio communications become solid and reliable. Had there been communications problems, Dukes or Carter would make it a point to check the UCC-1.

Rigney checks the Reuters teletype. An interesting story prints while he checks signal quality. Spanish authorities have closed the Political and Economic Science College in Madrid.

Chapter 53

Rigney's watch relief does not arrive until 2350. Everyone else in his watch section has already departed. He exits the MAIN COMM door. In preparation for walking the outside decks and ladders, he puts on his watch cap and pulls it over his ears. He zips the foul weather jacket to his neck and pulls up the collar. He proceeds down the ladder. When he reaches the 04 Level, he contemplates entering the fan room to verify the presence of one of the two 9mm Berettas.

He stands facing the fan room hatch. The *darken ship* condition allows only a few red lights along the passageway. Rigney sees no one; he hears no one. He worries about being caught. No reason exists for him to enter that fan room. Nevertheless, he rotates the four dog levers that hold the hatch shut. He pulls the hatch open, and he steps inside. Darkness masks the room. Rigney uses the little light penetrating through the hatch to locate the light switch, which he locates just a few inches outboard from the hatch. When he flips the switch, a bright light fills the fan room and casts light into the passageway for ten feet. He quickly shuts and dogs the hatch.

He finds himself in a rectangle shaped room about ten feet by fifteen feet. A maze of round and square air ducts passes through the room at varying angles. The duct that holds the fan assembly is large and square. The top of the fan assembly rises from the deck and comes waist high to Rigney. The noise from the large fan drowns the sound of his steps.

He walks to the aft, port corner and searches the overhead for an access plate on the exterior of an air-conditioning duct. He sees an oblong access plate in a twelve-inch-wide air duct just a foot above his head. He pulls on the access-plate release lever and slides the access plate back as far back as it goes. Cold air pours through the eight-inch-long by four-inch-wide access opening. Rigney removes his gloves and sets them on top of the fan assembly duct.

He probes the interior of the duct with his right hand. He finds nothing. A moment of concern overcomes him. Then, he stands on his toes to allow deeper penetration. His fingers feel leather. He grabs a hold and pulls a leather pouch out of the duct.

Rigney holds the leather pouch in his palms. He can tell from the weight and feel that the bag contains a pistol. He sets the pouch on top of the fan assembly housing. He reaches inside the pouch and pulls out an ankle holster that holds a 9mm Beretta. The holster has two side pockets that hold an extra magazine and a suppressor.

Rigney unsnaps the holster and removes the Beretta. He verifies that the thumb safety is engaged. He ejects the magazine and inspects it—

fully loaded. He pulls back the slide to verify no round rests in the chamber. No round ejects. As he inspects the weapon, he notices a smooth shinny surface where the serial number should be. He studies the muzzle and verifies the modification for the suppressor. He holsters the Beretta. He removes the spare magazine, inspects it, and finds it fully loaded. Rigney feels comfortable knowing that he has twenty rounds at his disposal.

Satisfied, Rigney puts everything back in the leather pouch and stores the pouch back inside the air-conditioning duct. He pulls the access plate forward so that it covers the access hole. He pushes the lever, which locks the access plate in place.

He walks to the hatch. He leans forward in an attempt to hear if anyone is moving about on the other side of the hatch—futile attempt. The noise from the fan drowns out all other noise. Rigney flips the light switch and the room becomes total darkness. Through touch and feel, he un-dogs the hatch and steps into the 04 level passageway. The sound of the fan dampens after he closes the hatch.

As he dogs the hatch, Rigney hears steps behind him. He turns to leave and finds himself face-to-face with an officer, a full lieutenant. The officer does not wear a hat or coat. It is obvious that the officer has just come out of some compartment on the 04 Level. He holds a cup of coffee in his right hand. The officer stands a foot shorter than Rigney.

"Everything okay in that fan room, sailor?" the officer inquires.

Rigney does not know what to say. The officer did not challenge him; he just asked if everything is okay. *Good! He thinks I belonged in there.* "No problems in the fan room sir."

"Good." responds the lieutenant, "We wouldn't want to lose air-conditioning to the Combat Information Center."

"No, sir. We wouldn't," Rigney agrees with a smile.

"Carry on, sailor," the officer orders.

"Aye, aye, sir."

Rigney turns, takes a few steps, and opens the portside hatch to the outside ladder. He steps onto the small landing at the top of the ladder. He closes and dogs the hatch behind him.

He pauses on the landing and stares outboard. The moonlight shimmers over the water. The cold night air bites into his face. The clear night permits millions of stars to shine bright in the night sky. The *Columbus* glides over small ocean swells, the pitch and roll barely noticeable.

As he stands on the landing, Rigney ponders the events of his watch. *Could Bollier be Python?* His preconceived image of Python was someone dark and sinister looking. He wants to reject Bollier as a suspect. However, he cannot dismiss that Bollier is the only person so far to do anything unusual.

Why did Bollier push in those channel drawers? Why did channels three and four have teletype keying? Where did the teletype keying come from? I must learn more about Bollier's background. Maybe Larry Johnson knows something.

Rigney decides to talk to Larry about it tomorrow morning. He also decides that he must search Bollier's Teletype Repair Shop on the 05 Level.

Five minutes later, Rigney enters the dark CR Division berthing compartment. No one stirs or moves about. He notices Bollier sleeping soundly in a middle rack. Rigney notes that Bollier's dungaree trousers hang from the rack frame. The key chain with a dozen keys that always hangs from Bollier's belt is not there. *He must keep his keys in his rack-locker.*

Rigney stands at his rack. He considers vacating the middle rack and moving into the bottom rack. He knows that the infamous Rouché will come aboard tomorrow after docking in Rota. His concern is not what Rouché will do. His concern is will Rouché's actions and his own actions best suit the needs of Operation Jupiter. He wonders if his willingness to confront and fight Rouché will show that he does not scare easily. That could be a problem because it may alert Python. On the other hand, his willingness to face Rouché could be seen as the immature act of a prideful boy. Rigney also considers that if Rouché attacks him, Rigney could become disabled and may not be able to complete his mission.

Rigney thinks back to the behavior training he received from Brad Watson and Doctor Williamson. They stressed that the more he behaves like a supercilious wiseass and flagrant attention getter, the less likely he will look like a counterintelligence agent. Python would have been advised to be on the lookout for someone new aboard who is quiet, unassuming, and does not bring attention to himself.

Rigney decides not to move racks. He undresses and stows his clothes in his rack-locker. He climbs into his rack. He attempts sleep, but thoughts of Rouché race through mind. He also thinks about how he will get into Bollier's Teletype Repair Shop.

The continuous snoring contests and ongoing farting contests always make it difficult to sleep. Because of the annoying contests and because of all that is on his mind, he sleeps little this night.

Chapter 54

"NOW REVEILLE! ALL HANDS HEAVE TO AND TRICE UP! NOW REVEILLE!"

Rigney awakes abruptly at the loud blast over the 1MC. He looks at his watch—0530. He calculates that he only got three hours of continuous sleep.

"THE SMOKING LAMP IS LIT IN ALL AUTHORIZED SPACES!"

"MAKE ALL PREPARATIONS FOR ENTERING PORT!"

The CR Division Berthing compartment remains dark. All the radiomen remain in their racks. The division will remain in Underway Watch Bill status throughout the port visit in Rota. The next watch for CR Division does not begin until 0730. The *communications messenger of the watch* will not come to the compartment for another hour to wake the ongoing watch.
Rigney lies awake, thinking about Rouché and Bollier.

"CLEAR THE MESS DECKS!"

Annoying!
Rigney wonders why the 1MC speaker in the compartment has never been disabled. He decides to make it his mission in life to disable the 1MC speaker.
Larry Johnson jumps from his rack, retrieves his shaving kit, and makes for the head.
Rigney knows that Larry plans on going to breakfast before he relieves the watch. Larry eats four meals a day. Larry eats mountains of fattening foods, does not exercise, and stays thin. *Go figure!*
Shipboard food disappoints Rigney. He always took for granted the variety and quality of food at shore stations. On *Columbus*, fresh fruit and vegetables were gone after the first five days underway. However, canned fruit and canned vegetables are plentiful. *Yuk!*
Rigney decides to eat chow with Larry. *This will be a good time to pump Larry for information about Bollier.*
Twenty minutes later, Rigney and Larry pass through the steam line. Rigney selects wheat toast and oatmeal. Larry heaps on a mound of powdered eggs, a half-pound of bacon, four sausage patties, a mountain

of home fries, and the largest cinnamon bun ever created.

Rigney leads them to the aft mess deck. He looks for a spot away from other sailors. He selects a dimly illuminated area in the aft, port corner. A subdued noise level hovers over the mess deck. Most of the sailors talk about what to expect in Rota. All those going on the bridge watch wear Service Dress Blue uniform because the ship is entering port. Everyone else wears dungarees.

Larry Johnson shovels food into his mouth.

Rigney says to Larry, "I have wanted to ask you a question since Radioman 'A' School."

"Shoot, Rig."

"How is that you can eat so much fatty foods and never gain any weight? You don't exercise. How do you stay so thin?"

"It's in my blood," Larry responds with a smile. "It's the same with everyone in my family. My Dad, who's fifty, eats like I do. He can drink beer by the barrel, just like me. He wears the same size clothes as he did when he was eighteen. My grandfather and my brothers are the same way."

Rigney thinks about what Larry said. "Do they all smoke three packs of cigarettes a day, like you?"

"Yeah. They all smoke, except for my Grandfather. He had a lung removed last year. He's eighty-three."

"It will all catch up with you someday," Rigney responds. "You will pay the price on the end."

Larry lays down his spoon and looks directly into Rigney's eyes. "Well, Rig, that's it, isn't it? Death waits for everyone. Why not enjoy the journey?"

"The journey will be longer if you take care of yourself."

"What should I do? Eat twigs and berries and drink nothing but water for the rest of my life? I can see myself on my deathbed. My last words will be 'look everyone, I hated my life, but I made it to ninety-four.'"

Rigney does not agree with Larry, but he nods his understanding of Larry's reasoning.

Larry resumes his shoveling.

Rigney just shakes his head and continues stirring his food. In all, he has only taken a few bites of toast and a few spoonfuls of tasteless oatmeal.

Rigney asks Larry, "Did you pass your JFKs last quarter?" JFKs is the term sailors apply to the physical exercise test that must be passed each quarter. The term comes from the exercise requirements specified by John Kennedy when he was President of the United States.

"No, I just missed; the senior chief passed me anyway."

"Why's that?"

"Because he knows I'm a lifer. He knows that I will stay for thirty."

Rigney wonders how Senior Chief Bulldoone passed the JFK's over the years. *Bulldoone could not possibly have met the JFK standards. He must have been given passing marks for the same reasons that Larry got passing marks.*

Rigney asks, "Why does being a lifer make a difference?"

"Shit, Rig. You haven't got it yet. If you're a lifer, other lifers lookout for you. You can get away with a lot more than the young punks with an attitude."

Rigney shakes his head in puzzlement. He attempts to understand why the requirements are not enforced equally.

Larry points his spoon at Rigney and advises, "Speaking of attitude, you need to watch yours."

"My attitude? What are you talking about?"

"Guys in the division say you are a know-it-all showoff who thinks he's better than the rest of us."

"All of them think that?"

"No, not all of them. I have heard some talk. I heard Dukes tell Carter that he was going to speak to the senior chief about your attitude."

It's working! Rigney proclaims proudly to himself.

"But why do they think I am a know-it-all showoff?" Rigney asks. "I hardly speak to anyone except on watch, and that's only watch stuff."

"First off, I want you to know that I don't think that. I know you. I am happy to call you a friend. You helped me and a couple other guys get through Radioman 'A' School. Nobody asked you to. I will be eternally grateful for that. You are who you are. It's just that others perceive you differently than what you really are."

"I am not responsible for how people perceive me!" Rigney says frustratingly for thousandth time in his life.

"Yeah. Yeah. You've said that before," Larry responds and with a wave of his hand. "But you must understand that you need to get along with these guys. We're all part of the same team."

Rigney stares quizzically at Larry and challenges, "Are you telling me that I must change my behavior?"

"Yeah. That's what I am saying."

"Like how?"

"Well, you could take longer to qualify in your watch stations. You qualified at fleet broadcast in two watches . . . takes most guys a month at sea. And, stop going to MAIN COMM in your spare time for self-training. You irritate those on watch with your continuous questions about how things work. Frank Carter is afraid that you will take his Technical Control position away from him."

Rigney expresses disbelief. "How can he possibly think that? He knows more about it than I do."

"Some think you're getting special treatment from the senior chief. It makes them think you're brown nosing."

Rigney shakes his head and rolls his eyes.

"Well, that's what people think, anyway."

"Anything else I should change?"

"Well, yeah. You could stop doing those one-handed pushups in the compartment."

Rigney hits the table with his fist as he responds impulsively and loudly, "This is ridiculous! I am not changing the way I am just because others feel threatened or uncomfortable!"

Rigney's outburst causes sailors at other tables to turn and look in his direction.

Gunny Bronston and another Marine, who are walking nearby, turn their eyes toward the outburst. Gunny Bronston stops abruptly and stares at the dimly illuminate corner that hides the faces of the two sailors sitting there. The second marine walks into the back of the Gunny.

"Sorry, Gunny," the marine apologizes.

"Shut up!" Bronston barks.

Out of the corner of his eye, Rigney catches the abrupt stop of the two marines. He turns his head toward Gunny Bronston and sees that Bronston stares directly at him. *Oh, shit!*

Larry asks Rigney, "What's happened to you since Radioman 'A' School? You've changed."

Rigney does not respond to Larry. His heart begins to race as he watches Gunny Bronston.

That voice sounds like that fuckin' squid's voice, Bronston says to himself. Bronston walks toward Rigney.

Larry notices that Rigney stares across the mess deck, and he turns to see what has Rigney's attention. He sees Gunny Bronston coming toward them. Another marine follows Bronston.

All eyes on the mess deck follow Bronston as he makes way to the aft port corner. The Gunny still walks with a limp as a result of the beating he took from Rigney, and he still bears bruises and stitches on his face.

Rigney continues to stare at Bronston's face. *Does he recognize me? Think fast!*

This is too easy, Bronston reasons. *Too much of a coincidence for that fuckin' squid to be aboard Columbus!*

285

Rigney decides to feign humility and apologize for his outburst.

As Gunny Bronston arrives at the table, Rigney jumps to his feet. His sudden movement causes Gunny to step back.

He stepped back. He may fear me more than I fear him. I will play the respectful sailor and see how this develops.

Larry does not stand. He has no respect for this marine.

Rigney apologizes. "Sorry about the outburst, sir. I didn't mean to cause a disturbance."

"You know who I am, sailor?" Bronston asks with a slightly suspicious, calm tone.

"I know you're a marine, sir."

"I'm not a *sir*. I'm a Gunnery Sergeant. You saying you don't know who I am."

"No, sir. I . . . I mean no, Gunnery Sergeant." Rigney stutters the words. He tries to sound uncertain and apprehensive, which makes his voice sound less similar to the voice Gunny Bronston remembers from New Year's Eve.

Bronston moves his eyes to Rigney's third class crow; then, he moves his eyes to Rigney's name stencil. Then, he looks back into Rigney's face and says, "How long you been assigned to *Columbus*, Page?"

"I came aboard last week, Gunnery Sergeant."

Bronston remains silent for a few moments. Then, he looks over at Larry; then, he returns his stare back to Rigney. Then, he asks, "Where were you on New Year's Eve?"

The question takes Rigney by surprise and he expresses surprise, and he knows Gunny observes the expression of surprise. *Why shouldn't I be surprised? Bronston asked a strange question.*

"Well?" Bronston questions impatiently.

Think fast! Rigney says to himself. Then, he thinks of an alibi. "I was at the Enlisted Club at the Norfolk Naval Station. Why do you ask, Gunnery Sergeant?"

"Can you prove that?" Bronston challenges.

Rigney looks down at Larry's face; then, he looks back into Bronston's face.

"Yes, Gunnery Sergeant. I was with Johnson." Rigney nods toward Larry.

The two marines are looking at Rigney, and they do not notice the startled look on Larry's face.

By the time Bronston looks at Larry, Larry has recovered. Larry decides to play along. He remains seated in disrespect toward Bronston.

"Is that right, Johnson."

"Yes, Gunny. That's correct."

Bronston asks Larry, "What time did you leave the club?"

Rigney responds, "We left at 0100."

Bronston takes his eyes off Larry and looks into Rigney's face. Then, he turns back to Larry and asks, "Is that right, Johnson?"

"That's right," Larry replies.

Larry wonders why Rigney lies about New Year's Eve. *But why does Bronston want to know what Rigney did on New Year's Eve? Wait a minute! New Year's Eve was the night Bronston was beat up. Did Rigney have something to do with that? Does the Gunny think Rigney was involved somehow?*

"Where did you go after that?" Bronston asks Larry.

"What's this all about, Gunnery Sergeant?" Rigney interrupts. Rigney plays it up.

"I'm asking the questions, squid! Just answer!" A loud belligerent tone enters Bronston's voice.

"We went to my place," Larry informs. "And we spent New Year's Day watching the football game. My wife cooked us a traditional New Year's Day meal."

Bronston thoroughly scrutinizes Rigney from head-to-toe. He attempts to determine if this boy is capable of the brutality inflicted on him. Bronston decides it would be too much of a coincidence. He turns and walks away. The other marine follows closely behind.

Larry stares suspiciously into Rigney's eyes.

Rigney sits and asks, "Wonder what that was all about?"

"Why did you lie?" Larry asks, eager to know.

"I don't know. Why did you?"

"Don't change the subject, Rig. Did you have anything to do with Gunny's beating?"

"No, I just didn't think it was any of his business what I was doing. I didn't want to reveal that I spent New Year's weekend with my friend. You know, the first class WAVE that you saw me with that morning." Rigney avoids looking into Larry's face.

Larry does not buy it. He remains skeptical.

"Look, Rig, the word is that Gunny was beaten up by a third class on New Year's Eve. Was that you?"

"Where do such rumors come from?" Rigney responds nonchalantly.

"From the captain's yeoman. He's my next-door neighbor. He told me that he read both the medical report and the shore patrol report. He also told me that Bronston could not identify his attacker . . . only that he was a young sailor . . . a third class. Bronston reported he could identify his attacker's unique voice if he heard it again. Your voice is unique. You know how people always comment on that."

"Be sensible," Rigney argues. "Do you think I am capable of beating up a tough marine like the Gunny?"

"Yes, I do. I saw that big bruise on your arm. Where did you get it?"

"Okay, Larry. Quiet down. You cannot reveal to anyone what you think about this."

"If you admit that you beat up the Gunny, I promise I will be quiet about it."

Rigney sits quietly while he considers the resulting problems of revealing this secret to Larry. *Would Larry really talk to anyone about it? Fucking captain's yeoman. No wonder America's secrets are being revealed to the enemy. People talk too much.*

"Larry, there is more at stake here than the Gunny finding out that it was me. You must be absolutely sure that you speak to no one about this. Do I have your promise?"

"Yeah! You have my promise. So, it was you, then?"

"Yes."

"Tell me all the details!"

Rigney tells Larry the details of the incident on the Virginia Beach Boardwalk.

"Rig, you must be careful. Bronston is devious and dangerous. Last MED Cruise a sonarman insulted Gunny, and Gunny was pissed off. Well, Bronston did not go after the sonarman; he sent two of his marines to do it when we were in Athens. They almost killed the kid. The two marines lied and said that the sonarman was crazy drunk and attacked them with a knife. A switchblade was found at the scene."

Rigney shakes his head while exhibiting disbelief. "Larry, I continue to wonder about this navy. First, you tell me about this Rouché who beats on people and everyone knows it. Now, you tell me about Bronston. I don't understand how everyone knows what they do, but the captain does not put a stop to it."

"It's not what you know, Rig. It's what you can prove. Besides, the captain will avoid making a deal of it if no one else does. He won't want his superiors knowin' about it."

"How do you know these things, Larry?"

"Remember. I'm a navy brat. My Dad is a lifer, a master chief."

Rigney and Larry sit quietly for a few minutes while they continue their breakfast.

Larry is curious. "Aren't you worried about Bronston and what he could do to you?"

"Why should I worry?" Rigney replies flippantly. "You confirmed my alibi. He does not think it was me."

Larry's face goes blank while he thinks about Rigney's words. "I hope you're right; because if Bronston finds out it was you, he will know I lied . . . and that bothers me. I have a wife to take care of."

Rigney expresses regret as he realizes how his actions negatively affect his friend.

Larry looks at his watch; then, he gathers his silverware and cup and places them on his tray.

"Larry, can you stay for a few more minutes. I need to talk to you about something."

Larry looks at his watch again and says, "Sure. What do you want to talk about?"

"Bollier."

"What about him?"

"Please tell me what you know about him."

"Why? What's he to you?"

"I had a brief confrontation with him last night on watch. I just want to try and understand him."

"He's a complete asshole," Larry states firmly. "I can tell you that with certainty."

"People aren't born assholes. What made him one?"

"Part of it could be that he can't get a recommendation for advancement to chief. I've heard him bitching about it. He gets low marks in Leadership, Military Bearing, and Military Appearance. He's been in the navy for seventeen years. He made first class in six years. He's been a first class for eleven years."

Rigney concludes, "Six years is good time to make first class. He must have been totally squared away back then."

"I don't know about that. Anyway, the senior chief takes care of him. *Columbus* is their third command together. The senior chief defends Bollier to the division officer and communications officer."

The last two comments cause Rigney's eyes to widen.

"What, Rig?" Larry asks after seeing the expression on Rigney's face.

"Oh, nothing. Well, it just seems that I have encountered too many unmilitary lifers aboard *Columbus*. I just continue to wonder about an organization that allows people like BM1 Genoa, Gunny Bronston, and RM1 Bollier to be in the navy. I mean, how can the navy expect me to have respect for it when it allows such unmilitary types to be career men?"

"It's the Vietnam War," Larry responds. "The armed forces can't draft enough people fast enough. Like I said before, if you're a lifer, you get away with a lot more."

Rigney spends a few moments evaluating Larry's words; then, he asks, "Knowing all that, you still want to be a lifer?"

"Rig, the navy's not perfect. No organization is. I have been around the navy all my life. It's all I have ever known. I never considered any other line of work."

Rigney does not respond. His face reflects deep thought. He attempts to place logic in Larry's reasoning.

Larry advises, "I must go on watch now. I'll see ya later. Don't relieve me late." Larry stands and carries his tray to the scullery.

Rigney stays behind. He spends five minutes mulling over the conversation he had with Larry. He feels guilty about getting Larry involved in the Bronston incident and hopes that someday he can tell Larry the whole story.

I think I will have another cup of coffee . . . and I'll have one of those gargantuan sized cinnamon buns!

PART II

EVOLUTION OF A TRAITOR

Chapter 55

Thomas arrived in the world on June 18, 1932. He was the youngest child of Richard and Jane Bollier. When he was a boy, Thomas's sisters often told him that his birth was a disappointment to their mother and father. His parents did not want more children, but Thomas came along anyway.

Thomas's ambitionless parents lived a lower class existence in Dearborn, Michigan. Refusal to accept responsibility for their situation in life was a Bollier family trait. Richard and Jane Bollier blamed conspiring coworkers and unsympathetic union officials for Richard's continuing string of low paying autoworker jobs and periodic layoffs. Having four children during the first six years of marriage contributed to their inability to move away and seek better paying opportunities. "*We wanted to move to California*," they would complain. "We didn't want children until we established ourselves, but the children were born anyway. It's not our fault."

The Bollier family faulted the federal government for allowing all those immigrants into the country. Richard and Jane Bollier blamed uneducated non-English speaking immigrants for taking *all the good paying jobs*.

All this lack of self-accountability passed to the Bollier children. Low grades in school and lack of achievement by the Bollier children were the fault of uncaring teachers and devious schoolmates.

Of course, the ultimate fault of their failures belongs to God. *Why does the Lord punish us!*

The life of the Bollier family changed drastically in 1942. Richard Bollier easily avoided the WWII draft because of the large family that he had to support. However, Richard could not endure what he perceived as the ridicule of others. He misperceived that others ridiculed him for using his family as an excuse to avoid military service. However, no one ridiculed him. Richard Bollier suffered from such low self-esteem that he worried constantly about what others thought of him. As a result, Richard enlisted in the Marine Corps in March of 1942. Seven months later, the telegram arrived advising that Richard Bollier was killed in action. Thomas was ten years old at the time.

In addition to the emotional stress over the loss of Richard Bollier, Thomas and his mother and his three older sisters were surviving on the little amount of money that Richard had been sending home each month. However, all money was gone within a few months after Richard's death. Thomas's uncles helped some, and so did grandparents. It was not enough.

Richard never enrolled in the Serviceman's Life Insurance Program. He attended training on the advantages of the insurance program, but he distrusted the government. He thought the program was a devious trap to reduce his pay.

The Bollier family grew bitter toward government. They reasoned that Richard Bollier volunteered to go to war, and the government did not take care of the financial needs of the family left behind. Every day, Jane Bollier spoke venomously about an uncaring government. Within a short time, Thomas and his sisters echoed their mother's words.

With most of the young men in uniform, Jane Bollier had no difficulty finding work at a local automotive plant. With Jane Bollier working, the responsibility of raising Thomas passed to his teenage sisters. As the baby of the family, Thomas received continuous attention. His mother and sisters waited on him hand and foot. When he was younger and sensed that attention toward him lessened, he would throw a temper tantrum to regain attention. As he progressed into his teenage years, his attention gathering antics became increasingly clever. He would perform some comic action or say something funny.

The flood of male labor into the job market at the end of World War II caused Jane Bollier to lose her job at the local automotive plant. Jane worked two waitress jobs to make ends meet.

By the time Thomas was a junior in high school, only Thomas and his mother lived in the Bollier house. He performed all household chores, except for the washing and ironing of his mother's clothes. Performing the chores and taking care of himself was time consuming at first. Then, he learned how to organize and plan specified chores each day.

Thomas's attraction to females and vice versa developed at an early age. By the time he started high school, he learned that he gained the attention and respect of others through proficiency at sports and achieving high academic grades. His sole motive for sports activities and grades was to gain attention to himself. How such activities would improve the quality of his life never occurred to him. Whenever he did not win or succeed, he reverted to the family trait—it was someone else's fault or some conspiracy.

Thomas Bollier excelled during his senior year of high school— 1950. He was on the track team and the swimming team. When he was a teenager, Thomas was broad shouldered and muscular. His thick black hair and dark eyes endowed him with a mysterious aura that girls found attractive and seductive.

His charm and mild sarcastic wit won admiration from all. His senses were quick, and he often added humor with original quips. He

293

had no problem with getting dates, and he easily seduced the girls he dated.

Thomas's mother and three sisters focused on his happiness. Thomas reveled in the limelight. He enjoyed being the center of attention. If he found himself in a situation where he was not the center of attention, he would perform some action that would divert attention to him. His maneuverings to become the center of attention were not perceived as self-centered behavior; his behavior was perceived as part of his charm.

Thomas's sisters followed the tradition of marrying men who were irresponsible losers. Family gatherings always evolved into excuse making and blaming others for their own lack of accomplishment. The Bollier sisters complained about their non-achieving and ambitionless husbands. Their husbands complained about being cheated by cold-hearted rich people. Jane Bollier would cry about the government. And, all distressed over God's reason for allowing it all to happen. Interestingly, none of them went to church or practiced any ritual of religion. Nevertheless, they believed stubbornly in God. They had to believe in god because there must be an all-powerful force that controlled the events of human beings. Otherwise, what would account for the failures of the Bollier family members.

After his high school graduation, attention on Thomas diminished. He attempted to regain the spotlight, but fewer and fewer noticed. Attention-getting tactics that worked in high school no longer worked. Depression overcame Thomas. He started smoking. Each day he just went through the motions of existence. He had thrived on attention, and now it was gone.

Thomas had lain around the house and seldom dressed or went out. His mother forced him to take a job. Because of his 1A draft status, employers did not want to invest money and training time. A part-time job hauling boxes at a local hardware store was the best he could find that summer after high school graduation. The job paid enough to keep him in cigarettes and gas money for when he used his mother's car. At the hardware store, he attempted his attention-gathering antics. The storeowner saw Thomas's actions as immature and childish and put a stop to it. Even his mother and sisters grew weary of his behavior.

Thomas, anticipating that he must soon consider military service, talked with the navy recruiter and coast guard recruiter.

Chapter 56

As required by law, Thomas Bollier registered with the Selective Service System when he turned eighteen in late June of 1950, which was the same month the North Koreans invaded South Korea. He knew he would be inducted soon. In all, the Cold War turned hot. Although his high school grades and college entrance scores were high, his family had no money for college. In mid-September, his military draft notice arrived in the mail. To avoid the foxholes of Korea, he immediately enlisted in the navy. The navy recruiter conspired with Thomas to backdate the paperwork and backdate the *Oath of Enlistment*.

Thomas hated boot camp because everyone was treated the same. He received no special attention. He attempted to gain attention through exaggeration of his high school accomplishments and exaggeration of his sexual conquests. The other recruits were not interested. As time passed, other recruits laughed and joked openly about Thomas's obvious lies and fabrications. Then, to avoid ridicule, he retreated inward. He stopped talking and stopped gathering with others. He became a loner. After a few weeks, the other recruits did not notice his presence. He became just another face in the crowd of thousands of recruits. An inner loathing toward others, especially toward chiefs and officers, burned inside him.

Blind idiots, Thomas thought of them. *They cannot see that I'm special and they don't understand my worth. I'll prove it to them, not now . . . later. I must get through boot camp first. There are no intelligent people in this place.*

The results of the Navy Classification Tests revealed that Thomas would excel at electronics and Morse Code. That surprised him; he did not think he knew anything about radios. After boot camp, the navy sent him to radio school at the Naval Training Center, Bainbridge Maryland.

While attending radio school, he strengthened his opinion of himself that he was special and different from the other sailors. Thomas discovered that he easily gained understanding of radio electronics faster than other sailors. He knew his mind worked faster. He also discovered that he knew more about most things than the others around him. Most of them were high school graduates, like him; but he seemed to have retained more of his education. Also, during radio school, he discovered that he had a natural and creative ability to solve technical problems. After six months of radio school, he graduated at the top of his class.

During June 1951, Thomas reported to the USS *Grant, DE-420*. The *Grant*, a Destroyer Escort, was home-ported in San Diego. The *Grant* made three Western Pacific—WESTPAC—cruises with most of her time patrolling the coast of Korea. Thomas considered his work interesting and he discovered the foreign ports to be exiting.

When in San Diego, he was never lonely. He had several girlfriends that he dated on a regular basis.

Thomas proved his excellence as a radioman. Mostly, he sat the CW ship-to-shore circuit. He copied Morse Code at 52 words-per-minute. His CW sending skill was flawless. For Morse Code transmission, he used a speed-key when others were only skillful with a traditional manual-key.

Most importantly, he was awarded a commendation for fixing a radio transmitter during a crucial firing engagement off the coast of North Korea. After the so-called experts gave up on the repair, he used non-radio parts to repair the transmitter. After that, when the captain wanted to send an important message, the captain insisted that Bollier sit the radio position.

Thomas advanced quickly to second class petty officer. During his first two years on the *Grant*, his performance evaluation marks were 4.0. He maintained his teenage physique, and he took extreme care to ensure his military appearance was always perfect.

Thomas smoked two packs of Camel cigarettes per day. The tar and nicotine stained his teeth, which destroyed his engaging smile. Eighty percent of the *Grant's* crew, including officers and enlisted alike, smoked one-to-two packs of cigarettes per day. In 1951 the hazards of smoking were just becoming widely known; smokers were in denial.

During the last year of Thomas's enlistment and during his third year aboard *Grant*, his marks in military bearing and leadership dropped to 3.6. The comments accompanying the lower marks stated that Bollier *on occasion displays disrespect toward his seniors and sometimes shows contempt for his peers.*

Bollier was fully aware of his growing disrespect and contempt for others. The traditional processes frustrated him. He did not understand why his superiors could not overlook his behavior infractions. *After all, I am the hero of that firing engagement off the Korean coast. Am I not the fixer of all problems big and small?*

He did not understand why he had to wait the required time-periods between pay-grade advancement. The time in rank requirements would not allow him to compete for advancement to first class until he had five years of service. Bollier openly displayed contempt for the lackluster performance of the senior radioman, a first class petty officer with twelve years' service. Bollier was aggressive and consistent with gaining knowledge and experience. The senior radioman did not seem to care about anything and was never the focal point of problem solving.

Don't I know more, and don't I perform better than the radiomen that are senior to me? Am I not the captain's number one radioman?

Inwardly, Thomas enjoyed his work as a radioman, although he openly expressed loathing toward navy policies, navy procedures, and shipboard life. None of it made sense to him. Everything was always in a constant state of change. *Planning and order are nonexistent! Lifers issue orders that make no sense. Orders given one day are reversed the next. Lifers error seriously and are not held accountable. Contrarily, junior enlisted men are punished severely for minor infractions. The food is bad and the hours atrocious. Lifers never seemed to care about the disrespect and bad attitudes they instill in others.*

Thomas was not aware that his negative attitude was fired by his underlying distrust of government that he learned from his family. His distrust for government evolved into contempt toward any structured organization or figure of authority.

Thomas's contempt for others extended to the *Grant's* leadership. He felt the ship's leadership protected the *incompetent lifers*. He did not trust the senior petty officers or the officers. His seniors lied to him too many times. His seniors would specify a radio technical fact or a navy policy. Later he would discover their specifications were erroneous.

The *Grant* had two commanding officers during Thomas's time aboard. Neither CO seemed cognizant of the incompetence cover-ups. Thomas had drafted several letters to the Chief of Naval Operation. He was sure that if the CNO knew about what was happening aboard *Grant* the CNO would do something about it. But Thomas never sent the letters because, on paper, his complaints looked minor and looked like a weak and unsubstantiated attempt to discredit his superiors.

Near the end of his enlistment, the reenlistment sales pitches started. They started with the division officer, who had already announced his intentions to leave the navy at the end of his obligation. Then, the department head took a shot. Thomas thought both of their attempts to be halfhearted and insincere. Neither officer could provide any incentives to continue his service other than pride and patriotism. The promise of retirement and medical benefits after twenty years of service contained no value for the twenty-one-year-old Bollier.

Then, the commanding officer talked with Bollier. The CO asked Bollier a question that the previous two officers had not asked. "What do you want in return for reenlisting?"

Since Thomas never seriously considered shipping-over, he had never given the subject any thought. On several occasions, he proclaimed to seniors, peers, and subordinates alike, "Only losers reenlist in the navy!"

Thomas declared to the CO, "The navy has nothing to offer me."

"You are eligible for shore duty," the CO advised him. "How about some advanced technical schools to go along with that shore duty. And a fourteen-hundred dollar reenlistment bonus will be paid."

"Not interested," Thomas responded.

"What will you do when you leave the navy?"

"I will go back to Dearborn and get a job in one of the automobile plants there."

"Sounds exciting," the CO commented dryly. "Look, Bollier, the navy offers eight months of advanced electronic repair and teletype repair courses, plus some choice shore duty afterward. Would you like a three year shore tour in Europe or maybe Hawaii?"

"No, sir. You cannot offer me anything that will change my mind."

The meeting ended with the CO asking Thomas to think it over.

Thomas went back to his division and boasted to anyone who would listen how he had told off the captain.

The captain knew that Bollier would eventually reenlist because Bollier enjoyed his status as a quality radioman. He enjoyed the spotlight. The captain saw Bollier's enjoyment and excitement every time that the captain asked Thomas to perform some special task. The captain also knew that Bollier's technical ability would benefit the navy. However, the captain also knew that unless Bollier changed his immature and contemptuous attitude, Bollier would never advance beyond first class petty officer.

The captain was proud of his ship's 83 percent reenlistment rate, which always received favorable comments in his fitness report. He would do all he could to change Bollier's mind. The captain planned to call BUPERS during the next in-port period. He would ask BUPERS to issue orders to Bollier for schools and shore duty.

The closer Thomas Bollier came to the end of his enlistment, the less the life as an autoworker in Dearborn Michigan appealed to him. A letter from his uncle said he must join the union to get a job in the auto plant. His uncle explained in the letter that Thomas's name must go on a waiting list. When his name came to the top of the list, he would be considered for the next open position.

Thomas's mother offered Thomas to live at home and work at temporary or part time jobs until the auto plant job became available. His mother also proposed that Thomas could attend the local junior college until the union job became available.

Bollier reevaluated his whole situation. He hated the idea of joining a labor union. He considered labor unions as a safe-haven for low skilled workers who could not survive on their own merits, and he believed *lifers* fell into the same category. He believed union membership as protection to maintain a job that anyone could perform. His pride had developed beyond that. Bollier knew that his successes so far in life were of his own doing. He considered his navy life and navy job as a success. The only reason he wanted to leave the navy was that he could not stand the label *lifer*. He was offended and frustrated by the thought that he need not perform any better than the *Grant's* Leading Radioman for advancement to first class.

Thomas ruled out college. He liked the technical work that he performed; he found it satisfying. He sent resumes to twenty-two electronic companies in the Detroit area. None of the companies responded.

With a month left on his enlistment and while the *Grant* was docked in Pearl Harbor, orders arrived. The orders read for RM2 Thomas Bollier to report to Naval Training Center, San Diego for advanced electronics schools and Teletype Repair School. Upon successful completion of the schools, he would transfer to the United States Consulate in Edinburgh, Scotland via indoctrination at the American Embassy, London. The orders stipulated that to qualify for the schools and Scotland, Bollier must be found suitable for overseas duty as prescribed by BUPERS Directives, and he must reenlist for six years.

Upon hearing the contents of the orders, Bollier became exuberant. He had thought that there was nothing the navy could offer. *I never considered this! I never imagined!*

Bollier's trust in the navy's judgment improved rapidly. "See how bad they want me to reenlist!" he announced to everyone in his division. "These orders prove the navy knows my value."

His whole outlook changed. He went to the Commanding Officer and agreed to reenlist, but only if he transferred immediately. He did not want to hear his peers and subordinates call him *lifer,* especially since he had previously proclaimed *lifers* to be losers.

Two days later, the captain officiated the reenlistment ceremony. The only other attendee to the ceremony was the communications officer. The next day, Thomas transferred to San Diego to start his schools.

Chapter 57

After arrival in San Diego, RM2 Thomas Bollier spent some of his reenlistment bonus for a deposit and first month's rent on a furnished apartment near Ocean Beach. He also used some of his bonus to purchase a three-year-old car, a 1951 Buick.

Thomas could not have been happier. He had no worries. He breezed through each course and finished at the top of each class. He experienced a comfort level never felt before—no stress. He received a steady paycheck. School hours were constant and did not change. He kept expenses low by using on-base facilities. He did not need to study. Instead of going back to a barracks every afternoon, he drove to his apartment at Ocean Beach. He spent most nights and weekends with his various girlfriends. Life was good. *What a great time!*

He was especially pleased with his instructors. The first class petty officers and chief petty officers were quality instructors and quality leaders. All the instructors were professionals who were proud of their place in the navy. *These lifer instructors know what they are talking about—unlike the lifers on the Grant. These lifers genuinely care about my success—unlike the lifers on the Grant. These instructors are not like those idiots back on the Grant.*

Thomas's orders to Scotland were the envy of his classmates and his instructors. No one could remember knowing anyone who served on consulate duty in Scotland.

Thomas anxiously anticipated a leisurely train trip to the east coast and a more leisurely cruise across the Atlantic.

Then, with two months of school remaining, Thomas was informed by the personnel office that he had never been screened for overseas duty, which was required before he reenlisted. "Before your travel orders can be issued, you must pass the suitability screening for overseas assignment," the personnelman told him. "If you're found unsuitable for overseas, you will not be allowed to go to Scotland, and you will probably get orders to a stateside shore duty."

What the fuck is this! Isn't this typical of this chicken shit outfit? They make me ship-over; then, they tell me I might not get the duty! Jesus Christ! Don't the lies and incompetence ever stop!

Thomas complained loudly about the overseas screening to his classmates. The lead instructor, a chief radioman and veteran of WWII destroyer duty in the Atlantic, overheard RM2 Bollier's complaints. He called Bollier into his office and talked to him about his complaining behavior. Bollier expressed his frustration over this latest development. The chief instructor promised to help Bollier through the screening. The chief had gone through the screening himself prior to being sent to duty in Italy in 1950.

The chief soothed Bollier's frustrations, "All the navy wants to do is make sure that you're not an embarrassment in front of foreign citizens. The screening includes medical and dental checkups. That's to ensure that you're physically fit and to ensure that you do not expose a mouth full of black-rotting teeth when you smile. I don't think you will have a problem with the medical, but I am concerned about the dental exam."

"Who interviews me?"

"The Commanding Officer of Schools Command. He has the responsibility to verify that you are mature and well behaved and that you won't act like a rude idiot in front of foreign nationals."

"But what about my CO on the *Grant*? Why didn't he do this? He was supposed to! It would have been no problem aboard the *Grant*! They wanted me to ship-over real bad."

"Listen Bollier. If you want to pass the CO's screening, you can't come across with anything negative. Don't dwell on what happened aboard your last ship. You must come across to the CO as mature and positive about everything. Do you understand?"

"Yes, I understand, Chief; but why does the navy allow all these fuck-ups? *Lifers never get punished for fucking-up!*"

"Like I said, Bollier, do not get all excited with negative words, not if you want to pass the screening."

Thomas understood the chief's advice. He would put aside his negative feelings and comments until after the screening.

"One more thing, Bollier, your dental health must be good to pass the screening. Before you see the CO, you must go to the dental clinic and get that black stuff off your teeth."

"Okay, Chief. No problem. I will do as you say."

"I will guide you through all the screening steps. I have been through it myself. I want to see you succeed here. Do you believe me?"

"Yes, Chief. I believe you." Thomas sincerely believed the chief.

"Good. Now, do you have an inspection quality set of Service Dress Whites?"

"Yes, I always have an inspection uniform ready."

"Good for you," praised the chief. "That says something about your pride in wearing the uniform. Wear that uniform when you interview with the CO."

The screening took four days. Thomas Bollier followed the chief's direction through the whole process. The following week, RM2 Thomas Bollier was advised that he was found suitable for overseas assignment.

Thomas gained more respect for the chief. No one in the navy had shown that much interest in his success. The chief also convinced Thomas not to be bitter toward the *Grant's* CO for what happened. "Remember, it was that CO who got you choice orders."

The chief had a long talk with Thomas about the enormous responsibilities carried by a ship's captain. Thomas came away from the situation with a better understanding of the navy and with an increasing respect for navy chiefs.

Chapter 58

During late May 1955, Thomas was in his last weeks of technical school. He prepared for transfer to Scotland. The personnelman told Thomas that he could only take his regulation seabag and regulation uniforms to Scotland. Thomas sold his car and moved out of his apartment. He put all his personal items in storage.

His travel orders directed that he report to the Naval Air Station, San Diego and await transport via military aircraft to the Naval Air Station Norfolk, Virginia. He was required to wait in the San Diego Naval Air Station passenger hanger day and night until an opening for his travel priority became available. Several times, he was number one on the list, just to be bumped by someone with higher travel priority. He waited for two days while catching catnaps in uncomfortable chairs and eating bad food from the hanger canteen. Other than the sink faucet in the head, there were no bathing facilities. Thomas became irritable. His contempt for navy processes resurfaced after lying dormant for eight months. The reenlistment honeymoon was over.

RM2 Bollier finally boarded a two-prop engine transport airplane at two in the morning. The passenger compartment was full. The trip to Norfolk was totally uncomfortable. The plane was not heated, and the air became cold at flight altitude. Thomas was wearing his Tropical White Long uniform and had to pull his peacoat, gloves, and extra socks from his seabag. The passenger seats were nothing but metal benches. No food was available. The airplane made one refuel stop at an Air Force Base in Texas. Thomas worried about the stop because he could get bumped. When the plane landed in Texas, he asked the crew chief if he could get off the plane and get some food. He was told no because some food would be brought aboard. He did not get bumped. The flight crew forgot to pick up the food.

Thomas was miserable and hungry when the plane landed at the Naval Air Station in Norfolk. The trip took a total of fourteen hours. He stepped off the airplane into a hot and muggy May afternoon. His cotton tropical white uniform did little to keep him cool. The effort of carrying his seabag resulted with him being drenched in sweat.

Hot, sweaty, dirty, hungry, and in a foul mood, Thomas dragged himself wearily into the passenger terminal. The terminal was just as hot and muggy as the outdoors. He handed his orders to the petty officer behind the Check-In Desk.

"Those West Coast guys never get it right!" the Check-In Petty Officer remarked with a slight frustration in his voice.

What now! Thomas screamed into his own mind. *Don't lose your temper, Thomas ole boy. Whatever the problem, it's not the Check-in Petty Officer's fault.* "Is there a problem?" Thomas asked with a constrained voice and with a thin smile on his face.

"That London Embassy flight no longer passes through Norfolk, discontinued about six months ago. You must go to Andrews to catch the flight."

"Andrews?"

"Yes, Andrews Air Force Base . . . Washington D.C."

"Gee, how unfortunate for me." Sarcasm seeped from Bollier's voice. "What do I do, now?"

"I book you on the next flight to Andrews. That's at 0800 tomorrow."

"I suppose I must sit around here all night, waiting." It was more a statement than a question.

"Not at all! You stay in the transient barracks for the night. It's out the door and to the left . . . just down the block."

"Can't I get bumped, if I am not here?"

"Of course not. You're booked Priority One. All Embassy Permanent Change of Station travelers are Priority One."

RM2 Bollier considered the petty officer's words. "Why wasn't I Priority One from San Diego?"

"I don't know," replied the petty officer. "Like I said, those West Coast guys never get it right."

Thomas Bollier knew it had nothing to do with West Coast versus East Coast. He knew that it had everything to do with superiors not properly training their sailors, and those sailors not taking enough pride in their work to seek out self-training to learn their jobs the best they can on their own.

Fucking navy! What a bullshit outfit!

"What about some food?" Thomas asked anxiously.

"The chow hall is not far from the transient barracks. Here, take this." The petty officer handed a piece of paper to Bollier. "Give this to the barrack's master-at-arms and a copy of your orders. He will assign you a billet for the night. Be back here at 0700 tomorrow morning."

"Thanks!" Bollier responded enthusiastically. "I appreciate it." He was sincerely appreciative.

"No problem, sparks. We're here to serve."

Thomas swung his seabag onto his left shoulder and departed the passenger terminal. His mood became more cheerful as he realized that he would have a meal and a good night's sleep. The fact that his body was drenched with sweat and his uniform a mess did not diminish his growing good mood.

Forty minutes later, Thomas had shaved and was standing in a shower. He stood there with cold water running for twenty minutes. Afterwards, he dressed in a clean Tropical White Long uniform. He looked at his watch—1715. He departed the barracks and went to the chow hall to eat supper. By 1930, he was asleep. He slept in a noisy open-bay barracks, but nothing disturbed him that night.

The next morning, reveille sounded at 0600. Thomas awoke refreshed. The cool morning air filled the barracks. Thomas felt comfortable. He dressed quickly in his uniform from the night before and went to the chow hall for breakfast. He checked into the Passenger Terminal at 0650. The Check-In Petty Officer from the previous day was not on duty. However, the on-duty Check-In Petty Officer looked at Bollier's paperwork and advised that everything was in order. The aircraft, another two-prop transport, took off at 0800.

The flight to Andrews Air Force Base lasted one hour.

The Andrews passenger terminal was air-conditioned and had plenty of padded chairs. The air-force-blue colored tile floor was clean and freshly waxed. This time, Thomas found himself standing at a Check-In counter with an air force sergeant standing behind it. The sergeant shook his head disapprovingly as he studied Bollier's orders. The sergeant studied Thomas's orders for a full five minutes, before he finally said, "Those navy guys never get it right."

"Is there a problem?" Bollier tried to sound casual.

"Yeah. All the codes are wrong. It will take forever to straighten out the paperwork." The sergeant continued to shake his head disapprovingly while staring at the paperwork.

"So, what's next?" Thomas asked cheerfully, although he wanted to reach across the counter and rip the head off this air force puke.

"Oh, you will board the embassy flight this afternoon at 1400. You will be in London by tomorrow morning. Just because the paperwork is all messed up does not mean your Priority-One status changes. This flight is specifically for embassy business . . . lots of diplomatic stuff onboard and supplies for the embassy. As of right now, it's you and three other passengers. The plane allows for twenty passengers."

"No chance of me getting bumped then?"

"It's not that kind of flight. You got a confirmed reservation."

"*Great!* What do I do now?" Bollier fantasized that he was putting the sergeant's head back on.

"Just take a seat, sailor. We'll announce when we are ready to board. You can get something to eat in the cafeteria in the next building."

Well! Things are getting better!

Chapter 59

The airplane for the embassy flight was more like a commercial passenger airplane than like a military aircraft. A stewardess actually served meals and drinks. Thomas had a short conversation with the other three passengers. They were State Department civilians going to London for several weeks to conduct an audit of some kind. After a good meal and a few drinks, Thomas leaned back in a first-class style seat and went to sleep.

The flight landed at London's Gatwick Airport at 11:00 a.m. Several U.S. Embassy representatives and a British Immigration official met the airplane.

After departing the airplane, the passengers were led into a small building to undergo processing. Bollier's arrival took the Embassy representatives by surprise. They were not expecting him. An issue developed over Bollier not having a diplomatic passport.

"Those Department of Defense people never get it right," commented the senior U.S. Embassy representative.

Bollier rolled his eyes on that comment.

After viewing Bollier's Military I.D. card and receiving a copy of Bollier's orders, the British immigration officer agreed to allow Bollier into the country. The senior U.S. Embassy representative promised that Bollier would be processed for a diplomatic passport as soon as possible.

While the officials continued working on the visa paperwork and the logistic paperwork, Thomas looked out a large window and watched men in U.S. Air Force uniforms unload the plane's cargo into a truck. Luggage and Thomas's seabag were also loaded into the truck.

The senior U.S. Embassy representative called the Embassy's Defense Attaché's office and informed them of Bollier's arrival. Then, he told Bollier to report to the Defense Attaché's office when they arrived at the embassy.

Twenty minutes later, the new arrivals and the embassy officials climbed into a minibus. Ninety minutes later, they arrived at the U.S. Embassy at Gosvenor Square.

Thomas grabbed his seabag from the bus. A marine helped him find the Defense Attaché's Office. A receptionist directed him to Commander Logan's office.

After introductions, Commander Logan briefed Thomas. "A communications center has been built at the U.S. Consulate in Edinburgh, Scotland. Plans are in the works to build a U.S. Navy submarine refit base at Holy Loch, Scotland and U.S. Navy transmitter station near Thurso in northern Scotland.

"The increased flow of messages to and from the consulate will require a communications center that can send and receive dispatches electronically. Since the navy funded the consulate's communication center, it was built to a navy model.

"Your assignment is to operate the communications center, repair broken equipment, and train State Department civilians on how to operate it. Currently, online encryption systems are not part of the operation. All classified messages to and from the consulate require offline encryption with the Adonis Crypto System. Are you familiar with Adonis?"

"I watched the Communications Officer on the *Grant* operate the Adonis equipment," Bollier told Commander Logan. "Only officers are allowed to operate it."

"That's correct. Communications Security Regulations prohibit enlisted men from operating Adonis, except during periods of extreme operational need. An officer-grade DOS civilian at the consulate has been designated as Crypto Security Officer. He will operate the Adonis equipment. He will encrypt and decrypt all coded messages."

"DOS?"

"Department of State," the commander explained.

Thomas nodded his understanding.

Commander Logan continued the briefing. "You should not expect more than a dozen encrypted messages a week. Your primary responsibility is to perform scheduled preventive maintenance on the Adonis devices and to repair the devices when required."

Thomas does not offer that he was never trained on the Adonis devices. He did not want to endanger his duty assignment before it began. *If a tech manual exists, I can figure it out.*

Commander Logan spent an hour explaining Bollier's duties at the Edinburgh Consulate. Bollier affirmed understanding.

Commander Logan studied Thomas for a few moments; then, he asked, "Bollier, why are you in uniform?"

Thomas blinked his eyes and jerked his head back with a confused look. "Uh . . . well . . . I don't understand your question, sir. The personnelman back in San Diego said I was only allowed to take my seabag and regulation uniforms. We always travel in uniform. It's the rules. Right?"

"Normally, yes," Commander Logan said. "However, the personnel requisitions we sent to BUPERS authorized travel in civilian clothes. We also authorized shipment of a car and authorized shipment of 2000 pounds of your personal property."

"Sir, the personnel office back in San Diego said I could only bring my seabag and regulation uniforms. I put everything in storage, including my civvies."

Commander Logan pulled some papers from a file folder and studied them. He shook his head in disgust. His manner revealed that this was not the first time such mistakes have occurred.

"The personnel requisition is clear on the civilian clothes and personal property. Well, no matter now. Do you have any money to buy some clothes?"

"I have about forty dollars. The rest of my money is in a bank back in San Diego."

"Hmmm," the commander vocalized as he opened a desk drawer and pulled out an envelope stuffed with British currency.

"Here's 150 pounds." The commander reached across the desk and handed the money to Bollier.

"You will be in London for a week for check-in and indoctrination. You can go shopping for clothes while you are here in London. You can go shopping now. Be back here tomorrow at 0800 and be in civilian clothes. A suit would be best. The yeoman made reservations for you at a hotel down the street. The hotel will bill the embassy directly. You can charge meals to your room.

"I know that you must have a lot of questions; hold them for now. You will be totally briefed over the next couple of days. Now, go see the yeoman and he will give you directions to the hotel."

Bollier totally enjoyed his four days in London. His hotel room was spacious, and he fell immediately in love with the food and pub culture. He discovered the theater district and saw his first stage play.

Thomas had visited foreign cities before, like Hong Kong, Rangoon, and Manila. But that was as a sailor in uniform. He felt totally at home in London. Yanks were highly respected and appreciated. And he spoke the language.

To top it all, the Edinburgh Consulate had already found Thomas an apartment. Thomas would get an additional per diem and housing allowance of $163.00 per month. He would also receive an additional $50.00 per month to maintain a civilian wardrobe.

Thomas would be the only navy person at the consulate. There were official discussions about assigning navy officers at the consulate; however, no officer billets had been established. Thomas Bollier was on top of the world. He would be away from the *navy bullshit* and on his own. *I guess I made the right choice by staying in this outfit!* The reenlistment honeymoon was back on.

On June 5th, 1955, Thomas boarded a train for Edinburgh, Scotland. The train ride from London took twenty-two hours. Thomas enjoyed the trip. The train passed through green and lush countryside with intermittent stops at several large cities. He mixed with the locals and engaged in small talk about American and British customs. All the Brits he met treated him like a hero. All remembered the war years and gratefully revered Americans. Thomas laughed deeply every time a Brit affectionately spoke about the Yanks during WWII as *over fed, over sexed, and over here!* Thomas Bollier was the center of attention; he was happy again.

Chapter 60

Thomas arrived in Edinburgh the next morning. No one met him at the train station. He loaded his newly acquired suitcases and seabag into a taxi. He told the taxi driver to take him to the United States Consulate.

Upon arriving at the consulate, Thomas went directly to the information desk. He asked for the chief of the Administration Section.

After making a phone call, the Information Desk Attendant told Thomas to take a chair, and someone would be with him soon.

An hour later, a man in his mid-thirties arrived in the waiting area and introduced himself to Thomas as Edward Stanley, Chief of the Administration Section. Stanley was a frail looking man of medium height. He combed his thinning black hair strait back. Owl glasses perched on the end of his pointed nose.

Stanley told Thomas to leave his bags where they lie and follow him. Stanley took him on a quick tour of the consulate, which ended in the newly built Communications Center.

During their discussions, Stanley's attitude about the Communications Center came to light. Stanley told Thomas that in all his years of diplomatic service, he had never encountered a situation where the navy funded and operated the Communications Center. The Department of State never requested the Communications Center. The navy insisted on it because of the plans to build U.S. Navy installations in Scotland. Finally, DOS agreed to the Communications Center, but only if funded by DOD and made operational by DOD.

"The Communications Center has been ready for months. We've been waiting for you to arrive and start operations." Sarcasm and accusation edged Stanley's tone.

Thomas felt defensive.

Stanley told Thomas, "Two State Department employees are assigned as teletype operators. One of your assignments is to train them on all aspects of operating and maintaining the Message Center. Commander Logan was specific on that. *But I want no navy nonsense established in my Communications Center!* You are to operate it in the same manner as other DOS Communications Centers. *Do you understand that?"*

Stanley's confrontational behavior confused Thomas. He decided it best to nod his head in understanding and not argue.

With an air of superiority Stanley explained, "The consulate staff is not pleased that the navy sent an enlisted man, instead of an officer."

"I can do this," Thomas defended confidently.

Stanley studied Thomas for a few moments; then, he said,

310

"Regardless of what you may have been told, DOD and DOS agreed that you would not be in charge. Your status is that of technical adviser and trainer. I am in charge here. Nothing is done without my approval." Stanley lied. Stanley believed DOD to be staffed with incompetent morons; therefore, he justified his lying as to what was best for DOS.

Stanley's revelation conflicted with Commander Logan's instructions, but Thomas did not argue the point. He would talk to the commander about it later.

Stanley released Thomas to the consulate driver, who drove him to his apartment a few blocks from the consulate. The apartment was fully stocked with everything he would need. Other than purchasing food and personal hygiene items and paying the rent, Thomas had no need to purchase anything for his apartment.

The next morning, Thomas dressed in a civilian suit and went to work early. He was anxious to get started. His primary motivation was to impress everyone that he was more than capable to get the Communications Center operational.

The Communications Center consisted of three rooms. The Message Center occupied most of the space. The second largest room served as the Repair Shop, and the smallest room served as the Crypto Vault. The Crypto Vault had a metal door with a tumbler combination lock.

The publications library included all the current navy and DOD Operating Manuals and Technical Manuals. Department of State telecommunications manuals were not included in the Communications Center technical library. When Thomas queried Stanley regarding DOS telecommunications manuals, Stanley informed that he would verbally direct Thomas on all that conformed to DOS procedures.

Without difficulty or delay, Thomas activated the two-teletype circuits. One circuit connected over British telephone lines to the U.S. Air Force Message Relay Center at Croughton, near London. The other connected over British telephone lines to the navy communications center at the navy headquarters building in London, which was located a few buildings away from the United States Embassy.

Since the Communications Center operated only during normal working hours, Monday through Friday, the communications circuits were shutdown at 5:00 p.m. each day and reactivated at 8:00 a.m. each morning. For the first week, only a few messages flowed through the Communications Center, which allowed plenty of time for Thomas to train the two DOS teletype operators. Both operators were former members of the Army Signal Corps. They already knew the basics and they learned quickly.

Thomas was disappointed that he was not in charge of anything or anybody. He served only as a technical expert. Edward Stanley, who seldom followed Thomas's advice, made all decisions. Thomas would justify his recommendations by pointing out the applicable specifications in the communications manuals. Edward Stanley would respond that those were DOD Manuals and not DOS manuals. "*We do it different in DOS,*" Stanley would assert.

The reality was that Stanley did not know how DOS was supposed to do it. Stanley would deny implementation of any procedure that would cause him extra work or attention to the Communications Center. Stanley saw himself as a potential diplomat. All these Communication Center duties interfered with his real job.

Six weeks into his Edinburgh tour, Thomas was standing outside Edward Stanley's office door. He overheard Stanley telling someone on the phone how the consulate staff was disappointed regarding Thomas's performance. "We thought Bollier would come in and take charge of this Communications Center. He didn't. He waits to be told to do things."

Petty office politics influenced all internal activities in the consulate. Thomas perceived the consulate staff as over-educated civil servants. Their elitist behavior held Thomas in contempt and they never left him in doubt that he was an essential burden who had to be tolerated. He often found himself in conflict with his civilian supervisor and civilian coworkers. One thing all the civilians made clear to him was that the consulate was Department of State, not Department of Defense. *Stop telling us how you do it in the navy.*

Thomas decided to keep a journal. He perceived the consulate staff capable of deceit and conspiracy. When he came back to his apartment each afternoon to change clothes before going out for the evening, he would make entries in his journal. He recorded every instance of when his recommendations for improving procedures or security were denied by Edward Stanley. Thomas put his recommendations and justifying references in memorandums. He filed a carbon copy of all these memorandums in his journal. Thomas also recorded everything he perceived as inappropriate behavior by the consulate staff. His journal contained information regarding all the internal conflicts that he witnessed. He also recorded every circumstance of what he perceived as favoritism. Eventually, Thomas added gossip, speculation, and innuendo. His journal became his outlet to vent anger and frustration.

Edward Stanley was the designated Crypto Security Officer. His duties included safeguarding the small number of crypto key lists. He also performed manual encrypting of outgoing classified messages and the manual decrypting of all incoming encrypted messages. Stanley made no secret that he found these Crypto Security Officer duties a burden. He often complained to others that he anxiously waited for the navy officers to arrive so that he could be relieved of these extra tasks that interfered with his diplomatic duties.

Each morning, Stanley busied himself in the Crypto Vault with the setup of the two Adonis rotor baskets with the current day's key list. Two rotor baskets were required because the consulate expected to receive encrypted messages from both DOS organizations and DOD organizations. The two organizations used different key lists. Monday setups were especially time consuming because DOD sent messages that were encrypted on Saturdays and Sundays, which required him to process Saturday and Sunday messages before he could setup for Monday. Each morning he grumbled and complained aloud while he sat at the Adonis cryptographic equipment. Thomas and the two teletype operators would just smile and chuckle at Stanley's complaining.

Thomas observed that Stanley would leave the Crypto Vault door open and unlocked during the day, even when he was not working in there. Thomas commented to Stanley that vault door should be locked with the vault was unoccupied. Stanley replied with irritation in his tone that the Communications Center was a Controlled Area, and everyone assigned to the Communications Center was cleared for whatever was in the Crypto Vault.

Thomas knew Crypto Vault security regulations and knew that Stanley was wrong. Thomas decided not to make it an issue. Thomas knew he was on a *choice* duty assignment, and he did not want anyone angry with him. That night he recorded the event in his journal.

As the weeks passed, the number of incoming and outgoing Adonis encrypted messages increased from twenty per week to more than fifty per week. Government organizations that needed to send classified messages to the Edinburgh Consulate discovered that communications circuits had been established. They no longer needed to use the time consuming process of sending classified messages via diplomatic courier. The consulate staff became educated on how to use this new resource. As time passed, Thomas became less the source of information regarding how to use the new communications facilities. Thomas saw his importance dwindle.

After four months, the two civilians were operating the communications circuits without assistance from Thomas. Stanley insisted that the civilians operate the Message Center.

Thomas spent most of his days sitting in the Repair Shop reading manuals, performing preventive maintenance, and repairing equipment. He set his own hours, and no one questioned his coming and going.

Chapter 61

Thomas escaped into an active and thriving social life. Most of the Scots he encountered found him friendly and interesting. He made numerous Scottish friends. He attracted many Scottish women, and he had ongoing romantic relationships with three or four Scottish women at the same time.

He found himself the center of attention again. A plentiful sex life kept him happy and satisfied.

He was careful. During indoctrination in London he was told to use precautions against impregnating any Scottish women. According to the Embassy Indoctrination Program, Scottish women used pregnancy as a way to snare an American husband. Thomas had no desire to become tied to married life. He was extremely cautious. The local chemist shops stocked many brands of condoms.

Thomas lay naked on his side in his bed in his apartment. Maggie, his favorite girlfriend lay next to him. She was on her back and naked.

"Oh Thomas, you are not going to wear one of those again?!" Maggie referred to the condom that he pulled from the nightstand drawer.

"You don't want to get pregnant, do you?"

"No, Thomas, but I want us to be intimate. I want to feel you inside me, not that rubber thing."

Thomas judged the veracity of Maggie's words. *Does she truly want this, or is she only looking for an American husband?*

He slowly moved his eyes over her body. Her fair skin, reddish-brown hair, and green eyes typified her Scottish genes. Her oversized breasts detract only slightly from her otherwise perfectly shaped body.

"You are such a good looking man. I want to feel you inside me."

He wanted to enter this woman bare-skinned. He wanted to feel the pleasure of his naked penis inside her. She had told him that she loved him. He liked Maggie, although he did not love her. He definitely did not want to marry her. *Someday I will love someone and get married, but not Maggie.*

Better judgment prevailed. He slipped on the condom and rolled on top of her. He wiggled the lower half of his body between her legs. Maggie spread her legs wider.

"You are so good at this Thomas," Maggie rasped into his ear. Her Scottish brogue added sensuality to her words. "It would be better if you did not wear the rubber."

Thomas did not answer her. He pressed his lips to hers. Then, Thomas pumped faster and a little harder. Maggie moaned again, and she wrapped her legs around Thomas's buttocks. She pumped her hips up and down to match Thomas's movements.

Most of Thomas's time outside the consulate was spent in the local pubs. His social life centered on the pubs. He consumed too much beer. He ate too much kidney pie, too much lamb and potatoes, and too much haggis.

His breakfast, always taken at a local restaurant, included three eggs, sausage, potatoes, and heavily buttered toast, and all washed down with a pint of the local cream laden milk.

The food is delicious!

Thomas adopted a new pastime—betting on horse races. His Scottish friends showed him how to track a horse's history and how to read the daily racing paper. At first, he bet only one pound at a time. Then, he moved to betting parleys. As each week went by, Thomas bet more and more, and he lost more and more. In the beginning, he made his bets at the legal and legitimate off-track betting parlors. When his losses mounted and the legitimate parlors stopped taking his bets, he turned to the illegal bookies and loan sharks.

One area of Scottish life totally irritated Thomas—the drycleaners. Thomas wore a suit every day to the consulate. Every time he sent his suits to the drycleaners, the suits came back with some shrinkage. He would complain to the drycleaner that the cleaning processes were shrinking his clothes. The drycleaner assured Thomas that they used the latest processes. "It must be the materials." the drycleaner would explain. Thomas kept changing drycleaners in search of one who would not shrink his suits.

Chapter 62

Edward Stanley observed that Thomas spent most of his time reading manuals in the Repair Shop. Thomas's free time at work annoyed Stanley, although all Thomas's free time was due to Stanley's policies.

In an effort to relieve himself of the continually increasing demands of the Communications Center on his time, Stanley requested permission from the Defense Attaché Office in London to allow Thomas to perform the encryptions and decryptions on the Adonis machine. Stanley made the request officially through the Department of State channels.

When the request reached Commander Logan, the commander disapproved the request. He cited security regulations that specified only officers and officer grade civilians were allowed to operate Adonis.

The Edinburgh Consulate appealed to CINCUSNAVEUR—Commander in Chief U.S. Naval Forces Europe—with reasoning that the navy had not yet staffed its requirement of officers, and that the shortage of navy officers caused adverse diplomatic circumstances. The consulate further reasoned that RM2 Thomas Bollier held a top secret clearance and had crypto access on the USS *Grant*.

CINCUSNAVEUR overruled Commander Logan and directed Commander of Naval Activities UK to provide a Special Waiver. The Special Waiver specified that the consulate Crypto Security Officer must continuously monitor Thomas's activities in the Crypto Vault. The Waiver forbade Thomas to be a witness or a participant in the destruction of superseded crypto material.

Stanley took seriously the waiver that allowed Bollier to perform the duties, but Stanley ignored the continuous monitoring requirement. Stanley justified to himself that *"the navy has its priority, and the Department of State has other priorities."*

During his sixth month at the consulate, Crypto Operator became one of Thomas's duties. Operating procedures for the Adonis offline Crypto Equipment were classified. Cryptographic procedures were not complicated, and Thomas learned the procedures from Stanley in less than two hours.

Adonis was the codename for a typewriter like device that was used to encrypt messages offline before they were transmitted over online circuits. Daily encryption settings were keyed into eight rotors. The rotor settings were specified in paper keypads that were created and distributed by the National Security Agency. Separate keypads were used for each classification level: confidential, secret, and top secret.

Each keypad had 31 slips of paper, one for each day of the month. On each slip of paper was printed the rotor settings for that day.

Each rotor was approximately one-third-inch thick and four inches in diameter. The eight rotors were inserted in predetermined order into a cylindrical basket, about the size of a one-pound coffee can. Then, the basket was inserted into the typewriter device. As each plain language character was typed at the keyboard, the disks would rotate and an equivalent encrypted character printed to a quarter-inch paper tape. After the message was completely typed, the tape was pasted to a sheet of paper to form the message page.

On the receiving end, the encrypted character was typed at the keyboard, the disks would rotate, and the plain language character printed on the quarter-inch paper tape.

Thomas faced this new duty seriously, and he spent half his time in the Crypto Vault. When Thomas departed the vault, he would shut and lock the door. *They will never find me violating any crypto procedures!*

Shortly after assuming his cryptographic duties, Thomas found months of superseded key lists sitting in piles around the Crypto Vault. He knew that crypto security manuals required daily key lists to be destroyed within 24 hours of being superseded. Thomas also discovered that Mister Stanley was not performing the daily crypto inventory. The inventory sheet was six weeks behind. Thomas thought about reporting what he found then decided against it. He did not want to rock any boats or make anyone angry with him.

While reading classified messages during his cryptographic activities, Thomas became informed of CIA activities in Northern Scotland. He did not know there were any CIA agents at the consulate until he started working in the Crypto Vault. In fact, it was the CIA Agent, Bob Hopkins, who generated most of the classified messages. Bob Hopkins also received most of the incoming messages requiring decryption. Thomas delivered messages to the CIA agent several times a day. Thomas and the CIA agent, an ex-Naval Intelligence officer, became friendly. Occasionally, they went pub hopping together.

Chapter 63

Thomas had little contact with the navy. Occasionally, he would receive some form to sign from the Navy Personnel Office in London. Commander Logan forwarded copies of the Navy Times each week and All Hands Magazine each month. Thomas appreciated the commander's attention. Thomas immediately consumed the information in these publications. He did not want to admit it, but he missed the familiar day to day routine of navy life. Thomas was required to call Commander Logan at the London Embassy at least twice a month. The purpose of the call was to keep the commander up to date on Thomas's activities.

Then, one afternoon near the end of his sixth month in Edinburgh, Thomas answered the phone in the Repair Shop.

"Hello, Bollier. Commander Logan here."

"Hello, Sir. What's up?"

"You are eligible to take the First Class Exam. Personnel Office says you have all the requirements completed. All I need to do is write the recommendation. Personnel Office said that we missed submitting your last performance evaluation. They want me to submit one now and include my recommendation for advancement to first class."

There was a long pause.

Bollier asked cautiously, "Uh, sir. Is there a problem with the recommendation?"

"Well, Bollier, it appears you are doing your job up there. However, I did have a complaint a while back from Mister Stanley. He says your lack of attention to your duties causes late delivery of messages and too many errors in messages."

Anger flared within Thomas, but he managed to respond with an even tone. "Sir, anyone else complain?"

"No, just that one time from Stanley."

"Sir, I do not supervise the Communications Center. Mister Stanley does. He made that quite clear to me. I know that problems with message processing exist. I have made recommendations for improvements to Mister Stanley. He always rejects them and tells me that he is the Communications Officer and things will be done his way. I recommended adding traffic checking processes and second-person proof reading. He said no . . . he said there was no time for it. Actually, I do not process messages anymore. Stanley said he wants only the DOS teletype operators to process messages. I spend half my time in the Crypto Vault decrypting and encrypting messages and the other half in the Repair Shop with preventive maintenance and repair actions."

"So why would Stanley make such a report about you?"

"To cover his ass," Thomas replied. "A few months ago, several of the consulate secretaries came to me and asked why so many errors were being made. They thought I was running things. I told them I did not know about the problems because I am not in charge of the Communications Center. I referred them to Mister Stanley. I think Stanley is blaming me for everything that goes wrong."

Commander Logan took a few moments to consider Bollier's words. He knew that such conflicts often occur when DOS and DOD personnel work together. He decided to give Bollier the benefit of the doubt.

"Okay, Bollier. I'm giving you 3.8 across the board. Those are good marks and more than necessary to qualify you for an advancement recommendation."

"Four-O across the board would be better sir . . . would give me more advancement points."

"No, Bollier. Everyone needs improvement. Just do your best on the exam."

"Yes, sir," Thomas responded evenly.

"Someone up there needs to administer the exam to you. Must be a GS-11 equivalent or higher. Who should I tell the Personnel Office to send it to?"

"Have them send it to Mister Hopkins in the consulate Public Affairs Office."

"Okay, Bollier. I will do that. You should take the exam two weeks from now. I wish you success," the commander said sincerely, and he meant it.

That same afternoon, Thomas Bollier satisfied his anger against Stanley's lies by detailing in his journal all of Stanley's crypto security violations. Thomas marked in the journal page margin the numbered paragraph references of the Crypto Security Manual that Stanley violated.

I need insurance. Thomas convinced himself that Stanley wanted to destroy him. He often found Stanley whispering with others. Thomas knew that they were conspiring against him. *That the nature of government employees,* he would tell himself. He remembered that shortly after his father was killed in the war, his mother pleaded with the government for assistance. None came. Her letters to the War Department went unanswered. He remembered the many nights that his mother cried herself to sleep.

Thomas gathered as much detrimental evidence against Stanley that he could find. *When the showdown comes, I can prove that Stanley is the guilty one. The evidence in my journal will prove that Stanley caused all the problems within the Communications Center.*

Two weeks later, Thomas took the First Class Radioman Exam. He felt confident that he did well. He needed the highest score possible on the exam to compete successfully against those RM2's who had more time in service and more time in rate than him.

Thomas knew how the advancement process worked. First, the navy determined who passed and who failed the exam. The exam was graded on a curve system. Those who failed the exam were no longer candidates for advancement. For those who passed the exam, points were added to their test score for years in the navy, time spent as an RM2, and for medals awarded. Then, the navy created a list of all the candidates in order from highest points to lowest points. Then, the navy would check its manpower requirements and determined how many candidates could be advanced. The navy would count down the list by that number and draw a line. Those above the line were declared *passed* and *advanced*. Those below the line were declared *passed*, but *not advanced*.

As time passed, Thomas concluded that his assignment to the U.S. Consulate was nothing special. Except for the occasional piece of interesting classified intelligence to which he was exposed, his job lacked importance and excitement.

The only nagging sore points in his life were his growing debt to illegal bookies and the drycleaners who continued to shrink his suits and shirts.

A disturbing incident occurred that Thomas did not understand. Maggie, his favorite girlfriend, ended their relationship. She told Thomas that he got fat and he was losing his sexy looks. Thomas attempted to explain to her that he was not getting fat. "The dry cleaners are shrinking my clothes," he would tell her.

"Look at yourself in the mirror," she advised him with a chuckle. "Stop fooling yourself!"

A bright point to Thomas's professional existence occurred during his eighth month in Scotland. He received notification that he had been advanced to first class petty officer. He was jubilant. However, he had no one to share his joy. Advancement ceremonies are an honored naval tradition. All members of the command usually attend these ceremonies, which are happy occasions with abundant congratulations and wishes for continued success. No such ceremony took place for Thomas. The only person at the consulate who took any interest in Thomas's achievement was the CIA Agent, Bob Hopkins. When Thomas informed others at the consulate, he got uninterested shrugs. He discontinued sharing his good news. No one else showed interest that the unseen uniform hanging in his bedroom closet gained one additional stripe.

During March of 1956, two additional teletype operators joined the Message Center staff. Stanley was ordered to extend the Communications Center operating hours to include an evening shift.

Stanley openly objected to his superiors any orders that required more of his time be spent in the Communications Center. He argued to his superiors that he could not rely on Bollier to properly train and supervise additional personnel. However, Stanley's accusations against Thomas Bollier were no longer credible with his superiors. Stanley's superiors had uncovered Stanley's plot against Bollier.

Edward Stanley's nature became clear to the senior consulate staff. Stanley's last evaluation included comments that he spent too little time on the Communications Center and too much time on what Stanley incorrectly perceived as *his diplomatic duties*.

Chapter 64

During the first Monday in April 1956, RM1Thomas Bollier sorted through the disorganized stacks of Adonis crypto keypads. Edward Stanley had not marked which keypad versions became effective on the first of April. In the past, Stanley had always marked the keypads with the month for which they were effective. *Another thing he isn't doing!*

Thomas needed this information so that he could key the Adonis rotors. He had a backlog of seven messages to encrypt before transmitting. He called Stanley's office. Stanley's assistant said that Stanley called in sick and would probably not be in the office until Wednesday. Thomas searched the crypto files for information that listed which keypads were effective during which months. In a stack of papers at the bottom of a desk drawer, he found what he needed. A single sheet of paper marked SECRET CRYPTO listed the effective dates of all Adonis keypads for the current year, 1956. He carried the classified sheet of paper over to the shelf where piles of disorganized and unmarked keypads were stored. He found the keypad versions for April. He marked April 1956 on the cover of the two key list pads.

Just as Thomas turned to put the sheet of paper back in the drawer, one of the teletype operators distracted him by calling his name through the vault door. The operator asked Thomas to come into the Message Center and help with a problem. Thomas walked out of the Crypto Vault and into the Message Center. Thomas was not aware at the moment that he still held the SECRET CRYPTO paper in his hand. I few minutes later while standing in the middle of the Message Center and talking to the operator, Thomas noticed that he had the classified paper in his hand. Knowing he should not be in the Message Center with this paper and not wanting the operators to see him with it, he folded the paper and put it in his back trouser pocket.

Later that afternoon while at his apartment and changing clothes to go out for the evening, Thomas reached into his back pocket for his comb. He pulled out his comb and the SECRET CRYPTO paper. Thomas's heart pounded in his chest. He began to sweat. *I never committed a security violation before!*

He sat down at his kitchen table and thought about what he should do. Then, he saw his journal on the table. He thought about that *incompetent idiot* Stanley. He thought about all he had written in the journal about Stanley. Then, the idea hit him. *I can really nail Stanley!*

Accounting for crypto material was Stanley's responsibility. Thomas saw this as an opportunity to further document Stanley's continuing crypto violations. Thomas opened his journal and transcribed from the SECRET CRYPTO paper all the effective dates of the keypad versions for the entire year. *Now that should take care of Mister Edward, this is DOS—not DOD, Stanley!*

Thomas returned the document to the Crypto Vault the next day.

The incident gave Thomas additional ideas about gathering evidence against Stanley. Every day, he brought back to his apartment the paper slips from the keypad that contained the daily Adonis rotor settings. Thomas wrote the daily rotor settings in his journal. As was his practice, he would write in the margin the numbered paragraph reference of the Crypto Security Manual that Stanley was violating.

Thomas became obsessed with gathering evidence against Stanley. He discarded thoughts that he also violated Crypto Security Procedures. He justified his actions in his own mind. *It's not like I am giving away secrets to the Russians. I am gathering evidence against a government official . . . an uncaring, deceitful, and incompetent government worker . . . like the ones that got us into the war and, later, ignored my family after my father was killed.*

Chapter 65

Javier Ramirez enjoyed the cool air of summertime Scotland. He found walking the streets of Edinburgh an interesting trek. The brownstone buildings appeared ageless. The structures could have been built last year or three hundred years ago.

Javier came to Scotland to gather intelligence regarding the U.S. Navy bases soon to be established in Scotland. He prowled the pubs looking for Americans who could become sources of information.

The United States Consulate contained the largest concentration of Americans in Edinburgh. Javier watched the entrance of the consulate for a week. Using a camera with a telescopic lens, he took pictures of people entering and departing the consulate. After following some of the consulate employees to lunch and listening to their conversations, Javier learned that he would find many of them in certain pubs at night.

One evening during his third week in Edinburgh, Javier entered the pub most popular with American Consulate personnel. The pub was larger than most. Cigarette smoke hung like a fog throughout the entire room. The pub was three quarters full of patrons. The pub décor was typical with dark polished wood everywhere. Scottish Coats of Arms and pictures of handsome horses hung on the walls. Pint size mugs containing varying quantities of dark beer sat on the bar and all the tables. Unfinished plates of food littered the tabletops. The occupants were an equal mix of men and women. Laughter filled the room. Occasionally, a boisterous male voice rose above the din. In the far corner, five men played darts. Javier recognized one of the dart players from the consulate photographs.

Javier ordered a beer at the bar; then, he casually walked to the area of the dartboard. He drew stares from a few of the patrons. Javier's black hair and dark complexion was out of place in this land of milk-white faces and light colored hair. He found an unoccupied, small two-chair table about ten feet from the men playing darts. The dart players laughed, cheered, and jeered as shots were made and missed. The five men were inebriated. Javier concentrated on their conversation. The one from the consulate photograph spoke with an obvious American accent. His friends called him Thomas. As Javier observed the activities in the pub, he concluded that no other Americans were in the Pub.

The American, a medium height, pudgy man with thinning black hair and a black mustache, was whining about another one of his girlfriends dumping him. The American did not take the rejection of the woman lightly. Oddly, the American seemed more offended than saddened. The American's companions consoled him and assured him that there were plenty more women in the world.

Javier pretended not to listen. His eyes were on the dart game, but his ears were on the words of the American. Javier brought the beer mug to his lips, but he did not drink. The American, named Thomas, complained about his boss, *Mister Stanley*. This Stanley was out to get him.

"But I have insurance," Thomas declared in a drunken slur. "Stanley does not know who he's up against. I have the goods on him!" Thomas slammed his beer mug on the tabletop. Then, he looked around him to get assurance from his friends. His eyes briefly landed on Javier, who pretended not to notice Thomas's stare. Thomas, however, had definitely noticed Javier.

Several minutes later, Javier left his table and exited the pub.

The following afternoon, Javier Ramirez waited down the street from the entrance to the consulate. When he saw the American from the night before exit the building, Javier followed. The American entered an apartment building just a few blocks from the consulate. Javier waited across the street. An hour later, the American emerged from the apartment building. Javier looked at his watch—5:50 p.m. Javier concluded the American was going out for the evening.

Javier walked across street and stopped at the door of the apartment building. The door was not locked. He stepped into a small foyer. Eight mailboxes hung on the wall. Javier read the names. *Thomas Bollier - # 6* was written under one of the boxes. He climbed the stairs to the third floor where he found Thomas Bollier's apartment. As he approached the door, he pulled his key set from his coat pocket. After several minutes, he conquered the door lock and entered the apartment.

Javier previously searched the apartments of three Americans from the consulate. He hoped to find something of value regarding the plan to establish U.S. Navy bases in Scotland.

He checked the closets in Thomas's bedroom first. He was surprised to find a navy uniform hanging in one of the closets. *He's an American sailor!* Javier had been briefed that there were no military personnel assigned to the consulate. *So much for the value of Soviet intelligence*, Javier opined to himself. He found nothing of value in the closets. In a drawer, he found two letters from Bollier's mother. He read the letters several times. The mother had not seen her son in six years. She wanted to know if he was ever coming back to Dearborn.

When Javier entered the kitchen, he immediately noticed the journal on the table. He turned the cover, not expecting to find anything important. His heart beat faster with every turn of a page. He stopped reading and just scanned the pages. Then, he skipped to the last page with an entry. *Today's date! The rotor settings are there!* Javier went back to the bedroom closet to find the suit the American wore earlier in the day. He searched the pockets and found the paper slip from the keypad. *Today's rotor settings! I am searching for morsels, and I discover a royal feast!*

Javier removed a miniature camera from his coat pocket and took a picture of the slip of paper with the rotor settings. He stuffed the slip back into the suit pocket. He hurried to the kitchen and photographed pages of the journal. He ran out of film. *No problem . . . I will come back . . . many times!*

Javier exited the apartment and stood on the landing, listening for footsteps. No one moved about. He slipped quietly down the stairs and out the building. No one noticed him.

As he walked down the street, he looked like someone out for a casual stroll. However, his mind raced with thoughts about the value of the treasure he had just discovered.

Javier Ramirez was not a Soviet citizen and was not an employee of the Soviet Government. He was an independent. He gathered information of value and sold it to the highest bidder. At the moment, the Soviets were bidding high for information regarding the establishment of American navy bases in Scotland, especially any information about placing America's recently developed nuclear submarines in Scotland.

Javier evaluated which source to pursue—Bollier or Stanley. He considered that if he used the information from Bollier's journal to blackmail Stanley, Stanley would know the information came from Bollier. If he attempted to blackmail Bollier and Bollier said no, then Javier would surely lose both as a source. He needed to determine which one of the two Americans would be the easiest to turn. Javier decided to follow each man for several weeks before he made a choice.

Chapter 66

By August 1956, the volume of encrypted message traffic had increased to the point where RM1 Thomas Bollier spent ten hours a day, six days a week in the Crypto Vault. He spent half the seventh day in the Repair Room fixing and maintaining equipment. Four weeks previous, he started making calls to Commander Logan in London advising that the consulate needed online crypto equipment. The commander asked Bollier to send him traffic volume statistics to include percentage of encrypted messages.

During the first week in September 1956, tragedy struck the United States Consulate. Edward Stanley was found dead in his apartment. The police report stated that Stanley committed suicide. The police concluded that Stanley was extremely saddened over the breakup with his homosexual lover and decided to take his own life. A local newspaper revealed that Stanley's lover, embarrassed by his exposure as a homosexual, moved away. If any of the consulate staff knew that Stanley was a homosexual, they kept it secret.

Stanley's sudden demise left Thomas Bollier with a dilemma. The crypto account was in total disorder. Stanley had stuffed superseded keypad slips in burn bags, but never destroyed any of it. The Crypto Custodian file was full of false destruction reports signed by Stanley. The file also contained correspondence from the Crypto Material Issuing Office asking for clarification of destruction records.

Thomas knew he was safe from any responsibility. The Letter appointing him as a Crypto Operator emphasized that Thomas was not to be involved with destroying crypto material. However, Thomas knew that Stanley would be replaced, and Thomas knew he would be asked why he never reported the violations to Stanley's superiors.

While sitting in the Crypto Vault and staring into space, the way out came to him. *No one knows that I have read the Crypto Security Publications. I was never directed to. My sole duty was encrypting and decrypting messages, no more, no less. I will claim ignorance. I will say that I did not know what Stanley was supposed to do. I'm just an operator.*

Thomas deliberated over what to do with his journal. He thought of destroying it. But then thought, *what if something surfaced later that would require proof of Stanley's mishandling of the Crypto Account.* He decided to keep the journal for a while. He stuffed the journal in his seabag, which was located deep in back of a packed closet. As the weeks passed, the existence of the journal faded from his thoughts.

During an afternoon in the third week in September 1956, RM1 Thomas Bollier sat at his workbench in the Repair Room. He was replacing the spring on a teletype print hammer when he heard the shuffle of feet behind him. He turned to see Commander Logan with two other navy officers. All three officers wore their Service Dress Blue uniform.

Mister Reynolds—the consulate Security Officer, and Mister Hopkins—the resident CIA agent, were also standing there.

Bollier slipped off the workbench stool and walked over to the group of men.

"Bollier, nice to see you again," said Commander Logan as he stretched out his arm to shake hands.

Thomas wiped his hands on his lab coat. "It's a pleasure to see you again, Commander," Thomas replied sincerely as he shook the commander's hand.

"RM1 Thomas Bollier, I want to introduce Lieutenant Commander Hampton," Logan nodded toward the officer.

They shook hands and exchanged greetings.

"And this is Lieutenant Benton," Thomas turned toward the lieutenant. They shook hands and exchanged greetings also.

"And, of course, you know Mister Reynolds and Mister Hopkins."

"Yes, sir."

An awkward silence fell over the group of men.

Thomas stared passed the group and saw the two civilian teletype operators sneaking glances through the door to the Repair Room. Commander Logan noticed the onlookers, and he went to the door and closed it.

Commander Logan said to Thomas, "Lieutenant Commander Hampton and Lieutenant Benton will inspect the crypto account. It should take several days."

"Sir, I need to spend most of my time in the vault. We process a lot of offline-encrypted messages. It will be crowded with the three of us in there."

Mister Reynolds, the consulate Security Officer, responded, "We will transport all the files and all the key lists, except for the current month, up to Mister Hopkins's office."

Thomas became confused about this action. The Crypto Vault was the only area within the consulate that complied with Exclusion Area specifications. Thomas did not question the order because he did not want to reveal his understanding of Exclusion Areas.

Thomas did not know that a secret Exclusion Area was attached to Hopkins's office, which was accessed through a false wall in the back of a closet in the CIA agent's office.

Commander Logan said to Bollier, "Mister Hampton needs to ask you a few questions regarding crypto operations and the recently deceased Mister Stanley."

Thomas turned his attention to Lieutenant Commander Hampton.

"Did you ever see Mister Stanley remove material from the Crypto Vault and return it sometime later?"

"Sir, for the last six month, I only saw Mister Stanley a few times in the Crypto Vault. I didn't see him remove anything or bring in anything."

Hampton stared into Bollier's eyes for a full 30 seconds. Then, he asked, "Why didn't you report that Mister Stanley was violating crypto security?"

"I did not know that he was," Thomas replied innocently.

The look on Hampton's face conveyed doubt as he asks, "Didn't you notice all the bags of old keypad slips?"

"Sir, I am not involved with destruction. Never was. My Appointment Letter as Crypto Operator specifically prohibited me from being involved with the destruction part of it. I never worked with this Adonis system until I came here. Mister Stanley taught me how to operate the Adonis, and he made it a point several times that I was to do only what I was told to do—no more, no less."

"Do you have a copy of your Appointment Letter?"

"Yes, sir. I will get you a copy."

Thomas went over to his workbench and opened the file drawer on the bottom left side. He pulled out his personal correspondence file. He had the original and two carbon copies of his Crypto Operator Appointment Letter. He pulled a carbon copy and scanned the statement regarding destruction of material. *It's crystal clear! I am not in trouble here!*

Thomas returned to the group of officers and handed the carbon copy to Mister Hampton, who quickly scanned the letter. He nodded confirmation when he found the restriction regarding destruction of crypto material.

"Lieutenant Benton has been assigned to the consulate," Commander Logan advised. "He will assume duties as Communications Officer and Crypto Security Officer."

This news disappointed Thomas. He had been the only military person at the consulate. *Now, not only will there be another navy man, that navy man is an officer!*

Commander Logan stated, "I'm sure you're pleased that another navy man will be at the consulate."

Thomas glanced at Lieutenant Benton and smiled. "Yes, sir . . . will be great to have someone else here I can relate to."

"Good! I have other good news," Commander Logan said with enthusiasm. "The online encryption equipment for both teletype circuits will arrive this week. You are to install them and get the circuits working with online crypto devices. Do you think that you can do that?"

"Sir, I spend most of my time encrypting and decrypting messages with the Adonis system. Is there a deadline for getting the new crypto equipment online?"

Commander Logan nodded toward the lieutenant and said, "Lieutenant Benton will take over your Crypto Operator duties while you install and make operational the new crypto equipment."

That is good news! Thomas thought to himself. "Which type of online cryptographic equipment, sir? I don't think there are any keypads or keycards in the Crypto Vault for anything other than the Adonis. At least, I don't think there is. Mister Stanley never showed me anything else."

Commander Logan responds, "It will be Romulus Crypto System equipment. We are getting the prototypes. NSA agreed to let us have two identical systems with no charge to our budget because the navy agreed to the consulate being prototype test location. Two tech-reps will arrive with the equipment to help you get the system setup and operational. The keycards will arrive the following week. Are you okay with supervising the installation?"

"Yes, sir. I should have no problems with it."

During the next month, Thomas worked eighteen hours a day with the tech-reps to get the new Romulus equipment installed and operational. The installation was technically challenging, but Thomas met all deadlines. Each fully loaded Romulus rack was the size of a refrigerator. A lot of muscle was needed to get the equipment in place. Thomas realized that he had lost some physical strength. Even with assistance from the tech reps, Thomas would be sweating and breathing hard after positioning system components. He had concerns that the prototype Romulus systems would not work. However, there were no problems circuit activation and the Romulus came up operational on the first try.

Two additional teletype operators were assigned, and the Message

Center went operational 24 hours a day. Thomas trained all the operators on how to operate the new Romulus cryptographic equipment. Because the Romulus keycards were classified SECRET, all SECRET and below classified messages would be sent and received over the Romulus circuits. Only TOP SECRET message would require Adonis offline encryption, reducing the Adonis workload by ninety percent.

Lieutenant Benton was pleased with Thomas's work and assigned Thomas as the Communications Center Supervisor. The assignment as supervisor gratified Thomas.

However, the shift-working teletype operators were not happy about Thomas being their supervisor. They complained through their administrative channels that they would be supervised by a military person and not by a qualified DOS Communications Officer.

Such pettiness surprised Lieutenant Benton. The lieutenant explained to the teletype operators that the Communications Center was established and funded by the navy. Agreements between DOD and DOS specified that the navy would supervise the Communications Center, and DOS would provide the teletype operators. The navy funded the cost of the DOS teletype operators. The explanations did not satisfy the DOS teletype operators, and they continued their petty bickering.

Overall, Thomas was pleased with his new role. He was the Communications Center Supervisor, and he was the only repairman. He was happy that he no longer performed Crypto Operator duties. Lieutenant Benton and an officer grade DOS civilian now handled the few top secret messages that required Adonis processing. Thomas had not been in the Crypto Vault since several days after Lieutenant Benton arrived.

However, the quality of Thomas's private life deteriorated. Because of his debt to a local loan shark, Thomas was living payday to payday. As a result, he had to cut back on his social spending. Instead of eating meals out, he bought inexpensive groceries at the local shops. He prepared breakfast and dinner in his apartment, and he started brown bagging his lunch. He had his suits dry-cleaned less often, and he did his own laundry and ironing. He was not always timely with washing and ironing, and his appearance became sloppy.

When he went to his favorite pubs, he no longer bought rounds of pints for his Scottish friends. His social manner became sullen and snippy. Believing that the locals had taken advantage of him, he would make derogatory comments about Scottish people in general. His Scottish friends noticed and stopped including Thomas when one of them bought rounds. His dart-game companions stopped inviting Thomas to join their games. The last woman he considered a girlfriend dumped him; she said his irritable manner and recently thrifty behavior made him a bore. He no longer received invitations to home parties and gatherings. When he went to the pubs, he sat by himself. No one initiated conversation, and Thomas stopped seeking companionship. Eventually, he stopped going to pubs and would just sit in his apartment at night and read. His disposition became increasingly gloomy as his clothes continued to shrink.

Occasionally, Thomas would make a big bet on a long shot to try and get even. Of course, he continued to lose. He started shorting his weekly payments to the loan shark. The loan shark would threaten to expose Thomas's gambling problem to consulate management. Although the loan shark did not specifically threaten physical harm, the innuendo to do so grew stronger.

Thomas panicked. He owed over 2800 pounds. The consulate conducted training and counseling on a regular basis regarding the hazards of gambling on the horses. If Thomas's gambling debt were to be discovered by his superiors, Thomas would be relieved of his duties and transferred. His gambling problem would be placed in his personnel record. He would never be recommended for advancement to chief petty officer, and he would never again be recommended for choice overseas duty. Thomas continued to pay weekly, but he seldom paid the amount necessary to reduce the debt.

Chapter 67

On an afternoon during the second week in March 1957, Lieutenant Benton called Thomas to his office. When Thomas entered the lieutenant's office, he saw that the officer was in Service Dress Blue uniform. The lieutenant had not worn his uniform since the first day he came to the consulate.

"Bollier, come on in. Please sit." The lieutenant's voice was serious and official and not the usual casual tone.

Thomas sat in the chair in front of the lieutenant's desk.

"I need to talk to you about some areas of your performance that need improvement."

Thomas stared at the lieutenant. He accepted the bad news as just another adverse event in his life.

"First, I want you to know that your technical knowledge of Communications Center operations is first rate, and your upkeep of the equipment is four-oh."

"Thank you, sir," Thomas replied in a sulky tone, knowing the praise was a lead into some criticism.

"But like I said, some areas need improvement. Your appearance has deteriorated. You continue to gain weight and you always look like you're ready to bust through your clothes. Your clothes often look wrinkled and dirty. I have made an appointment for you with the consulate contract doctor to put you on a diet and to provide you with an exercise routine. I hope you take advantage of this opportunity to improve. You will, won't you?"

Thomas realized that he must finally face the truth about his weight gain. The drycleaner had not been shrinking his clothes. *I'm fat!*

Thomas thought of arguing the applicability of his fatness. *After all, my technical knowledge and technical ability and what I've accomplished in the Communications Center should make my appearance irrelevant?* Thomas decided not to argue. He knew it was a time to listen and time to be agreeable. "Yes, sir. I will see the doctor and do what he tells me."

"And you will see the contract dentist and follow his treatment?"

"Yes, sir."

"Good." The lieutenant responded flatly. "Now. Let's talk about your leadership ability and military bearing."

What the fuck is he talking about! My leadership ability! My military bearing! I supervise a bunch of idiot civilians! Thomas did not share his thoughts with the lieutenant. "Okay, sir. Let's talk about it."

"As I said before, Bollier, your technical knowledge is excellent; but you don't use it effectively. You talk down to those you supervise. You often and openly ridicule the input of the teletype operators, and you berate their knowledge and performance in front of others."

Thomas did not understand this criticism. He remembered a number of discussions with the teletype operators regarding their ideas on how to do things. He remembered showing them communications publications and proving that his direction was by the book. The teletype operators' justification to do it their way was the same old reason. "We have always done it that way in DOS." Thomas's response to that invalid reason was to always say, "Show me a DOS Communications Publication that specifies your way, and I will change it. Until then, we do it the way these DOD communications pubs say to do it."

Lieutenant Benton was never present during those discussions. The teletype operators must have complained to him. Typical, they can't prove me wrong, so they lie and make false accusations about my behavior. But why is the lieutenant buying it?

Thomas did not to argue the point and responded, "Sir, just tell me what you want me to do, and I will do it."

"You can start by implementing some of the procedures that the teletype operators recommend. This will convey that you believe their contributions to our operation are valuable."

"Even if what they want to implement is contrary to the communications pubs?"

"Bollier, bend the rules a bit. If we can form a cohesive team does it really matter if some minor procedure does not comply with publications?"

Does it matter! Of course, it matters! The pubs don't say use these procedures only if you want to. What's wrong with this officer? You can't pick and choose which regulations or procedures you want to follow! What about all the training that I have had that tells me to follow orders?

"Sir, the procedures they want will increase the chance of nondelivery of messages."

"You don't need to implement everything they want. Just implement enough to make them feel they are part of the team."

"Yes, sir. I will start doing that. Should I pass it through you first? I think we both need to agree on the publications that we will violate."

"No, use your own judgment. I will know if you are successful when I see a change in the team spirit in the Communications Center."

"Yes, sir." *Idiot!*

"I'm pleased that you are agreeable to these improvements. Your Performance Evaluation is scheduled for next month, and I want to reflect your improvements in your marks. Okay?"

"Okay, sir." *God damned double idiot!*

"Good. Just one more thing to cover. New direction from London orders us to start wearing our uniforms to work. You know . . . show the colors kind of thing. London wants the local populace to understand the increasing U.S. military presence in Scotland. Wear your Dress Blue uniform tomorrow. Oh, and you need a haircut."

Why does this fuckin' navy continue to give no notice? So typical! Make a change and implement immediately, regardless of the havoc! Thomas does not share his thoughts with the lieutenant for concern over affecting his Adaptability marks. Thomas responds, "Yes, sir."

"And stop here tomorrow morning on your way to the Communications Center. I want to see how you look in your uniform. Sort of like an informal inspection."

"Yes, sir." *Fuck you, sir!*

Later that afternoon, Thomas got a haircut at the local barbershop. Then, he went home to his apartment. He pulled his Service Dress Blue uniform from the closet. He had not put on a uniform in twenty months—since coming to Scotland. He removed his uniform from the drycleaner packaging. He slipped on the trousers. He had to suck in his belly and hold his breath to fasten the waist buttons. He looked at himself in the mirror. His belly and love handles bulged and hung over the waist of the trousers. His t-shirt would not stay tucked in the trousers. His arms had lost muscle tone.

Christ! What has happened to me? Who did this to me! I'm just a young man, and I am fat, and . . . and I am losing my hair too!

He put on his Service Dress Blue jumper. It barely covered his belly. As he moved, the jumper rode up and exposed his t-shirt. *I cannot wear this! I will be a laughingstock!* But Thomas knew he had to wear it.

He pulled his uniform shoes from the closet. *Still has a spit shine!*

He pulled one of his white hats from a drawer—*immaculate!*

His neckerchief was still perfectly rolled.

He removed his peacoat from the drycleaner packaging and slipped it on. Fortunately, he was issued an oversized peacoat in boot camp. It was snug, and he had some difficulty with the buttons. Wearing the peacoat hid his midriff from showing. *Maybe I can wear the peacoat all the time . . . until I can get new uniforms.*

Suddenly, he had a brainstorm. He shucked the uniform, put on his civvies, and dashed out of the apartment.

The next morning while standing naked in front of a full-length mirror, Thomas wrapped a corset like device around his bare belly. He spent several minutes of sucking in and holding his breath before he connected all the snaps.

He had purchased the device the previous evening at the local chemist shop. The device was designed to assist those with back pain. Thomas had a short disagreement with the chemist regarding the size of the device that Thomas would need. The chemist insisted on *extra-large*. Thomas settled only for a size *large*.

He slipped on his boxer shorts and t-shirt. He used safety pins to attach the bottom of his t-shirt to the top of his boxer shorts.

Then, he donned his Service Dress Blues. The trouser buttons fastened easer, and the uniform looked more like a fit but not by much. The uniform still felt like a vise around his middle torso waist, crotch, and thighs. He made slow and calculated movements so as not to over stress the seams. The constricting clothes allowed him to take only short and shallow breaths. The safety-pinned t-shirt attempted to rise out of his trousers, but a chokehold on his crotch prevented the t-shirt from doing so.

He called the Navy Uniform Store located at the Headquarters of Commander Naval Activities UK in London. He called from his apartment instead of from the consulate because he did not want anyone to know that he needed larger uniforms. He became angry when the clerk told him that the size he wanted was a special order back to the United States and would take six weeks to deliver.

When Thomas arrived at the consulate, he went directly to Lieutenant Benton's office. The lieutenant stood as Thomas entered the room.

"Take off your peacoat so I can see how you look," the lieutenant directed cheerfully.

Thomas removed his peacoat and laid it over the back of a chair. Then, he did a three hundred and sixty degree turn.

"Tight fit, huh?"

"Yes, sir."

"Well, as you lose that weight, the fit will get better."

"Yes, sir."

Thomas despised Lieutenant Benton. The lieutenant was not fat and not balding, and he was an officer. Thomas concluded that Lieutenant Benton was part of the privileged class that denied others their just due. The same privileged class that denied his parents those good paying jobs. The same privileged class that God favors.

336

Thomas went to his Repair Shop and put on his lab coat. He decided to stand at his workbench instead of sitting for apprehension over splitting the seams of his trousers.

For the first couple of days that Thomas wore his uniform, a number of consulate personnel snickered and commented about the fat boy in the crackerjack sailor uniform. The amusement of his uniform dissipated after a week, and there were no more comments about it.

Chapter 68

Three weeks later, Thomas stood at his workbench—still standing because his larger uniforms had not arrived. He answered the phone on his workbench after the second ring.

"Are you RM1 Thomas Bollier?"

"Yes."

"This is Personnelman First Class Conklin at the NAVACTS UK Personnel Office in London. I'm calling to let you know your orders arrived. I will send you some copies. The week before you are due to transfer, you will need to come to London for out-processing."

Thomas was stunned. "What are you talking about, Conklin? I have another year before I'm due for orders."

"Your two year tour is up in June," PN1Conklin declared.

"No, I am on a three year tour."

"What makes you think that?"

"I was told that by my captain when I reenlisted for orders."

"I don't know why he would tell you that. It's a three-year tour for married personnel and a two-year tour for single personnel. Maybe your captain didn't understand that."

"There must be a mistake," Thomas insisted. "I was guaranteed a three year tour in Scotland as a reenlistment incentive."

"Hold on. I got your personnel record right here. Let me check."

Thomas sat irritable and anxious as he heard the shuffle of papers through the phone.

"Bollier, I am sorry about all this, but nothing in your reenlistment papers or your orders to Scotland say anything about a three year tour. Your transfer orders are in, and we got copies of the orders for your replacement. So am afraid that's it."

"Where am I going?"

"USS *Shangri-La*. She's an aircraft carrier home-ported in San Diego, and your orders specify that you are being sent to a sixteen-week Romulus cryptographic repair school in San Diego prior to going to *The Shang*. Anyway, I will send you copies of your orders. I will be calling you to schedule your out-processing."

Then, Conklin hung up.

Thomas's astonishment and irritation turned to anger. *This fucking navy, why did I let them suck me in! The navy has made my life miserable! I don't deserve this. Mom was right. Never trust the government. They will ruin your life and . . . and I definitely do not deserve The Shitty Shang!*

Several hours later, Thomas's phone rang again.

"Hello, Thomas. This is Charlie Moriarty."

Thomas recognized the strong, Scottish brogue voice of the loan shark. In the past, Charlie had always called Thomas's apartment. This was the first time Charlie had called him at the consulate.

"Hi, Charlie." Thomas attempted to sound cheerful and glad to hear from Charlie.

"Thomas, you are not paying enough on your debt to me. You owe me over 2800 pounds. If you don't make a payment that brings your account current by Monday, I must take action."

Thomas worried that the consulate operator may be listening.

"What kind of action?" Thomas asked apprehensively.

"It will not be pleasant," Charlie threatened. "And your superiors at the consulate will know what you have been doing."

"Please don't tell anyone. I will make a payment on Friday."

"Not good enough, unless it pays you up to date!"

"Okay! Okay! Please don't do anything until Friday!" Thomas pleads.

"Okay. Friday!" Charlie hung up the phone.

Thomas felt desperate and afraid. He had been threatened with physical harm, possibly deadly harm. He didn't know for sure. That was Charlie's way—never specific about what he would do—keep you in fear.

His heart pumped rapidly and out of control. Sweat flooded from every pore. He felt dizzy. He had to sit down. He flopped his ass down on the workbench stool, which resulted in a loud ripping noise as the seams in his trousers gave way, and his fat butt burst through the new opening in search of freedom.

His fear turned to anger, and he snarled a deep growl. *The navy is to blame for all this! I have sweated blood for this place. What have I gotten in return? Threats on my life and the navy fucking me out of a year of shore duty! And on top of all that, the navy orders me to The Shitty Shang!*

Thomas remained angry and desperate throughout the day. He could not think of a way to pay Charlie what he owed him.

The day's distressing events preoccupied Thomas's thoughts as he unlocked the door to his apartment. He removed his peacoat and hung it on the coat rack next to the door. When he turned and entered the living room, he became startled and apprehensive when he saw a man standing near the fireplace. He recognized the man but could not place him. The man wore an expensive dark gray suit with a red silk tie and a white silk shirt. The man was trim and solidly built. He had brown skin and short, jet-black hair. His mustache was thick and neatly trimmed.

Some objects on the coffee table caught Thomas's attention. He saw three rectangle boxes, the kind that clothing stores use when packaging purchases.

"Do not be afraid, Thomas," the man said softly. "You know me. We frequent the same pubs, although I have not seen you in the pubs recently." The man spoke with an indefinable accent.

"Yes, I have seen you around. Who are you? Why are you here?"

"My name is Javier. I have come to help you." Javier spoke in a comforting tone and with smile on his face.

"What can you help me with?" Thomas asked doubtfully.

"Open those boxes on the coffee table. I'm sure that you will be pleased."

Thomas hesitated. He glanced quickly back and forth between Javier and the boxes on the coffee table.

"Why should you want to give me anything? What do you want?" Thomas's voice reeked of suspicion and apprehension.

"Please. Just open the boxes and you will be happy with my gifts."

Thomas walked over to the coffee table and removed the lids from the three boxes. Two boxes contained the Service Dress Blue uniform of a first class radioman with one hash mark and a pair of suspenders that were the same color as the uniforms. The third box contained a navy peacoat with a first class radioman chevron.

"You are pleased. Yes? You are choking in the uniform you wear. Please remove your uniform and wear one of these. I had them handmade by a tailor in London, near Gosvenor Square. The tailor specializes in U.S. Navy uniforms."

"How did you know that I . . . what is your name again?"

"Javier, Javier Ramirez."

"Javier, how did you know that I needed uniforms?"

Javier responds with a fatherly tone, "I know many things about you, Thomas."

"You want something from me! What is it?" Thomas demanded.

"We will discuss that, but first, please try one of these uniforms. Use the suspenders. You will find the uniforms comfortable."

Javier's melodious voice was hypnotic and calming, which caused Thomas's apprehension to subside.

"I will take them into the bedroom and put them on."

"Yes, please do."

Thomas went into the bedroom and peeled off his constricting uniform. He unpinned his t-shirt from his shorts. He removed the corset.

First, he put on the trousers. The waist was snug but not tight. He fastened the suspenders to the waist of the trousers and slipped the suspenders over his shoulders. He tugged the waist of the trouser up and down. The suspenders brought the waist of the trousers right back to the best fitting position.

The jumper slipped easily over his shoulders and torso. He looked in the mirror. The uniform fit comfortably. He walked and turned at the waist without the jumper riding up over his belly.

Yes, I like his gift.

Thomas went back to the living room, still wearing the new uniform.

Javier was leafing through the daily horse racing form. "Do you know what this is, Thomas?" Javier holds up the racing form.

"Yeah. It's the daily paper for horse racing," Thomas answers, less apprehensive than he was earlier.

"No, Thomas, this is a guide for human destruction. Do you not agree?"

Thomas paused to consider Javier's words; then, he said somberly, "Yes, I do agree with that."

"It destroys you. Correct?"

"You know, then?" Thomas bows his head, shamefully.

"I know about your gambling problems. I can save you from that destruction."

Javier took an envelope from his inside coat pocket and handed it to Thomas.

Thomas knew what was in the envelope, before he even looked. He knew it would be enough money to pay off his gambling debt. Thomas opened the envelope and pulled out a wad of one hundred pound notes. He counted out three thousand pounds.

Thomas sat down into an overstuffed chair by the fireplace. He stared at the wad of money. He knew the money would save him from harm, from embarrassment, and from scandal. "What do you want for this money?"

"Nothing for that money, Thomas. That money is payment for something that I took from you."

"What?"

Javier reached into his inside breast pocket, pulled out several photographs, and handed them to Thomas.

Thomas's eyes widened. He uttered a gasp in response to what he saw in the photographs. They were pictures of pages from his journal. He looked up at Javier, who was standing five feet away. The man did not look like a spy, at least not Thomas's idea of a spy. The man was well dressed, polite, and had a sophisticated manner about him.

Thomas rose from his chair and went to the closet where his seabag was stored. He dug down until he found his seabag. He opened the seabag and dumped the contents on the floor. The journal was missing. He stared at the pile of seabag objects for several moments. Then, he walked back to the overstuffed chair and sat down. He again considered what he should do. Knowing that he possessed the money to clear his debt exorcised the fear of destruction from his heart.

Javier stood quietly and waited. He already knew the outcome of Thomas's deliberations. The classified information that Thomas had recorded in the journal was proof that Thomas had committed crimes against his county. Javier considered his advantage. *Thomas will commit to me. He has no other options. Well, except the option that Edward Stanley decided to take after I approached him with the contents of Thomas's journal. Stanley left a suicide note and named Thomas and me as spies. Fortunately, I found the suicide note in Stanley's apartment before his body was discovered. Stupid behavior! Why didn't he mail the note or put it on his desk at the consulate?*

Thomas queries, "Since the money is already mine, you must have future plans for me, right? I mean, you'll hang that journal over my head like a guillotine blade, right?"

"Such a draconian description. I would prefer to consider our future as partners."

"Partners?"

"Yes, Thomas, partners."

"And you as the senior partner, directing operations. Right?"

"I think that we can have a mutually beneficial partnership. I will tell you what I need, and you provide it. You will be appropriately compensated. When you are resourceful and provide valuable material that I have not specified, the compensation will be double. When I am especially pleased, you will receive gifts appropriate to the situation, like the uniforms."

Thomas became calmed by the soft flow of Javier's voice and the knowledge that his gambling debt was resolved. Thomas took comfort in the understanding that he only had one logical direction to go, and that was with Javier. His only other option was exposure and life imprisonment. He rationalized that collaborating with Javier would revenge the miserable life that the U.S. government dealt him. Being revenged and being paid for it appealed to him. He reasoned that if he refused this partnership, Javier would expose him; and he would go to jail. He also reasoned that if he partnered with Javier and was later caught, he would be sent to prison. Thomas concluded that there was no downside to becoming Javier's partner.

With a conspiring tone, Thomas asked, "How much money are we talking about?"

For a few moments, Javier stared at Thomas and thought, *how easy I recruit this fat, pathetic American. He has no principles, and he has no honor. He has no will power and no self-respect. Such human beings disgust me.*

"The quality of what you provide decides the amount. In the beginning, your compensation could be as high as several thousand dollars a month.

Thomas snapped his head back in surprise at the possibility of having so much money. "What do you want?" Thomas asked.

"Do you have access to dispatches?"

"In my job as Communications Supervisor, I get a copy of every message sent or received. My job is to ensure the messages were processed completely and accurately."

"Do you have access to any other sensitive material? What about your access to cryptography material?"

"I don't have access to the crypto stuff anymore. A navy officer took over all that."

"What do you do with your copies of the dispatches when you are finished reading them?"

"I put them in a burn bag. We take all the burn bags to the consulate incinerator three times a week."

"Can you take your copies from the consulate?"

"Sure. I could hide them under my uniform jumper or in my peacoat. No one is searched when they leave the consulate."

"How many dispatches—messages—do you have each day."

"About one hundred. Which ones do you want?"

"All of them."

Thomas jerked his head and blinked his eyes as he understood the volume. "That's a lot of messages!" he blurts in a raised tone.

"Bring your new uniform overcoat to me and bring scissors and some black thread. I will show you how to make a pouch for carrying papers."

Fifteen minutes later, the pouch was made.

"You must resume dining at the *Highlands Angus* restaurant. During dinner on Tuesdays and Friday nights, you will go to the water closet where you will give me the dispatches. You will receive your compensation at that time. After a month, we will change the meeting place. Do you understand?"

Thomas nodded. Then, he remembered. "*Oh!* I will only be in Scotland and the consulate for another two months. Then, I transfer stateside."

This revelation confused Javier. He had overheard Thomas tell friends that his tour at the consulate would end in the spring of 1958 and that Thomas would apply for a tour extension. Javier thought that Thomas lied.

"Are you truthful, Thomas? I have heard from your own lips a different story."

"It's the truth. No shit! I thought my tour was three years, but I got orders today."

"Where do you go from here?"

"San Diego, California . . . to the USS *Shangri-La*."

"The aircraft carrier?" Javier raised his eyebrows.

"Yes."

"What will be your work on that ship?"

"I won't know until I get there. Before I report to the *Shangri-La*, I will attend an eight week crypto equipment course."

"The school is before you go to the aircraft carrier?"

"Yes."

"Do you know the cryptographic system?"

"Yes, it's the same one we just installed at the consulate. It's a prototype and still under test. It has been working without problems."

"Can you provide me copies of the technical manuals?"

Thomas took a few moments to think about that. "The publications are registered and inventoried daily. I would need to bring you sections to photograph, and I would need to return the sections the same day."

"Your way has too much risk. I can teach you to photograph pages. Are you willing to photograph the pages yourself?"

Thomas gulped and felt nervous over the possibility of being discovered in the act of photographing pages of classified manuals. However, he did spend hours at a time in the Repair Shop with the door shut and no one entering. Thomas nodded his head as he said, "I should be able to do it."

"Excellent!" Javier emphasized and beamed a smile. "Tomorrow evening I will come here and show you how to use the camera and how to arrange light for taking photographs."

Thomas nodded.

Javier studied Thomas's face; then, he asked, "This school you will attend, will you be educated on how to repair the crypto equipment?"

"Yes."

Appreciation spreads across Javier's face. "Thomas, I foresee a profitable partnership for both of us. We will discuss how to meet in San Diego."

During the remaining two months of his Edinburgh tour, Thomas took no interest in his work. He lost his desire to *stick to the book* and keep the Communications Center organized. Whenever teletype operators requested a change to procedures that was contrary to official procedures, Thomas complied and made the change. He made several changes a week based on the teletype operator's recommendations. When he posted the change, he would specify the name of the teletype operator who recommended the change. After a few weeks, he was changing recent changes. The teletype operators all had different and conflicting recommendations. After Thomas made a change, the teletype operators began bickered among themselves as to the validity and value of recent changes. There was no resolution to the bickering because no recommendation could be substantiated by authorized publications.

When teletype operators came to Thomas for resolution, he would tell them, "Understand that you cannot have it both ways. You guys complained to the lieutenant that your recommendations were being ignored, and the lieutenant ordered me to start implementing your recommendations. Now you bicker amongst yourselves because there is no way to prove your recommendations are valid. Now, maybe you understand why procedures should be in accordance with *the book because the book* settles all arguments."

Eventually, some of the teletype operators went directly to the lieutenant and to high-level consulate officials and complained that the changes were causing confusion and disorder in the Communications Center. The teletype operators claimed that Bollier had lost control.

During his last months at the consulate, he showed an increasing disrespect for authority as demonstrated when the lieutenant called Thomas to his office again to discuss the teletype operator's complaints.

"I did what you told me, sir. I implemented their changes. Now they complain about the changes. The reason for so much confusion is that the changes are in conflict with each other, and all the changes are in conflict with authorized communications publications. As an officer you should be supporting authorized publications and not the misperceived concepts of low-grade, inexperienced DOS personnel." Thomas's voice became loud and frustrated as he continued. "Frankly, I don't understand your order not to follow the book! And with such a short time left here, I don't care to try!"

The lieutenant decided to micro-manage Thomas. Thomas was ordered to meet with the lieutenant twice a day to discuss all decisions. The lieutenant no longer trusted Thomas. The lieutenant made all decisions and had Thomas implement them. The conflict and confusion in the Communications Center became worse.

345

Lieutenant Benton never came to understand that the problem was not Thomas's supervisory ability. The problem was the perennial and petty conflict between DOS and DOD when they operated jointly and the lack of leadership on the part of Lieutenant Benton when he did not support Thomas's position to operate *by the book*.

The conduct of Edward Stanley and the conduct of Lieutenant Benton convinced Thomas that the navy and the U.S. Government in general is managed and directed by inane and inept fools.

Thomas focused on sneaking messages and photos of the technical manual pages out of the consulate and passing them twice weekly to Javier. At first, Javier paid Thomas $500.00 for each delivery. The material must have been of increasing value because the payments later increased to $700.00.

Thomas's Transfer Evaluation was his worst evaluation ever. His marks in Military Bearing, Leadership, and Adaptability were all unsatisfactory. Justification for his bad marks was constant criticism of his superiors and coworkers and the discontent and disorder in Communications Center. Thomas's unsatisfactory mark in Military Appearance was attributed to his gross weight gain and lack of dental hygiene.

Chapter 69

Thomas traveled to San Diego via military aircraft. As happened before, he encountered the same finger pointing between Air Force and navy personnel regarding the preparation of the paperwork. He did not get angry or exhibit frustration because he understood that incompetence is the nature of government employees—military and civilian.

Thomas scheduled some leave so that he could get to San Diego two weeks ahead of his class start date. He had some things to do before he checked in with the navy. He wanted to spend time at the beach. He loved summertime at the beaches in San Diego, especially the beach at Coronado Island.

Before leaving Scotland, Javier had directed Thomas to rent an apartment, but keep it a secret from the navy. Javier gave Thomas a bonus to ensure he had the money to get the apartment and to buy a car.

As Javier had directed, Thomas bought a used and common looking automobile; he bought a 1954 Chevrolet. He rented a two bedroom furnished apartment in Ocean Beach, close to the one he had rented several years prior.

Thomas also needed time to find, or have made, some *adequately* sized dungarees and Summer White uniforms. He found a tailor on Broadway who specialized in tailor made uniforms.

During the last week in June, Thomas reported to the San Diego Naval Training Center. He was assigned to a two-man room in the barracks, which he shared with another first class petty officer. Thomas pretended the barracks room to be his only residence. He claimed he had family in San Diego, and that is why he did not spend much time in the barracks.

Javier had given Thomas a contact address—a post office box in Madrid, Spain in the name of one Maria Sanchez. Thomas assumed the name was fictitious. Javier directed Thomas to send a letter to that post office box and provide the apartment address and telephone number. Thomas wrote the letter and mailed it at a civilian post office. Javier's instructions were not to write again until Thomas knew the *Shangri-La's* schedule.

Thomas contacted some of his former girlfriends. Some agreed to see him. However, once they saw how he had let himself go, they told him that he had changed too much and were no longer interested. Thomas, like anyone else, had feelings, and those feelings were hurt. He finally accepted the fact that he had lost his good looks. He did find some women who were interested. They were similar in girth and hygiene to Thomas.

Thomas started school. He had an advantage on the others in his class because of his experience with installing and operating the Romulus system in Scotland.

He had a social life and he was comfortable with his lifestyle. He knew that he should not get too comfortable because he knew that Javier would soon knock at his door.

During October 1957, Thomas reported to the aircraft carrier, USS *Shangri-La*. Shortly after reporting aboard, he learned that *The Shang* was scheduled for local operations for the next six months and was scheduled to depart in March 1958 for an eight-month deployment to WESTPAC. Thomas was one of twenty-three first class radioman assigned to *The Shang's* Communications Department. He was assigned to the Teletype Repair Shop where he and two others would repair and maintain over eighty teletype machines.

Thomas would be assigned to the Teletype Repair Shop until the Romulus equipment came onboard—three months away. Then, he would be transferred to the Crypto Repair Shop. Thomas would be responsible for working with the tech reps to get the Romulus cryptographic equipment installed and made operational before departing on the WESTPAC cruise.

Thomas sent a letter to the Madrid address. The letter explained his duties and listed the ship's schedule. As directed by Javier, Thomas did not use any part of the military postal system and he used his apartment as the return address.

Thomas's life aboard *Shangri-La* was routine. His rack was located in a 100-man berthing compartment that, no matter the time of day, was noisy and filled with sailors moving about. Thomas stayed aboard only during working hours and duty days. The rest of the time he spent at his apartment, the beach, and nightclubs.

Javier's orders to Thomas were to become anonymous and inconspicuous. He was not to attract attention to himself, either in his navy life or his social life.

The next few months were uneventful and routine. From time to time, the *Shangri-La* would go to sea for a week or two in the San Diego Operating Area. Thomas earned the reputation of being a quality technician who could solve any teletype related problem, whether the problem resided with teletype machines or with the associated equipment.

348

Maintaining his apartment became financially difficult. Thomas wrote a letter to the Madrid post office box and explained that he was short on funds and would have to give up his apartment in two month unless he received some money.

Five weeks later, he received a checkbook and a letter from a local San Diego Bank. The letter thanked Thomas for opening an account. The checkbook showed a balance of $2000.00. Every month after that, Thomas received confirmation in the mail that an additional $500 had been deposited.

Two days after receiving the checkbook, Thomas received a letter from the Madrid Post Office box. The letter directed him to mail a copy of his apartment key to the Madrid address.

Thomas used the extra money to purchase a quality bed and sofa for his apartment. He also bought a few Heath Kits; he built a short wave radio and a stereo record player.

The Romulus crypto equipment arrived onboard *Shangri-La* during the last week of January 1958. Thomas transferred to the Crypto Repair Shop where he was assigned to assist and supervise the civilian tech reps with installing and making operational the Romulus equipment. By the last week in February 1958, the Romulus equipment was installed and tested satisfactorily online over high frequency radio circuits with Naval Communications Station San Diego.

Chapter 70

Two weeks prior to *Shangri-La* departing for WESTPAC, Javier finally showed up in San Diego. Thomas entered his apartment one evening and there sat Javier.

"Hello, my partner!" Javier said enthusiastically as he rose and extended his hand. Thomas shook Javier's hand reluctantly and without enthusiasm. Javier noticed.

"You are not glad to see me?" Javier still sounded cheerful.

"Well, I am not *unhappy* about it. But you always greet me as if we are friends. You know we are not. We have a business relationship that at your whim I could be sent to jail for the rest of my life."

Javier paused and carefully considered his next words. "You are correct, Thomas. We are business partners with me having the upper hand. However, I do not plan ways to expose you to your government. Such actions would not benefit me. You are most valued when you are free to move about your navy without suspicion. You agree?"

"Yes, I guess so." Thomas was not convinced.

"Have I not kept you in good living style with monthly compensation deposits?"

"Yes . . . Yes, you have."

"I see that you still wear the uniform that I had made for you. Do you always wear that uniform?" Javier was referring to the Service Dress Blue uniform that Thomas was wearing.

Thomas grew embarrassed and explained. "It's not the same uniform. I had to have bigger ones made. The ones you gave me are in the closet."

Javier shook his head in disapproval. "Thomas, you must take control. Your navy will dismiss you if you become very large. Is that not true?"

"Yes, that's true, but I got a long way to go. Some sailors on *The Shang* make me look like a slim gentleman."

"Your government has no physical standards for its military?"

"Sure, if you're a marine or a soldier, I guess. But what I do requires brains, not a thin waistline. If a standard exists for people like me, it's not enforced."

"I see," Javier responded, but he really did not. "Why do you wear your uniform when you are away from the navy?"

"I just left the ship. I can't go on liberty without being in uniform. Pay grades E-1 through E-6 are not allowed civvies onboard. I'm an E-6."

"Civvies?" Javier asked.

"Civilian clothes."

Javier nodded his understanding.

"Anyway, you probably want the up to date tech manuals on the Romulus crypto system, right? It will not be easy like the last time."

"Yes, we must talk about the Romulus. What other sensitive materials are you in contact?"

"Not much. Until recently, I was working teletype maintenance. I have access to spaces that process top secret material, but I have no reason to view that material. So, if someone saw me looking at or touching most classified material, questions would be asked. Primarily, my only authorized access is what's stored in the Crypto Repair Shop. That's mostly classified tech manuals for the crypto equipment. I have no access to key lists or codes or messages."

"Are you ever alone with any of this material?" Javier asked.

"Yes, in port on duty days. Only one repairman is on duty at a time. After working hours, I'm the only one aboard who has the combination to the cipher lock on the door to the Crypto Repair Shop. I could spend the whole night in the shop and no one else would come in."

"How much can you take off the ship?"

"That's a problem. The master-at-arms force performs random body searches with pat-downs of body and clothing. All bags are searched. They are looking for people who are trying to steal supplies or equipment."

"What about a camera? Would one be confiscated?" Javier considered options.

"Sailors are always coming aboard and departing with camera cases over their shoulders. If I went aboard or left the ship with a camera case over my shoulder, there would be no problem."

"When do you have duty again?"

"Two days from now."

"I will come here tomorrow evening. I will provide you with camera technology much better than the last time."

"I thought you would," Thomas responded with resignation in his tone.

Thomas stood duty every four days, which allowed him five nights alone in the Crypto Repair Shop before the *Shangri-La* departed for WESTPAC. He managed to photograph all of the technical manuals. The only other items that Javier requested were lists of all the radiomen assigned to *Shangri-La* and the ship's in-port schedule during the WESTPAC cruise. Both were easy to obtain. Both were posted in the

351

Message Center.

Thomas introduced Javier to the manager of the apartment complex. Thomas told the apartment manager that Javier was a second cousin from Spain who would be living in Thomas's apartment and driving Thomas's car while Thomas was on the WESTPAC cruise. The manager had no problem with that as long as the rent was paid.

"No problem with the rent," Javier assured the manager as he paid three months in advance.

A few days prior to the *Shangri-La's* departure for WESTPAC, Thomas explained certain chores that needed to be done and how to pay utility bills. Javier asked Thomas what do about the tape-player recorder that was in pieces on the kitchen table.

"That's a Heath Kit that I am putting together. I will have it finished before I leave. I will wire it into my stereo system."

On his last evening before departure, Thomas showed Javier how to use the stereo system and how to record and play music on the tape-player recorder.

Javier told Thomas, "My stay here will be pleasant. I promise to watch and care for your belongings. I must go to Europe twice, no longer than two weeks each time."

Chapter 71

The *Shangri-La* deployed to WESTPAC. Thomas's duties were that of both teletype repairman and Romulus repairman. His workload was moderate, allowing him time to experiment with some electronic devices that he thought would be beneficial to his partnership with Javier. He sought to increase the monthly payments to his bank account.

The Romulus crypto system was designed for land based seventy-five baud, point-to-point circuits using reliable telephone lines for connectivity. When *The Shang* was in port in San Diego or underway in the San Diego Operating Area, solid and reliable radio connectivity existed. However, the Romulus system design did not consider the effects of radio interference and adverse atmospheric that resulted from long distance connectivity, which drastically reduced circuit up time.

During the transit to WESTPAC, *The Shang* shifted radio connectivity to NAVCOMMSTA Hawaii and ultimately to NAVCOMMSTA Philippines. Radio Circuit outage time increased as *The Shang* sailed farther from its connected NAVCOMMSTA.

The Romulus operational concept required only one crypto keycard change per day. The keycard change procedure was referred to as *Hotel Juliet* or HJ for short. However, the design also required a keycard change every time crypto synchronization failed. When atmospherics or radio interference caused radio signal distortion of more than 25 percent, crypto synchronization failed, and frequent HJs were required.

When a ship was at sea, reestablishing crypto synchronization was a frustrating, time-consuming task. Usually, contacting the shore station via the CincPAC High Command Voice Net was necessary, which was also a high-frequency radio circuit that also fell victim to the same interference and atmospherics as the Romulus circuits. Information regarding the next keycard number or frequency changes had to be first encoded using the Numerical Code, NUCO. The most common delays were caused by incorrect numerical coding. Outages up to twenty-four hours were common. Such outages drastically affected ships operations.

Often, *The Shang's* Technical Controllers were quick to point a finger at electronic problems with the Romulus equipment, and Thomas would be called to the Crypto Center to investigate. Thomas was too experienced with the Romulus system to become occupied with needless troubleshooting. His diagnostic tools, some that he designed himself, would quickly prove distorted radio teletype signals were the problem.

He would say to the Technical Controllers, "Get the radio teletype signal distortion level below 20 percent. If you still have a problem after that, call me back up here."

Later, when the shipboard and shore Romulus synchronized because of reduced signal distortion, the Technical Controllers would log the cause of outage as UNKNOWN and CLEARED WHILE TROUBLESHOOTING. Logging the cause as poor quality radio frequencies would infer that the Technical Controllers were not properly managing frequency changes to ensure the best quality signal. However, way too often and no matter how much attention was exercised managing radio frequencies, quality frequencies were not available. No one in the highest levels of navy echelon wanted to hear that crypto systems not suited for shipboard use were purchased and installed anyway.

Thomas enjoyed the WESTPAC cruise. He went on liberty at every port of call. He enjoyed visiting the same ports as when he was on the USS *Grant*. He frequented his favorite bars and frequented the same brothels in Subic Bay, Philippines and Bangkok, Thailand. In those ports, no onstage sexual act was deemed too bizarre or too deviant, and Thomas enjoyed it all.

Twice, Thomas came down with gonorrhea, *the clap*. Fortunately, so many sailors came down with *the clap*, that Sick Bay was always well stocked with penicillin. Some sailors came down with severe cases and had to be hospitalized in sickbay for several days, placing a burden on their work centers. *Sailors will be sailors* was an often excuse for not taking severe nonjudicial actions. However, until a sailor was cured of *the clap*, he was restricted to the ship and could not go ashore during the next liberty port. CINCPACFLT directives required that every time a sailor was afflicted a notation must be entered into the sailor's Service Record. Documented counseling by the division officer was also required.

During the entire cruise, Thomas received two letters from Javier. Both letters were short and stated that all was well with the apartment and car. Javier wrote that a few ladies had called, and Javier told the ladies that Thomas would be away until the fall. During the cruise, Thomas sent only one letter to Javier. The letter was to inform Javier of the date that the *Shangri-La* would be back in San Diego.

When Thomas arrived at his apartment complex, he noted his car was freshly cleaned and waxed. When he entered his apartment, he found a note from Javier. The note advised that Javier was in Europe and would return in two weeks. Next to the note was Thomas's checkbook. He looked at the balance. He was pleased to see that the $500 deposits per month continued while he was gone. Thomas appreciated his situation. Obviously, Javier did consider Thomas a valuable member of their partnership. Thomas was anxious for Javier's return. Thomas wanted to show Javier his electronic invention.

Two weeks later on a Saturday afternoon while Thomas was sitting at his kitchen table eating lunch, Javier arrived. The two men shook hands and greeted each other cordially—no fake enthusiasm from Javier this time.

They sat at the kitchen table and chatted. Javier had many questions about the WESTPAC cruise. Javier quizzed Thomas thoroughly on Thomas's work during the cruise. Javier showed concern that Thomas still had limited access to classified information. Then, Thomas told Javier that he had designed some electronic components that allowed him access to thousands of classified messages.

"Tell me about it, my partner!" Javier's tone reflected anticipatory enthusiasm.

"Have you ever heard of a modulator-demodulator? Some people abbreviate the term as modem."

Javier thought for a moment. "Modulator-demodulator . . . modem . . . hmm . . . *yes!* . . . devices used in telecommunications. Is it not?"

"Yes, it is. Do you know its function?"

"No, I do not," Javier admitted.

"A modem converts voice frequency signals to digital signals and vice versa."

"And how is that to our advantage?" Javier asked with raised eyebrows.

Thomas said proudly. "I got the idea during the cruise when I was working on a D.C. loop problem between a modem and a teletype machine."

"Okay. Continue."

"It's better if I demonstrate. Come into the living room."

Thomas directed the two of them to sit near the Heath Kit tape player-recorder. Thomas picked up the microphone.

"Javier, what happens when the machine is set to record, and you speak into the microphone?"

"Your voice is recorded onto the tape."

"Exactly . . . your voice is an audio signal, and a teletype signal is a digital signal."

Javier's eyes widen. He immediately grasped the technical concept.

Thomas continues the explanation. "So, if you take a teletype circuit and connect it to the digital side of a modem, and you take a tape recorder and connect it to the audio side of a modem, you will record the messages that flow over that circuit."

"*Yes!* I understand the possibilities! What have you done to help us?!"

"Aboard *The Shang,* I am known as a music loving kinda guy. I've had a Heath Kit record player and tape player-recorder on my workbench since day one. I am always recording records to tape and often have earphones on listening to music while I work. Also, everyone sees me up in the Communications Center wiring things. The Communications Center wiring isn't compatible with all the new communications gear. I was tasked to run cable and wire equipment. New equipment comes onboard faster than the shipyard can install the appropriate cable. I was assigned to install whatever cable is necessary to get the new equipment operational. No one knows what I am doing. They leave it up to me. And, several cables run between the Communications Center and the Crypto Repair Shop." Thomas paused for questions.

"Continue, Thomas. I am following you," Javier said with exuberance.

"I had to modify the modem's output voltage to the tape recorder. I burned up a few circuits while I was experimenting. I eventually got it right."

"Got what right, Thomas?! What were you able to do?!" Javier's excitement increased.

"I wired my modem and tape recorder into the teletype circuitry on the ship-to-shore termination. It's the radio teletype circuit that uses the Romulus crypto equipment. I'm always in MAIN COMM fixing things with the wiring. No one knew what I was doing. The chiefs and officers were just happy that I could make the new stuff work. For the last four months of the cruise, I copied to magnetic tape every message transmitted and received on the Romulus radio circuits."

Javier sat back with an amazed look on his face. None of his other partners had been so creative. He wondered if the U.S. Navy knew that Thomas was a technical wizard. Javier gained some respect for this American. Then, Javier asked, "No one asked you about the device connected to your tape recorder?"

"No, I keep the modem in a locked drawer under my workbench. I drilled a hole in the back of the drawer for the cables."

"How do you know it works?"

"One day when no one was around in the Crypto Repair Shop, I patched everything into a teletype machine. I watch three messages print. Then, I stopped."

For a few moments, Javier stared at Thomas in astonishment. Then, he asked, "What is the highest classification of messages on that circuit?"

"The keycards are top secret, but I don't think any top secret messages were processed. Plenty of SECRET messages, though. This Romulus stuff is new. People don't trust it yet, and they still offline encrypt the top secret stuff."

"Explain the purpose of these keycards that you speak of."

"Ever see an IBM punched card?"

"I have seen pictures in magazines," Javier replies. "There have been articles about these new computers. The punched card is essential to the operation of the computer."

"That's right. The keycard has punched holes that provide the encryption key. Both the ship and the shore station must have keycards with identical holes placed in the Romulus card reader. Identical keycards are necessary for crypto synchronization between the ship's Romulus and the shore station's Romulus."

For clarity, Javier asked, "The teletypes connect to the Romulus and the Romulus connects over radio circuits between ship and shore?"

"Yes, that's right," Thomas confirmed.

Javier spent a few moments to collect his thoughts; then, he asked, "Where are the tapes with the messages?"

"Right there," Thomas nodded toward a stack of 100 tape reels under the table.

Javier picked up a few of the tapes. The writing on the labels listed names of classical composers.

"Where is the modem?"

Thomas pointed to a corner of the living room. In that corner sat a metal container about the size of a large breadbox.

"How did you get it off the ship?"

"Just carried it off in plain sight. I told the master-at-arms at the quarterdeck that I was taking it to the maintenance facility for repair."

Javier was impressed with Thomas's deceitfulness.

"Thomas, if I provide some teletype machines, can you wire up the modem and tape recorder and make the messages print?"

"Sure can."

Several days later, Thomas and Javier loaded the tapes, modem, and tape player-recorder into Thomas's car. Javier drove the two of them to an office building in La Jolla. They unloaded the car and took the items into a first floor office. The sign on the office door read *SANCHEZ IMPORTS and EXPORTS*. The office contained two tables and some chairs. Two teletype machines sat on the tables. Some tools and rolls of thick gauge wire lie on the floor. In the corner were cases of teletype paper and teletype ribbons.

Thomas went to work with wiring up all the equipment. Two hours later, messages were printing.

After that first day at the La Jolla office, Javier told Thomas not to return to the office. Javier told Thomas that some associates were taking care of the printing.

"Can you provide more modems?" Javier asked Thomas.

"No problem! I can order what I need out of the Heath Kit catalog."

Three weeks later, Thomas gave Javier two more Heath Kit tape player-recorders and two more modems.

"Thomas, my resourceful partner, you are a paradox. I had underestimated your ability. You are more valuable to our partnership than I ever imagined."

At the end of the month, Thomas's checkbook statement revealed a $4,000.00 increase over the previous month.

Chapter 72

Thomas continued his message harvesting aboard *Shangri-La*. Once a week, he would pass the tapes to Javier.

Thomas was concerned that a TEMPEST inspection of the communications spaces and repair shops could result in recommendations that personal tape recorders must be removed. Thomas had read the TEMPEST regulations and understood how a personal tape recorder could be viewed as a TEMPEST security hazard.

Navy issue tape recorders with TEMPEST protections were connected to CW and voice circuits in *The Shang's* communications spaces. The tape recorders were used for copying the CW Morse Code radio broadcasts and for recording important voice circuits. Thomas assumed that since there were already tape recorders copying radio signals, no one thought a tape recorder on a workbench was a problem. Thomas must have been the only one in the Communications Department who had read and understood the TEMPEST regulations. No one suggested or ordered that he should remove his Heath Kit tape player-recorder.

Javier advised that he was moving his operation back to Europe. He instructed Thomas to mail the tape reels to the Madrid address.

They both concluded that using the mail system was safe. First, who would suspect that sensitive U.S. classified material would be sent unregistered mail in a small box labeled *stationery supplies*. Second, even if someone acquired the tape reels and attempted to play them, only low level clicking noises would be heard. Third, fake return addresses would always be used.

They also concluded that only engineers who knew what they were looking for could discover what was on the tapes. If it ever got that far, Thomas's activities would have already been discovered.

Thomas mailed tape reels to Madrid on a regular basis, and monthly $500 deposits to his checking account continued.

Several months after Javier departed San Diego, Thomas drove out to La Jolla to the SANCHEZ IMPORTS and EXPORTS office. The office had been vacated and the sign removed from the door.

During March 1960, USS *Shangri-La* moved to its new homeport at Mayport, Florida. Thomas drove his car from San Diego to Mayport. After arriving in Mayport, Thomas quickly rented an apartment and mailed his new address to Javier.

The *Shangri-La* deployed to the North Atlantic and to the Mediterranean. When in liberty ports, Thomas smuggled the tape reels off the ship in a self-constructed false bottom of his camera case. Thomas would hire a taxi to take him to a post office.

Thomas adjusted to being a loner. He lost his desire to be the center of attention. He discovered that anonymity was essential to his success as Javier's partner. Thomas was always agreeable and cooperative with his superiors.

His hatred of the U.S. Government and the U.S. Navy no longer surfaced in emotional outbursts. His hate was a quiet and methodical hate. He achieved revenge by doing his navy job well and performing well as Javier's partner. His bank account reflected the success of his revenge. *All those message I send to Javier must cause damage somewhere to the U.S. Government!*

Thomas did continue one bad habit. Whenever one of his peers or juniors challenged the validity of something he was doing or would tread into his territory, he would let loose with eloquent insults that attacked the offender's judgment, technical ability, and any unusual physical characteristic. Thomas's shipmates became accustomed to his insulting outbursts and became hesitant to approach him. Thomas was careful not to exhibit such behavior in front of chiefs and officers.

His Performance Evaluation marks improved. His expert technical ability gave him the *halo effect*, which resulted in no mark being *Unsatisfactory*. Professional Performance continued to be his highest mark. His other marks were the lowest they could be and stay in the *Satisfactory* category. *Evaluation Comments* applauded his technical accomplishments and how his technical actions improved *Shangri-La's* mission effectiveness. On the negative side, his *Evaluation Comments* stated that RM1 Bollier tended to be a loner and did not take the lead of juniors when appropriate to do so. *Evaluation Comments* also stated that RM1 Bollier's uniforms were always immaculate, but his continually increasing body weight and lack of attention to oral hygiene detracted from his military appearance. Thomas had gained an additional twenty-three pounds since reporting to *Shangri-La*.

During 1961, his last year on *Shangri-La*, a chief radioman reported aboard who Thomas developed a cordial and agreeable relationship. Thomas considered RMC Sean Bulldoone to be his technical equal. They worked on many projects together. Thomas liked Chief Bulldoone so much, he did not object when credit went to Bulldoone for some of

Thomas's successful ideas.

During early 1962, Thomas received orders to the Naval Communications Station in Rota, Spain. This surprised Thomas because his Performance Evaluations would not qualify him for overseas shore duty. All personnel ordered to overseas shore duty had to go through a screening to ensure they were suitable examples of American citizens. The *Shangri-La's* Commanding Officer sent a letter to BUPERS advising that RM1 Thomas Bollier was not suitable for overseas shore duty. To everyone's surprise, BUPERS wrote back and overruled the suitability screening. BUPERS advised that *'needs of the service'* required RM1 Bollier's skills and experience at NAVCOMMSTA ROTA.

During his last few weeks onboard *The Shang*, he removed all electronics that may later reveal his traitorous deeds. He disconnected the modified modem from his tape-recorder. He disassembled the modem and put the various components in parts bins. One of his final tasks was to remove the wiring that routed the classified teletype signals to his workbench in the Crypto Repair Shop. His division officer wrote a note explaining that RM1 Bollier was allowed to remove his personal tape recorder from the ship. With the note, he had no problem at the quarterdeck.

Thomas wrote to the Madrid address and advised that he was transferring to Rota, Spain. He sold his car and the few pieces of furniture that were his own. The navy packed his personal items and shipped them to Spain. His personal items were mostly stereo and radio equipment that he had built from Heath Kits. He sent a change of address to his bank, and he made the last mailing of tape reels to the Madrid address.

Three days before his departure from Mayport, Thomas received a letter from a housing rental company in Rota, Spain. The letter, written in English, thanked him for his deposit and for the first three months' rent in advance. The letter said to come to the rental agency to get the keys when he arrived in Rota.

Javier thinks of everything!

Chapter 73

During July 1962, RM1 Thomas Bollier reported to the U.S. Naval Communications Station at Rota, Spain. He was assigned to the Crypto Repair division as a Romulus technician. The Crypto Repair Shop had a cipher lock on the door and only a few people had the combination. He was given his choice of workbenches. He chose the workbench against the far wall—the one with cable tray running above it and a vertical cable tray running behind it.

A maze of overhead cable trays ran through every room in the Communications Station. The metal labels affixed to each cable identified where the two ends of the cable were located. The translation of the label codes was filed away somewhere in the EMO's office, where mountains of disorganized technical diagrams gathered dust.

Seldom did anyone need to look at cable diagrams, so no one was assigned to keep it organized. Whenever someone needed to know a cable's routing, they never attempted to find the applicable diagram in *that trash heap*. Instead, they would attach a tone-tester to one end and trace the tone along the cable until the other end was found. Chiefs and officers believed that hundreds of old, unused cables lie in the cable trays. No adverse operational impact resulted from the lack of cable management, so no one cared much. Thomas discovered the disorganized condition of the cable trays during his first week. *Typical and very much to my advantage!*

On his third day in Rota, Thomas went to the rental agency and picked up the keys to his house, which turned out to be a two-bedroom bungalow near the beach. He bought a 1957 Citron from a departing chief. Thomas would rather have purchased a new sports car, but that would have drawn too much attention to him and would have drawn definite disapproval from Javier.

When his division officer discovered that Thomas had moved off base and into a beach bungalow, he asked Thomas how he could afford it. Thomas explained that he had just spent five years on sea duty, and he had saved all his money. Now that he was on shore duty, he planned to live it up. The division officer accepted Thomas's answer.

Installation of twelve Romulus cryptographic systems was scheduled during the next three months. Thomas was assigned to assist the NAVELEX technicians with the installation. One of the technicians was from the installation at the Edinburgh Consulate. The technician did not recognize Thomas at first.

"You have changed a lot," the NAVELEX technician commented to Thomas.

"No shit," was Thomas's irritated reply.

Thomas installed his Heath Kit tape player-recorder and record player on a table next to his workbench. He placed his custom-made modems in a large drawer of his workbench, which he kept locked. He placed the speakers atop the overhead cable tray above his workbench. From the beginning, he had the tape player-recorder reels turning and low volume classical music flowed from the speakers.

No one objected because no one considered the possible hazard. Again, tape player-recorders were used elsewhere in the Communications Station as logs for CW and voice circuits.

The Crypto Repair Shop was a designated *Black Area*, which meant that only unclassified or encrypted electronic signals were allowed to pass through it. Thomas did not worry about anyone snooping around his workbench. A repairman's workbench is sacred ground—no trespassing allowed.

The Romulus installation kept Thomas extremely busy. He had short timelines to get the twelve Romulus systems installed. The Electronics Material Officer constantly looked over Thomas's shoulder and nitpick the installation. The EMO was an experienced Mustang lieutenant who knew his business. Thomas remained cordial and agreeable and did not show his annoyance of the EMO's interference.

Thomas had routed Romulus signal cables through the cable tray above his workbench, and he was concerned that the EMO would discover the security violation. To avoid the EMO's scrutiny, Thomas volunteered to pull the cables during the evening hours when less people were around, including the NAVELEX technicians, EMO, and other crypto repairmen. Although classified signals passed through the cables above his workbench, Thomas purposely marked the cables with *Black Area* identification markings, which was another Communications Security Violation. The cables that Thomas routed over his workbench were not include in any of wiring diagrams produced by the Romulus installation project manager.

All the watch standers in the Communications Station became accustomed to seeing Thomas working with cables in the overhead. They all assumed the evening work was necessary to meet installation deadlines.

Thomas spliced wiring plugs into the cables above his workbench. The plugs would allow easy connect and disconnect of his custom wiring harness into the teletype signal wires. He routed the custom harness through a vertical cable tray that ran from the overhead tray to the floor behind his workbench. Thomas routed the custom harness through an access hole in the back of his workbench and connected the harness to a modem.

Thomas placed six speakers on top of the cables in the overhead tray. To an observer, the harness appeared to be the wires for the six speakers to his tape player-recorder.

Thomas's two-bedroom bungalow was located at the end of a row of pastel colored bungalows in a coastline community several miles north or Rota. The casual atmosphere of the community caused most people to wear shorts and sandals from early May until late September. The local populace was a mix of Spanish citizens and British citizens. This area of Spain was a favorite retirement location for British citizens. Patio parties were common during the evenings of the warm season. Thomas's front patio faced the dark blue of the Atlantic Ocean. He could hear the surf pound against the rocky coastline just 100 yards away.

On a sunny Saturday afternoon in September, Thomas sat on his patio eating tapas and drinking ice cold San Miguel. He had finished one bottle and was taking another from the ice chest at his feet when Javier pulled up in a white Mercedes sedan with Spanish license plates.

Javier wore expensive European-cut casual clothing—a light blue silk shirt and white cotton-silk trousers. Javier had never revealed his nationality to Thomas, and Javier always inferred he was Spanish. Thomas did not believe Javier was Spanish. For some reason that Thomas could not identify, Spanish just did not fit and European did not fit.

Javier never spoke Spanish in Thomas's presence. Javier's educated and sophisticated manner hid his origin. He could have originated from any of the countries that border the Mediterranean Sea.

"Hello, Thomas. Welcome back to Europe."

Thomas waved hello in an enthusiastic manner.

Javier sat down in a lounge chair opposite Thomas.

"Can I get you anything?" Thomas asked. "I know you do not drink beer. I have some cokes and some lemonade."

"Yes, some lemonade, please."

Thomas went into the bungalow. A few minutes later, he returned with a tall glass of iced lemonade and handed it to Javier.

"Thank you, Thomas."

"You're welcome," Thomas responded cheerfully.

"Thomas, my friend, you are in a good mood today."

"I am seldom in a bad mood, Javier. However, I always have worries on my mind."

"What worries do you these days?" Javier asked as he looked directly into Thomas's eyes.

"I worry that someday my partnership with you will be discovered. Then, my life is over. I will spend the rest of my life in jail."

"Thomas, if I were to give you unconditional freedom today, would you accept it?"

Thomas answered immediately, "No! Please do not confuse my worry with a desire to end what we do. In the beginning, I did what you wanted out of fear. Now, I have my own motivations for what I do, and I enjoy a comfortable lifestyle as a result. Only if I thought my activities were about to be discovered would I request an end to it."

"Good! I am pleased to hear that. As I have told you before, I will protect you should you be discovered. Now, Thomas, tell me what you are doing that is beneficial for our partnership."

Thomas explained what he accomplished so far at the Naval Communications Station.

"I am waiting for some Heath Kit components from The States. Once they get here, I can build several modems."

Javier said, "I can be of assistance with the modems."

Thomas's face reflected doubt.

Javier went to his Mercedes and returned with two metal boxes, each the size of a small toaster.

"My associates have improved your design. They call it *reverse engineering*. They made the modem unit smaller by one-third. Hiding the modem will be easier."

Thomas examined the exterior of each modem. Except for their smaller size, they looked identical to the modem that he gave Javier several years before. Thomas went into the house and returned with a small tool kit. He removed the metal cover of one of the modems and expected the inside.

Javier explained, "See, no vacuum tubes. My associates call it *solid-state* design. Are you familiar with *solid-state* components, Thomas?"

"Yes, I am. It's expensive but less power consumption and less heat dissipation. The newest navy communications equipment includes more and more solid-state components."

"I am not surprised that you understand these things. I do not understand the electronics. My contributions lie in the human element."

"Yes, Javier, and you do that part just as well as your associates do their part with designing the components."

365

Javier smiled and said, "I appreciate the compliment."

Thomas did not mean it as a compliment. *If Javier misinterprets, that's okay.*

Thomas advised, "I think I can increase the previous volume by 300 percent, and the messages will be from more than one radio circuit. All messages will be to and from a number of the heavies in the MED."

"Heavies? MED?" Javier queried.

"Sorry. I should not use jargon. I should remember English is not your first language."

"I would appreciate that," Javier responded.

"Heavies are big ships like aircraft carriers and heavy cruisers. When I say MED, I mean the Mediterranean."

"I understand, now."

Thomas chose his next words carefully. He was apprehensive about how Javier would respond. "Javier, I often wondered what you do with all those messages. Do you read them? I mean, how are they used?"

"If I answered your questions truthfully and completely, I would reveal too much about myself. That would not be good for our partnership. Let it be sufficient to say that you provide valuable documents."

"Okay. I will not ask you about it again."

"Yes, we will not talk about it again. When can you start providing the classified message tapes again?"

"Next month. By then, I will have all my equipment in place, and the first of the aircraft carriers will be establishing radio links."

"Will you be able to do some photographic work?"

"Only of technical manuals. The Crypto Repair Shop is the only place where I can be locked in and alone for any period-of-time."

"That is sufficient. I will bring the camera equipment tomorrow. I think you will be amazed at the advancements in small cameras since the last time."

"I'm sure that I will be astonished," Thomas said calmly and without enthusiasm.

Chapter 74

Thomas pursued romantic relationships with some Spanish women. Women wanted nothing to do with him. Thomas's mannerisms, oral hygiene, and obesity repulsed most women. Some of the less attractive women who were also equal in size to Thomas showed some interest. But Thomas was not interested in them. For female companionship, Thomas drifted to the Rota Gut. His favorite haunt was the *El Toro Blanco* bar and whorehouse. He preferred the *El Toro Blanco* because it was situated on the edge of *The Gut* farthest from the Naval Station, which resulted in low volume patronage by fleet sailors.

By the end of his first year in Rota, Thomas had settled into a daily routine. His work became an eight to five day job with a duty day every six days. He developed a reputation as a repairman that could solve any problem. His Performance Evaluations improved. His sarcastic comments lessened, and his marks in Military Behavior improved. After years of neglect, he finally started seeing a dentist again. The *halo affect* improved his marks in Military Appearance. Thomas received a recommendation for advancement to chief. Thomas took the Chief Radioman Test. He passed the test, but his evaluation marks were too low for him to be advanced.

Each week, Thomas mailed tape reels to the Madrid Address. He would go to a Spanish Post Office in El Puerto De Santa Maria, a port city located on the Bay of Cadiz halfway between Rota and the city of Cadiz.

Thomas continued to receive monthly deposits to his bank account. Most months, the deposit was $500. Some months the deposit was as high as $800. Thomas never asked Javier why some months the deposit was higher. Thomas just assumed that the messages he provided had some higher value at times.

During November 1963, Thomas was pleased that his old friend, Chief Radioman Sean Bulldoone from the *Shangri-La*, arrived in Rota for duty. Sean Bulldoone was assigned as chief in charge of the Repair Division and was Thomas's supervisor. Bulldoone was on an accompanied tour, and his wife was with him. Thomas and Sean renewed their friendship but did not spend as much time together as they did back on *The Shitty Shang*. Occasionally, Sean would invite Thomas over for dinner or cookouts. Often, they would stop at the Chief's Club after work for a few beers.

After several months, Sean Bulldoone entered into an extramarital affair with a Spanish woman. Thomas allowed them to use his bungalow from time to time. Bulldoone was appreciative and often overlooked Bollier's shortcomings in their work environment. Sometimes the favoritism was so obvious that other sailors complained to their division officer.

During his twentieth month in Rota, Thomas submitted a request to have his tour extended for a year. The request went to BUPERS with a strong and positive endorsement from Thomas's commanding officer. BUPERS approved Thomas's request. Thomas was surprised at the approval. *The navy finally did something positive for me.*

Chapter 75

During a Monday morning in March 1964, one of the Teletype Repairman, RM2 Bennett, came to Thomas with a question about cabling. "They tell me around here that you're the expert on the Fleet Center cabling,"

Bennett reported aboard two weeks prior and was fresh out of Teletype Repair School. Teletype Repair School and assignment to Rota was Bennett's reenlistment incentive.

Thomas gained his thorough knowledge of the Fleet Center wiring during the Romulus installation. All others who were involved in that installation had transferred. Thomas still had the NAVELEX cabling diagrams locked in a drawer of his workbench—no one knew that.

"Yeah, I know something about it," Thomas responded with a superior tone. "Whadda ya need?"

The medium height, slim, sandy-haired, blue-eyed sailor explained, "I'm troubleshootin' a teletype problem out there, and I've come across somethin' that I don't understand. Can ya come out there for a minute and take a look?"

Bollier shook his head in disgust and annoyance. However, he wanted to be involved in everything regarding the station cabling.

"Okay. Lead the way."

As Bollier and Bennett entered the Fleet Center, the sounds of clacking teletypes, radio teletype signals, and CW signals caused them to raise their voices over the din of operations. A dozen radiomen moved about and engaged in tuning radio receivers, operating teletype circuits, and operating CW circuits. Yellow colored teletype tape and teletype paper hung from most of the teletype machines. The Fleet Center was that area of the Communications Station where radiomen operated radio teletype circuits and radio CW circuits with U.S. Navy ships at sea. Bennett led them to a bank of teletype machines in the middle of the Fleet Center.

"I was troubleshootin' that teletype. I think there is a problem with the signal cabling. I traced the cable back to the teletype patch panel. I'll show you what I found."

Bennett pointed at the overhead cable tray and said, "Now, you see where the cable tray splits. One tray goes toward the patch panel and the other goes through the bulkhead into the next room."

"Yes, I see that," Thomas replies impatiently.

"Well, the signal cable for that teletype goes into the next room, instead of going over to the teletype patch panels in this room. I checked some of the other cables for the Fleet Center teletypes. All the teletypes that have circuit loops with Romulus crypto have a cable that goes into the next room instead of going directly to the patch panel."

"Not to worry," Thomas said with a slight shake of his head. "There's lots of cable runs around here that make no sense. The room next to this was the Fleet Center at one time. It probably has something to do with that. I am always finding cable runs that don't make sense. Everything works, anyway. My recommendation is to not waste your time."

"But I think the cabling is causing the problem."

Thomas deliberated for a few moments; then, he asked, "When was the problem with the teletype first reported?"

Bennett pulled the Repair Ticket from his pocket and read it. "Last night. The Fleet Center Watch Supervisor said they went to use it, and it would not print, no matter what teletype loop they patched in."

"When did it last work?" Thomas queried.

Bennett looked back down to the Repair Ticket. "Watch Supervisor says they were using it the night before. Ticket doesn't say why they stopped using it, though."

Thomas pondered this information for a few moments; then, he stated, "I think I know. Come with me."

Bennett followed Thomas into the Teletype Repair Shop. Thomas went to the wall-mounted Preventive Maintenance Schedule. He ran his finger down the date column for two days ago.

"Just what I thought," Thomas announced as he glanced at Bennett. "According to the Preventive Maintenance Schedule, two days ago someone performed a quarterly PM on that teletype." Thomas paused and with a raised brow looked questioningly at Bennett.

Bennett expressed bewilderment for a moment; then, his eyes went wide, and he said, "You think that the tech who did that PM *fucked up* the teletype?"

Thomas rolls his eyes at the young sailor and declares with arrogance, "Yes, that's what I think."

"I never thought to check the Preventive Maintenance Schedule."

"Instead, you thought that somehow the cable, an item with no moving parts, went bad all of a sudden when no other equipment connected to the cable went bad."

"Okay. What now?" Bennett asked. "I'm in the learning mode here."

Thomas shook his head and stared at Bennett. Then, with a sarcastic tone he said, "Fuckin' boot camp rookies! Get your tool bag and the PM card. If you do the PM, I bet you'll discover the problem. I'll watch."

Fifteen minutes later, Bennett found the problem. Whoever had previously performed the PM, did not properly connect the signal relay.

Bennett concludes, "That means the tech that performed the PM didn't test the teletype after he worked on it, as the PM card says to do."

With a disgusted look on his face and a sarcastic tone in his voice, Thomas said to Bennett, "Don't be surprised. Most people in this canoe club only do a half-assed job."

"I won't be that way!" Bennett declared.

"Right!" Thomas responded sarcastically. "Anyway, you do not need to trace cables. Just always expect that the last technician that touched the equipment probably fucked it up."

"I think I will trace cables, anyway," Bennett stated enthusiastically.

Bennett's intentions startled Thomas. He gave Bennett a head-to-toe appraisal. Thomas remembered that he was better built and more handsome than Bennett is when he was Bennett's age. "Why would you want to trace cables?" Thomas asked in a condescending tone.

"My goal is to make first class during my Rota tour. You know. Do something extra that's not required. Besides, the knowledge will help me in my work."

"When are you going to trace cables? If you can wait a few days, I can help you."

Thomas hoped his offer would buy him some time to think about what to do. Thomas also knew that he must inform Javier. Javier had promised to protect Thomas should Thomas be in danger of being discovered. Javier promised to give Thomas a new life and new identity.

Bennett advised, "I get off watch soon, and this is my last watch in the string. I will be off for three days. I will start when I come back on my next watch string. I want to find out where those cables go."

After work, Thomas drove to the Naval Station Telephone Center, which provided long distance pay telephone service. He gave the Madrid telephone number to the operator.

Javier had directed Thomas to call the telephone number only in the case of an emergency. Javier had been specific and adamant about that.

"Please take a seat in booth nine," the operator said.

Thomas sat in the booth and picked up the handset. He heard a dialing signal followed by ringing for the distant end.

"Hola!"

"May I speak to Charles, please?" Thomas spoke the codewords.

"Charles is gone for the day. May I give him a message?" The woman spoke the correctly coded response.

"Yes, tell Charles that Thomas called. Please tell him that I cannot come to Madrid tonight." The codewords translated to "*Javier, I need to see you immediately!"*

"Yes, Thomas. I will give him the message."

"Thank you. Goodbye."

During late evening, Thomas sat next to the fireplace in the living room of his bungalow. He had lit a fire to burn off the winter chill. His bungalow did not have central heat. He wore a double-layered sweat suit. He sipped brandy and lit a cigarette from his third pack of the day. He sat on the couch with his head bowed and deep in thought as he waited for Javier to arrive.

Thomas raised his head as he heard a car come to a stop. He lifted his immensity off the couch and waddled to the window.

Javier exited his white Mercedes and walked to the bungalow door.

Thomas opened the door and got right to the point. Anxiety lined his words. "We have a problem. One of the teletype repairman is about to discover my cable splices."

"Okay, Thomas. Let me take off my coat and sit. I hope you have some tea brewing?" Javier responded; his tone casual.

"Yes, I have hot tea. Hold on." Thomas went to the kitchen.

Javier removed his coat and sat on the couch near the fireplace.

Thomas retuned from the kitchen with a small tray holding a pot of tea, a teacup, and a small container of sugar. He sat the tray on the coffee table in front of Javier. Then, he pulled over a chair and sat down directly across the coffee table from Javier.

Javier poured the tea and stirred in some sugar.

Thomas stared at Javier and wondered how the man stayed so trim and solid. Over the years Javier's dark face aged a bit, but he never gained an ounce of weight and never lost a strand of his black hair.

Javier took a sip of tea and smacked his lips. "Good! Thank you. Now, tell me about our problem."

"Like I was saying, there's a teletype repairman who plans on tracing cable runs. He wants to learn where the cables are routed. He is sure to find my splices and the connections to the tape recorder."

"Could he be a counterintelligence agent?" Javier asked seriously.

The question surprised Thomas. He never considered that. "I don't think so. How would I know? He's like any other sailor."

"What is the sailor's name?"

"Bennett . . . why? Is that important?"

Javier took out a notebook and wrote the name. Javier asked, "Does this Bennett have access to your Crypto Repair Shop?"

"Not normally. He could get access under certain circumstances. I would know if that happened."

"How long have you known him?" Javier asked.

"A couple of weeks. He just reported aboard."

"What does he look like?"

"Pale skin. Blond hair. Thin."

"Age and height?"

"Twenty-two, I would say . . . height about five-eight."

Javier wrote Bennett's description in the notebook.

"Why do you need his description?"

"Pass it around to my associates. See if any of them recognize this Bennett."

Thomas expressed understanding.

"Is it unusual for someone to want to trace cables?"

"Yes, it's unusual. I've never known anyone anywhere who wanted to do that."

"Is there anything else about his work that is unusual?"

Thomas sat back and thought. He lit a cigarette and sipped some brandy. After more than a minute, he responded, "Yes, the problem on the teletype today, he should have known to check the signal relay before thinking it was a cable problem. It's basic week one, day one teletype troubleshooting. He should have known. So, I guess I should wonder why he came to me about cabling." Thomas looked to Javier for an answer.

"To see how you would react, possibly."

"But why would he wait for a couple of days to start tracing the cables? If he wanted to see if I got scared about cables, he should have started tracing right away."

"If he is a counterintelligence agent, he or his associates would want to observe your behavior for a couple of days . . . to see if you contacted anyone."

"Oh my god! I called you! I wasn't thinking!"

"Did you call me immediately after talking with this Bennett?"

"No, I waited until after work. Must have been six hours between the time I talked with Bennett and when I called you."

Javier stroked his chin while he evaluated the situation. Then, he said, "I do not think this is a problem, Thomas. If an investigator traced that phone number, he would find Charles, a British national, and his Spanish wife, Maria. If asked, they would speak very well of their American friend, Thomas."

Thomas shrugged his shoulders and looked questioningly at Javier.

"Thomas, surely you remember Chuck and Mary who spent the last two summers in the bungalow two doors away. The three of you attended many patio parties together."

Thomas was stunned by this revelation. He would never have

suspected. "Chuck and Mary work for you?"

"No one works for me. I have partners and associates. They are associates of mine."

"So, their friendliness toward me was staged, not real?" Disappointment showed on Thomas's face and in his voice.

Javier had not considered that Thomas's feelings could be hurt by this situation. Not that Javier cared, but he did not want his operation put in jeopardy. Emotion can destroy an operation.

"Not staged, Thomas. They told me they always had a good time with you and the other neighbors."

Thomas thought about that for a moment. Then, another thought came to his mind. "Do you have people following me?"

"Following is not the correct word. Looking after you is a better description. I cannot always be near you. I occasionally have associates check to ensure you are still safe."

"What should I do, then? Is it time for me to run away from the navy and go into hiding and start that new life?" Thomas was anxious for a course of action.

"I will explore possibilities. Do nothing until I get back with you."

"Okay," Thomas responded with concern in his voice.

Javier gulped down the remainder of his tea. Then, he stood and put on his coat. He attempted to comfort Thomas again, "Do not worry, my friend. I will take care of you."

Thomas was hopeful and doubtful at the same time.

Javier opened the door, exited, then faded into the dark.

Over the next few days, Thomas went about his normal work routine. He expected Javier to arrive Thursday night with some solution to the Bennett problem because Bennett would be back to work Friday morning and start tracing cables.

When Javier did not arrive, Thomas became fearful for his future. He did not sleep a wink on Thursday night.

On Friday morning, Thomas sat at his workbench, waiting for Bennett to knock on the door of the Crypto Repair Shop. At 1100, Thomas wondered why Bennett had not come by. He went looking for him. *Maybe Bennett had started the cable tracing without me.* Thomas went to the Teletype Repair Shop, but Bennett was not there.

"Where's Bennett?" Thomas asked the only repairman in the shop.

"Don't know. He hasn't come in yet. He was supposed to relieve me at 0800. Chief Bulldoone sent someone to the barracks to look for him or find a relief for me, I hope."

All sorts of morbid thoughts raced through Thomas's mind. *Could this be Javier's doing.* Thomas had not considered that Javier would harm Bennett. *My god! This can't be happening!*

As the day progressed, Thomas checked the Teletype Repair Shop for Bennett several times. Another repairman had replaced the one from this morning.

During late afternoon, Thomas went searching for RMC Bulldoone. He found the chief in the coffee mess. Thomas pretended a chance encounter.

"Hey, Chief, what's up?"

"Frustrated!" RMC Bulldoone declared with a deep sigh.

"Why? What's going on?"

"Do you know RM2 Bennett, the Teletype Repairman?"

"Yeah, I've seen him around . . . thin, blond kid . . . new guy, right?"

"Yeah, that's him. He reported aboard several weeks ago. Anyway, he didn't report for duty this morning. Master-at-arms searched the barracks. No one has seen him since yesterday. Now, the Shore Patrol is out looking for him."

Bennett never appeared. As the weeks went by, many speculated as to where he had gone. No one knew him except for the two weeks he was at Rota. After thirty days, Bennett was declared a deserter. Two months later, Bennett was no longer a topic of conversation, and he was forgotten.

The Bennett incident unnerved Thomas. He knew that Javier must have eliminated Bennett—*killed Bennett!* Thomas had always suspected that Javier could become a killer, if he wasn't already. Thomas was frightened. More than ever, Thomas feared that he was playing a dangerous game.

Thomas had always viewed his *activities* as revenge against the United States Government. Until the Bennett incident, Thomas never thought of the cost of his revenge in human life. Thomas dreaded his next meeting with Javier. Both men would look at each and know that Javier had killed. Thomas worried that he would breakdown in front of Javier.

Months went by and Thomas had no contact with Javier. Thomas continued to mail tape reels. The deposits continued to Thomas's bank account.

Chapter 76

Javier Ramirez sat at one of the outside tables. He frequented this restaurant on Via Veneto every time he came to Rome. He shed his coat and tie earlier in the day, during the heat of the afternoon. A light breeze cooled the evening air. While looking over the menu, he ordered some *aqua minerale* with ice and lemon.

Javier watched the people on Via Veneto. At 9:30 p.m., the Romans were just coming out for the evening. Tourists crowded the sidewalks, looking for excitement. The young Italian gigolos pursued men and women alike with offers to satisfy the tourist's search for excitement. The restaurants were just starting to fill. Tourists flooded the world-renowned shops. Young adults from all over the world formed lines outside the more popular nightclubs. Small Italian automobiles darted, zigzagged, and honked up and down the street. The drivers obviously from a culture that considered traffic signals and traffic signs as nuisances to be ignored.

"Hello, Javier, always a pleasure to see you. Too much time separates our visits," Andrei said in English. His Russian accent slightly detectable.

Javier looked up and into the suntanned face of the middle aged Russian. Andrei, dressed in a summer weight Italian-cut gray suit, looked more European than Russian. Daily, rigorous exercise resulted in the Russian maintaining his athletic build, and he was fortunate enough to have kept a full head of sandy colored hair.

Javier responded sincerely to the Russian KGB operative, "Hello, Andrei. Yes, it has been too long. Our visits are always a pleasure for me."

Javier and Andrei had been associates for ten years. They were both educated men who spoke several languages, and both were sophisticated in the ways of the world.

The waiter, dressed in the traditional white shirt, black tie, and black pants came to their table and took their orders. Javier ordered the sea bass, and Andrei decided on the cannelloni.

Andrei and Javier engaged in small talk until the waiter delivered their food. Then, they got down to business.

Andrei advised, "My superiors are very satisfied with the material that you have gathered from the United States Navy communications channels, although they think the amount of money you demand to be excessive."

Javier responded with a smile, "As the capitalists say, *whatever the market will bear.*"

Javier knew that Andrei's superiors were more than satisfied with his price. He also knew that Andrei's words were a maneuver to request additional information and not at an increased price.

Andrei informs, "The information you provide is useful, but recent activity from the Americans indicate that they know we must be reading their mail. In addition, this Bennett business . . . very distasteful . . . we do not enjoy resolving problems in that way. It had to be done, of course. Had Bennett actually been an American counterintelligence agent, we could not have eliminated him. It would have told the Americans that Bennett had discovered something. Unfortunately, for Bennett, he was just a patriotic boy who wanted to do his duty better than others. My superiors almost disapproved your request to have us resolve the Bennett problem for you."

More maneuvering, Javier thought. However, he believed that Andrei's KGB superiors found the Bennett resolution distasteful.

"Yes, I agree," Javier lied. He had no reservations about eliminating an American for the benefit of his cause.

The KGB had considered removing Javier as the intermediary and deal directly with Javier's sources. However, Andrei had wisely informed his superiors that Javier's network would fall apart if Javier were removed. Javier promoted that his partners worked with him because he was obviously not Russian. Javier's partners deceived themselves into thinking little harm could come from their spying as long as they were not spying for the Russians. As Javier explained logically, *they will spy for me, but not for the Russians. If they knew the Russians were involved, too many of them would rediscover their patriotism; even at the cost of being jailed.* KGB headquarters agreed with Javier's logic.

The KGB did not want to risk losing the valuable intelligence that Javier provided. Just recently, information in U.S. Navy messages assisted the KGB with discovering a Soviet diplomat who spied for the Americans. The KGB suspected seven diplomats. To identify the spy, the KGB gave false information to each of the seven diplomats regarding future Soviet warship patrol areas in the Mediterranean. The location information was different for each diplomat. The diplomat was identified when the information provided to him appeared in U.S. Navy intelligence messages.

Javier asked, "Andrei, you asked for this meeting. What task do you have for me?"

"The Americans have a new crypto system that they call Orestes. We need to know more about it. We need to understand its concept of operation and we need the technical manuals."

"Same price," Javier announces.

"My supervisors ordered that I negotiate for a lower price because of our assistance with the Bennett problem."

Javier responded, "Andrei, you know that I would have handled the Bennett situation myself, except that all my resources were committed elsewhere. I needed action within a few days. Anyway, we all benefited from Bennett's elimination, especially your government."

"My superiors appreciate that you came to us regarding Bennett. We handled it better than you handled that situation in Athens last month. You should have come to us on that one also. My superiors are furious over the way you disposed of those two intelligence operatives then openly displayed to the world what you did. We seldom do business that way. When we do, it is only as a last resort, and we never broadcast our actions to the world. Bennett was one of those last resort situations. If we been given more time, we may have come up with an alternative. It was not necessary for you to kill those operatives Athens, and it was not necessary for you to broadcast your actions. Now, our enemies want revenge. Our enemies think the Soviet Union is responsible for the death of those two operatives."

Javier countered, "Athens was necessary. Our enemies must know that it is dangerous to get too close to us."

Andrei had always understood that Javier's motives were money to pay for an extravagant lifestyle. Andrei thought that Javier cared only for himself and had no cause. After Athens, Andrei reevaluate Javier's motives. Andrei directs, "Someday you must explain to me why you thought it necessary to be so brutal and so obvious. But now, we must talk about this American Orestes cryptographic system."

"Same price," Javier stated firmly.

Andrei hesitated. His supervisors would not be pleased. However, he was authorized to agree to the same price but no higher.

"Yes, same price," Andrei agrees with a reluctant tone. "So, you can get us the Orestes information?"

"I will tend to it." Javier smiled triumphantly.

Chapter 77

On a cool September evening in 1964, Javier arrived at Thomas's bungalow. He wasted no time on pleasantries. "Thomas, do you know of these Orestes crypto devices?"

Thomas did not answer right away. He searched Javier's face for some hint that Javier did not kill Bennett.

"What bothers you, Thomas?"

Thomas was afraid to ask and also afraid not to ask. He needed to know. He could not be in doubt about what happened to Bennett. He knew that he could not be comfortable in Javier's presence without knowing the truth. Thomas finally asked, "What happened to Bennett?"

Javier looked into Thomas's eyes while evaluating the effect of telling Thomas about Bennett.

After what seemed an eternity of silence to Thomas, Javier finally spoke. "Bennett was a danger to our partnership. He could not be allowed to discover what you are doing."

"But we could have let him find it. I could have disappeared and started a new life with a new identity, like you've said before."

"We are beyond that, now. Some of my associates would not react compassionately to a halt in the flow of the information that you provide. Believe me when I tell you that your contribution is too valuable to be discovered by a curious boy."

"So, he was not a counterintelligence agent?"

"We do not believe so."

Thomas felt trapped and afraid. He could not resolve Javier's explanation as justification. At this point, Thomas became aware of the danger to him. In the past, he had only considered the possibility of being discovered and going to jail for the rest of his life. Being killed by Javier or one of Javier's *associates* had not been a consideration until now.

Thomas's voice quivered, his heartbeat accelerated, and his eyes misted as he challenged, "You told me that when I wanted to quit you would protect me and hide me."

"That promise was a long time ago. We cannot retire from this. The stakes are too high, now. What we do is of great value to my associates."

Thomas detected acquiescence in Javier's tone. Thomas thought that Javier might also have no choices. *The Russians must be in charge of all this.* Thomas relaxed a little when he thought that Javier and he were in the same boat. Maybe killing Bennett was not Javier's idea.

Both men paused.

Thomas broke the silence. "Can I make you some tea?"

Javier expelled a sigh of relief and replied, "Yes, thank you."

Ten minutes later, they sat before the fireplace. Javier sipped tea. Thomas took gulps of brandy and opened his third pack of cigarettes for the day.

"We must discuss the Orestes cryptographic system. Are you familiar with it?"

"Yes, NAVELEX installed a bunch of Orestes devices last year. I wasn't involved in that."

"Do you have access to any of the technical manuals?"

"They are in the Crypto Repair Shop. I can do the same as before. On my duty night I have the place to myself."

"Good. I have the camera equipment in the car. You will be surprised at the technology improvements since the last time.

"I'm sure I'll be amazed."

During March 1965, Thomas requested another year extension to his tour. Again, the request was forwarded to BUPERS recommending approval. Again, BUPERS approved the one-year extension. The approval letter also stated that this was the final extension.

Chapter 78

Thomas continued to spend most of his liberty time in the Rota Gut at his favorite bar and brothel, *El Toro Blanco*. He became a regular. All the employees knew his name. He developed a relationship with a prostitute named Rosa. Thomas and Rosa would go to the beach and have picnics. She had an apartment in town, and sometimes Thomas would sleepover. Occasionally, Rosa would sleepover at Thomas's bungalow. These sleepovers were private for Rosa and provided her with opportunities to show her affection for Thomas. She was a good friend to Thomas, and she was not a prostitute when they were away from *El Toro Blanco*. She truly thought Thomas Bollier to be a nice person, and she never suspected the secret side of his life. Rosa was the first woman in years to show true affection and interest in Thomas. To show his affection, Thomas bought Rosa expensive gifts.

One night while they lay in his bed at the bungalow, Thomas handed Rosa another gift in a wrapped box. With the excitement of a child on Christmas morning, Rosa tore the wrapping from the box. She opened the box slowly and whistled softly as she removed a gold bracelet. "Thomas, not need you pay for me when we no in Gut. I much like you. We honey friends."

"I want to give you gifts, Rosa. I don't think gifts are payment. My gifts show how much I like you and how much I want to be with you."

The remainder of Thomas Bollier's tour at NAVCOMMSTA Rota progressed without additional threats to his espionage activities. No one showed any interest in cables or interest in the elaborate audio system components that Thomas installed around his workbench, and no one showed any interest in the cable tray above his workbench. He continued his monthly shipment of tape reels, and the balance in his bank account continued to increase.

During the month of April 1966, Thomas received orders to the USS *Columbus*, CG-12. Norfolk, Virginia was the homeport for the Guided Missile Cruiser.

During May 1966, Thomas received a letter from the *Columbus's* communications officer. The letter contained the usual *Welcome Aboard* information. The COMMO advised that Thomas would be assigned to the Communications Department as teletype repairman and Romulus repairman. Thomas would be the only repairman. He would have the

Repair Shop on the 05 level all to himself. The COMMO also advised that Thomas was scheduled for a three-week UCC-1 Repair School that he would attend shortly after reporting aboard *Columbus.*

Thomas sent a letter to the Madrid address and wrote about his pending transfer and the details he knew so far regarding his work aboard *Columbus.* He had previously told Javier that he must depart Rota during July 1966. He also wrote that his last shipment would by on July 4th.

Thomas disconnected the teletype cables from the modems. He removed the plugs from the overhead cables and spliced all the wires back together. Then, he fastened splicing clamps around the cable. Thomas speculated that should anyone ever look at the cables and see the splicing clamps, they would just assume that during the initial cable installation the cable pull was too short, and additional cable had to be spliced to complete the pull. *Considering the number of idiots in this canoe club, they probably won't even know what the clamps are.*

Thomas destroyed the wiring diagrams from the Romulus installation. He concluded, correctly, that should anyone ever trace the Romulus cables, the discoverers would conclude that the cable installers were unsupervised. Thomas correctly concluded that the danger of *red signal cables* passing through a *black area* would be dismissed as a harmless mistake by incompetent installers who were directed by equally incompetent superiors.

Thomas removed all his sound system equipment from the Crypto Repair Shop and put it in his bungalow for packing by the navy movers. He shipped the modems to the Madrid address.

Thomas went to the *El Toro Blanco* to say goodbye to Rosa. Thomas became emotional when Rosa's eyes misted.

"Do not worry Rosa. I will be back in six months. I will come to see you when my ship stops here."

Rosa hugged him tightly and said tenderly, "Señor Thomas, me hurt with you no here. I will want for you much when you gone."

Two nights before Thomas's departure from Rota, Javier came to see him.

"I have a gift for you." Javier handed a thick envelope to Thomas.

The envelope contained a map, a key ring, and papers from a bank in the Bahamas. The map was to a street address in Virginia Beach, Virginia.

"What's all this?"

"The map provides directions to your house, and the keys are for that house. The house is yours to occupy at no expense to you. There will be no rent payments. The house does contain some HAM radio equipment that you will be required to use from time to time. You are not to tell your navy about this house."

"Well, I guess that's a gift," Thomas responded appreciatively.

Thomas studied the documents from the Bahamian bank. A letter explained that Thomas was approved for a Secret Numbered Account. The remaining documents explained the procedures for obtaining the secret account number.

"And this?" Thomas questioned as he raised his hand containing the bank documents.

"You must hide your money from your government. Only you can withdraw by presenting your secret number. The documents include a form for transferring your money from your American bank account."

Javier lied regarding Thomas being the only one knowing the secret number. Javier's arrangement with the bank was that both Javier and Thomas had access to the funds. Javier learned this lesson well. He remembers Jonathan who was a former associate who decided to run away from Javier and disappear. Eventually, Javier tracked Jonathan to Barbados and with some difficulty extracted the secret number from Jonathan. The account number was the last words ever spoken by Jonathan.

"Okay. I will take care of it when I get to Norfolk."

"Excellent!" Javier responded with enthusiasm in his tone. "Now, we need to talk about your contributions to our partnership while you are aboard this USS *Columbus*. What do you think you can do?"

"As I said in my letter, I will have a repair shop all to myself. I will be able to provide technical manual updates for sure. I will not know about messages until I get there."

"What about cryptographic key lists and code books?"

"Sorry, only the people who do daily code changes and operate the radio circuits would have access to that, and those people are always double checked. I just won't know much until after I get there."

"You are a resourceful person, Thomas. I am sure that you will develop a valuable contribution."

"I will do my best," Thomas responded without enthusiasm.

"Good! Now, we must talk about something of considerable importance to some of my associates. The messages you provided for the last four years here in Rota were timely and very useful. But we remember when you were on *Shangri-La*. Sometimes two months would pass before we received tapes from you. Much of the information was out-of-date."

"The ship was at sea during those times."

"I understand that. I ask you to use your abundant technical skills to get the messages to me faster and without using your navy postal system."

"I will do my best."

"I am sure that you will, Thomas."

PART III

APOLLO
RISES

The ancient, culturally rich beach town of Rota rests on the southwestern coast of Spain. The town sits on the north end of the Bay of Cadiz halfway between Gibraltar and the border of Portugal. A Spanish Naval Base spans thousands of acres immediately to the east of the town. The Spanish Navy controls access to the base, and the United States Naval Station occupies areas within the Spanish base.

Javier Ramirez sits on the balcony of his hotel room, which faces Rota's southern shoreline. He sits in a comfortable lounge chair and wears a heavy jacket to protect him from the chilling wind coming off the Bay of Cadiz. Binoculars sit on a small table next to him. Room Service has delivered his breakfast to the balcony. He easily views the channel leading to the naval station. The binoculars aid his view. In between searches through the binoculars, he takes bites of his continental style breakfast and enjoys sips of the strong French roast coffee.

He enjoys the view through the binoculars. The choppy, dark-blue and white-capped water of the Bay of Cadiz sharply offsets the multi-pastel colored buildings along the shoreline. This clear and sunny day reveals a spectacular view of the bay and surrounding shorelines.

On his next search through the binoculars, Javier sees a large warship steaming north up the channel toward the Spanish Naval Base. Eventually, he identifies the hull number 12 on the bow. Javier watches the warship for more than an hour as it makes its approach. About midmorning, he loses sight of the *Columbus* as buildings and other structures close to the naval base block his view.

Although the time is late morning and the *Columbus* is in port, the CR Division berthing compartment overhead lights remain off. The division remains structured in the Underway Watch Schedule. Light shines down the ladder from the First Division Berthing compartment above. The light prevents a comfortable darkness for sleeping. Thirty percent of CR Division attempts to sleep off the mid watch. Others lie awake in their racks and read under the dim illumination of their low wattage bunk lamps. Occasionally, loud noises and shouts funnel down the ladder from above, and the never-ending blasts of announcements over the 1MC make an undisturbed sleep impossible. The deep snoring by some and the occasionally loud and odorous farting by others increase the difficulty of sleeping soundly.

The rest of the ship conducts normal working-hours routine and seem not to have any regard for those *fuckin', privileged, pussy twidgets* in the compartment below.

A loud, vibrating bang from the deck above jerks RM3 Rigney Page awake. The luminous dial on his watch reveals that he must get up in twenty minutes for the afternoon watch.

He focuses on several of his fellow division mates putting on their Service Dress Blue uniforms. They are going on liberty. One of them says in a soft tone that he knows *the best places in Rota to get laid.*

These sailors only slept for a few hours off the mid watch. They must be back at 1730 to stand the eve watch. These sailors are known as *steamers*. When in port and still in Underway Watch Schedule, they only have an eight-hour window between watches to go on liberty. These sailors have a reputation for being able to *steam* for three days with only a few hours of sporadic sleep.

Rigney eats a light lunch prior to going on the afternoon watch. As he walks forward across the ASROC deck, he enjoys the view of the Bay of Cadiz and the view of sun-bleached buildings with red tiled roofs that line the shore. The crystal-clear day and chilly breeze invigorate him.

He stops on the 04 Level landing at the top of the ladder. He looks aft and easily views the submarine tender, *USS Canopus*, and two SSBNs—Nuclear Ballistic Missile Submarines. The size of the submarine tender dwarfs the two sleek and low-lying submarines. Rigney knows that those submarines are larger than they appear from this view. He knows that when a nuclear submarine is on the surface only one-third of the submarine rises above the waterline.

Rota is homeport for the submarine tender and a number of SSBNs. Rigney takes a moment to reflect on the way his life will be after this ONI assignment. He wonders if his work onboard a submarine will be more interesting than onboard *Columbus*. He knows one thing for sure. If he were on one of those submarines, he would be deep into working on his Basic Submarine Qualifications. He yearns for the submarine duty for which he waited and trained so long.

He sighs deeply, turns, and enters the superstructure. As he walks past the fan room, he thinks about the weapon hidden within. Thinking about that weapon in the fan room causes him to think about the second pistol. He decides to verify the presence of the second weapon sometime tonight.

As he performs his duties on the afternoon watch as Fleet Broadcast Operator, he frequently glances at the UCC-1. The transmit channel three and four drawers are pushed in. He checks the teletype patch panel. The DC meter shows keying on those channels, but no teletypes operating in MAIN COMM are generating that keying. Rigney continues to wonder about the source of that keying.

The Naval Communications Station Rota and USS *Columbus* sit only a few miles apart. All radio signals are *five-by-five*—loud and clear. The soft clickity-clack of the fleet broadcast teletype and the sound of the ventilation fans are the only noise in MAIN COMM. Most of the watch standers are up on the Signal Bridge breathing fresh air and enjoying the view of Rota.

With no radio frequency problems to fight, Rigney easily keeps pace with the incoming message volume. He enjoys a watch where he does not struggle against a rolling and pitching deck under his feet.

Rigney's relief arrives at 1700.

After watch, Rigney goes to the mess decks for dinner. He takes advantage of the fresh fruit and vegetables that were delivered after arrival in port. He piles fleshly sliced tomatoes, cucumber, and broccoli on his plate.

After dinner, he goes to the Signal Bridge on the 07 Level. Most of the MAIN COMM watch standers loiter about the Signal Bridge, instead of sitting at their watch positions in MAIN COMM.

Rigney discovers that loitering around the Signal Bridge while in port when you should be at your MAIN COMM watch station is common practice among CR Division radiomen. He discovers *big eye liberty*, which is using the fifty-power binoculars to scan the streets and buildings along the shore for any interesting activity. He spends more than an hour exchanging small talk with the other members of his division.

Chapter 80

Near the Rota harbor waterfront, an economic zone exists that American sailors call *The Gut*. For most establishments in *The Gut*, a sleazy bar occupies the first floor, and a cheap whorehouse operates in the upper floors. Ageless, rundown stucco buildings with fading pastel colors line the narrow streets. The road surface is a patchwork of brick and cobblestone and zigzags at irregular angles around oddly shaped buildings. Alleyways dart into the darkness and can end without notice. Windows caked in decades of grime and the smell of rotting garbage contribute to the *unwashed* atmosphere.

The Gut exists in most foreign ports visited by the American Navy. Business names like the *California Bar* and the *Texas Bar* attempt to defraud American sailors into a sense of belonging in a place far away from home. However, sailors are not attracted by the names of these enterprises. They are attracted by the honesty of those businesses' marketing techniques. Sex is for sale, and no business attempts a subtle *soft sell*. Sailors are more than willing to buy, and no sailor considers haggling the price.

On this evening, U.S. Navy sailors crowd the streets of the *Rota Gut*. These sailors, all in Service Dress Blue uniform, white hat, and peacoat, linger outside the doors of their favorite bar. They came ashore with their friends in groups of three or four. More than half the sailors are smoking and when they inhale the night appears to be invested with fireflies. Many, who started drinking earlier, stagger along the sidewalk. The occasional inebriated sailor who wanders from his friends and staggers alone becomes the target of muggers and thieves.

Radioman First Class Thomas Bollier walks the main street of the *Rota Gut*. He weaves in and out and between the groups of sailors on the sidewalk. His destination is specific. He has an appointment. He enters *El Toro Blanco* bar, located near the west border of *The Gut*. The bar, not one of the favorites of visiting sailors, has only a dozen sailors sitting at the bar and at the tables. Several prostitutes sit at the tables and they chat and laugh with the sailors.

The darkened interior of the bar is typical for *The Gut*. Stains of varying concentrations from a century of spilt drinks cover the floor. Cigarette butts and ashes litter the floor and tables. The place smells of beer, cigarettes, and sewer. On the right are the stairs to the upstairs brothel. The splintered and worn wooden bar runs along the far wall. The bartender, dressed in the Southern European traditional white shirt and black pants, moves back and forth behind the bar. As are his orders from the bar's owner, the bartender often short-changes the inebriated sailors.

Bollier scans the interior. He spots Javier sitting alone at a table in a front corner. To the casual observer, nothing looks unusual about the Spanish man sitting at the corner table.

After Thomas sits, Javier stares into Bollier's face for a few moments; then, he asks, "Anything to report?"

"No, everything is the same. No problems."

"Anyone new that I need to investigate?"

Bollier considers if he should tell Javier about RM3 Page. *During the last year, Javier has become unfriendly and confrontational. Javier becomes annoyed and angry when he thinks I hide things from him. Page is just a boy who cannot be a threat. Why take the chance with Javier becoming annoyed?*

Javier sees hesitation in Bollier's eyes and says, "I told you to never leave anyone out. Who is it, and why to you hesitate?"

"I don't want to needlessly bother you about people that can't possibly be a problem to us," Bollier justifies weakly.

"I will be the judge of that," Javier states firmly and in an agitated tone.

"Okay," Bollier relents. "His name is Rigney Page. He's an RM3, just reported aboard a couple of days before we left Norfolk. He's just a boy, a dumb jock, cannot be more than twenty or twenty-one."

Javier pulls out a wallet-sized notebook and writes the name.

"Where did he come from?" Javier asks without looking up from the notebook.

"He was stationed at Bethesda Naval Medical Center," Bollier replies casually. He shrugs his shoulders to convey Page's unimportance.

Javier looks up from the notebook. He has a quizzical look on his face. "Why would a radioman be assigned to medical duties?"

"Bethesda is the largest navy hospital in the world. It has its own Communications Center. He must have been assigned to the Communications Center."

"You are not sure?" Javier challenges.

"Where else would he be assigned?" Bollier knows he made a mistake by not verifying the details of Page's previous duty history. He knows this Page is unimportant and not a threat, but he fears that Javier will make a big deal over nothing.

Javier studies the man in front of him. In the early years, Thomas was more concerned and more cautious. During the last year, Javier has noticed that Thomas appears to care less about the security of their partnership. Experience tells Javier that this change in Bollier's behavior is a sign of a partner who is about to run. He remembers Jonathan's behavior. "You have become less concerned about our safety, my friend."

"I'm concerned," Bollier assures. "I just don't think we need to consider this RM3 Page a problem."

Javier is not assured. "Where is this Bethesda?" He questions.

"It's near Washington DC," Bollier states evenly.

"Washington!" Alarm creeps into Javier's voice. "All the intelligence agencies are headquartered there—are they not?"

"Easy, Javier. Many sailors aboard *Columbus* were stationed in Washington at one time or another, nothing unusual about it. The Pentagon is in Washington."

"Do you have a picture of this RM3 Page?" Javier's questions with a demanding tone.

"I will get one," Thomas promises.

"Good. Make sure that you do. I want the picture before your ship departs, and I want you to observe this Page more carefully. Report to me anything unusual about this man. You want to keep those monthly payments coming, don't you?"

"Yes, of course."

Javier changes the subject. "Do you have the new devices in place?"

"Yes, they are connected and ready for use."

Javier smiles and appears to be satisfied. "Okay, my friend. We shall meet here again tomorrow night at the same time. Make sure tomorrow night you have a picture of this RM3 Page." Javier stands, nods goodbye, and exits the bar.

Bollier remains seated. He worries that Javier is displeased about his lack of detail regarding RM3 Page. Over the years, Javier has been good to Bollier. Nevertheless, Javier occasionally sounds threatening. During the last year, there were those two times that Javier did not make the monthly deposit into Bollier's Bahamas bank account. Javier said it was punishment for Thomas not doing exactly as Javier directed.

Bollier catches the eye of his favorite prostitute, Rosa, sitting at the bar. She smiles at him. She orders a beer from the bartender. Then, she walks over and sits next to Thomas. She hands him the bottle of beer.

Rosa is thirty-one. She has the dark skin and black hair of her Moorish ancestors. Her facial features are plain and hard. She has been selling herself since she was fifteen. She escaped the life of a poor fisherman's daughter and the inevitable future as a poor fisherman's wife. Her first ten years as a prostitute were her most profitable years. Now, as she ages and puts on more weight, fewer men want her services.

Some of the younger prostitutes find ways to trap American sailors into marrying them. When she was in her early twenties, Rosa had considered this tactic to improve her life. She wanted to be selective, and the best time passed. Now, she must hustle more and provide extra services, and she must depend on established clientele. Fortunately, she lives a frugal lifestyle and saves most of her income. She knows that at best she has five years remaining in the business.

Rosa likes *Señor* Thomas. She has known him for five years. He has always been kind to her and always pays her extra. When *Señor* Thomas was stationed in Rota, they often had long talks and she would spend nights with him in his bungalow on the beach. Occasionally, they would go on beach picnics. Neither had considered taking the relationship beyond that. Rosa knows that *Señor* Thomas is a troubled man. He never speaks of the trouble. She knows that other sailors do not like him. She always found him likable and agreeable.

"*Señor* Thomas, you not be here long time. We miss you this place. We think you always friend."

"Hi Rosa, it's nice to see you again," Thomas greets happily.

"Where you been?" Rosa is equally happy to see *Señor* Thomas.

"The States."

"Someday, I will go to States and see my friends married to sailors."

"Maybe someday you can come to The States and visit me."

"Yes, I will like." Rosa smiles but doubts that *Señor* Thomas will follow through.

"*El Toro Blanco* has not changed much," Thomas comments as he looks around the bar. "I see that Jose is still the bartender."

"Yes, place never change. Rota never change. You change, *Señor* Thomas. Me change," Rosa declares in a deflated tone.

"You look the same to me," Thomas responds. "How am I different? Fatter?"

"*Señor* Thomas, me not worry you fat. You always nice man."

"Gracias, Rosa. You have always been nice to me also."

"Yes, we nice both. How much time you be Rota?"

"Two more days."

"I no work tomorrow. You like beach picnic?"

"Yes, I would like beach picnic but isn't it too cold?"

"We take blankets to wear us."

"Okay. Sounds great!" Thomas is enthusiastic. "Are you still in the same apartment? What time should I come?"

"Yes, same apartment—one o'clock time. You not wear uniform tomorrow."

"Okay. I will bring some civvies with me. I will change in your apartment."

392

"Good! I like."

Rosa studies Bollier's face for a few moments. Then, with a sexy smile on her face, she asks, "You want same again blowjob topside? It two dollar more before last time. If no, I must go work more."

Rosa knows that *Señor* Thomas will pay double, which she never reveals to the *Señora* who supervises topside operations.

Thomas smiles. "Yes, I want same again."

He follows Rosa up the stairs to topside.

Chapter 81

Rigney lies awake in his rack. He looks at his watch—0320. The hours have passed slowly as he waited for activity and movement within the berthing compartment to cease. All the noisy, stumbling, and drunken liberty hounds finally settled down and fell into a deep sleep. The compartment is finally dark and quiet.

He quietly lowers himself from his rack and puts his feet on the deck. He reaches under his mattress, retrieves his shower shoes, and slips them on his feet. Dressed only in his boxer shorts, he walks to the head, which is located in the aft port corner of the berthing compartment.

As he opens the head door, the glaring lights momentarily blind him. The lights are always on bright; no *soft glow* feature exists.

If you need to use the head while trying to sleep between watches, you must walk through the dark compartment then be harshly awakened by the head's bright lights. The experience violently shakes your senses and always diminishes your chances of falling back to sleep.

The radioman strikers, who are at the bottom of the divisional pecking order, are always assigned the racks closest to the head. They do not complain because they are very happy not to be in the deck divisions where they would be unappreciated as deckhands.

The head, of course, does not have the comfortable atmosphere of home. The functional shipboard décor includes a maze of piping in the over-head. Two stainless steel sinks and two stainless steel urinals are affixed to the forward bulkhead. Against the aft bulkhead are two shower stalls and two stainless steel toilet stalls. Shower curtains are rigged across the front of each toilet stall to provide privacy for its occupants. The deck is made from a substance called terrazzo. The bulkheads, overhead, and deck are sea green in color, or more affectionately known as *puke green* to the sailors of *The Tall Lady*.

Rigney closes the door behind him. He wishes there were a lock to ensure his secrecy. He knows that anyone can come through that door and discover his actions. This time of morning provides the least risk of discovery. He steps into the outboard toilet stall and pulls the shower curtain closed. He lowers the wooden toilet seat; then, he steps up onto the toilet seat. He reaches into the maze of piping in the overhead and finds the small oval cover plate on the air conditioning duct. He unsnaps the cover plate and moves it sideways. He reaches into the opening and pushes his hand six inches into the duct. He feels the leather bag. He pulls the bag out of the opening, and he steps down from the toilet seat. He lowers his butt onto the seat and places the leather bag on his lap. He feels the outside of the bag. The shape and weight of the bag's contents are familiar.

Rigney *freezes* when he hears the head door open. By the sounds, only one person enters. He hears the shuffle of shower shoes sliding toward the urinals. Then, he hears the sound of a urine stream hitting stainless steel, and he hears the deep sighs of a person who is in dire need of relief. The voice sounds like Larry Johnson, but Rigney cannot tell for sure.

Larry was one of the *steamer*s who did not get back from liberty until late. Larry had boasted to no one in particular that he drank a barrel of Spanish beer.

Rigney looks at the shower curtain and verifies that when the person turns around, he will only see legs from mid-calf down inside the toilet stall.

He hears the person flush the urinal, and the shuffle of feet tells Rigney that the person has turned around to exit.

"Hey, Rig!" Larry says too loudly and with an inebriated voice. "What's up?"

The recognition startles Rigney; however, he recovers quickly.

Rigney responds softly, "Wadda ya think, Larry. I'm using the crapper . . . keep your voice down. People are trying to sleep."

"Okay, Okay," Larry responds softly with resignation in his voice.

"Hey, Larry, how did ya know it was me?"

"No one, 'cept you, has that much reddish brown hair on his legs," Larry slurs.

"Oh."

After hearing the door open and close, Rigney rapidly opens the leather bag and pulls out the holster. The contents are the same as the other bag in the fan room on the 04 Level—one 9mm Beretta with a ten-round magazine inserted, one extra magazine fully loaded, and a suppressor.

Rigney quickly repacks everything into the leather bag and stores it back into the air-conditioning duct. He flushes the toilet for effect. He washes his hands to remove the lightweight oil that rubbed onto his hands from the Beretta.

He returns to his rack and lifts himself onto the mattress. He looks at his watch—0342.

"REVEILLE, REVEILLE, ALL HANDS HEAVE TO AND TRICE UP! THE SMOKING LAMP IS LIT IN ALL AUTHORIZED SPACES!"

Rigney awakens and turns slowly in his rack. He opens his eyes and looks at the luminous face of his watch—0600. He has the morning watch and must be in MAIN COMM by 0730.

The lights remain off in the compartment. Rigney notices a few men rolling out of their racks. After a few moments, he sees flashes from cigarette lighters. I few moments later, the acrid smell and feel of cigarette smoke saturate his senses. The annoying cigarette smoke bothers others still trying to sleep, and they ask the smokers to take it topside.

The smokers answer simultaneously with a loud, clear, and sarcastic, "Fuck you!"

One of the smokers, RM1 Dukes, announces, "The smoking lamp is lit, and we are authorized to smoke. Those of you who are bothered by the smoke can take your complaining asses topside."

Rigney lies in his rack and ponders this smoking incident. He wonders why in such close quarters cigarette smokers practice their annoying habit. Rigney reasons that since 75 percent of the division smoke—annoying the other 25 percent is acceptable behavior.

He thinks about all the rack-lid slamming and loud talking while others are trying to sleep. He also thinks about the First Division sailors on the deck above purposely pounding the deck with tools to annoy those below. *Team spirit does not exist aboard this ship. Life aboard ship is not what I expected.* He hopes that life aboard submarines will be more pleasant.

He turns on his side. The smell and taste of cigarette smoke in the air and the noise and shouting coming from the First Division Berthing Compartment above makes sleep difficult.

"SWEEPERS, SWEEPERS MAN YOUR BROOMS. GIVE THE SHIP A SWEEP DOWN FORE AND AFT. TAKE ALL TRASH AND GARBAGE TO THE PIER, NOW SWEEPERS. NOW MUSTER A SIXTY MAN WORKING PARTY ON THE PIER."

Rigney opens his eyes and looks at his watch—0642. He rolls out of his rack, lifts the lid of his rack-locker, retrieves his shaving kit, slips into his shower shoes, and quietly closes the rack-locker lid. He pulls his towel from the towel rack mounted inside his rack space. He walks to head.

Cigarette smoke hangs heavily in the air. Dukes, Bollier, and two others sit at the card table; all four are puffing away.

Fifteen minutes later, Rigney exits the head, dressed only in shower shoes and a towel around his waist. As he comes abreast of the ladder,

BM1 Genoa steps off the bottom rung.

Genoa reaches over Dukes's head for the light switch and turns on the compartment lights. Complaining moans about the lights echo through the compartment.

Genoa wears his M.A.A. armband. He is red faced, and his breathing labored. His Undress Blue uniform stretches at the seams. He constantly tugs at the bottom of his jumper to keep it from riding up over his belly. "Who's the fuckin' senior twidget here?" Genoa booms angrily.

Genoa blocks Rigney's path. Rigney just stands next to Genoa, facing the card table where the four smokers sit.

Although Bollier has eleven years in grade and is senior to Dukes by six years, Bollier turned down the Leading Petty Officer position when first reporting aboard. The chief radioman at the time agreed and was pleased that he would not need to deal with such a poor leader in the LPO position.

"I'm the division LPO," Dukes responds. "What brings you out of the master-at-arms shack and out of hibernation?"

Rigney and everyone at the card table chuckle at Dukes's disrespectful remark.

Genoa steams. He looks menacingly at Rigney who stands beside him. Genoa orders, "Page, get dressed and report to the working party on the pier."

Rigney looks at Dukes for guidance.

"No, Genoa. Page is going on watch. I am not sending anyone on a working party. CR Division is exempt from working parties and you know it. Besides, you're out of your jurisdiction here. We are attached to the admiral's staff and not to ship's company."

"Bullshit!" Genoa retorts. "Ship's Organization and Regulation Manual says CR division must provide three men to a sixty man working party!"

"I'm not going to argue about this again, Genoa," Dukes replies calmly.

"Do I have to bring the chief master-at-arms down here to kick ass?" Genoa snorts.

"Bring whomever you want," Dukes replies as he looks at his watch. "I will call the Staff Operations Officer to come down here and discuss the matter with the chief master-at-arms."

Some of those trying to sleep request, "Quiet, please."

Genoa looks around the compartment and says sarcastically, "Fuckin' pussy twidgets!"

Bollier, who has been sitting quietly next to Dukes, lifts a camera from the tabletop and aims it in the direction of Genoa and Rigney; he snaps a picture.

"What the fuck is that about!" Genoa snarls loudly at Bollier. "You some kind of fuckin' tourist?"

"It's my new camera," Bollier replies. "Just testing it out."

"There have been some cameras stolen recently. Maybe I should confiscate the camera and check it against the list of stolen ones."

Bollier utters in a despising tone, "Yeah, and maybe you should suck my dick you pathetic excuse for a cop!"

As Rigney listens to the disrespectful exchange between the three first class petty officers, he cannot help but think what poor examples of leadership these three men provide. They all sound like children arguing over rules in a playground game. Rigney has known many senior enlisted men during his two-and-one-half years in the navy. He has never seen any act like this. He also remembers his parents' navy friends back in Seal Beach. *They were never like this.* He wonders if the stress of living in such close quarters aboard ship brings it about. He also wonders why the officers do nothing about it. *Maybe officer inaction or apathy is the cause of this problem.*

Genoa, frustrated from his lack of ability to get his way, pushes Rigney aside and storms up the ladder.

The four men at the table exchange glances and chuckle. They resume smoking.

Dukes flips the light switch; the compartment darkens.

Rigney goes to his rack and dresses for watch.

After dressing, Rigney steps toward the ladder. He is stopped by a question from Dukes, "Hey, Page, how is it that Genoa knows your name?"

"During my first day aboard, he came down here and ordered me on a working party. It was during stand-down, just before the New Year. We got along well, and, now, we are life-long friends."

The men at the table exchange glances. Dismissive expressions appear on their faces.

"Did you go on the working party?" Dukes asks.

"Yes."

"Why?"

The cloud of cigarette smoke around the card-table area engulfs Rigney. The acrid substance stings his eyes and nostrils. He waves his hand in front of his face, which displays annoyance. Then, he replies, "He's a master-at-arms and a first class. Even if I had known that CR Division was exempt, I would have gone anyway. Navy regulations require that I obey orders of seniors. Besides, it was no big deal. I wasn't doing anything else."

The smoke continues to bother Rigney. He steps back a few feet and waves his hand in front of his face again. This time, a more intense and disapproving look appears on his face.

"Does the smoke bother you, Page?" Bollier asks with an uncaring tone.

"Yes, it bothers me. It's extremely annoying."

"We have the right to smoke," Dukes challenges. "The smoking lamp is lit."

Rigney shakes his head in defeat and responds, "Did you ever consider that your so called right to smoke stops when it violates the rights of others."

"If you can't hack it, leave!" Bollier orders with a raised and impatient voice.

Rigney's face is expressionless and he does not comment. He turns and walks up the ladder.

Rigney sits in thought at the fleet broadcast position. He contemplates the smoking incident and the Genoa incident earlier this morning. He shakes his head in bewilderment.

Senior Chief Bulldoone enters and tells Rigney, "Report for the evening watch later today." The senior chief gives no reason.

"Why the shift change?" Rigney asks Bulldoone.

Bulldoone replies, "Because I need to rearrange the watch sections for the upcoming fleet exercises. The traffic load will be heavy, and we need to be consolidated from three watch sections to port and starboard watch sections."

Rigney does not embrace the rotating eight-hours-on and eight-hours-off work schedule because he will have less time to hunt for Python. He knew it was coming. Larry Johnson told him to expect port and starboard most of the time during the MED Cruise.

Larry Johnson had explained, "We're always in port and starboard in the MED because the traffic load is so heavy for ships in the Sixth Fleet. The only real break we'll get is the week we are in Naples. There's a local U.S. Naval Communications Unit in Naples that will take our communications guard."

Later in the morning, Rigney sits alone in MAIN COMM at the fleet broadcast position. All other watch-standers are up on the Signal Bridge. Rigney decides this is a good time to see if he has any messages from ONI.

All the R-1051 single-sideband radio receivers are in the Technical Control Room. He double-checks the MAIN COMM areas to make sure no one is around. He enters the Technical Control Room, then grabs an earphone set. He patches a high-frequency antenna to an unused R-1051. He slips the earphones over his ears and plugs the set into the AUDIO jack of the receiver. He sets the selector switch on the R-1051 to LSB— Lower Side Band. Then, he tunes the receiver to an ONI carrier frequency. The first few carrier frequencies he tries are hit severely with static and interference. The ONI broadcast frequency in the nine megahertz range provides the best signal. He retrieves the code card from his wallet. He listens carefully to the recorded ONI voice broadcast. Several minutes later, he hears his codename—*Apollo*. As he hears the codewords, he runs his finger up and down the columns of codes with their translations. *They want me on the pier at 1100 tomorrow! Shit! I will be on watch at that time. The ship gets underway at 1300. That's cutting it close! How the hell can I be on the pier at 1100?* Rigney churns ideas through his mind as to how he can comply.

Chapter 82

RM1 Thomas Bollier sits at his favorite table in the *El Toro Blanco* bar. He had changed into his Service Dress Blues after the day at the beach with Rosa. He looks at his watch—2043. He waits for Javier, who is forty-three minutes late.

He reminisces with pleasure the day at the beach with Rosa. He had a good time and so did Rosa. They talked for hours about their lives. She was always truthful about her life. Thomas would fabricate events to make his life sound better than it is.

Rosa's English continues to improve.

Although the Rota Naval Base continually offered Spanish courses when he was stationed in Rota, Thomas never bothered learning the language.

Throughout the afternoon, they held each other. From time to time, they would kiss. Their kisses are never passionate. Their kisses are more of friendship than of lovers.

Thomas feels a bond with Rosa. She accepts him as he is, or as he deceives to be. He knows that she genuinely likes him. She never tried to trap him into a marriage so that she could become an American citizen.

As Thomas was about to leave her apartment, Rosa handed him an envelope. He pulled a letter and a picture from the envelope. On the back of the picture, Rosa had written, "Forever Friends."

Thomas came directly to the *El Toro Blanco* from Rosa's apartment about two hours ago.

Thomas looks at his watch again—2105. *Where the hell is he!*

Thomas orders another beer.

Finally, Javier sits down across the table from Thomas. Javier wears a cheap suit so that he fits in with the cheap atmosphere of the bar.

Thomas hands a roll of film to Javier. "There's only one picture. Page is the one with a towel wrapped around him."

Javier raises his brow.

I caught him coming out of the shower. There are others in the photo.

"Very good, Thomas. You are a cooperative partner. Thank you."

Thomas nods.

"Thomas, I must ask you again if you put the new devices in place as I have instructed."

"Yes, I have, and I threw the old devices overboard in mid-Atlantic as you instructed."

"Good!" Javier responds good-heartedly.

"Anything else?" Bollier asks wearily. "It's late, and I must have four teletypes repaired and in place before we get underway tomorrow."

"No, nothing more," Javier responds. "By the way, I will not see you in Palma. I have important matters elsewhere. However, I will see you in Naples. In Naples I will tell you how well our new devices work for us."

"Okay—first day in Naples—same place and time?" Thomas queries for confirmation.

"Yes, same place and time," Javier answers. Then, he stands and departs the bar.

After finishing his beer, Thomas departs the bar. At the edge of *The Gut*, he finds a taxi and negotiates a fair price for a ride back to the naval base piers.

Chapter 83

Rigney sits, restless, at his Fleet Broadcast Operator position. He looks at his watch—1048. He arranged for Larry Johnson to relieve him at 1050. Senior Chief Bulldoone approved it. Rigney gave the excuse that he had given his Dress Blues to the Navy Exchange Laundry Van, which will return the cleaned uniforms at 1100.

Larry arrives at 1055. Rigney gives him a quick turnover and races from MAIN COMM. He glides swiftly down the various ladders. He renders all proper honors at the gangway. He arrives on the pier at 1059.

Rigney scans the area. Vehicles and sailors move up and down the pier. The wind whips back and forth over the pier. He must hold his white hat on his head as he walks toward the head of the pier.

A sailor falls in step beside him. "Keep walking to the head of the pier," a familiar voice orders.

Rigney smiles as he recognizes John Smith's voice.

John directs, "Let's go around to the other side of that dumpster."

On the other side of the dumpster, the two sailors stop and face each other.

Rigney now sees that John Smith wears dungarees, and John's Blue Working Jacket has a first class crow on the left arm.

"John, great to see you! You're a first class, now! That's some advancement program that ONI has!"

"Get serious, Rig. You got anything to report."

"No, except that life sucks aboard that bucket." Rigney nods toward the *Columbus* on the other side of the pier.

"That so-called bucket is paradise compared to the jungles of Vietnam," John responds, his eyes distant in remembrance.

"You've been to Vietnam?"

"No time for that, now. Do you have anything to report?"

Rigney previously decided not to say anything about Bollier and the UCC-1. He believes that he does not know enough about the UCC-1 and what Bollier is doing to know if it is out of the ordinary. He does not want to look foolish by sending ONI to *General Quarters* over nothing.

John's experience tells him that young and inexperienced ONI agents are hesitant to report anything for concern that they are wrong. John detects that hesitancy in Rigney. He uses an alternative approach.

"Is there anyone aboard that ship that you would like to know more about? If you have more information about people, you can better evaluate their actions."

Rigney takes a few moments to consider that question. "Yes, I would like to know about RM1 Bollier and Senior Chief Bulldoone."

"Why those two?" John asks. He knows that Rigney must have observed something unusual about those two men. Otherwise, he would not have mentioned them.

"Bollier has been a first class for eleven years. He does not act like a career navy man should. Well a lot of them don't. I mean . . . I just don't know what to make of some of these lifers. Well, anyway, Bollier just seems to get away with things, and the senior chief does nothing about it. That's what people say. The rumor is that Bulldoone and Bollier go way back."

"Do you think either of these two could be Python?" John asks while looking directly into Rigney's eyes for any sign of agreement.

"Possibly, but anyone could be. I just don't know yet."

The wind whips up behind them. They both grab for their white hats. A few sailors chase their white hats along the pier.

John advises, "I will have the information on those two when you get to Palma. That's a week from now."

Rigney asks, "Where should I meet you in Palma?"

"Go to a district called *Sa Llonja*. I will find you."

"Okay. Anything else?" Rigney asks. "I must get back on watch. I don't want Senior Chief Bulldoone to catch me in a lie."

"Have you had any encounters with Gunny Bronston?"

"Yeah, one time during chow. He heard me talking on the mess decks. He challenged me as to where I was on New Year's Eve. I lied, of course, and my friend Larry Johnson substantiated my story."

"Does Bronston suspect you?"

"I don't think so."

"One more thing, Rig. Can you get access to the ship's high-frequency transceivers without anyone knowing?"

"That will be difficult while at sea. Those transceivers are located in Radio II, which is continuously manned at sea. The only time the watch leaves that space is to go setup transceivers located in other spaces. The watch would not normally be gone for more than fifteen minutes. In port, those spaces are not manned."

"Brad wants to know if you can start making radio reports."

"I will see what I can do."

John responds, "Good. See ya in Palma." He turns and walks to the head of the pier, turns right, and disappears on the other side of a building.

Rigney reappears from behind the dumpster and walks along the pier toward the gangway.

Captain Saunders, commanding officer of USS *Columbus*, tours the decks of his ship prior to getting underway. As he looks over the rail on the starboard side of the ASROC deck, he notices RM3 Page walk off the gangway. Saunders sees Page start his walk to the head of the pier. Then, he sees a first class petty officer who seems to appear from nowhere and who now walks along side of Page. Saunders observes the two men walk behind the dumpster on the far side of the pier. After several minutes, the first class petty officer appears from behind the dumpster and walk off the pier. Then, RM3 Page walks from behind the dumpster and comes back aboard the ship. The captain makes a mental note to schedule a meeting with Page.

Chapter 84

One hour after *The Tall Lady* sails from Rota, Rigney feels the *Columbus* mildly pitching and rolling under his feet. He stands the day watch and will not be relieved for several hours. Occasionally, he glances at the UCC-1 in the Technical Control Room. Channel drawers 3 and 4 are still pushed in and powered up. As long as the ship-to-shore termination frequencies stay solid, Dukes will probably not notice.

Most messages received over the Rota Fleet Broadcast are for *Columbus*. Rigney's scan of messages tell him that after *Columbus* transits the Strait of Gibraltar, *Columbus* will proceed directly to the EXERCISE DAWN PATROL area and join the USS *Shangri-La* Task Force.

Admiral Melton who is aboard *Columbus*, now designated as Commander Task Group 62.2, will be in operational command of a task group that includes *Columbus* and three destroyers.

As CTG 62.2, Admiral Melton will be under operation command of Commander Task Force 62, whose flagship is the aircraft carrier USS *Shangri-La,* CV-38.

Rigney checks a map of the Mediterranean, which hangs in the Message Center. The EXERCISE DAWN PATROL area lies between the island of Mallorca and the island of Sardinia. Other messages tell Rigney that *Columbus* should arrive in the exercise area two days from now.

From his scan of fleet broadcast messages, Rigney concludes that Admiral Melton will command the EXERCISE DAWN PATROL Orange Forces. Rigney also concludes that the ships comprising the Orange Forces are the only ships copying the Rota Fleet Broadcast. He also notices that the number of Adonis offline-encrypted messages has decreased significantly.

Rigney checks the news printers. The first story reports that East Germany, a Soviet Bloc country, has adopted a penal code that includes the death penalty for political offenses.

After watch, Rigney proceeds directly to the mess decks. After passing through the steam line, Rigney finds a seat next to Dukes on the aft mess deck. The smoking incident from yesterday seems forgotten.

"What time do you think we will go through *The Strait* tonight?" Rigney asks Dukes.

"About 2200," Dukes answers.

"I was thinking about going to the Signal Bridge to see it."

"Waste of time—too dark," Dukes informs. "All you'll see is some lights far away. You're better off getting some sleep before the mid watch tonight. After we enter the MED, frequencies will go to shit. Keeping the fleet broadcast *synched* and the ship-to-shore termination up and passing traffic will be a continuous chore."

Rigney decides to take Dukes's advice and hit the rack after dinner.

Rigney dumps his tray in the scullery. Then, he walks carefully along the pitching and rolling second-deck, portside passageway. He hesitates at the top of the ladder as he peers down the ladder into CR Division Berthing. He sees a seabag standing upright near the table at the bottom of the ladder. Bedding is stacked on top of the seabag. Sitting at the card table next to the seabag is a sailor in Service Dress Blues. The sailor wears a RM2 rating badge on his sleeve. *Rouché! Shit! I forgot about him!*

Rigney knows that he has the amount of time it takes to go down the ladder to decide whether to participate in a confrontation with Rouché or to back off. As Rigney starts down the ladder, Rouché stands and stares into Rigney's eyes and continues to stare as Rigney comes down the ladder.

As Rigney reaches the bottom of the ladder, he notices about ten members of the division standing around and watching him intently. Rigney stands about three feet from Rouché.

Rouché's tailored Dress Blue uniform accentuates his broad shouldered boxer's physique. Scars mar his dark complexion. His hands are scarred and calloused. He stands twelve inches shorter than Rigney.

Rigney has no doubt that Rouché is hard and tough and is no stranger to fist fighting.

Rigney sweeps the crowd with his eyes. First class petty officers are not present. The scene reminds Rigney of those who watch car racing for hours on end. They do not find the race stimulating or interesting; they are waiting for the crashes. These sailors have gathered to watch the fight. Rigney has not yet decided how he will handle this. Rigney chuckles and shakes his head while expressing amusement.

"Are you Page?" Rouché asks with a singsong southern drawl.

"Yes," Rigney answers with a raised eyebrow and an impatient tone in his voice.

"You're in my rack, and I want you out of it . . . *now!*" Rouché demands with a menacing look on his face.

With a smirk on his face, Rigney looks Rouché up and down. Then, he leans forward so slightly, towering over Rouché. Rigney detects Rouché stiffening, as if bracing himself against an attack. Rigney becomes anxious as his adrenal glands shift to high speed, and his heart pounds at an increasing rate in his chest. His face becomes red and the arteries in his neck visibly pulsate. He does not fear this Rouché, although he is concerned about putting his mission in jeopardy by becoming physically disabled as a result of a fight.

Rouché thinks that Page is about to hit him. Some of the radiomen told Rouché that Rigney has a tough look but has a mild manner. However, Rouché is not prepared for what he sees as a tall, muscled, tough, and powerful looking man that now towers over him. He feels fear, which he did not expect to feel.

Ever since Rigney took Rouché's rack, the radiomen debated whether Rigney will standup to Rouché or back down.

Rigney detects that Rouché feels uncertain and threatened. Suddenly, Rigney jumps forward half a step and blurts, *"Boo!"*

Rouché steps backward and stumbles over the chair behind him. He quickly regains his balance and recaptures his stance. Rouché's manner becomes defiant, and he looks like he is ready to pounce.

"Okay, I will move out of your fuckin' rack, now," Rigney states agreeably as a satisfied smile breaks out on his face. Rigney turns and struts confidently away from Rouché and toward his rack. His expression and manner announce to everyone that he won this confrontation.

Although he gets his rack back, Rouché feels that he is the loser in this confrontation. He also sees it in the face of the onlookers. His objective was to scare and intimidate this Page character, which is his objective with all new junior members of CR Division. Rouché now knows that Page will not be intimidated or scare easily. *So why did he give me back my rack?*

Rigney busies himself with moving out of the center rack and into the rack beneath it. He accomplished his task of acting like a smartass showoff. Now, he hopes that Rouché is satisfied with getting his rack back and there will be no more problems. Rigney understands that the rack has little to do with anything. Rigney knows that Rouché is a bully, and Rigney knows that down deep he wants Rouché to attack him. Then, he will be justified in teaching another bully a lesson.

Rouché drags his seabag across the compartment to the forward starboard corner where Rigney changes racks. Rouché parks himself and his seabag about two feet from Rigney.

Rigney looks over at Rouché, who stares menacingly at Rigney. Looking beyond Rouché, Rigney sees members of the division watching, obviously expecting to see some action. Rigney says nothing. He returns to moving his belongings from the middle rack to the bottom rack.

"You're not as tough as you look, are you?" Rouché challenges loud enough for everyone to hear.

Rigney does not respond.

"I had you pegged the moment I saw you. You look tough, but you're just a scared pussy." Rouché's tone turns nasty.

Rigney does not respond. He remembers Larry's comments that Rouché becomes belligerent when ignored.

"You were mouthy a few minutes ago . . . too scared to talk now?" Rouché's nostrils flare and his face flushes red with anger.

Rigney continues to ignore Rouché's comments.

Rouché becomes angrier. He attempts a different attack. "At least your mother talked the last time I fucked her!"

Some of the onlookers chuckle at Rouché's crude remark.

Rigney remains silent as he completes moving the last item from the middle rack to the bottom rack.

"But then your mother couldn't talk after I rammed my cock in her mouth. She loved it so much, she sucked it for hours."

Rigney continues to be silent. He slips his own combination lock through the hasp of the bottom rack-locker. He removes the bedding from the middle rack and throws it on the bottom rack with intentions to make it up later. He decides to go to the ship's library for a while. He wants to give Rouché time to move into his rack and get over this confrontation.

Rigney turns to leave. Rouché blocks Rigney's path. Only two feet separate outboard racks and the inboard racks. Usually, two people must walk sidewise to pass each other. Rouché does not stand aside to let Rigney pass.

"Looks like you will have to move me," Rouché dares with a sneer.

The onlookers joust for better viewing positions. They all know this is when Rouché's victims make the mistake of trying to push past him.

Rigney stands fast between Rouché and his beloved rack. He flashes a knowing smile at Rouché as he crosses his arms and leans casually back against the rack frame.

A full minute passes, which seems like an eternity to everyone watching. Then, Rigney stands aside with his back against the outboard racks, waves his hand in the direction of the inboard racks, and says, "Mister Rouché, your royal rack waits."

Rouché blinks his eyes. He was not expecting this. He expected that Page would try to push him aside. Then, he would have justification to beat Page to the deck and claim self-defense. He could never justify hitting Page now.

Rigney tells Rouché, "I will not move until you pass."

Rouché warns, "No one makes me look like a fool and gets away with it."

Rigney responds, "Fools expose themselves to the world, Rouché. No one has to do it for them."

Rigney's insulting quip prompts chuckles from the onlookers.

It takes Rouché a few moments to understand Rigney's words. When understanding comes to him, he becomes enraged. After a few moments, he calms himself as he exerts self-control. He knows that he can payback this asshole some other time, when no one else is around. He thinks about the switchblade that he bought in *The Rota Gut.*

"Don't let me find you on the beach. I will teach you some respect." Rouché warns in a lowered voice that only Rigney can hear. Rouché grabs his seabag then drags it behind him as he walks past Rigney.

After Rouché passes, Rigney straddles the space between the two stacks of racks where Rouché stood a few moments before. He now stands facing Rouché, and his back is to the onlookers. Rigney says in a calm and confident tone, "You are vile and uncouth. You are an uncivilized bully, which makes you the lowest form of human."

Rouché turns his head and looks at Rigney, unconcerned and unmoved by Rigney's words.

Rigney continues, "You can say anything you want anytime you want. I have no concern or cares about what you say. I find your testosterone-laden idiocy to be the behavior of a farm animal. I will not respond to your words; but lay a hand on me, and you'll discover that I don't fuck around. I'll put you down hard."

Rouché conceals his slight apprehension at Rigney's words. To get in the final word, he responds confidently, "Stay prepared. Your chance to put me down will come without warning."

Rigney turns and leaves the compartment.

Rouché goes about making his rack and stowing his gear.

The onlookers disperse.

Rigney sits, bending over a book, at a table in the *Columbus's* library. He attempts to absorb himself with reading about the building of the Panama Canal, but his focus will not shift from the confrontation that he had with Rouché several minutes prior. He knows that his safety is at stake, which puts the mission at risk. He fears Rouché's ability to interfere with the mission. He also fears Rouché's ability to hurt him. He considers that he should carry one of the Berettas when on liberty, just in case Rouché comes after him.

Rigney understands his violent nature regarding bullies. As a young boy, he was often the target of bullies. They would gang up on him in the schoolyard and on the beach. Bullies would boast about their assaults on Rigney to his classmates.

The attacks came more often when he reached his early teens, especially when he and girls were together. He would always try to avoid a fight, but the bullies would start pushing and hitting. He would try to fight back; but the bullies were always bigger and stronger, and they always attacked in numbers.

One incident when he was thirteen is especially painful to remember. He was surfing on Huntington Beach and had just come out of the water when a couple of girls came up to him and started talking with him. A few minutes later, three juvenile delinquent types who hung around the beach and were always picking on smaller kids jumped in and started pushing him around. They punched him in the face a couple of times. Then, two of them held his arms and the third pulled off Rigney's Surfer Baggies. They took his Baggies with them. He had to run bare-assed across the beach through the crowds of people to get his towel to cover himself. He painfully remembers how little girls, teenage girls, and grown women stared and gawked at his flopping up and down penis as he ran across the sand toward his towel.

During the following year, he grew four inches in height and developed muscle tone. Rigney added weightlifting to his daily routine. He wanted to become too tough looking for bullies to find him an easy target. All the incidents of bullies hitting him and embarrassing him lie etched in his memory.

By the beginning of his high school freshman year, Rigney's muscles were hard and strong. When the bullies came after him, he fought back. His punches had more effect. He discovered that he was becoming more powerful—more than just powerful. After puberty, he sensed an extraordinary physical strength within him. When he told his father about that extraordinary strength, his father nodded and commented, "It's a Page trait. Sometimes it passes over a generation. My father had it. I don't. I was wondering if you would have it. You need to keep it a secret."

Rigney never went looking for a fight; but when he encountered a bully picking on someone else, he stepped in. He would never be the aggressor, only the defender. As a defender, he only used the force necessary to fend off an attack. *But there was that time in the boxing ring with the gym teacher . . . I went too far that time . . . and with Gunny Bronston I certainly went beyond being just a defender.*

Rigney distresses that the boxing ring incident and the Bronston incident more accurately defines his true nature than his knightly actions as a defender.

Philippe Rouché lies in his rack. The earlier incident with Page angers him and gnaws at his gut. He learned early in his life from his father how to scare and intimate people. *To get your way, you need others to fear you.* Rouché knows that if people do not fear him, they take advantage of him. Page made him look like a stumbling fool in front of others. *He will pay for that!*

Rouché realizes that at first glance, Page comes across as lean, hard, and tough looking. A closer look at Page's smooth and unmarred features reveals that he is not an experience and hardened fighter. Rouché knows that he will easily beat and stomp Page to the ground, and he will do so at the first opportunity. *I must prove to everyone who is the toughest and meanest. Otherwise, they will lose their fear . . . their respect for me.*

Chapter 85

Lieutenant Commander Brad Watson sits at the desk in room 4 of the ONI Cheltenham building. He studies the record of ONI's second recruit to his special program. The new recruit is a fire control technician second class, FTM2, that specializes in the submarine based Polaris A-1 Missile System. Brad designed a condensed four-week training course for the FTM2.

During a raid on the apartment of suspected terrorists in Manila, American agents found unauthorized copies of classified Polaris A-1 Maintenance Manuals. ONI traced the manuals to the Submarine Tender, USS *Hunley* in Guam. The FTM2's mission will be to discover who made the copies and removed them from the ship.

Brad's superior officer, Captain Willcroft, Chief, ONI Counterintelligence, authorized Brad to recruit and train the FTM2. However, Brad could not send the FTM2 on his mission unless RM3 Rigney Page proves successful on his mission. Brad's special program has few supporters among the Chiefs of the various military intelligence organizations. ONI must prove success with Page's mission as a milestone in gaining acceptance within the intelligence community.

Brad's Secure Telephone Unit beeps. Brad picks up the handset, "Lieutenant Commander Watson."

"Hello, sir. Lieutenant Cranston here. I wanted to inform you that Magnolia has departed for Naples. She will arrive in Naples two days from now."

"How did she react to your brief regarding her ONI duties in Naples?"

"Enthusiastic, sir. Actually, too enthusiastic, I believe."

"Why's that?" Brad asks.

"She happily accepts her expanded ONI role. She wants to join ONI permanently, but you already know that. Anyway, when I told her she must contact Apollo when the *Columbus* arrives in Naples, her eyes lit up and she was joyous. Sir, I think she has fallen for Apollo. We all know how dangerous a personal relationship can be to an operation."

Brad responds, "In this case, it's necessary. It's a calculated risk that I had to take. They need to look like a couple. They need to meet often, so information can be easily passed from Page to ONI."

"Yes, sir."

"Anything else to report?"

"No, sir. That's it."

"Okay, talk to you later."

The door to Brad Watson's office opens. The yeoman enters and places a folder on Brad's desk. The folder contains the daily message traffic. The two-inch-thick stack of messages contains numerous intelligence related reports, which Brad must study and analyze.

One hour later after finishing half the stack of messages, Brad finds a single page message from the ONI Field Office at SUBASE New London. The message markings are SECRET NOFORN INTEL. The message is a surveillance report regarding the person with the codename of Debutante, which is the codeword for Sally Macfurson. The report states that Debutante has departed for Europe to pursue her doctoral studies. Her destination is the archeological dig near *Lago Patria*, Italy.

Brad goes to the Mediterranean wall map. He runs his finger all over the map of Italy. He cannot find *Lago Patria*. He walks to the bookcase and pulls a volume that contains detailed maps of Italy. After ten minutes, he finds *Lago Patria*.

Damn! No! Double Damn! The area known as *Lago Patria* is located ten miles north of Naples, Italy.

Brad analyzes his logic regarding his new program. The old, accepted practices seldom resulted with so many unknowns and so many variables. Most events were predictable. However, in recent years, the old methods produce few results. The counterintelligence community searches for a new approach. As is the nature of government, implementation of new ideas and the threat of turf invasion cause improvements to occur at a snail's pace.

Unpredictability has become the rule for this operation. Now, he must burn precious time while actualizing counter actions. Brad's superiors demand daily reports. Brad must sell patience and understanding that their agent is at sea with little chance of unfettered access to communications facilities.

Chapter 86

The *USS Columbus* cuts a menacing silhouette against the clear, moonlit night. She moves smoothly at eighteen knots through a calm sea. The *darken ship* condition allows only her running lights to be lit. From horizon to horizon, millions of bright stars form a canopy over *The Tall Lady*.

Lookouts stand watch on the bow and stern and on the port and starboard bridge wings. The cold, January air causes the lookouts to shiver inside their insulated jumpsuits. The lookouts wear two watch caps snug over their ears. A sound-powered phone set, which provides direct communications to the bridge, hangs around the neck of each lookout. The earphones of the phone set cover both ears. Periodically, the lookouts report to the OOD on the bridge the condition of the running lights and position of any visible contacts.

Inside the *Columbus's* Bridge, sailors stand their watch in the dark. At various spots on the bridge, a soft green glow emanates from indicators and repeaters. After several minutes on the darkened bridge, their eyes become acclimated to the dark. They can actually see across the length of the bridge.

The *Columbus* departed Rota two days ago. She steams on a northerly course. The Balearic Islands lay 75 miles to the west, and the island of Sardinia lay 175 miles to the east. *Columbus* steams toward a sunrise rendezvous with the USS *Shangri-La* Task Force and the other ships of the EXERCISE DAWN PATROL.

The OOD stands on the port side of the bridge. He glances at the luminous face of his wristwatch—0112.

"Bridge, CIC, sonar reports a submerged contact at 14,000 yards . . . bearing 155 . . . designate contact as Sierra One . . . still trying to classify and determine course and speed."

The OOD presses the talk lever on the MC unit and replies, "CIC, Bridge, aye."

The QMOW, Quartermaster of the Watch, enters the contact report into the Deck Log.

The OOD lifts the handset of an interior phone unit. He sets the switch to the captain's sea cabin and cranks the call lever.

"Captain."

The OOD states, "Sonar reports a submerged contact to the southeast at 14,000 yards."

Captain Saunders looks at the illuminated ship's control indicators mounted on the bulkhead at the foot of his bunk. He notes that *Columbus's* heading is 358 degrees and that she steams at eighteen knots. He orders the OOD, "Call me with the contact's classification, heading, and speed as soon as you have it; and verify that the CIC Watch Officer is preparing a Submarine Contact Report."

"Aye, aye, Captain."

As the OOD cradles the handset, CIC provides the additional information over the MC, *"Bridge, CIC, classify Sierra One as Soviet Whiskey Class submarine. Distance to the Whiskey has increased to 14,500 yards. Appears that she is attempting an intercept course but cannot catch us with her maximum submerged speed. Anticipate we will lose contact in another hour."*

"CIC, Bridge, aye," the OOD responds. Then, he queries CIC, "What is the status on the submarine contact report?"

"On its way to MAIN COMM for transmission," CIC Watch Officer replies.

The OOD calls the captain and advises him of the contact falling behind and that the Submarine Contact Report has been sent to MAIN COMM.

One hour later, CIC reports that sonar lost contact on Sierra One.

At 0345, another section assumes the Bridge watch.

"Bridge, CIC, sonar reports submerged contact at 11,500 yards ahead of us on a bearing of 358. Designate contact as Sierra Two and classify her as a Soviet Whiskey Class submarine. Sonar verifies that the contact has not changed course. She is waiting for us. Also, both sonar and radar confirm that we have a Russian Trawler at 19,000 yards at a bearing of 005. Designate this contact as Romeo Three Five. The Trawler is on an intercept course. She's waiting for us also."

"CIC, Bridge, aye."

The OOD looks at his watch—0403. He walks to the quartermaster's table to ensure the QMOW logged all the contact information. Then, the OOD walks to the internal phone unit and calls the captain.

Three hours later, *The Tall Lady* steams at six knots on a course of 358. The Soviet Whiskey cruises submerged at a distance of 4,000 yards off the *Columbus's* aft port quarter. The Russian Trawler is visible in the early morning light at a distance of 2,500 yards off the *Columbus's* forward starboard quarter.

In MAIN COMM, the watch standers take turns going to the Signal Bridge to observe the Russian Trawler through the 50 power binoculars. Rigney cannot get anyone to relieve him so that he can go up on the Signal Bridge. He calculates he will be relieved in 30 minutes. Then, he can go to the Signal Bridge.

Rigney has been on watch since midnight. He witnessed the flurry of contact message reports. Both the Operations Officer and the

Communications Officer made various visits to MAIN COMM to verify quick and accurate processing of the contact messages. Each contact message does not have a subject of EXERCISE DAWN PATROL. Rigney understands that the contacts are real.

Most messages received over the fleet broadcast list *Columbus* or CTG 62.2 as an addressee. Contrary to Dukes's prediction, high-frequency communications have been solid since entering the MED. Except for occasional frequency changes and daily crypto keycard changes, both Dukes and Carter have been mostly idle. Neither Dukes nor Carter appears to notice that UCC-1 transmit channel drawers three and four are pushed in and have been so since departing Rota.

In Rear Admiral Melton's stateroom, Captain Saunders expresses his concern over the early morning contacts. He stresses the increasing threat of Soviet knowledge of the admiral's task group movements.

"Bill, I am as concerned as you are about this. We did agree with CNO that we would let ONI have their chance."

"Yes, Admiral, but that was ten months ago. ONI should have discovered something by now, and, frankly, I have doubts regarding this latest action with this young man, Page."

"I have doubts also" Admiral Melton responds.

"Admiral, I will schedule another meeting with Page. I want to know if he has discovered anything."

"Advise me of what Page says."

"Aye, aye, Admiral."

Admiral Melton glances at his watch and asks Captain Saunders, "Do you have anything else to discuss?"

"Yes, I have drafted this message. I think we should send it from you to ONI and info CNO." Captain Saunders hands the message to Admiral Melton.

The admiral reads the message. "Yes, I think it's time we did this. We should use a one-time encryption pad. Do you have any of those onboard?"

"Yes, Admiral."

Admiral Melton directs, "This information is too sensitive to get my communications staff involved. The fewer that know about this, the better. Have your Crypto Security Officer make an appointment with me today."

"Aye, aye, Admiral."

On the Signal Bridge, Rigney takes his turn observing the Russian Trawler through the large, high-power binoculars. Rigney has read about these intelligence-gathering vessels. Although these trawlers are disguised as fishing boats, the dense field of antenna arrays about the decks and superstructure reveal their true nature. Rigney observes a few deckhands cleaning and repairing various pieces of equipment. He imagines technicians scurrying about below decks quickly gathering and recording ELINT about the *Columbus*.

Rigney walks to the port side of the Signal Bridge. He stares toward the southwest. He sees a helicopter about five miles away. He gets on the *big eyes* and watches the actions of the SH-3 Sea King helicopter. The Sea King, from the carrier USS *Shangri-La*, hovers one-hundred feet above the surface with a hydrophone line lowered into the water.

Python caused this situation, Rigney concludes. He considers that if the United States were at war with the Soviets, Python's actions would cause a battle where many of his shipmates would be killed or injured. Rigney strengthens his resolve to catch the *traitorous bastard!*

LTJG Richard Rowing sits at the Adonis offline encryption machine in the Crypto Vault of USS *Columbus*. Following an unusual string of events this morning and a meeting with Rear Admiral Melton, he keys the Adonis rotor settings to the appropriate one-time pad.

From the content of the message, LTJG Rowing learns about the presence of an ONI agent onboard as part of an operation called *Jupiter*. In the message, the admiral advises ONI and CNO that allowing the Russian spy to continue operating aboard *Columbus* puts the admirals task group at increasing risk. The admiral references the Contact Report messages from this morning, and the admiral emphasizes that the Russian submarine and trawler were waiting at the task force rendezvous point, which endangers the entire USS *Shangri-La* Battle Group, not just Admiral Melton's cruiser-destroyer task group. The admiral reminds ONI and CNO that they all agreed months ago that Admiral Melton or Captain Saunders have authority to terminate Operation Jupiter onboard *Columbus*. The message states that if the ONI operative is not successful by February 15th, which is one month from now, Captain Saunders will initiate his actions. The message also informs that Captain Saunders witnessed the meeting between the ONI agent and another agent on the pier in Rota. Captain Saunders and Admiral Melton want to know what transpired.

The plain language version of the message is classified TOP SECRET NOFORN INTEL. The Adonis equipment turns the top secret information into an unclassified message of alpha character code groups.

In its unclassified form, no one can understand the message content. The Crypto Officers at ONI and CNO will have the equivalent one-time pads to translate the code groups back to the top secret clear-language version.

LTJG Rowing takes the encoded version to Admiral Melton for release. Then, he takes the released message to MAIN COMM to have it transmitted.

LTJG Rowing considers all the newly reported officers and speculates as to which one is the ONI operative.

Chapter 87

"Hey, Page, time to get up," the *communications messenger of the watch* orders as he shakes Rigney's mattress.

Rigney awakes and looks at his watch—1630. As usual, Rigney did not get eight hours of continuous sleep.

When he came to the berthing compartment after his watch this morning and after spending time on the Signal Bridge watching the trawler, he quickly shed his uniform and climbed into his rack. He noticed that Rouché was still sleeping at 0840. On one hand, he was thankful that Rouché was still in the rack so that he would not have another confrontation. He also considered that Rouché, the Division Police Petty Officer, and the compartment cleaners should be up and about performing their duties.

Now, still groggy from lack of adequate sleep, Rigney forces himself out of his rack. He looks around the compartment and sees only the ongoing watch up and about.

Rouché is not in his rack or present in the compartment.

Rigney goes to the head takes a cold shower to help revive is brain. The cold shower works. He returns to his rack and dresses in dungarees and ball cap. He pulls his foul weather jacket from his rack-locker and slips it on. He hasn't eaten since yesterday; so, he decides to go to chow and have a good meal before going on watch.

On the mess decks, Rigney finds an open seat at a table occupied by other members of his watch section. Then, Rouché sits down next to him.

"Hey, Rig-ass, I understand that you're the one to thank for me gettin' PPO. You must be some kind of fool to turn down that job. It's the most skatin' job in the division. What's wrong with you, Rig-ass?"

The whole table watches Rigney to see how he responds.

Rigney looks at Rouché and says, "Well, *Roach*, the berthing compartment is a dark hole. I knew you were coming back aboard. I assumed you would easily adapt to hiding in that dark hole because that is what *roaches* do, right?"

All eyes at the table shift to Rouché. Rouché's face flushes and anger shows in his eyes. Everyone expects the always wisecracking and sarcastic Rouché to have a clever or scolding comeback, or at least some threat as to how he will *even the score* during the next liberty port.

Rouché cannot think of anything to say. Not being accustomed to others insulting him and showing no fear of him, his mind cannot react fast enough.

"What's the matter, *Roach*? Nothing to say?" Rigney challenges in a sarcastic tone. "No threats as to how you are going to kill me when we get to Palma? Are you going soft? Have you lost your will to be fearsome?"

Rouché responds in a constricted and threatening tone. "You'll find out how fearsome I can be."

"So, your only comeback is a threat!" Rigney raises his tone. "*Roach*, you need to read up on your cleaver and witty comebacks. You can read, right?"

Angry, Rouché wants to take Rigney down right now, but he exercises his best self-control. He puts a self-knowing smile on his face, stares at Rigney, and says quietly and confidently, "See you in Palma, Rig-ass."

"Yeah! See ya in Palma. Always great to see you, anywhere, *Roach*," Rigney announces enthusiastically and with a happy look on his face.

Rouché leaves the table with a knowing sneer on his face.

All eyes at the table turn to Rigney.

Rigney winks at those at the table. He takes a bite of his steak and quips, "Always great to see *Roach*, isn't it? Must be something bothering him, though. Don't ya think?"

A few at the table just shake their heads over the knowledge of Rigney's pending disability. Others are gratified to see someone standup to Rouché.

Twenty minutes later, Rigney relieves Larry Johnson on the fleet broadcast.

"Heard you really let Rouché have it down on the mess decks . . . verbally, I mean." Larry's voice conveys concern.

"You heard about that already?"

"Yeah. When Carter came on watch a while ago, he told everyone up here. Will the fight be in Palma? You gonna rip him a new asshole like you did Gunny Bronston?"

"Quiet about that, Larry." Rigney looks around to see if anyone is listening. "And, no, I will not fight Rouché."

"Rig, you suffer under a major misconception. Rouché won't ask your permission. He will give you no choice. He'll come after you. You will have to defend yourself."

Rigney bows his head in thought. He just does not understand how the chain of command can be aware of bullies like Rouché and Bronston and do nothing about them.

During the watch, Rigney becomes preoccupied with what might happen with Rouché in Palma. He must go on liberty in Palma as ordered by John Smith. He worries about Rouché following him. Again, he considers carrying one of the Berettas. He believes that he can scare off Rouché by displaying the weapon to Rouché from a distance. There is no doubt in Rigney's mind that as long as Rouché is around, his mission is in jeopardy. During his next report to ONI, he will explain the Rouché situation to his superiors and recommend they do what is necessary to get Rouché quickly transferred.

Rigney keeps an eye on the UCC-1. Drawers three and four are pulled out. Makes sense, high-frequency communications have worsened over the past ten hours. The last watch must have had Bollier pull the channel drawers.

Rigney casually wanders into the Technical Control Room. Dukes and Carter are busy with frequency changes and the new crypto day procedures. He maneuvers himself so that he can see if Bollier's cables are attached to the back of the UCC-1. They are.

Rigney goes back to the Fleet Broadcast Room and checks the UCC-1 teletype patch panel. He puts the meter switch alternately to the UCC-1 CH3 and CH4. The meter shows teletype keying on those channels.

"Bewildering?" Rigney says to himself.

"Hey, boot camp, you know what the fuck you're looking at?!"

Rigney turns around and sees RM1 Bollier.

Bollier has a suspicious look on his face.

Rigney thinks fast. "I am trying to patch that teletype over there so that I can get additional copies of fleet broadcast messages."

A disgusted look appears on Bollier's face as he says to Rigney, "Get qualified, Page! You're looking at the wrong patch panel! You fuckin' kids! Didn't you learn anything in RM 'A' school?"

Rigney fakes embarrassment and asks, "Can you help me out here? What am I doing wrong?"

Bollier grunts his annoyance, grabs a patch cord from the supply on top of the patch panel, and plugs each end of the patch cord into the appropriate jacks. The teletype starts printing fleet broadcast messages. Bollier flashes a satisfied and all-knowing smile at Rigney. Bollier turns to enter the Technical Control Room. Then, he stops and turns back to face Rigney and says, "I hear you're gonna be killed in Palma." He chuckles; then, he enters the Technical Control Room. Bollier shakes his head and wishes the world understood his burden. *That kid's no threat!*

Javier is wasting our time.

Rigney sits down at the fleet broadcast position. He keeps an eye on Bollier's actions.

Bollier pulls the cover off a teletype machine. Then, Bollier takes some screwdrivers and a multimeter from his tool bag. Bollier powers on the multimeter and starts making checks on the teletype power supply.

Rigney continues to watch Bollier, and he notices from time to time that Bollier glances at the rear of the UCC-1.

Chapter 88

Lieutenant Commander Brad Watson walks into the office of Captain Willcroft, Chief of ONI Counterintelligence. He takes a chair in front of the captain's desk.

Willcroft lifts a piece of paper off the center of his desk, reaches across his desk, and hands the paper to Brad.

Brad reads the message from Admiral Melton. A look of concern crosses his face. After reading the message twice, Brad looks up and stares into space while considering the implications of the message.

"Brad, has there been any progress since your last report?" Captain Willcroft asks.

"Yes, sir. Page has given us the names of two radiomen to investigate."

"I assume Page provided those names during the meeting on the pier?"

"Yes, sir."

"So, Admiral Melton and Captain Saunders know about Page. I don't recall you reporting that to me."

"Page was assigned to compartment cleaning." Brad explains. "He needed assigned to radio watches. Since Captain Saunders and Admiral Melton already know about Jupiter, I thought it low risk to seek Captain Saunders's help in getting Page advantageously assigned."

Captain Willcroft raises an eyebrow as he comments, "The CO *Columbus* directing his Communications Officer as to where to assign a newly reported RM3 must have raised some questions."

"I'm sure it did, sir."

The ONI Counterintelligence Chief has never found reason not to trust and believe in Brad Watson. He allows Brad more leeway than others in his department. Allowing Brad to implement his new approach by recruiting Page is evidence of that trust.

"Who did Page meet on the pier?"

"Smith, sir."

"Who?"

"Galahad, sir."

"Oh." Captain Willcroft nods his head in recognition.

"Page and Galahad will meet again in Palma."

"When will that be?" questions Captain Willcroft.

"Four days from now. By then, I hope to have a complete history on the two sailors reported by Page."

"Who are they, and what information do you have so far."

"A Senior Chief Bulldoone is one of them. A review of his record shows his career as mostly routine, nothing out of the ordinary, good evaluations."

"Why did Page name this senior chief?"

"Page says he wants to know why the senior chief doesn't hold RM1 Bollier accountable."

"What's with this Bollier?"

"Bollier is one of those never-go-higher than first class. You know the type, 4.0 technical skills, but 3.0 and 2.8 in all others. His marks are too low for a recommendation to be advanced to chief petty officer. Looks like Senior Chief Bulldoone stands up for him and gives him marks just high enough to stay in the navy. Bulldoone and Bollier were stationed together twice before. The first time was the USS *Shangri-La*, and the second was NAVCOMMSTA Rota, which was just before *Columbus*."

"Do you have any reason to pursue these two?"

"I need to find out why Senior Chief Bulldoone favors this Bollier. I have the resident agent in Rota looking into it. I have also scheduled an appointment with Vice Admiral Logan."

"Admiral Logan?" Captain Willcroft questions with surprise. "What does the President's National Security Adviser got to do with this?"

Brad advises, "Back in the mid-fifties, Bollier was on independent duty at the consulate in Edinburgh, Scotland. Admiral Logan who was a commander at the time was Bollier's immediate superior and wrote Bollier's Performance Evaluations. Admiral Logan was headquartered at the United States Embassy in London. The two had little contact. Admiral Logan recommended Bollier for first class. Bollier made first class on his first attempt."

Captain Willcroft cautions, "Brad, you need to tread carefully. Why do you think it necessary to question Admiral Logan?"

Brad explains, "Bollier's record contains little information for that time in Scotland. I think some official letters generated during Bollier's Edinburgh tour require investigation. One letter from *State* requests that Bollier be appointed as an Adonis Crypto Operator. Admiral Logan denied the request because security regulations at the time did not allow enlisted men such access. Then, a letter comes from the COMNAVACTS UK authorizing the appointment of Bollier as an Adonis Crypto Operator.

"Also, the last two Performance Evaluations on Bollier while he was in Scotland were written by a different officer, who gave Bollier much lower marks. I want to see if Admiral Logan can provide some insight."

"Brad, didn't you review the service records of all radiomen on *Columbus* when we first suspected a traitor aboard? You didn't find anything on Bollier, then?"

"Sir, until Page's report, I had no reason to single out Bollier or Bulldoone. Bollier is the teletype repairman. He has less access to classified information than most of the other radiomen, but, now, I am taking a closer look."

"Okay. Let me know immediately about the outcome of your talk with Vice Admiral Logan."

"Yes, sir."

"Now, what about this February 15th deadline given to us by COMCRUDESFLOT EIGHT? That's not too far away."

"I will put more focus and more manpower on it. I have already directed Page to use ship's communications equipment to make reports. With this deadline, I think we will need to take a few more risks."

"I agree," Captain Willcroft responds. "I want daily reports, even if there is no progress."

"Yes, sir."

Captain Willcroft says, "Another interesting development has come up."

"What's that, sir?"

"Remember your proposal to use Python's treachery to force a showdown between Soviet submarines and selected U.S. Navy ships in the MED."

"Yes," Brad responds curiously.

"Well, as you know, the President issued an order to SECNAV to actively confront the aggressive actions of Soviet submarines against our ships. We know the Soviets are reading *Columbus's* messages. The time and location of EXERCISE DAWN PATROL flowed over the Rota Fleet Broadcast during the past week. This morning, *Columbus* and other DAWN PATROL ships sent several FLASH precedence Submarine Contact Reports from the EXERCISE DAWN PATROL location. Those Soviet submarines are on a collision course with the *Shangri-La* Task Force and specifically with Admiral Melton's task group. We should have a showdown sometime today."

Brad puts his hand to his chin in contemplation of what he just heard. Then, he asks, "Does Admiral Melton and CO *Columbus* know that this confrontation is being orchestrated?"

"No. SECNAV also wants to test senior officer's resolve and commitment to follow orders, even if it means a shooting conflict."

"What will happen if Admiral Melton passes the test?"

"The involved Soviet submarines must comply with international treaties or die."

Chapter 89

Rigney looks at his watch—1135. He has been on the day watch since 0730. The message traffic load is heavy. Every message coming over the fleet broadcast is for *Columbus*. Thirty outgoing messages backlog the ship-to-shore termination. NAVCOMMSTA Rota advises over the coordination channel that NAVCOMMSTA has a 150-message backlog for *Columbus*, and Rota asks to activate extra traffic circuits on UCC-1 channels three and four. On top of all that, interference and jamming trash frequencies in the HF band. All HF communications circuits, which include the ship-to-shore termination and the fleet broadcast, are experiencing 60 percent outage time. The vacation is over—today is a typical communications day in the MED.

In the Technical Control Room, LTJG Rowing, Senior Chief Bulldoone, RM1 Dukes, and RM1 Bollier discuss activating additional traffic circuits on UCC-1 channels three and four. Rigney and RM2 Carter stand in the doorway and listen to the discussion. All except Bollier are in favor of activating channels three and four as overload traffic circuits. Bollier recommends channels five and six.

"That's crazy!" Dukes objects loudly. "Five and six are farther out in the sideband. If we use three and four, and pull the drawers on 5 through 8, we get maximum power advantage on channels one through four."

Dukes looks at Senior Chief Bulldoone for agreement.

"Dukes is right, Thomas. Why should we do it your way?"

RM1 Thomas Bollier shakes his head slowly and the expression on his face foretells that he must suffer incompetent fools.

Bollier responds in a superior tone. "If you check the Equipment Status Log, you will see that I have reported channels three and four as unusable and awaiting parts."

"Bullshit!" Dukes blurts. "I check those channels several times a watch. QA checks show that three and four can pass signals with little or no distortion."

Again, Bollier's face tells of his continually increasing burden of having to educate the ignorant. He says, "If you checked the Equipment Status Log as required by the Standard Operating Procedure, you will see that I wrote that channels three and four are out of tolerance, not that they won't pass signals, which means we are better off using channels five and six."

RM1 Dukes shakes his head in disbelief at what he hears. He looks at senior chief and pleads, "Senior Chief, I read the Equipment Status Log every time I come on watch. I've seen those entries that Bollier talks about. Up 'till this morning when we started having HF problems, drawers 3 and 4 have been pushed in with diagnostic keying on them. That's why I have performed QA checks every day. There are no problems with those channels, and I have told Bollier that."

Senior Chief Bulldoone must make the decision—channels three and four, or channels five and six. He considers the opinions of both Dukes and Bollier.

LTJG Rowing, not understanding the technical issues, asks Bulldoone, "Senior Chief, if Dukes is correct, why don't we proceed with using channels three and four?"

Bulldoone glances at LTJG Rowing then glances at Bollier and Dukes. "Because, sir, no matter what channels we use, we will spend hours trying to make them work. We won't know if the problems are atmospherics or tolerance problems with the channels. If we do have tolerance problems, we will not be able to maintain crypto synchronization. The risk with using channels five and six is that they are farther out in the sideband and more susceptible to atmospherics."

LTJG Rowing scans the faces of the three senior radiomen; then, he says, "Senior Chief, make a decision. I will stand behind whatever you decide. We must do something, even if it's wrong."

Rigney intently watches Bulldoone. Rigney does not believe Bollier. He understands that the others have not seen what he has seen regarding Bollier and the UCC-1. Rigney also understands that the senior chief must make a difficult decision. If he makes the correct decision, he is a hero; if he does not, he will probably get a negative comment in his next evaluation. Rigney also realizes that Bulldoone could make the right decision and still be unsuccessful, which would look like he made the wrong decision. Rigney wants Bulldoone to choose channels three and four because he wants to see Bollier's reaction.

Bulldoone orders, "Dukes, activate channels three and four as overload traffic circuits."

"Aye, aye, Senior Chief!" Dukes turns to the Rota coordination channel teletype and arranges activation of extra traffic channels.

Bollier grunts his disapproval and storms out of the Technical Control Room. To avoid being bulldozed down by Bollier's mass, Rigney and Carter step quickly out of Bollier's way.

Rigney returns to his fleet broadcast position. He continues to track the activity in the Technical Control Room.

"Page!"

Rigney looks up from scanning fleet broadcast messages on the teletype machine. He sees the Communications Watch Officer, LTJG Rowing, standing in the doorway between the Message Center and the Fleet Broadcast Room.

"Yes, sir?"

"The Messenger is gone with the message boards. The *bunny trail* is *broke dick*. I need you to run this Operational Immediate precedence message up to the captain on the bridge. I will have Carter watch the fleet broadcast while you are gone, shouldn't take you more than ten minutes."

"Yes, sir," Rigney responds and grabs his foul weather jacket.

"No, don't need your jacket, just your white hat."

"Don't have my white hat, sir. Just my ball cap."

"That will have to do. Here, put on this guard belt." Rowing hands Rigney a white guard belt.

Rigney buckles the guard belt around his waist.

"When you get to the bridge, announce to the OOD that you have an Operational Immediate message for the captain. I will call the Bridge on the bitch-box and tell the OOD that you're coming."

Rigney has no idea how to recognize the OOD, but he does not tell Rowing that. *I'll figure it out when I get there.*

Two minutes later, Rigney stops at the door to the bridge and searches for the OOD. The bridge has a dozen people moving around. Then, he realizes that it is change of watch time for the bridge. He sees Captain Saunders sitting in the captain's chair. Rigney worries that no one notices him, and he cannot determine which officer is the OOD. He announces loudly, "Communications Messenger with an Operational Immediate message for the captain!"

Many heads turn toward him including Gunny Bronston, who Rigney did not see during his first scan of the bridge. The Gunny is on the far side of the bridge inspecting the ongoing Marine Sentry. Rigney catches the Gunny's eye for a split second. Rigney hopes that he does not look startled or afraid. That would be a dead giveaway.

"Over here, messenger!"

Rigney turns his head and looks in the direction of the voice. Captain Saunders motions for Rigney to come over. Rigney walks across the bridge.

The captain stares through the bridge window and appears focused on some object in the distance. At this point, he does not know that Rigney is the messenger.

Rigney stops and stands by the captain's chair. He waits for the captain to ask for the message board.

A few moments later, Captain Saunders extends his hand, indicating he wants the message board.

Rigney reads the message over Captain Saunders's shoulder. The message reports that a P-3 Orion aircraft tracks a Soviet November Class nuclear submarine. The P-3 is an antisubmarine warfare aircraft out of the Naval Air Station in Naples. The P-3 first detected the November at the western approach to the Strait of Bonifacio. The P-3 uses SONOBOUYS to track the November. The November travels submerged on a southwest course at flank speed. The November moves directly toward the *Shangri-La* Task Force.

A few moments later, Captain Saunders pats his breast pocket looking for a pen. The captain needs to initial the message to indicate that he has read it.

Rigney pulls a pen from his breast pocket and offers it to the captain.

Captain Saunders looks at Rigney's face as he takes the pen. Recognition appears on the captain's face. Then, Captain Saunders looks past Rigney and checks to see if anyone on the bridge is watching them. The only person whose eyes are on them is the Marine Sergeant on the other side of the bridge. The Gunny is too far away to hear anything that Captain Saunders or Rigney say.

The captain advises, "I will arrange a meeting. I want to talk to you about a few things."

"Yes, sir."

Captain Saunders initials the message and hands the message board back to Rigney.

Rigney does an about-face. Out of the corner of his eye, he can see Gunny Bronston staring at him. *My voice! Damn my unique voice!*

Back in MAIN COMM, Rigney resumes his watch position at the fleet broadcast. His curiosity regarding the extra traffic channels on the UCC-1 draws him into the Technical Control Room. He walks up to Dukes who is typing away on the coordination channel teletype. Dukes smiles and jokes with RM2 Carter.

"How's it going with the overload traffic channels?" Rigney asks.

"Came right up!" Dukes reports happily. "Got crypto synch on the first try. The signal is taking some static hits, but we are accepting the message traffic."

"Senior chief must be happy about that," Rigney comments.

"Sure is," Carter confirms.

Rigney asks, "Dukes, mind if I ask you a few questions about the QA checks you were talking about?"

"Okay. We're busy here. Make it quick."

"You said that you made QA checks with diagnostic keying. What generates the diagnostic keying?"

Dukes points to a toaster-size metal box at the rear of the QA rack.

"That box is a key generator. I can patch it to any teletype loop and check signal quality."

Rigney leans closer to study the box. Red, black, and green wires connect to sixteen terminal posts on the front of the box. One thick black cable exits a hole on the side of the box. Rigney reasons the thick black cable to be the power cable.

"Looks like a jury-rig, not navy issue," Rigney observes.

"That's right," Dukes confirms. "Bollier made it last MED cruise. It's really been a help, allows us to monitor and fine-tune the UCC-1 channels before we need them. That's how I knew channels three and four are okay. The diagnostic keying is always patched into unused channels."

Rigney studies the equipment in the QA rack. Then, asks Dukes, "So if you patch the key generator into the UCC-1 channels, that keying will appear anywhere that you can monitor the teletype loop for those channels?"

"Correct," Dukes replies.

Well, that explains why the patch panel shows keying and UCC-1 CH3 and CH4 loops when nothing is physically patched in.

Rigney asks, "What about when the channel drawers are pulled out?"

Dukes replies, "Pulling a channel drawer will put an open on the teletype loop. If you monitor the channel, you won't see keying, zero milliamps."

Rigney has observed keying on UCC-1 CH3 and CH4 when the drawers are pulled, which contradicts Dukes explanation. Rigney does not want to reveal his observations to Dukes because Dukes might investigate and bring these unusual events into the spotlight.

Dukes queries, "Anything else, Page? We need to get back to work here."

Rigney pauses to consider if he has anything else to ask. He does. "Yes, one last question. Why does Bollier need to connect his jury-rigged cables to the back of the UCC-1 when channels three and four drawers are pulled out . . . and why just channels three and four? When channel drawers five through eight are pulled out, which is all the time, why aren't Bollier's cables needed for those channels?"

"That's a good question," Dukes admits. "Bollier says it has something to do with balancing voltages across the channels. It doesn't make sense to me, but Bollier convinced the senior chief. So now, whenever we want to pull channel three or four drawers, we must get Bollier to attach the cables."

Rigney has his head bowed in thought.

Carter asks, "Why you so interested in the UCC-1 operation and QA procedures?"

"Oh, I want to know as much as I can about communications. The more I know, the better I can do my job. Plus, I am preparing for the RM2 Exam."

"You're eligible for RM2, *already*?" RM2 Carter challenges. "You've been working as a radioman for less than a month. How can you know your rate well enough?"

"I've been an RM3 for more than a year. I have completed all prerequisites, except for the recommendation, which I hope the senior chief forwards this week."

Rigney returns to the Fleet Broadcast Room.

Carter turns to Dukes and comments, "Took me five years to make RM2. How can a kid that has less than a month at his first command be eligible for advancement to RM2?"

Dukes stares questioningly at Carter and queries, "Wadda ya mean first command? Thought he was stationed at the Bethesda Communications Center before coming here?"

"Don't think so" Carter replies. "Johnson told me that Page was in Submarine Radiomen School prior to reporting to *Columbus*."

"That doesn't make sense," Dukes states confidently. "How does a submarine radioman end up on a cruiser?"

"Beats me," Carter responds.

Chapter 90

Messages regarding the inbound Soviet November Class Submarine flood the fleet broadcast. Rigney quickly processes high-precedence messages and passes them to the Message Center. Rigney reads the file copies in detail. The messages are of two types— position updates and intelligence analysis.

As each position report is received, Rigney goes to the wall-mounted map of the Mediterranean in the Message Center. He can see that the November moves closer. Currently, the November's position is fifty miles to the northeast. Rigney understand the threat. The map shows the diesel powered Whiskey ten miles away to the southwest.

Intelligence messages report that the November advances at flank speed, periodically slows, and shoots a water slug. That means the submarine floods a torpedo tube and impulses the water with compressed air. The flank speed and shooting water slugs make loud noises in the water, which is easily sensed by sonar. Because the next shot could be an actual torpedo, shooting water slugs near U.S. warships is considered aggressive, provocative, and dangerous behavior. The November purposely announces its presence and its impending arrival. The November dares the U.S. ships to do something about it.

A SECRET NOFORN message from COMSIXTHFLT advises Admiral Melton of the political situation. The Soviet tactic of sending submarines to penetrate U.S. task force operation areas at flank speed and shooting water slugs started six months ago. The tactic's purpose is to test U.S. commanders' resolve to maintain position in international waters. The Soviets want to determine just how far they can push U.S. warships. The COMSIXTHFLT message informs that during the early days of the Soviet tactic, U.S. policy was to avoid any possibility of an international incident. U.S. warships would be within their international rights to fire upon the Soviet submarines, but U.S. policy has been not to be an aggressor. The policy to move U.S. ships out of the way of the Soviet submarines is to show other countries that the U.S. is the victim, not the aggressor. When the U.S. moves its ships out of the way of the Soviet submarines, it openly protests the incident in the United Nations and in the press. The U.S. releases edited sonar recordings to the international community as proof of the Soviet's aggressive behavior. The U.S. wants to dampen the misperception of other countries that the U.S. is an aggressor. The final paragraph of the message informs that the U.S. Government has warned the Soviets through diplomatic channels that as of January 10, 1968, U.S. ships will no longer move out of the way of Soviet submarines. The message says that the Soviets have been warned that when Soviet submarines approach U.S. ships with torpedo tube outer doors open, firing water slugs or not, U.S. Ships will give the offending submarines one warning via underwater telephone to close outer doors. Should Soviet submarines fire a water slug or not close outer doors after the warning, U.S. ships will fire on those Soviet submarines with intentions to sink them.

The Fleet Broadcast top secret alarm sounds. Rigney reads the message as it prints. The message is from COMSIXTHFLT and is marked TOP SECRET NOFORN. The subject line reads ADDENDUM TO THE RULES OF ENGAGEMENT. The message orders Admiral Melton to stop the November from shooting water slugs and to stop the November from penetrating the task force perimeter. COMSIXTHFLT authorizes Admiral Melton to exercise all necessary actions including deadly force to stop the November. Additionally, COMSIXTHFLT authorizes Admiral Melton to use the same deadly force to prevent the Whiskey that stalks the task force to the southwest from penetrating the task force perimeter. If the Whiskey opens her torpedo tube outer doors, Admiral Melton is authorized to sink it, whether inside the task force perimeter or not.

Troubled by what he reads, Rigney worries about the possible outcome of these events. He remembers Captain Saunders's words. "How can you possibly understand the role this ship, and the role the admiral's task group plays in our National Security Program. Do you really understand?"

Rigney admits that he does not fully understand. He knows that standing up to the Soviet Union is important. America is part of NATO, and NATO must protect itself. He wonders if it really makes any difference if U.S. ships move out of the way of Soviet Submarines. *Yes, it is dangerous that Soviet submarines are shooting water slugs in proximity of U.S. ships. How can the U.S. feel safe and secure if it allows such action?*

Yes! That's it! The U.S. has every right to move about the seas and feel safe. The Soviets have no right to bully anyone in international waters. How can the U.S. Navy protect U.S. shipping and American citizens if it allows the Soviets to conduct dangerous, unsafe, and provocative actions in places where the Soviets have no right to do so?

Chapter 91

"BONG! BONG! BONG! BONG! BONG!" The General Alarm blasts over the 1MC.

"THIS IS NOT A DRILL! THIS IS NOT A DRILL! GENERAL QUARTERS! GENERAL QUARTERS! ALL HANDS MAN YOUR BATTLE STATIONS!"

Shocked surprise overcomes everyone in MAIN COMM. Each person's eyes jump from one person to the next looking for confirmation that they heard correctly . . . that they are at General Quarters—Battle Stations—for real!

Rigney's adrenalin glands shift to fast speed. His heart pounds harder and faster. Sweat seeps from his forehead and armpits. *Am I feeling fear?* He wonders if the *Columbus* is under attack. He feels isolated inside MAIN COMM, he wants to rush to the Signal Bridge and see what's happening. His Battle Station is the fleet broadcast position. He must stay at his Battle Station.

Rigney wonders about ground troops in Vietnam. *Do they feel as I do before going into battle? Can this type of battle even compare to a soldier or marine who is face to face with enemy soldiers in a hot sweltering jungle . . . a thick, wet jungle infested with insects and snakes . . . a jungle that is enemy to all soldiers. What about sailors on Swift Boats and PBRs? They must feel fear all the time when patrolling.*

Rigney remembers those he knew in high school who died in Vietnam. He cannot help but wonder if he dies in a naval battle in the Mediterranean, will his death be thought of in the same way as those who die in Vietnam? *What would those thoughts be? Would Diane and her hippie companions think my life was wasted and my death valueless? Would anyone think of me as a hero? Would anyone care ten years from now?*

On the *Columbus's* Flag Bridge, Admiral Melton communicates with his task group ships over the Primary Tactical, PRITAC, voice radio circuit. Admiral Melton also communicates over PRITAC with the P3 aircraft that circles above the sea at the November's position.

PRITAC voice signals are encrypted with the NESTOR cryptographic system. Even if the Soviets are monitoring U.S. radio frequencies, they will not understand what is being said.

The P3 reports that the November is ten miles northeast of the destroyer, USS *Patrell*. The P3 also reports that the November has just shot another water slug. The *Patrell* patrols the northeast perimeter of the task force. The USS *Patrell* reports she has the November on sonar.

Admiral Melton orders the *Patrell* to steam toward the November. The admiral also orders the *Patrell* to warn the November via underwater telephone that if the November shoots another water slug or does not close her outer doors within twenty minutes the *Patrell* will fire on her and sink her. The admiral tells *Patrell* to send the warnings in both English and Russian.

Admiral Melton orders the destroyer, USS *Richardson*, to move closer to the Soviet Whiskey Class submarine that maneuvers southwest of the task force. The admiral instructs *Richardson's* captain to fire on and sink the Whiskey, if the Whiskey opens her torpedo tube outer doors. The admiral further directs that if the Whiskey enters the task force perimeter, *Richardson* is to warn the Whiskey to depart within ten minutes or risk being fired upon.

Admiral Melton orders *Columbus* to proceed east to intercept the November.

On the *Columbus's* Bridge, Captain Saunders has assumed The Conn, and The Operations Officer has assumed The Deck. In CIC, the Executive Officer has assumed the functions of CIC Watch Officer.

In MAIN COMM, the remainder of CR Division personnel, who were off watch when General Quarters sounded, assume their Battle Stations. 25 percent of CR Division personnel do not have a specific Battle Station; they muster in Radio Central for further assignment by Senior Chief Bulldoone.

Larry Johnson enters the Fleet Broadcast Room and gets a briefing from Rigney. Both Larry and Rigney have the Fleet Broadcast Watch during Battle Stations.

On the *Columbus's* Bridge, Captain Saunders orders flank speed, and he orders the Helm to put his rudder hard right and to come to course 084. Captain Saunders also orders all conventional ASROC missiles and all torpedo tubes be made ready for firing.

As *Columbus* makes the turn and increases speed, she vibrates harshly and leans twenty-eight degrees to starboard.

In MAIN COMM, Larry and Rigney hold onto the equipment racks to maintain their balance.

"Rig, did you know that the *Columbus* and the other two ships of her class have a top-heavy superstructure. The scuttlebutt is that she cannot recover from a lean to port or starboard of more than forty-five degrees."

"What would make her lean more than forty-five degrees?" Rigney asks. "Is forty-five degrees hard to obtain?"

"I don't know. It's just a scary detail."

Rigney just shakes his head and rolls his eyes as he dismisses such scuttlebutt.

Admiral Melton orders *Columbus* and *Patrell* to transmit one sonar ping once every two minutes. Admiral Melton orders the pings so that the November's captain absolutely knows that the U.S. ships are closing. Admiral Melton reasons that when the November's captain detects *Columbus* and *Patrell* bearing down on her, the November's captain will close the submarine's torpedo tube outer doors and depart the area.

In MAIN COMM, Rigney and Larry feel the *Columbus* come upright. The vibration of the ship has lessened. They feel the ship lightly pitching and rolling at rapid rate.

"We're steaming at flank speed," states Larry.

"How can you tell," Rigney asks.

"Felt it before . . . during drills."

"If we shoot at that submarine, what weapons do you think we will use?" Rigney asks, but not expecting Larry to know.

"Not sure."

"We'll probably fire an ASROC," Rigney concludes.

"Yeah. Maybe," Larry responds.

Seventeen minutes remain until the warning deadline.

PRITAC speakers are positioned on the bridge and in the CIC of all the task force ships. All personnel within hearing range of a PRITAC speaker, including those on the *Columbus's* Flag Bridge and the cockpit of the P3 wait for a report that the November has closed her outer doors. They all look hopefully at the PRITAC speaker. Everyone wants to hear that the November has shut her outer doors. No one wants to fire at the submarine and sink her.

The P3 Orion aircraft has the best sonar contact on the November. The aircraft flies directly over the November's position. The P3's most recently dropped SONOBOUYS encircle the November.

On the Soviet November, the submarine's captain hears garbled voice coming over the underwater telephone unit. Because of the submarines high speed, the voice signals are unintelligible.

The November's captain knows that an American P3 using SONOBOUYS is tracking him. *That's the whole point!* These high-speed approaches while shooting water slugs is designed to draw the attention of the Americans and intimidate them and cause them to move their task force elsewhere.

The latest dispatch from Submarine Command advised that the Americans warned they would no longer tolerate these *illegal, aggressive, and dangerous actions*. The dispatch said that starting January 10th, the Americans would give a twenty-minute warning to close outer doors. If outer doors are not closed by the end of twenty minutes or if another water slug is fired before the end of those twenty minutes the Americans will fire weapons with intention of sinking the offending submarine.

The dispatch directs submarine captains to continue the aggressive actions, but the captains are counseled not to place their submarines in danger or any compromising situations. *Such vague and contradictory guidance from Submarine Command is typical,* the November's captain says to himself. *No matter what you do, you can be charged with being derelict in duty.*

The November's captain wonders if the underwater telephone signals are warnings. He is close to the American task force. He is due to fire another water slug. He decides to reduce speed and listen to the underwater voice signals.

USS *Patrell*, which is the closet U.S. ship to the November, cruises eight miles southwest of the November. At its current course and speed, the November will penetrate the task force perimeter in 25 minutes at a distance five miles north of *USS Patrell*.

Columbus still steams at flank speed toward the November class submarine. Admiral Melton's Flag Plot advises that if the *Columbus* and the November maintain the same course and speed, *Columbus* will pass over the November at the task force perimeter boundary. *Columbus* has two ASROCS ready to fire.

The P3 aircraft reports, *"Tango Golf this is Papa Three. November has slowed to twelve knots."* Tango Golf is Admiral Melton's voice call sign.

All in hearing range of a PRITAC speaker become nervous. The November's behavior has been to slow to twelve knots and shoot a water slug.

Fifteen minutes remain until the deadline.

On the Soviet Whiskey, which cruises submerged to the southwest of the task force, the captain prepares to come to periscope depth. The previous day he received a message from Submarine Command to come to periscope depth at this time and these coordinates. The message did not say why he is to do this. The boat needs to come to periscope depth and snorkel, anyway.

Twelve minutes remain until the deadline.

The SH-3 helicopter that hovers over the Whiskey's location reports over PRITAC, *"Tango Golf this is Sea King. The Whiskey has come to periscope depth and is snorkeling."*

Admiral Melton asks back, "Sea King this is Tango Golf. Has the Whiskey changed course or opened her outer torpedo tube doors?"

"That's a negative, Tango Golf. Whiskey is on same course and has not opened outer doors."

Admiral Melton evaluates the tactical situation and reviews the position of all ships and aircraft on the Flag Plot displays.

On the task force northeast perimeter, *Columbus* and *Patrell* cruise at five knots. Both ships have the November targeted and triangulated at a distance of five miles, and they are ready to fire ASROCS or torpedoes on Admiral Melton's order.

The P3 antisubmarine aircraft circles the November and is ready to drop a torpedo on Admiral Melton's order.

On the task force southwest perimeter, USS *Richardson* circles slowly at five knots. *Richardson* has the Whiskey targeted at four miles and is ready to fire ASROCS on Admiral Melton's order.

The SH-3 Sea King hovers over the Whiskey and is ready to drop a torpedo on the admiral's order.

Admiral Melton also considers that the Whiskey had not been to periscope depth for eighteen hours. The Whiskey is too far away to have the November on sonar and too far away to have heard the underwater

439

telephone warnings. A submarine preparing to go to battle would not involve itself in housekeeping chores such as snorkeling. Because of the Whiskey's distance and her nonaggressive actions, Admiral Melton surmises that the Whiskey is unaware of the November's presence and that there will be no coordinated actions between the two Soviet submarines.

Nine minutes remain until the deadline.

The November has slowed to eight knots. Her outer doors are still open. The November's captain listens and understands the warnings. The November's sonar picture shows that two U.S. warships are on different bearings and both are at a distance of five miles. An American P3 flies above. The Soviet captain orders his Fire Control Officer to ready torpedo tubes 2 through 6 for firing.

Although he has no sonar verification, the November's captain assumes that another Soviet submarine is about thirty-five miles to the southwest and should be coming to periscope depth to provide a distraction that complicates the tactical scenario for the Americans. That is the tactical plan executed by submarine command.

His Fire Control Officer reports that tube one is ready to shoot the water slug. *Will the Americans really fire on me?* His superiors know where he is located and what he is doing. If he backs off, he will be reprimanded. His superiors will know if he has been successful because the Soviet trawler to the south will report on whether or not the American task force moves to the west or northwest to avoid the November.

The November's captain knows he violates international law with his fast approach on the U.S. task force while shooting water slugs. Surely, the Americans are copying the sonar situation to tape.

Five minutes remain until the deadline.

The November's captain stands in the control room of his submarine. He looks into the face of his second in command who says nothing, but his eyes say *I support whatever decision you make.* However, the faces of the other crewmembers in the control room plead with him to shut the outer doors. Apprehension consumes some of them, and some of the crew physically tremble.

So young, the captain thinks to himself. They do not even consider that the Americans may be bluffing. The young ones are so impressionable and not educated in the political maneuvering of nations.

The November's Fire Control Officer reports that tube 1 is ready for firing a water slug and tubes 2 through 6 are ready to fire torpedoes, and he has firing solution on both U.S. warships locked into the computer.

The November's captain has only a few minutes to decide whether to comply with the warning that ensures preservation of his life and the lives of his crew but will end his naval career; or not comply with the warning and take a chance that the Americans are bluffing, which would make him a hero. He also considers shooting torpedoes at the two U.S. ships when the deadline expires. The Americans announced they would fire at the deadline if outer doors were still open. *If the Americans are going to sink me, maybe I should take the two U.S. ships with me. Would my superiors agree with that!* He continues to consider which option to choose.

Two minutes remain to the deadline.

Hands are trembling and stomachs are churning on the bridges, weapon firing stations, and Combat Information Centers of *Columbus* and *Patrell*. Firing triggers have been unlocked and fingers are poised over buttons that will fire conventional ASROCS. All are confident that they can sink the November but worry that the November may fire torpedoes. Some search their memories for the location of their Abandon Ship Station.

Admiral Melton continues to run the tactical scenario through his mind. In a few minutes, he must comply with what his orders tell him to do, which is to launch ASROCS or fire torpedoes. His duty does not trouble him. He will not hesitate. Thirty years of navy training and conditioning have made him mentally and morally ready. He has been in battle before—during World War II. Admiral Melton feels some fear, but his actions will be fearless.

The P3 aircrew is nervous and tense but not afraid. They are not in danger, but none of them wants to be part of the actions that kill an entire submarine crew. Each of them knows that they will not hesitate to drop a torpedo when ordered to do so.

In MAIN COMM, the radiomen go about their work. The tempo of operations does not change during Battle Stations. The message traffic load is heavy and keeping the high-frequency radio circuits reliable is a continuous chore. Few in MAIN COMM sense the impending danger. Rigney, Larry, and Mister Rowing are the only ones who have read the messages and understand why they are at Battle Stations.

441

One minute remains to the deadline.

Hearts pump faster on the U.S. warships, P3 aircraft, and Sea King helicopter. Sweat glands shift to high speed. Some are overwhelmed with their deadly responsibility.

Admiral Melton stands on the *Columbus's* Flag Bridge. He has the PRITAC handset to his ear, his finger poises over the push to talk button.

Time's Up!

Admiral Melton presses the push to talk button on the PRITAC handset. He must wait for the NESTOR synchronization tone before speaking. He does not hear the synchronization tone. He releases the push to talk button. He hears a rush of noise. He waits five seconds and presses the push to talk button again and gets the same result.

At First, he thinks something has gone wrong with the radio equipment. He worries that he is losing precious seconds. The November might have shot torpedoes in anticipation that the Americans have fired. Then, he remembers the problem is symptomatic of two stations trying to communicate at the same time. He releases the push to talk button and waits.

"Tango Golf this Papa Three! The November has shut its outer doors! I say again! The November has shut its outer doors!"

A tidal wave of relief flows throughout the task force. CIC operators and Fire Control Operators slump in their chairs. Bridge watches let out a loud and collective sigh.

Confirming reports from each ship's sonar room reach Admiral Melton. The confirming reports also state that the November has reversed course and has gone deep. The admiral smiles with relief and satisfaction as each report reaches his ears.

In MAIN COMM, the watch standers are not aware that anything significant has happened. They go about their communications duties as usual.

Admiral Melton orders all ships and aircraft to stay on station and keep weapons ready. They will stay at Battle Stations for another two hours to guard against the November from suddenly emerging from the deep and shooting water slugs, or possibly a torpedo.

Aboard the Soviet November Class submarine, now submerged to 250 meters and heading northeast, the captain secures his submarine from Battle Stations and relinquishes The Conn back to the OOD. The captain goes to his stateroom and starts writing his report to Submarine Command. He begins to feel bitter about what will happen over the next couple of weeks. He spent his adult life dedicated to the Soviet Navy, only to be placed in an impossible situation by his political superiors.

Occasionally, he looks up from writing his report and stares at his wall-mounted memorabilia that speaks of his eighteen-year career. His eyes linger on the picture of his family, and he feels guilt for the shame that his actions today will bring upon them.

On the *Columbus's* bridge, the *boatswain mate of the watch* announces over the 1MC, "NOW SECURE FROM GENERAL QUARTERS. SECURE FROM BATTLE STATIONS."

Rigney looks at his watch—1618. *We were at General Quarters for over four hours.* His thoughts are stimulated by his anxious curiosity about what happened. *Why doesn't someone explain what happened? Shouldn't the captain say something over the 1MC? Now is the time to use that damn annoying 1MC!*

Forty-five minutes later, Admiral Melton's Staff Communicator delivers the SECRET NOFORN report of the afternoon's actions.

Everyone in MAIN COMM gathers around the Message Center Supervisor's desk and attempts to read the message. LTJG Rowing shoos everyone away with a promise that the message can be read after it has been transmitted over the ship-to-shore termination and NAVCOMMSTA Rota has acknowledged receipt of the message.

Larry Johnson relieves Rigney at 1725.

Rigney stays in MAIN COMM for another twenty minutes because he wants to read Admiral Melton's report. He is the only member of the previous watch section to do so.

At 1800, Rigney departs MAIN COMM and climbs the ladder to the 07 Level. He opens the hatch and steps into the night. He dogs the hatch behind him. He stands on the starboard side of the Signal Bridge. The cold air causes him to zip his foul weather jacket all the way to his neck and to pull his collar around his neck. He removes his ball cap, which provides no protection against the cold. He pulls his wool watch cap out of his jacket pocket, puts the watch cap on his head, and pulls the wool cloth down over his ears.

He waits until his eyes adjust to the darkness. Then, he walks around to the aft end of the superstructure to the darkened Signal Shack. He opens the door to the Signal Shack, steps in, and closes the door behind him. He exchanges a few pleasant words with the *signalman of the watch*, who is always happy to have a visitor on these lonely night watches. Rigney studies the compass mounted on the forward bulkhead. *Columbus* steams westerly toward Mallorca.

Rigney exits the Signal Shack and walks to the port side. He looks aft, past the stern, to the east, and ponders the near deadly situation that occurred out there this afternoon. He wonders about the military, political, and social value of what occurred today. *Has the cause of democracy been strengthened today?*

He affirms his reasoning that America has the right to feel safe on the open sea. *However, does that right extend to justification for sinking a Russian submarine?* Rigney troubles himself about such questions. He attempts to understand his value as an ONI agent in the midst of this large scale maneuvering between nations. *I just don't know for sure.*

Chapter 92

RM1 Bollier sits on a stool at his workbench. The wooden stool audibly moans under the strain of his weight. His wide butt droops over the edges of the seat. From time to time, he finds it necessary to reinforce the joints of the stool with additional screws.

The action of sitting causes his dungaree shirt to pull from his trousers. The top of his butt and underwear are exposed. The forceful air-conditioning chills the exposed flesh of his butt.

He scrutinizes the toaster sized metal square box under a magnifying glass. *"New and improved,"* Javier had said. Bollier sighs and lifts his head from the magnifying glass.

Two Heath Kit tape player-records sit on the back of Thomas's workbench. He built the kits himself last year. He reaches for the PLAY knob and switches it to the right. Classical music fills the shop.

The Teletype Repair Shop serves as a haven for Thomas Bollier. He possesses the only keys to the door. The day after he reported to *Columbus*, he changed the door lock. He did not notify the master-at-arms shack of the lock change. *They have no need to enter my shop without me present*, he justifies to himself. Although he had considered the safety and security aspects of violating the compartment locks regulation, he has convinced himself that the security of *his* tools and his parts take precedent. *Besides, no one aboard knows enough about teletypes and the UCC-1 to be in my shop by themselves. They would only screw something up. I am saving them from their own incompetence!*

When material inspections of O5 level spaces occur, Bollier always ensures he is present. He has not taken leave in two years for concern that someone could discover the secrets he hides in his shop.

"NOW SET THE SPECIAL SEA AND ANCHOR DETAIL."

Rigney awakes and curses the 1MC. The berthing compartment remains dark. He looks at the luminous dial on his watch—0915. Rigney cannot feel *The Tall Lady* moving. She must be in calm waters near the coast of Mallorca.

He was sleeping off the mid watch and must go back on watch at noon. Senior Chief Bulldoone rearranged the watch bill so that everyone would have at least 24 hours off in Palma. *Columbus* will have three full liberty days in Palma. *Columbus* will depart on the fourth morning.

Today, Rigney must stand port and starboard watches of four hours on and four hours off through tomorrow morning. Then, he is off for 24 hours, which will be his only opportunity to go on liberty in Palma and meet John Smith.

He turns over and goes back to sleep.

A shrill whistle blasts over the 1MC, signifying the first mooring line has been tossed to the line handlers on the pier.

Rigney awakes. He looks at his watch—1120. He looks to the far aft end of the compartment. The illumination coming down the ladder from the above compartment allows Rigney to see RM1 Bollier toss his key ring into his rack-locker. A loud clunk sounds throughout the compartment as the keys hit metal. A few men stir in their racks.

Instead of quietly lowering the lid of his rack-locker, Bollier lets gravity slam it shut with a vibrating bang.

Several sleepers jerk awake. "You fuckin' asshole, Bollier!" Bollier snaps-shut the combination lock to his rack-locker. He wears Service Dress Blues. He puts on his peacoat and white hat and departs the compartment.

He's going on liberty. This provides an opportunity to search the Teletype Repair Shop. I must find a reason for leaving MAIN COMM sometime during my watch.

From where he sits in the Fleet Broadcast Room, Rigney easily views the Technical Control Room. He cannot take his eyes off the UCC-1. The drawers for transmit channel three and channel four are pushed in and the patch panel meter shows teletype keying. Dukes deactivated the overload traffic channels just prior to arriving in Palma.

Rigney verified earlier that the QA equipment was powered down. He attempted to disrupt the keying by inserting a dummy plug into the CH 3 and CH 4 jack on the patch panel, but the keying was not disrupted. *That's abnormal. The wiring must be rerouted, bypassing the channel jacks. What the hell is being keyed on those channels, and where is it originating? Bollier must have the answers. I must search the Teletype Repair Shop.*

RMCS Bulldoone steps into the Fleet Broadcast Room and says, "Page, the Personnel Office wants to see you about your paperwork for the RM2 Exam. I will have Carter watch the fleet broadcast for you while you're gone."

Chapter 93

Rigney enters the door to the Personnel Office on the Main Deck. He stands at the counter waiting for his turn. Two sailors stand in line before him.

"Are you Page?" asks a second class personnelman from a desk in the middle of the office."

"Yes."

"Open the counter door there and come this way. The Personnel Officer wants to see you."

Rigney follows the personnelman to a door in the center of the forward bulkhead.

"Just knock. When you enter, remove your cover, and go through the door. Remember to shut the door behind you."

The personnelman walks off.

Rigney knocks.

"Enter!"

Rigney removes his white hat, opens the door, steps through, and closes the door behind him. A lieutenant stands in front of a desk. Rigney is about to say *reporting as ordered*, when he notices Captain Saunders sitting behind the desk.

Captain Saunders says to the lieutenant, "Thanks, Steve. You can have your office back in forty-five minutes."

"Aye, aye, sir," the lieutenant replies. Then, the lieutenant departs through his office's private door that exits to the Main Deck starboard passageway.

"Sit!" Captain Saunders orders as he points to a chair at the side of the desk.

Rigney lowers himself into the chair.

"Page, you witnessed the events two days ago with the Soviet submarines. You have access to messages. If you are any kind of competent intelligence agent, you have read the admiral's reports. Correct?"

"Yes, sir. I have read them."

"Do you also understand that those Soviet submarines knew where to find us, and their knowledge was probably gained from the spy you seek?"

"Yes, sir. I understand that."

"Do you understand the global impact had we sunk that Soviet submarine?"

Rigney contemplates the question for a few moments; then, he answers honestly, "No, sir. I don't think I do."

Captain Saunders studies the *boy* in front of him. He considers that Page is too young and too inexperienced to understand the politics of Cold War maneuvering. He also struggles with the wisdom of ONI sending this uneducated and untrained sailor amidst an environment that he does not understand.

"Page, I have drafted a classified message to ONI. I haven't decided to send it. First, I want to see the outcome of this meeting. In the message, I express my objections to ONI for sending such an inexperienced and uneducated operative. I have known a number of ONI operatives over the years. All of them clearly understood the political situation and their actions were always compatible with that understanding. You must help me understand your value."

Rigney knows that the international political issues are outside his total understanding. He feels inadequate and intimidated with communicating directly with senior officers like Captain Saunders. He wishes he could get advice from Brad Watson.

When Brad instructed me to reveal as little as possible, could Brad have imagined the events of the last few days? Should I blindly follow Brad's instructions? If I do not reveal anything, I will have one pissed-off navy captain, who is also my Commanding Officer. Brad also said that unpredictable occurrences could make your orders irrelevant and nonsensical. Therefore, sometimes you must act on your own judgment and hope your ass is in one piece when it is all over.

"Answer me, Page. I am your Commanding Officer. I am responsible for you and all who serve on *Columbus*. I can remove you from this ship, today, and send you back to ONI. My actions in these matters are final. As the Commanding Officer, I have that authority. If you do not want me to do that, you must prove to me that you are accomplishing something here."

Rigney explains, "Captain, I was selected for this mission because the old, traditional methods of undercover work did not produce any results. One of the reasons ONI chose me to come aboard *Columbus* is because I *am* so young. A lot of my ONI training was to teach me how to act like some kind of smartass, showoff kid. Enemy agents will dismiss me as possible threat because traditional undercover agents do not act immature and bring attention on themselves. Therefore, ONI sees my youth as an advantage.

"Another reason that I was selected is my technical knowledge of communications systems. I spent two years learning how to operate and repair many of the same systems that are on this ship. I probably know these communications systems better than others my age, but no one in the Communications Department knows my skills. That's the advantage.

I can go through all the communications spaces and study the communications systems for irregularities. I tell everyone that I am working on watch station qualifications and studying for advancement.

"My mission is to discover who the spy is and how he is doing it. Then, I am must report my findings to ONI. I just need the time and freedom to do it."

Captain Saunders writes notes during Rigney's explanation. He will brief the admiral. He puts his pen down. Then, for about a minute, he looks back and forth between his notes and Rigney. Then, he makes a few more notes.

Rigney sits quietly while Captain Saunders writes.

"Page, several days ago, before the action with the Soviet submarines, the admiral sent a message to CNO with copy to ONI stating that they have a deadline of three weeks from now to uncover this spy. After that, the admiral and I will take our own actions to stop this spy. Do you know what those actions will be?"

"I was briefed at ONI that you will bring a TEMPEST team aboard and some Naval Investigative Agents and try to smoke out Python. ONI predicts Python will run, and we will lose our chance to get him."

"Python?"

"That's the ONI codename for our spy."

Rigney realizes that he probably should not have revealed that information.

"Interesting codename," Captain Saunders says with a grin on his face.

"Yes, sir. I think so too," Rigney replies with a grin equal to the captain's.

Captain Saunders advises, "Because of what happened with those Soviet submarines, the admiral plans to move the deadline up to the day we pull into Naples."

"Please don't do that, sir! I think I discovered something! I need more time!" Rigney blurts without thinking. As soon as he said it, he knew he did wrong.

The captain shakes his head and expresses dismissal of Page's words. He advises, "Page, we are in a serious situation here. Three days from now, we depart Palma and steam for Naples. We will transit over the same area where we encountered those Soviet submarines. We could find ourselves in the same conflict as before. The CNO has directed the admiral and me to be cooperative with ONI. However, the admiral and I have the final say. The safety and security of my ship and the safety and security of the admiral's task group are at stake. If you—ONI—do not want the deadline moved up, you must provide me an incentive. You must tell me what you have discovered, if anything."

"Sir, what if my discoveries are not sufficient for you to stick to the original deadline?"

With an aggravated tone, Captain Saunders replies, "As Commanding Officer, I am the best judge of how to proceed."

Again, Rigney struggles with how much he should tell Captain Saunders. If he tells the captain nothing, the deadline moves up. If the deadline moves up, Rigney must endure increased risks to uncover Python. Rigney decides to be truthful.

"Captain, I observed RM1 Bollier do things that do not make sense to me. His actions may be nothing more than the ego of a stubborn technician who wants things his way. Also, Senior Chief Bulldoone seems to cater to Bollier . . . well . . . some of the time. I have passed both of their names to ONI. I want them investigated to see if they have some sort of unusual past."

"Was that an ONI contact who you met on the pier in Rota?"

The captain's knowledge of the meeting causes Rigney to jerk his head back and blink his eyes.

"I was on the ASROC deck when I saw the two of you. Is that first class a member of my crew?"

"No, sir."

Captain Saunders feels confident that Page is telling the truth, and he wants more details.

"What has RM1 Bollier done that is so unusual?"

"It's kind of technical, sir."

"Humor me," the captain orders tightly.

"It has to do with teletype channels on the AN/UCC-1 multiplexer. Bollier seems to be manipulating the use of them."

"Explain the use of the UCC-1 to me."

"It's a device used for putting multiple teletype signals on one carrier frequency, primarily used for the ship-to-shore termination."

"Aren't those teletype channels covered with online crypto devices?"

"Yes, sir. They are."

"And you think that Bollier is doing something unusual with the teletype channels?"

"Yes, sir."

"If the channels are covered by crypto devices, what could he do with them?"

"I don't know, sir. That's why I need time to investigate."

"What is holding you up? Is it something I can help you with?"

"I don't think you can help, sir. I need to trace out all the cables and equipment that has anything to do with the UCC-1. I need to do that when no one is around, and it will take several hours. My instructions are to find out who Python is and how he is doing it, without Python knowing that I have discovered him. I am looking for an opportunity to do that while we are in Palma."

Captain Saunders recalls events of ten months ago when staff members from CNO N2 and N3 briefed him that the national security operation encompassed a lot more than what is happening on *Columbus*. He was not briefed on the details. He was only told that there was more to the counterespionage operation than stopping the spy's actions on *Columbus*.

"Okay, Page. You have more time."

Rigney waits for Captain Saunders to say more.

"That's all, Page."

"Yes, sir." Rigney stands and exits the office.

Before leaving the Personnel Office, he stops by the desk of the second class personnelman who guided him to the Personnel Officer's door.

Rigney notices the nameplate on the desk. "Excuse me, Taylor. The lieutenant told me to check with you to see if I am all set to take the RM2 Exam."

"RM3 Page, right?" asks Taylor.

"Yes."

PN2 Taylor goes to a filing cabinet, retrieves Rigney's Service Record, and brings it back to his desk. He thumbs through the pages.

"Yup! You're all set to take the test on February 10th. That's a couple of days after we leave Naples."

"Okay. Thanks!"

Captain Saunders continues to sit at the Personnel Officer's desk and studies his notes from his meeting with Page. He writes a few more notes.

The Personnel Officer sticks his head through the office's private door. "Should I come back later, Captain?"

"No, I am done." Captain Saunders stands and says, "Steve, have someone deliver to my stateroom the Service Records of Senior Chief Bulldoone and RM1 Bollier."

"Yes, sir." The Personnel Officer writes down the names.

"Steve, do not reveal to anyone my meeting with RM3 Page."

"Aye, aye, Captain. I will not say anything."

Captain Saunders exits through the private door.

451

As Rigney climbs the ladders back to the 06 Level, he chuckles at himself. *We chase Soviet submarines and are seconds away from blasting them from the water! I'm chasing a spy who probably put us in that position, and I am worrying about whether or not I am all set to take the RM2 Exam.*

Chapter 94

"NOW MAIL CALL. ALL DIVISION MAIL PETTY OFFICERS PICK UP MAIL AT THE SHIP'S POST OFFICE."

Gunnery Sergeant Christopher Bronston walks through the chief's mess dining area on the way to the chief's berthing compartment. He opens the door. He notices that a couple of the CIC chiefs are sleeping off one of their eight-hour port and starboard watches. Instead of closing the door quietly, he lets it slam shut. The chiefs jerk awake and glare a Bronston, but they do not say anything.

"Chicken-shit squids," Bronston mumbles under his breath.

Bronston has one of the choice racks—a center rack at the opposite end of the compartment from the door. He finds two letters on his rack. He opens the letter from a judge in Norfolk, Virginia. The judge orders Bronston to court to answer charges that he violated the judge's restraining order. The judge had issued the restraining order that forbade Bronston to come within one-hundred feet of his ex-wife, Mary.

Fuckin' cunt! She will get what's coming to her when I get back to Norfolk.

The other letter is from the Norfolk private detective that he hired to find out who attacked him on the boardwalk in Virginia Beach. The letter states that the detective has not yet discovered the name of the sailor, but he has identified the WAVE who was with the sailor as Yeoman First Class Barbara Gaile, who recently transferred to the Naval Support Activity in Naples, Italy.

I will convince that bitch to become cooperative.

Rigney feels drained and frustrated as he steps down the ladder into the CR Division berthing compartment. He hopes that he may get some hours of uninterrupted sleep. He finds three letters on his rack. He feels so tired that he considers sleeping before reading the letters. Instead, he takes the letters to the table near the ladder where the light is better. He sits down and looks at the return addresses. One letter is from Diane Love, one is from Sally Macfurson, and one is from Barbara Gaile. All three letters are perfumed. The letters from Sally and Barbara are pastel pink in color, and the letter from Diane is light blue.

Rigney opens the letter from Diane Lobe first. She starts by writing how much she enjoyed their time together over Christmas. She does not want their different political and social ideologies to harm their friendship. As he reads the letter, he notices out of the corner of his eye that Rouché comes down the ladder.

Rouché stops at the bottom of the ladder, which is next to the table. Rouché scans the compartment to see who is watching. A few of the junior radiomen are in their racks or standing near their racks. None of the first class petty officers are present. He sits down directly across the table from Rigney.

"Nice looking letters, Rig-ass!" Rouché says with a sneer. "And two of them are pussy pink. You'd better not let any those women see me. They'd drop you in a second just so they can suck my cock."

Diane's letter had lifted Rigney's spirits. Rouché's crude words destroy the moment. He glares angrily at Rouché and warns, "I'm in no mood for your uncouth and vulgar conversation. Now, back off!" He raises his voice loud enough that others in the compartment turn their heads in Rigney's direction.

Rouché chuckles and looks around the compartment. He sees an audience forming. He grabs one of the sealed envelopes and starts to open it.

Rigney quickly grabs both of Rouché's wrists, pins them to the table, and starts bending them back toward Rouché. Rouché grunts in pain. Rigney wants Rouché to drop the letter; he increases his vise like grip on Rouché's wrists and bends his wrists a little more. Rouché feels severe pain but does not let go of the envelope.

Witnesses to this incident will later say that Rigney's arm movements were a blur. They will say that Page moved so fast that one-second his hands were flat on the table and the next second he had Rouché's wrists pinned to the table.

Rigney's face flushes red with anger. His voice is coarse and harsh when he rasps, "Let go of the letter you mother-fuckin' son-of-a-bitch, or I will break both your wrists!" Rigney has lost control. Total anger overcomes him.

Rouché attempts to stand and pull away.

Rigney increases the backward pressure on Rouché's wrists, forcing Rouché to sit back down.

Rouché attempts to kick Rigney from under the table, but the distance and angle will not allow him to make contact.

Rigney squeezes with all his strength with the intent of breaking both of Rouché's wrists.

Rouché moans and releases the letter.

Rigney lessens his grip slightly, glad that he did not need to break Rouché's wrists.

Someone in the audience comments, "Did ya see that? Page made him let go of the letter. That's gotta be one for the record books."

The comment from the onlooker, more than the pain, angers Rouché.

Rouché tries to pull away, but Rigney easily pulls Rouché toward him, as easily as he lifts barbells. Rigney pulls Rouché halfway across the table and threatens loudly, "If you ever touch anything of mine again, I will rip out your mother-fuckin' throat and leave you choking on your own mother-fucking cock roach blood!"

Rigney shakes with anger.

"Fuck you! Rig-ass!" Rouché hisses. "Never go on liberty if you want to live!"

At that moment, RM1 Dukes comes down the ladder. He sees that Page grips Rouché's wrists and has Rouché pulled over the table.

Rigney glances up and sees Dukes. He releases his grip on Rouché, and Rouché falls back in his chair.

Rouché concentrates hard to suppress moans of pain.

"Is there a problem here?" Dukes questions with authority.

"No problem," Rouché replies with a smile. "Page and me were arm wrestling. He won!"

"You two need to quietly settle whatever conflict exists between you. Rouché, you have been in trouble before for fighting. You cannot afford any more trouble like that. Page, you've gotten a good start here on *Columbus* and you are about to take the Second Class Test. You don't want to do anything stupid."

"Okay. Good advice," Rouché says as he walks toward his rack.

Dukes looks at Rigney for agreement.

Rigney nods his head and says, "I will do my best."

"Good," Dukes responds. Then, he walks off toward his rack.

Rigney returns to reading Diane's letter. His anger against Rouché still burns within him. He focuses on Diane's letter. Finally, his mood improves as he grasps the meaning of her words. Her letter is pleasant and reassures him that he has a comfortable lover back in Seal Beach who thinks about him often.

He opens Barbara's letter next. She wrote the letter before leaving Norfolk. She explains how surprised she was to see him standing high up on the ship when *Columbus* departed Norfolk. She had gone to the pier just for the spirit of the event. Her letter also says that she received information from Naval Support Activity, Naples. The information explains that she will be the captain's yeoman. She promises Rigney to check port schedules so that she can meet Rigney when his ship visits Naples. She promises a romantic and sexual experience equal to or better than their last. Rigney feels himself getting hard just thinking about it.

Then, he opens Sally's letter. The letter was written two weeks ago. She hopes Rigney is doing well aboard his ship. She writes that she departs New London on January 3rd for Naples, Italy. She will work at an archeology dig in a place called *Lago Patria*, which is ten miles north of Naples. She provides the exact address. She asks Rigney to come and see her if his ship comes to Naples. She says she misses him and hopes they can renew their relationship sometime in the future.

What a coincidence! I will make time to see her. I hope Barbara is not offended if I want to spend some time with Sally. Yep, Rigney is clueless as to how women feel about such things.

Rigney gathers the letters and walks toward his rack. Both Dukes and Rouché stand at their racks. Rigney slides past Dukes and comes within two feet of Rouché who puts on his Service Dress Blues in preparation for going on Liberty. Rouché continues to massage his wrists.

"Going on liberty tonight?" Rouché asks Rigney.

"No, I am on duty."

"How about tomorrow?" Rouché persists.

"I don't know . . . probably."

"Good. I am looking forward to it," Rouché responds cordially. "Maybe we can have a beer and mend this conflict between us."

As he walks along the Main Deck toward the gangway, Rouché admits to himself that he had underestimated Page. He had thought Page to be all mouth and no substance. Rouché now realizes that not only is Page willing to get physical, Page is incredibly strong. Rouché puts his hand to his throat as he thinks about Page's threat. Rouché decides that if he is going to hurt Page, he must have some help.

Rouché's friends, his gang as some refer to them, wait for him near the gangway. They obtain permission to leave the ship and walk down the gangway. After they have walked halfway up the pier, Rouché stops and conspires with his friends.

"You guys know that smartass, Page?"

"Yeah," says one of them. "He's that guy who's always doing pushups and chin-ups in your compartment."

"That's him," Rouché agrees. "He brags to everyone that we are just a bunch of pussies and have no balls to fight him. He brags about how tough he is, and no one can take him. Our friends expect to us to bring this loudmouth asshole down to size. We can do it, and we must do it right."

Rouché explains to his gang what weapons to bring with them tomorrow and how they will use those weapons.

Rigney would like to keep his mind on the sexual promises of Barbara Gaile, but he cannot rid his thoughts of the physical confrontation that he had with Rouché. Rigney feels frustration that he lost his temper and thinks that he has gone too far with his *tough* behavior. He knows that Rouché will attack. Rigney must go on liberty tomorrow so that he can meet John Smith. Rigney comprehends the reality that when he goes on liberty, he must go armed.

Chapter 95

Brad Watson sits in his office at the ONI Headquarters in Suitland, Maryland. His unclassified phone rings.

"Extension 8925"

"John Smith here."

Brad pauses. Galahad would only make an unscheduled call from Europe if there were something wrong.

"How's your vacation?" Brad Asks.

"Okay, until today. I was planning to take the ferry to Palma. Unfortunately, I was in a taxi that was involved in an accident with two other cars and a bus. Many people hurt and three were killed. I wasn't hurt. My taxi had minimal damage. Now, I am stuck in Valencia while the police investigate. The police took my passport. They will not give it back until they have finished questioning me. The police say it will take another three days."

"Sorry to hear that. You will miss your friends in Palma, then?"

"Yes, I will miss them. I will go directly to Naples."

"Okay. Thanks for updating me on your schedule."

John Smith hangs up.

Brad considers what needs to be done to recover from this latest twist. He must send a message to Apollo who will go on liberty in Palma expecting Smith to meet him. Smith has instructions for Page to focus on RM1 Bollier as the number one candidate to be Python.

Brad learned from Admiral Logan that during Bollier's tour at the U.S. Consulate in Edinburgh, there was a serious incident regarding missing crypto material. The crypto custodian, Mister Edward Stanley, had committed suicide. When the admiral and his team went to Edinburgh to verify the status of the Crypto Account, they found the account to be a mess. There were dozens of burn bags filled with undestroyed key lists and crypto documents, most of which had been reported as destroyed by Stanley. Stanley was suspected of passing crypto material to unauthorized persons. According to Admiral Logan, Stanley was falsifying destruction records. The classified report on the incident speculated that Stanley's was being blackmailed to hide his homosexuality, and he committed suicide as the only way out of a scandalous and embarrassing situation.

Admiral Logan had informed, "Stanley and Bollier were the only two authorized access to the Crypto Vault. RM1 Bollier was assigned as Adonis Crypto Operator, and he spent most of his time in the Crypto Vault encrypting and decrypting messages. Bollier said that Stanley seldom came to the Crypto Vault. The teletype operators reported that

Stanley would go into the Crypto Vault at night when Bollier was not around. Written navy orders forbid RM1 Bollier to participate in crypto material destruction. Therefore, he paid no attention to Stanley's actions regarding destruction. Bollier said he did not know the destruction regulations. Facts revealed during the investigation substantiated Bollier's statements."

Brad worries about the mid-February deadline laid down by Admiral Melton. Brad has read the intelligence messages regarding the confrontation between Admiral Melton's task group and the Soviet November Class submarine. He knows that the *Columbus's* CO would be totally justified to move up the deadline. Brad must instruct Apollo to become aggressive and to take some risks. He decides to send a message over the ONI Radio Broadcast.

Larry Johnson relieves Rigney as Fleet Broadcast Operator.

Larry asks Rigney, "You going on liberty today?"

"Yeah, probably this afternoon. I'm gonna get some sleep first. Do you know anything about the Sa Llonja district?"

Larry answers, "Yeah. Plenty of nice restaurants, bars, and nightclubs. The locals there love American sailors . . . and lots of female tourists who are friendly to American sailors. Just go to the head of the pier, jump in a taxi, and tell the driver to take you to *Sa Llonja*. When you're ready to come back, grab a cab and tell the driver to take you to fleet landing."

"Okay. That's where I will go. Thanks, Larry."

"Uh. Rig. There was talk in the compartment that some of the radiomen will follow Rouché today, hoping he meets up with you. Those guys think you're a smartass with a superior attitude and they want to see it knocked out of you."

Rigney shakes his head, smiles, and chuckles lightly.

Larry says, "Yeah, I understand. It doesn't take much to entertain those guys. But you must take Rouché seriously. I've seen him in action. He is one mean son-of-bitch."

"Thanks for the warning. I can take care of myself. Besides, I will avoid a fight. I will be on the lookout for him. If I see him, I will run in the other direction."

Rigney stops at the fan room hatch on the 04 Level. He looks around and listens. He sees no one and hears no one. He enters the fan room and dogs the hatch behind him. He retrieves the ankle holster and Beretta from the air conditioning duct. He slips the pistol from its pouch. He pulls back the slide and chambers a round. He checks the thumb safety engaged. He sets the weapon to semiautomatic mode. He pulls the suppressor from its pouch and screws it on the Beretta's barrel. Then, he removes the suppressor and puts it back in its pouch. He slips the pistol into the holster. He verifies all pouch covers are snapped shut. He puts the holster in the right side deep pocket of his foul weather jacket.

Rigney enters the dimly lit berthing compartment. He observes that no bunk lights are on and no one is awake. Because of the Cinderella Liberty regulation, all E-6 and below were back on the ship by midnight.

He steps quietly to his rack in the forward starboard corner. Rouché snores away in the middle rack. Rigney kneels down, enters the combination of the lock, and opens the lid to his rack-locker. He takes off his foul weather jacket and stuffs it into his locker. He undresses and crawls into his rack.

Falling asleep is difficult for Rigney. He worries about being discovered with the Beretta when he departs the ship. He also worries about Rouché catching up with him. *I must meet up with John Smith, regardless of the risks with carrying the pistol and running into Rouché.*

Later, loud chatter in the berthing compartment causes Rigney to awake. He looks at his watch—11:23 a.m. A dozen sailors, including Rouché, are dressing to go on liberty.

"Think Page will go on liberty?" one of the radiomen asks another.

"Shit, man! Would you?" is the response.

Rigney goes back to sleep.

Chapter 96

During midafternoon, Rigney crawls out of his rack and prepares to go on liberty. When he comes out of the head, he observes that he is the only one in the berthing compartment. *Fortunate!*

He quickly slips into his Service Dress Blue uniform. He retrieves the holster from his rack-locker. He rolls down his bulky knee-high sock on his right leg and straps the ankle holster to his bare leg. He pulls the sock over the holster so that it is covered should his pant leg rise. He thinks of the other Beretta in the head. He wonders if he should take that one also. Then he dismisses the thought as overkill.

Outside on the Main Deck, Rigney moves aft toward the gangway. As he approaches the gangway, he sighs with relief when he sees that no one is searched prior to departing the ship. The chief at the gangway checks I.D. cards and liberty cards; then, he grants permission to depart the ship.

A gust of chilled wind sweeps across the pier. Although the temperature ranges in the mid-forties, the sun shines bright. Rigney raises the collar of his peacoat around his neck. He retrieves sunglasses from an inside pocket and slips them on.

A few moments later Rigney stands at the head of the pier with a group of deck apes waiting for a taxi. When a taxi arrives, Rigney enters a taxi and shares a ride with three other *Columbus* sailors.

Fifteen minutes later, Rigney walks along a street in Sa Llonja. Young people pack the streets as they speak in a dozen different languages. Traditional Spanish music mixes with American Rock and Roll. The architecture is a mix of what Rigney thinks to be medieval and modern European.

Rigney feels hunger. He has not eaten since mid-rats last night. As he walks along the street, he stops and reads the menus posted on stands outside each restaurant's door. Most of the menus are in Spanish with English translations under each menu item. When he looks through the door of these restaurants, he always sees a dozen or so *Columbus* sailors inside. He wants something typically Spanish.

He enters a small restaurant whose outside menu does not have English translations. The warmth of the interior causes Rigney to remove his peacoat. Only two other sailors sit among the many Spaniards and tourists. A mixed aroma of cooking onions and garlic permeates the air. He takes off his white hat, rolls it, and sticks it in his peacoat pocket. Then, he sits down at a small table near the window. A waiter hands Rigney a menu. Rigney orders a San Miguel beer.

Rigney does not bother to read the menu. Instead, he looks at the dishes that others have in front of them. A plate that has a mixture of sausage, beef, olives, cheese cubes, and mushrooms, all covered with a red sauce, grabs his attention. When the waiter returns with the San Miguel, Rigney points to the dish. The waiter understands and writes the order on his pad.

Less than ten minutes later, the waiter brings his food. He quickly shovels down the first four bites and takes a gulp of the beer. For the remainder of his meal, he slows down to enjoy the food.

As he chews, Rigney stares out the restaurant's window. He becomes fascinated by what he sees. The crowd is a mixture of people his age from different countries around Europe. The crowd includes the well dressed and the not so well dressed. Many of them are dressed like American hippies. Some stand in groups and engage in conversation. Some sit at tables at outside cafés, despite the cold temperature. He continually scans faces while looking for John Smith.

He stiffens as he sees Rouché and two other sailors walking along the opposite side of the street. He recognizes the other two sailors as Rouché's *friends* from First Division. About twenty feet behind Rouché, walks five radiomen from CR Division. Rouché and his friends look in the doorways and windows of the bars and restaurants, as if they are looking for someone. Rigney figures it is just a matter of time until they start working his side of the street.

As his ONI training taught him, he stands and walks to the rear of the restaurant, looking for the rear exit. He finds it and makes sure he can open it.

He returns to his table and decides not to rush his meal. He continues to eat slowly and sip his beer. He will not allow himself to be anxious, rushed, or intimidated.

Rigney considers what he will do if Rouché attacks him. All the factors tell Rigney that he should not engage in a fistfight with Rouché. Rigney knows that even if he were to come out on top of the fight, he could still be hurt bad enough to put his mission out of business. His ONI training taught him what to do if attacked by Python or his associates. The training never covered what to do if attacked by someone else. *Rouché is not alone. He has two of his gang with him.*

Rigney knows what Brad Watson would advise. *Don't give any of them a second chance to disable or kill you. Put them down—permanently!* Rigney doubts that he has the will to point a gun at another human being and pull the trigger. *So why did I bring a gun with me?*

When he finishes his meal, Rigney conducts a final scan of the street through the restaurant window. He does not see Rouché or any of Rouché's groupies.

As he exits the Restaurant, he immediately looks up and down the street to see if Rouché is around. He does not see him. The dark of night approaches and the temperature is dropping. He raises the collar of his peacoat to protect his neck from the chill. He walks away from the restaurant in the opposite direction from where he last saw Rouché walking.

He continually scans all directions. Not only does he need to stay away from Rouché, he needs to find John Smith. Several times, he stops at a small café and has a cup of coffee. By 7:30, he gives up on trying to find John Smith. The night makes it too difficult. *He'll just have to find me.*

Rigney enters a café. The café is half-full of people, mostly civilian tourists. Only four sailors sit in the café. Rigney does not recognize any of them. He decides to sit for a while and have a beer before returning to the ship. He finds an empty booth in the back corner farthest from the door. He rolls his white hat and sticks it in his peacoat pocket. He unbuttons his peacoat but does not remove it because he plans to be in the café for only the time it takes to drink one beer.

The booth is dark. He can see the front door, but those entering through the front door should not be able to see him. He orders a San Miguel and asks the waiter where he can find the bathroom. The waiter points behind Rigney to the rear of the bar.

Rigney glances toward the direction the waiter points. He sees the sign to the water closet. The rear exit is ten feet beyond the water closet. Rigney goes to the water closet and relieves himself. After that, he checks to ensure that he can open the rear exit door. The door opens easily.

As he walks back toward his booth, a sexy looking woman tourist passes him on her way to the toilet. She gives Rigney a big smile, which Rigney returns. Instead of scanning the café as he returns to his booth, Rigney stares after the woman.

His beer is on the table. He sits, grabs the beer, and lifts the bottle to his lips. Not until he puts the bottle to his lips, does he look toward to the front area of the café. Then, he sees them.

Rouché and his two friends stand twenty feet away. All three show a satisfied, smiling sneer on their faces.

Rouché stares past Rigney toward the rear exit. He speaks some words to one of his friends and the friend departs through the front door.

Rigney cannot hear what Rouché said. He speculates that Rouché sent his friend to find the radiomen groupies.

Rouché and his other friend continue to exchange words. They continue to look at Rigney while they sneer and chuckle arrogantly.

463

Rigney puts his hands in his lap. From where Rouché and his friend stand, they can only see Rigney from his mid torso up. Rigney wants his hands hidden in case he needs to get the Beretta into his right hand.

Rouché puts his hand into his peacoat right side pocket. He pulls a closed switchblade three-quarters of the way out of his pocket.

Rigney wonders what they are waiting for. *Is Rouché waiting for a Columbus audience?* Rigney watches while Rouché reaches into his pocket and exposes the switchblade. Rig has never seen a real switchblade, only the ones he saw in the movies. Rigney has no doubt that Rouché showed a switchblade.

Rigney raises his right leg up until it hits the underside of the table. He pulls the Beretta from the holster and sets the pistol on his lap. Then, he removes the suppressor from its pocket in the holster. He holds the Beretta with his left hand while he screws on the suppressor with his right hand. All this he does under the table without looking. *Hats off to my ONI training!* Faking that he is looking for his white hat, he sticks the Beretta into the right side pocket of his peacoat.

"What's he doin'?" Rouché's comrade asks.

"Shittin' his pants, probably," Rouché responds confidently.

Rigney considers, *Rouché must be waiting for me to leave or he is waiting for his audience. If I go out the front door, I must walk by him. What will he do when I walk past him? Jump me and claim I attacked him.*

What do I do if they come toward me? I can't pull out the Beretta and start shooting. I can't pull the trigger if I don't feel a deadly threat, and I don't feel that threat.

I will never get away with shooting them in here, too many witnesses. I could miss and hit innocent people. If I do shoot, will ONI protect me from prosecution? I must shoot if they attack me. Rouché showed his intentions when he flashed the switchblade. Well, I am not going to give him the chance.

Rigney jumps from the booth and runs for the rear exit.

Rouché's friend jumps forward to start running after Rigney. Rouché throws his forearm in front of his friend and says softly, "We don't want to attract any attention. Jack will stop Page out there."

Rigney slams through the rear door and bursts into an alley. He starts to run to the left where he sees the main street. He stops when he sees Rouché's friend running toward him. *Damn! I should have realized that Rouché sent his friend to guard the rear exit!* He turns and runs in the other direction. The alley turns ninety degrees to the right. Just after he makes the turn, he sees that the alley is a dead-end fifty feet away. He hears Rouché say loudly, "Where is he?"

"He ran down there!" reports an excited voice.

Rigney hears running feet. He starts to panic. His heart pounds rapidly in his chest. He begins to sweat. He fights for breath. He steps behind a stack of wooden crates at the end of the alley. He attempts to regain control of himself. *Relax. I know what I must do. I must let my ONI training direct me to take care of this situation.*

"It's a dead end," says a voice.

"Okay. Slow down. Don't let him get past us," Rouché orders.

Rigney hears the footsteps coming closer. *I must do this, and I must do it calmly and confidently. Damn it, John Smith, where are you?!*

The footsteps stop.

"Hey Rig-ass!" Rouché hisses. "Come on out here. We know you're behind those boxes."

Using his right hand, Rigney pulls the Beretta from his peacoat pocket. He flips off the thumb safety and cocks the hammer. He holds the pistol down and toward his back. He does not want them to see the pistol. Once they see the pistol, Rigney knows he must use it. *There will be no second chance once they see the gun.*

Rigney steps from behind the stacked boxes and faces them.

The alley is adequately illuminated. Rigney sees them well enough. All three have their right hands in their peacoat pocket.

At the same time, they pull weapons from their pockets. Rouché and the sailor on Rouché's right flip open six-inch switchblades. The sailor on Rouché's left snaps his hand forward and the object in his hand extends out to two feet. It looks like a telescoping metal rod.

"Okay, Rig-ass! It's payback time!" Rouché snarls. "We ain't gonna kill ya. We're just going to cut you up some and give you some bruises. Don't fight it because we could make a mistake. If you tell anyone who did this to you, we will finish the job. Understand!"

Rigney extends his left hand with palm facing them as a motion for them to stop. "Please don't do this, Rouché!" Rigney pleads. "Please just go away and leave me alone!"

"No way Rig-ass. Your beggin' ain't gonna save you. You're not so tough, now. Are you? You don't fuck with me and get away with it!" Rouché's voice is cold and fearless.

Rouché and his two comrades start walking toward Rigney.

Rigney evaluates that Rouché and the other guy with a switchblade are the most threatening. *Rouché first then the other guy with a switchblade then the guy with the rod.*

Rigney brings up his right arm fully extended with the Beretta aimed toward Rouché. He brings up his left arm extended and steadies his gun hand in the palm of his left hand.

Rouché and his friends stop dead in their tracks, incredulous. They never expect their prey to be armed.

Rigney lines up the front and rear sights of the pistol on the middle of Rouché's chest and fires one round. Before Rouché falls, Rigney shifts his angle of fire to the left, lines up the sights, and fires a round into the chest of his second target. Rigney shifts to the right. The sailor with the metal rod runs away. Rigney takes careful aim and fires two rounds into back of the running sailor. The sailor falls forward on his face.

He put down all three in less than six seconds.

Rigney stares at the three men who lie dead on the alley's surface. He feels exited. He feels satisfied. He does not feel guilt or remorse.

Then, he listens carefully for any sign that anyone else is around. The sound of each shot had been no louder than a light slap, thanks to the suppressor. The most audible sounds were the mechanical noises of the ejected 9mm casings hitting the pavement. He hears no one.

As he ponders what to do next, Rigney hears one of his victims moan. His ONI training was clear about what to do next. He walks over to Rouché, aims, and fires two rounds into Rouché's head. He turns to his second victim, aims at the victim's head, and fires two rounds. He walks the short distance to the third man. He aims at the man's head and fires two rounds.

He turns and starts walking, half running, out of alley. He stops as a thought occurs to him. He goes back to the bodies and takes their wallets and he takes their I.D. cards. He had read in Navy Times that stolen U.S. military I.D. cards are sold in black markets around the world. He also takes their watches and rings.

Rigney knows his three victims will be identified by the stenciling on the inside of their uniforms and by the ship's name patch on the upper sleeve of their uniforms. He formulates a plan to dump their I.D. cards and valuables into the sea while *Columbus* transits to Naples.

He turns and walks slowly to where the alley makes the ninety-degree turn toward the street. With himself butted up against the corner of the wall, he sticks his head beyond the corner of the building and scans the alley from his position to the street. He sees no one in the alley. A wave of people walks across the alley's entrance on the street. No one glances into the alley.

Rig looks back at the three bodies on the ground. Their weapons and white hats are scattered about. They are hidden by the right angle turn in the alley.

He looks down at the Beretta. The slide is back all the way, indicating an empty ammo magazine. He holds the slide, releases the catch, and guides the slide shut. Then, he unscrews the suppressor. He bends down and puts both the suppressor and the pistol back in the holster. Then, he snaps shut all pouch covers. He pulls his sock over the holster.

He stands upright and buttons his peacoat. He pulls his white hat from his peacoat pocket, unrolls it, and pulls it down tight on his head.

Rigney exits the alley and merges with the crowd on the street. Two unoccupied taxis sit a short distance from the alley's entrance. He looks at his watch—8:03 p.m. *I must get back to ship and hide the pistol before the bodies are found.*

He considers taking one of the taxis then rejects the idea. This close to the alley, a taxi driver may later remember his passenger when questioned by police. Rigney passes many unoccupied taxis. The demand for taxis is low at this early hour. The high demand for taxis will come between 11:30 p.m. and midnight when sailors rush back to the ship to beat the Cinderella Liberty deadline.

Four blocks from the alley, Rigney climbs into the backseat of a taxi. He keeps his head lowered. "Fleet landing," he tells the taxi driver. The taxi speeds out of the Sa Llonja district.

As he walks along the pier toward the gangway, he searches for recognition of any of the sailors he passes. Rigney does not recognize any of them, and none of the sailors pays attention to him. He gets behind a line of sailors going up the gangway. Additional sailors fall in line behind him. Some of the sailors are drunk and talking loudly.

When he arrives at the top of the gangway, he salutes the chief and requests permission to come aboard. After permission is granted and he steps onto the Main Deck, he shows his I.D. card and Liberty Card. He also does not recognize the chief or petty officer standing the gangway watch. No record is kept of ship's company personnel as they come and go for liberty. Rigney does not believe that the chief or petty officer will identify him as a sailor that came aboard during their watch.

As he enters the berthing compartment, he observes only a few radiomen asleep in their racks. No one moves about the deck. He opens his rack-locker and pulls out his dungarees. He scans the compartment to ensure no one watches him. With the ankle holster still strapped to his leg, he quickly changes into dungarees. He needs to hide the weapon, wallets, I.D. cards, and jewelry as soon as possible. He puts on his foul weather jacket and ball cap and walks toward the ladder. He stops when he realizes that the compartment will be searched thoroughly after Rouché's death becomes known. Investigators will search for anything that will give them a lead.

He goes to the head, steps up on the toilet, opens the panel to the air conditioning duct, and retrieves the leather bag. He tucks the leather bag inside his foul weather jacket and under his arm.

After stepping through the hatch onto the Main Deck, he turns and dogs the hatch behind him. He walks quickly toward the ladder to the ASROC deck.

"Stand fast, Page!"

Rigney stops and turns. Master-at-Arms Genoa walks toward Rigney and stops two feet away.

Genoa growls, "Page, why are you out of uniform?"

Rigney does not understand the question. He wears his dungaree uniform.

"I don't understand what you mean."

"Fuckin' twidget! You radiomen are so unmilitary! You don't know nothin' 'bout ship's routine!"

Rigney still does not understand and shrugs his shoulders. "Please explain, Genoa. I really don't understand what you mean."

"In port, you must be in the Uniform of the Day after 1800. That would be Undress Blue for you. You're in dungarees. I have to write you a speedin' ticket."

"A speeding ticket . . . what's that?"

"Christ sakes! Where you fuckin' been boot camp! It's like putting you on report, only you don't go to captain's mast. You just do some EMI as specified by the executive officer."

Rigney shakes his head slightly and exhibits bewilderment. "I must apologize for my lack of knowledge regarding these things. This is my first ship. So, I must also ask you: What is EMI?" Rigney attempts to sound apologetic.

"Extra Military Instruction you fool!" Genoa expresses he is about to burst with anger and frustration.

Rigney decides not to ask any more questions.

Genoa starts writing on a pad of preprinted forms. Then, he orders, "Let me see your I.D. card."

"It's in my locker," Rigney advises.

Genoa drops his hands to his sides and shakes his head in disbelief. He gives Rigney one of those *you are hopeless* stares.

"Alright, I won't even talk to you about it. I'll just write you another speedin' ticket for not havin' your I.D. card. I'll look up your service number in the Personnel Office."

"Oh. My service number is—"

"Don't bother," Genoa interrupts. "I can't take your word for it."

Genoa continues to write on the pad.

Rigney contemplates how strange all this is. *BM1 Genoa is a master-at-arms—a ship's policeman. I killed three people tonight. I have their I.D. cards, wallets, and jewelry in my pocket. I stand before Genoa with two deadly weapons hidden in my clothes, and he is writing me up for being out of uniform and not having my I.D. card.* Rigney chuckles.

Genoa snaps his head up and snorts, "What's so fuckin' funny?"

"Sorry. It's not funny. I just think how odd it is that every time we meet, you're chewing my ass for something."

Genoa responds by trying to sound like a marine drill instructor. "That's right sailor. And if you don't square away soon, you ain't gonna have any ass left."

Rigney suppresses a laugh. He does not want to enrage Genoa any further.

Genoa hands Rigney two slips of paper, which are carbon copies of the speeding tickets.

"Your division officer will tell you when and where to report for EMI." Genoa stomps off muttering about *unmilitary pussy-ass twidgets.*

Rigney moves quickly up the ladder and across the ASROC deck. He climbs the ladders on the port side of the superstructure to the 04 Level. He steps inside the hatch and dogs the hatch behind him. He now stands in front of the fan room hatch. He listens for anyone moving about. With half the crew on liberty and fewer watches being stood, there is much less chance of people moving about on the 04 Level.

Rigney hears no one.

He opens the fan room hatch, steps in, and dogs the hatch behind him. He stuffs the I.D. cards, jewelry, and currency into one of the leather bags. He unbuckles the holster straps around his leg. He stuffs the holster into the leather bag. He stows both leather bags into the overhead air conditioning duct.

After exiting the fan room, he climbs the ladders to the 06 Level and enters MAIN COMM. The only sounds he hears is one fleet broadcast teletype clacking away and the steady hum of ventilation fans and equipment fans. He enters the Fleet Broadcast Room to chat with Larry Johnson.

"Hey, Rig, back from liberty so soon? It's early."

Exhibiting nonchalance in his response, Rigney says, "Yeah. I had a good meal, saw the sights, and stopped at a few bars. I wish I had more time to tour the whole island. I would like to engulf myself into the culture."

"Rig, with our watch schedule the extent of the culture you'll have time to *engulf* is the best looking whore in the best whorehouse in town.

Well, that satisfies most swabbies, anyway."

Rigney chuckles lightly and nods his head in understanding.

"You didn't see Rouché, then?"

"Nope. Never saw him." Rigney lies. "Never saw any of the radiomen."

Larry offers, "In Naples, we'll hit the beach together. I'll show you the Naples Gut."

"I'll look forward to it," Rigney replies sincerely. "Well, think I will hit the rack. I think had one drink too many."

"Yeah, right!" Larry says doubtfully. He wonders why Rigney exaggerates how much he had to drink. Larry knows that Rigney purposely exercises self-control to ensure he never over consumes anything.

Chapter 97

Rigney cannot sleep. Uncertain as to how he will react to the inevitable questioning, his thoughts jump from one answer to the other as he formulates the possible questions. At first, he considers lying about the time he returned to the ship—like around 7:30 p.m. Anyone who knows him could have seen him from a distance as he walked the streets looking for a taxi and when he returned to the ship.

He finally settles on telling the truth about being in *Sa Llonja* and the times he was there and the time he got back to the ship. *I was back on the ship around 9:00 p.m. No, I don't remember if I was on the street or in a bar at 8:00 p.m. No, I do not remember the name of the cafés or bars. No, I never saw Rouché. I do not know Rouché's friends. No, I never saw anyone who can substantiate where I was and when.*

His eyes open wide as a revelation hits him. *Oh, shit! There must be burnt gunpowder residue on my clothes—maybe blood too!*

Rigney looks at his watch—0245. He climbs out of his rack and opens the lid to his rack-locker. He pulls out the Service Dress Blue gabardines and peacoat that he wore to Sa Llonja. He also pulls out his shoes. He pulls the sleeves of his jumper and peacoat to his nose. The smell of burnt gunpowder is unmistakable.

He takes his shoes and uniform items to the head. He inspects the shoes, including the bottom of the soles. He sees no blood. He decides to clean them, anyway. He opens the gear locker in the corner of the head. He pulls out a can of scouring powder and a scrub brush. He thoroughly cleans the shoes. He retrieves his shoeshine kit from his locker and spends fifteen minutes reapplying the spit shine.

He inspects every inch of clothing. He sees no blood. He pulls the various pieces of clothing to his face and sniffs. Only around the sleeves does he smell gunpowder. Using liquid soap and cold water, he washes the sleeves of his gabardines and of his peacoat. Afterwards, he wrings them dry.

He removes the ironing board and iron from the gear locker. While ironing the sleeves of his gabardines, RM1 Dukes enters the head. Dukes nods in Rigney's direction.

"Good morning," Rigney says cheerfully.

"Ga'morning," Dukes replies sleepily as he walks toward the urinal.

As he stands at the urinal, Dukes watches Rigney iron. When he finishes, he flushes the urinal and washes his hands.

Dukes starts to leave, then turns and asks, "You're not going on liberty today. right? Aren't you in the duty section startin' at 0800?"

"I'm just squaring away my uniforms," Rigney responds. "Master-at-Arms Genoa issued me speeding tickets last night for being out of uniform."

"Tell me what happened."

Rigney describes his encounter with Genoa.

"He's always doing that to the radiomen. Don't worry about it. I'll have the senior chief take care of it."

"Thanks!" Rigney responds appreciatively.

"No problem," Dukes responds. Then, he exits the head.

After he finishes the ironing, Rigney smells the sleeves of his gabardines and his peacoat. The gunpowder smell is gone.

He stows all the cleaning items, iron, and ironing board back into the gear locker.

He returns to his rack. He retrieves aftershave from his shaving kit and splashes some on the sleeves of his gabardines and peacoat. He stows his gabardines in his rack-locker and stows his peacoat in one of the peacoat lockers installed against the port bulkhead.

He goes back to the head. He shaves. Then, he showers and washes his hair. After drying off, he splashes aftershave into the palms of his hands and applies the aftershave to his face and neck. He does not wash the aftershave from his hands.

He climbs back into his rack and looks at his watch—0408. He closes his eyes, but he only sleeps in short naps. His mind continues to thread through all the possible scenarios that can occur after Rouché and his friends are found. One of the more disturbing scenarios that he visualizes is police officers leading him off the ship in handcuffs.

"NOW REVEILLE! ALL HANDS HEAVE TO AND THRICE UP!"

"THE SMOKING LAMP IS LIT IN ALL AUTHORIZED SPACES. NOW REVEILLE!"

"SWEEPER! SWEEPERS! MAN YOUR BROOMS. GIVE THE SHIP A CLEAN SWEEP DOWN FORE AND AFT. NOW SWEEPERS!"

"TAKE ALL TRASH AND GARBAGE TO THE PIER."

Rigney awakes at the sound of reveille. He notices a few radiomen rolling out of their racks. He listens, waiting for someone to comment about Rouché's absence. After five minutes, no one has said anything.

472

He closes his eyes and attempts sleep, but the acrid smell of cigarette smoke fills his nostrils. His mind fills with possible scenarios. He knows that he cannot sleep.

After rolling out of his rack, he senses people staring at him. He looks to his left and sees three of his division mates shifting their stares between him and Rouché's rack. The three are some of those in Rouché's groupie entourage yesterday afternoon. The look on their faces say *thought you would be in sickbay licking your wounds by now.*

"What's up?" Rigney asks casually. He begins to dress.

"Not much," says one of them. "We're looking for Philippe. Have you seen him?"

Rigney glances at Rouché's rack; then, he looks at the group and replies, "No, I haven't seen him in a couple of days."

"His rack doesn't look slept in," observes another groupie.

Rigney glances at Rouché's rack again; then, he returns his look to the group, shrugs his shoulders, and says, "Maybe he went on liberty early this morning."

"I don't think so" another groupie responds. "Those two letters were on his mattress yesterday afternoon."

Rigney shrugs again and responds, "Beats me. I don't have the Rouché watch." Rigney turns away from the group and resumes dressing.

The three groupies walk off. Rigney hears one of them say, "You can't go on liberty until after 0800. Rouché must have stayed on the beach last night. He'll be put on report for that." Then, the three disappear up the ladder.

That went well, Rigney thinks to himself. *I established that I thought it possible that Rouché was in his rack last night.*

As Rigney passes down the galley steam line, a deep hunger growls in his stomach. He wants to eat more than normal. He orders a three-egg cheddar cheese, mushroom, and onion omelet. He piles some sausage patties and two cinnamon buns on his tray. Today, he ignores the apples and bananas.

As he exits the chow line, he sees a seat open at a table with all CR Division radiomen. The occupants include all the Rouché groupies from the previous afternoon.

This is not the time to avoid members of my division.

As he sets down his tray, the conversation at the table stops. Rigney goes to the coffee urn and draws a cup of coffee. He sits down at the table. The conversation starts back up. The sailors speculate about

473

Rouché's absence.

Rigney has eaten half his omelet and one sausage patty when Senior Chief Bulldoone comes up to the table.

Bulldoone orders, "I want all of you to report to the CR Berthing Compartment, immediately. Open the lids to your rack-lockers and stand by them. Stay there until I tell you to leave."

"What's up, Senior Chief?" a radioman asks.

Another radioman informs, "Some of us have the next watch."

Bulldoone responds, "I don't know what's up, and I have already told the watch that they will be relieved late. Go now! All of you!"

All eight sailors get up and take their trays to the scullery. They scrape the food off their trays into the garbage cans and toss their trays on the shelf of the scullery window. They proceed forward in single file along the port passageway. As they pass through the First Division berthing compartment, they see most of the First Division sailors standing by their racks with their rack-locker lids raised. They also see two armed marines standing guard in the compartment. A master-at-arms petty officer stands ready with a bolt cutter tool.

Rigney and his watch section file down the ladder into the CR Division berthing compartment. When Rigney arrives at the bottom of the ladder, he sees an armed marine and Master-at-Arms Genoa standing in the compartment. Genoa holds a bolt cutter tool in one hand and a large canvas bag in the other hand. Everyone in the division, except for Rouché and those on watch, are dressed and standing by their racks.

Rigney weaves his way through the others as he proceeds to his rack in the forward starboard corner. As he passes RM1 Dukes, Dukes asks Rigney if he has seen Rouché. Rigney shakes his head in the negative.

Rigney stoops, enters his lock combination, opens the lock, and props open the lid to his rack-locker. The odor of aftershave greets him.

A few of the radiomen grumble about snap inspections. A second class radioman, one of Rouché's groupies, complains that CR Division is exempt from ship's inspections. A few others vocally agree.

"Stow the bitching," Dukes orders.

"Hey, Dukes, doesn't Rouché have to stand this inspection?" another asks, more of a complaint than a question.

"Focus on your own situation," Dukes dictates.

Then, two uniformed Spanish policeman and a German Shepherd dog on a leash come down the ladder, followed by a middle aged Spanish gentleman in a light gray suit. The Spanish civilian has a policeman's badge hanging from his breast coat pocket.

Commander Remington, the *Columbus* Executive Officer, comes down the ladder. LTJG Rowing and Senior Chief Bulldoone are the last two down the ladder.

The radiomen become silent as they realize that this situation is more than a snap inspection.

BM1 Genoa orders, "Okay, twidgets. Stand fast at your racks. The police here are gonna have this dog sniff you and your racks."

One of the radioman comments humorously, "The dog will need a vet after that."

Several of the Radiomen chuckle.

"Quiet!" Genoa orders.

A policeman starts the dog at the aft end of the compartment. The policeman must lift the dog to the top racks. After ten minutes, the dog gets to Rigney, who is second from last to be sniffed. Both Rigney and his rack pass the sniff test.

When the sniffing is over, BM1 Genoa advises, "The policemen are now gonna search your racks. Give them your name when they ask."

The civilian policeman in the light gray suit turns and speaks to LTJG Rowing.

Rowing asks, "Dukes, which rack belonged to Rouché?"

The question causes a stir of whispers throughout the compartment, especially the use of the past tense '*belonged.*'

"Over here, sir, in the forward starboard corner."

The Spanish policeman in the gray suit directs one of the uniformed policemen to search Rouché's rack.

The policeman, Genoa, and the Executive Officer weave their way through the sailors and stop next to Rigney.

"Stand aside, Page," Genoa orders.

Rigney moves a few feet and stands against the forward bulkhead.

Genoa places the cutting edges of the bolt cutter around the elbow of Rouché's combination lock and severs it. Genoa removes the destroyed lock, lifts the lid of the rack-locker, and lifts the holding rod to keep the lid raised.

Rigney clearly views the interior of Rouché's rack. He watches with interest the policeman's methodical search procedure. Rigney is not surprised when the policeman discovers brass knuckles, a large hunting knife in a sheath, and one of those heavy expanding metal batons.

The policeman passes all three weapons to Genoa.

Genoa pulls some twist wire identification tags from his pocket. He twists a tag onto each item. Using an indelible fine tipped marker, Genoa writes identifying information on each tag; then, he hands the marker to the Executive Officer. The XO signs his name on each tag.

The policeman searches Rigney's rack; nothing is found. They move to the next rack. The rack search takes an hour. The only other items of interest found are bags of marijuana in two racks.

The Executive Officer orders, "Mister Rowing, have the Medical Department verify that those two bags contain marijuana. When you have the verification, place those two men on report for possession. Bring the report chit to me, and I will sign as a witness. Have Genoa sign as a witness also."

"Aye, aye, sir," Rowing responds.

Senior Chief Bulldoone orders, "Lower your rack lids and lock your lockers. Those who should be on watch, go relieve the watch. Remind the person that you relieve that they are to come directly to the compartment. The rest of you are to muster with Dukes on the ASROC deck and stay there until I or Mister Rowing say it is okay to secure."

Rigney closes his rack-locker lid and snaps the combination lock shut. He proceeds to MAIN COMM to relieve Larry Johnson.

"You must go directly to the berthing compartment after I relieve you," Rigney tells Larry Johnson.

"What's going on?"

"I don't know for sure. I think it has something to do with Rouché. The Spanish police are searching all the racks in the compartment . . . and in First Division compartment, I think."

"Why do you think it has something to do with Rouché?" Larry queries.

"Doesn't look like Rouché slept in his rack last night. Mister Rowing asked which rack *belonged* to Rouché, not which one *belongs* to Rouché. And Rouché's rack was the only one they searched of those who weren't in the compartment. They cut off the lock. I saw the policeman pull out a large hunting knife and brass knuckles."

"Sounds like Rouché," Larry responds. "I wonder what kind of trouble he's gotten himself into now."

"Probably something really serious."

"Rig, do you relieve me?"

"Yes, I relieve you."

"I stand relieved."

Three hours later, RM2 Carter walks into the Fleet Broadcast Room and tells Rigney, "I'm relieving you for chow."

Rigney glances at his watch—1205. His stomach growls with hunger. Rigney asks Carter, "Have you heard anything as to why we had the locker search this morning?"

476

"Lots of rumors. I just came from the mess decks. I've heard everything from Rouché has been murdered by the Spanish Mafia to Rouché murdered the local Mafia leader and is in jail. Sailors who don't know Rouché are claiming lifelong friendships. Rumors are rampant that the Spanish Government will not let us leave port, and the Spanish Navy has blockaded the harbor to make sure that we don't."

"Do you believe any of it," Rigney asks.

"I've been in this outfit too long to believe anything I hear, and I don't believe anything I see until it's verified by two other people."

Rigney chuckles and nods his understanding.

Rigney moves quickly down the ladders and passageways. He bypasses those standing in line for chow and reports directly to the mess decks master-at-arms who stands at the beginning of the steam line.

"Hey, Gunner. I am on watch relief in MAIN COMM."

The first class gunners mate recognizes Rigney as a member of CR Division and lets him pass to the steam line.

Rigney loads his tray with sliced roast pork and fresh sliced tomatoes and sliced cucumbers. He spots Larry Johnson and a couple of radiomen at a table in the starboard mess deck. Rigney takes a seat across from Larry.

"Hey, Rig, it's official! Rouché and members of his gang were killed in a shootout with Spanish mobsters. And during the rack search, everything from switchblades to sniper rifles to hand grenades were found." Larry laughs and shakes his head at such ridiculous scuttlebutt.

"Seriously, Larry, have you heard anything that may be truthful? I've been stuck on watch for the past three hours."

"The only thing I know for sure is that no one has seen Rouché today. Anyway, the truth will be in the messages that the CO sends to COMSIXTHFLT. Read those messages and you will know what the captain knows."

Rigney and Larry engage in casual conversation for the rest of their meal. Between words with Larry, the image of being led off the ship in handcuffs flashes through his mind.

Larry asks, "Rig, did ya see the new watch bill?"

"Yeah, I lucked out. I get off watch at 1700 and don't have another watch until tomorrow morning at 0700, just before we get underway."

"If we get underway," Larry says pessimistically.

"You think we won't?"

Larry shrugs.

477

Chapter 98

During the afternoon watch, a number of messages regarding Rouché are transmitted and received. Rigney scrutinizes each message for any detail that could lead to him.

The first message reports that three *Columbus* sailors were found shot to death in an alley in the Sa Llonja area of Palma de Mallorca. The name, rank, and service numbers of Rouché and his two associates are listed. The message further states that the bodies were discovered around 1:00 a.m. by a young German couple that were looking for some privacy. Ten 9mm casings were recovered at the crime scene. The Spanish police suspect robbery as the motive because the victims' I.D. cards and valuables are missing. The message also reports that although the Spanish police suspect the local criminal element to be responsible, a complete search of the CR Division and First Division spaces were conducted. No 9mm pistols were found. The police did specify an irregularity. Each of the dead sailors had a weapon beside their body. Two of them had switchblades and one had an expandable metal baton. The police have not yet determined if the sailors drew the weapons in defense, or if they initiated an attack on a person who had a gun. The last paragraph of the message advises that the police will forward to the American Consulate the results of the autopsies and ballistics tests.

Another message reports that the Spanish police requested *Columbus* stay in port so they can continue their investigation. The Spanish police want to continue interviewing *Columbus* crewmembers and continue their search for a 9mm pistol. Captain Saunders denied the request because of ship's operational commitments. However, Captain Saunders invited the Spanish police to ride the *Columbus* to Naples. The Spanish police accepted the invitation. The message also requests that NIS agents be dispatched to *Columbus* to assist the Spanish police with their interviews and to ensure that the U.S. Navy part of the investigation is properly performed.

Rigney becomes concerned. *Someone is sure to mention that there was conflict between Rouché and me. I must stick to my story. I must be casual and confident. I must concentrate on looking into their eyes when they ask me questions and when I provide answers.*

Rigney frets about the police and NIS having ten full days to search the ship for the 9mm pistol. He wonders what the odds are of them finding his weapons in the 04 Level fan room. He cannot throw them overboard because Brad will later ask for them. Disposal of the weapons would be an admission of guilt to ONI that he was the killer.

Additionally, his ONI training taught him *never perform any actions that prevent access to your own weapons.* Brad Watson had said that you never know when you will need them. At the time, Rigney had thought he would never need them. He thinks of relocating the weapons. *But what location would be safer than any other location? There must by tens of thousands of nooks and crannies onboard. Only luck will get them to the 04 level. And even if they did, they still might not find them. And what if they did find them, the only way to connect me is by my fingerprints.*

Because the police are coming aboard tomorrow morning, Rigney decides that he must dispose of the I.D. cards, wallets, and jewelry tonight. He will wipe the Berettas clean of fingerprints at the same time.

Forty-five minutes prior to Rigney's scheduled watch relief time, a message comes over the fleet broadcast from the NIS office in Naples. Two agents will be dispatched. They will fly out of the Naval Air Facility at Capodichino to the USS *Shangri-La*. The *Shangri-La* will helicopter the agents to *Columbus*.

Rigney notices that *Office of Naval Intelligence, Suitland, Maryland* is an Information Addressee on each message.

I wonder what Brad will think of all this. I wonder if he will know I did it. There must a good reason why John Smith never contacted me.

Rigney decides to check the ONI Radio Broadcast for any messages addressed to him. The duty Technical Controller, RM1 Dukes, is not standing a scheduled watch. Rigney has the Technical Control Room to himself. He grabs an earphone set and patches a high-frequency antenna to a R-1051 radio receiver. He maneuvers the earphone set so that the foam cushioned speakers fit firmly around his ears. He searches for the best quality ONI Broadcast frequency. He finds the best frequency in the 27 megahertz range. He listens carefully for several minutes to the recorded voice of the ONI broadcaster. Then, he hears his codename. He writes down the message.

Rigney translates the codes in his mind. ONI wants a report on Rigney's best guess as to the identity of Python. The ONI message also states he is to make the report via radio.

The only way he can make a radio report is to go down to the Radio II compartment on the Main Deck where all the high-frequency transceivers are located. Radio II is not manned while in Port. The on-call Technical Controller makes all required transmitter changes. The Leading Petty Officer, RM1 Dukes, has the keys. Fortunately, Radio II is equipped with several URC-32 transceivers. Rigney had extensive URC-32 training in Submarine Radioman School, and it is the same transceiver taught in the ONI Field Communications course.

But first, I must get into Bollier's Teletype Repair Shop and see what I can find.

RM2 Rosen relieves Rigney at 1715. Rigney exits MAIN COMM through the forward door. Just outside the door and to the port side, a ladder leads down to the 05-Level. Rigney looks down the ladder. Then, he looks across the passageway at the closed door to Radio Central. Then, he looks to starboard at the closed door to the Signal Flag Locker. He sees no one and hears no one. He quietly descends the ladder to the 05 Level.

The door to the Teletype Repair Shop is under the ladder. Rigney tries the doorknob. The door is locked. He looks around for a place where Bollier might have hidden a key. Hundreds of nooks and crannies exist for hiding a key. Rigney searches for ten minutes. He finds nothing. He hears voices coming closer. He scurries down the ladder to the 04 Level.

Rigney understands that whatever he does, he must do it tonight. He cannot wait until tomorrow morning because there will be too many people up and about preparing the ship to get underway. *I will wait until after midnight. I will break into the Teletype Repair Shop and Radio II, if I must!*

Chapter 99

At 2345, Rigney lies in his rack. His reading lamp is off. Other light sources allow him to see most of the starboard side of the CR Division berthing compartment. Dukes sleeps soundly. Rigney sees the keys to Radio II hang from a belt loop on Dukes's dungaree trousers, which hang on Dukes's rack frame. *One problem solved.*

Rigney fights sleep. He knows that he must wait until after midnight to do anything. He considers ways in which he can break into the Teletype Repair Shop.

Then, opportunity presents itself. RM1 Bollier, back from liberty, stumbles drunkenly toward his rack. He switches on his reading lamp. He works the combination lock to his rack-locker. After four attempts, he gets the combination right. He lifts the lid to his rack-locker and props the lid open.

Rigney can see Bollier clearly.

Bollier fumbles with removing his uniform. He leans against his rack frame to keep his balance. He clumsily folds his uniform and puts it in his rack-locker. He grabs his shaving kit and a towel and goes to the head. Going to the head with his shaving kit means that Bollier will be in there for a while.

Bollier left his rack-locker open!

Rigney rolls out of his bottom rack and furtively moves toward Bollier's rack. He checks each rack that he passes to ensure the occupant is asleep. He is confident that no one sees him. Bollier has a center rack. As Rigney approaches Bollier's rack, he can identify the contents. Bollier's keys lie in the center of the rack-locker. Rigney grabs the keys, dashes back to his own rack, and rolls in.

Fifteen minutes later, Bollier returns to his rack. He puts his shaving kit in the rack-locker and closes lid. Then, he climbs into his rack and turns out the reading lamp. Bollier is asleep within minutes.

Rigney waits for another hour. No one moves about in the berthing compartment. He quietly slides out of his rack and dresses in his Undress Blues and white hat. *I don't want Genoa stopping me tonight.*

As he walks past Dukes's rack, he removes the Radio II keys from Dukes's belt.

He encounters no one during his journey through the ship, across the weather decks, and up into the superstructure.

He enters the 04 Level fan room and retrieves the two leather bags from the air duct. He dumps the contents of both bags onto the deck. He removes all weapons components from their holster, then ejects the ammo magazines from both Berettas. He takes two handkerchiefs from his back pocket. Using the handkerchiefs as gloves, he wipes down all weapon components to remove fingerprints. After that, he runs the handkerchiefs over the leather bags and leather wallets.

Continuing to use the handkerchiefs as gloves, Rigney loads full magazines into the Berettas. He pulls back and releases the slide of each weapon, which causes a round to be chamber. He holsters all the weapon components and inserts each holster into their respective leather bags.

He picks up the three I.D. cards and puts them in his pocket.

He spreads out one of the handkerchiefs flat on the deck. He places the three watches, wallets, and two rings in the center of the handkerchief. He ties the opposite corners together to form a bag. He sticks the handkerchief bag into his pocket.

He stuffs the leather bags back into the air duct.

After leaving the fan room, Rigney goes down the ladders to the Main Deck, port side. He walks slowly along the rail and stops facing the water. He looks forward and aft to ensure no one is near. He pulls the handkerchief with the jewelry and wallets from his pocket. He bends down as if tying his shoe. He makes one final look forward and aft, puts his hand under the bottom rail chain, and releases the handkerchief bag. He hears a barely audible splash.

Rigney climbs the ladders to the 06 Level. He enters Radio Central and steps quickly to the table-mounted paper shredder. Radiomen use this crosscut shredder each day to destroy the previous crypto-day keycards and codes. The crosscut shredder reduces paper to one-eighth-inch wide by one-half-inch-long unrecognizable shreds. After passing through the blades, the shred drops through a hole in the tabletop and into a burn bag. After being shredded, the material is considered unclassified and may be disposed of as trash.

Rigney flips the power switch. The shredder comes to life, making a humming noise as the blades mesh and rotate. Rigney removes the three I.D. cards from his pocket and feeds them through the shredder. The shredder utters crunching noises as the blades cut through the laminated I.D. cards.

He pulls the burn bag from under the table and scoops up a handful of the shred residue. The residue gives no indication that it contains shredded I.D. cards.

He departs Radio Central and walks down the ladders to the 05 Level. He stops in front of the Teletype Repair Shop door and listens for anyone who may be about. He hears no one. The shop door unlocks with the fourth key he tries. The overhead lights are on and the shop is well lit. He steps inside and locks the door behind him.

He visited the Teletype Repair Shop only once before. The shop looks like it did the previous time. The space measures eighteen feet long fore-to-aft by ten feet wide port-to-starboard. The space smells of machine oil and stale cigarette smoke. All the bulkheads are painted a light gray. Oil stained, gray-colored rubber mats cover the deck. Cigarette ashes lie everywhere about the shelves and the deck.

Rigney slowly walks the length of the shop. His eyes make a quick scan of all objects. The overhead is a maze of cables, conduits, and pipes. Parts bins and a teletype gunk tank stand against the port bulkhead. Bookcases, over-stuffed with teletype and UCC-1 technical manuals, stand along the forward end of the starboard bulkhead. The remainder of the starboard bulkhead contains tool drawers and test equipment storage racks. As he walks down the center of the shop, he touches some items on the shelves, hoping that if the object has a secret that secret will be revealed.

A large workbench extends the width of the aft bulkhead. A swivel stool with a large cushioned seat stands in front of the workbench. Bollier's two Heath Kit tape player-recorders sit on the left side of the workbench. The player-recorders stand upright, not on their backs. Two stereo quality speakers are mounted near the overhead above the workbench. Wires between the tape player-recorders and the speakers loop and interweave with the ship's cabling into the overhead above the workbench.

An oscilloscope, a multimeter, and a distortion analyzer sit along the backside of the workbench. A soldering kit sits on the right side of the workbench.

Rigney closes the distance to the workbench. He sits on the swivel stool. Bits of wire, solder droppings, and cigarette ashes litter the workbench tabletop. An ashtray overflowing with ashes and cigarette butts sits in the middle of the workbench. He pushes the ashtray to the far left of the workbench tabletop. He slowly swivels 360 degrees and scans the contents of the shop.

What am I looking for? Will I know it when I see it? Well, I guess I will look at everything. Brad Watson always emphasized to look for something unusual, even if it does not seem related.

A teletype printer sits on a bulkhead-mounted shelf two feet above the left end of the workbench. A black teletype patch panel mounts to the bulkhead next to the shelf. One patch panel jack is labeled PRINTER.

He focuses his attention on the two tape player-recorders. The tape reels on both player-recorders are turning. The selector switch on both player-recorders point to PLAY. He notices the speaker wires plugged into the speaker jack on both player-recorders, but he does not hear music coming from the speakers. One at a time, he turns the volume control fully clockwise on each player-recorder, but no sounds come from the speakers.

Rigney stops the reels on both player-recorders. He reads the sticky labels. The reel label on one player-recorder reads yesterday's date and in large letters next to the date is written *B-2 of 2*. On the other player-recorder, the reel label reads *T-1 of 1* and yesterday's date. Rigney flips the PLAY switch and the reels are turning again.

He swivels on the stool and looks for more tape reels. A large drawer mounts to the underside of the workbench tabletop on the right hand side. He tugs on the handle and discovers it locked. He tries a number of keys from Bollier's key ring. The sixth key he tries unlocks the drawer. Dozens of reels stand in neatly aligned rows inside several shoeboxes. He pulls out a few reels from the nearest shoebox. The reels are labeled with the names of classical composers such as *Bach*, *Haydn*, and *Vivaldi*. Rigney puts the reels back as they were. He reaches into the other shoebox and pulls out four reels. They are all labeled like the reels on the player-recorders. Only the dates are different.

He removes both shoeboxes from the drawer and sets them on the workbench.

He looks deeper into the drawer and sees a small wooden box that is the size of a cigar box. He pulls the box out of the drawer and sets it on the workbench tabletop. He opens the lid and jerks with surprise at what he sees. A small automatic pistol and a box of ammunition lie in the box. The safety is off. He carefully lifts the automatic out of the box. He ejects the magazine, which appears fully loaded. He pulls back the slide and a small caliber round ejects. Rigney closely inspects the firearm. He estimates the weapon to be .25 caliber. The manufacturer and serial number are filed off.

Rigney places the automatic on the workbench. He stares at the pistol while considering the ramifications. *Radioman First Class Thomas Bollier are you Python. This gun sure makes you look like Python.*

The weapon is a threat to him. *I need to throw it over the side. No. Wait! If Bollier notices that it's missing, he will know someone is onto him. I will disable it.*

He checks some of the tool drawers and finds a heavy file. He disassembles the slide mechanism. He files down the firing pin. He reassembles the slide mechanism. Then, he reloads the automatic.

I must test fire it. I cannot be sure otherwise.

He searches around the shop and finds a metal wastepaper can. He searches for clean rags and finds some in a parts bin. He stuffs the rags tight into the bottom half of the wastepaper can. With the wastepaper can sitting in the middle of the floor, Rigney leans over and pushes the barrel of the gun against the top of the rags.

Even if it fires, the sound of the shot will be muffled.

He pulls the trigger. The automatic does not fire.

Satisfied, he stows the gun the same way he found it. He places the shoeboxes full of tape reels back into the drawer—the same way he found them. He stores the rags back into the same bin that he found them. He puts the wastepaper can back to where he found it.

He returns to the workbench and sits on the stool. He refocuses his attention on the tape player-recorders.

Okay Mister and Mrs. Player-Recorders, what is your secret? Why doesn't sound come from your speakers when I turn up your volume?

Rigney traces the speaker wires with his eyes. The twisted red and black wires run from the speaker jack and disappear behind the player-recorders. The black and red twisted wires appear again running from behind the player-recorders and up the bulkhead. The speaker wires are intertwined with ship's cabling and spread in opposite directions toward the two speakers mounted in the overhead.

Rigney slips off the stool with intention to trace the speaker wires into the overhead. Immediately, something unusual catches his eye. *Wait a minute! Hold on! What's this?* His eyes follow the red and black twisted wires that thread up the bulkhead from behind the player-recorders. Eight twisted wires thread along the cables where there should be only four. Rigney reaches over the player recorders and feels the wires with his fingers. He discovers that in addition to the four red and black low-voltage speaker wires, there are four black and red high-voltage wires. *Now why would he have high-voltage wires twisted with the speaker wires?*

He climbs onto the workbench so that he can get a better look at the wires. He looks over the top of the player-recorders. He uses his fingers to trace the high-voltage wires. He looks down behind the player-recorders and notices that the thicker wires actually come from down below the workbench tabletop. He looks down behind the workbench but cannot see where the wires go.

He looks around the workbench for a flashlight and finds one. He points the beam of light down the wires and sees that the wires enter a hole in the back of workbench on the left hand side, just beneath the Heath Kit tape player-recorders.

He steps down from the top of the workbench and looks under the tabletop. An enclosed metal cabinet is mounted to the underside of the tabletop. The door on the front of the cabinet has a handle and key lock.

Rigney tries the handle. The cabinet door is locked. He tries the smaller keys on the key ring and unlocks the door on the second try.

The cabinet has two shelves. On each self, two toaster-sized metal boxes sit in a nest of red and black wires and power cables. The red and black wires are a mix of both low-voltage and high-voltage gauge. The four boxes have no markings other than INPUT and OUTPUT.

Rigney puts his hands on the boxes on the top shelf. The boxes are warm to the touch. He lifts the boxes from the top shelf. The slack in the wires allow him to pull the boxes all the way from the cabinet and place them on the workbench tabletop.

Rigney investigates all the wires and how they are connected. He begins to understand their purpose. In the mix of wires and cables are several teletype patch cords.

He unplugs one end of one of the teletype patch cords from the metal box and plugs it into the teletype patch panel. The teletype printer comes alive. Rigney moves closer to the teletype printer so that he can see what it is printing. He is not surprised to see yesterday's fleet broadcast messages printing. He watches several messages print. One SECRET message lists the schedule of several ships, including the *USS Shangri-La*.

Bollier is recording the fleet broadcast and storing it to tape. The box connected to the player-recorder must be some kind of modem that converts the player-recorder analog signal to a teletype DC signal. So, what does the other box do?

Rigney reaches across the workbench and turns the selector switch on the player-recorder to stop. The teletype printer stops printing. Rigney looks at the reel label. *The large B must mean Broadcast.*

Rigney puts the switch back to the play position. The teletype starts printing again.

For the next hour, Rigney conducts tests. He traces the high-voltage wires into the overhead where he finds them spliced into cables that run to MAIN COMM. He goes to MAIN COMM twice to verify his suspicions. On both trips, only Larry Johnson and the Message Center Supervisor are in MAIN COMM. Rigney assumes that the rest of the watch standers are up on the Signal Bridge. Rigney tells the Message Center supervisor that he could not sleep, and he came up to MAIN COMM for some self-training.

By 0300, Rigney finishes his investigation in the Teletype Repair Shop. He exercises extreme care to put everything back to their original positions. He rips the yellow teletype paper from the printer, rolls the paper, and stuffs it under his jumper. *I must dispose of the classified messages that printed.*

He locks the door to the Teletype Repair Shop and proceeds to MAIN COMM. He enters MAIN COMM. This time the Message Center Supervisor is absent. He can hear the fleet broadcast printer in the next room. Rigney locates a half-full burn bag near the Message Center Supervisor's desk. He removes the teletype paper from under his jumper and stuffs the paper into the burn bag.

When he is done, he turns to leave MAIN COMM. Larry Johnson stands in the doorway between the Message Center and the Fleet Broadcast Room. Rigney is startled. He does not know what to say. Larry walks over the burn bag and takes out a few of the teletype paper sheets that Rigney had just stuffed into it. He looks back and forth several times from the teletype paper to Rigney.

"What are you doing, Rig? Why are you up here? You've been coming in and an out of here for the last two hours." Larry jerks his thumb toward the Technical Control room and says, "I saw you in there, tinkering with Bollier's QA equipment. He got anything to do with this? What is it with his equipment that has you so interested?"

"Larry, please trust me. I cannot tell you what's going on. You must trust me."

"Rig, these are classified messages. You took them out of your jumper and stuffed them into the burn bag. I should report this."

"Larry, I ask you as a friend not tell anyone. Please give me some time."

Larry studies Rigney's face for a few minutes. He wants to believe Rigney, but he is duty bound and obliged to report Rigney's actions.

"Does this have anything to do with Gunny Bronston?"

"No!" Rigney retorts.

"How about Rouché? Does it have anything to do with him?"

"No! Absolutely not!" Rigney's voice is shaky and he cannot look Larry in the eyes.

"Look, Rig, I want to believe you, but you've changed. You're not the same person I knew back in 'A' School. You need to give me something. You could be stealing classified messages, and I could be accused of something for not reporting you."

"I'm not stealing messages!"

Larry pleads, "You must tell me something. I need a good reason not to report this."

"Okay, but you must not tell anyone about what I reveal to you. And you must not tell anyone that I was checking out Bollier's QA equipment."

"Okay. What is it?" Larry's manner turns curious.

"You cannot tell, even if I disappear, or I'm found dead."

"My God, Rig! What are you into?"

"I cannot tell you what I'm doing. I can tell you that the captain and the admiral know why I am here. The captain can vouch for me, and I ask that you only go to him as a last resort. If you want to report me, please go see the captain first."

Larry's face expresses absolute puzzlement. His eyes are wide and dazed. Then, Larry stutters a question, "Are . . . are you a . . . a . . . spy?"

"I am not a spy," Rigney responds mildly with a friendly smile. "I must go now. I need to do something."

"Where are you going at 0330 in the morning? Are you leaving the ship? You're my relief in four hours. Are you going to be here?"

"I cannot tell you where I'm going. I will be here on time to relieve you." Then, Rigney declares impatiently, "I must go, now!"

"Okay! Okay! Go!" Larry responds with resignation and a wave of his hand.

Larry disappears through the door to the Fleet Broadcast Room.

Chapter 100

Five minutes later, Rigney unlocks the door to Radio II and enters. He locks the door behind him. He checks the status board. URC-32 transceiver #3 is not in use. The URC-32 is both a radio transmitter and a radio receiver.

Rigney steps in front of URC-32 #3. The transceiver is in standby mode, as it should be. He patches an antenna suitable for nine megahertz to URC-32 #3. Then, he dials the frequency into the URC-32 frequency window. He flips the mode switch from STANDBY to TUNE. The transmitter now emits a low wattage signal needed to pre-tune the antenna.

Down in the CR Division berthing compartment, the *communications messenger of the watch* wakes RM1 Dukes.

"What is it?" Dukes responds irritably.

"Rota wants us to change our transmit frequency on the Ship-to-shore," the seaman responds with a whisper.

"Why?"

"I dunno. The Message Center Supervisor sent me down here to tell ya. He said you would know what to do."

Dukes knows he is the only one in the duty section who knows how to setup *the 'mitters*. He must go to Radio II and change frequencies on the ship-to-shore termination transmitter. He could wake someone else who is not in the duty section, but that would be taking advantage of his rank. *I'm on duty, and It's my responsibility.*

After tuning the transceiver, Rigney puts the mode switch to OPERATE. Then, he listens in the handset to hear if anyone else is transmitting on the frequency. He hears an occasional burst of static, but no one is transmitting.

He looks at his watch—0355. As specified by ONI communications procedures, he must wait until 0400 before he can transmit in the voice mode.

RM1 Dukes approaches the Radio II door. He reaches to his belt for the key ring and does not find it. He comes up to the Radio II door and just stands there considering options to gain access. He tries the doorknob. The door is locked. He knocks on the door.

The knock on the door startles Rigney. He looks at his watch—0359.

More knocking—louder this time.

Rigney holds his breath.

"Is anyone in there?" Dukes voice sounds loudly through the door.

Rigney sees the doorknob rattle again.

Dukes decides to go to the master-at-arms shack to get the master key. The master-at-arms shack is much closer than the CR berthing compartment. *I will search for my key ring later.*

Rigney glances at his watch—0402. He listens in the handset. No one is transmitting. He places the handset back in its cradle. He goes to the door, puts his ear against the door, and listens. He carefully unlocks the door and opens it just a crack. No one stands immediately in front of the door. He opens the door wider and sticks his head out and looks both ways in the passageway. No one is present. After locking the door, he returns to the URC-32. He picks up the handset and listens to make sure no one is transmitting. He looks at his watch again—0403.

He pulls his ONI code card from his pocket. With the handset held to his mouth, he pushes the handset transmit button with his right index finger. Indicators illuminate on the transceiver. Rigney speaks into the handset, "Apollo Zero One, break, message follows . . ."

He speaks the codewords of his message. He repeats the message twice. With each repeat, he speaks louder to increase the power output of the URC-32. His last repeat pegs the power out meter. His voice is loud enough to be heard through the door and into the passageway. Fortunately, the passageway is still empty. He releases the pressure on the handset transmit button. The transceiver indicators go dark. The power output meter returns to zero.

Rigney's coded message to ONI translates to "*I know Python's identity, and I know how he is doing it.*" The last part of the message is Bollier's name spelled out in the coded equivalent. He considers sending his message again on the ONI five-megahertz frequency, but Dukes may come back and interrupt him.

Rigney places the URC-32 transceiver in STANDBY and dials in a random frequency.

RM1 Dukes comes around the aft corner of the Main Deck passageway. He catches a glimpse of a sailor in Undress Blues turning a corner near the forward end of the passageway. *Was that Page?* He is not sure that it was Page.

Dukes comes to the Radio II door. He unlocks the door with the master key and enters. By the time he closes the door behind him, the thoughts of RM3 Page possibly being in the passageway have vacated from his mind. He now focuses on changing the frequency on the ship-to-shore transmitter.

Rigney enters the CR Division berthing compartment. No one appears to be awake. All reading lamps are off. Rigney walks to Bollier's rack. Bollier lies on his back and snores mildly. Rigney slips the key ring under Bollier's blanket. *Hopefully, Bollier will think he was too drunk to remember where he put his keys.*

Rigney walks forward toward his own rack. Dukes is not in his rack. Rigney stuffs the Radio II key ring under Dukes's blanket. He hopes Dukes will have no memory either.

Rigney strips off his clothes, folds them, and places them in his rack-locker. He lowers himself into his rack and slips beneath the sheets. He cannot sleep. His thoughts are on the possibility that ONI did not get his transmission. He will not know until he goes back on watch at 0730. He lies awake in his rack knowing that the next major event in his life will be the *communications messenger of the watch* shaking him for the next watch.

Chapter 101

Rigney relieves Larry Johnson early at 0655. He wants to listen to the ONI broadcast before his own supervisor, RM1 Dukes, arrives for watch.

Larry comments, "I think I will have a leisurely breakfast before climbing into my tree."

Rigney and Larry exchange a few casual words about Palma. Larry's nonchalant manner dismisses their early confrontation regarding Rigney possibly being a spy.

After Larry departs, Rigney proceeds to the Technical Control Room. As he walks by the UCC-1, he notes that channels three and four are still pushed in. He grabs an earphone set, puts them on, and moves quickly to the same R-1051 radio receiver that he used before. He dials the ONI Broadcast frequency and plugs the headset into the audio jack of the R-1051. He instantly hears the recorded voice of the ONI Broadcaster. For several minutes, he listens to a string of acknowledgements. Then, he hears the acknowledgement to the message he transmitted earlier. *"Apollo Zero One acknowledged. I say again, Apollo Zero One acknowledged."*

He returns to his watch station in the Fleet Broadcast Room and focuses his attention on the duties of Fleet Broadcast Operator. All the fleet broadcast signals are five-by-five.

The ringing telephone disturbs the quiet dark of the bedroom. Lieutenant Commander Brad Watson awakes. Before answering the phone, he glances at the luminous clock on his nightstand—0318.

"Watson," he says sleepily into the phone.

"Sorry to wake you, sir," the ONI Communications Watch Officer apologizes. "But the message you are waiting for has been received."

"Okay, just read the coded text."

Brad flinches and his eyes go wide with astonishment as he hears the coded message.

"Thank you," Brad says, then hangs up the phone.

Brad lies on the bed. His astonishment slowly turns to warm, smiling satisfaction. He must double check his code card, but he feels confident that the codewords translate to *Bollier*. Then, he feels doubt. He wonders if Apollo made a mistake.

Thinking about all the possibilities, Brad cannot go back to sleep. He remembers that during training, Apollo recited the code flawlessly without use of the code card. He feels more confident that Page actually

492

did discover Python's identity and activities. Page's success validates Brad's new program for recruiting a different type of field agent.

Brad drags himself out of bed and prepares to go to the office. He contemplates what he must do today. He knows that *Columbus* departs Palma today and spends a week at sea before making a seven-day port visit to Naples, Italy.

Brad ponders the events of the last few days and the possible outcome of those events. *Admiral Melton's plan to advance the deadline required ONI to scramble and take additional risk. That risk required Apollo to take quick actions that probably resulted in Python—Bollier— knowing that he was discovered. Hopefully, Bollier will not know until after the ship is underway. If John Smith were in Palma, the risk of losing Bollier would be less. Now, if Bollier runs while in Palma, there will be no one to tail him. Bollier's presence aboard will be easily determined. If Bollier misses ships departure from Palma, there will be message reports to BUPERS. If Bollier did not run in Palma, then he will run when Columbus arrives in Naples. I must assemble surveillance teams for Naples. I need Bollier followed everywhere he goes in Naples.*

We have never before come this close to Lucifer. We cannot let Bollier disappear.

Chapter 102

In CR Division berthing, Bollier has his body half buried into his rack-locker as he frantically searches for his key ring. He searched his rack-locker twice. *Where the fuck is it? I know I tossed it in here last night!* He grunts and groans as he turns and tosses everything in his rack-locker for the third time.

"Has anyone seen the Radio II keys?" RM1 Dukes asks loudly so that everyone in the compartment can hear him. No one answers.

Alarms sound in Bollier's head when he hears Dukes question. He pulls back from his rack-locker and stares suspiciously in Dukes direction, not suspicious of Dukes but suspicious of the coincidence.

Bollier waddles over to Dukes and asks, "Strange thing, my keys are missing too. How long have the Radio II keys been missing?"

Dukes turns his head and looks into Bollier's face. He contemplates why Bollier is interested. Bollier never talks to him or shows interest in anything or anyone other than himself. Dukes sees no harm in telling him.

"Maybe it's a conspiracy," Dukes replies with a smile.

Bollier fakes a chuckle.

"Anyway, last night when I hit the rack, I thought my keys were on my belt. I had to go to Radio II about 0400. When I couldn't find the keys, I thought that maybe someone needed them to set up a 'mitter. *Oh, wait a minute!* Maybe it was Page. I thought I saw Page near Radio II around 0400."

Bollier focuses on Dukes comment about Page and asks, "Why would Page take the Radio II keys? Does he know how to setup transmitters?"

"Don't know. Maybe we should ask him," Dukes responds absently; his mind obviously occupied elsewhere.

"Good idea. Let's ask him," Bollier responds, trying to appear uninterested.

Dukes and Bollier look over at Page's rack and sees that it is empty.

"He's on my watch," Dukes advises. "I will ask him when I get to MAIN COMM."

Dukes turns his attention back to his rack and searches for the key ring. As an afterthought, he runs his hand under his blanket. "Son-of-bitch! Here they are!" Dukes pulls his hand from beneath his blanket. The key ring is around his index finger.

Bollier stares at the small key ring around Dukes's finger. He wonders about the coincidence of Dukes's key and his own key ring going missing at the same time.

"Gotta go," Dukes advises. "Good luck with finding your keys."
Dukes disappears up the ladder.

Bollier goes back to his rack. He runs his hand under his blanket and finds his key ring. His heart starts pounding. His face flushes. Beads of sweat appear on his face. *Someone knows! Could it be Page? How could it be Page? He's just a kid! I must get a message to Javier. How will I do that? The ship departs in less than an hour.*

Then, Bollier realizes that getting a message to Javier does not protect him. *I must get the hell off this ship before she sails!*

Bollier grabs his checkbook from his rack-locker and darts up the ladder. He weaves through the maze of passageways and exits the superstructure on the port side Main Deck. He runs toward the gangway. He pushes people out of his way as he runs. He grunts and groans as he attempts to move his bulk quickly aft along the port side. He arrives at the gangway just in time to see it lifted away from the ship by a small crane on the pier. He stares open mouthed at the gangway as it moves through the air to its place on the pier.

"NOW SET THE SPECIAL SEA AND ANCHOR DETAIL!"

Bollier panics. He does not know which way to run. He feels trapped. That gangway was not just his escape; it was the rest of his life.

For a moment, he thinks about jumping overboard but quickly dismisses that. *Too dangerous!* Well, too dangerous for him considering his physical condition. The effects of large amounts of alcohol that he consumed the day before clouds his thinking. He barely notices that someone is talking to him and tugging at his sleeve. After a few moments, Bollier comes around to be aware of his surroundings. He notices an officer talking to him.

"You need your cover to be on deck, sailor. If you don't have your white hat, you must go below."

Bollier recognizes the officer as a member of the Deck Department. "Yes, sir. I will go below."

Bollier enters the superstructure at the nearest hatch. Just inside the hatch, he leans against the bulkhead. He tries to clear his mind and focus on a plan. He does not notice the multitude of sailors running past him to get to their *Special Sea and Anchor Detail* stations. He cannot think clearly. He decides to go to his shop where he can make some coffee and think in quiet surroundings.

Several minutes later, Bollier checks the Teletype Repair Shop door. The door is locked. *No forced entry.*

He unlocks the door, steps inside, and locks the door behind him.

Locked inside his safe haven, he relaxes and feels more comfortable. His heart rate slows, and he stops sweating.

He opens a cabinet door that hides his unauthorized coffee mess, and he makes a pot of coffee.

He checks his shop for any signs of an intruder. At first glance, nothing looks out of place. Then, he concentrates on his tape player-recorders; the reels are turning, as they were when he departed the ship yesterday. When Thomas built the player-recorders, he had wired them so that when the reel came to the end of the tape, it would automatically rewind and start playing again.

He carries his cup of coffee to his workbench. He sits on the stool. His enormous butt spills over the sides of the stool seat. The seams of his dungaree trousers stretch to the breaking point. He pulls a pack of camel cigarettes from his breast pocket. He removes one cigarette and puts it between his lips. He retrieves a cigarette lighter from the other breast pocket and lights the cigarette. He tosses the lighter and cigarette pack on the workbench tabletop.

While he inspects every inch of the tabletop, he takes puffs on his cigarette. *Nothing looks out of place.*

He removes the cigarette from between his lips and starts to lay it in the ashtray. Now, he detects something out of place. The groove in the ashtray that holds the cigarette is on the far side, away from him. He always keeps the ashtray groove on the side closest to him. He moves his head closer to the ashtray and inspects it. *The position of the ashtray is where I left it, but the groove is on the wrong side!*

Then, he sees a barely noticeable smear of ashes, a trail, stretching away from the ashtray to the far right of the tabletop. *Looks like someone pushed the ashtray to the right; then, put back in its original location and didn't do a good job of covering-up.*

Bollier checks the cabinet under the tabletop. The door is locked. He unlocks the door and inspects the cabinet's contents. The devices are in their proper place, but the wires are not coiled the way he normally coils them. His breathing becomes heavier. Sweat seeps from the pores on his face, neck, and armpits. He locks the cabinet door.

He stretches his left hand to one of the tape player-recorders. He feels the position of the knobs and switches on each player-recorder. He finds the volume knobs not fully counterclockwise to the stop, as they should be, as he always sets them. *Someone has been here. No doubt about it! But who? Whoever tampered with the equipment must have seen the metal boxes. So why haven't I been arrested?*

Bollier checks the drawer containing his tapes and pistol. The contents of the drawer are organized as he had left it. He pulls out the pistol case and opens the lid. The interior of the gun case looks the same. He cannot determine if the drawer was searched or not.

He relaxes. He reasons that if someone had come into his shop and discovered his secret, he would have been arrested by now.

Maybe the intruder doesn't know about my secret. Maybe he came in here for a different reason. Maybe it was a routine search by someone just checking everything. Maybe they know someone is passing secrets but don't know who. Yeah, that's it! The shop was searched as a matter of routine. Even if the intruder saw all my gear, he would not understand its true purpose. No one aboard could understand this setup. That's it! The intruder doesn't think he saw anything unusual. He probably thinks it's just an elaborate music system. No one, other than me, is smart enough to design this setup and disguise it as a music system. So, who searched my shop? Was it Page? But he doesn't know anything. He doesn't even understand teletype patch panels.

Bollier decides not to question Page about the keys to his shop. He reasons that asking Page about the keys would put too much emphasis on caring about who was in the shop. *I must appear that I don't care about the keys or the shop.*

Thomas concludes that the navy suspects someone on *Columbus* is passing classified information but does not know who or how. He also concludes that eventually the trail will lead back to him. He decides to dump his gear over the side at night while the *Columbus* transits to Naples. He also decides to remove all the wiring and mend the splices.

The next deposit to his Bahamas bank account is due the same day that *Columbus* arrives in Naples.

When the Columbus arrives in Naples, I will leave the ship and never come back. I will escape to a remote tropical island where they will never think to look. Even Javier will not be able to find me.

Chapter 103

With the *Columbus* back at sea, the radiomen are back on a port and starboard watch schedule of eight hours on and eight hours off. *The Tall Lady* has a full schedule, which consists mostly of short duration exercises with other U.S. ships.

Ninety percent of all messages coming over the fleet broadcast are for *Columbus*. Most of the messages contain garbles because of radio static and interference. The continual course changes and position changes of *Columbus* make it difficult for Rigney to find lasting, quality signals across the high-frequency band. The Technical Controllers, RM1 Dukes and RM2 Carter, have equal difficulty with atmospherics on the ship-to-shore termination.

From his angle of view, Rigney sees that Bollier's special cables are attached to the back of UCC-1. Earlier in the watch, Rigney watched Bollier attach the cables and pull Channels three and four.

Curiosity grips Rigney's thoughts. *I know that Bollier is Python, and I know how he passes classified messages. Why are we letting Bollier continue? Maybe ONI has not had enough time to react. Maybe the real reason the Naval Investigative Service agents are coming aboard is to arrest Bollier. Maybe John or Brad will be posing as one of the NIS agents.*

In the Teletype Repair Shop, RM1 Thomas Bollier considers his options. He settles on waiting until the night before arriving in Naples before breaking down his equipment and throwing it overboard. He knows that after he is found missing, his shop will be searched. *I want them to think me a deserter and not a traitor. As a deserter, few will care. As a traitor, however, the U.S. Government will not rest until they find me.*

Bollier still believes that whoever searched his shop did not know what he was looking at and, therefore, does not suspect Bollier of anything.

Brad Watson sits at the desk in the ONI building on the Cheltenham, Maryland Naval Communications Station. He thumbs through the afternoon message stack. The message stack includes five messages regarding the killing of three *Columbus* sailors in Palma. The 9mm casings found at the scene grab Brad's attention.

This must be a coincidence. Nine millimeter is a common caliber in

Europe. Besides, what reason would Page have for killing these three sailors? Brad knows from Page's psychological evaluation that Page is capable of killing. Page has insisted that he cannot kill. *Incorrect Apollo, Dr. Williamson concludes otherwise.*

Brad writes down the name and serial numbers of three dead sailors. Brad calls the yeoman into his office.

"When's the next run to BUPERS?"

"The messenger left thirty minutes ago, sir."

Brad looks at his watch. "I doubt that he got there yet. The messenger's vehicle has a radio, doesn't it?"

"Yes, sir."

"Okay, call him on the radio and tell him to pull over so he can write down these names and serial numbers. Tell him to check out the service records of these three. Oh, look up Page's service number and add his name to the list. I want his record too."

Brad hands the yeoman the list of names.

"Yes, sir. I will do that right away."

On the USS *Columbus*, the chow line backs up the ladder to the Main Deck and wraps around the passageway past Radio II. Rigney stands at the end of the line. He estimates 20 minutes in line.

Rigney focuses his mind on what he should do next about Python— Bollier. Brad Watson's instructions for this mission were clear. *When I discover whom and how, notify ONI and take no further action.*

The current situation appears anticlimactic. My mission is complete. I could be on a submarine by the end of February.

"How ya doin', Page?" a familiar voice asks behind him.

Rigney turns and sees RM1 Dukes standing behind him. First class petty officers have head of line privilege, but Dukes only takes advantage of that when he eats prior to going on watch or on chow break from watch.

Rigney replies, "I'm okay. How are you doing?"

"Looking forward to eating some warm chow and hitting the rack. I had to get up at 0400 this morning and retune a '*mitter.*" Dukes pauses for a minute while he remembers something.

Dukes asks, "Was that you I saw in this passageway this morning about 0400? I was wonderin' why you were here. When I thought I saw you, I thought you might have taken the keys to Radio II."

"Wasn't me," Rigney replies instantly. "I slept through the night."

"Not important, now. I found the keys in my rack."

Rigney just smiles in response.

Then, Dukes bows his head and utters a slight chuckle.

"What's funny," Rigney asks politely.

"Well, Bollier lost his keys too. We joked about it being a conspiracy. When I told Bollier that I thought I saw you up here last night, he thought we should ask you about the keys. Anyway, he later told me he found his keys in his rack."

Anxiety swells through Rigney's body. He hopes Dukes cannot see it.

Rigney steps down the ladder into the berthing compartment. He sees Bollier sitting at the table reading a magazine.

Bollier looks up casually at Rigney; then, he lowers his head down to continue reading the magazine.

Bollier's action confuses Rigney. He thought there would be some kind of panic on Bollier's part. *Bollier must not know I searched his shop. Maybe he does not know that his shop was searched.*

At the ONI building in Cheltenham, YN2 Randson sets three service records on Lieutenant Commander Brad Watson's desk. He explains, "They could not find Page's record. The record was not filed where it was supposed to be, and there was no tickler. I called BUPERS a few minutes ago to see if they found it yet. They're still looking for it."

Brad Watson looks at his wristwatch and says, "It's too late to do anything more about it today. Call BUPERS first thing in the morning. If they found it, send the driver to get it."

Brad needs to verify some details of Page's past. Brad has plans for Page after this mission, and Page will need additional security clearances. Page's success on this mission will result with Brad receiving full approval to continue with his new recruiting program and condensed training program.

Brad opens each service record. He compares each page of Rouché's, Lemare's, and Robichaux's service records for any similarities. After a few minutes, Brad discovers that all three graduated from the same high school in New Orleans. *Interesting!*

Brad's crypto covered phone rings.

"Watson," Brad speaks into the handset.

The voice on the other end says, "Going secure. I will initiate."

Brad waits and listens to the tones while the two secure voice units synchronize.

"Brad, this is Howard Worthington in the New London Field

Office."

"Hello, Howard. What's up?" Brad expects Worthington to provide some new detail regarding Debutante—Sally Macfurson.

"Brad, you wanted to know if anyone asked any questions about Sally Macfurson or RM3 Page."

"Yes, what's occurred?"

"I had asked Commander Driscoll who is The OIC of Submarine Radioman Schools to let me know if anyone asked any questions about Page. Commander Driscoll came to see me this morning. He says that he received a call from a loan company in Norfolk. The caller claimed that Page applied for a car loan and Driscoll was listed as a reference. The loan company wanted to verify Page's background. The caller asked if Page had attended Submarine Radio School from March 1966 through December 1967. Driscoll confirmed the dates. When the caller asked to where Page had been transferred. Driscoll replied that navy policy did not allow him to release that information. The caller thanked him, and that was all there was to the call."

"Thank you, Howard. Anything else?"

"No, that's it."

After he hangs up, Brad sits back and stares into space while he thinks about coincidental events. *Page's personnel record goes missing, and someone pretending to be a loan officer investigates Page's background. And both events occur on the same day. The Soviets are investigating Page, and the Soviets have a resource in BUPERS!*

Brad makes a note to inform the appropriate ONI section regarding his suspicion of a Soviet agent at BUPERS.

The next morning, YN2 Randson enters Brad Watson's office and advises, "I called BUPERS this morning, and Page's record is back in its proper place. The checkout sheet for Page's record is not signed for the period that it was missing."

Chapter 104

Two days after *Columbus* departs Palma, two NIS agents arrive by helicopter. The two Spanish police detectives and the two NIS agents setup an interview room in the ship's library. They organize into two teams with one Spanish detective and one NIS agent on each team. While one team interviews crewmembers, the other team, with the aid of the master-at-arms force, searches for a 9mm pistol.

The Spanish detectives and the NIS Agents consider their interviews and gun search to be routine. They view their time on *Columbus* as an interesting diversion while performing the perfunctory actions of any homicide investigation. Neither the Spanish detectives nor the NIS agents believe anyone on *Columbus* to be the killer.

On the third day after departure from Palma, Senior Chief Bulldoone orders Rigney to report to the ship's library.

Rigney feels ready. He spent days rehearsing his answers and his mannerisms.

Rigney enters the library. Two men sit at the far end of the reading table. He recognizes one of the men as the Spanish policeman who searched the CR Division berthing compartment. Stacks of papers and file folders clutter the end of the table where the two men sit.

"Please sit there," the Spanish policeman says in heavily accented English. He points to a chair at the opposite end of the table from the two men.

The two men run their fingers down a list of names.

"You are Rigney Michael Page," the NIS Agent asks.

"Yes, sir," Rigney responds cordially.

"Page, I am Special Agent Kirkwood from the Naval Investigative Service. This gentleman is Detective Gallego of the Spanish Police."

"A pleasure to meet you," Rigney says with a smile.

Agent Kirkwood asks, "Page, we are investigating the deaths of RM2 Rouché, Seaman Lemare, and Seaman Robichaux. Did you know them?"

"I knew Rouché. I didn't know the other two."

Kirkwood states, "We have reports that you and Rouché did not get along, and that you both threatened each other on a number of occasions."

"Rouché did the threatening. I just advised him of how I would respond should he try to fulfill those threats."

Kirkwood questions, "Then, you're saying that Rouché was the aggressive one?"

"That's right. I never initiated any of the situations where he threatened me."

Detective Gallego asks, "Why did he threaten you? What did you do to him?"

Rigney replies in an even, mild tone, "I didn't do anything to him. I don't know why he wanted to hurt me."

"What did he threaten to do to you?" Gallego inquires.

"He never said exactly . . . just that whenever I left the ship, he would teach me a lesson that would be bloody and painful."

Detective Gallego picks up a file folder, opens it, and reads a few paragraphs. Then, he asks, "Do you know others who are enemies of the three dead men?"

"I've only heard rumors," Rigney responds. "I understand that Rouché bullied people around. He would coerce money from people pretending that it was a loan."

Detective Gallego asks, "Where were you at approximately 8:00 p.m. on January 21st?"

"Was the 21st the day of the killings?" Rigney speaks his practiced response.

"Correct."

"I was on liberty."

"Where?"

"In Palma."

"Yes, of course!" Gallego responds impatiently. "Where in Palma?"

"I don't really know. At the pier, I jumped in a taxi with some other sailors. One of the other sailors gave the directions."

"Was it the *Sa Llonja* district?" Gallego queries with more patience.

"Yes, I think that was it," Rigney replies calmly and with a nod.

"We have a witness that says you were seen entering the *El Greco Bar and Café* at approximately 8:00 p.m. Is that correct?"

Detective Gallego has no such witness. He states this to everyone he interviews. If the interviewee was at the stated place and time, this tactic usually results with an admission of being there.

"I have no idea where I was at any time. If I was seen going in there, I guess I did. I cannot verify it. Is that where Rouché was killed?" Rigney had rehearsed this response also.

Gallego does not respond. He just writes in the folder in front of him.

Gallego stares into Rigney's eyes and asks, "Do you have a pistol hidden on this ship?"

Rigney puts a quizzical look on his face that he hopes conveys *why would you ask me such a question.* He looks directly back into the eyes of the Spanish Detective and says, "No." He shakes his head slightly as he answers. He had practiced this particular answer many times in the mirror.

Detective Gallego nods toward Special Agent Kirkwood and pushes the file folder to Kirkwood.

Kirkwood stares at Page. Then, he says, "We have witnesses that say you threatened to break Rouché's wrists and threatened to rip out Rouché's throat. Do you deny this happened?"

"I don't deny it. I was tired and testy, and my words were in response to his continuing string of threats."

Kirkwood says, "Page, we found a gun on this ship of the same caliber as the murder weapon. Preliminary tests show a high probability that the gun has your fingerprints on it. Do you want to change your answer about the gun?"

Rigney jerks back slightly and blinks his eyes. He had not anticipated this. *Even if they found the Berettas, they would not have my fingerprints. Kirkwood is trying to trick me into a confession.*

"I do not have a gun. Someone made a mistake." Rigney looks directly into Kirkwood's eyes.

Agent Kirkwood writes in the file folder before him.

Rigney correctly assessed the purpose of questions regarding the gun and fingerprints. Those questions are interview tactics designed to trap a guilty suspect. Rigney does not believe he is a suspect. He knows from reading the message traffic that the Spanish Police suspect local criminals in Palma, and the onboard investigation is merely routine investigative actions.

Kirkwood says cordially, "Okay, Page. That's all. Thank you for your cooperation."

Rigney departs the interview with the understanding that the Spanish Police and the NIS Agents are nobody's fool. *I will not go near my weapons until they all leave and go back to where they came from.*

Chapter 105

Several hours later in MAIN COMM, Rigney reviews the Communication Center File for messages relating to Rouché. A message from the Spanish Government contains the findings of the autopsies and the ballistics analysis. The United States Consulate in Barcelona relayed the message to *Columbus*.

All three died from gunshot wounds. Rouché and Lemare were shot once in the chest and twice in the head. Robichaux was shot twice in the back and twice in the head. The three men were standing or walking when they were shot in the torso. All three lay on the pavement when they were shot in the head.

The bullets were designed to explode once they enter the body. Because ten 9mm casings were found at the scene, the ballistics lab concludes a 9mm weapon was used. The ballistics lab also believes that the weapon had a suppressor.

The message also reports that Palma police investigated a local, illegal gun dealer. The gun dealer had dozens of guns in his house. Some of those guns were 9mm Berettas. Suppressors were found in the house that fit the 9mm weapons. The illegal dealer also had four hundred rounds of 9mm exploding cartridges. The gun dealer was arrested and is being questioned.

The following day, the onboard NIS agents and Spanish policemen send a message stating they completed their investigations and found no evidence linking any of the *Columbus* crew to the homicides.

Several days remain before pulling into Naples, so Admiral Melton arranges for a helicopter to transport the NIS Agents and the Spanish policemen to the *Shangri-La* for further transport to shore.

Relief flows through Rigney as he reads the message. *Well I can finally put that behind me!*

Rigney continues scanning the Communications Center File for messages of interest since his last watch. Worry returns as he sees that the message containing the autopsy and ballistics results was forwarded to a number of addresses, including ONI SUITLAND MD.

If Brad had any doubts that I did it, the report on the exploding bullets must have removed those doubts.

Bob Mater and Brad Watson sit in Bob Mater's office at ONI Headquarters in Suitland, Maryland.

"Commander, our analysis reveals that this RM1 Bollier was always in the Theater of Operations when the Soviets knew the positions of our ships. However, this is not true for this RMCS Bulldoone. The only occasions that correlated with Bulldoone were when Bollier and Bulldoone were at the same command at the same time. I don't think this Bulldoone is in on it. If Bulldoone does not hold Bollier accountable for his actions, it must be for another reason."

Bob Mater shuffles through his papers for other points he needs to tell Brad. "Oh, here is an interesting revelation by one of the junior analysts. In previous years, Soviet ship movement indicates that the Soviets were getting some information several months after the fact. The Soviets were looking for our ships in areas where our ships had previously been. Many of these areas were standard patrol areas. In recent years, especially in the MED, the Soviets are waiting for our ships as our ships arrive in their patrol area." Bob Mater removes his glasses and looks at Brad Watson says, "If this Bollier is our Python, I will be very interested to know how he is doing it."

Brad responds, "Page says Bollier is Python, and Page says he knows how Bollier is doing it. We need to meet with Page so that he can give us the details. We hope that Bollier will lead us to Lucifer. We are forming several surveillance teams to tail Bollier in Naples."

Bob Mater bows his head and shakes his head in annoyance. "Ya know, Brad, you would think with the advances in communications systems we would have come up with some way to get real-time detailed classified reports from our Field Agents."

"It's coming Bob. The U.S. is sending up another communications satellite in the near future. ONI will have its own channel. We will have portable satellite radios and voice encryption equipment in the field."

A satisfied look appears on Bob's face as he says, "None too soon from my point of view."

Chapter 106

Andrei and Javier finish their dinner in a restaurant close to Rome's Spanish Steps. Andrei hands Javier a large envelope and informs, "The envelope holds results of our investigation on this Rigney Page."

Javier opens the envelope and removes three sheets of paper. He scans the report for evidence that Page is a counterintelligence agent. His concern about Page increases when he reads that Page was never stationed at Bethesda Hospital and that Page was stationed at the Submarine Base in Connecticut, instead. *Not that where Page was stationed is significant. Thomas's misperception about Page's background is significant.*

The report states that Page was in Washington for two weeks and stayed at the Bethesda Patients Barracks. The doctors found Page medically unfit for submarine duty. Then, Page was transferred to the USS *Columbus*.

Javier stares into space as he evaluates the report. *Why does Thomas think this Page was assigned to Bethesda?* Then, he asks, "Andrei, this report says Page attended radio school for two years. Why would it take so long to learn how to operate radios and learn the Morse Code? Was he really attending radio school all that time?"

Andrei concedes, "Yes, that does seem a long time, even for their submarine radio training."

Javier focuses on Andrei's words. "What is different about training for their submarine radio operators?"

"Their submarine radio operators are also trained to repair their radio equipment. They are instructed how to integrate the systems and how to fix those systems. The initial training for their surface navy radio operators is less technical."

Javier feels anxiety, but he does not let Andrei see it. *Page's technical training could be the qualifying factor that makes him a counterintelligence agent.*

"What about this Sally Macfurson?" Javier asks. "Do they truly have a romantic relationship, or could she be his field contact for their intelligence agency. This report says she now works near Naples . . . too convenient to be a coincidence."

"She worked as a librarian on the submarine base while Page was there," Andrei informs. "She is an academic. She belongs to a family of wealthy aristocracy capitalists. They have much influence in the United States. She probably arranged this so she could be close to him while this *Columbus* cruises the Mediterranean."

Javier responds, "Possibly, but too many unusual coincidences have occurred for me to feel comfortable."

"Javier, my friend, this report looks the same as all the others. This Rigney Page does not appear to be a problem. Why do you trouble yourself over it?"

Javier answers, "This Page situation concerns me. How does an American sailor train for over two years for submarine duty, and at the last minute become medically unsuitable?"

"Yes, unusual," Andrei admits. "But he is just a boy. He is too young. You should not worry." Andrei's tone is dismissive.

"Andrei, you saw his picture, the one where he had only a towel to cover him. Does he look like an ordinary American boy to you? Does he look similar to their typical enlisted sailors? Does he look like he is medically unsuitable?"

"No, he does not," Andrei acknowledges. "He looks like an Olympic swimmer."

"So, you see why I think it wise to be cautious."

"Do you need any assistance from us?" Andrei offers.

"No, not presently."

Javier has already formed a plan. He previously arranged to have Thomas Bollier followed in Naples. Javier will form another team of associates to follow Page in Naples. He also decides to have a team follow Sally Macfurson.

On the USS *Columbus*, Lieutenant Junior Grade Rowing sits at the Adonis machine in the Crypto Vault. He keys the Adonis rotors to one-time-pad settings for an offline-encrypted message received from the Office of Naval Intelligence.

Rowing types the first line of the code groups. As regulations dictate, he checks the first few words of decrypted text on the paper tape for any EYES ONLY instructions. He looks at the tape and sees FOR COMMANDING OFFICER EYES ONLY.

Regulations forbid him from continuing. He marks the last encrypted character that he typed. He must now notify Captain Saunders of the COMMANDING OFFICER EYES ONLY message. Regulations dictate that the commanding officer must decrypt the remainder of the message.

LTJG Rowing locks the Crypto Vault and starts his search for Captain Saunders.

Chapter 107

The sun rose into a clear sky over the Mediterranean forty minutes ago and now sits just above the horizon. A chilly twelve-knot wind causes whitecaps to form on the chop of the sea.

Rigney stands on the port side of the Signal Bridge. He wants to absorb fresh air and sunshine before relieving the watch. He compares the position of the sun to the direction in which *Columbus* steams, and he approximates *Columbus's* course as southerly. He looks through the big-eyes at the aircraft carrier *USS Shangri-La* that cruises three miles to the east of *Columbus* on the same course. Two miles behind the carrier, the destroyer, USS *Patrell* sails the same course.

Rigney moves away from the big-eyes. He removes his ball cap and grips the rail. He faces the sun, closes his eyes, and lets his mind wander. *We will be busy on watch today with shifting our communications guard to Naples. I must copy both the Rota and Naples Fleet Broadcast most of the day.*

With his ONI mission over and the Rouché homicide investigation behind him, Rigney has become tranquil. He sleeps better, and he resumed his exercise regimen.

The only thing left to do is brief ONI on Bollier's methodology. Occasionally, he finds himself in close proximity to Bollier. If Bollier suspects anything about Rigney, Bollier does not show it.

What happens to me after we arrive in Naples? Rigney hopes that ONI does not whisk him back to Washington. He looks forward to spending time with Sally and Barbara. He has requested leave for the entire Naples port visit. Senior Chief Bulldoone forwarded the leave request recommending approval. Few sailors request leave while deployed; they reserve leave time for the first month after returning to Norfolk from a deployment.

He hopes there will be no conflict with seeing both Sally and Barbara. If he must, he will be honest with both of them. He will tell them, *"no commitments this early in my life. I must experience as much of life as I can in my youth."*

During his watch, Rigney shifts to the Naples Fleet Broadcast. The frequencies are clear, and he has no problem maintaining good print quality.

As part of his duties, he retunes the frequencies for the Associated Press teletype printer. He takes time to read some of the stories. The first story he reads provides details regarding 5000 women demonstrating on

Capitol Hill against the Vietnam War. The next story reports that Britain, France, and the United States announce their willingness to relinquish their remaining World War II Occupation Rights. Another story reports that President Johnson says the Vietnam War costs the U.S. 25 Billion Dollars per year. Another story quotes the New York Times as reporting that North Vietnam is massing a large troop force in Laos for a possible onslaught against the U.S. Marine Base at Khesanh. The final story reads that the United States Navy suspects that the North Koreans knew exactly where to find the USS *Pueblo* on January 23rd.

The San Germano Hotel in Naples, Italy stands on Via Beccadelli, which is the road that runs between the Naval Support Activity at Agnano and the NATO Headquarters of Allied Forces Southern Europe at Bagnoli. The San Germano Hotel is midway between the two bases.

Javier sits by the phone in room 212. He waits for a call to Barcelona that he placed more than two hours ago with the hotel operator.

The phone finally rings.

After exchanging pleasantries with his associate in Barcelona, he asks, "Do you have anything to report?"

"The signals have stopped," the man in Barcelona reports.

"The signals have stopped before," Javier responds.

"Yes, Javier, but usually resumed after several hours. Ten hours have elapsed since the last signals."

"Continue to monitor the channels," Javier directs. "If the signals resume, call me here. If I am not here, leave a message with the hotel operator that the signals have resumed." Javier provides the telephone number and disconnects the call.

Javier evaluates the possibilities. For the last year, Thomas's behavior has been that of one who is ready to flee. Javier knows the symptoms. One of his other U.S. associates ran away nine years ago. Javier spent two years hunting Jonathan down and eventually found him in Barbados. Javier eliminated Jonathan, but not before Javier forced Jonathan to reveal the secret number of his bank account.

Javier considers that Thomas plans to flee when *Columbus* arrives in Naples. He suspects that Thomas disconnected his equipment and dropped his equipment into the sea.

Javier dismisses the possibility that Thomas's traitorous activities have been discovered. If Thomas had been discovered, the U.S. Government would not have terminated the signals. Terminating the signals would be a sure sign that Thomas had been discovered and the termination of signals would alert Thomas's coconspirators.

The U.S. Government would not want to chase me away. They would want me to believe Thomas is operating as normal then follow Thomas in an attempt to catch me.

Javier concludes that Thomas will desert the U.S. Navy when *Columbus* arrives in Naples.

But this Rigney Page snips at my instincts!

Chapter 108

"See Naples and die!"

The *Columbus* newsletter attributes the origin of the saying to *Johann Wolfgang von Goethe* who visited Naples in the late eighteenth century. Popular belief holds that *Goethe* coined the flattering phrase to convey his belief that once you have seen and experienced the beauty and magnificence of *bella Napoli,* all of life's joys have been fulfilled—nothing else in life is worth experiencing.

A short visit to the city of Naples will reinforce and enhance your belief in the saying. However, those who entrench themselves into the daily routine of living and working in the congested and polluted city of Napoli also understand the less flattering description of the city as the *Calcutta of the West*. The more flattering phrase is on Rigney's mind as he stands on the Signal Bridge.

The *Columbus* cruises northeast at nine knots as she transits the Gulf of Naples toward her destination of the Port of Naples. The most visible landmark is the towering Mount Vesuvius to the east, which appears to stand guard over the gulf. The shoreline arcs around the gulf, starting with the Isle of Ischia on the northwestern tip of the bay to the Isle of Capri on the southeastern tip of the bay. The dozen cities on the Gulf of Naples continually grow and expand up the slopes of Mount Vesuvius.

The smoggy brown haze that hovers over the entire area disappoints Rigney. The books in the ship's library characterized Naples as Italy's most beautiful city. The photographs of large ornate buildings and sprawling piazzas certainly made it look so.

The Tall Lady enters Naples harbor, turns to port, and slows.

Rigney notices the color of the water changes from sea green to a dirty brown. He also notices a significant increase in floating debris.

Commercial tankers and freighters line the piers. The *Columbus* passes a number of outbound commercial vessels, all with flags of nations that Rigney does not recognize. The foreign vessels are a mix of those that are filthy and rusty to those that are immaculately clean and in good repair. The sailors of the foreign vessels line the rails of their ships to get a close look at the powerful United States Navy Guided Missile Cruiser.

As the ships come abreast, the foreign sailors point and gawk at the *Columbus's* TALOS and TARTAR missiles. Those missiles are mounted on their launchers for display during the Naples visit. Some of the foreign sailors wave as the *Columbus* passes. Rigney waves back.

Two tugboats meet *Columbus*. Rigney watches with interest as *Columbus* deck hands toss lines to the tugs. The tugs guide the *Columbus* stern first to the Fleet Landing pier. Then, the anchor drops, followed by a shrill whistle over the 1MC.

"THE OFFICER OF THE DECK IS SHIFTING HIS WATCH FROM THE BRIDGE TO THE QUARTERDECK."

Rigney remains on the Signal Bridge to enjoy some big-eye liberty. An hour later while focusing the large binoculars on the passenger cruise ship across the harbor, he hears someone calling his name. He turns to see Larry Johnson standing at the hatchway.

"Hey, Rig! Mister Rowing sent me looking for you. He wants to see you right away in the Communications Office."

"What for?" Rigney ask.

"He didn't say."

"I hope he is not planning on canceling my leave."

"When you going on leave?" Larry questions.

"As soon as the liberty goes down."

"I thought you and I were goin' steamin' together."

"Sorry, Larry. Something else came up."

"When ya comin' back?"

"The morning we get underway."

"Well, have a nice leave."

"Thanks."

As Rigney approaches the Communications Office, he sees the COMMO, Lieutenant Conner exiting the door of his office.

"They are inside waiting for you," LT Conner says as he passes Rigney.

They who? Rigney wonders as he watches Lieutenant Conner walk away.

Rigney stands facing the door to the Communications Office. He hopes that whoever is behind that door will not stand in the way of his leave. He opens the door and steps in.

Lieutenant Commander Brad Watson sits at the COMMO's desk. John Smith leans against a filing cabinet in the corner. Both Brad and John wear the Service Dress Blue Uniform of a lieutenant commander.

Rigney moves his eyes back and forth between the faces of the two men. Rigney is somewhat surprised that the two men came aboard. He thought that Barbara Gaile would advise him of a meeting.

Rigney fixes his attention on John Smith and says, "You were supposed to meet me in Palma. What happened?"

513

"Ancient history, Rig. No value in discussing it now," John replies.

Rigney looks John Smith up and down and says, "John, I must get into the same organization as you. The advancement system is fantastic."

John Smith smiles but does not respond.

"Sit and be quiet," Brad Watson orders as he points to a chair beside the desk.

Rigney sits.

After a few minutes, Rigney gives Brad a questioning look.

"We are waiting for Captain Saunders," Brad informs without inflect or emotion.

Several minutes later, the door opens. Captain Saunders enters.

Rigney jumps to his feet, stands at attention and announces, *"Attention on deck!"*

Brad rises and snaps to attention. John is slower at coming to attention; his body language says this ritual is unfamiliar to him.

"Stand easy, gentleman, and relax," Captain Saunders says as he shuts the door behind him.

Brad Watson says, "Page, tell us how Bollier is doing it. Use that blackboard to diagram the process."

Rigney walks to the bulkhead-mounted blackboard and picks up the chalk.

Captain Saunders sits down where Rigney previously sat.

Rigney glances at each of the three men, takes a deep breath, and begins. "Bollier tapped into the teletype signal lines for both the fleet broadcast and the ship-to-shore termination. Those tapped lines run down to his Teletype Repair Shop. He uses a modem like device to convert the teletype signals to audio signals, which allows messages to be recorded on magnetic tape reels using his tape player-recorders."

Rigney sketches a block diagram on the blackboard to illustrate the connectivity.

Captain Saunders asks, "Where are these modems and recorders located?"

"The recorders are on his workbench. The modems are locked in a cabinet below his workbench."

"Continue," Captain Saunders directs.

"He records messages. Then, later, he reverses the process. He puts the tape player-recorder in PLAY mode and routes the signal back through the modem to convert back to teletype signals. Then, he runs the signal through another device, which I think is some sort of encryption device. The encrypted signal routes back up to MAIN COMM over wires that tap into the UCC-1 circuitry. Bollier's messages transmit over channels three and four of the UCC-1. The UCC-1 multiplexes multiple teletype signals onto one radio frequency. Channels one and two are used for *Columbus* traffic channels and coordination for the ship-to-shore termination."

Rigney again sketches on the blackboard to show connectivity from the tape player-recorder to the UCC-1 and to the radio transmitter.

"And where is this encryption device," Captain Saunders asks.

"In the same cabinet as the modem devices."

"Why didn't anyone notice that channels three and four were in use?" Brad Watson asks.

"Bollier created a device he calls a Teletype Generator. He mounted this device in the QA rack in the Technical Control Room. He told the Tech Controllers that they could use the Teletype Generator to test signal quality on spare channels. Actually, the Teletype Generator is just a pass-through device for the signals coming from his shop. Since the signals were encrypted, anyone who might patch channel three or four to a teletype machine would only see random characters print, which according to Bollier is what the Teletype Generator creates."

"Let me see if I have this correct," Captain Saunders comments. "Normal ships message traffic is sent on channels one and two, and the messages from Bollier's shop are sent on channels three and four . . . and all four of those channels are transmitted on a radio frequency to the Shore Communications Station. Is that Right?"

"Yes, sir," Rigney confirms.

"Okay, so what did the Shore Communications Station do with channel three and four?" Captain Saunders asks.

"Probably nothing," Brad Watson responds. "The Shore Communications Station isn't expecting anything on those channels, so they probably didn't even look."

Captain Saunders pauses for a few moments of thought; then, he asks, "So you think that someone else copies our frequencies and decrypts channels three and four?" Captain Saunders looks to Rigney for the answer.

"Yes, sir. Anyone with a Single Side Band radio receiver and equivalent equipment that Bollier has could decrypt the messages and print them. Or even copy them to magnetic tape reels like Bollier does."

Brad Watson asks, "How do they know which radio frequencies to copy?"

"All the authorized transmit frequencies are posted in the Technical Control Room. Anyone with that list and knowledge of our general location and use of direction finding equipment could easily find our transmit frequencies. I've looked at the list. It's only thirty-some frequencies."

Captain Saunders sits in thought. Then, he looks at Brad Watson and asks, "Mister Watson, how do we proceed from here?"

"Captain, we believe Bollier will run, desert, when Liberty Call is announced. ONI asks that you wait a few days to ensure Bollier is gone. Then, you can call in NAVELEX to repair the cabling. Page will provide a diagram as to where all the cable taps are. You can give that diagram to NAVELEX when they get here. NAVELEX will be here under the guise that they are making electrical grounding modifications."

"Why can't Page show them?" Captain Saunders asks.

"Sir, we have other plans for Page, and his cover would be blown if he helped NAVELEX. We plan to have Page back aboard before you sail so that his cover is preserved. Can you arrange something that makes his absence look normal?"

Rigney interrupts, "Sir, I already have leave approved for the whole week, starting today."

"Perfect," Brad says with a satisfied smile on his face.

Captain Saunders asks, "What about the equipment that Bollier leaves behind? Should we arrange a shipment to ONI?"

"Captain, if Bollier runs, his equipment will not be onboard. He will not want any evidence left behind as to what he was doing. His equipment probably sits on the bottom of the sea somewhere between here and Palma."

"I suppose that you have made arrangements to follow Bollier when he leaves the ship?"

Brad answers, "Correct, sir. We want to see who he contacts."

Captain Saunders's attention shifts from Brad to Rigney to John Smith. For a few seconds, Captain Saunders wonders about Mister Smith's involvement. Then, he focuses on Brad and comments, "Mister Watson, I am relieved that you and your team have finally brought this situation to closure."

The captain stands and walks to Rigney. He smiles warmly as he says, "Page, I had doubts about you. Obviously, ONI knew what it was doing by sending you here. It's a pleasure to have you as a member of my crew."

The captain sticks out his hand and Rigney takes it. The captain's handshake and manner exude enthusiastic appreciation.

Rigney's face beams with pride.

Captain Saunders turns and walks toward the door. He stops short of opening the door and turns to Brad Watson and orders, "Mister Watson, I want to be kept informed regarding any situation that affects my ship and my crew."

"Yes, sir," Brad responds.

Captain Saunders exits the office and closes the door behind him.

Rigney turns toward Brad and asks, "Why would Bollier desert? He doesn't know I searched his shop and figured out his gear."

"He knows someone searched his shop. That alone gives him enough reason to run."

"I don't think he knows," Rigney insists.

Brad counters, "My experience tells me that he suspects, which is enough to make him run. Anyway, this subject is moot. I need to extend your mission. If you accept, it means you must spend a few days with Barbara Gaile at a beach house north of Naples."

A devilish expression spreads over Rigney's face. He says to Brad with a glance toward John Smith, "I dunno Brad, sounds dangerous to me."

"Seriously, this situation has an element of danger. I believe that Bollier's Soviet Controller suspects you. Your background was investigated. I think that you will be followed when you leave the ship. We want to follow your followers. With you being stationary at the beach house, your tails will be stationary. We have setup a command center in an apartment a half a block from the beach house. The apartment is on the top floor and gives maximum view of the beach house. We will see anyone who approaches that house. We will have the opportunity to follow your tails when they are relieved and see where they go and to whom they report. When they are stationary watching the beach house, we can detect their radio frequencies and listen in. We hope that by following Bollier and following your followers, we will find Bollier's Soviet Controller. If anyone attempts to make a move on you, we will be there to protect you.

"Bollier's Soviet Controller will not think that we have discovered Bollier for three reasons. One, the signals have stopped because Bollier dumped his equipment over the side when he discovered someone searched his shop. Two, Bollier's Soviet Controller will conclude that if U.S. authorities know about Bollier, we would have continued the signals so as not to advertise that we know about their operation. Three, When Bollier easily and freely walks off this ship, his Soviet Controller will be convinced that we don't know about Bollier. When Bollier goes to the airport or train station, the Soviet Controller will be convinced that Bollier has not been discovered."

Rigney asks, "Won't the spies consider the possibility that the U.S. Government will follow Bollier?"

"No, because they won't think Bollier has been discovered. But even if they look for tails, they won't detect any. Our Surveillance teams are trained professionals. They will not be detected."

"Won't Bollier tell his Soviet Controller that his shop was searched?"

Brad replies, "No, because Bollier will be running away from us and from his Soviet Controller. Bollier knows his Soviet Controller is no friend. Bollier knows he has more to fear from his Soviet Controller than from the U.S. Government."

Rigney asks, "Won't Bollier think that he might be followed by us or his Controller?"

"Yes, he will," Brad affirms. "But he has no choice. He knows his only chance is to run."

Rigney stands; then, he expresses thoughtfulness for a few moments. He asks, "Since I was investigated, won't those spies think that someone from the U.S. Government will follow me?"

"No, because they don't know that we know you were investigated."

Rigney nods his acceptance of the explanation. Then, he remembers about Bollier's gun and says, "I found a gun when I searched Bollier's shop. I filed down the firing pin; so, it won't fire. I don't know if Bollier knows his gun was disabled."

John Smith asks, "What does the gun look like."

"It's a small caliber automatic with a white handle. I think it's a .25 caliber."

John says, "I will tell the ONI surveillance teams about Bollier's weapon."

Brad asks Rigney, "Are you okay with this expansion of your mission?"

"Yes, I am." Then, he asks, "Has Barbara agreed to this?"

Brad replies, "Yes, she received a limited briefing and was told about the possible dangers, and she agreed."

"So, what do I do?" Rigney asks.

"It's 1100 now," Brad says while looking at his watch. "Liberty call will go down at 1200. I don't want you to be in the initial liberty rush. I want your followers to easily identified you and I want to make it easy for them to follow you. At 1445, go out to the street at the head of the pier. A shuttle will arrive at 1500. Take the shuttle to the Naval Support Activity at Agnano. Go to the Commanding Officer's office. That's where Barbara works. Barbara will depart with you. Walk out the Navy Exchange parking lot gate. When you walk out the gate, stand around for a few minutes so that your followers have time to react. Then, take a taxi to the beach house in *Lido di Licola*. Barbara knows where it is."

"Sounds easy enough," Rigney comments. "Where's the danger?"

"Whoever follows you could rush the house without warning. You need to be prepared."

"Prepared?"

"Yes, I want you to carry."

"Carry what?"

John Smith speaks up. "Come on, *Rig!* Carry your weapons—both of them."

"Oh," Rigney responds in a low voice as he diverts his eyes.

Brad gives Rigney a calculating stare and says, "You should have no problem using your weapons if you need to, right?"

Rigney cannot answer. If he says yes, he confirms he committed the killings in Palma. *But they already know I did it, don't they?* By not denying it, he admits to it.

Brad says, "Look, Rigney. It was easy for us to figure out you killed those sailors in Palma. Did those three sailors attack you with switchblades?"

"Yes."

"Why?"

"Because they didn't like me."

Brad and John exchange looks.

Brad sighs deeply and asks, "Why didn't they like you. What did you do to make them dislike you to the point they wanted to kill you?"

"I openly displayed no fear of Rouché. He didn't like that."

Brad says in a dubious tone, "So he and his two friends attacked you, and you were lucky enough to have your weapon."

"Brad, it's a long and complex story."

Brad sits in thought for a few moments; then, he says, "After this mission is over, you need to tell me what happened and why. John and I are the only two that know. John is the one who prepared your weapons and hid them here on *Columbus*."

"So, I ask you again, Rig. Will you have any problem using your weapons if you need to?"

"Sir, if I am attacked, I will use them."

"Good!" Brad responds with finality in his tone.

John Smith just nods a knowing smile.

"Anything happen with Gunny Bronston? Have you seen him, or has he recognized you?"

"I saw him several times and talked with him once. I don't think he suspects me."

Brad stands and says, "One last thing before you depart. You probably know that Sally Macfurson is here in Naples?"

"Yes, I know she is here."

Brad orders, "Stay away from her until this is all over."

"Yes, sir."

After Rigney departs the Communications Office, John Smith turns to Brad and comments, "You didn't tell him that you have a team watching Sally Macfurson."

"It's only a safety precaution, just in case the Soviets discovered her relationship with Rig. If they know she's here, they may put a tail on her. It's another possible lead to Lucifer."

John considers Brad's words and comments, "Sally Macfurson is an unwitting and innocent participant in this game. The other side could see her as a bargaining chip."

"That's why I have Delta Team watching her. We'll ensure no harm comes to her."

Chapter 109

"NOW LIBERTY CALL—LIBERTY COMMENCES FOR
SECTIONS ONE AND TWO—LIBERTY EXPIRES ONBOARD AT
MIDNIGHT."

RM1 Thomas Bollier stands in the long liberty line on the fantail.
He plans to take a taxi to the train station and board a train to Rome
where he will take a flight to the Bahamas. His .25 caliber pistol and
five-thousand dollars in cash are the only personnel items he carries. He
carries the pistol for protection of the money. He plans to ditch the gun
just prior to getting on the airplane.

The liberty line moves quickly and Bollier departs the ship without
incident. He exits the fleet landing area and walks to *Via Christoforo
Columbo*.

The scene on the street is typical Naples. Small Italian cars zigzag
and weave in all direction with drivers paying no attention to the traffic
lanes or the traffic signals. Honking and screeching tires are the
prevalent sounds. Magnificent buildings with artfully detailed façades
stand dignified against the disrespecting, chaotic traffic.

Sailors load into taxis, which whisk them off to their desired
locations. Bollier walks across *Via Christoforo Columbo* and enters the
Piazza Municipio. On the other side of the *Piazza*, he hails a taxi.

"*Napoli Centrale* Train Station," Bollier tells the driver.

"Ten thousand lire, signore."

"Yes. *Bene*. Go quickly."

The taxi driver presses down on the accelerator and merges with the
traffic.

Javier's two men follow the taxi.

Robert and Oscar, who comprise ONI Alpha Team, follow Bollier's
taxi in their fifteen-year-old Mercedes.

At this time, neither tail team knows that the other tail team exists.

Thirty minutes later, Bollier's taxi pulls to the curb in front of the
train station. Javier's men pull to the curb fifty feet behind the taxi. The
ONI car pulls up directly behind Javier's men.

About thirty people linger around the outside of the train station.
Several travelers pass through the front swinging doors.

Bollier pays the taxi driver thirty dollars, which includes a sizeable
tip. He exits the taxi and walks toward the door of the train station.

Javier's man, the one in the passenger seat, exits the car and follows
Bollier.

Oscar exits the ONI vehicle from the passenger seat and follows

Bollier.

As Bollier opens the door, Oscar identifies Bollier's tail, causing Oscar to drop back another fifty feet.

Bollier enters the train station and proceeds to the ticket windows. Javier's man stands behind Bollier at the ticket window.

Oscar stands back thirty feet to observe the actions of the two men.

Bollier purchases a one-way ticket to Rome. When the ticket clerk advises that an open round-trip ticket is only 50 percent more, Thomas declines.

The purchase of the one-way ticket convinces Javier's man that Bollier plans to flee. Javier's instructions were clear. *If your evaluation of Thomas's actions makes you think he is fleeing, abduct him and take him to the house in Lago Patria.*

Bollier turns and walks toward the gates. Javier's man walks behind him.

The ONI agent remains close enough to observe and back far enough not to be noticed.

Javier's man is five feet behind Bollier when he says, "Thomas, stop."

Bollier stops and stiffens. His breathing becomes heavy. He starts to sweat. He slowly turns to see who spoke to him in heavily accented English. He sees a medium sized man with a dark complexion and with a thick mustache walking slowly toward him. The man has his hand in his jacket pocket.

When the man is two feet away, he says, "Thomas, look at my hand in my pocket."

Bollier looks down and sees the butt of an automatic pistol. His heart skips a beat, and he gulps hard.

"You must come with me," the man orders in a tough, threatening voice.

Thomas considers reaching for his own pistol, which is stuck deep down in the inside pocket of his peacoat. *I would never beat him to the draw. I will wait for a better opportunity.*

As Bollier and his abductor walk through the train station swinging doors, Oscar follows fifty feet behind.

Robert, who sits in the driver's seat of the ONI Alpha Team vehicle, observes Bollier exit the train station. He becomes alarmed when Bollier and another man get in the backseat of the car in front of him. Robert looks toward the train station door for Oscar. His partner walks casually in the direction of their car. He does not hasten his approach toward their car until the car with Bollier speeds off.

"Follow that car with Bollier," Oscar orders as he gets into the passenger seat. "Stay five or six cars back. I need to tell the Command Center."

Oscar picks up the microphone and calls the Command Center. "Charlie this is Alpha, over."

A familiar voice comes over the radio. "This is Charlie, go ahead, over."

Oscar uses prearranged codewords to advise the Command Center of Bollier's abduction. He also tells the Command Center that Alpha Team is pursuing. He also reports the make, model, and license number of the abductor's car.

Dave and Greg, who comprise ONI Bravo Team, sit in a Fiat sedan not far from the fleet landing entrance. They scan the busy street looking for Lucifer's men, who they believe will tail Page. They cannot use binoculars or be obvious in their search. There are hundreds of people on the street. Many parked cars have people sitting in them. Any of them could be waiting for Page. The ONI advantage is that the enemy should not expect American intelligence agents to be watching.

Dave and Greg stare at the radio as they hear the report of Bollier's abduction.

"Looks like this assignment might get dangerous," Greg says from the driver's seat.

"Yup!" Dave agrees.

Both men pat their sides to verify the presence of their weapons.

Greg suggests, "Will be awhile before Page comes out. What say we grab a bite to eat and be back here at 1430?"

Dave agrees. Both men exit the car and enter the closest café.

Chapter 110

Gunnery Sergeant Christopher Bronston parks his rental car at the Naples Navy Exchange parking lot. He places the visitor's pass for his vehicle on the dash so that it is visible through the window. He pushes his .45 automatic under the driver's seat. He exits the car, locks all doors, and walks into the Navy Exchange.

Inside the Navy Exchange, Bronston purchases some nondescript casual clothes and an equally nondescript jacket. He enters the men's room, removes his uniform, and dresses in the civilian clothes he just purchased. During his search for Barbara Gaile, he wants to be anonymous. His large size makes him noticeable enough. When in uniform, he is conspicuous.

He checks his appearance in the mirror and convinces himself that he looks ordinary. The only evidence remaining of the beating he took on New Year's Eve is a small amount of black and blue around one eye and a scar across the bridge of his nose. Five stitches were required to close the cut. He still walks with a slight limp. Light pain remains in his testicles.

Bronston departs the Navy Exchange and returns to his rental car. He drives through the Naval Support Activity complex and pulls into a parking spot in front of the Administration Building. From his parking spot, he has an unobstructed view of the building's entrance. He steps out of the car and verifies all doors locked. He walks through the Administrations Building front door and finds himself on the quarterdeck.

He looks around and thinks about what to do next. Then, a voice to his left asks, "Can I help you, sir?"

He looks in the direction of the voice and sees a young female third class petty officer sitting behind a large counter.

"I hope so" Bronston replies. "I am looking for YN1 Barbara Gaile."

The petty officer looks through a roster and replies, "She is on the third floor in the captain's office. You can take that elevator over there."

"Thank you." *That was too easy!*

Bronston exits the elevator on the third floor. An office directory on the wall across from the elevator directs him to the left. He slowly walks along the hall and looks in each office as he walks by. He finally comes to a closed door with a sign announcing COMMANDING OFFICER.

He stands at the door and considers entering when the door suddenly opens and a woman with a YN1 chevron exits. Her head is bent down, preoccupied with a hand full of papers. Her nametag identifies her as YN1 Gaile. She walks right into Gunny Bronston.

"Oh! Excuse me!" she apologizes, not even looking into Bronston's face. Then, she walks down the hall while thumbing through the papers in her hand.

She's a looker, Bronston says to himself. *I will have a good time with this bitch.*

Bronston returns to his rental car where he sits and waits for Barbara Gaile to exit the building.

Chapter 111

In the fan room on the 04 Level, RM3 Rigney Page straps on both ankle holsters. Both holsters are fully equipped with Beretta and suppressor. He again wonders why they are called *ankle* holsters because each holster runs halfway up his calf. He pulls his knee high stretch socks over each holster. He stands up straight. His uniform hangs perfectly over his body. The bellbottom trousers of his Service Dress Blue uniform give no hint that two pistols hide beneath.

He walks around the fan room to become accustomed to a holster strapped to each leg. As he walks with the holsters attached to his legs, he remembers the ankle weights he wore when he was a teenager jogging around Seal Beach.

He buttons his peacoat and puts on his white hat. He picks up his gym bag and proceeds to the fan room door. He listens at the hatch. Fan noise makes it difficult to hear if anyone is in the passageway. If anyone senior sees him exiting the fan room wearing his Service Dress Blues, questions will be asked. The best answer he can concoct is that he thought he heard some loud noises and entered the fan room to investigate. He opens the hatch in a manner as if to say, *I am not hiding the fact that I was in the fan room. I had good reason to be in there.*

The passageway is empty. He quickly descends the ladders to the Main Deck and walks aft to the quarterdeck. He hands his leave papers to the *Petty officer of the Watch* for entry in the quarterdeck log. Then, he salutes the OOD and requests permission to depart *on leave*. The OOD grants permission. At the top of the gangway, Rigney salutes the ensign and walks down the gangway to the pier.

After exiting fleet landing, he finds himself on a busy street like no other that he has ever experience. In the Piazza across the street, the scene reminds him of the demolition derby he watched on television, except no crashes occur. The cars dart in all directions and often come close to crashing into each other but at the last second dart off in a different direction. He looks to the west and sees Castle Nuovo, a large brick and marble structure dating back to the thirteenth century. Rigney decides that when he has time, he must walk the streets of this city and experience its culture.

Javier's associate, Carlos, becomes alert when he identifies Page exiting the fleet landing building. He lays his miniature binoculars on the passenger seat. He looks at the photo of Page who is dressed only in a towel. He studies the face in the picture and confirms his identification of Page. Carlos was beginning to think this was another one of Javier's dead-end assignments. Carlos has been waiting down the block from fleet landing since 10:00 a.m. this morning.

Carlos exits his Mini-Minor and steps onto the sidewalk. He walks toward Page then stops when he realizes that Page is standing still, as if he is waiting for someone. Carlos stays distant by one-hundred-fifty feet. He mentally prepares to follow Page on foot.

A gray U.S. Navy bus stops in front of the fleet landing building. The sign in the front window of the bus says *Naval Support Activity Shuttle*.

Rigney climbs into the bus.

Carlos returns to his Mini-Minor and starts the engine.

Fifteen minutes later, the bus departs for Agnano.

Carlos drives his vehicle directly behind the bus.

ONI Bravo Team follows one-half block behind the bus. They know where the bus is going. They have not yet spotted the Lucifer tail. As soon as they do, they must radio the Command Center and confirm that Page has a tail.

The city of Naples fascinates Rigney. The last time he had seen so many beautiful and ornate buildings was during his visit to Washington D.C.

The bus passes the San Germano Hotel and turns left onto the street leading to the Naval Support Activity.

Carlos still drives directly behind the bus.

ONI Bravo Team now follows a full block behind the bus, and they now suspect the Mini-Minor is the Lucifer tail.

The bus enters the Navy Exchange gate.

Carlos has no access permit to the U.S. facility. Cars occupy all on-street parking spaces near the gate. He performs a U-turn; then, he double-parks near the gate.

ONI Bravo Team passes the Mini-Minor. Two-hundred feet later, the ONI car does a U-turn and pulls into a marked parking space. Greg, the ONI driver, can easily see the double-parked Mini-Minor and the Navy Exchange gate.

Rigney does not exit the bus at the Navy Exchange. He exits the bus at the next stop, which is the Administration Building.

"I fuckin' knew it! I should have trusted my instincts!" Gunny Bronston utters tightly as he sees RM3 Rigney Page exit the shuttle bus and enter the Administration Building. This development changes Bronston's plans. Not sure how he will now proceed, he decides to follow Page and Gaile for the time being. He does not want to act too quickly. *Torturing those two requires a planned course of action.*

527

Fifteen minutes later, Rigney and Barbara exit the Administration Building and walk across the parking lot toward the Navy Exchange.

Gunny Bronston drives out of the parking space and follows slowly at a far distance.

"We are supposed to exit at the Exchange parking lot," Rigney tells Barbara.

"I know," she replies. "I was briefed."

They walk another twenty feet and Barbara asks, "Do you need to get anything at the Exchange?"

"I don't know. I have a three-day supply of socks and underwear. Can you think of anything else that I would need?"

"Well, do you plan on wearing that uniform all the time? We could be at the beach house for some time."

"Actually, I was planning on being out of this uniform most of the time," Rigney says with a devilish smile on his face.

"I mean other than that," Barbara snaps back with a smile and slap to his forearm.

"I guess I will need something to lounge around in," Rigney concedes.

"I have already moved in the stuff I need," Barbara advises. "and I have stocked it with food, drinking water, and wine. This house does not have central heat. Gas bottle space heaters called *boombalas* provide heat. Maybe you want to get a sweat suit and a pair of tennis shoes and some thick socks. The Exchange is right there." Barbara points to a building ahead of them on the left.

"Good idea."

Gunny Bronston pulls into a parking space that gives him a good view of the front door to the Navy Exchange.

Twenty minutes later, Rigney and Barbara stand outside the gate. They look about and chat trying to look undecided about what to do next. They both see the double-parked Mini-Minor across the street, and they both concentrate on not staring at it.

Carlos becomes anxious. He feels exposed being this close to Page. He watches Page out of the corner of his eye.

"There they are," Greg observes from the driver's seat of the ONI Bravo Team vehicle.

A taxi stops in front of the gate and several sailors exit the taxi. Barbara walks to the taxi and talks to the driver. After a few moments, she waves Rigney over. They both get into the backseat, and the taxi takes off. The Mini-Minor takes off right behind it.

"That cinches it," Greg confirms. "Radio the Command Center and tell them we have sighted the Lucifer tail."

Greg drives the ONI car out of the parking space and follows.

As the ONI car comes abreast of the gate, Gunny Bronston accelerates his car out the gate without looking both ways. Bronston's eyes focus on the taxi as he cuts off the ONI car.

Greg slams on the brakes and comes to an abrupt stop. He takes a deep breath and says, "I guess after you have been here a while, you start driving like the natives."

In the passenger seat, Dave has both hands on the dash and does not say anything. He has been in Naples too long to get upset over the driving habits of the natives.

At the San Germano Hotel, the taxi turns right and proceeds west toward the beach areas of *Lido di Licola* and *Lago Patria*. In succession, Carlos, Bronston, and ONI Bravo Team make the turn and follow the taxi.

When ONI Bravo Team observes the car that rushed out the Exchange gate make the same turn, they suspect a second Lucifer tail.

The taxi and three tailing vehicles drive through Pozzuoli and proceed north on Via Domitiana. The congested rush hour traffic on Via Domitiana moves slowly, and neither Carlos nor Gunny Bronston considers that they are being tailed.

At the signs pointing to *Lido Di Licola*, the taxi turns left onto Via Ariete. Before making the turn, Rigney notes the road sign that advises *Lago Patria* is six more kilometers north on Via Domitiana. He remembers that *Lago Patria* is where Sally Macfurson lives and works.

The taxi and three tailing vehicles mix with a dozen other cars on Via Ariete.

When the same car that nearly hit them back at the Navy Exchange gate also turns onto Via Ariete, Dave writes down the vehicle's make, model, and license number.

The taxi stops at the beach house.

Carlos drives past the taxi and pulls to the curb on Via Del Mare one block north of the beach house. He can see the activities at the taxi through his rear view mirror.

Bronston sees the taxi stop ahead. He pulls to the curb on Via Ariete east of the beach house and across the street from the apartment building that houses the Command Center on the top floor. Bronston immediately sweeps his eyes in surveillance of his surroundings.

Out of the corner of his eye, Rigney watches the Mini-Minor pass them and stop about a block away.

Rigney does not notice Bronston's car.

The ONI Bravo Team car passes Bronston and pulls into the underground parking lot of the apartment building that houses the

Command Center in an apartment on the top floor.

Rigney and Barbara exit the taxi. Rigney looks to the west and sees the sun setting over the Tyrrhenian Sea. The chilled air causes both to raise their coat collars around their necks. Barbara pays the driver. Rigney stands and inhales deeply. He enjoys the familiar sounds and smells of the beach. He looks between the buildings and sees the shoreline. He can hear the surf pounding the sand. They walk arm in arm into the beach house.

"Quiet," Rigney observes.

"Yeah," Barbara responds. "This area of *Licola* is peaceful during the winter months. During the summertime, city dwellers swarm the roads and beaches."

Chapter 112

John Smith parts the curtain and looks out a window of the Operation Jupiter Command Center. He watches Rigney Page and Barbara Gaile walk into the beach house. *Right on time*, John says to himself.

The apartment serving as the Operation Jupiter Command Center occupies half the top floor of a five-story apartment building. Except for an eight-foot-wide blind spot along the beach side of the beach house, the Command Center has an unobstructed view of the beach house and all the approaches to the beach house.

Every room of the beach house has a hidden microphone wired back to the Command Center. In the Command Center, an ONI Radio and Acoustics Engineer monitors all audio coming from the beach house. The Command Center also has direct-line telephones to the beach house. In the beach house, the telephones are located in the living room and the bedroom.

"Randy, do you have a clear view of Lucifer TWO?" John Smith asks from the living room to the ONI agent on the balcony.

Randy, an ONI photographer, stands on a Command Center balcony that faces the beach house. He shifts his position several times behind the telescopic camera on a bipod. He hides behind some tall plants and latticework, which they installed on all the balconies as camouflage. The telescopic lens protrudes through a hole in the latticework and points toward the street where Carlos sits in the Mini-Minor.

Randy replies, "Yes, there is only one person in the car. I got him. I'm snapping pictures of him now."

Greg and Dave, the two ONI Bravo Team agents, enter the apartment.

John Smith looks at Greg and Dave and asks, "Any problems?"

"Not a problem, really," Dave responds. "Apollo has two tails."

"Two tails?"

"We just confirmed it a few minutes ago."

"Where's the second tail now?" John Smith asks.

"He's parked on *Via Ariete*, just below us."

John tells Dave, "This apartment has balconies on three sides. Check to see if the second tail is visible from the south balcony."

Dave is back in less than thirty seconds. "Yeah, I can see the car. The guy is still sitting in it."

"Randy," John calls to the agent with the camera. "Get some pictures of this second car and who is in it."

"ROGER! WILCO!" Randy replies and moves his bipod and camera to the south balcony.

531

John directs Greg, "Setup a binocular station on the south balcony to watch the actions of the second tail."

Greg acknowledges Johns order with a casual salute.

John Smith hands all the details regarding the tail cars to Dave. "Update the blackboard with all the tail information. Designate this second tail on Page as Lucifer THREE. Then, get on the phone to the local ONI office. They have a liaison with the Italian Police. Have them trace these cars. Tell them we need to know the names, addresses, and nationalities of all the car owners. We need to know within the hour. If the cars are rentals, we need as much information as possible on who rented them."

Barbara and Rigney enter the beach house through the front entrance, which is on the street side. After entering the house and closing the front door behind them, Barbara slides the two dead bolts to the locked position.

The décor of the house immediately impresses Rigney. He has never seen anything like it. Sea green colored ceramic tile covers the floor of every room. The furniture is Mediterranean contemporary. All the tables and bureaus are made of elaborately carved wood. Oil paintings of nautical scenes adorn all the walls. Carved marble statues of varying heights and ranging from three feet to six feet stand throughout the house. A six-foot-high marble statue of Neptune stands against the wall in the front foyer. The Neptune statue causes Rigney to pause and study it. He wonders why Neptune's trident is stainless steel and not carved marble like the rest of the statue.

Both the couch and armchair in the living room are made of marble and wood. Over-stuffed, blue colored cushions cover the seat, arms, and back of both pieces of furniture.

In front of the marble and wood couch stands an ornately carved wood coffee table. Inlaid glass serves as the tabletop. The theme of the carved wood appears to be sailing ships in full sail.

The living room and master bedroom face the water and have seven-foot-high double-glass doors that open to a courtyard. Rigney walks to the center of the courtyard. He enjoys the familiar sights, sounds, and smells of the beach. On the other side of the courtyard, a large sandy beach stretches for miles to the north and south. A low, four-foot-high wall surrounds the courtyard and allows a spectacular view of the sun setting over the dark green Tyrrhenian Sea. To the southwest, the Island of Ischia rises above the sea.

"Beautiful, isn't it?" Barbara says as she comes to stand beside him.

"I think this is the most beautiful ocean view that I have ever seen. Nothing in Southern California compares to this. How did ONI become so fortunate to own this house?"

"ONI doesn't own it," Barbara informs. "It's the summer home of a cooperative Italian navy captain. ONI leased it from him."

"Spectacular!" Rigney declares.

"We must get back inside and seal up the house," Barbara advises. "ONI orders."

Barbara shows Rigney how to close and lock the roll-down shutters that cover all windows and courtyard doors. Slide bolts on the bottom of each shutter slip into holes on the metal frame. With all the shutters rolled down and locked, no light escapes from the inside of the house. From the outside of the house, the house looks dark. The front door is the only entrance without roll-down shutters.

Barbara ignites the *boombala* space heaters in several rooms.

They are both drawn to the bedroom.

They remove their uniform overcoats. For the first time since meeting each other in Naples, they embrace and kiss tenderly.

"I'm really glad to see you," Rigney whispers into Barbara's ear.

"Not too loud," she whispers back. "They wired this place with listening devices."

"Brad didn't brief me on that," Rigney replies with a whisper.

"Who's Brad?" Barbara continues to whisper.

Rigney just assumed that Lieutenant Commander Brad Watson had briefed Barbara.

"Uh . . . if you don't know him, I guess it's a secret." Rigney's whispering tone is apologetic.

"It's okay, Rig," she whispers back

"Who briefed you?" Rigney asks, still whispering.

"Lieutenant Commander Smith," Barbara whispers softly. "I assume his name is a fake. At first, I thought he might be your brother. He's a hunk too, and he is more my age! I can't get over how much you two look alike."

"I know John Smith. You can stop dreaming. You are not allowed to fraternize with officers, anyway."

"Fraternize, no . . . fantasize, yes!" Barbara responds in a low sexy tone.

They pause as they both wonder what to do next. Then, Barbara looks up into his eyes and whispers softly, "I want to make love to you. Is it okay with you that the Command Center is listening?"

"Where's the microphone in this room?" Rigney whispers.

"Behind the painting above the bed," she whispers in his ear.

Rigney looks at the large rectangular painting of a stormy sea pounding against a rocky coast. He walks to where the bed meets the wall and pulls the bottom of the painting forward. He sees the microphone, which is easily reachable.

"What are you going to do?" Barbara asks.

Rigney puts his finger to his lips as a signal for her to be quiet.

He retrieves a thick athletic sock from the bag of items he purchased at the Navy Exchange. He doubles the sock over and wraps it around the microphone.

"They will not hear us now," Rigney says while exhibiting a mischievous grin.

"Is that okay? Won't they come over here to find out why it isn't working?"

"They will not come over here unless they see someone approaching the house, which is unlikely. ONI wants to follow those who followed us. Anyway, they'll know what I did when they see the only microphone not working is in the bedroom."

Barbara presses her body against his. "What now, sailor?" she asks sexily as she starts unbuttoning the thirteen buttons of Rigney's uniform trousers.

"I guess we find something to occupy our time," he replies and starts unbuttoning the white blouse of her uniform.

They take their time undressing each other. They hang their uniforms in the wardrobe closet. After a few minutes, Barbara wears only her bra and panties. Rigney wears only his undershirt and boxer shorts. The Berettas are still strapped to his ankles.

Barbara laughs. "You look like a cowboy who has dropped his pants!"

Rigney looks down and chuckles. "Looks ridiculous, huh?"

He sits down on the bed and loosens the holster straps.

Barbara's face turns serious, and she asks, "Why do you have those guns?"

"I was told to bring them."

"Why?"

"In case some bad guys get to us before the posse can get here." Rigney attempts to be comical and unconcerned about the remote possibility of danger.

"Mister Smith told me it might get dangerous, but I didn't feel any fear until now. I was thinking too much about being with you again."

"Don't be concerned," Rigney comforts. "They're just a precaution."

Rigney lays both holsters on the bed.

Barbara sits on the bed. The holsters are between them. She looks down at the holsters and runs her hand over the leather. She abruptly looks up at Rigney's face; her eyes are wide. "Have you ever had to use these?" she asks in a horrified tone.

He looks at her. He did not expect the question. He has no lie ready. He does not know how to answer.

His hesitancy gives her the answer.

"Oh, Rigney," she says apologetically. "I'm sorry. I should not have asked."

"No problem. Let's not talk about it."

She nods and smiles.

Rigney moves the holsters from the bed to the floor next to his gym bag. He removes his undershirt and boxer shorts. Barbara removes her bra and panties.

At the sight of Barbara's naked body, Rigney's penis stiffens and he becomes flushed.

At the sight of Rigney's naked body, Barbara feels a warmth wash over her body, and her nipples become hard.

They slip under the covers and hold each other. At first, their kissing is light and tender. Their hands explore each other, rediscovering the other's pleasure zones. Their bodies slowly heat, flaming their passions.

Rigney positions himself over Barbara. He keeps his weight off her by resting on his elbows.

Barbara spreads her legs.

Rigney lowers himself and pushes his penis into her.

Rigney moans with pleasure.

Barbara inhales sharply and moans with pleasure as she feels Rigney's penis slip inside her.

They kiss passionately.

For three minutes, they grunt and moan as they match hip movements. Then, Rigney feels the pressure in his penis.

"I'm going to come Rigney whispers in Barbara's ear."

"Hold off. I'm not ready yet," Barbara pleads back.

"Rigney tightens his pelvic muscles and prevents ejaculation. He maintains his pumping action at the same pace. Holding off the ejaculation takes all his concentration and muscle power.

Ninety seconds later, Barbara squeezes Rigney hard and blurts loudly, "Yes! Now! I'm coming now. Oh Rigney, keep me coming!" She mentions God in several utterances of pleasure.

He relaxes his pelvic muscles and allows his penis to pump semen. His moans become softer with each contraction. He keeps his hip-pumping action constant.

Barbara feels pulsating pleasure spasms from her thighs to her abdomen. She utters deep passionate moans.

Both are captured in sexual ecstasy. They both moan and groan loudly as their orgasms overtake their senses and control the movement of their bodies.

Chapter 113

Gunny Bronston sits in his rental car. He has been parked in the same spot for two hours. Night has fallen. The drop in temperature chills his hands and feet. He can no longer see the beach house clearly.

He has not formed a plan of action. He thought about walking to the beach house and check for entrances, but he does not want to be seen by anyone. He decides to sit for another hour and see what develops.

Thinking that he might need his weapon at a moment's notice, he reaches under the seat, pulls out the .45 automatic, and puts it in his jacket pocket.

Lieutenant Commander Brad Watson enters the apartment serving as the Operation Jupiter Command Center. Like all the ONI agents, Brad wears casual, Italian style clothes. He walks to a back bedroom that serves as a briefing room. A quick scan of the status board informs the location of the ONI Teams and the locations of the Lucifer tails. He notices that some details regarding the Lucifer vehicles are missing.

Brad walks to the living room area, which is the side of the apartment facing the beach house. Except for a few low wattage lamps near the floor, lights are extinguished. Randy, the photographer, loads film into a camera. Dave has the phone to his ear and talks to the local ONI office regarding details on the Lucifer vehicles. Brad steps through one of the balcony doorways and finds John Smith scanning the beach house and surrounding area with night vision binoculars.

"Something going on?" Brad asks John.

"No."

Brad enters the dining room where Harry, the ONI Acoustics and Radio Engineer, sits with earphones over his head. Harry monitors the microphones in the beach house and operates the radio detection equipment. Brad walks back to the living room and motions to John Smith to come to the briefing room.

"John, give me a brief as to assignments and as to what we know so far."

John steps to a map of the local area posted on the wall next to the chalkboard. John points at the chalkboard and the map as he briefs Brad.

"Lucifer One abducted Python at the Naples Central Train Station. ONI Alpha Team followed them to a house in *Lago Patria*. The *Lago Patria* house is designated location Lima. We replaced Alpha Team's car with the surveillance van. Alpha Team is still watching the house from the back of the van. They reported that a number of people have entered the house. None have departed. The Lucifer One car is a rental and was rented by a Madrid company named *Sanchez Imports and Exports.*

"Lucifer Two started tailing Apollo at Fleet Landing and is now parked on Via Del Mare just one block north of us. The Lucifer Two car is also a rental and rented by *Sanchez Imports and Exports* of Madrid. When Lucifer Two departs, we will have Bravo Team follow. We expect Lucifer Two will go to the house in *Lago Patria* where Python is being held.

"Lucifer Three is parked on *Via Ariete*, just below us, and also arrived at the same time as Page. This target has a weapon. About an hour ago we saw him put an automatic in his coat pocket. We have traced his vehicle to the car rental agency at the Navy Exchange, which closed at 1700. We have the NAVSUPPACT duty officer tracking down someone to open the agency so we can see who rented the car."

Dave enters the briefing room and reports, "Hey, John, I just got that info from the Navy Exchange car rental. A Marine Gunnery Sergeant named Christopher Bronston rented the car."

"Oh, fuck!" Brad blurts.

John Smith shakes his head in disbelief; then, he asks Brad, "Should we have Bronston arrested?"

"No, the last thing we want is a lot of commotion down on the street with someone being arrested. We don't want Bronston to know that Page is a target of interest. We might blow Page's cover. We know Bronston has a gun, and I have no doubt that he plans to use it on Page and Gaile. We can arrest Bronston when this is all over. That beach house is a fortress. He won't get in there easily. If he tries to break in the door or break through one of those shutters, shoot him. Shoot to kill. Any questions?"

John asks, "Should we put a tail on Bronston?"

"No, we know where to find him. Besides, when he comes around here, we can track his moves."

John nods his understanding.

"What about the Marine's Fast Reaction Force?" Brad asks.

"They are on standby. They can be at Lucifer's *Lago Patria* house within one hour of us notifying them."

Brad nods and says, "Call Apollo and tell him about Bronston. Tell Apollo he is not to let Bronston or anyone else in that house under any circumstances, unless first notified by you or me. Tell Apollo to have his weapons ready. Tell him that if anyone enters that place without clearance from you or me, he must shoot, and he must shoot to kill. Emphasize that he must shoot without hesitation. Make sure he understands that."

"Yes, Brad. I will do that," John replies seriously.

"And change Lucifer Three on that board to read Bronston One.

"Will do," John replies.

"Okay, continue with the brief."

John Smith glances back at the chalkboard and continues, "We have designated the Command Center as Charlie Team."

Brad nods his understanding.

"Delta Team tails Sally Macfurson. Delta reports nothing unusual."

"Anything else?" Brad asks as he looks around the room.

"Yeah. Harry says that Lucifer is not using radios. Anyway, there have been no radio transmissions from the Lucifer automobile."

"That's odd," Brad comments.

"Sure doesn't make sense," John adds.

"Anything else," Brad asks.

"That's all we have so far," John summarizes. "Oh. Shortly after our lovebirds entered the house, the bedroom microphone stopped working."

"Make that call to Page immediately. Tell him everything I told you to tell him and tell him he must undo whatever he did to that microphone."

"I'm starving," Barbara says as she pushes her naked body from the bed.

Rigney turns on the nightstand lamp and says, "We only did it twice . . . one more time before we eat . . . please?"

The phone on the nightstand rings. Barbara stops and turns toward Rigney. He lets it ring. He is not sure if he should answer it.

"Answer it, Rig. That phone is a direct line to the Command Center."

Rigney picks up and says, "Hello."

He listens to the voice on the other end. Occasionally, he says, "Yes, I understand."

Rigney cradles the phone. He climbs out of bed. He pulls forward the bottom of the painting above the bed and removes the sock from around the microphone.

He turns to face Barbara so that he can brief her on the call. When he sees the full length of her naked body, he is immediately aroused. He inhales sharply and deeply.

She does the same. She looks down and watches his penis rise from flaccid to erect. Her breathing becomes heavy.

They step quickly toward each other and throw their arms around each other. They kiss hard and passionately. Their hands moving rapidly over each other's body.

She pulls her head back and whispers, "But I am so hungry."

"Just a quickie?" he begs in a whisper.

"Okay, but we must do this quietly.

They fall to the bed.

"Lucifer Two is driving off to the north on *Via Del Mare*," Randy reports from the Command Center window where he has night vision binoculars to his eyes.

John Smith picks up the radio's microphone, keys the radio, and says, "Bravo this is Charlie, Lucifer Two moving north on *Via Del Mare*."

A voice responds over the radio, "This is Bravo—roger—out."

Thirty seconds later, Bravo reports over the radio, "Charlie this is Bravo. We have Lucifer Two in sight and are following."

Gunny Bronston looks at his watch – 7:50 p.m. He decides to check the house for entry points. He will only enter if he finds a door or window unlocked. Otherwise, he will go back to the ship and formulate a plan.

He exits the car and starts walking toward the beach house.

"Bronston One is out of his car and walking toward the house," Randy reports from the south balcony.

John Smith picks up the telephone handset.

Barbara and Rigney stand in the kitchen of the beach house and prepare dinner. Barbara makes omelets and Rigney tosses a salad. They wear sweat suits and heavy wool socks to overcome the chill.

Rigney tells Barbara about Bronston.

"So how did Bronston find out you were the one who beat him up?"

"John didn't say."

Barbara wonders if it was the Norfolk private detective. Her Norfolk Controller had briefed her on the private detective that Bronston hired.

They place the food on the kitchen table and start shoveling it down.

The phone rings. Rigney goes to the living room to answer the phone. Barbara follows.

"Got it!" Rigney becomes nervous and fidgety. He hands the phone to Barbara.

"Bronston is walking toward the house. They want you to stay on the phone and relay messages."

Barbara sits on the couch and puts the telephone to her ear.

Rigney dashes to the bedroom to get one of the Berettas.

"Randy, take the phone," John Smith orders. "Relay Bronston's position as I give it to you."

John goes to the corner of the living room and selects a XM21 sniper rifle with a night vision scope. Then, he steps onto the west balcony. John raises the rifle to his shoulder and looks through the scope.

"I have Bronston in my sights," John reports. "He is approaching the front of the house—the street side."

"He's approaching the front of the house. That's the street side," Barbara reports to Rigney.

Rigney stands in the living room and looks at the front door, a distance of twenty-five feet. His right arm is fully extended, and the Beretta is in his right hand. His left hand cups his right hand for support. The thumb safety is off, and he looks down the Beretta's sights to the center of the door. His heart thunders in his chest and sweat seeps from his face, neck, and armpits. He feels fear. Anxiety takes over his body. His arms tremble slightly and the gun waivers in his hands.

Barbara has the phone handset to her ear. She stares at Rigney who stands in the middle of the room with his pistol aimed at the front door. She detects his fear. She begins to realize the danger. She understands that if Bronston comes through that door, Rigney will start shooting. However, she surprises herself because she does not feel fear. She only feels excitement.

Barbara concentrates on the voice on the other end of the line. She reports to Rigney, "Bronston has taken a gun from his pocket, and he is walking up to the front door."

Bronston attempts to turn the doorknob. *Locked!*

Rigney sees the doorknob move slightly. The door vibrates slightly. Then, nothing happens for thirty seconds. He hears one of the window shutters rattle slightly. He turns his stance in the direction of the rattle.

"He's trying the window shutters," Barbara reports into the phone. "Rig, he will never get those shutters open. All those shutters have locking slide bolts. The easiest and quickest way for him to get in here is through the front door, and its solid wood with two dead bolts."

Rigney tracks Bronston's walk around the house as each shutter rattles.

"He just stepped over the courtyard wall on the beach side," Barbara advises. "Command Center has lost sight of him behind the house . . . the beach side."

Barbara and Rigney flinch as the living room courtyard door shutter rattles and vibrates. Rigney turns and aims at the patio door. One minute later, they hear the bedroom shutter rattle.

Bronston continues around the house in search of an entry point. He thinks that someone would come out to investigate the cause of the noise. He hopes someone does. *Then, I'll have them!*

"Okay! The Command Center has him in their sights again!" Barbara whispers excitedly.

Rigney nods his acknowledgement.

Now, silence.

"Bronston is walking back to his car," Barbara whispers, relieved.

Rigney relaxes his stance. He sets the thumb safety on the Beretta. He drops his gun hand to his side.

Barbara rises from the couch and stands next to Rigney. She stares down at his gun. Then, she stares at the front door. "What did they mean that they had Bronston in their sights? Do you think they had guns pointed at him?"

"Most definitely," Rigney responds. "Probably sniper rifles."

Barbara gazes into Rigney's eyes and says, "I do not know what this is all about. Mister Smith asked me to accompany you here. He told me it could be dangerous. I said okay because I want to be with you, and I would like to go with ONI full time. I had no idea what he meant by dangerous. I believe this is about spies. Then, Bronston shows up . . . Sniper rifles you say! I hope someday I'm told the whole story about this because I find this whole thing exciting and fascinating. I don't see how I could go back to shuffling papers."

Rigney just stares back at Barbara. *I am frightened and doing this out of a sense of duty. She finds it exciting!*

"Let's finish dinner," Barbara says with a smile.

Bronston sits in his car. He knows that the only way he will get in that house is through the front door. *They must be in there. Why didn't one of them come out to see what the noise was about? I've got to figure a way to get in that front door.*

Bronston starts his car and drives off.

In the Command Center, everyone lets out a sigh of relief.

John Smith checks with Harry, the acoustics expert. "What are Page and Gaile doing?"

"They're finishing dinner."

"Anything I need to know?" John Smith asks.

Harry Responds, "Yeah. Barbara Gaile is excited about this assignment. She embraces the danger."

In *Lago Patria*, Alpha Team sits in the ONI van and continues their surveillance. From the back of the van, they look through one-way glass with binoculars. They wear headsets so they can listen to the ONI radio reports to and from the Command Center. The reports on the radio tell them that Page's tail is coming to their location. A few minutes later, a car pulls up to the *Lago Patria* house. A man with a dark complexion and thick mustache departs the car and enters the house. Their total count of the people inside the house is eight, including Bollier.

A few moments later, the Bravo Team car drives past the Alpha Team van. Bravo Team radios the Command Center for instructions. John Smith orders Bravo Team to park two blocks away from the *Lago Patria* house and wait for further instructions.

Chapter 114

In Javier's *Lago Patria* house, Thomas Bollier and Javier sit across from each other at the dining room table. Two of Javier's men stand behind Thomas, and another two men stand at the doorway. Thomas's pistol and envelope with five-thousand dollars lie in the middle of the table.

Thomas sweats and breathes heavily. Fear contorts his face. He spent the last two hours explaining his planned trip to Rome.

Javier's manner has been confrontational and threatening.

Bollier knows that he has not convinced Javier. He fears for his life.

"Thomas, your lies make the situation worse!" Javier shouts at Bollier as he slams his fist on the table.

Bollier trembles in his chair.

In a less agitated tone and manner, Javier says, "Thomas, I must know why you stopped transmitting the messages."

"I told you, Javier. We had a fire in MAIN COMM and the cables to my shop were damaged. Everything should be up and running when we go back to sea." Bollier's voice is a desperate plea for Javier to believe him. Bollier has decided that if he can somehow get back aboard *Columbus*, he will turn himself in. He now realizes that life imprisonment will hide him from Javier.

The front door opens and closes. Carlos walks into the dining room.

Javier stands and follows Carlos into the kitchen.

Javier and Carlos converse in Spanish.

Carlos reports, "I followed Page to the navy base. He met a military woman there."

"An officer?" Javier asks.

"No, she wore an enlisted uniform with red stripes like Page, but more. She is a pretty woman. She looks much older than Page."

"Where did they go?"

"They took a taxi to a house in *Lido Di Licola*."

"How did they act toward each other?"

"Affectionate. They acted like lovers."

"What did they do when they arrived at the house?"

"They went inside the house. They had their arms around each other."

"How long did you watch the house?"

"Two hours. After that, I thought I should come and tell you about the woman and the house."

"Did anyone else enter or leave the house?"

"No."

Javier bows his head in thought. *Today's events only make sense if in fact Thomas has not been discovered, but he thought he was discovered and decided to run. The Americans would not let Thomas just walk off his ship. If Thomas was discovered and he agreed to become a double agent, they would not have stopped the messages, and Thomas would have come to our scheduled rendezvous instead of fleeing to Rome. If Page were an American agent and suspects Thomas, Page would be following Thomas and not romancing this navy woman. And today's events only make sense if neither Page nor Sally Macfurson knows the other is here. All logic says this must be true, but my instincts tell me there is more to this Page. I cannot be satisfied about all this until I know for sure about Page. I must know if Page knows about Thomas.*

"Thank you, Carlos. You may get some food now."

Javier walks back into the dining room and sits down next to Bollier. Javier takes a deep breath. He stares at Thomas while trying to decide how to get the truth. He reaches for Thomas's pistol and picks it up. He holds the pistol in both hands and rotates it while thinking about what to do.

"Thomas, why take your pistol to Rome for the day?"

"The last time I was in Rome I was robbed and beaten. I took it for protection."

Javier shakes his head; his disbelief evident.

Thomas shifts in his chair. He looks at Javier and the other men in the room for some indication someone believes him. He sees no indication.

"We were scheduled to meet tonight at our Naples rendezvous. What about that?" Javier asks.

"I thought that was tomorrow night," Thomas says quickly.

Javier shakes his head in dismissal of Bollier's answer. He resumes thinking about how to proceed. He still rotates the pistol in his hands. He ejects the magazine and counts the number of rounds. He pulls back the slide and the chambered round ejects. *Fully loaded.* Then, he places the ejected round back in the chamber and closes the slide. He inserts the magazine.

Javier looks over at Bollier and asks, "Thomas, do you know how to use this pistol?"

The change of subject surprises Bollier. He spends a few moments wondering why Javier would ask that question. Then, he answers, "Yes, I know how to use it. The gun club I belong to in Norfolk has a firing range. I went there once a week and practice."

"When was the last time you practiced?" Javier asks.

Thomas shakes his head slightly and blinks his eyes in bewilderment about these questions. "The weekend before we left Norfolk. Javier, why do you—"

"Because you can redeem yourself, if you are willing to use your pistol."

Javier formulates a plan that has nothing to do with Bollier redeeming himself. A plan that will be useful in determining if Page is an American counterintelligence agent.

Javier assumes a fatherly manner. "Thomas, you must be truthful with me. Tell me why the signals stopped. If you tell me the truth, no harm will come to you. Otherwise, I cannot guarantee your safety. Please understand that I do not wish you harm. I am under the influence of powerful associates that do not always agree with my nonviolent principles. You remember what happened to Bennett in Rota several years ago. That was not my doing. My powerful associates insisted that either Bennett or you be eliminated. They worried about our organization being exposed. I argued in your favor. I only want to know the truth so that I can determine what must be done. By knowing the truth, I can better protect you from my more violent associates."

Desperate to believe that Javier will not harm him, Bollier tells Javier the truth. "Someone took my keys and entered my shop while we were in Palma. I don't know who it was. I could tell someone moved things around on my workbench. Whoever it was did not discover my setup. The concept is too technical and too well disguised. He would have looked right at it and not detect anything out of the ordinary. I think the shop was searched as a matter of routine, and nothing was discovered. Otherwise, I would have been arrested."

"Then, why did you run away?" Javier asks curiously, taking care not to sound confrontational.

"I figured it was just a matter of time before the shop was searched again, and by someone who could understand my setup. The fact that my shop was searched means that they suspect something is happening onboard *Columbus*. So, I disassembled everything and threw it overboard when we were at sea."

"Why did you not come to me, Thomas? I understand perfectly. No one can fault your actions."

"I didn't think you would understand. I have told you previously that I wanted to quit and run away. You wouldn't let me."

"I understand, Thomas. Considering the circumstances, I do not object."

Javier pats Bollier on the shoulder and stands up. He motions to one of his men, Pedro, to follow him into the living room.

Javier and Pedro converse in Spanish.

"Pedro, you know the location of the Hotel Angela here in *Lago Patria*?"

"Yes, Javier, not far from here."

"A young American women named Sally Macfurson lives at the Hotel Angela. She is a short woman with long red hair. She drives a dark green Fiat convertible. She departs her hotel every morning at 7:00 a.m. Tomorrow morning, I want you and Fernando to follower her to the *Ristorante Lago Patria* where she eats breakfast. When she exits the *ristorante,* stop her before she enters her vehicle. Show her your pistol and force her to drive here. You sit in the passenger seat of her vehicle. Fernando can drive our vehicle back here. Do you understand, Pedro?"

"Yes, Javier. I understand."

Barbara and Rigney stand at the kitchen sink in the beach house in *Lido Di Licola.* Barbara washes. Rigney dries.

"You must show me how to use those guns," Barbara insists.

"Why."

"Because I want to know. You never know what kind of situation could arise where I'll need to know how."

"I am not sure that ONI would allow it," Rigney rationalizes. "If ONI wanted you trained on small arms, they would have trained you. Have you had weapons training?"

"During my NATO tour, I was on the Repel Boarders Squad. I was thoroughly trained on the .45 automatic."

"They assigned a woman to a combat squad?"

"You don't think a woman can hold her own in a combat situation?" Barbara challenges.

"I think you can, but I thought it was against government policy to assign women to combat roles."

"It's against American Government policy. I was assigned to a NATO staff. I volunteered. It was mostly ceremonial."

"How often did you fire the .45 automatic?"

"I had to requalify every six months."

The phone rings. Rigney goes into the living room to answer it.

"Hello."

"Rig, John here. Teach her how to load and fire those Berettas."

"No problem with that, then?" Rigney asks for clarification.

"No problem. Just make sure she understands that if the occasion arises that she has to point the weapon at one of the bad guys she must pull the trigger. She cannot hesitate. Make sure she understands that."

"Okay, will do."

Rigney spends the next hour showing Barbara how to use the Berettas. He teaches her how to load the magazine and how to chamber a round. He explains the difference between automatic and semiautomatic mode. He shows her the proper firing stance and how to aim the weapon. He instructs her on how to set and release the thumb safety and how to cock the hammer. Lastly, he trains her on how to screw on a suppressor.

"That's it?" she questions. "No big mystery here. Not much difference from the .45 automatic."

"I taught you the mechanics," Rigney replies seriously. "The tough part is pulling the trigger when you know that you will kill the person you're aiming at. Do you think you can do that?"

"If I know the person will kill me, yes, I will shoot," Barbara says confidently.

"No, Barbara. You don't understand. If a bad guy gets in here, you must shoot to kill. Even if the bad guy appears not to have a weapon pointed at us, his intentions are to harm us. You cannot hesitate."

"I will remember that," Barbara affirms. "But I don't think anyone will get in here. This place is locked down."

Rigney looks at the coffee table where both Berettas lie. Both weapons have suppressors attached. "Let's leave one of the pistols here in the living room, and we can keep the other in the bedroom."

"Sounds good to me," Barbara replies with a deep yawn. Now, let's go to bed. I'm tired. Okay?"

"Okay!" Rigney responds enthusiastically.

Gunny Bronston sits in the chief's mess aboard *Columbus*. He thinks about how to get into the beach house. His eyes dart around the mess. His eyes occasionally focus on an object in hope that the object will spark a good idea. The need for revenge burns in his gut. The more he thinks about those two cuddled up in that house, the more his revengeful anger sizzles.

Not only does he feel hate and the need for revenge, he envies their intimate relationship. After two failed marriages and a string of failed relationships, he still does not understand why women leave him. Most of them had restraining orders issued against him.

Bronston sees himself as a strong and dominating male who is attractive to women. Battering women about when they displease him is part of the natural order. *After all, women are inferior to men and beating up on them is the only way to control them and the only way to gain their respect. It's like training a dog. Equal rights! Fuck those liberal ass*

Jewish bastards!

Bronston plans to kill them both, but not before he puts them through torture. He fantasizes what he will do to the woman while he forces Page to watch.

He stands; then he walks around the Mess and studies the pictures and plaques that hang on the bulkheads. He stops on a drawing of several marines stalking the enemy in the jungles of Vietnam. A plan formulates in his head.

Chapter 115

No other incidents occurred in the area of the beach house after Bronston departed last night. The command center is quiet while the morning shift drinks coffee and eats a continental breakfast.

A call comes over the radio in the ONI Command Center. "Charlie this is Delta. Over."

John Smith grabs the microphone and responds, "This is Charlie, go ahead. Over."

"This is Delta. Debutante has picked up a tail. Over."

"This is Charlie. Where are you now? Over."

"This is Delta. Heading toward location Romeo. Over."

John looks at his watch—7:10 a.m. *Sally is on her way to breakfast.* Romeo is the designator for *Ristorante Lago Patria.*

"This is Charlie. Keep following, avoid detection. Over."

"This is Delta. What if they take Debutante? Over."

"This is Charlie. I say again, do not get detected. Just follow. Over."

"This is Delta. WILCO. Out."

John Smith considers that Sally Macfurson will be abducted. However, Brad was clear last night when he gave instructions. "Until we identify Lucifer, we don't risk being detected."

Sally Macfurson sips her coffee while reading the newspaper. She has no problem reading the articles because Italian is one of the four languages that she speaks fluently. On page four, she reads a lead-in about a U.S. Flagship making a port visit in Naples. She reads the article and finds that the USS *Columbus* arrived yesterday for a seven-day visit.

She digs through her purse, searching for Rigney's letter. She finds it and confirms that Rigney said in his letter that he was assigned to the *USS Columbus. I wonder if he got my letter about me coming to Naples.* She decides to go to the harbor this afternoon and find him.

Sally pays her bill and walks out of *Ristorante Lago Patria* and into the parking lot. As she approaches her car, she sees two men sitting in a car next to hers. Their car sits six feet from her driver's side. The men stare at her as she walks across the parking lot.

During the few weeks that she has been in Naples, she has become accustom to the bold flirtations of the Italian men. This morning, she is not concerned because she believes daylight protects her, and others are walking about.

As she comes around to the driver's side of her car with keys in hand, the man in the passenger seat of the other car rolls down his window and calls to her in heavily accented English, "Miss Macfurson."

Surprised that he knows her name, she turns to face him. She studies his face to see if she knows him. Then, she notices the barrel of a gun pointed at her. She sucks in air, and her heart starts pumping harder. Her face flushes, and she expresses horror.

The man with the gun steps out of the car. The gun is now in his jacket pocket. He still points the gun in her direction through the cloth. In a menacing tone, the man with says, "Drive your car, Miss Macfurson. I will sit on the passenger side."

"Charlie this is Delta. Lucifer Three has taken Debutante. We are following . . . looks like we are going to Lima. Over."

John Smith glances at the *call signs and codenames* list and verifies Lima is Lucifer's house in *Lago Patria*. "This is Charlie. Advise when you reach your destination. Out."

John goes to one of the bunkrooms in the back of the apartment to wake up Brad Watson.

"Charlie this is Delta. Lucifer Three has arrived at Lima with Debutante. Request instructions. Over."

Brad Watson picks up the radio handset. "This is Charlie. Stay two blocks from Lima and within view of Lima. Over."

"This is Delta, WILCO, Out."

Brad looks at John and orders, "Dispatch Bravo Team to sit about two blocks from Lima but within view of Lima. If Lucifer takes either Sally Macfurson or Bollier away from there, I want our teams following."

"Will do." John goes to wake Bravo Team.

John returns ten minutes later and reports to Brad, "Bravo is awake and will leave in five minutes."

Brad looks at his watch—7:30 a.m. He turns to John and asks, "Did we get the pictures back yet?"

"I called the lab at seven. They will have the photos here by 8:00 a.m."

"Good," Brad responds. "Now, let's pull out that picture file of possible Lucifer candidates."

Javier Ramirez should have accepted Andrei's offer of assistance. Andrei's advice would have been to dispose of Bollier and take no further action.

Andrei would have said, *"To go after Page is nothing more than ego running amuck, especially since you are not certain that Page is an agent."*

Andrei would have also advised, *"Cut your losses. Your information resource is lost. Whether the American Navy knows about Bollier's activities or not makes no difference. They don't know about you. If you go after Page and he is an agent, you risk exposing your identity."*

Javier never accepted Andrei's offers of assistance. Javier peddles information to make money for his cause and to harm America, NATO, and Israel. His actions focus on manipulating people, not conducting covert operations. The Soviets provided him with his initial intelligence training, but he had declined the full course of instruction. He also declined the annual seminars designed to hone espionage skills. Javier did not want to be obligated to the Soviets. He wanted the Soviets to be obligated to him. Had he attended the full course and attended the annual seminars, he would have learned how to recognize situations that put him in jeopardy. Javier is an intelligent and educated man with a degree in International Law. Nevertheless, he does not understand, nor is he cognizant of the technology, strategies, and processes being used against him.

Javier plans to trap Page. Javier cannot tolerate loose ends and he sees Page as a loose end. He plans to torture Page for information that he can sell. Then, he will kill all of them. The killings will serve as a warning to the Americans not to come after him. He has killed in the past to send the same message and he will not hesitate now.

He reasons that the Godless and decadent American people are beneath his theological and cultural intelligence. His arrogance and faith prevent him from believing that any American Intelligence Service is smart enough to find him, let alone put him under surveillance.

Javier concludes *I am safe because my cause is Allah's will.*

Chapter 116

Terror consumes Sally Macfurson. She breathes heavily and her heart beats rapidly. Tears run from her eyes. The men who abducted her said nothing during the ten-minute drive from the *Ristorante.*

They took her at gunpoint to this house. Now, she sits at a dining room table. A pistol sits in the middle of the table. Five swarthy looking men stand around the room. All the men ravage her with their eyes. Their stares increase her fears about what will happen to her.

A grossly fat, unshaven man in a rumpled and lint-laden U.S. Navy uniform sits at the other end of the dining room table. She notes the first class radioman chevron on the sailor's sleeve. For a brief moment, she wonders if this has anything to do with Rigney.

The men who stand around the room speak to each other in a mixture of Spanish and another language that she thinks to be a middle eastern. Mostly, they speak Spanish, which she understands. Their manner indicates that they do not know she understands what they say in Spanish. Sally does not let on that she understands. Mostly, they talk about a man named Javier. They wish Javier would soon finish his business in Italy, so that they can all go home and spend time with their families.

Javier enters the room. The other men around the room stop talking. Javier sits down at the table midway between Sally and Bollier. For reasons that she cannot understand, the presence of this well dressed and dignified looking man causes her fear to lessen.

Javier speaks in English. He does not know that Sally speaks and understands most of the Romance Languages.

"Sally, my name is Javier. Are you comfortable? May I get you anything?"

Sally exhibits bewilderment. She was kidnapped, and now this man treats her as a guest. Her voice trembles, and she chokes back sobs as she asks, "I just want to know what you want from me. Why am I here?"

"Sally, you should not feel afraid. If you do as I say, you will be back in your hotel room tonight."

Javier sounds convincing to Sally. However, Javier is lying. If all progresses as Javier plans, Rigney Page, Thomas Bollier, and Sally Macfurson will not survive the day.

Javier continues, "I must speak with Rigney Page, and I need you as security. When I face him, he must know that your safety is in my hands."

Suddenly, Sally is less frightened for herself and more concerned about Rigney's safety. Sally looks around the room again. She looks at all the men more closely. When she was first abducted, she thought these men were thieves and rapists. After that, she dismissed the thieves and rapists theory and thought they were kidnappers with the intention of extorting money from her father. Now, she thinks they are neither because Rigney is involved. *How could Rigney be involved with such men? What has Rigney done?* Sally glances at the sailor sitting at the far end of the table. *What's going on here!*

Sally no longer sobs. Javier's manner conveys that he is telling her the truth, and she begins to understand that this situation is about Rigney, not her.

Sally returns her attention to Javier. "I don't know where Rigney is and I don't think he knows I'm in Italy."

"I know where he is," Javier states. "He stays with a woman at a beach house in *Lido Di Licola.*"

Javier studies Sally's face for a hint of jealousy.

Sally's expression is more surprise than jealousy. Rigney had never mentioned that he knew anyone in Italy. When they parted last November, they congenially agreed that they were not obligated to each other. They both agreed that should they come together in the future, there would be no obligation to continue their romantic relationship.

"What woman?" Sally asks.

"Her identity is not important. What is important is that you and Thomas follow my instructions." Javier nods toward Bollier.

Sally looks at Bollier and wonders about his involvement.

"We will go to the beach house in *Licola.* I will place you in Page's view but too far away for him to talk with you or assist you. He will speak to me when he understands that you are under my control."

Sally knows that Rigney is his own person, and he is obsessed with not allowing others to manipulate him. She considers that Rigney might not respond as this Javier predicts. She feels compelled to tell Javier this.

"Rigney might not do what you want. He knows when someone attempts to manipulate him. He will not respond to manipulation. He can be very stubborn."

"When he sees you next to one of my men, he will do what I ask. I am sure that he has more concern for you than you say. You two are intimate lovers. You have shared your bodies. He will not want to see you harmed."

Javier's description of the relationship between Rigney and Sally causes a stir among the men in the room. Javier's words cause each man, including Javier and Bollier, to visualize lying naked with this attractive and fair-skinned American woman. Each fantasizes his penis pumping in and out of the orifice of his choosing.

Sally hears the breathing of the men becoming faster and heavier. She quickly looks around the room. Their penetrating stares betray their thoughts. Fear comes back to her. She visualizes the horror of these men violating her. She becomes weak and slumps in her chair. She begins to sob.

Javier now realizes the effect of his words on his men. Although Javier and his men consider themselves religious, disciplined, and civilized, rape might be considered an acceptable action against nonbelieving women. Javier sees the fear of rape in Sally's manner. He decides to use her fear against her. Fear of rape will allow Javier to control her.

Javier promises, "Sally, you have nothing to fear from us as long as you are cooperative."

Javier's calm and soothing voice comforts Sally. She wants to believe him.

Javier looks at one of his men and says, "Pedro, take Miss Macfurson upstairs and lock her in the large bedroom. Stand guard outside the door."

Pedro nods acknowledgement. Sally stands, and Pedro leads her upstairs.

As she walks up the stairs, she realizes that she will be alone in the bedroom. She hopes to find a window. She hopes to escape.

Sally enters the bedroom. The room is four bare walls. Unmade single beds stand against the walls. The room smells of dirty clothes. The only window has jail like bars.

Javier stares across the table at Thomas Bollier. Javier finds Thomas's appearance disgusting. *Running away is the only option for this Godless and pathetic human being.*

Javier does not want to display his loathing toward Thomas. Today, he wants Thomas to get inside that beach house.

Javier reaches to the middle of the table and pushes the pistol toward Thomas.

Bollier's eyes intently follow the motion of the pistol.

Javier stops the pistol just inches from Thomas's grasp.

Thomas looks up from the gun and stares into Javier's eyes and asks—almost pleads, "What do you want me to do? I will do anything to prove my loyalty to you!"

Javier snaps his head back in revulsion of the foul smell of Bollier's breath. He moves his chair back to distance himself from Thomas's odor.

"I want you to convince Page to come out of that house and sit in my car so that I talk with him."

"How will I do that?"

"I will position a car with Miss Macfurson and one of my associates down the street from the beach house, which will allow Page to easily see them from the door or window. You will tell Page that if he does not come out and talk with me, he risks Sally's safety."

Thomas responds, "If Page is what you think he is, he will be too smart to come out of that house and get into a car with you. If he is not what you think him to be, I will have exposed myself as a participant in a spy conspiracy. Either way, I am dead meat. Page will report me. The U.S. Government will know what I did, and they will hunt me down."

Javier demands softly and firmly, "You must force Page and the woman with him to come out of that house. You can use your pistol to force them out of the house. After you do this for me, you are free to run and hide wherever you wish."

A spark of hope flashes through Bollier's mind. He looks down at his pistol.

"Take your pistol," Javier offers.

Javier's offer startles the other men in the room. They all place their hands on their own weapons.

Javier notices his men's actions. He stops them by raising his hand with his palm facing out and saying, "Do not pull your pistols. I trust Thomas not to turn on us. He is one of us now."

Thomas's eyes dart from face to face looking for reassurance from the other men in the room. He sees only blank stares. He looks into Javier's face. He sees encouragement; he also knows that Javier can be dangerously deceptive. He spends a few moments contemplating his situation. He doubts Javier's promise to let him go. He concludes that he has no control. He must do what Javier demands. He has no choice. Thomas picks up the pistol.

Javier smiles.

"How do I get Page to listen to me? What do I say to him to make him leave that house?"

"Knock on the door. If he does not come to the door, call to him. Tell him who you are and that if he does not cooperate, he risks the safety of Sally Macfurson. Tell him you want to come inside and explain the situation to him."

Bollier considers what can go wrong with this. Then, he asks Javier, "What if he won't come out to meet with you?"

"Point your pistol at him and force him to come."

Bollier dislikes the idea of pulling a gun on Page. If Page is an American agent, which he doubts, Page could have a gun of his own.

After some consideration, Bollier realizes that he has no choice. He must do as Javier demands.

"What about the woman with Page?" Thomas inquires.

"Bring her out with Page."

"Okay, Javier. When will I do this?"

"This morning, but first you must shave and shower and wash your mouth."

Chapter 117

Gunnery Sergeant Christopher Bronston moves stealthily through the thicket located on the south side of Via Ariete and spans the length of the distance from the Via Domitiana to the *Licola* beach, approximately 300 yards. The dense growth prevents him from seeing more than fifteen feet in any direction. He carefully and cautiously pushes branches to the side so that his movement in the thicket cannot be seen from the road, Via Ariete, which he calculates to be fifty feet to the north. The thicket's vegetation is high enough to form a canopy over him that hides him from anyone's view in any of the multiple story apartment buildings on the other side of Via Ariete. His combat knife, which he carries sheathed in his left hand, has a compass at the top of the handle. He periodically checks the compass to ensure he maintains a westerly direction toward the beach.

He wears his olive green combat uniform. He removed all the insignias, name patches, and chevron patches. He wears a web belt and a holstered .45 caliber automatic.

Bronston glances at his watch—8:50 a.m.

"That must be Lucifer," Brad Watson declares as he points to three pictures he separated from the rest.

John Smith looks at the photographs spread over the table in the Command Center dining room. He nods his head in agreement.

For the last hour, Brad and John studied photos taken of the men entering and leaving the house in *Lago Patria*. They compared those photographs to others taken over the years of suspected espionage agents who could be Lucifer. Only one man's photograph from *Lago Patria* matches those from previous years.

Brad picks up the best quality photograph. He studies the image of the man who wears expensive clothes and jewelry and who portrays a sophisticated and worldly appearance. Brad shares his analysis with John. "CIA believes this person killed their operative and that Mossad operative in Athens four years ago. Those killings made no sense to U.S. Intelligence. The Soviets would not kill two agents who were about to discover one of their operations. It's an unwritten rule of the game. If you know that the other side is about to discover your operation, you move it, or close it down. You don't kill the operatives because others will easily replace them. Even the Soviets understand that such tactics are a waste of human life. If killing were part of the game, we would be focused on revenge and not discovery. Killing does not serve either side.

Mossad reported that the assassinations looked more like a terrorist attack than chance killings. Now, I do not believe that Lucifer is the Soviet agent that we always thought him to be. In any case, Lucifer is a kidnapper and dangerous killer. We must deal with him accordingly."

"I agree," John responds.

"Charlie this is Alpha. We have movement of two Lucifer vehicles. Debutante is in a blue Fiat sedan with two men. Python is in a red Mercedes with three other men."

Brad picks up the radio handset and orders, "Delta, follow Debutante. Bravo, follow Python. Over."

"This is Delta. WILCO, out."

"This is Bravo. WILCO, out."

Brad looks at his watch—9:25 a.m.

Gunny Bronston crouches behind a large bush at the edge of the thicket. He looks across a clear patch of sand and easily views the front door to the beach house. He calculates the distance to the door to be fifty feet. Considering the sand, he knows he can dash across the space to the door in about five to eight seconds. *Now, I must wait until someone opens that fuckin' door!*

Bronston cycles his plan in his head. He had parked his rental car behind some trees on the west side of the Via Domitiana. The vehicle has Italian license plates instead of the Allied Forces Italy—AFI— license plates. Therefore, the car should not attract any attention. It took him forty-five minutes to transit the thicket. He plans to depart the area through the thicket when he is done with Page and Gaile. He wears his battle uniform to camouflage himself in the thicket. He removed all Marine Corps insignias and patches from his combat uniform.

Bronston looks at his watch—9:35a.m. He becomes anxious. He needs to get into that house. He thinks of the torturous pain that he will inflict on Page and Gaile. His heart pumps faster, and he breathes harder when thinking of the sexual acts he will make the woman perform on him. His penis aches as it gorges with blood.

Bronston concentrates on nonsexual thoughts. *I can't be running across that space with a stiff dick!*

Delta Team reports over the radio, "Charlie this is Delta. Both Lucifer vehicles have turned toward your location—should arrive in ten minutes, over."

"Charlie this is Bravo. I concur, over."

"Delta and Bravo, this is Charlie, drop back and stop following. Return to Charlie. Over."

"This is Bravo. WILCO, out."

"This is Delta. WILCO, out."

Brad lays down the radio handset and looks at John Smith. "This is unexpected."

Brad spends a few moments considering the possibilities. Then, he concludes aloud to John, "Lucifer must be coming to get Page, and he's gonna use Sally Macfurson to lure Page out of the house."

"That's a stupid move," John Smith declares. "Lucifer is playing right into our hands. He will place himself in our line of fire. Lucifer could not possibly know for sure that Page is an intelligence agent. Why is he risking exposure?"

Brad concludes, "Bollier might have told Lucifer that he thinks Page is an agent, or Lucifer suspects Page is an agent as a result of their investigation. In Lucifer's mind, he must make sure. The logical move for Lucifer would be to eliminate Bollier and disappear. Lucifer has not considered the possibility that we are watching and guarding the beach house. We have been passive so far. Lucifer must think that if Page had discovered Bollier's activities, Bollier would have been arrested. Lucifer must think that Page has not discovered anything because Page went on vacation and locked himself and Barbara in a love nest. Lucifer might think that if he eliminates Page and Page is not an ONI agent, then no harm done to Lucifer. Page just becomes another deserter statistic. If he eliminates Page and Page is an agent, Lucifer sends us a strong message that he is dangerous and clever, and we should not fuck with him."

"But that would be stupid and vain on his part," John Smith reasons. "I've never known the Soviets to kill agents just to send a message. There's no value in it."

"You're preaching to the choir, John. As I said before, we might have been wrong as to Lucifer's affiliation. He does not act like an experienced and trained Soviet operative. As I said before, he might not be what we have always thought him to be. Lucifer is a kidnapper and a murderer, and we must treat him as such."

John nods his agreement.

Brad tells John, "Get on the radio and order the Marine Fast Reaction Force to deploy here. Have them standby at the intersection of *Via Domitiana* and *Via Ariete*. We don't want the Marines storming in here until the situation warrants. Also call the local ONI office to coordinate actions with the Italian police. The Italians should know that we will eventually cordon off this area."

John acknowledges the order and picks up the radio handset.

Brad picks up the handset to the phone unit that connects with the beach house.

Rigney Page and Barbara Gaile sit on the couch in the living room of the beach house. The phone rings. Barbara picks up the handset.

"They want to talk to you." Barbara passes the handset to Rigney.

He listens and recognizes Brad's voice.

Rigney listens for a few moments. Then, he jumps to his feet and expresses anger. "They have Sally!" Rigney says loudly into the handset. "How did they know about her?"

"You must calm down, Rigney," Brad cautions over the phone. "We have a mission to complete, and you cannot afford to become emotional. I promise you that no harm will come to her. We are watching their every move. If they try to harm her, we will take them out. Can you calm down and listen to my instructions?"

Rigney demands in an agitated tone, "Why didn't you take them out before? Why didn't you stop them from taking her in the first place?"

"We didn't have the opportunity," Brad Watson explains. "And, you must remember that aspects of this operation were not made known to you. You must trust me on this."

Rigney feels the need to take personal action to rescue Sally. He believes that she is more at risk unless he is personally involved in the rescue actions. He also comprehends that he must follow Brad's orders, but he will disobey Brad's orders if he sees an opportunity to save Sally.

"Okay. What are we going to do?" Rigney conveys irritable agitation.

"They will try to lure you and Barbara out of that house. I think that Bollier will come to the door and try to talk you out of that house. They will probably place Sally up the street where you can see her from the door. You must not come out of that house unless I specifically order you to. We have four sniper rifles up here in the Command Center. We will have them targeted from the moment they arrive. The only way to ensure Sally's safety is for you and Barbara to stay inside that house. We will get Sally away from them."

"So, what do you want me to do when Bollier comes to the door?"

"I want you to be armed but conceal your weapon. Attach the suppressors. If you must shoot, I don't want anyone outside the house hearing the shots.

"Get Bollier to come inside. After he is inside, show him your weapon. Tie him up and gag him. Put him somewhere out of the way. Then, just sit tight, and we will do the rest. If anyone besides Bollier comes through that door, you are to shoot to kill. Have Barbara on the phone with us, so that she can relay instructions and reports."

Rigney does not respond right away. He thinks about how Sally got involved in this and what can happen to her.

Brad barks into the phone, "Page! Acknowledge what I just told you to do. We don't have much time!"

Rigney comes back to the moment and warns, "Brad, you promised that no harm will come to Sally. I will hold you to that. If any harm comes to her, I will hold you responsible."

"They are pulling up." Rigney hears someone say over the telephone from the background in the Command Center.

"I will take care of Sally, Rig. You just do your part. Now, hand the phone to Barbara and get ready."

Rigney hands Barbara the phone. He starts for the bedroom to get the other Beretta.

"Who is Sally?" Barbara calls after him.

"I'll tell you in a second," Rigney replies back over his shoulder.

Rigney returns to the living room with the Beretta, his sneakers, and Barbara's sneakers. "Put these on, quickly," he orders as he hands Barbara her sneakers.

Barbara remains seated on the couch. She puts on the sneakers as Rigney directs.

Rigney stands by the couch next to Barbara. He flips off the safeties for both Berettas. He puts one of the pistols in the pouch of his hooded sweatshirt. The other weapon he places at Barbara's feet. The pistol lies between her feet and the ornate coffee table, which hides it from view anywhere else in the room.

Barbara remains seated on the couch. Her eyes lock on Rigney's every movement. She waits anxiously for him to explain what's happening.

Finally, Rigney explains, "Something unexpected has come up. In a few minutes, a fat sailor who happens to be a Soviet spy will knock on the door. He will try to lure us outside with the threat that Sally Macfurson will be hurt if we don't. Our orders are not to leave this house. I will bring Bollier in here, bind him, and gag him. If anyone else comes through that door, my orders are shoot to kill. If a bad guy gets past me, pick up that Beretta and start shooting. Do not hesitate to pull the trigger. Can you do that?"

"How will I know a bad guy when I see him?" Barbara's eyes are wide, and her breathing becomes heavy. She feels anxiety. She was not expecting this. When she asked Rigney to show her how to use the Berettas, she never thought she would really need to kill anyone . . . *and not so soon!*

Rigney stares at Barbara with a concerned look and says, "Anyone who comes through that door has the intention to do us harm. Shoot to kill!"

A worried and confused look overcomes Barbara's face.

"Barb, you must do this. Our lives are at stake here."

She nods her head and stammers, "Yes . . . I . . . I can do this." Barbara stares into space as she thinks about the possibility of killing someone.

Rigney understands what is going through Barbara's mind. He has been there.

Barbara comes back to the moment and asks, "Who is Sally?"

"She's a woman I know from New London."

"Are the two of you more than friends?" Barbara hopes not.

"We were romantically involved, but we broke it off last November."

Barbara thinks for a few moments; then, she asks, "How did she get involved in this?"

"Coincidental happenstance."

Chapter 118

Out on the west balcony of the Command Center, Brad Watson and John Smith look down through the balcony camouflage at the two cars parked on Via Del Mare. The two cars sit two hundred feet north of the beach house. The Fiat sedan is parked directly behind the red Mercedes.

ONI Bravo Team and Delta Team come through the front door of the Command Center.

Brad directs, "Dave, Greg, bring all the sniper rifles out here."

Javier exits the backseat of the red Mercedes and walks to the Fiat sedan and talks to the driver.

Brad and John have their sniper rifles aimed at the Fiat sedan. Through the scopes, they recognize the man who exited the Mercedes as the one they have identified as Lucifer.

After a few minutes, Lucifer returns to the backseat of the Mercedes.

The Fiat sedan pulls away from the curb and repositions itself on the south side of Via Ariete, about halfway between the beach house and the entrance to the Command Center apartment building. The car points to the east and is in direct view of the beach house front door. Both the Mercedes and the Fiat are in view of each other.

Brad could not have asked for better positioning of the Fiat sedan that holds Sally Macfurson. He looks at the Fiat sedan through the scope of his sniper rifle. Three people sit in the Fiat. Brad clearly sees Sally in the backseat, directly behind the driver. He also has a clear view of the driver through the windshield and driver's side door window. Because of the car's roof, Brad does not have a full view of the man in the backseat with Sally. He can only see the man's body from the chest to his lap.

The man in the backseat points an automatic pistol at Sally, but his trigger finger is around the trigger guard and not the trigger. The man obviously thinks he is in no danger.

Brad turns to John Smith and asks, "How's your targeting on the Mercedes?"

John looks through the scope of his sniper rifle. "I have a clear view of the driver and Python. I have a good shot on the guy sitting directly behind the driver, but I only have a partial view of Lucifer. He is in the backseat directly behind Python."

"Do you have a kill shot on Lucifer?" Brad asks.

"Yes, I have the crosshairs on his heart."

Brad considers the targeting situation and who should do what. He looks at Dave and Greg who stand just inside the balcony door. Fredrick and Sammy of Delta Team stand behind Dave and Greg.

Brad orders, "Sammy, go get Randy. Oh, and bring the beach house phone out here."

Sammy returns with Randy and the beach house phone a few moments later.

Dave and Greg hold the other two XM21 sniper rifles.

Brad explains the targeting plan. "John and Dave target the Mercedes. John, you take out Lucifer, and Dave takes out the driver. Dave, your second target is the guy behind the driver.

"Greg and I will take the Fiat. I will target the guy holding the gun on Sally Macfurson. Greg, you take out the driver. We are all going for kill shots. I will give the order to fire. We all pull our triggers at the same time."

Brad instructs Fredrick and Sammy. "I want you two to go down to the street and get as close to the Fiat as you can without exposing yourselves. When you see that we have fired, I want Sammy to get Sally and bring her here. Fredrick, you cover Sammy."

Brad gives instructions to Randy, "Randy, I want you on the balcony with us. Your job is to watch the front door of the beach house and to be on the phone with Barbara and relay reports and instructions.

"In a few minutes, I expect a sailor to get out of that red Mercedes and go to the front door of the beach house. Page will let the sailor in. Now listen, Randy. The rest of us will be focused looking through the scopes of our weapons. You must describe what you see as it happens. Speak softly into the phone. The rest of us will hear you."

Brad picks up binoculars from a small stand and hands them to Randy.

Brad looks around the group of operatives and asks, "Any questions?"

Each agent shakes his head.

"Okay. Take your positions."

Sammy and Fredrick leave the Command Center and proceed to the parking garage.

Brad, John, Dave, and Greg take up their positions behind the camouflage on the west balcony. All four point their suppressor equipped, XM21 sniper rifles through the camouflage and down toward the street. Each has the scope's crosshairs on their assigned target. Randy stands on the same balcony with the phone headset to his ear, and he watches the red Mercedes through the binoculars and waits for the sailor to exit.

Gunny Bronston becomes impatient. *Isn't anyone ever gonna open that fuckin' door!* His impatience makes him more angry and hateful toward the couple inside the beach house.

He looks at his watch—10:05 a.m. He contemplates rushing the house and using his ramming weight to crash through the door. From where he hides, he cannot see much of the street. He heard a few cars go by. He has not seen anyone walking around. He estimates little chance exists that anyone will see him. He thinks about the possible failure of crashing the door. If he is not successful on the first try, Page will be alerted and, therefore, be on guard. Bronston does not fear Page. He knows that Page surprised him last New Year's Eve. He never thought that a squid could fight. Now that he knows Page's capabilities, he will only face Page with a gun or knife. Gunny Bronston is proficient with both weapons.

Bronston hears footsteps on the street. He looks through the brush northward on the Via Del Mare. He can only see a small portion of the street. A sailor in crackerjack Dress Blue uniform walks into his view. A surprised look appears on Bronston's face when he recognizes the fat radioman from the *Columbus*.

What the fuck is he doing here? This new development increases Bronston's agitation.

When Bollier knocks on the door of the beach house, Bronston realizes that this is his chance to get in. *Okay, so I must kill one more person.*

"Bollier is coming to the door," Barbara reports.

Rigney walks to the door.

Bollier knocks.

"What do you want, Bollier?" Rigney asks loudly through the closed door.

Surprised that Page knows who is on the other side of the door, Thomas looks for a peephole. He does not see one.

"What do you want, Bollier?"

"I must talk to you about Sally Macfurson. She's in danger."

Rigney slides back the two dead bolts and opens the door slightly. He has his hand in his sweatshirt pouch; he grips the handle of the Beretta. He looks around quickly to see if anyone stands near Bollier. He does not see anyone. Then, Rigney gives Bollier a look from head to toe.

"What do you know about Sally?" Rigney asks with a defiant look on his face.

"Look past me to that dark blue car up the street. You will see Sally." Bollier turns halfway around and looks in the direction he just described.

Rigney looks east on Via Ariete and sees a man exit the rear door on the passenger side of the car. The man holds a pistol pointed at the ground. The man walks around the rear of the car and opens the rear door on the driver's side. Sally steps out of the car.

The man positions Sally to stand in front of him. Sally looks frail and vulnerable as she stands in front of the large and sinister looking man. The man's pistol still points to the ground.

Rigney's heart skips a beat, and he becomes angry at the thought of Sally being at the mercy of these despicable, evil men. He glances upward toward the Command Center balcony. Rigney clearly sees sniper rifle suppressors protruding from the latticework. Two of the suppressors point down to where Sally and the man stand.

Bollier notices Page's glance upward. As a reaction, he looks in the same direction but does not know what Page is looking at.

Rigney notices Bollier looking in the same direction. Rigney quickly brings his eyes back to look at Bollier. Rigney pulls the Beretta from the pouch and holds it hidden behind the door. Rigney waits for Bollier to turn back toward the door. He plans to open the door, show Bollier the gun, and force Bollier to come into the house.

On the Command Center balcony, Randy has the binoculars to his eyes; he speaks softly into the phone. His voice is loud enough for all the men on the balcony to hear.

Randy reports, "Bollier is knocking on the door."

A few seconds pass.

"The door is opening but only a few inches."

A few seconds pass.

"Page is half hidden behind the door. He is speaking with Bollier. They are now looking up the street. Uh oh! Page is looking up here. Bollier is looking in our direction. I don't think he grasps what Page is looking at."

A few seconds pass.

"The door is opening wider."

From the edge of the thicket, Gunny Bronston waits for the right moment to sprint across the open, sandy space. He sees the door open slightly. Bollier's body blocks his view of the person at the door. He assumes it is Page.

Bronston's groin area is still sore for the beating he took from Page. He is confident that he can shutout the pain of running for the few seconds it will take him to get to the door.

Bronston now sees Page's head sticking out from the door. Both Page and Bollier are looking up the street.

Bronston pulls his .45 automatic from its holster and cocks the hammer. He will run the distance with the pistol in his right hand.

The door opens wider. Bronston crouches and is ready to sprint.

On the Command Center balcony, Brad Watson and his team have their fingers on the triggers of their sniper rifles. Brad plans to give the order to fire when he hears the report that Bollier has gone into the house, or when Lucifer's man attempts to put Sally Macfurson back in the car, whichever occurs first.

From his position in the backseat of his Mercedes, Javier looks through the windshield. He has a clear view of his other car. He sees Pedro standing behind Sally. The scene is exactly as he had planned it.

Although he can only see Thomas Bollier on the doorstep, he is sure that Page is suffering through guilt and rage at the sight of his lover in the hands of a violent stranger.

Rigney is about to show Bollier his Beretta and force Bollier inside when Bollier says, "Let me come inside, and I will explain the situation to you. But remember, if any harm comes to me, Sally will be dead meat."

Rigney becomes enraged by Bollier's threat. He fights the impulse to put the Beretta to Bollier's head and pull the trigger. Instead, he puts the Beretta back in the pouch of his sweatshirt, and he opens the door wider so Bollier can enter.

As he crouches at the edge of the thicket, Gunny Bronston concentrates on the activities at the door of the beach house. He is oblivious to the approaching climax of international intrigue closing in around him. He cannot see the red Mercedes, or the blue Fiat, or the four men on the balcony aiming sniper rifles toward the street.

The beach house door opens wider.

Bronston springs from the edge of the thicket and sprints across the sandy open space. He feels weak shooting pains in his groin but not enough to slow him down. Bronston carries his automatic in his right hand. The automatic is cocked and ready to fire.

On the Command Center balcony, Brad Watson sees through the scope that Sally is being directed to get back into the car. The crosshairs of his sniper rifle are just over the man's right ear.

At the same moment, Randy reports, "Bollier is going inside."

"Fire!" Brad orders succinctly.

As all four sniper rifles sound off at the same time, Randy blurts, "Who the fuck is that?!"

The balcony is awash in mechanical sounds of moving ejection slides and spent cartridges hitting the tiled balcony deck.

One-second later, Dave fires on his second target in the Mercedes.

"Who is that?!" Randy asks excitedly as he watches Bronston run from the thicket to the beach house.

John Smith continues to fire—three shots—then—another—and another.

Chapter 119

Javier is first to see the soldier spring from the bushes. He sees Bronston three seconds before Randy sees him. Those three seconds are just enough time for Javier to understand he has entered a trap.

Javier leans forward to tell the driver, Carlos, to drive away quickly. Just as he leans forward, the driver's side window shatters and Carlos's head explodes. Bloody brain pieces and skull fragments spray across Javier's shoulders and face. At the same time, a bullet creases Javier's left bicep and slams into the backseat cushion.

Javier quickly opens the door and dives out of the car at the same split second that the backseat window on the driver's side shatters and Fernando's head explodes and another bullet slams into the seat where Javier was just sitting one second ago. Less than a second later, another bullet hits the inside panel of the open car door.

Javier scrambles to hide behind the front part of the Mercedes where he hopes the vehicle's engine block will protect him from incoming bullets. For the time being, the bullets have stopped coming.

Sally Macfurson looks west along Via Ariete toward the front of the beach house. She can see the fat sailor who sat with her at the dining room table back at that house in *Lago Patria*. Then, she sees Bollier turn and look at her. She can see Rigney standing in the partially open doorway looking in her direction.

"You must get back into the car, miss," Pedro says to Sally Macfurson.

Sally feels the urge to resist. She feels a sense of freedom on the outside of the car. She also senses a measure of compassion from this stranger standing beside her. She stands still and does not move. She believes that if she does not get back in the car, everything will be okay.

Pedro opens the back door of the car. He grips Sally's arm and pushes her toward the backseat.

Then, Sally feels Pedro's grip loosen at the same time that she sees the driver's side window shatter and blood sprays on both the outside and inside of car. Pedro begins his fall beside her. She turns and watches him fall; half his head is missing. She looks down at her coat and sees it splattered with blood. Panic floods her thoughts. She fears someone shooting at her. She puts her hands to her face and starts screaming. The events have occurred so fast that Sally has not yet discerned that she is not a target.

Sally looks toward the beach house and sees a soldier with a gun in his hand running to the front door of the house and pushing the sailor and Rigney inside. Then, she sees a man exit a parking garage and step into the street. The man calls her name. She walks backward; then, she turns and runs east on Via Ariete.

Sammy shouts, "Wait, Sally! Don't run!"

Sally does not stop. She concentrates on fleeing. Sammy runs after her. Sally looks over her shoulder and sees the man running after her. She knows he will catch her, and she decides to put up a fight this time.

"Sally, please stop. You don't understand. I am here to help you."

Sally keeps running. She blocks out Sammy's words.

Sammy catches her ten seconds later. He grabs her forearm and forces her to stop. Sally screams louder and starts hitting Sammy on the chest with her free arm. She attempts to kick him in the groin but cannot get the correct balance or angle. She looks around frantically hoping someone will come to her aid. She weakens with frustration at not being able to overcome this man. Sammy grabs her flailing arm. Sally twists and turns in attempts to free herself.

"Sally, I am here to help you, not harm you," Sammy says in a comforting and warm tone. "I am an agent with the Office of Naval Intelligence. Rigney works for ONI. Rigney is here because of ONI. You are safe now. We are the ones who shot your abductors."

Sally stops fighting as she begins to understand Sammy's words. She looks up into Sammy's face. Her eyes pleading that he is telling her the truth.

"Yes, Sally. You are safe now." Sammy is smiling.

Sally believes him. Relief overcomes her. She becomes relaxed and she falls against him. She buries her face into his chest and starts bawling her heart out. Sammy gently puts his arms around her to make her feel more protected.

On the Command Center Balcony, John Smith still has his sniper rifle aimed at the red Mercedes. Brad has binoculars to his eyes and looks down at the Mercedes.

"What happened?" Brad asks.

"Lucifer moved at the last second," John Smith explains. "I have him pinned down behind the front of the car. I think I did wound him, though."

"Dave, keep your weapon on the Mercedes also. Keep Lucifer pinned down. If he tries to escape, shoot to kill."

Dave puts his eye back to the scope and adjusts his aim to the front of the Mercedes.

Brad turns and looks at Randy and asks, "What did you see?"

"Just as you gave the order to fire, some big guy in a fatigue uniform jumped out of those bushes ..." Randy points to the area of the thicket near the beach house. "... and ran to the front door of the house. He had a large automatic in his right hand. He pushed Bollier and Page inside."

"Must be Bronston!" Brad concludes aloud, exasperated at himself for not predicting Bronston's actions. For a moment, Brad is angry at Rigney for not controlling himself back in Virginia Beach last New Year's Eve.

Brad calculates that two minutes has passed since Bronston crashed the door of the beach house. *More than enough time for Bronston to kill everyone in that house.*

"Anyone on the other end of that phone line?" Brad asks Randy.

Randy speaks into the phone, "Barbara, are you still on? Is anyone on?"

No response.

"No one answers," Randy reports.

"Do you hear anything?"

Randy listens again and reports, "I hear shouting. I also hear crashing sounds, like someone is busting things on the floor. Barbara is one of the people shouting."

"What is she saying?"

"She's yelling at Rigney to get out of the way."

Brad and John sigh with relief at the same time.

"Someone just yelled, *don't shoot!*"

"Rigney is no match for that marine," John Smith advises as he continues to look through the scope.

"I think I just heard two shots," Randy reports with the phone headset still to his ear.

The sound of two shots echoing from the beach house is loud enough to be heard on the Command Center balcony.

"God damn it!" John Smith spits angrily while still looking through the scope. He understands that the shots were fired by Bronston's gun because Rigney's Berettas have suppressors attached as Brad had earlier ordered.

Brad concludes that Bronston has killed Rigney and Bollier. He shudders at the thought of Rigney's death and what Bronston probably plans for Barbara Gaile.

Brad must decide his priorities. Does he send a team to the beach house to help Barbara, or does he go down to the Mercedes and capture Lucifer before Lucifer finds a way out of here. Brad considers that until Lucifer is captured, Lucifer has a wide firing zone on the access to the beach house. Brad knows that he cannot risk sending someone through that firing zone. An additional risk is that Bronston has the advantage in that house. An ONI team would need to knock down the door and proceed into the house looking for a killer who knows they are there and could easily shoot from hiding.

Brad decides that after he captures Lucifer, he will devise a plan to rescue Barbara.

"The front door just closed," Randy reports while looking through binoculars.

Brad explains the plan. "Greg and I are going down and arrest Lucifer.

"Dave, as soon as you see that we have Lucifer in cuffs, I want you to take a rifle and a handgun and go down to the beach side of the house. Take a handheld radio and set it to channel two. If Bronston tries to escape through the rear, you are to shoot him—shoot to kill.

"John, as soon as you see that we have Lucifer in cuffs, shift your aim to the front of the house. If Bronston comes out—shoot to kill."

Brad pauses. Then, he advises, "Now, I will call in the Marines."

Brad and Greg depart the balcony and go inside to use the radio.

Guilt and regret about not putting a tail on Bronston nags at Brad's thoughts. *Damn, Rigney, why did you need to kick Bronston's ass!*

Chapter 120

Rigney sees Bronston only one second before Bronston heaves his shoulder into the middle of Bollier's back. The force of Bronston's forward momentum into the middle of Bollier's back causes Bollier to lose his balance and fall forward and crash into Rigney.

To keep his balance, Rigney quickly steps backward into the middle of the living room.

Bollier begins to fall. He grabs the arm of a man-sized marble statue of Neptune in an attempt to keep from falling, but he fails. He topples the statue.

Just before the falling statue hits the floor and breaks into pieces, it catches Bronston across both shins, tripping him. Bronston falls forward, and he throws his hands out to brace his fall. The force of his right hand hitting the ceramic tile floor causes the automatic to spring from his hand, slide across the floor, and come to rest under the marble and wood couch on the other side of the living room.

Bronston, Bollier, and pieces of the statue spill into the living room.

Barbara still sits on the couch. She is stunned by the unexpected appearance of Gunny Bronston.

When Bollier's head hits the floor, he is knocked unconscious.

Rigney reaches into the pouch of his sweatshirt and pulls out his Beretta.

Bronston looks up and sees Rigney pulling a gun. Bronston's hand-to-hand combat training engages his reflexes. Before Rigney can put his finger around the trigger and aim, Bronston jumps to his feet and slams his right shoulder into Rigney's midsection. At the same time, Bronston grabs Rigney's gun hand wrist and points the gun hand away toward the ceiling.

Reacting instinctively, Rigney repeatedly slams his left fist down on Bronston's kidneys. Rigney's punches have little effect and the tough and committed marine.

Bronston drives Rigney into the courtyard door. The glass shatters. The closed shutters prevent them from spilling out of the house and into the courtyard.

Bronston, using both his hands, grabs Rigney's gun hand wrist and twists Rigney's arm in an attempt to flip Rigney to the floor. Bronston's balance and Rigney's position are not as it should be for the maneuver to be successful. Instead, Bronston's attempt causes Rigney to spin on his feet 180 degrees and be thrown toward the couch. Bronston keeps hold of Rigney's wrist and is pulled by Rigney's weight in the same direction.

Barbara glances at the Beretta at her feet. She is about to reach for it but stops when she sees Rigney and Bronston crashing toward her. She quickly jumps from the couch.

Rigney trips backward over the coffee table, and he and Bronston crashes down on it. The glass tabletop shatters and the ornate wood breaks and splinters. Rigney's gun arm smashes across the edge of the coffee table, and with Bronston's downward pressure on that arm the pain causes Rigney to drop the gun.

Bronston is on top of Rigney, and Rigney lies in the broken glass. Rigney's thick pullover sweatshirt protects his back and shoulders.

Bronston sees two Berettas under the pile of glass shards and broken wood. Bronston reaches for one of Berettas. Rigney stops him by wrapping both hands around Bronston's throat and pushing Bronston back. Rigney locks his elbows and squeezes both his thumbs with all his strength into Bronston's larynx. Bronston instinctively grabs Rigney's forearms. Bronston attempts to pull Rigney's hands from his throat, but Rigney has a death grip on Bronston's neck.

Bronston panics as he realizes that he cannot pull Page's hands from around his throat. Bronston cannot breathe. He chokes, and his face turns blue. As a defensive move, Bronston throws punches into Rigney's face.

Rigney feels the stunning and painful punches to his nose and mouth. Because of the distance that Rigney holds Bronston and because of the pressure on Bronston's throat, the blows to Rigney's face lack sufficient force to cause Rigney to release his grip.

The blows are forceful enough to fracture Rigney's nose and cause Rigney's teeth to cut the inside of his lips. Blood flows from his nose and mouth.

Bronston reaches for his combat knife. He has difficulty finding it. He frantically pats his left side in search of the knife handle.

Rigney sees Bronston's search for the knife. He knows that he is dead if Bronston gets a hold of the combat knife. He pushes up and throws Bronston backward, releasing his grip on Bronston's throat.

Bronston falls on his back, and he makes loud sucking sounds as he refills his lungs.

Rigney scrambles to get one of the Berettas, but both guns are now under the couch and behind sharp shards of glass. He knows he must have a weapon to stop Bronston. He starts picking away at the glass so he can get to the Berettas. He cuts his fingers during the attempt, but he keeps picking.

Barbara feels vulnerable and helpless without access to a Beretta. She looks around the room for something to use as a weapon.

"Barbara!" Rigney yells. "Get his gun from under the couch and shoot him!"

Barbara had seen Bronston's gun slide under the end of the couch. She steps quickly to the end of the couch, gets on her hands and knees, and looks beneath the couch to locate Bronston's automatic. All she can see is sharp pieces of glass and broken pieces of coffee table. She stands and attempts to move the marble couch. The weight of the couch defeats her attempts. She gets back down on her hands and knees and starts picking away the glass in search of the automatic.

Bronston recovers. He stands up and unsheathes his combat knife.

Rigney jumps to his feet and moves away from Bronston. He walks backward and trips over broken pieces of the Neptune statue. He falls to the floor on his back.

Bronston stares at Rigney like a wild man. "You're a dead fuckin' squid!" Bronston yells like a maniac and screams in rage. "First I will gut you. Then, I will rape and kill her!"

Rigney is on his back and looking up at Bronston.

Bronston charges toward Rigney with the knife held over his head ready to plunge down into Rigney's belly when at the correct distance.

Rigney desperately looks around for something to use as a weapon. Neptune's trident lies two feet away. He reaches out for the trident and grabs the shaft.

Bronston dives toward Rigney.

Rigney swings the trident in an upward arc from the floor.

Bronston sees the three barbed tines of the trident coming at him. His mind tells him to stop, but he cannot stop his diving-forward motion.

Bronston screams a moment before Rigney plunges the three barbed tines of the trident into Bronston's neck. An outer tine severs a jugular vein. The middle tine and the other outer tine rip away Bronston's larynx. With no voice box attached, Bronston's scream abruptly stops.

Bronston collapses to the floor. He jerks violently. Gurgling sounds come from the gaping hole that was once his larynx. Blood gushes from Bronston's wounds and spreads over his uniform and over the floor.

Rigney releases his hold on the trident. He stares coldly at the dying Bronston.

With the trident still stuck in his neck, Bronston's body jerks less frequently as life flows from his body.

Rigney stands and circles around to the other side of Bronston. He wants to remove the combat knife from Bronston's hand; he fears that Bronston still has enough strength to stab him.

Then, Bronston stops jerking. His eyes are open and lifeless.

Rigney picks up a coffee table leg from the busted pieces on the floor. He jabs the coffee table leg into Bronston's side—no reaction from

Bronston. He jabs the coffee table leg into the hand that holds the combat knife—still no reaction. The combat knife is covered in Bronston's blood.

Rigney stands over Bronston's dead body. He feels nothing for the passing of this despicable life—no sympathy—no compassion. He does feel that again he has accomplished something. He feels satisfied. He has rid the world of one more evil person. He reaches down and removes the combat knife from Bronston's dead hand.

"Got it," Barbara says as she stands with Bronston's gun in her right hand. She had been consumed with looking for the gun and not aware that Rigney had killed Bronston. Horrified by what she now sees, she cannot help uttering a ghastly, "Oh my God!"

Rigney hears a moan from the other side of the room. He sees Bollier rising to his feet at the foyer entranceway that leads to the front door.

Bollier rubs his head and moans.

Barbara stands next to the west wall of the living room. Bollier stands on the opposite side of the living room from Barbara. Rigney stands over Bronston in the middle of the living room between Barbara and Bollier.

Bollier takes in the scene in the living room. Still dazed from the knock on his head, he does not think clearly. He sees Page standing over what appears to be a dead man on the floor. Blood is everywhere. Page holds a bloody knife in his hand. Thinking that Page killed the man on the floor, Bollier senses danger to himself. Then, he recognizes the dead man as Gunny Bronston. Thomas fears that Page will kill him.

For a few seconds, Bollier thinks about how to protect himself. Then, he remembers why he is here. He remembers the gun in his pocket. He reaches into his peacoat pocket, pulls out his small caliber automatic, and points it at Page. He pulls the trigger twice.

Rigney hears the two metallic clacks of the ineffective hammer hitting metal. He recognizes the automatic as the one that he disabled. Rigney feels no threat.

Barbara sees the sailor pull the gun and aim the gun at Rigney. She does not know it has been disabled. She does not distinguish the two metallic clacks from the sounds of crunching glass and splintered wood under her feet. She fears Rigney being shot. She lifts Bronston's automatic to aim at the sailor.

Rigney notices Barbara's movement. He turns to tell her no danger exists. As he turns, he steps into Barbara's line of fire. He waves his hand to stop her and orders sharply, "No! No!"

"Get out of the way, Rigney!" Barbara shouts.

Rigney shouts, "No! Don't shoot!"

Barbara ignores Rigney. *Doesn't he understand that he is about to be shot!* She focuses on the sailor at the other end of the room.

Bollier stares questioningly at his pistol. His dazed mind works slowly. *I know I pulled the trigger.* He carefully aims at the middle of Page's back.

Barbara does not understand Rigney's actions. Her instincts tell her that she must act quickly and that there is no time to understand Rigney's actions. She takes two steps sideways to remove Rigney from the line of fire.

Bollier pulls the trigger, and nothing happens. He pulls it again— still nothing. All three of them are stepping on broken glass. The sound of the pistol's hammer action is now lost in the sounds of crunching glass.

Bollier notices a woman against the wall on the other side of the room. She has a gun in her hand. He sees the woman raising the gun in his direction. Bollier instinctively shifts his aim toward the woman and pulls the trigger.

Using both hands and taking the firing stance, Barbara quickly aims to the middle of Bollier's torso and pulls the trigger twice.

Two thundering shots vibrate the walls of the house.

Bollier feels the two bullets slam into his chest. He is knocked backward. He utters only a short painful scream as he feels the searing pain. One bullet enters his left lung. The other bullet enters his heart, which stops functioning. He falls to the floor.

Bollier lies on the floor and attempts to speak. He wants to ask what is happening to him, but those parts of his body that allow speech are no longer working. He realizes he is dying. Knowing there is no chance to repent and change, he questions futilely: *What went so wrong?* The searing pain in his chest subsides. Five seconds later, Thomas dies.

Rigney's shoulders droop in frustrated resignation as he stares at Bollier. He looks around for any more threats. He sees that the front door is still open. He walks through the foyer, shuts the door, and slams the two deadbolts home to their locking position.

Brad and Greg go into the adjacent room where Harry, the acoustics man, listens intently.

"What's going on?" Brad asks.

"There was one hell of a fight in that house. Two shots were fired. Now, I don't hear anything."

Brad and Greg go into the dining room and pick up weapons. They each take a .45 caliber automatic. Brad walks to the south balcony and looks down to Via Ariete. He sees Sammy holding Sally's arm and walking her toward the apartment building. Fredrick walks behind them.

Brad shouts down to the street, "Come back to the Command Center and hurry!"

The two ONI operatives look up and wave in acknowledgment. They quicken their pace.

Brad and Greg exit the Command Center. They rapidly descend the five levels of stairs two and three steps at a time. The building does not have an elevator. On the first level, Brad and Greg meet Sammy, Fredrick, and Sally entering the building.

"Where you two going?" Fredrick asks.

Brad explains, "Lucifer is pinned down behind his car. We are going out to capture him."

Brad orders, "Sammy, after you get Sally to the Command Center, suit up and get weapons for an assault on the beach house. Take a handheld radio with you. Set it to channel two. As soon as you see that we have Lucifer in handcuffs, take a position in front of the beach house but out of the front door's line of fire. I have John up on the balcony targeting the front door to the beach house. Dave will take position on the beach side of the house. I will give further instructions over the radio after you are in place."

"Will do!" Sammy responds.

"Fredrick, I want you to come with us."

During the conversation, Sally fixes her eyes on the large automatic pistols in the hands of Brad and Greg.

Sammy nods his understanding. He turns and leads Sally to the stairs.

As Brad exits through the door, he hears Sally ask Sammy, "What is ONI? Is Rigney okay?"

Sammy responds, "Can't explain it to you now; maybe later."

Javier holds his pistol tightly. He crouches behind his Mercedes, afraid to raise his head for worry of being shot. A few minutes ago, he heard the sound of two shots come from the beach house. *They killed Thomas. Was he foolish enough to pull his gun against that armed soldier?*

Javier concludes that he was fired upon from the upper floor balconies of the apartment building to the east of him. He looks to the beach area and sees the shore between two houses. He considers dashing for the beach. However, he is not confident the houses will block the shooter's aim. He sees no escape from this. He worries that if he stands with his hands up to surrender, he will be shot.

Javier hears a voice. "You, behind the red Mercedes. Throw your weapon over the car and into the street. Five guns are pointed at you. If you try to run or fire your weapon, you will be shot dead."

Javier challenges, "How do I know you will not shoot me? You killed my associates, and they posed no danger to you."

"You and your friends held two American citizens as hostages. Those Americans are now in our protection. We have no reason to kill you now."

Javier now believes that whether he surrenders or takes a stand and goes down in a hail of bullets, his network of spies and associates will crumble. *Without my leadership, my organization is nothing.* He knows he has failed his cause. If he takes a stand and dies, he will not be praised as a martyr for the cause. The details of his disappearance will be known only to a select few in the American government. The manner of his death will be a closely guarded secret. If he surrenders, he understands that the Americans will try everything short of torture to extract information from him. *What a paradox. I and anyone else in my cause would not hesitate to torture our enemies, but our enemies will not use torture. Torture is against their law, and they are repulsed by the idea of torture.*

Javier reasons that he always has the chance of escape or the chance of prisoner exchange. *I have influential friends in the leadership of the PLO. If they know I am alive, they will take actions to free me.*

Javier sets the safety on his weapon. Then, he tosses his weapon over the car. The weapon lands in the middle of the street.

"What do I do now?" Javier shouts.

"Raise your hands above the hood of the car and stand."

Javier raises his hands. He waits a few seconds before standing. He still fears being shot when he stands. Then, he rises to his feet.

Brad, Greg, and Fredrick walk into the street. All three have their .45 caliber automatics aimed at Lucifer.

Brad orders, "Greg, pick up his gun and stay in the middle of the street until we have him handcuffed."

Brad and Fredrick walk closer to the red Mercedes. When Brad sees that Dave has picked up the gun, he says to Lucifer, "Come out from behind the car. Keep your hands raised."

Javier comes out into the street and stands three feet from Brad and Fredrick.

Brad directs, "Fredrick, shackle and handcuff him; then, search him for weapons. I will keep him covered."

As Fredrick performs the handcuffing and the body search, Brad and

Greg stand three feet away with their automatics pointed at Lucifer's chest.

Up on the Command Center Balcony, John shifts his aim from Lucifer to the door of the beach house.

Randy no longer has the phone to his ear. He watches the beach house through binoculars.

Javier stands only four feet from the driver's side door of his red Mercedes. While he is searched, he stares at the bodies of Carlos and Fernando. Looking at the grotesque brutality of their deaths, he reassures himself that he acted correctly by surrendering.

Brad's eye catches movement near the beach house. He turns his head slightly just in time to see Dave dart toward the back of the beach house. Sammy takes up a position in front of the beach house.

In the beach house, Rigney and Barbara sit at the dining table. Barbara, using contents from a well-stocked first-aid kit, tends to Rigney's wounds. Rigney flinches every time Barbara applies stinging blood coagulant.

He stares into space and replays the last twenty minutes in his mind. Then, he glances at Barbara and asks, "Barb, have you ever heard of the poet William Ernest Henley?"

"No," she responds as she applies a bandage under his eye.

Rigney explains, "I am the person I am today because of a poem he wrote. We won today because of how Henley's words motivate me."

Barbara stares curiously into Rigney's eyes. She expresses curiosity as she attempts to look into his soul. "What poem?"

"Do you want to hear it?"

Barbara shakes her head while expressing astonished befuddlement. "You want to recite poetry?! Now?!"

"In the past I have recited the poem when I have overcome a powerful force. Sometimes I recite it in my head. I prefer to recite it aloud."

Barbara still holds a medicated swab in her hand. She sits back in her chair and says, "Go ahead."

"The poem is titled Invictus, Latin for *unconquerable*."

"Out of the night that covers me,

Black as the pit from pole to pole,
I thank whatever gods may be
For my unconquerable soul.

In the fell clutch of circumstance
I have not winced nor cried aloud.
Under the bludgeonings of chance
My head is bloody, but unbowed.

Beyond this place of wrath and tears
Looms but the Horror of the shade,
And yet the menace of the years
Finds and shall find me unafraid.

It matters not how strait the gate,
How charged with punishments the scroll,
I am the master of my fate:
I am the captain of my soul."

Barbara declares, "That fits you to an extent!"
"It is a standard by which I want to live," Rigney states.

Chapter 121

Harry, the ONI radio engineer, steps out onto the Command Center's west balcony. He sees Randy looking through binoculars toward the beach house. He also sees John Smith aiming a sniper rifle toward the beach house. Harry observes the phone handset being ignored and on the deck.

"Hey you two!" Harry beckons. "Barbara Gaile is trying to get you on the phone."

John smiles happily at the report but does not take his aim off the front door.

Randy picks up the phone handset and starts talking.

"I have Barbara on the phone!" Randy says with excitement and a sense of relief. Randy keeps the phone to his ear. Then, he reports, "Barbara and Rigney are okay. Bronston and Bollier are dead!"

John Smith lowers his XM21 sniper rifle and sets the safeties. They all sigh deeply and stand relaxed.

"Thank God!" a female voice says with relief from the balcony doorway.

The three ONI agents turn to see a petite and attractive redhead standing at the doorway. She wears rumpled khaki pants and shirt. Her eyes are red and puffy. She sighs in deep relief and starts sobbing again.

John turns back to Randy and says, "Let me talk to Barbara."

Randy hands the phone to John.

"Barbara, this is John Smith. Are you harmed in any way?"

"No, sir," Barbara answers over the phone. "But Rigney's nose and mouth are bleeding. I think his nose is broken."

"Put Rigney on," John directs.

"He is in the bathroom getting some wet towels to wipe off his face." Rigney walks back into the living room.

"Oh, here he is."

"It's John Smith," Barbara says as she hands the phone to Rigney. "Hi John."

"Are you sure that Bronston and Bollier are dead?"

"Absolutely," Rigney responds confidently as he stares down at the two bodies on the floor. "How's it going outside? Is Sally safe?"

"Sally is safe. She's up here in the Command Center. The bad guys have been neutralized. There's a bloody mess on the street. The Marines are blocking off the area."

"So, what happens next?" Rigney asks.

"The whole scene will be investigated. We need to extract as much detail about this group of spies as we can before we bring in the cleanup crew to carry off the bodies."

"Can Barbara and I come outside? It's pretty gruesome in here."

"It's pretty gruesome outside too."

"Blood is everywhere in here! We need to get outside!" Rigney insists.

"Okay, but give me five minutes to call off the two agents we got in front and back of the house. Then, you can come out. Oh, and carry a weapon with safety off, as a precaution against any more surprises."

"Will do. Thanks." Rigney hangs up the phone.

"We can go outside," Rigney tells Barbara.

Rigney and Barbara step onto the sandy area in front of the beach house. A chilly, light breeze blows off the sea and refreshes them. They breathe deeply and fill their lungs with fresh cool air.

Barbara carries Bronston's automatic in her right hand, which hangs at her side. Blood covers her sneakers. Blood drops spot the front of her sweatshirt.

Rigney has a gauze bandages on his right hand and has small bandages over the bridge of his nose and around his eyes. Several patches of wet blood stain his sweatshirt. His face has puffed up. The blood is drying on his face cuts. His nose throbs and hurts severely when he touches it. Blood covers his sneakers. In his left hand, he carries one of the Berettas with suppressor still attached.

Rigney and Barbara quietly watch the activities of the ONI agents and the Marine Fast Reaction Force.

Marines setup a roadblock on Via Ariete. Near the roadblock, a body lies next to a blue Fiat. A Marine with a rifle in his hands stands over the body.

On Via Del Mare, Rigney and Barbara see several armed ONI agents, including Brad Watson, guarding a man in handcuffs. They also see the bloody shattered windshield of the red Mercedes. Beyond the Mercedes, the Marines have setup another roadblock.

Sally Macfurson stands on the Command Center balcony. She observes the activity on Via Del Mare and Via Ariete. She sees a group of armed Marines setting up roadblocks. Mostly, she watches the ONI agents guarding Javier. She picks up the binoculars to get a better look. She inhales deeply and lowers the binoculars when she scans the red Mercedes and sees the two dead bodies with half of their heads blown away.

Sally watches Rigney and a woman exit the beach house. She lifts the binoculars to her eyes to get a better look at the slender woman who stands beside him. *She has a pretty face.*

Sally sees that Rigney and the woman hold guns. Rigney and the woman look at ease and look natural with gun in hand. She wonders if Rigney knew all along that he was leaving New London and going to work for ONI. Sally also wonders what relationship Rigney has with the woman.

Brad Watson finally notices Barbara and Rigney standing outside the beach house. A sense of relief overcomes him. His feelings of regret and guilt subside. He realizes that Rigney must have killed Bronston. *What about Bollier?* Brad motions for Rigney and Barbara to come to him.

Brad pulls Rigney and Barbara over to the side and out of Lucifer's hearing range.

Brad asks, "Tell me about Bollier and Bronston. What's their condition?"

"They are both dead," Rigney responds without emotion.

"You're sure they're both dead? You killed them both?"

"No doubt about it," Rigney answers. "They're both dead. I killed Bronston. Barbara killed Bollier. Bollier pulled a gun on us. Barbara had to shoot him."

Brad stares at the tall, slim, and attractive Barbara Gaile who looks drained and disheveled. He sees what must be Bronston's automatic in her hand. He observes the blood on her shoes and the blood drops on her sweatshirt.

Brad thinks that the description of the battle that went on in that house will be an interesting one—probably the type that John Smith drools over.

Brad looks at Rigney and says, "Your hands and face are bleeding. Several ambulances will arrive shortly. I want you to take one back to the navy hospital at Agnano. Gather up whatever personal items you have in the house. You will not be coming back here. Also leave your weapons in the house. You will not need them at the hospital."

"Yes, sir."

"May I go with him?" Barbara asks.

"Yes," Brad replies.

Brad turns and walks back to the area of the red Mercedes and talks with the ONI agents who have just begun their search of the car.

"Who's that?" Barbara asks.
"Brad Watson, my boss."
"Oh."

"May I speak to Rigney Page," Javier asks.

Brad motions for Rigney and Barbara to come over.

Rigney walks toward Lucifer and stops three feet away. Barbara stands behind Rigney.

Javier looks at the Beretta in Rigney's hand. Then, he looks into Rigney's eyes. Javier smiles as he accepts Rigney's identity. Then, he asks, "Is Thomas dead?"

Rigney does not say anything. He assumes that Brad wants him to remain silent.

Lucifer spends a few moments looking into the faces of Brad, Barbara, and the other ONI agents. With an omnipotent expression on his face, he threatens, "Today, you successfully deceived me. My associates and I have long memories. You might sleep well for a while, but not for long."

Rigney feels the chill of the threat. He hopes he does not show fear.

Later in the day, ONI agents and U.S. military police surround Javier's *Lago Patria* house. When Javier's two remaining associates step out the door, they are captured.

Chapter 122

Rigney lies in a hospital bed at the Agnano Naval Support Activity Hospital. For security reasons, he was put in a single bed VIP room. A thick gauze bandage covers his nose. Several stitched cuts, black eyes, and bruised and swollen lips mar his face. Bandages cover his hands.

Brad Watson, John Smith, Barbara Gaile, and Sally Macfurson stand around Rigney's bed. Brad and John have shed their Command Center civilian attire. Now, they wear their lieutenant commander uniforms. Barbara wears civilian clothes.

Brad Watson speaks, ". . . and when you are discharged tomorrow, you are to report to the local ONI office and start writing your report."

Rigney raises his bandaged hands.

"No excuse," Brad says. "You will dictate your report to a stenographer who will type it up."

"How long should it take?" Rigney asks, thinking about getting back to *Columbus* before she departs Naples.

"Should take a week," answers Brad.

"A week!" Rigney objects. "What all do you want in the report?"

"Everything from the time you reported aboard *Columbus* to when you climbed into that ambulance two days ago."

Rigney considers the scope of the report. Then, he asks, "Even things that happened on liberty, like liberty ashore in Palma?"

"No, just include everything that happened aboard ship and everything that happened since arriving here in Naples."

Rigney nods his understanding.

Brad looks at Sally and says, "Sally, the navy thanks you for your cooperation in providing a report of what you observed and heard in Lucifer's *Lago Patria* house."

Brad shifts his attention to Barbara and says, "Barbara, you are to report to the ONI office tomorrow. Your report must include everything that happened after arriving at the beach house."

"Aye, Sir," Barbara replies. A contented smile crosses her face when thinking about events in the bedroom that she will exclude from the report.

Brad, John, and Rigney notice Barbara's smile and understand it. The three men blush.

Sally Macfurson sees the blushing smiles on the three men. She knows the four of them are sharing something. She pretends not to notice.

Rigney looks at Brad and says, "Sir, I will miss *Columbus's* departure."

"Not a problem, Rig. We have informed Captain Saunders that you will not be aboard when *Columbus* sails."

"But if I don't sail with the *Columbus*, I will miss the Second Class Exam on the tenth."

Brad smiles. John shakes his head, expresses amusement, and John starts chuckling.

"What's so funny," Rigney asks.

John looks at Rigney, shakes his head, and says, "After all the important and significant events in which you have been part, you are still thinking about going back to the pomp rituals and military correctness of navy life? Don't you understand? If you come to work for ONI, rank doesn't matter. You will be given whatever rank is required to get the job done."

"I don't understand," Sally interrupts. "I thought Rigney was already an ONI spy."

"Well, spy isn't the right word," Rigney explains.

Sally frowns at Rigney's response. Then, she asks, "What word best describes you, then?"

"I am more like a . . . well a . . . I guess you would call me a *spy catcher*."

Chapter 123

Sally Macfurson and Barbara Gaile sit at a table in the *Ristorante Lago Patria.* They have a corner of the *Ristorante* to themselves. Not many people dine in the *Ristorante* on this cold, winter night. Their conversation cannot be heard by anyone.

Sally says, "This whole incident has awakened me to military activities I never imagined existed. When I thought of the military, I thought only of Vietnam and the waste. I believed military leaders to be dunderheads because of their insistence that America needs to be in Vietnam. Because of Vietnam, I considered the American military to be totally engaged in an irrelevant war. Therefore, I thought the military to be irrelevant."

Barbara interrupts, "You said that you worked on the submarine base at New London? Didn't that help you understand?"

"When I thought of submariners and submarines, I thought of them as boys with powerful, unnecessary toys who deployed on unnecessary missions. I just didn't understand the need for it all."

"Unnecessary missions?"

"Yes, unnecessary. I believed that the Soviet Union is no enemy. I thought that the Cold War is a big exaggeration—an exaggeration perpetuated by American big business and the military. I thought that those who led our country and led our military during World War II created the Cold War because they need wars to fight to feel important and significant. I have spent most of my adult life attending universities. What I believed is what many university faculty and students believe."

"But you have changed your mind?" Barbara asks.

"Not totally. Having been kidnapped by those spies causes me to question what I believe. When I thought of spies, I thought of James Bond movies. I never thought that men really died. Now I understand that there are countries led by evil men who send other evil men to kill innocent people. I now understand our government's responsibility to protect Americans from such evil . . . evil that I didn't know existed until recently.

"When I was held hostage by that man they call Lucifer, I suffered total terror. When I saw all those dead men around the beach house, I came to understand what it takes to protect people like me from people like them.

"I now have an appreciation for the military that I didn't have before. I think I understand, now, why America has a military draft. Our leaders know and understand the evil in this world. Our leaders know what it takes to protect and defend America from that evil. The common, every day American does not understand. If America had to wait for young men to enlist voluntarily, our military would never be strong enough to protect us from evil.

"I once told Rigney that I thought *The Draft* to be unfair because it doesn't apply equally to everyone. I still believe that, although I no longer think it justified for young men to avoid *The Draft*. I now think all Americans, men and women, have an obligation to perform some level of government service. Hundreds of thousands of American men have died to preserve American freedom. A few years of service is not too much to ask to preserve that freedom. I no longer believe that my brother, Willie, was justified when he fled to Canada to avoid *The Draft*.

"I went to Agnano two days ago and signed up with the navy reserve. The chief there told me that I must go to Officer Candidate School six months from now, which will be followed with two years of active duty. Six months gives me enough time to finish my doctoral work here."

Barbara asks, "Do you know what your officer specialty will be?"

"Brad Watson thinks with my educational background and my fluency in European languages that I would do well in cryptology or intelligence. Brad wrote an endorsement that I gave to the recruiter."

Barbara lifts her wine glass and toasts Sally's commitment.

Sally smiles appreciatively and says, "Thank you for letting me have Rigney to myself for a couple of days before he left."

"Not my place to deny permission. Rigney and I have no committed relationship," Barbara explains with a deep sigh.

Sally hears the passionate sigh and understands it.

Barbara continues, "Too much difference in our ages. Anyway, I'm finally getting what I want. I transfer to ONI headquarters in Washington next month."

Sally thinks about Rigney for a few minutes; then, she admits, "There is no commitment between Rigney and me, either. Rigney wants travel and adventure . . . and there is that side of him that . . ." Sally pauses while trying to form the correct words, finds them, and continues, "That brutal side to him that I did not know existed."

"Brutal side?" Barbara lowers her fork and raises her eyebrows. "Are you talking about Rigney killing that marine?"

"Yes."

"Believe me, Sally. He killed Bronston in self-defense."

"I know that," Sally acknowledges. "I heard the ONI agents describe how Rigney did it. That thing with the trident—how horrible! But that's not what I mean by brutal."

"What, then?" Barbara questions.

Sally looks sadly into Barbara's eyes and says, "He was not affected by it. During the three days we spent together, it was like the killing had not taken place. It was like we continued from where we left off back in New London. I mean, you told me that you were reflective and depressed about killing Bollier, not at first, afterwards, when you had time to think on it."

"Yes, I was, but I had never killed anyone before."

Sally's eyes go wide with disbelief and her heart beats faster. "You mean Rigney has killed before?"

Barbara realizes that she should not have made that comment. She and Sally have become friends. Barbara believes she should be honest. "Yes, Rigney killed before."

Astonishment overcomes Sally. *How can that be?! When could he have done it?! Before I met him in New London?! Could Rigney have possibly hid that from me!*

"When? Where? Are you sure? How do you know?"

"I don't know when and where. It was something he said that night we spent in the *Licola* beach house. He did not want to explain it, and I didn't push it."

Both women sit quietly for a few minutes. They take a few bites of dinner and take a few sips of wine.

"Oh, Rigney," Sally moans sorrowfully.

"What?" Barbara asks with a sympathetic tone.

"Don't you see? Rigney is in danger. We must help him."

"I don't understand." Barbara shakes her head with a bewildered look on her face.

With a frightened look on her face, Sally stares directly into Barbara's eyes and explains, "Don't you see? A brutal and ruthless demon possesses his soul."

Chapter 124

Brad Watson sits at his desk at the ONI Suitland, Maryland Headquarters. He studies preliminary analysis of the data seized at the *Sanchez Imports and Exports* offices. The unique ringing sound of his secure telephone breaks his concentration.

"Lieutenant Commander Watson," he announces into the phone.

"Brad, any new information on the Lucifer data since we last talked?" ONI Chief of Counterintelligence asks.

Brad recognizes Captain Willcroft's voice. "Yes, sir. Information seized at Lucifer's *Lago Patria* house led investigators to search the offices of *Sanchez Imports and Exports of Madrid Spain. Sanchez Imports and Exports* has offices in Madrid, Rome, Athens, San Diego, and Norfolk.

"Records at *Sanchez Imports and Exports* showed that Lucifer had received classified information from contacts in all three U.S. Military Services. Lucifer had also recruited personnel from the military services of Italy, Greece, and The United Kingdom. The records also list the names and location of each military man turned traitor. Within two weeks of seizing the *Sanchez* records, all traitors were arrested, and their operations shut down." Brad pauses to give Captain Willcroft a chance to ask questions or make comments.

"What about Lucifer himself. Have we been able to trace his origin and background? Anything that could lead us to more like him?"

"Yes, sir. Turns out that Lucifer is one Javier Ramirez, and he is not what we thought him to be all these years. Lucifer is Palestinian by birth. His father is Spanish by birth and traveled to Palestine in his youth as part of an archeology team. In Palestine, Lucifer's father met and married a Palestinian woman. Lucifer's mother was Muslim. Lucifer's father refused to convert from Catholicism, although he allowed their children being raised in the Muslim faith.

"During 1948 when Lucifer was 22, his entire family fled the Israeli takeover of Palestine and went to Spain. The Ramirez family settled in Madrid and became active members in the Palestinian immigrant community.

"During the late 1940s and early 1950s, Lucifer joined a number of Palestinian nationalist organizations. Lucifer originated the concept to raise money for his organizations by recruiting servicemen of NATO countries to steal classified information then selling that classified information to the Soviets."

"When did he recruit Bollier?"

Brad thumbs through some papers. "1957, while Bollier was

stationed at the consulate in Edinburgh, Scotland."

"My god, more than ten years! Is that when Admiral Logan was a commander and was Bollier's Division Officer?"

"Yes sir."

"Brad, none of this information must leak out. Admiral Logan has made some powerful political enemies while serving as the President's National Security Advisor. Those enemies would use this information to destroy him."

"How's that sir? Bollier was appointed Crypto Operator over the admiral's objections, and Bollier's appointment letter stated he was not to be part of the accounting for destroyed cryptographic material. Besides that, hundreds of miles separated the two of them. All that can be proved with unclassified documents that I have in front of me."

"Brad, you've never been savvy about Washington politics. When people are out to discredit you, facts and truth are irrelevant. Your enemies spray half-truths and innuendo in all directions. By the time the truth surfaces, the target has been destroyed and has retired to a rabbit farm in Oklahoma."

"I am beginning to understand that, Sir. I have friends who work at IBM and NCR. They tell me that corporate politics is no different."

"I can believe that," Captain Willcroft responds. "Anyway, where are those documents filed?"

"My copies came from the BUPERS copy of Bollier's service record. The requests for Bollier to be assigned as crypto operator and his appointment letter were originated by Department of State and the National Security Agency. So those organizations will have copies filed somewhere, probably in archives."

Captain Willcroft says, "We can't do anything about copies at DOS and NSA. We can do something about the copies in Bollier's service record. Remove from Bollier's BUPERS service record all documents that have Admiral Logan's name on them and file them in the TOP SECRET LIMDIS file for *Operation Jupiter*. Also send a CAPTAIN'S EYES ONLY message to Captain Saunders on *Columbus* and tell him to send Bollier's shipboard service record to you. When you get that record, pull all documents that have Admiral Logan's name on it and file them away in the *Operation Jupiter* file."

"Yes, sir."

After a short pause, Captain Willcroft advises, "The Director and I had a meeting this morning with Admiral Vernier, Commander Naval Communications. He was quite embarrassed to discover that his Inspector General staff never discovered the lack of Tempest adherence. Admiral Vernier will issue a number of directives to tighten Tempest inspections. He will also order all private tape player-recorders removed from all offices and communications centers."

Brad responds, "I'm sure we will see major changes in communications security."

"I'm sure we will," Captain Willcroft says in a concurring tone. "New subject. I want to congratulate you on the success of your new recruiting program. RM3 Page brought home the bacon. I have just finished reading Page's report. Discovering Bollier's communications setup was superior technical investigating."

"Yes, sir. It was."

"I also read Page's and Gaile's reports on the battle in the beach house. They both demonstrated brutal skill and resourcefulness in taking care of business."

"Yes, sir! They sure did!" Brad Watson answers enthusiastically.

Captain Willcroft asks, "The ballistics report says that Bollier's pistol was neutralized—the hammer had been filed down. Do you know anything about that? I don't see anything in Page's or Gaile's report about that."

Brad responds, "Sir, we believe that Lucifer gave Bollier that pistol."

"Does Barbara Gaile know that the pistol was neutralized?"

"No sir. I see no reason for telling her."

Brad pauses and waits for Captain Willcroft to continue the discussion.

Captain Willcroft asks, "Did you offer both of them fulltime assignment to ONI?"

"Yes, sir. Barbara Gaile accepted right away. She will report here next month to begin the full-length counterintelligence course. Page says he must think about it."

"So, Page has not yet accepted his true nature?"

"Sir, I think that Page suspects his true nature, and he does not like what he suspects."

"Where is he now?"

"He's on his way back to *Columbus*. He will stay on *Columbus* until he decides what he wants to do. I promised him that if he decides *not* to join ONI, I would get him assigned to a submarine out of Pearl Harbor."

"Okay. Keep me posted."

"Yes, sir."

Chapter 125

Thomas Bollier's family had not seen or heard from him since 1953. Family members seldom thought of him. They felt that Thomas had abandoned them for a life inside an uncaring, oppressive, and fascist government. Two of Thomas's sisters lost sons in Vietnam. His sisters believed that Thomas had betrayed them because he belonged to that government that conscripted their sons and sent them to a foreign land to be killed. When Bollier's mother died in 1964, no one in his family made the effort to find Thomas and inform him.

The permanent home address listed in Bollier's service record was no longer valid. When the letter from the U.S. Navy advising of Thomas's death eventually found its way to the Bollier family, the response from his sisters was that *he got what he deserved.*

Rosa Ruiz looks curiously at the envelope. The return address reads Commanding Officer USS *Columbus*. She wonders why Thomas's commander would send her a letter.

She opens the envelope and reads the letter. The letter advises that her address was found in Thomas's locker, and the United States Navy thought she might want to be informed of Thomas's death. The letter states that Thomas was murdered, and his death is being investigated.

Rosa is devastated. Thomas was her friend. She often thought that she loved Thomas. She falls onto her bed and weeps. She is the only person to mourn Thomas's death.

Chapter 126

The Tall Lady steams at six knots through a choppy, white capped Ionian Sea. An eight-knot wind blows across the weather decks. The *Columbus* is at Flight Quarters. A helicopter from the U.S. Naval Air Facility at Sigonella, Sicily descends from the overcast sky and hovers forty feet above the *Columbus's* fantail.

The helicopter crew chief operates the cable winch and lowers a large gym bag to the *Columbus's* deck. The *Columbus's* deck crew disconnects the cable from the gym bag. Then, the helicopter crew chief reels in the cable.

Next, the sole passenger, RM3 Rigney Page, descends on the end of the cable to the *Columbus's* deck. When his feet are solidly on the rolling deck and he feels the cable go slack, Rigney quickly unbuckles the cable harness.

The helicopter crew chief reels in the cable. The helicopter moves away from the fantail and hovers over the *Columbus's* wake for a few moments. Then, the helicopter darts into the overcast sky.

"NOW HEAR THIS—SECURE FROM FLIGHT QUARTERS."

Rigney picks up his gym bag. He proceeds to the closest hatch and enters the superstructure. He descends the ladder to the aft mess deck. When he gets to the bottom of the ladder, he sees RM1 Dukes and Larry Johnson sitting at a table and drinking coffee. He looks at his watch—1445.

Larry Johnson sees his friend Rigney Page and queries in a happy and excited tone, "What the hell happened to you, ole friend? Where you been for the last month?" Larry points to the thickly padded bandage across Rigney's nose. "She slam her legs shut at the wrong time?"

Rigney and Dukes chuckle at Larry's comment.

Rigney takes off his peacoat and lays it across the back of a seat. "Give me a second to get some coffee. I will be right back and tell you details."

Rigney goes to the coffee urn and draws a cup of coffee. He returns and sits down at the end of the table. Larry Johnson sits to his right, and Dukes sits to his left. Rigney unbuttons and folds back the cuffs of his Service Dress Blue gabardines to avoid spilling coffee on the white piping.

"Anything interesting happening?" Rigney asks casually.

Swinging his tone in sarcasm, Larry responds, "Oooohhhh nnnnoooo, nothing out of the ordinary! Rouché and his two buddies from

596

First Division are killed in Palma! NAVELEX comes aboard the day we depart Naples and tests cables and removes Bollier's QA equipment! The ship departs Naples with three crewmembers missing ship's movement—you, Gunny Bronston, and Bollier! Then, we hear that Bollier and Gunny Bronston are murdered in Naples, and you are in the hospital! Now isn't all that more than coincidence?"

Dukes looks over at Larry and asks, "Why is that more than a coincidence?"

In his excitement, Larry forgot about Dukes sitting there. Larry's face flushes.

Rigney's heart pumps faster over worry that Larry revealed information that he promised not to reveal.

Larry attempts to recover, "Well . . . well . . . I mean . . . I just think that . . . that . . . well with so many radiomen involved in all these strange happenings. I mean . . . well ya know . . . Rouché, Rigney, and Bollier. Of course, I am just guessing . . . I mean . . . well, I don't want to start any scuttlebutt."

Dukes Asks, "So why would Gunny Bronston's murder factor into your guessing?"

"Oh . . . well, I . . . well, I guess he doesn't. Forget what I said. I'm just rambling."

Dukes is doubtful. He still wonders why Johnson would relate all these events as more than coincidence.

Dukes turns his head toward Rigney and states, "Page, since you reported aboard, you have been at the center of unusual events. First, you are given special treatment by not being assigned to PPO. You qualify as Broadcast Operator in only three days, and you've never been to sea before. Then, you're in the middle of several confrontations with Rouché before he is murdered. Then, I see messages yesterday saying you've been granted special permission by BUPERS to take the Second Class Exam later than the grace period allows . . . tomorrow, if I remember correctly. Then, another message I see says that a helicopter is flying out from Sigonella with its sole mission being to return you to the ship. Maybe Larry is right. Maybe all these events are more than coincidence."

Rigney shakes his head in denial and replies, "It's all coincidence. I don't know about Rouché's murder. I don't know anything about Bollier or Bronston or their murders. Larry just wants to start some rumors."

"Yeah, that's right," Larry lies. "You know . . . that I . . . well, yeah. I admit it. I'm a rumor monger."

Dukes is still doubtful. He knows that Johnson and Page know each other going back several years. He surmises that Johnson inadvertently let go of some information that was private between them. "Listen up you two," Dukes commands. "If you two know something about all these killings, you need to report them. Now!"

Dukes, with a stern look on his face, glances back and forth between Larry and Rigney. "Well, do you guys have anything to report?"

Rigney responds, "I have nothing to report. I have no involvement in any of it. I missed ship's movement because I was in the hospital after getting mugged in Naples. If I had just given up my wallet instead of fighting those punks, I would have been here when the ship sailed."

"Yeah. Rig is right," Larry agrees. "I can't really say all of this is more than coincidence."

RM1 Dukes has a skeptical expression on his face when he rises to his feet and says, "You two are in my watch section. We have the eve watch. Page, you will be Broadcast Operator. Johnson, I am moving you to Ship-to-Shore Termination Operator."

Rigney and Larry acknowledge with a nod.

Dukes looks at Rigney and says, "That means we have the day watch tomorrow when you are scheduled to take the Second Class Exam. Don't worry about that, the senior chief has arranged a relief for you."

"Great! Thanks!" Rigney responds appreciatively.

Dukes walks off.

Rigney and Larry follow Dukes with their eyes.

When Dukes is out of hearing range, Rigney chastises Larry. "You must never say anything about any of this! The price of you knowing about me is your silence!"

"Sorry Rig. I was excited about seeing you. I sort of forgot about Dukes sitting there."

"I don't think we convinced Dukes," Rigney speculates. "I think he still suspects something, but without proof he cannot do anything about it."

"Okay, Rig. You got my silence. Now tell me what happened in Naples."

"I would tell ya, Larry, but then I would have to kill ya," Rigney replies jokingly.

"Come on, Rig, 'fess up, man!"

"No, I can't. I have already told you more than I should. National security is at stake."

"I will settle for just a piece," Larry pleads.

"Okay, Larry," Rigney says smugly. "Tell me just a piece of the last TOP SECRET LIMDIS message that you read."

Larry's collateral duty is Top Secret Control Clerk.

"You know I can't do that," Larry replies firmly.

"Well I can't tell you about Naples for the same reason you cannot tell me about the TOP SECRET LIMDIS. Now, do you understand?"

Larry nods his understanding.

Rigney urges, "Let's talk about something else. What's our next port? We can go steamin' together."

"Souda Bay, Crete . . . two weeks from now. Oh yippee!" Larry declares sarcastically.

They continue to talk about Souda Bay and sip their coffee.

"What the fuck you twidgets doin' sittin' on the mess decks during working hours!" shouts Master-at-Arms Genoa as he storms across the mess decks toward Rigney and Larry.

When Genoa arrives at the table, he pulls out his speeding ticket pad and starts writing.

Rigney and Larry just look up at Genoa and continue to sip their coffee.

"You goddamn twidgets know the mess decks is secured during working hours, but you stupid asses keep doing it."

"Hey, Genoa!" Rigney calls.

Genoa pauses his writing and looks down at Rigney. "What!" he spits.

"It hain't our working hours," Rigney says condescendingly.

"Always the smartass, Page. In addition to the speeding ticket, I am writing you up for insubordination."

Rigney and Larry sit quietly and drink coffee while Genoa fills out the paperwork. When Genoa is done, he requires Rigney and Larry to sign the speeding tickets.

"Now get your twidget pussy asses out of here!"

Rigney and Larry stand and gather their coats and gear.

Genoa turns and walks away.

Rigney watches Genoa waddle across the mess deck. Rigney spurts a laugh and shakes his head as if remembering the punch line of a joke.

"This is hardly funny, Rig."

"Oh, I am thinking of something that someone said to me several weeks ago."

"What's that?"

"It was about me wanting to get back to the pomp rituals and military correctness of navy life.

Rig's Next Adventure

NEA MAKRI

The Office of Naval Intelligence, ONI, assigns Petty Officer Rigney Page undercover to a small U.S. Navy Communications Station on Greece's Aegean coast.

Page's mission: Surveil a scheming master chief who is suspected of espionage.

ONI planned Page's mission to be a routine monitor and report operation. But his mission becomes complicated when he encounters violent and unethical sailors and a mentally disturbed commanding officer.

Rigney's romance with the commanding officer's niece is the talk of the base and incurs the wrath of the commanding officer.

The mission turns deadly when enemy operatives make their move to silence Page and the master chief he is surveilling.

*For Mature Readers

Rigney Page Adventure #2

NEA MAKRI

MICHAEL R. ELLIS

U.S. NAVY RETIRED

Conquering Those Poker Room Forces Against You

MIKE'S POKER NOTEBOOK

The author shares what he has learned during 30-years playing poker in America's casinos.

MIKE'S POKER NOTEBOOK:
1. Explains the strategies that made the author a winning player.
2. Focuses on limit poker.
3. Was written for casino poker players who want to improve their game.
4. Assumes the reader already knows poker structure, rules, and terminology.
5. Explains those poker forces against the player and how to overcome them.
6. Debunks the concept of pot odds and explains why calculating pot odds is not a winning process for limit poker.
7. Explains why drawing to a strait or flush is not a wise play in most situations.

MIKE'S POKER NOTEBOOK

"FROM VICTIM TO VICTOR"

STRATEGIES FOR WINNING AT CASINO POKER

MICHAEL R. ELLIS

GLOSSARY OF NAVY TERMS

1MC - Ship's announcing system; ship-wide reports and announcements made over this sound system; announcing general quarters, chow time, ship's time by bells, flight quarters, reveille, taps, commence ship's work, liberty call.

2-Kilo - A 3-M form used for reporting technical problems and repair actions for all navy equipment by serial number. Also used as a work order. The information on the form is entered into central computer databases. An accurate, up-to-date, and centralized 2-Kilo database is crucial to rapid equipment improvements, legitimate manpower authorization levels, parts and maintenance support, and assignment of trained technicians.

3-M (Maintenance, Material, Management) - The U.S. Navy system for managing maintenance and maintenance support in a manner that will ensure maximum equipment operational readiness. The 3-M system standardizes preventive maintenance requirements, procedures, and reports on a fleet-wide basis.

4.0; four-oh - 4.0 was the highest numerical value a sailor could be assigned in a performance evaluation.

96 - The number of hours between watch strings. For most navy watch standing [shift work] organizations, watches are organized as two day watches, two mid watches, and two eve watches; then 96 hours off until the next watch string.

ACP 127 - Allied Communications Publication 127 – Tape Relay Procedures

Adonis Crypto Machine / device - An electromechanical typewriter style machine used for offline encryption and decryption of military messages of all classifications and accesses. Codes changed daily.

ARI / GCT - Scores resulting from navy enlistment tests for math, knowledge, and reasoning skills.

ASC - AUTODIN Switching Center; Communications complexes located throughout the world that provide interface with tributary stations to AUTODIN and perform computerized relay of messages from one ASC to the other and to distant tributaries.

ASROC - Antisubmarine Rocket; launched from ship, parachuted into sea, motor and guidance systems activate, seeks to destroy submarine

ASW - Anti Submarine Warfare; systems and processes used to combat enemy submarines

BAQ - Basic Allowance for Quarters; Expense paid by navy when sailor authorized to live off base.

Baudot code - A character set predating EBCDIC and ASCII and the root predecessor to International Telegraph Alphabet No 2 (ITA2), the teletype code in use until the advent of ASCII. Each character in the alphabet is represented by a series of five intelligence bits; sent over a communication channel such as a telegraph wire or a radio signal. Example: Baudot code for the alphabet character "A" = 11000; for "E" = 10000

Blue Jacket - navy slang for a U.S. Navy sailor; a junior enlisted sailor

Boatswain's mate of the Watch (BMOW) – Bridge watch position; responsible for rendering bridge related ceremonies and traditions; armed when needed for additional bridge security; makes announcements and sounds bells over the ship's announcing system

BOQ - Bachelor Officer Quarters.

BUPERS - Bureau of Naval Personal; assigns personnel to ships and shore stations; establishes manpower requirements; maintains central personnel records

burn bag - A paper bag used for storing discarded classified paper.

burn run - Communicator jargon for the action of destroying classified material – normally paper bags full of classified paper.

Captain's Mast - Navy terminology for Uniform Code of Military Justice (UCMJ) Article 15 punishment. Process by which commanding officers punish sailors for minor infractions.

CASREP; casualty report - Report of un repairable equipment onboard; tells the senior chain-of-command that ships personnel unable to fix equipment. Report will request outside technical help and / or parts.

CDO - Command Duty Officer – 24 hour duty. Represents Commanding Officer after normal working hours

CIC - Shipboard Combat Information Center; central location on warships that funnel all battle and combat information.

CINCEUR - Commander in Chief of all U.S. military forces in Europe

CINCUSNAVEUR - Commander in Chief U.S. Navy forces in Europe

CINCLANT - Commander in Chief U.S. military forces Atlantic area

CINCLANTFLEET - Commander in Chief of U.S. Navy forces Atlantic area

CINCPAC - Commander in Chief of all U.S. military forces Pacific area

CINCPACFLT - Commander in Chief of U.S. Navy forces Pacific area

cleaning bill - Specifies what is to be cleaned, when it is to be cleaned, and who is assigned to clean it.

CMS - COMSEC (cryptographic) Materials Systems – manages distribution and accountability of crypto devices, codes, key-lists, and ciphers for both online and offline communications security systems.

CO - Commanding Officer

COMDESRON - Commander Destroyer Squadron

COMMO - Communications Officer; Communications Department Head

COMNAVCOM - Commander Naval Communications; predecessor

to COMNAVTELCOM

Communications Watch Officer; CWO - The person who supervises all command-wide communications operations during the shift. Originally, junior officers were assigned. As navy manpower lessened, the position was assigned to chiefs and, then, to first class petty officers.

Communications Watch Supervisor; CWS - The senior enlisted technical advisor to the Communications Watch Officer. Originally, chiefs were assigned. As navy manpower lessened, the position was assigned to first class petty officers and below.

COMNAVACTS UK - Commander U.S. Navy Activities United Kingdom; located in London.

COMRATS - Commuter Rations; expense paid by navy for food when sailor authorized to live off base.

COMSIXTHFLT - Commander Sixth Fleet; operational commander of U.S. Navy ships in the Mediterranean

COMSUBPAC - Commander Submarines Pacific

COMSUBRON - Commander Submarine Squadron

CONUS - Continental United States

CR Division - Communications Radio division; Shipboard division with all the radiomen

crow - navy slang for rating chevron.

CW - continuous wave; a mode of radio communications using Morse code.

Chief Warrant Officer; CWO2; CWO3; CWO4 - Officer rank between chief petty officer and ensign. Sailors in this rank are selected from the senior enlisted ranks.

DCA - Defense Communications Agency

Deck and Conn - Deck: At sea, in charge of ship navigation and safety; Conn: control of ship's engines and rudder.

DNI - Director, Naval Intelligence

dungarees - U.S. Navy working uniform; denim fabric shirt and trousers; phased out during the1990s

ECM - Electronic Counter Measures; electronic equipment used to detect and combat radiated signals from the enemy.

EMI - Extra Military Instruction; a process used by midlevel leadership to punish sailors for minor infractions. Called "instruction" to get around the legalities that only a commanding officer can award punishment. Usually a dirty job loosely related to the infraction.

EMO - Electronics Material Officer; officer responsible for maintenance, repair, allocation of electronic equipment

ET - Rating designator for navy electronics technician

ETOW - Electronics Technician of the Watch; submarine control room watch position

eve watch - Navy communicator jargon for the swing shift

Exclusion Area - a Security Area defined by physical barriers and subject to access control; where mere presence in the area would result in access to classified material.

field day - Organized and scheduled activity to clean decks and spaces

FITREP - Annual report of officer performance

five by five; fivers - A radio communications term meaning loud and clear, high-quality radio signals.

fleet broadcast - Shore based teletype, one-way transmit system that ships at sea are required to copy.

frock; frocked - The process by which a sailor who has been selected for advancement is allowed to wear the uniform and rank of the next pay grade before the official advancement date.

galley - chow hall; dining facility;

Galley Master-at-Arms - A navy petty officer who enforces regulations and provides crowd control in the navy dining facility.

GMG / GMM - Rating designator for navy gunners mate; GMG – guns; GMM - missiles.

GMT - Greenwich Mean Time; Zulu time zone.

gut; the gut - The area of a port city with a heavy concentration of bars and brothels catering mostly to visiting sailors.

Helmsman - Mans the steering control on the bridge of ships

HF; High Frequency - Radio frequency range 3 – 30 Megahertz

HM - Rating designator for navy hospital corpsman

IFF - Radio system that receives interrogation signals from air, surface and land IFF-equipped units and automatically replies with a coded response signal that provides own ship identification.

JANAP 128 - Joint Army Navy Publication 128 – AUTODIN

JASON Crypto – An electronic inline crypto device used for encrypting and decrypting teletype signals. Primarily used for fleet broadcasts.

JOOD - Junior Officer of the Deck; assists the OOD (Officer of the deck)

KGB - The security agency of the Soviet Union government, which was involved in nearly all aspects of life in the Soviet Union since March 1954. Yet its roots stretch back to the Bolshevik Revolution of 1917 when the newly-formed Communist government organized Cheka, a Russian acronym for "All-Russian Extraordinary Commission for Combating Counter-Revolution and Sabotage. Headquartered at dom dva (House Number Two) on Dzerzhinsky Street in Moscow, the KGB had numerous tasks and goals, from suppressing religion to infiltrating the highest levels of government in the United States. They had five main directorates into which their operations were divided:

- Intelligence in other nations
- Counterintelligence and the secret police
- The KGB military corps and the Border Guards
- Suppression of internal resistance
- Electronic espionage

LDO - Limited Duty Officer; previous first class petty officers and chief petty officers advanced to officer rank; duties normally involve managing departments related to previous enlisted specialty

LF; Low Frequency - Radio frequency range 30 – 300 kilohertz

MC - circuits 1MC through 59MC; transmit orders and information between stations within the ship by amplified voice communication by either a central amplifier system or an intercommunication system.

MED – Mediterranean

Message minimize - A period of time when non-essential messages are prohibited from entering the military communications networks; usually initiated during periods of high-level defense alerts.

MI6 - British Military intelligence

mid watch - Navy communicator jargon for the graveyard shift

MS - Rating designator for navy Mess Management Specialists; cook

mustang - A sailor who was advanced to officer rank from senior enlisted rank.

MWR - Morale, Welfare, and Recreation (department); a non-appropriated fund activity on military bases used to provide recreational services that is directed to improve the morale and welfare of personnel; usually includes baseball fields, basketball courts, swimming pools, sports equipment check-out, gymnasiums, bowling alleys, enlisted clubs.

NATO - North Atlantic Treaty Organization; multinational coalition of mostly European countries.

NAVCAMSMED - Naval Communications Area Master Station; located in Naples Italy.

NAVCAMSWESTPAC - Naval Communications Area Master Station Western Pacific; located on Guam Mariana Islands.

NAVCOMMSTA - Naval Communications Station

NEC - Navy Enlisted Code; Code assigned to navy enlisted personnel that defines technical specialties and skills

Nestor – Mythological designator for KY-8 encrypted voice devices

NOFORN - No foreign dissemination

NTP - U.S. Navy Telecommunications Publication

ONI - Office of Naval Intelligence; Located near Washington DC

OOD (underway) - Officer of the Deck; captain's on watch representative; in charge of ship's maneuvering and operations during watch (shift); the OOD underway is designated in writing by the commanding officer and is primarily responsible, under the commanding officer, for the safe and proper operation of the ship. The OOD under way will: 1. Keep continually informed concerning the tactical situation and geographic factors that might affect the safe navigation of the ship, and take appropriate action to avoid the danger of grounding or collision according to tactical doctrine, the Rules of the Road, and the orders of the commanding officer or other proper authority.

OOD (in port) – Officer in charge of quarterdeck; controls access to ship in port

orderwire - A channel within a multichannel radio teletype configuration used to facilitate radio circuit management. Usually channel 1 of the multichannel configuration; normally operated from the technical control facility at the shore station and technical control room on the ship.

Orestes crypto - An electronic inline crypto device for encrypting and decrypting teletype signals. Usually used for ship-to-shore two way communications circuits.

peak loader - Additional operators assigned during busiest message volume periods.

PMs - Preventive Maintenance actions; part of the 3-M system

port-and-starboard watches - A situation when those who work shifts are required to stand watches for 12 hours on and 12 hours off.

PPO - Division Police Petty Officer (aboard ship); supervises cleaning and maintenance of divisional spaces.

PRI-TAC – encrypted voice radio circuit used to issue tactical orders and responses

Quartermaster of the Watch (QMOW) – Bridge watch position; primarily assists with ship's navigation while on watch; enters deck log entries

quarters - An event when divisions gather prior to start of working hours for muster, reading of the plan-of-the-day, and to hear other announcements.

Restricted Area - Access controlled to specifically authorized personnel only.

RM - Rating designator for navy radioman.

RMSN - Navy rate *radioman seaman*; E-3 Radioman

Romulus crypto - An electronic inline crypto device (KW-26) for encrypting and decrypting teletype signals.

Routing Indicator - A four to seven alphabet character sequence; every military unit is assigned a routing indicator; similar in function to an email address.

SACEUR - Supreme Allied Commander European NATO forces

SCP - Ship's Control Panel; located in submarine control room; a panel containing controls and displays for steering and driving the submarine.

Sea and Anchor Detail – Sailors assigned to specific positions to perform actions and to be held responsible for getting ship underway and for entering / departing port.

Seabee - A person in the navy construction ratings

SEA; Senior Enlisted Advisor - Advises commanding officer on enlisted matters. Usually, the senior enlisted man in the command, and usually a collateral duty. SEA was the predecessor to the Command Master Chief position / program.

ship over - navy jargon for reenlisting

ship to shore circuit - A radio teletype or radio Morse Code circuit in the high-frequency range between a U.S. Navy ship and U.S. Naval Communications Station. Used to transmit and receive messages to and from the ship.

SOP - Standing Operating Procedure

Sound-Powered Phone – Intercommunications device aboard ships; normally used during battle stations; powered by the sound of human voice. Consists of earphones and microphone that rests on a chest plate.

squared away - Navy terminology for situations or people that significantly exceed minimum performance and uniform requirements.

SSN - Submersible Ship Nuclear; fast attack nuclear-powered submarine

SSBN - Submersible Ship Ballistic Nuclear; nuclear-powered submarine carrying intercontinental ballistic missiles; boomer.

synching - Military telecommunications slang for cryptographic synchronization between transmit and receive electronic cryptographic machines

TAD - Temporary Assigned Duty

Tape Relay - A teletype message relay system in which the paper tape punched by a re-perforator is torn off after each message is received and manually transferred by an operator, who examines the tape for the destination address and feeds it to a transmitter-distributor connected to a teletype line leading to that destination.

Technical Control - Facility within Naval Communications Stations responsible for radio circuit management and quality control

Tempest - Electronic specifications for minimizing classified information riding on electromagnetic waves.

Tender / Submarine Tender / Destroyer Tender - U.S. Navy ships specializing in providing maintenance and repair facilities

The East - Cold War term referring to the communist countries; primarily, Eastern Europe and the Soviet Union

The West - Cold War term referring to the democracies and republics of Europe and North America

tracer(s) messages(s) - Official messages that request information regarding processing, handling, and disposition of other official messages. Usually initiated after or non-delivery or delayed delivery of important official messages.

traffic channels - Channels within a multichannel radio teletype configuration that are used to transmit and receive specifically formatted military message.

UCMJ - Uniform Code of Military Justice; the foundation of military law in the United States; established by U.S. Congress in accordance with U.S. Constitution, Art I, Section 8.

VLF; Very Low Frequency - Radio frequency range 3 – 30 kilohertz

Watch - Shifts to cover 24 / 7 work schedule

watch bill - Document, usually updated monthly, that lists who is in which watch section, specific watch positions by name, and the dates and times watches are stood.

WESTPAC - Western Pacific

WILCO - Radio telephone abbreviation for "will comply"

XO - Executive Officer (second in command)

ZULU - Military communications operates on the same time worldwide. All communications clocks are set to ZULU (GMT) time zone.

NAVY RANK STRUCTURE

Pay Grade	Rank	Abb.
E-1	Seaman Recruit	SR
E-2	Seaman Apprentice	SA
E-3	Seaman	SN
E-4	Petty Officer Third Class	PO3
E-5	Petty Officer Second Class	PO2
E-6	Petty Officer First Class	PO1
E-7	Chief Petty Officer	CPO
E-8	Senior Chief Petty Officer	SCPO
E-9	Master Chief Petty Officer	MCPO
W-1	Warrant Officer	WO1
W-2	Chief Warrant Officer	CWO2
W-3	Chief Warrant Officer	CWO3
W-4	Chief Warrant Officer	CWO4
O-1	Ensign	ENS
O-2	Lieutenant Junior Grade	LTJG
O-3	Lieutenant	LT
O-4	Lieutenant Commander	LCDR
O-5	Commander	CDR
O-6	Captain	CAPT
O-7	Rear Admiral (one star)	RDML
O-8	Rear Admiral (two stars)	RADM
O-9	Vice Admiral (three stars)	VADM
O-10	Admiral (four stars)	ADM

Made in the USA
San Bernardino, CA
12 March 2020

65582245R00350